A
BLADE
of
BLACK
STEEL

'All is forgiven, sister. The sun sets on the Day of Becoming, and the Sunken Kingdom rises from the deep. The Fallen Mother has returned, and she awaits us away to the living paradise she has brought us. The reign of mortals has expired, Indsorith; our duty is complete.'

The words struck the ... 's ears but floated there for a time, ye... religious babble ... without real meaning. What did register was Pope ... Shona holding up Indsorith's crown to catch the last ray... then casting it toward the edge of the throne room...skipped several times on the obsidian, then slow...it might stop just short of the precipice, or jut out over the edge like a piece in some noble's lawn game. It didn't, though, slipping neatly over the edge and vanishing, the Carnelian Crown tumbling down to the streets of Diadem like the heaviest symbol ever wrought by a mother's metaphor.

And finally, the Black Pope's words made some kind of feverish sense to Indsorith, but her tongue was too sticky to ask the obvious question: if the reign of mortals had truly ended, who would rule the Star in their stead?

By Alex Marshall

The Crimson Empire
A Crown for Cold Silver
A Blade of Black Steel

A
BLADE
of
BLACK
STEEL

ALEX MARSHALL

Orbit
An imprint of
Little, Brown Book Group
Carmelite House
50 Victoria Embankment
London EC4Y 0DZ

An Hachette UK Company
www.hachette.co.uk

www.orbitbooks.net

ORBIT

First published in Great Britain in 2016 by Orbit

1 3 5 7 9 10 8 6 4 2

Copyright © 2016 by Alex Marshall
Map copyright © Tim Paul

Excerpt from *Hope and Red* by Jon Skovron
Copyright © 2016 by Jon Skovron

A CIP catalogue record for this book
is available from the British Library.

ISBN 978-0-356-50571-8

Printed and bound by CPI Group (UK) Ltd, Croydon, CR0 4YY

Papers used by Orbit are from well-managed forests
and other responsible sources.

MIX

This one goes out to all the musicians, artists, writers, filmmakers, actors, family, and friends who inspire me – the magic users, in other words

LEGEND
City/town
Gate Location
Road
Reh
FLINTLAND
Frozen Savannahs
THE SEA of DEVILS
The Raptor Wood
Bal-Amon Jungle
New Slair
The Worst Marsh
Yennek
Geminides
Temple of the Black Vigil
EMERITUS, THE FORSAKEN EMPIRE
The Witch Wood
Agalloch
Old Slair
THE LOST WATERS
N
W
E
S
© Tim Paul 2014 timpaulmaps.com

PART I

THE HOURS OF MORTALS

My candle burns at both ends;
It will not last the night;
But ah, my foes, and oh, my
friends—
It gives a lovely light!
—Edna St Vincent Millay,
'First Fig'

CHAPTER

1

The girl slept in her nest of flannel sheets and heavy down, dreaming the honeyed dreams of the few and the privileged, but awoke in the early hours to find her world aflame.

'Come,' her mother called in the dark of her daughter's bedchamber, backlit by the unsteady lanterns of the servants who waited at the door. 'Quickly, Sori, you must see.'

Yet Sori already saw, a faint glow creeping over the casement of her picture window with dawn still many dreams distant. She scrambled out of bed and went toward the window, the chill granite floor beneath her feet warning her this was no nightmare. Before she reached the stained-glass panes in the likeness of their blocky family crest, her mother slid off her beaver-lined cloak and cast it like a net over the girl's shoulders, steering her toward the door.

'I said quickly,' said her mother, and more startling than the glint of Lady Shels's breastplate in place of her gold-threaded nightgown was the trembling hand she pressed into her daughter's back. That hand ought to be as firm as the steel the woman wore at her belt and, for the first time since her parents had told her that trouble might descend on their tranquil kingdom, Sori found herself afraid.

'Wait,' said the girl, turning toward her vanity, and when her mother's fingers tightened to draw her away, she said, 'I need Moonspell.'

Her mother hesitated, then released her, and when Sori hurried back with her sword she saw her mother's teeth shining as bright as her golden war paint in the flickering light. Sori knew better than to ask questions as they strode upward through the keep, the tumult echoing through the halls and up from the courtyard making her heart pound; were they actually under attack? As they reached the spiral staircase leading to Father's observatory, her mother stopped and addressed her daughter's hovering handmaids.

'Go and pack, the lot of you, and be sure blades are brought as well as bonnets. Take only what you can carry on your own backs, then go to my chambers and help yourselves to whatever you wish from my closets and jewelry boxes. Do not tarry, though, and leave from the southern gates fast as you can. It may be safer if you travel in twos and threes, but neither all together nor alone.'

Tristessa, who had braided Sori's hair for as long as she could remember, burst into tears, and Halfaxa shook her nearly bald head, meeting Lady Shels's eyes as she said, 'No, m'lady, we will not desert this house when—'

'You will do as you're told,' said Sori's mother in a stern tone she had heretofore reserved only for her children. 'I should have dismissed you from the first, pray do not compound my crime by lingering a moment longer. They will be here by dawn, and there is nothing more you can do.'

'But Sori—' Tristessa began, but again Lady Shels interrupted her maids.

'It will be better for all if Sori goes with Corben.' Before Sori could recover from the shock of hearing she was to be sent away with her fencing instructor, a yet more confounding sight met her watering eyes in the lantern-bright corridor: her stiffly formal mother stepped forward and threw her arms around Halfaxa, the two women embracing. Then her mother stepped back and, bowing to her servants, said, 'It has been an honor to have you wait upon my family. Now flee while you still may.'

Before, Sori had not spoken out of customary obedience, but as she followed her mother up the tower staircase she found herself unable to speak out of sheer panic. Even after the lecture Father had given her the previous week about preparing herself for some very big changes, she had never imagined such chaos. Her mother took her hand as they climbed the stair, and though she was almost fifteen years old, Sori still found herself choking back tears.

Father, Arkon, and Esben were already on the rampart when they emerged onto the level roof of the tower, Corben holding the door open for his mistress and pupil. The stars Lord Shels would contemplate from this roost were drowning beneath waves of smoke, the grey sheets hanging thick above them like exiled clouds that had gathered to muster their strength before retaking the heavens. Father turned from the glow to the north, and upon seeing his wife and daughter tried to smile but couldn't quite pull it off.

'Time to go, boys,' he told his sons, but their mother shook her head, joining them at the low wall.

'Take them below,' she said, planting a hand on each of their heads and ruffling their hair. 'We'll be down soon, but Sori has to see.'

'We have no time,' said Father, his voice cracking. 'They must leave, now, before—'

'We'll be down soon,' Lady Shels said gently, hands lingering on the scalps of her sleepy boys as though they might float away if she released them. Then she said a word Sori had never heard her use before: '*Please*, Mervyn. She must see.'

Father yielded, as he always did, but he seemed just as embarrassed as Sori was at Lady Shels's requesting instead of ordering. 'Come along, boys, it's time. Who's ready for an adventure?'

They might be young, but neither nine-year-old Arkon nor six-year-old Esben seemed to buy whatever tale he had told them as they left their mother and went to the stair, looking at their sister with wide eyes. She shrugged and smiled, hoping if she put forth a firmer façade than their father they might not be as scared as she was. Esben flung his little arms around her hips, and she pulled Arkon in, too, when he seemed reluctant to hug his big sister. Their father joined them, a knot of arms shivering in the early chill, and beyond them Sori saw her mother turn away from her family, planting her hands on a battlement as she looked out onto the ruddy horizon. Then her brothers and father went back down into the keep, Corben following to give Lady Shels and her daughter their privacy.

'Come here,' Lady Shels called, and Sori dragged her cold feet over to the battlement, dreading whatever hellish sight must have consumed their lands. Yet when she put her own goose-pimpled arms on the granite rampart, she saw the fires were still distant and, stranger still, almost beautiful as they danced against the bruise-dark curtain of night at the northern end of the valley. 'Do you know what's happened, Sori?'

'The Cobalts,' said Sori, the hated word almost catching in her tight throat. 'They're . . . they're burning our fields.'

'Yes and no,' said Lady Shels, her low voice carrying more fury than any shout or cry could have. 'They're on the far side, looking upon the same fires. But we set them, as soon as we spied their advance.'

'*We* did?' Sori remembered riding with her family along the wide track that cut through those fields, picnicking along the river, hiding in the labyrinth of corn with her brothers, plucking berries with her maids. Tears quivered in her eyes, but she held them back, as she knew her mother expected. 'Why?'

'Why do you think?' Lady Shels was looking down at her daughter, her successor, and Sori could scarce believe her mother would take even such a terrible occasion to deliver another of her endless lessons.

'To buy us time to flee,' Sori decided, her heartbreak giving way to relief, however mild. 'To keep them at bay long enough to—'

'No,' said her mother, 'that is not why. Do you know what a symbol is?'

'Yes?' said Sori, and knowing her mother expected further proof, tried to think of an example. 'Like our crest. It's a symbol for our province, and our history. The corn is gold because our gold grows from the earth. The bear is our family, guarding the realm. It's all in a star, because food for the people and strength to protect them is what holds up the Star.'

'Very good,' Lady Shels said, and pointed to the distant fires. 'I ordered that our fields burn as soon as the Cobalts came to take them because that's a symbol, too. Do you know what it symbolizes?'

'No,' said Sori, embarrassed by the wetness on her cheeks. To ignite thousands of acres just before the harvest as some kind of a symbol frightened her nearly as much as the prospect of the Cobalts burning them.

'It's a symbol that we will never, ever give up,' said Lady Shels, wiping away Sori's tears with the back of her glove. 'That we would sooner destroy our world than let our enemies rob us of it. That if thieves seek to take our lands from us, they will find themselves poorer for having made the effort. That what we labor to build is ours alone. Do you understand?'

Sori's hand tightened on the scabbard in her shaking hands, and she shook her head.

'You will,' said Lady Shels, and now she sounded sad instead of angry, another unprecedented and upsetting change in her temperament. 'I told you they ordered our surrender, yes? It would have been easier to accept their terms. It would have been safer, for our family, for our friends and vassals. But that would have been a symbol, too, and not a good one. Our enemies would use our surrender as a symbol to strengthen themselves, even as we were brought low. Instead our fall will be a symbol to our allies, to all just people of the Star, that might does not make right, that hope is not lost so long as good people stand strong by their principles instead of taking the easier path, when they know it is wrong. Now do you understand?'

'Our fall ...' Sori gulped, the orange horizon no longer seeming pretty at all. 'You don't mean we ...'

'We lost a long time ago, Sori,' said her mother, the gold flake of her war paint shimmering in the dark. 'But even when one has lost, there is still a choice to be made – to stop fighting, or to carry on even when the odds are impossible, because you know that your fight is righteous. Our fight is righteous, Sori, and even if we cannot win this day, we may still be a beacon of hope for others, trusting that tomorrow the odds may be different. Our courage will not die, even if we do, and that is why the songs still speak of heroes long past – because true courage is only found when victory seems beyond reach but we stretch for it all the same. This will be my legacy, and when I am gone, you must uphold it, even when you are scared, even when you doubt yourself, even when all seems lost. We are not simply people, Sori, we are symbols, every one of us, and so we must ensure that our symbols are worthy.'

Sori was relieved her mother's gaze stayed on the burning fields so she could not see her daughter's weakness as she tried to digest this heavy lecture. Sifting for meaning in all the talk of symbols, she said quietly, 'If we're supposed to fight, why are you sending me away with Corben?'

'Because today we need but one martyr,' said her mother, and it finally sunk in all the way, what this was all about. Lady Shels, golden chin held high, looked down at her daughter and said, 'When we go downstairs I will lead our people north, and we will fight the Cobalts to the last. I will die with my boots on the soil our ancestors have tilled for generations, and after I am gone, child, it will be up to you to avenge me. To lead whomever remains. To fight on, and not stop until you reclaim our lands, our legacy. In time you will rule from this keep, just as I did, and my mother before me, and her father before her. You must live, so that you may become a symbol of righteousness.'

'But you might not die,' said Sori, not caring that her voice was rising. 'You've fought before, plenty of times, even against the Cobalts, and you always ... you always ...'

'Strength, Sori!' her mother snapped. 'Everyone dies; our doomed fate is the very thing that unites mortals against the First Dark. Two centuries hence no one who draws breath this morn will still be alive, not one mortal in all the Star, and all that will remain are the symbols they left for their heirs. I must die, and so I will die fighting for what I believe in. And when the time comes, so will you. Won't you?'

'Yes.' Sori blinked away the last of her tears and met her mother's firelit eyes, and though it wasn't quite true, not yet, she said, 'I understand.'

'Good,' said her mother, leading her away from the ramparts, down into Junius Keep. 'You will be strong, Indsorith, and in time even the Cobalt Queen will learn to fear your name. Now come, I ready for my last charge, and you must watch your mother ride to claim her fate. We shall not meet again, my child, and so let our parting be worthy of the songs of our heirs!'

Lady Shels's final proclamations had been so fiery the words were branded into her daughter's skull. Through all the hardships young Indsorith endured over the following weeks as she and her fencing instructor fled across Junius and into the Witch Wood, the words shone through like a beacon revealing the only safe path through the perilous night. Even when the agents of the false queen braved the Salted Crypts and discovered her and Corben hiding in that unhallowed place, Indsorith believed in her mother's words the way feebleminded folk believed in the Burnished Chain. She and Corben fought shoulder to shoulder until his was hewed open by an ax, and even then she battled on until they battered her down, too. She was ashamed to be taken alive, her injuries minor, and all along the snaking trails back through the Witch Wood she repeated her mother's words like a prayer, begging atonement for her failure to be a worthy symbol.

But then the girl was delivered to Karilemin, the work camp that the so-called Imperials had erected in the scorched fields of northern Junius, and she learned that her mother's claims had never been fulfilled. Every single oath had been undone by the machinations of the Cobalt Queen.

And while Indsorith knew that she betrayed her entire legacy by doing so, she gave thanks to the Fallen Mother to see her parents and brothers again. That they had all been captured by the forces of the usurped Empire stung her pride, but Indsorith truly believed that as a family they could weather anything, even such an indignity as this.

Her mother had different ideas, refusing to eat or drink or even speak to her family. The morning that she refused to take her turn in the fields, rebuffing the command with silent dignity, a guard casually caved in her head with his mace. It happened in front of the whole camp, Father and Arkon and Esben wailing as they ran to Lady Shels while Indsorith just stood there, staring, remembering how it had felt when Corben's arm had come off right beside her, spraying her face with its fading heat.

After that, none of them spoke very much.

Father died of a broken heart shortly after, or maybe it was just barrow plague.

And try as Indsorith did to protect her brothers from the vicious guards, to keep them warm through the blanketless winter and fed through the lean spring—

'Your Majesty?'

Indsorith didn't startle away from her memories at the intrusion, as though they were something to be ashamed of. Instead she drifted slowly back to the present, to the play of late afternoon sunlight on the obsidian floor of her throne room. She was the Crimson Queen, Regent of Samoth, Keeper of the Crimson Empire, and so she let herself linger over the memory of awaking to discover Arkon curled against her, hard and cold as the rocks they prised out of the stingy earth until their fingers bled.

'Your Majesty,' said the abbotess, 'I am sorry to intrude but—'

'What?' Indsorith snapped, perturbed to have her reverie interrupted before she could properly agonize anew over the yet worse fate that had met her younger brother, Esben. These meddling Chainites grew bolder by the moonrise, no longer content to harass her only when the Brat Pope sat in state on the onyx throne beside Indsorith's. Though really, now, if she only had to put up with one cultist at a time Abbotess Cradofil was far less obnoxious than Pope Y'Homa.

'Her Grace wishes to inform you that all is ready for your arrival in the Middle Chainhouse,' said the perpetually sweaty abbotess, even her voice sounding as greasy as collection-plate coppers. 'If you might be so good as to attend her now, she assures you that the procession shall be completed by midnight.'

'Oh, is that all?' Indsorith climbed down from her sable-padded throne, sore and weary from another long day of sitting. Twenty years and a hundred different combinations of bolsters and furs later, that fire glass chair was just as fucking merciless as when she'd first seized it from Cobalt Zosia – no wonder the evil old witch had been so keen to give it away to the first comer. 'I don't suppose I can cancel over something as trivial as awaiting word from the Fifteenth Regiment on what exactly the fuck is going on at the Lark's Tongue?'

'I would never presume to suggest what Your Majesty may or may not do, even under the most dire of circumstances,' said Cradofil, milky eyes everywhere but on her queen. What an answer! The old snoop must know as much about the unfolding situation on the Witchfinder Plains as Indsorith or any of her advisors; if she didn't, she surely would have tried to fish more details out of Indsorith instead of settling for noncommittal toadying.

'No, you're too smart for that, aren't you?' Indsorith stretched from side to side in preparation for the strenuous hike down to the Middle Chainhouse. 'Tell me, Abbotess, how many masters have you served in this chamber?'

'Your Majesty?'

'There's Y'Homa, and me, of course, now that the Black Pope and I share certain offices and honorifics, so that's two.' Cradofil was obviously having a hard time following, even though Indsorith was holding up only two fingers. 'And before his niece stepped into his slippers and mitre there was old Shanatu, whom you must have served before, during, and after his repeated attempts to depose me, yes?'

'Yesssss?' Cradofil fidgeted as Indsorith made a big to-do of retrieving Moonspell and her scabbard from their sheath in the arm of the throne. Her mother insisted Indsorith's first weapon be the ancient Bodomian spatha that had been in their family since the Age of Wonders, and while the sword had felt so heavy and unwieldy when she was a girl, she had grown into it, like so much else. Hard to believe that tracking down the Imperial who had stolen Moonspell when she'd first been captured had been the hardest part of her vengeance – escaping the prison farm hadn't taken much, and confronting Zosia even less.

'That's three, which isn't a bad run for a lackey, but old as you are I expect you may have had other masters before we youngsters came along – my predecessor, for example?'

'King Kaldruut would never have allowed a humble abbotess in the Crimson Throne Room,' said Cradofil.

'Ah, but he wasn't my predecessor, was he?' said Indsorith, allowing the pair of attendants who had glided into the room to help her into the absurd parade dress she was expected to wear. It was all garlands of garnets and rows of rubies held together with black velvet. 'You know who I'm talking about, don't you? Or will you force me to say her name?'

'Never, Your Majesty,' said Cradofil quickly. 'And no, I . . . I should not say I served her. She was a heretic, a butcher, and—'

'And why do you phrase it so?' Indsorith had only intended

to get Cradofil's goat as payback for the woman's disturbing her from her memories, but now her lazing curiosity was unexpectedly awakened. 'I don't give a good devildamn what you should or shouldn't say, I want the truth – did you serve Cobalt Zosia when she was queen?'

One of the attendants gasped and the other nearly tore off a gem-studded button at the use of the forbidden name, and Cradofil looked like a turtle who'd just realized she'd swallowed a fishhook. The abbotess looked down at the halo of the sun reflected in the obsidian floor as she said, 'I met with her once, yes. Here. Only a month before you cast the pretender down, Your Majesty.'

'Do tell!' said Indsorith, pulling herself free of her trembling handmaids and straightening the Carnelian Crown on her jaded brow.

'She . . .' Cradofil looked as nervous as Sister Portolés had, the night the disgraced war nun had been brought in here. 'The Stricken Queen . . .'

'Out with it, woman, I'm not very well going to punish you for something that happened twenty years ago.'

'It was the Stricken Queen who charged me with establishing the Dens,' said Cradofil, finally looking back up at Indsorith. 'Under King Kaldruut's rule any obvious anathemas were put to the stake on sight, and there was nothing the Chain could do to dissuade him from this position. When . . . *she* usurped Kaldruut she first tried to break the Chain entirely, to dismantle our noble church, but her sinful ambitions were thwarted by the will of the Fallen Mother. When we proved too strong for her to sunder, she made a number of egregious reforms, all but one of which were reversed as soon as you liberated the realm, Your Majesty.'

'And the one reform the Chain kept was the practice of

amassing an army of fervent weirdborn converts right under my feet?' Indsorith drained the glass of salt wine a page had brought her but waved away his squid pie, tempting though it smelled. 'For the life of me I can't imagine why.'

'It is only through my continued resolve and patience that the institution persists,' said the abbotess, her chest puffing out with more than a hint of that shameless pride Chainites were so big on. 'I know you have had your differences with the Holy See on the particulars of the matter, Your Highness, but of course that is not my purview.'

'Nor mine, at present,' said Indsorith, not caring to rehash the whole ugly business anew – when she'd found out just what methods the Chain used to 'heal' the weirdborn and tried to put a stop to it, Shanatu had refused to budge, and one thing led to another, and that was the most recent civil war. For all the good it had done her, or the weirdborn for that matter – the only ones who had benefited were mercenary guilds, blacksmiths, and, as always, the Burnished Chain . . . and now there was another war in the works, because there always was. To think there was a time not so long ago that Indsorith had thought getting Shanatu's young niece to succeed him was a minor coup for the future of the realm . . .

'I believe that not even the lowest devil is so lost that it cannot be brought into the Fallen Mother's grace,' Cradofil added, perhaps to fill the silence or perhaps because she thought there was an argument to win here. 'And it is only through the benevolence of the Chain that these poor wretches are made whole.'

'Or close enough,' said Indsorith, remembering how scarred the Chain had left Sister Portolés, and not just from their surgeons' removal of her weirdborn mutations. It was the deep emotional scars that had convinced Indsorith to trust the wretched war nun after knowing her for only an hour, and to trust her absolutely – one look in her scared eyes and Indsorith had known she had found the most powerful ally in all the Star, and also the most dangerous: a true believer in both good and evil. Of course she might betray her queen out of misplaced faith in the Chain, but Indsorith had wagered her life that the girl wouldn't, at least not intentionally. In a world of chance, deception, and deviltry, intention counted for something. It had to, because if it didn't, what did that say about Indsorith, and all the countless lives that had been snuffed out by Imperial soldiers over her twenty years of rule? What sort of a symbol had she grown into?

'News, Your Majesty, and what news it is!'

Indsorith squinted in the glare of the setting sun that washed out the only entrance to the Crimson Throne Room, recognizing the voice but scarcely expecting the girl would come to her.

'Your Grace!' Abbotess Cradofil exclaimed, confirming that the hazy silhouette striding out into the open terrace of the throne room was indeed Pope Y'Homa III herself. She wasn't alone, half a dozen of her personal guard accompanying the girl. She was naked under her loose cape of oily black fur, her pale cheeks and brow daubed with fresh blood, but far more disturbing than her ceremonial dress was the curved bronze dagger in her left hand, its rune-etched blade still dripping.

'Is the news that you have decided to get tossed over my balcony, stepping in here with a drawn weapon?' Indsorith demanded. 'I don't care what ritual I'm late to, you don't come in here . . . '

But she did, Y'Homa's bared teeth flashing brighter than her sun-kissed dagger as she advanced on the Crimson Queen, the Dread Guards stationed at the door who should have at least announced the pope and her retinue nowhere to be found, and Indsorith recognized the scene for what it was. Well she might, having welcomed forty-seven assassins over the course of her reign. Yet never in her wildest fantasies had she imagined Y'Homa herself daring to settle the matter with steel – the girl must have gone off her nut, if she thought this was going anywhere but south.

'I knew Your Grace was a loon, but I'll admit I underestimated your madness,' said Indsorith, snapping Moonspell out of her scabbard. As she did, her eagerness to duel the girl evaporated. Her hand was heavy, her arm sluggish, and her head floaty; something more than salt in the wine, and something strong at that to be hitting her so fast. 'I'll give Your Grace one last chance to reconsider, chalk it up as—'

'It's happened!' Y'Homa cried as she stopped a short distance away, her cape flapping over her wildly gesticulating arms like the wings of an oddly hairless owlbat. 'The Fifteenth's met the Cobalt Company on the Witchfinder Plains, and the war is ended! We've won!'

'We've . . . what?' Indsorith had assumed the girl's bluster about news of great import was just the preamble to a boast. Pieces began to materialize through the harsh sunlight, like interesting pebbles glimpsed at the bottom of a swift-moving stream. Too late, she gleaned the girl's plot. 'You . . . you've been working with Hjortt? You had him engage the Cobalts without my permission, and so his victory is yours instead of mine? And now you come to kill me?'

'*His* victory?' Y'Homa brayed with laughter, and began saying something else when Indsorith charged. Being drugged and betrayed came with the regency, but mockery did not. Would-be assassins could try to kill her or try to laugh at her, but they couldn't have both.

Even reeling from the poisoned wine, Indsorith's thrust

would have skewered the startled brat's heart if one of her guards hadn't gotten in the way. The big cleric's sword batted Indsorith's away as a second guard came in with a maul. Indsorith oozed around it and swept the swordsman's leg out from under him, her blade coming back down to bisect Y'Homa's snotty face. But that hammer again, coming in fast, and so she redirected her swipe, chopping off the fingers that wielded it and biting into the weapon's handle. Two more guards surrounded her, Y'Homa drifting back through the contracting ring of bodies, and Indsorith speared one under the chainmail cowl and elbowed another's face before the rest took her down.

To her mortification, neither the blows of their pommels nor the drugged wine were strong enough to kill her outright, and so she suffered the indignity of staring up at Y'Homa as the girl leaned down and tugged the Carnelian Crown away from her throbbing temples.

'Oh, Indsorith,' said Y'Homa dolefully and, instead of donning the crown she'd stolen, the girl slid down onto the slippery floor beside Indsorith, cradling the limp queen's head in her lap. The mad little pope stroked Indsorith's cheeks, but the queen couldn't lift a finger to stop her even had she wanted to . . . and the worst of it was that Y'Homa's touch was actually comforting, maternal. 'I fear you've got it all wrong, as usual. I didn't come to kill you, and Hjortt wasn't victorious. At least not to his primitive thinking. I'm talking about something much, much bigger, something that you're going to be a part of, the same as me. We each have our part to play, and I know that by the end of this we'll·be as close as sisters. Closer!'

Indsorith felt as though she were sliding down a chute, arms and legs bound to her side, and the farther she fell the faster she went, speeding toward the twin pits of Y'Homa's world-spanning black eyes. The Black Pope leaned down closer, and Indsorith saw that the blood on the girl's cheeks hadn't been anointed there, but dripped down from her shining eyes like war paint running in the rain. Her breath smelled of raw meat and vinegar as she tenderly kissed Indsorith's brow, then whispered in her ear.

'All is forgiven, sister. The sun sets on the Day of Becoming, and the Sunken Kingdom rises from the deep. The Fallen Mother has returned, and she awaits our journey to the living paradise she has brought us. The reign of mortals has expired, Indsorith; our duty is complete!'

The words struck the surface of Indsorith's ears but floated there for a time, yet more religious babble without real meaning. What did register was Pope Y'Homa holding up Indsorith's crown to catch the last rays of light, and then casting it toward the edge of the throne room. It skipped several times on the obsidian, then slowed so quickly it seemed it might stop just short of the precipice, or jut out over the edge like a piece in some noble's lawn game. It didn't, though, slipping neatly over the edge and vanishing, the Carnelian Crown tumbling down to the streets of Diadem like the heaviest symbol ever wrought by a mother's metaphor.

And finally, the Black Pope's words made some kind of feverish sense to Indsorith, but her tongue was too sticky to ask the obvious question: if the reign of mortals had truly ended, who would rule the Star in their stead?

CHAPTER

2

Everything was already ruined long before an entire regiment of Imperial soldiers lost their minds and started eating each other alive, but that didn't make the development any more pleasant. Walking through camp to the command tent the morning after the Battle of the Lark's Tongue, Zosia marveled at just how long the Burnished Chain must have been planning this shitshow. It was a quarter century since the devout Fourth Regiment had gone all cannibal crazy during their engagement with the Cobalts, and there was no way the similarities between two such nightmarish scenes were unrelated. What she and her Villains had witnessed all those years ago during the Fall of Windhand must have been a botched ritual, the faintest hint at the catastrophe that might have been ... the catastrophe that had now come to pass. And unlike after Windhand, there would be no debating the cause or results of the Imperials' sudden suicidal madness on the battlefield, because the consequences were as obvious as they were earthshaking: those nutty fucking Chainites had gone and raised the Sunken Kingdom.

Who even *does* that?

Well, they weren't the only ones to call back a power long absent from the Star, and the dearly departed young Efrain

Hjortt had summoned her back with a far lesser sacrifice – only the slaughter of her husband and village. Now she just had to prove that the return of one bad old broad and her mangy devil could be as momentous as an entire kingdom rising from the fucking ocean.

Assuming Choplicker ever came back. In a lifetime of bone-headed plays, telling her devil he could treat himself to any prize he wished had to be the boniest. What fiend doesn't desire its freedom above all else? And after being so meticulous in her wording back in Hoartrap's tent, too, rehearsing the language to make sure Choplicker couldn't slip through a loophole ... only to naively let him off the leash as soon as they were done interrogating the sorcerer. Small wonder she couldn't hack it as the Crimson Queen; with all her brilliant, noble impulses she couldn't even keep hold of a bound devil.

Try as she did to stop herself, she kept glancing down the rows between the frost-laced tents to see if Choplicker was trotting merrily back to his mistress. All she saw were soldiers wearily hauling themselves out to face a morning they wanted no part of. Miserable as most of them appeared, Zosia wryly wondered how they'd look once word got out about the Sunken Kingdom, or the much more immediate issue of a titanic Gate opening up at their doorstep. When the rank and file found out the Burnished Chain had lured the Cobalt Company into completing their ritual for them, the real question wasn't how many of these mercenaries and wide-eyed kids would desert; it was how many would convert. Ji-hyeon would have to put those ones down even harder than the deserters, lest religion spread like dysentery through the camp.

Come to think of it, Zosia supposed the awe-factor of the feat might have been what the church was after all along, something to inspire belief in even the hollowest heart. It would take a lot more than that to sway Zosia, who had met enough so-called gods to not think too highly of any cult, especially the Burnished Chain. She didn't know what else the Black Pope hoped to achieve with her monstrous miracle, what the legendary land's resurrection would mean for the Star, but it seemed pretty damn obvious anybody who wasn't a fundamentalist lunatic had a vested interest in figuring this thing out, and fast.

Well, obvious to some, anyway. A voice from inside rose alongside the guard's salute as he admitted Zosia into the command tent.

'I don't care if they brought back every citizen of Emeritus and every witch queen of the Age of Wonders, our goal remains the same,' said General Ji-hyeon, barely acknowledging Zosia's arrival. Hoartrap, Fennec, and Singh were already seated with kaldi and oatcakes on one side of the board, the general and Captain Choi on the other. Zosia sidled around to sit next to Ji-hyeon, but the girl was either too exhausted to care or actually welcomed the gesture instead of bridling at the imposition.

'Captain Zosia is already aware of the news regarding the Sunken Kingdom of Jex Toth?' Singh was tactful enough to direct the question to her new general instead of her old one as Zosia reached for the kaldi press. It was empty save for resinous dregs. Kind of how Zosia felt this morning, with nary a drop of satisfaction left to be wrung out from her ground-up ambitions.

'Yeah, I heard the whole sad song, though I guess we need to start calling Jex Toth the Unsunk Kingdom now—'scuse me, General, but any chance you've got some more beans, and a cupbearer to work them?' The girl's dark glare shifted to Zosia, her eyes more red than white, but from lack of sleep or weeping? Smart coin was on the former, and Zosia stood back up with a weary groan. 'No, don't get up yourself, I saw where you keep 'em. You all keep talking while I make up another pot.'

'Thank you, Captain, that would be delightful.' Ji-hyeon's voice was about as warm as a brass chamberpot on a midwinter's eve. 'In the future, Hoartrap, you will bring intelligence of such import to me before sharing it with anyone else. I didn't think that needed saying.'

'It doesn't,' said Hoartrap, sounding hurt by the insinuation. 'I planned on telling you first, of course, but Zosia cornered me with her devil and forced my tongue.'

'Is that so?' Ji-hyeon didn't buy it, but Zosia figured she'd be better served in the long run by yanking Hoartrap away from the cart she'd thrown him under. Especially with Choplicker nowhere around to protect her if the old warlock was sour over her forcing his confession.

'Yeah, but it's not as exciting as it sounds. What's this I heard about our goal being unchanged?' Zosia set the kettle on the woodstove and knelt with another groan to root under the kaldi table, shaking jars until she heard the mouthwatering rattle of beans. 'Remind me again what that goal was, because I think some of your captains have different notions of what that is, exactly.'

'I've set all confused parties straight,' said Ji-hyeon crankily. 'We're all here because we want to overthrow the Crimson Empire and the Burnished Chain in the same go, as quickly as possible. Those maniacs sacrificing their own people to dredge up an ancient isle is plenty weird, I'll grant you that, but it doesn't alter our aim.'

'Perhaps it does, and perhaps it doesn't.' Fennec sounded as tired as Zosia felt, though not so much as Ji-hyeon looked. 'But I believe Hoartrap's point was that the whole board has changed, so our strategies must adapt to suit it.'

'No matter how many times I ask you to knock it off, you grizzled old fusspots keep calling this war a game,' Ji-hyeon growled, perhaps failing to notice all the red and blue toy soldiers arranged on the map that covered the command table. 'Let us assume Hoartrap's right—'

'Which he is,' said the sorcerer, unable to resist.

'So fucking what!' Ji-hyeon was showing her age a little, but by Zosia's reckoning such a tantrum was long overdue. 'If the raising of the Sunken Kingdom really was the end of days those mooncalves have been preaching, don't you think we'd have a bit more to go on than your shaky word? Angels cleansing the land, devils set loose, all mortals judged, the iniquitous land of Jex Toth remade as a Chainite paradise – that kind of fairy-tale garbage? And yet here we sit, in defiance of their bullshit and yours.'

'I never alleged their prophecies were anything more than mumbo-jumbo,' Hoartrap said in the easy-breezy tone Zosia had always found so exasperating when she'd been the one in the general's seat. 'But the fact that they've managed to find a kingdom missing for the last half a millennium should at least give you pause, General.'

'Oh, you can bet your bottom devil it's giving *me* pause,' said Ji-hyeon. 'But a pause in our campaign is exactly what the Crimson Queen and the Black Pope want, and exactly what they expect. We flinch now, wait to see what the Sunken Kingdom's return actually means, then the next thing we know my dad will come riding back over the hill with terms of our surrender drafted by the Ninth Regiment.'

'Your dad?' Zosia looked up from her work, amazed that Kang-ho actually had the diamonds in his pouch to come here, now, after he'd sent Singh to kill her back in the Dominions. Unless Ji-hyeon meant her other father, King Jun-hwan . . .

'He's acting as envoy to the Imperial army out of Thao that's breathing down our breastplates.' Ji-hyeon pointed her bandaged hand at Zosia. 'And you don't lay a finger on my dad, not without my say.'

'Kang-ho was here?' Singh asked, looking over her shoulder at Zosia with a cocked eyebrow and an upraised biscuit.

'Was, and might be again,' said Ji-hyeon with a shrug. 'But right now he's sitting in a different command tent, one that belongs to a regiment big enough to slap us down without breaking a sweat. He had the Thaoans all juiced up to join us, to take back Linkensterne together, but after yesterday's massacre of the Fifteenth we'll be lucky if he convinces them to wait another day before laying into us. So that means we move. Fast.'

'In that, my general, we are agreed,' said Singh, 'but first a destination must be fixed, or else my dragoons and I will settle on west and move swiftly homeward, along with the purse you promised us for engaging the Fifteenth Cavalry.'

The mention of the unit that had erased Zosia's home from the Star curdled the fruity aroma of the crushed kaldi beans, making her teeth gnash harder than those of the grinder. The Imperial riders had all been sucked into the new Gate when the Chainite ritual had climaxed, and while she couldn't have hoped to deliver a more grisly end to those murderous bastards, it nevertheless felt strangely unfulfilling, perhaps because she hadn't seen it happen. It wasn't that Zosia wanted revenge, for she'd seen and done enough to know what comes of paying blood with blood, but she *needed* it, for her dead husband, Leib, and for her people, but mostly for herself. She had vowed to personally dispatch every single individual responsible for the massacre of Kypck, but instead the entire Azgarothian cavalry had escaped into death before she could seize them for herself. It left Zosia rudderless, half hoping it would turn out the Black Pope had given the order to attack her village, so that she could go back to pretending it was all somebody else's fault, that she was administering justice to a world in desperate need. Such succor smacked of stale smoke and spoiled meat, but it was better than nothing but the smell of your husband's blood on your own unrecognizably wrinkled hands, a stench that over-powered even the richest kaldi . . .

'*What*?' Ji-hyeon's voice went as high as the kettle, and Zosia looked over to see that Keun-ju had entered the tent and apparently whispered something unpleasant in his mistress's ear. Before, the half-pint general had looked too battered to sit up straight, but now she bolted out of her seat and followed her Virtue Guard out of the tent, addressing her captains as an afterthought. 'Something's come up. Let's reconvene at noon. Everyone out until I get back.'

'If I could have a quick word . . . ' Fennec called, harrying Ji-hyeon out as Zosia stuffed a salty cake in her pocket for the road and looked forlornly at the beautiful, brimming press she had just poured.

'If I told her once I told her . . . well, once, but trust that I made my reservations known,' Hoartrap murmured as he sidled up to Zosia. 'About using one's personal quarters as the command tent, I mean. Leads to all sorts of inconveniences like this. Let me help you with that?'

Singh had walked over as well but now glided past them, spotting her old partners' scheme and warmly addressing the bodyguards waiting for them to clear out. As Singh lay down the diversion, complimenting this one's sword and that one's cuirass, Hoartrap reached out and pocketed the hot kaldi press as smoothly as Kang-ho palming an opal bracelet off an oblivi-ous dancing partner. Wroth as she'd been at Hoartrap for his murdering Sister Portolés, and even worse, lying to her face about it, it brought a welcome smile to Zosia's lips to watch the old gang fall into their easy rhythms, even if it was just to filch the general's bean juice.

Her smile didn't last long. It never did, around Hoartrap.

'And how is Choplicker this morning?' The warlock breathed in her ear as they passed the blithely chatting Singh. 'It's not like him to be so far from your side.'

'He's close enough,' said Zosia, not wanting to give the old witch anything he could use against her. 'Too close, as usual.'

'You think so, do you?' Hoartrap frowned up into the iron clouds of the overcast dawn as they waited for Singh outside the command tent. 'Well, then I won't worry about it. So long as you feel safe, I'm happy.'

'Anyone else talked that way, I might think they were threatening me.' Zosia's heart wasn't racing but it wasn't exactly strolling at a leisurely pace, either ... which was exactly what the warlock wanted, and something he always seemed able to detect. She looked the hulking freak right in his eyes and said, '*Are* you threatening me, Hoartrap?'

'Heaven forefend!' said Hoartrap, the wavering tattoos on his neck going taut as he mugged for her. 'I would never, dearest friend, even after the shabby way you treated me last night.'

'You forced my hand,' said Zosia, willing her eyes not to water as she held his mirthful gaze. 'You don't like it, quit hitting yourself.'

'Ah, that does seem like the sort of game you would refine rather than abandon with age,' said Hoartrap, and to her surprise he flinched first, and fast, as far as their staring matches usually went. 'My concern, however, was sincere – what you did last night was very reckless, and could have gotten both of us in a lot of trouble. I would not advise you to play so loose with any devil, let alone ... *him*.'

'No, I figured you wouldn't,' said Zosia, resisting the urge to look around and see if Choplicker was trotting between the tents, back to her side. 'And so long as you're straight with me from here on out we won't have to worry about that again, will we?'

'I certainly hope not,' said Hoartrap, displaying his unnaturally white teeth as he removed the kaldi press from one cavernous pocket and two stacked bowls from another. 'I misspoke when I said what you did was reckless; it was *stupid*. And I don't just mean using your devil against me, but the offer you made him – to force the truth from me in exchange for his liberty, if I didn't willingly confess. Your wording was such that had I carelessly omitted some minor detail the fiend could have wriggled loose of his bondage through the loophole you left him, and then where would you be?'

Totally vulnerable to the witchery of a vengeful sorcerer, was one of several answers that went without saying . . . assuming Choplicker even left Hoartrap alive after gaining his freedom. Zosia took one of the bowls so Hoartrap could fill them as he went on. 'This is no time to be devil-less, Zosia, and certainly not for such a trifle as the truth.'

'That just proves the difference between us – I put a premium on honesty. I knew you were lying, so I called you on it, and I'll do it again if I have to.'

'You won't,' said Hoartrap, sloshing kaldi into her bowl and then his. 'Not where I am concerned, anyway. I pledge to be honest to a fault from this day forward. And my first hard truth for you is that risking your fiend's freedom in the course of an interrogation simply isn't worth it.'

'And what prize would Choplicker's liberty be worth, huh?' Zosia asked, feeling about as tired as she'd ever been. 'I'm beginning to think anything they can offer ain't worth the deal, seeing's how the rest of the Villains all cashed in their devils but still found their way right back here to where we all started. Excluding you and me, of course.'

'It's a sad commentary on the world, I'll grant you that,' said Hoartrap, raising his bowl in salute. 'If only devils could solve our problems we'd all be happier. Oh, and as part of my new oath to be forthright with you I suppose I ought to set you straight on that last count – I still keep a few minor devils on retainer, but loosed Lungfiller ages back, when I was helping dear little Indsorith solidify her rule. Which means of all of us Villains who took part in that last ritual, you're the only one sensible enough to hold on to your devil. It's almost poetic, given how reluctant you were to bind him in the first place, and now the two of you are inseparable.'

Was Hoartrap fishing? Did he suspect, as Zosia did, that Choplicker's absence from her side might be more than temporary? Did Zosia have a single sloppy fuck left to give? At least one of those questions had an easy answer, and Zosia scalded her tongue on the kaldi as she slurped from the bowl in a fruitless attempt to ward off the morning chill. It was even colder than when she'd stumbled over here from her tent, the Lark's Tongue blowing down the first waft of some bad mountain weather. She was exhausted, every bone and muscle muttering at her from the previous day's workout, but worse yet than the lead in her limbs was the weight on her humors, dragging her down, down, down . . . after everything she'd done to reach this point, there was nothing left for her but another interminable two-step in her endless verbal dance with Hoartrap the fucking Touch, on a morn as cold as her heart, on the ass-end of the Crimson Empire, without even a flea-harried devil to keep her feet warm when she plopped back down in her cot.

'I say, old girl, are you all right?' Hoartrap sounded almost genuinely concerned, and Zosia shook her head, too bushed to keep up with him for another round.

'Haven't been in so long I don't think me and all right would recognize each other anymore.' She poured out the rest of the kaldi and passed him back the bowl. 'I'm trying to work myself up about this return of the Sunken Kingdom shit, Hoartrap, I really am, it's just . . . I don't know anymore. Maybe Ji-hyeon's right, maybe Jex Toth coming back doesn't really change anything. Maybe the Star deserves whatever the Burnished Chain called down on it. Whatever it is, it can't be much worse than whatever red-handed salvation I'd bring them, you know?'

'Please, enough!' Hoartrap tried to pass her back the kaldi bowl. 'I think you might need this to catch all your tears.'

For just a moment there Zosia felt her fire again, ready to pop the ghoulish old fucker in the mouth, but fast as it came it was gone again, and she forced a smile to reward his valiant effort. 'I know, I know, boo frickin' hoo. I just wish . . . I just wish there was someone left to answer for Leib. For Kypck. It's more than I deserve, given how many I've widowed in my day, but still . . .'

'If we didn't wish, we wouldn't be mortal,' said Hoartrap, smiling sadly at his former general. 'And I know firsthand that wishing for what we've held and lost aches longer and deeper than idle dreams for that which we've never had at all.'

'Careful you two don't trip over each other's lips,' said Singh as she joined them in the thoroughfare between the tents, an empty cup at the ready. 'Apologies for the delay, another herald came in while I was chatting with the guards. Either Kang-ho's negotiation skills have waned or he's been spinning another long song for his daughter, because the Thaoans are already moving our way. Did you see which way the general went? I admire the child, so I believe I ought to have a quick counsel with her about the going rate of Raniputri dragoons before the next Imperial regiment gets any closer.'

'I'll find her for you,' said Hoartrap, filling Singh's cup as he gave Zosia a hopeful smile. 'See, we've cooked up another desperate fight against insurmountable odds, just for you! Doesn't that put a little spring in your step?'

'Hardly,' said Zosia, the very prospect of hoisting her hammer again so soon making her want to cry. 'I've said it before, and may not get a chance to say it again: we're fucked.'

'If we have to fight, yes,' said Singh, grimacing on the oversteeped kaldi. 'But for a nominal consulting fee I shall advise the general to do like we did back at Okkultokrati, and line up all the Imperials we captured between us and the Thaoans. If they want us they will have to ride down their own people.'

'Not bad,' said Hoartrap, as Zosia started to drift away from them, wanting an hour or two's peace back in her damp, drafty tent before things heated up again. 'Why don't we do one better, though, and line them up on the far side of that new Gate? It would take some doing but I daresay I could dispel that lingering fog at a dramatic moment, and reveal their fellows on the precipice – if that doesn't give them pause to reevaluate our power nothing will.'

'So long as you leave my name out of it,' said Zosia, waving her farewell. 'Don't let anyone harass me until it's unavoidable.'

'Safe havens keep you at your rest,' Hoartrap called after her, and by way of answer Zosia hawked up a grey clod of phlegm. The chill was rattling around her chest now, and as she trudged between the tents fat white flakes began to drift out of the low clouds overhead. Perfect. Just when a morning couldn't get off to a worse start, too, the weather had to go and match her mood. Run-down and sore as she felt, she would've assumed her period was blowing in on the winter wind, if it hadn't been several years since she was last in her moons. Thank the devils for that small mercy, at least, even if in old age she had become more prone to peeing a little when she sneezed or—

'Heard it was another three hundred Myurans, on top o' all that Azgarothian infantry,' one soldier was telling another as they ate their gruel outside a mess tent, the tired-eyed listener giving Zosia a half-assed salute as she passed. 'Those'd be decent hostages alone, peasants or no, but there was a few real officers to go with the petty ones. And cavalry's always better to do, some of 'em knights, even, and we got a good fifty of them in irons, so that's not just rabble, that's a serious chip of the bargaining persuasion.'

Zosia kept walking for a few numb steps, still ruminating on the petty victories and defeats of age, but then the words sank in. There was no hesitation, no moment of awareness as she stood in the snow, digesting the words. Instead she pivoted on her heel in one easy motion, descending on the two soldiers like an avenging angel in one of the Chain's fairy stories. She knew she was standing too close for comfort, but these humps would never know how much effort it took to keep herself that far back.

'You said cavalry?' she said, low and even. 'Captured yesterday?'

'Ah, um, yes Captain?' said the talker, turning paler than the snow landing on her threadbare blue cloak. 'Sorry, Captain, sorry, wasn't trying to gossip, but Mur here was down in the mouth, talking about all we lost, so I was just trying to be optimistic and—'

'I weren't gossiping at all,' Mur said, the second soldier scowling at his fellow. 'I was eating. Silent, like.'

'Who told you we captured the Fifteenth Cavalry?' It felt like there was a moth in Zosia's chest, fluttering perilously close to a candle . . .

'Nobody?' said the first soldier, but just as Zosia's tiny hope brushed that flame, burning out as fast as it had caught, the woman amended herself. 'That is, I was there when we took 'em in, so no one in particular told me, was just . . . common knowledge, Captain? Took a bit to sort 'em from the infantry, on account of most of 'em bein' thrown from their horses in the fight, and the whole lot of 'em bein' so addlepated from whatever black magic that Hoartrap the Touch called down on 'em they didn't know they names at first, let alone their position, but by the end of the night we'd gotten 'em sussed and – Captain?'

But Captain Zosia had stopped listening, a smile as hungry as any Kutumban leopard's splitting her face as she hastened away, down through the camp toward the prisoners' tents. Not such a bad morning, then, not such a bad morning at all – she might have finally lost her devil for good, but at least one of her wishes had actually come true.

CHAPTER

3

Everything was spectral, spooky, *otherworldly*, even before Princess Ji-hyeon's older sister Yunjin blew out the last candle, leaving the Mistward Balcony lit only by the Fisher's Moon above. It wasn't just the darkness that made Ji-hyeon glad for the comforting warmth of Hyori burrowing into the side of her thin robes, her little sister every bit as excited as she was, and it wasn't just Yunjin's throaty ghost song that made the girls shiver in the summer night. It was the faint cat's cradle of lightning that stretched above the Haunted Sea, like fox fire beckoning to them from across the moonlit waves.

To those who grew up on Hwabun, the ceaseless storm that rumbled to the north was as mundane a part of the landscape as the walnut planks beneath their feet or the blooming goblin vines that hung from the trellis at the back of the balcony ... but on rare nights like this one, when their fathers were away to other Isles and Yunjin let them stay up late so long as they listened to her off-key singing, the distant lights that burned like incense over the grave of the Sunken Kingdom took on a sinister cast. *A lighthouse for lost souls*, was one of Yunjin's better lines, a refrain that made Ji-hyeon squeeze her little sister tighter, the girls giggling together to ward off any wayward spirits that might be creeping up the cliff face beneath them. Everyone knew spirits were repulsed by human laughter, even little princesses all alone in a great big castle.

Except they were never really all alone, not on Hwabun. Besides the house staff who were never out of bell range, there were the three sets of three that minded the Daughters of Hwabun's Virtue, Honor, and Spirit, respectively, and these guards must always be close at hand, too, for one never knew when they might be called upon to defend their charges. If only it were Keun-ju cuddling up beside Ji-hyeon instead of her kid sister, the far-off beacon of long-lost Jex Toth would have had no thrall over her, and she could have turned her thoughts to more pleasant impossibilities than a drowned land populated by the dead and the damned. Of course she knew the likelihood of her gallant Virtue Guard reciprocating her highly inappropriate feelings ranked just under the odds of the Sunken Kingdom returning to the surface, but under a full moon with a little illicit soju tickling her imagination, any dream seemed attainable, if one but wished hard enough ...

If Ji-hyeon could have had one thing in all the world, it would have been time. A lot of it. Enough to sleep, then think, then sleep some more. Hustling uphill through the smoky camp of bedraggled and battered soldiers for whom she was entirely responsible, bandaged hand throbbing and back twinging and chest so tight she felt like she was drowning on the frigid morning air, she recalled how slowly time had seemed to move back on Hwabun, when she couldn't wait for her life to really start, how fervently she had wished she could escape the monotony.

Never, ever, *ever* make a wish, was the moral here, learned, as always, too late to be useful. It was positively chilling how foolish she had been, how childish, and just a short time ago.

Which begged the question of what she would think of her current outlook, if she lived long enough to be able to reflect back on it with a bit of distance. Was this the big secret of adulthood, that grown-ups actually became less and less sure of themselves as time went on? That you just had to charge ahead, knowing that as soon as it was too late to alter your course you'd realize how idiotic it was? Joy. Thank the devils who listen she had half a dozen experienced captains all offering her counsel; now if only she could get more than two of them to agree on something.

'You said a quick word, Fennec, not a slow thousand,' she said, interrupting the torrent of numbers he had been reciting at her ever since they'd left the tent, as though she didn't realize just how badly outnumbered they were by the looming Thaoan regiment. 'Is there a point?'

'The point is something I should prefer to relay to you in private,' said Fennec, his eyes fixed firmly on his general instead of straying to the pair of bodyguards ahead of them or the Virtue Guard who flanked her other side. 'It won't take more than a moment, if Keun-ju wouldn't mind.'

Before Ji-hyeon could protest on his behalf, Keun-ju surprised her by nodding curtly and stalking quickly ahead, her two other bodyguards keeping pace with him. Her lover had taken an even worse beating than she during the battle, and while he'd gotten a bit more sleep than she had the night before, he must be too tired to butt heads with Fennec on such a gloomy morn. Snow began to waft down as they climbed steadily up through the camp, the Lark's Tongue buried in cloud that hovered just over the plateau where Sullen, Zosia, and Hoartrap had captured the Myuran contingent that had sought to flank the Cobalt camp. The prospect of climbing that steep, frost-glazed escarpment filled Ji-hyeon with a knee-weakening melancholy.

'Now then, General . . . ' Fennec spoke quietly, and lowered his voice even more, despite Keun-ju being several tent-lengths ahead of them. 'My concern involves Kang-ho. I really wish you hadn't shared that message regarding Empress Ryuki and her murdered son with your father before allowing him to return to the Thaoans, or had at least kept him in camp a little longer.'

'And I wish I was already sitting on the Crimson Throne,' said Ji-hyeon, 'but we're both too old to waste time on wishes, so say what you mean.'

'What I mean is that your father knows the Empress of the Immaculate Isles has put a price on your head, and said price is the very prize he's coveted ever since we embarked on this quest of ours – control of Linkensterne. The quest that I presume you rejected to his face, yes?'

Ji-hyeon slowed their pace even more, a fresh wave of nausea cresting in her craw as she considered the implication. She had to hand it to Fennec; just when she thought there couldn't possibly be anything more to worry about he turned up something new. 'He's my second father. You really think he'd try to collect a bounty on my head?'

'I think he's a cautious man, and you've stuck him in a dangerous position,' said Fennec, and when she gave him a sharp look he easily deflected it with one of his gloved claws. 'Not entirely on purpose, I know, but it is what it is. If he sides with you, he has nothing but what you give him – he'll have lost his husband, his home, and any hope of claiming Linkensterne, ever. I think he could live with losing two of those, perhaps, but I'm not sure about all three . . . Not when he has an Imperial regiment ready to heed his advice, and a hostile, heedless daughter within easy reach, her beleaguered army no match for his Thaoan stooges. If—'

'Enough.' Ji-hyeon stopped entirely, closing her eyes and

taking deep gulps of cold air. She really might vomit, now that she saw the sum of Fennec's calculations. He was right. If her second father turned on her, he stood to gain everything she had cost him, and then some . . . in fact, it couldn't have worked out better for Kang-ho if he had killed Empress Ryuki's son himself, and framed Ji-hyeon for the crime. He wouldn't just have governorship of Linkensterne, but would also be praised as the hero of the Immaculate Isles, a subject so faithful that he'd sacrifice his own daughter to avenge the murder of Prince Byeong-gu of Othean.

Could he do such a thing?

Could he afford not to? He'd been keen enough to go behind his own husband's back when the stakes were a good bit lower, so what hope did a rebellious daughter have?

'I think our smartest option is to strike first,' Fennec murmured, a soft claw on her shoulder; every time she was reminded of how their trip through the Othean Gate had altered his hands she shuddered and resolved anew to never again risk that particular mode of transport. 'We lure Kang-ho and maybe even Colonel Waits back to our camp with the promise of a parley, and—'

'Enough,' she said again, though *enough* in this case really meant *too much*. Much, much too much. She was on the brink of total collapse, her mind, heart, and guts all swirling around at a frightening pace, and she half shouted the order to her unhinged organs: 'Enough!'

'I'll leave you, then,' said Fennec, squeezing her arm, 'and see you at the tent at noon, as ordered. I won't speak of your second father again unless provoked.'

She nodded, keeping her eyes closed until she was sure he had gone. When she reopened them, she saw several curious soldiers watching her from the mouths of the surrounding tents.

Most of them wore bruises or bandages to go with the cloaks of cobalt sackcloth she'd distributed to the new recruits after she'd broken the Siege of Myura. The youngest was a pug-faced girl who couldn't be more than thirteen years old, her left eye nearly swollen shut. Ji-hyeon knew she should tear off her own cloak of warm blue fox fur and offer it to this girl-soldier in exchange for the thin, ratty one that circled her squat shoulders, knew that was what the legends would expect of such a hero of the people, but it was too damned cold for such acts of valor, and it wouldn't benefit any of them if their general caught ill from the cold. Ji-hyeon saluted them instead, and found her uninjured right hand was shaking as she lifted it to these men and women who had risked their lives for her cause. She could barely meet their eyes as she hurried past them . . .

And caught herself in time, for a welcome change of pace. Unclasping the cobalt cloak, she shuffled back to the girl and handed it over, feeling less like a champion of the downtrodden and more like a thief guiltily returning something she'd stolen. Ji-hyeon felt everyone staring at her, and knew she should probably say something, but also knew if she tried she might burst into tears. The girl looked just as embarrassed as her general, and when she stiffly wrapped the fox fur around her shoulders on top of the threadbare cloak she already wore, Ji-hyeon gave her another salute. This time she was mostly shaking from the cold, at least, and she hustled after Keun-ju, toward yet another grim encounter that she was wholly responsible for.

'Everything all right?' Keun-ju asked quietly and, looking into his concerned eyes, and at the wide scabs forming at the edge of his beaded pink veil, she almost lost it. Her Virtue Guard shouldn't even be out of bed, badly as he was injured, but he'd insisted on serving her in any fashion that he could, and in all the chaotic, sprawling camp he'd managed to find

Sullen for her ... the man she'd almost betrayed his memory to, if fate hadn't reunited them in the nick of time. Keun-ju was too good for her. 'I didn't mean to pry, but I thought I heard Fennec say something about one of your fathers?'

'He's worried about Kang-ho,' said Ji-hyeon, putting on a brave face for her lover and finding his good hand with hers as they resumed their march through the upper edge of camp. 'He thinks the hard talking-to I gave him last night might not've been hard enough, and I'm thinking he's right. I don't give a damn what you say about letting bygones be long gone or whatever, after the way he tried to play Singh against you and Zosia back in the Raniputri Dominions my dearest daddy needs a serious ass-kicking. That fucking *snake*.'

Keun-ju's fingers wriggled a bit in hers, and Ji-hyeon realized she'd been crushing them at the thought of her treacherous second father. What a silly little girl she'd been, letting the old man off the hook so easily even after he'd almost gotten Keun-ju killed! She should have turned the crook over to Zosia, if nothing else – it would have been exactly what he deserved, after all the lies and schemes.

'Did he say anything about how Hwabun fares?' Keun-ju asked as they left the last row of tents and started up the steep escarpment at the camp's rear, the two bodyguards taking the lead. 'About King Jun-hwan and your sisters? I didn't know if after the empress ordered your arrest they were, you know, in any sort of trouble.'

Bless the sentimental boy's ever-loving heart.

'She didn't order my arrest,' Ji-hyeon panted as they slowly climbed the hill, frozen earth crunching underfoot. 'She ordered my murder. And no. Not a word from Hwabun yet, but it's only been a few hours since we heard about the empress's bounty. I'll send my family an owlbat. Soon. Need to ask if the

Sunken Kingdom's really back, anyway, and if so what exactly that means.'

They stomped onward, the snow coming down a lot faster than they were going up. As Ji-hyeon was trying to figure out what message she could possibly send her first father, what words could possibly soften the shame she would inevitably dump over his proud head, a rather nasty thought crossed her mind. She stopped hiking, still halfway up to the plateau.

'Spirits above and beneath, Keun-ju, you think she'll hold them accountable for my crimes? My *supposed* crimes, I mean? If Empress Ryuki knows I'm leading the Cobalts, and she thinks I killed her son, what does that mean for Hwabun? For my first father, my sisters?'

'I . . . I don't dare guess,' said Keun-ju, looking as pale and cold as the snow sticking to his tall, rectangular hat. He wasn't meeting her eyes. 'The truth is they are innocent, but the truth is not always enough, is it?'

'I'm not sure that it ever was, not even once,' said Ji-hyeon, chewing a piece of blue hair that slipped down her cheek as she looked out over the dismal camp and the fogbank beyond that still lingered over what Hoartrap insisted was the biggest Gate on the whole Star. What in all the foreign fucking devils of the Crimson Empire had she gotten herself into with this foolhardy adventure of hers? 'Damn damn damn. Listen, can you head back to the tent and have an owlbat sent over to the Thaoans, to my second father? See if he'll come back, say it's for another parley. I . . . I think I need to ask him how to play this, both with my first father and the empress. I shouldn't have sent him back to the Imperials so soon.'

'Certainly.' Keun-ju gulped. 'First, though, there's, well, can I tell you something? I should have, before, or rather, I never should have—'

'Can it wait?' Dear as her lover was, his constant need to share his feelings could be draining. 'I'm a little busy right now, you know?'

'Of course, yes,' he said, sounding as relieved as a condemned traitor receiving a stay of execution, but paused, clearly warring with himself. 'But I mean, we really, *really* need to talk. I tried to tell you, last night, but you were asleep before I could, and then this morning you were halfway out of the tent before—'

'We can talk soon, I promise.' Ji-hyeon felt like she might pop a tooth, hard as she was holding her smile. 'Now give me a kiss and scoot that cute rump back to the tent.'

You would have thought she'd asked him to come over and smoke a rat turd with her, the way he dragged his feet, and he practically flinched when she flicked up his veil to lay one on him. How fucking peachy. With her second father possibly planning a move on her and their innocent family stuck between the vengeful Empress of the Immaculate Isles and the resurrected Sunken Kingdom, a moody lover was exactly what Ji-hyeon needed to help her relax. Watching him slip and slide back down the scarp, she consoled herself by observing that his rump was indeed as cute as ever, but then her bodyguards called down the all clear and she resumed her miserable slog up the Lark's Tongue to where her next fun-filled encounter waited.

Ji-hyeon crested the escarpment and saw her two bodyguards talking with a small group of snow-blurred figures huddled partway across the narrow plateau. The group looked over at her, and just like that the warmth left her overheated legs and the cold air turned to scalding steam in her lungs. An ambush. Not twelve hours after she discovered there was an enormous bounty on her life and she had strolled right into it, wandering away from camp with only a pair of bodyguards whose faces were hidden beneath the bestial visors Fennec had commissioned for her personal retinue. What a brilliant tactician she was, sending Keun-ju away before she'd made sure the area was secure, and the ribbon on top was her decision to leave Fellwing dozing back in her tent rather than taking the weak devil out into the cold. She deserved exactly what she got.

Which might have been a tumble down the long, steep scarp as she fled back to camp if she hadn't caught ahold of her imagination in time. This wasn't an ambush; it was two of her most trusted bodyguards convening with the band of sentries she had ordered up to the plateau after yesterday's near fiasco with the Myurans sneaking around behind her army. Deep breaths of bracing cold air made things come back into focus, even if doing so also brought back the sting in her crippled hand.

'He's back in the trees there,' said Ankit, the bodyguard tugging up her frost-sticky visor to reveal a face only marginally less hard than that of the steel panther that protected it. 'And so's the sentries' fire, so if you'd like some privacy Qabil and me can watch you from there.'

'Or you can warm yourself at the fire and the rest of us can hang back,' said Qabil, though he didn't sound very hot on the notion himself.

'I don't think warmth is much of an option this morn,' said Ji-hyeon, leading the trek to the smudge of orange she now made out through the thickening snow. The plateau wasn't much more than a bump on the Lark's Tongue's knee, with a dozen wind-twisted pines rising from the rocky earth just before the mountainside resumed its thankless climb. On one edge of the grove, the paltry fire's smoke blurred into the clouds that had snagged on the low trees, and farther back Ji-hyeon saw two dark shapes, one sitting, one lying on a bed of branches.

'They were up here before the sentries, but one of 'em

recognized the barbarian from camp and so they let him stay,' said Ankit. 'Hasn't come over to the fire, just sits there. They're hoping you'll have him come down, or at least encourage him to dispose of the corpse.'

'It's creeping them out,' said Qabil.

'You two can wait by the fire,' Ji-hyeon told them, veering away from it before she brushed the edge of its warm perimeter. If she felt that welcome heat for even a moment she'd be unable to resist it and, after her thoughtlessness of the day before, a cold conversation seemed a light penance.

'Begging your pardon, general, but it's too cold for you to be out here without a cape, at least,' Ankit called after, and when Ji-hyeon turned to give the woman her most annoyed scowl for stating the obvious she saw the guard had already unclasped her blue wool mantle and was holding it out to her general. 'We've got blankets by the fire, so . . . please take it?'

Thanking her bodyguard and wrapping the ice-stiff cape around her, Ji-hyeon stepped under the leaky canopy of the pines, snow melting into her scalp, boots slipping on icy stones, and as she approached them the seated figure rose slowly to his feet. She didn't look at his face, not yet, knowing how hurt he must be, how frustrated he had to be that she hadn't come sooner. Yet another of her many failures – she couldn't have saved the old man, of course, but she could have noticed his absence sooner. *Should* have noticed, damn her selfish heart. That she had come now, to personally pay her respects, was too little too late, yet still more than she could do for most of the soldiers who had laid down their lives for her but a morning before.

Here under the branches, the white flakes had only just begun accumulating on the corpse, the awfulness of his rictus not yet veiled under a winding sheet of snow. Ji-hyeon knelt over the childlike body, because that's what it was, she saw now; these weren't the remains of a grown man, they were those of a puny boy, the sort to be teased for his slight build, his delicate limbs. Without the fire of life, and the man had certainly been all aglow with it, the once-ferocious Horned Wolf reminded Ji-hyeon of nothing so much as the fledgling sparrow she and her sisters had discovered at the base of one of Hwabun's olive trees. All that remained of his old vigor was his snarling mouth, frozen in a mute scream at the deaf heavens . . . or maybe locked in a final guffaw at the same.

'You came,' said Sullen from over her shoulder, and when he said it again his voice broke. 'You came.'

For all the good it would do any of them now. She turned to Sullen, and he swept her up in a great hug, sobbing into her hair, and she squeezed him as hard as she dared without reopening her injuries. Then squeezed him harder, knowing she owed him blood, and more than a little.

Holding each other there in the snow, it was almost warm. But not quite.

CHAPTER

4

Sullen had rooted around some dark corners in his time, for sure, but over the last day and night he'd explored the deepest fathoms a mind could reach while still hoping to someday make it back up to the light. And all that without leaving Grandfather, standing vigil and keeping his eyes pointed at the edge of the plateau, just *daring* a familiar face to come strutting up from the camp. After his fruitless search for Uncle Craven he'd cleared out his and Grandfather's tent, so he'd had some tough jerky to gnaw and syrupy mead to sip over the cold grey afternoon and the brutal black night that followed, but the hunger that constricted his bowel, the thirst that rasped in his craw, these weren't needs that could ever be filled by the food and drink of mortals. What he needed was the provender of devils.

But then he saw Ji-hyeon come haunting through the gnarled pines like the worthiest ancestor a Horned Wolf ever invented to flatter his vanity, a herald of Old Black come to fetch Grandfather to her Meadhall, and Sullen just totally lost his shit, crying into her tangled hair like a newborn whelp questing for its mama's dugs.

Soon as he thought about it that way, though, he got himself back together – like Grandfather always said, Sullen's imagination had a peculiar cast to it. Like Grandfather *had* always said, that was, before he ate a weakbow arrow fired off by a nervous boy. In a song the old wolf would've caught it in his teeth, spat it back at the runt, but . . . but . . .

It went like that for a long while, with Sullen unable to stop his mind from thrashing from one random thought to the next. Through it all Ji-hyeon didn't push him away or tell him to buck up, the way his mother used to when she'd catch him in one of his many unhappy childhood moods. And that, that *ickiness* right there of comparing the girl he was achingly keen on to his mother, if only for a grief-addled instant, was what properly brought Sullen back to some semblance of his senses. The Kid With Ten Thousand Tears needed to get his shit together but quick.

'Hey,' he said, self-consciously breaking off her embrace, and because thinking at all was hard and thinking in Immaculate was even harder, he just shrugged and shook his head.

'I know,' she said, and looking down at her red cheeks and runny nose and bloodshot eyes he figured she probably did. 'How . . . how did it happen?'

Sullen shook his head again, because there was no way to answer without exploding, and to feed the coals of sorrow was the shame that he hadn't even avenged the crime. The twitchy runt who had weakbowed Grandfather had only kept half the oath Sullen had made him swear, because while the old man was laid out here on the plateau just like Sullen had ordered, there had been no sign of the boy himself. That Sullen had sworn to hunt the kid down and murder him slow if he didn't arrive to find both his Grandfather and his murderer awaiting his further inspection hadn't been sufficient enticement – the kid must've hauled the old wolf up here and then hauled arse himself for fear that the crazy barbarian would murder him anyway, out here where there'd be no witnesses.

The truth was when Sullen arrived and found Grandfather's already ripe carcass left in the dirt and his killer fled there'd been a hot moment where he'd almost doubled back to camp to fulfill his threat, but just imagining what'd it be like to murder a boy that young, remembering how close he'd come to doing just that, Sullen gave up that oath in a flood of burning puke. Uncle Craven wasn't the only one who could play loose with his word, and the important thing was that the boy had carried Grandfather up here. That he'd like as not be glancing over his shoulder for the rest of his days would be punishment enough.

'I can't tell you anything that will help, but I'm so, so sorry, and honored he died fighting for me,' Ji-hyeon said softly, bringing Sullen back to the moment, to the dejected girl who sought to comfort him in his blackest hour. Maybe it was just the cold that made her look so tore up, but it was nice to know that at least for a little while now they both seemed in mourning.

Except no, damn Sullen's cast-iron skull, she was far more haggard than he, with bloody rags on one hand and bags under her eyes so heavy he could've used one for a bedroll. She should be dreaming in her tent, not hiking up frozen mountainsides . . .

And just like that he finally figured out the obvious. That kiss she'd given him back in her tent just before her old flame had returned hadn't been an idle smooch, something to pass the time on a chill night. This fierce Immaculate general must really care about him, and even if it wasn't in the same vein that he cared for her, even then it didn't matter, because she carried him somewhere in her heart, just as he carried her in his. Love, was the word for it, but the singers knew not a lot of good words rhymed with that one, whereas a heart, now, that was something you could work with.

And because you never really know anything, not until you've tested it, he looked deep into her dark eyes with what he hoped was his most enticing stare. She was certainly returning his gaze with curiosity, if not outright hope. Up came the arms he'd been awkwardly holding at his sides, landing stiffly on the shoulders he'd so naturally held once upon a time, before Keun-ju came back into her life. This was it. He wasn't going to swoop down like some thieving crow; he was going to glide in light and easy like a crowned eagle, giving her plenty of time to turn her head if those pale pink lips of hers didn't fancy a second meeting with his darker ones . . .

Yes, any moment now Sullen would get up the courage to kiss her.

Annnnnny moment.

Just not this one. Or that one. Or the next few, apparently.

'Do you . . .' Ji-hyeon licked her lips, her eyes darting downward. 'Can I . . . should we bury him? What's, um, your custom?'

Sullen the Romantic, trying to woo a girl next to his freshly dead kinfolk. Rakehell show mercy and grant a poor lost descendant some common decency, or failing that, some common sense. Following her gaze down to Grandfather's yawning mouth, Sullen half fancied the old man was laughing at him. But he only *half* fancied it, mind, having sworn off full fancies for good.

'The custom of the Horned Wolves is to leave 'em where they fall,' he said, willing his eyes not to fill anew as he stared down at Grandfather. Sullen's devil-touched eyes never did as he bid, so why should they start now? 'The thought is their spirit's gone on down to Old Black's Meadhall, or some less worthy place, so the meat and bones and all don't need special treatment. Best their remains nourish this doomed world of their kin, providing food for mortal beasts and the earth itself.'

'Is that what you want?' Ji-hyeon asked in that way she did that made Sullen feel like here at last at the end of the Star he'd found another soul who actually gave a care what he thought, what he felt.

'I . . . I don't know,' Sullen managed through gritted teeth. Each and every time he said that helpless mantra his tongue grew heavier, like a boot picking up mud on a trek through a half-thawed fen. He felt so pathetic, standing here unable to even give an easy answer to her easy question. His hands curled into fists, and he looked down on his grandfather with something a little like wrath but more like embarrassment. 'Story of my devildamned life, Ji-hyeon. I've traveled farther than most any ancestor of mine, or his, and I still don't know a fucking *thing*, do I? Not even how to get rid of my Fa, even after he went and left me. We aren't Horned Wolves no more, so I don't . . . I don't know what to do with 'im. Or what I'll do without 'im. I don't know a blessed thing.'

She stepped closer to him, the distant murmur of her guards and the sentries who had set up camp across the copse barely registering over the thunder of his heart, and like it was the most obvious thing in all the world, she said, 'You knew him best, Sullen, so what do you think he'd want you to do?'

Sullen considered it, then balked at the responsibility of her suggestion. 'I . . . I couldn't really say what he'd—'

'Yes you can,' said Ji-hyeon, her hand slipping into his and tightening round his fingers. 'Stop thinking so much, Sullen, and just tell me. What would he want you to do, if he saw you right here and now?'

'He'd want me to quit whining and start biting.' The words were out before Sullen knew they were even in him, but as soon as he said it he knew it was true. It gave him the chills, like Grandfather had reached in and used his tongue. And the aftertaste of it, like he'd just chipped his tooth biting down on an iron rasp, brought back something Grandfather had told him down in the Cobalt camp. Of course. Leave it to the old man to drop hints and riddles instead of making his wishes plainly known, trusting his starry-eyed grandson would eventually trip over the truth. Squeezing Ji-hyeon's hand in his, Sullen asked, 'You know much about blacksmithing? Weapon making?'

'Less than nothing,' said Ji-hyeon. 'But Keun-ju's a total bore about that stuff, and we've got at least three smiths working back in camp, so I'm sure someone can help. If cremation's what you want, though, we could build him a pyre up here, let him burn like the witch queens of the Age of Wonders. My first father said that was the custom in those times, from Jex Toth all the way across to Emeritus.'

Emeritus. Throughout the freezing night and into the bleak, snowy morning it had felt almost like being home on the Savannahs, Sullen having missed the wintry weather more than he'd known, but at the mention of the place the Outlanders called the Forsaken Empire he felt the chill in a way he imagined the Southern Armers must. Like the cold was something that could thrust its jaws through your cloak and chew you to the marrow. He glanced up into the icy pines, knowing it was foolish but all the same needing to make sure the Faceless Mistress hadn't poked her head down through the dark clouds to steal another kiss.

'Fa's not to burn like some witch, let alone the queen of 'em,' said Sullen, but thinking she might find his plans for Grandfather a touch savage, decided not to go into further detail at the moment. 'I'll come back to camp with you, if you got time to introduce me to one of the smiths, help me get my meaning across if they only speak Crimson or such. Don't need to worry your, um, Keun-ju with anything. It's the sort of last rites only a metalworker can do anyway. I think.'

'I'd be *delighted* to put in an introduction,' said Ji-hyeon, and while it took Sullen a second to figure out why she'd said it like that, he quickly remembered how he'd beat that poor overworked word near to death back in her tent. He met her wry smile with one of his own; not being a native speaker and all she ought to cut him some slack, and besides, everything did seem a mite delightful when he was in her company. Fast as her smile was out it'd fled again, though, as good things tended to do around Sullen. She nodded at Grandfather, and said, 'Does he ... should we carry him back to camp?'

'Nah, not till I talk to your smiths and see if they can do it. Might just be the kind of work the Horned Wolf metal makers do, I dunno. And if some critters gnaw on the old man while I'm gone that's still keeping with custom, so it'll be fine.'

'Is that so?' Ji-hyeon raised her eyebrows in that affected but still dead cute way she did.

'Sure,' said Sullen, mostly able to keep the raw, ravenous grief at bay so long as he kept his attention on her instead of on the dead man at their feet. And now that she'd distracted him from the immediacy of his loss, he could see plain as the snow in her hair or the freckles at her temples that she had her own devils squirming around in her heart, that talking to him about Grandfather had been a reprieve from her own troubles. Normally he'd leave it be, but on a sad, lonely morning like this it seemed important to press her a bit, if only to remind her that she, too, had a friend who saw she was hurting. 'But that's plenty of words about me and Fa, what about yourself? You, uh, you doing okay, Ji-hyeon?'

'Just lost a couple of fingers,' she said, trying to play it non-chalant but sounding panicked as a rumbled rabbit that he'd asked after her. She held up her rag-wrapped left hand so he could inspect it, her right shivering in Sullen's palm, her eyes everywhere but on his. 'Bruised bones and pulled muscles, nothing much else. With the bugs they give you you hardly feel it, so . . . so yeah. I'm fine. Everything's fine. Everything's fine.'

Sullen sucked on the inside of his cheek, ruminating on whether or not to keep pushing her. She finally met his eyes again and smiled, but behind the bared teeth and steady gaze he saw something she'd never before revealed, at least to him: real fear, or something close as kin to that old devil. That settled it, then, because if there was one thing Sullen was an authority on, it was feeling tangled up with all kinds of emotions but not knowing how to express them until someone, usually Grandfather, wrenched them out of him like a ghost bear digging the crunchy innards out of a frozen corpse.

'Ji-hyeon,' Sullen said quietly, 'I been all over the Star, and not once've I ever heard anyone say "everything is fine" unless it definitely wasn't.'

'No?' She was shivering from more than the cold, he saw that now . . .

'No. It's like, what you say when everything is totally, totally fucked, but you don't wanna talk about it for some reason.' As he spoke she bit her lip so hard he worried she'd cut it open, so he rushed to give her an out. 'And I know plenty of times it's better not to talk about something, so I ain't faulting, uh, anybody who said things were fine even when they weren't. I'm just sayin' . . . I'm just saying I've got your back, if there ever *is* anything you wanna talk about, I—'

'*I don't know what to do,*' Ji-hyeon said miserably, and though her bloodshot eyes were as dry as Sullen's mouth she sounded like her heart was breaking, and words came torrenting out in place of tears. 'I . . . I . . . I don't know what to do, and everyone

I talk to tells me something different, and I got so many people killed, and I don't know what I'm doing but I have to pretend I do or it'll all fall apart, and the Empress of the Isles wants me dead, and my second dad might try to sell me to her, and because I listened to Zosia and stayed to fight the Imperials the whole Sunken Kingdom's come back, apparently, and *a fucking Gate* opened up right in the middle of the battlefield, somehow, and ate so many people, it ate Chevaleresse Sasamaso, my bodyguard, my friend, and I don't know how or why or what the shit I'm supposed to do now, Sullen, I don't have any fucking idea, but I don't have any time, either. None. I have to go back and meet my captains and plan our next move and if I don't make the right move Chevaleresse Singh will leave and take her cavalry with her, and there's a whole other Imperial regiment on the horizon, and my dad might talk them into fighting us, and even if he doesn't as soon as word spreads that there's a bounty on me it won't be long before someone else comes to collect, and even if I make it out of this alive my whole family's on Hwabun, stuck between the empress's armies at Othean and whatever the fuck might be crawling around on Jex Toth, and I can't help them, and I don't know what to do. I . . . just . . . don't.'

Sullen let a little quiet roll back in after all that, but not so much that she'd think he didn't have an answer.

'I know exactly what you need to do,' he said without further delay, and the shining hope that bloomed in her eyes confirmed that he'd been right to force the issue. 'Funny that I do, since I never, ever, *ever* know what to do myself without somebody pointing me the way, but for once I'm dead sure I know the best course.'

'Yeah?'

'For sure.' Sullen gestured to the log he'd spent all night brooding on. 'The first thing we do is sit down there, burn one of Fa's beedies, and see if we can't sort through your troubles. Can't promise I'll have all the answers, or even any good ones, but I'll listen till you're done, I'll think hard on it, and we'll see what's what. Sound okay?'

'I . . .' She looked over her shoulder to where her guards waited by the nearby fire. 'I'd like that, but there's no time, there just isn't.'

'If you're too busy at present I'm ready anytime, right, but never forget you're the boss here. You say a lot of folk died on account of you, but I reckon a lot more would've if they didn't have someone clever as you leading 'em. And if more danger's coming, all those people who're looking to you for orders will want their general relaxed and ready, not overburdened with cares because she don't give herself time to take some of it off her shoulders. So if you want to sit a spell and talk, General, that's not just your right, it's maybe your duty? Yeah?'

She hesitated a beat longer, then nodded, and some of that panic had gone out of her eyes, the desperation out of her smile. 'Oh, Sullen . . .'

'Yeah?'

'I think you just said more than you have in the whole time I've known you.' Then she laughed and, though the sound was small and fragile as a wee bird, it felt like he'd caught the biggest game on the Savannahs, because he knew he'd got through to her. They sat down on the icy log and smoked, and he wriggled his arm under her scratchy blue cape and around her shoulder as she sung him everything that was nibbling at her. Or so it seemed, anyway; given how long she spoke, he couldn't imagine she'd left anything out. When she was finished and looked up at him, eager for his promised wisdom, her blue bangs hanging just above her reddish eyes, he nodded slowly, getting his thoughts in order before speaking.

'That's some shit, Ji-hyeon,' he said at last, and let out some of his anxiety over saying the right thing as she laughed again, stronger this time.

'That it is, Sullen,' she said, snuggling closer to him on their too-low, too-cold seat. 'That it is.'

'That ain't exactly helpful,' Sullen thought aloud. 'But if I start telling you what I think you should do, then I'm just another singer muddying the chorus with his version of the song. Don't wanna do that. But I'll tell you this: I can't pretend I've ever had that many riddles rolling around my nut at one time. I doubt most mortals have. So you'll be in for some rough times as you try to figure it all out, and you might make some mistakes . . . but I also know more times than not you'll do the right thing, so long as you trust yourself.'

'Gee, Dad, that sure is helpful,' she said, but before he could decide if that hurt his feelings or not she added, 'but for real, I appreciate your opinion, even when it's silent.'

'Hmmm,' said Sullen, not sure if he'd misunderstood what she was saying. 'What, now?'

'Just telling you everything . . . I feel a little better, I guess, just having said it all out loud,' said Ji-hyeon thoughtfully. 'No, I feel a *lot* better. Ever since yesterday's battle I've felt . . . kind of . . . crazy? And ever since then it's been one thing after another, with my second dad showing up, and then finding out about Empress Ryuki's vendetta, and then Hoartrap coming by to tell me that not only is there a Gate out on the valley but we also somehow resurrected Jex Toth . . . it's been too much, way, way too much. So I felt like there was this hurricane swirling around my head, of all the problems I have, that I *caused*, but there isn't. It's a stack of trouble, no doubt, but that's not the same as a storm – you can take things off a stack, one at a time. That's what I did to get this far, and I can't lose sight of that just because the stack is so much taller. Maybe?'

'Uh, yeah. Definitely.' Ji-hyeon, man – he had no earthly idea how she'd put all that together from his cheesy inspirational speech. 'And as far as all that stuff with a ... a new Gate opening up, and this Sunken Kingdom coming back up out of the sea, right next to your family's isle? *Damn*. That alone would be enough to freeze me up solid, and I don't have the same fondness for my home and kinfolk as you do for yours. Spooky stuff.'

'You told me ... you told me you maybe killed some of your clanfolk?' Ji-hyeon said cautiously. 'Is that why you left Flintland?'

'Not exactly,' said Sullen, hardly wanting to get into all of that now, because there was no way to sing that song without singing of Grandfather, and he didn't think he could manage it at present without his voice cracking. 'I'm gonna be really rude here, Ji-hyeon, and beg your leave to tell my story another time. Is that ... is that okay?'

'Of course!'

'It's just, I can't tell it without ... without ... ' Sullen kept his eyes firmly on her but nodded toward Grandfather's remains. Listening to her wild and harrowing tales of the battle and its aftermath, he'd almost forgotten about what had befallen him that day ... almost, but not quite. 'Without singing it all, though, I will say I know exactly how it feels to have your own blood turn on you, to have ... to have to wonder if a parent you'd lay down your life for wouldn't be a lot happier if you'd just disappear. And still missing her, worrying about her, hoping that nothing bad ever happens to 'er. Or him, I mean. Depending.'

'Oh yeah.' Ji-hyeon looked down, picking at the crust of

frozen blood on her bandaged hand. In a quiet voice, she said, 'If I could trust my second father, or if I knew everyone on Hwabun was safe, then the rest of it wouldn't be so bad. Not at all. But for now . . . ugh.'

Sullen squeezed her closer against him, the bravest Outlander he'd ever met trembling like a bur oak in a gale. She looked up at him and he looked down at her, this blue-haired girl from the Norwest Arm fair as any frost giant's daughter . . . too fair, in fact, like the kind of fair you went just before your skin blackened from frostbite. It was like a spell was broken and, though all he wanted was to tarry a little longer with the woman he adored, Sullen hauled himself up from the log. This sort of morning might be balmy by Frozen Savannah standards, but for a girl from the Immaculate Isles it must be about as comfortable as a dip in a glacier pool.

'We can talk more later, I hope, but for now let's get you somewhere warm,' said Sullen, taking her hand and helping her to her feet. He was careful not to squeeze her fingers lest they snap off like twigs. 'And long as I've kept you up here, get on with your day. There's no rush on introducing me to them blacksmiths – Grandfather's not going nowhere, and I've got two more days till I head out.'

Ji-hyeon had just started smiling again when his words seemed to hit her like the back of a hand. 'Until you what?'

'Oh.' Ever since he'd run into Hoartrap the day before and heard of Uncle Craven's most recent betrayal, Sullen had been thinking of little else but what he was going to do to the coward once he caught up with him. From Ji-hyeon's hurt expression he should've put at least a little thought into telling her he was leaving . . . but then he hadn't let himself hope she'd even much notice, now that her loverboy was back on the scene. 'I swore an oath, Ji-hyeon, to wait three days for that evil uncle of mine to come back to camp on his own. When he doesn't show, I hunt him down.'

'Oh,' said Ji-hyeon quietly, pulling her hand gently away from his. 'But if he returns of his own accord, then the matter will be settled?'

'He won't,' said Sullen, recognizing the naïve hope in her voice from all the years he'd nurtured it in his own heart, only to have his uncle uproot it once and for all. 'Notice I didn't have to ask if he'd come back already? He's run off, same as ever, only this time he won't be able to run far enough. An oath's an oath, though, so he gets another two days' lead on me. Hope he makes the most of them, 'cause once I get started he won't have another day nor night free of pursuit, till his arse is mine or mine is his.'

'Is that so?' Soft as she'd gone there, the Ji-hyeon who stood before him now was the hard-as-a-honey-badger general he'd met when he and Grandfather had first hooked up with the Cobalt Company. Close as they'd been before, she got closer, rolling up on the balls of her feet to get in his face ... or as near as she was able, being so much shorter than he. 'You swore an oath to serve me, did you not? Forgive a simple maid her ignorance, Master Sullen, but abandoning my army to go on a wild goose chase sounds an awful lot like desertion. Did you know the Cobalt Company hangs deserters?'

'I – what?' Sullen couldn't believe it, but looking into her unblinking eyes he supposed he had better. And as unexpectedly cold a play as it was on her part, she was dead right: without thinking it through he'd gone and sworn conflicting oaths, one to serve her without fail, and another to dip out the day after next. By Count Raven's unimpeachable honor, Sullen really needed to start thinking these things through before he ran off at the mouth – what in all the stars above was he supposed to do, now that he'd snared himself in such a bind? She looked like she might take a bite out of him.

'I hate deserters more than anything in all the Star,' Ji-hyeon said, her beedi breath hot on his chin, her bloodshot eyes burning even hotter. 'Which is why I charge you, Sullen of the Frozen Savannahs, with tracking down the deserter Maroto Devilskinner.'

There, at the left corner of her lip, hiding in plain sight, was that devilishly concealed smile of hers, the one that had made him first fall for her. And even as it widened into something obvious, escaping into the snowy morning, he darted forward and trapped it with his lips. There was an instant where he wondered if he was making the biggest mistake of his life, but then she convinced him he hadn't.

It was . . . it just was. Words are good for a great many things, and from the tongues of singers they can fill you with more emotions than there are stars above or devils below, but some things just are, and trying to catch them in simple words is like trying to catch smoke between your fingers. Why bother? It *was*, and that was enough for Sullen, and enough for Ji-hyeon, too, if he had to guess.

Their first kiss back in the tent had been something special, no doubt, but awkward and over before he knew what was even happening. This one, though, was worthy of the songs, the pair taking their time but neither giving up their ground, hands beginning to move, and legs as well, two dancers just starting up as she pushed into him and he backed up to let her take charge, and—

Sullen tripped over Grandfather, flailing backward and inadvertently pulling her down on top of him. The three of them sprawled out on the frosty ground, two blushing mortals and one dead man, and whatever it was before, it certainly wasn't anymore.

'Shit!'

'*Fuck.*'

'Sorry!'

'Nah, my fault.'

'Oh gods, Sullen, are you okay?'

'Yeah, definitely. You?'

'Yeah.'

'. . .'

'. . .'

'Yeah.'

They scrambled up like two necking youths interrupted by an elder, neither looking the other in the face. Sullen knelt to roll Grandfather back onto his bier and Ji-hyeon helped, her cheeks as red as fresh blood on snow. She said, 'We didn't, uh, mess him up, did we? Is he okay?'

'Sure, yeah,' said Sullen, eyeing the rigid corpse. 'Well, other than being dead.'

Which made her laugh a high-pitched nervous laugh, which made him join her, which turned into a guilty wail that stuck in his throat, which led to Ji-hyeon's bodyguards and sentries running up on them to make sure everything was all right.

Which all contributed to Sullen and Ji-hyeon's second kiss being even more awkward than the first. Maybe if he got a third chance with her the Faceless Mistress could put in an appearance. When Sullen Softskull made the scene, anything was possible . . . provided *anything* meant *the worst fucking thing imaginable*. Grandfather would be so proud, if only Sullen hadn't gotten him killed.

'Everything's fine, everything's fine!' Ji-hyeon swatted away her armored guards and gave Sullen a nervous smile. 'Let's, um, head back to camp now. Before you head after your uncle we ought to figure out what to do with your grandfather.'

'Yeah, great,' said Sullen, because right then the prospect of punching Uncle Craven into a pulp was about the only thing that could've cheered him up. That was something else about Ji-hyeon; she always knew just what to say. 'But no hurry, General, I know you're busy, and like I said I'm not leaving for another couple of days.'

'Right, right,' said Ji-hyeon. 'Well, until you can catch him let's hope he's having a shit time of it, wherever he is.'

'Nah,' said Sullen, forcing himself to look back at Grandfather's face once more before turning back to camp with her. 'I hope my uncle's having the best three days of his life, because once I get started the good times are over.'

CHAPTER
5

If it wasn't the best night of Maroto's life, it was bloody near close! Drunk as a lord and twice as rich, with a grand meal and grander company – what Flintland émigré ever dreamed such a dream, let alone lived one? And given the bawdy direction Singh had turned the conversation, it had seemed the perfect time to tell the gang about the nickname he had settled on for his cock.

'Charity?' Kang-ho said, the corners of his face twitching as he tried to hold in a smile. 'I thought that was what the whores were giving you!'

Laughter from the rest of the shit-faced gang crowded around the table. Laughter at Maroto's expense, the obtuse curs!

'Charity begins at home,' said Maroto, having considered the matter at length. 'It's a virtue of the Trve sutras, and requires a gentle heart. All the bright-eyed young consorts try to return my coin after they've felt its warmth, and though it pains me, I accept the refund – charity must be given freely, but when it is, both giver and receiver enjoy its benefit.'

More laughter, especially from Hoartrap, but Maroto could never tell if the big nasty beggar was laughing with him or at him.

Fennec poured another splash of Pertnessian lavajuice into Maroto's horn, the swaying Usban sticking up for him for a change. 'Now, now, I say we applaud our friend's wit, or that of the clever whore who put the notion in his head.'

'A fair point!' said Singh, spitting a red oyster of betel juice into the spittoon at her feet. 'I would have expected something like *clunge-plunger* or *bottom-borer* from the lug.'

Those were both pretty funny suggestions, Maroto had to admit, and he had indeed toyed with more elaborate titles before settling on *Charity*. What he really liked about it, though, was that you could take the word all sorts of ways. It was subtle. He adopted an enigmatic smile as he waved his horn and explained, 'Sometimes less is more, where these things are concerned.'

'I'll bet that's what they tell you!' Zosia hooted, the beautiful jerk punctuating her barb with a vicious punch to Maroto's shoulder, and the rest of them fell apart, braying with laughter. Maroto scowled, but soon joined in – it was either that or beat the lot of them, and he was far too drunk for that. It had been a grand night, celebrating some forgotten success in some nameless bar in some random town when they were all young, dumb, and convinced they'd live forever, or failing that, die together, back to back, standing as one the way only true friends can when the chips are down, the cards are a bust, and the First Dark beckons.

———

Sooner or later, it happens to everyone: instead of waking from a nightmare to find a bright morning, you stir from happy dreams to discover yourself in a stinky pickle.

For Maroto, the horror of consciousness did not merely stem from the confirmation that he had indeed been flung devils knew how far across the Star by the treacherous Hoartrap, that what he'd so desperately hoped were bug visions were in fact memories. That was bad, of course it was, with Purna dying on the ground and Zosia betraying them and all the rest of it, but it was not the sum of Maroto's horror. It wasn't even the fact that he had shifted in his sleep and almost fallen out of the high crotch in the eucalyptus tree where he had lodged himself before passing out, thinking it safer than sleeping on the squelchy jungle floor. No, what made him sorry he'd ever woken up was a tiny thing, not much bigger than the centipedes he used to abuse, and just as sinuous.

The snake had been slithering across the torn front of his padded leather vest when he awoke, but it froze just as he did, his mouth arrested midyawn, its head cocked up as if trying to hypnotize him with its beady gaze. It was close enough to look enormous, a wyrm ready to swallow him whole, but down past its colorful arrow-shaped head he saw its stubby tail barely reached his belt. Might have been a pretty specimen, spied from a safe distance, but this close the scales as bright as dew-slick autumn leaves didn't look so pretty at all ... looked rather fucking deadly, as a matter of fact.

Maroto didn't care for snakes, and not just because their bites were far more likely to kill you or make your parts rot off than give you a buzz. Well, truth be told that pretty much was the long and the short of it; he didn't have any personal vendetta against the horrible, legless, venom-injecting fuckers, but that didn't mean he had to like them. They were just animals, after all, and like most any wild creatures, if you didn't spook them and offered 'em an easy way out they'd take it nine times out of ten instead of throwing down on you ...

Maroto stared at the small viper, and it stared back at him, the only movement a fragrant breeze through the eucalyptus branches. The problem was Maroto really wanted to give it a little breathing room, but that was damned near impossible with it already in his face, and as far as breathing at all went, his chest was starting to go all hot and angry, since he hadn't taken in air since he'd seen the blighter. This, this right here? This was bad.

'Please don't bite my face,' was what he wanted to say but didn't, of course. Everybody knew snakes didn't give a shit what you thought, and even if they did, they didn't have ears. Still, he repeated the prayer in his heart: 'Please, please, *please* don't bite my face.'

At least he was finally alert, waking up to the snake flushing all the lingering grogginess of his epic bug hangover clear out of his system. Now he just had to do something. It was the hardest thing he'd ever done, or at least the hardest thing he'd done since Hoartrap had dumped him on this hellish rock, but Maroto forced his eyes off the snake, taking in his surroundings, trying to see just how bad off he really was.

Worse than he'd imagined, apparently. Woof.

His worthless, comfort-loving flesh had betrayed him. Instead of staying awkwardly – but safely – wedged in the gap where a wide bough broke from the main trunk, in his sleep he'd sprawled backward onto the branch, arms hanging over either side, his crotch barely meeting that of the tree. He didn't dare move his neck, and so couldn't look to see exactly how high off the ground he was, or if there was anything to break his fall, but he seemed to remember climbing quite a distance, so's not to be the low-hanging fruit for any predators. Another brilliant stratagem from the Mighty Maroto. Maybe if he knocked his bare foot against the tree trunk the noise would—

He felt the snake dart up his chest, fast, then stop again, and he slowly brought his eyes back to bear on the menace . . . and almost fell out of the tree when he saw it had come so close it'd gone blurry, reared up in a striking posture, its full attention on his right eye. Old Black, add an extra flagon at the Meadhall, because motionless as most of Maroto had stayed the movement of his eyeball had been enough to draw the serpent in. It probably thought it had found a nice little egg, a suspicion that seemed to be confirmed when the snake slithered forward again, now resting its head on his cheekbone, its neck sliding over his face. He raised his arm so slowly it hurt, not having any other choice but to make a grab for its tail and cast it away. It stopped, and so did he, the viper focusing on Maroto's eye from a scale's breadth away, as though appraising itself in a looking glass.

Maroto felt a tear forming as he waged the hardest staring contest of his life, his eyelid seeming to weigh more than all the steel or gold he'd ever hefted, his corked breath threatening to spill out any moment, his arm rising again but not even close to safe snatching distance . . . and then the snake came in, opening its coral-pink mouth wide to engulf his eyeball.

Maroto almost bit the snake then, doomed a move as it would have been, when the whole branch beneath him shook so hard he almost slipped over the side, and easy as that the snake lost interest in his eye. It was still right fucking there, its tongue flashing in and out, faster than a busy barber's needle through split flesh, and then another tremor rattled the tree, and the snake scooted up and over the rest of Maroto's face. Its lithe body swam along his scalp, bowing down the edge of his raggedy flattop, and finally it was gone down the branch, tickling his hair with the tip of its tail as it fled.

Maroto remained as still as he could, there being no fucking way to guess how far the snake had gone, but he slowly let the burning air out of his nostrils, and then gasped despite his best efforts not to. The air felt so blessed good in his burning lungs as he panted in place, the oily bouquet of the eucalyptus blending with the faint smell of cucumber that marked the snake's passage beside his flaring nostrils. The tree shook again, harder now, and Maroto abruptly sat upright, seizing the wide trunk in both hands as he finally allowed himself to believe he would live longer than however many beats it took for snake toxins to travel from his face to his heart.

The hasty movement made him swoon, as did the realization that he was still fifty feet off the ground. It wouldn't have been a bad climb, but the situation was somewhat complicated by the dozens of other rainbow-scaled serpents swarming the tree, one dropping from above, onto his shoulder, and then skating off his back and out along the branch after its fellow before he could even reassess the supremely dire nature of his circumstances. Must be a nest somewhere in the tree, which he would've thought was the worst fucking luck imaginable, if not for the other rather sizeable factor that occupied a branch slightly beneath his.

It wasn't an ape, that much was blatantly obvious from the thick, pink-skinned canine jaws that crushed a viper into mincemeat as it dropped one into its mouth, but the furry hand that snatched another fleeing snake was decidedly simian. Didn't seem to care much about the snakebites as it bit through this new one, either, so maybe it wouldn't care about Maroto ... but no, that was never how it went with monsters, and as Maroto slowly lifted his legs to get his feet under him, the creature's long, bald snout snapped up in his direction. It was barely ten feet below him and, as it hopped in place on its branch, shrieking at him with all the shrill hostility of alien jungles, the whole tree shook anew from its challenge, dislodging vipers from the higher boughs and causing a vibrant, deadly rain to fall around them.

Some days it just didn't pay to wake up, but what could you do?

Maroto hopped to his feet on the wide branch and matched its wild cry with a roar to be heard across all the seas and mountains that separated him from his vengeance. Unlike the creature's wordless scream, Maroto's battle cry had a name: that of the devil-eating fucker who'd banished him here for some sinister purpose. Or perhaps just for kicks.

'Hoartraaaaaap!'

And then, because the bough it crouched on was just off-center enough from his that there was a ghost-fart-faint chance this might work, Maroto jumped at the monster, leading with both feet. Because, really now: fuck this fucking shit in its fucking face.

Except instead of connecting with its ugly mug, which would have been nice, or feeling its sharp teeth break his ankles as it snatched him out of the air, which, real talk now, seemed a sight more likely, something utterly unexpected happened: it fled. The monster was a grey blur as it swung away through the close-knit trees, but Maroto barely registered this as his bare feet connected with the branch it had vacated.

Twenty-five years ago, he might've landed nimbly on the lower bough and watched the creature disappear through the forest. Twenty-five years is a long time. Even before he felt the agonizing earthquake of his impact jolt up his leg bones, he was falling forward again, arms instinctively spinning out to catch something, anything.

Nothing.

Maroto bellyflopped into a green and brown mosaic of vines and underbrush, then slammed face-first into a rock slab, and his world went black. The worst of it was that the pain set in a few moments later, even though he was obviously dead. This presaged extremely fucking poorly for one's fate after death, as the stinging agony that stretched all the way down from his face to the tops of his feet was only getting started, burning hotter and hotter with every moment . . . or every eternity, who could really tell? He tried to moan, because surely that wasn't asking too much from the afterlife, but as soon as he did, thick, sour sludge filled his mouth. Wasn't that nice, even dead men could taste things, even if it was just fermented arse?

His chest started burning again, and deceased or no, Maroto hoisted his heavy head in a vain reflex to reach good air. As he did, he felt warm fluid stir around him, and dim light crept in at the edge of one of his stinging eyes. Crumbsnatcher coming to taunt his former master in whatever hell he'd landed in, or some worse devil yet? As he wrestled his unhappy flesh out of the mire that weighed down his every limb, silt-thick water cleared his eyes and he saw it was the worst devil of all: the life he had made for himself. He should've known escaping it wouldn't be that easy.

Maroto thrashed about and pushed up through the blood-warm filth, coughing up muck and swamp water as his head broke the surface of the stagnant pool he'd landed in. Standing up was not happening, not even close, but the puddle was no more than a couple of feet deep so he was able to roll over and sit up in the rank stew, painfully gulping up lungfuls of humid air. It had only felt like he'd landed on a rock, then, when he'd actually smacked down into one of the countless stinking, leaf-clogged pools he'd waded through the day before during his aimless trek through the jungle. Oh, how he'd cursed these hollows, which were almost always hidden by foliage until he stumbled in one, sinking to his waist in warm water and warmer mud. The first had claimed his only remaining sandal, the next dozen his good temper, and now one had saved his life. That was the luck of Maroto, right there: why kill yourself outright when you could bruise a few ribs and near drown yourself in a bog because you were too stupid to realize you were still alive?

'That's right, Hoartrap,' he wheezed in his wallow. 'That's fucking right, you punk-arsed hedgewizard. I'm still coming, son, and coming hard.'

Just not right now. The morning sun bounced down through the dripping leaves, and with the odd viper in the underbrush retreating from his presence rather than forcing the issue, things almost seemed all right. Everything could still work out. He'd lived to fight another day.

Except Purna was dead, and try as he did to imagine her smiling and laughing and just fucking living, right, all he could picture was her washed-out face as she bled out on that dismal field.

And worse, far, far worse, Zosia could have saved her, but didn't.

And now he was here, which, wherever the fuck it was, definitely wasn't the Bal Amon jungles or any other wilderness he'd wandered.

So he was very lost and very alone, with nothing to his name, not even a pair of fucking sandals or a broken knife. His still-bandaged but befouled knee was even weaker than the rest of him, and he'd be walking on it for however many weeks or months or years it took for him to catch up to Hoartrap. And even then it wouldn't be the end of it, because obviously someone had put the old warlock up to the job – tight as he and the Touch had been, no way Hoartrap pulled a trick like this for no reason. Finding out who had forced his hand would involve beating it out of the sorcerer, but it had probably been Zosia . . . though there was the faintest possibility that his nephew was behind it, or hells, maybe even his father. Mad as Horned Wolves were, there really was no telling.

Maroto splashed some nasty bog juice in his face to clear his thoughts, but thirsty as he might be he knew better than to drink it. You just don't sip water that smells worse than you do, simple as that.

So he was exiled to devils knew where, for devils knew what reason. His best friend in the Star was dead, cut down by a fucking Chainite and then left to bleed out by Zosia. And for all he knew the rest of his new friends were dead, too – they'd become separated from Din and Hassan during the fight, and because they'd been so late to the battle he hadn't even seen where Choi had ended up in the fray.

The thought of the Immaculate wildborn twisted Maroto's stomach in painful knots – ever since they'd faced down a horned wolf together, he'd felt increasingly drawn to Choi, and had dared to dream that the side-eyed looks he sometimes caught her casting his way might be a sign that the attraction was, for the first time in a very, very long time, more than one-sided. She'd even agreed to come out and party with him and the crew once they'd returned to the Cobalt camp, but what had he done? Oh, not much, just stuck his tongue down Zosia's throat and grabbed her arse to boot ... right in front of Choi. He'd followed up that slick move by having his butt kicked by a justifiably pissed-off Zosia. And after *that*, he'd spent the whole party he'd invited Choi to camped out on a couch, having a bugged-out heart-to-heart with his former flame instead of chatting up the woman he'd spent weeks crushing on.

That was the last time he'd seen Choi, the wildborn beauty standing awkwardly by the bonfire and clearly looking for an opening to approach Maroto, just as Zosia had walked up to him instead. He'd been so intent on making up with his old general that his eyes had passed right over Choi, his worm-addled brain focusing not on the girl who might actually like him but the woman who would never love him. Sure, he'd had a lot on his plate that night, catching up with Zosia only to remember in a horrifying, bug-induced flashback that it was his freeing of Crumbsnatcher with the strung-out wish to be reunited with her that had presumably led to the destruction of her village and the murder of her husband, damn the fates, and the treachery of a devil's wish ... but that didn't change the fact that the last time he'd had the opportunity to see if he could build something new with Choi, even if it was only an agreeable evening, he'd spent the whole fucking time rehashing the past. And now for all he knew, Choi might be as dead as Purna, another casualty of the Battle of the Lark's Tongue ...

But no, the certainties of life were bitter enough without imagining tragedies that might not have been mounted. Choi could have survived the engagement, and good old Diggelby definitely had. There was still hope for some of his friends, and for himself. And hey, he might be as good as shipwrecked on an unknown shore, but at this point he was a full day off the bugs, so he was back on the wagon and no worse for wear. Other than sobering up to find himself in a snake- and monster-infested rain forest, of course, but he just had to keep his head, and remind himself it could be worse.

Which is what it became almost immediately, because really now, when had Maroto's luck ever been anything but blacker than a devil's arsehole?

The thick branches shook overhead, and Maroto looked up in time to see that ugly ape-monster swing back into view. Which was bad.

It hopped down onto a nearby bough, chattering angrily, and from this perspective he saw it was actually smaller than he'd originally thought, no more than four feet tall. Which was good.

It had also brought along its friends, at least a dozen equally grotesque ape-things scampering down from the treetops to surround him, which was so shitty a development as to cancel out the boon of their modest stature. Give Maroto one big beast over a pack of small ones any day. The monsters congregated in the low branches, their long bald snouts chirping and hissing at him with obvious malice. Some of them wore crude vine belts decorated with animal skulls, and the biggest wore a headdress of bright-plumed feathers. All of them brandished cudgels lined with serrated teeth. Which was just great, really.

'This is how you're gonna do me?' Maroto was addressing the gods and ancestors more than these scrub monsters, but when he spoke, the big one with the feathers held up a naked palm and the rest stopped their aggressive chattering. *That* was unexpected. Had it understood him? Maroto held up his open hands in what he hoped was a peaceable gesture and said, 'Hey, uh, I don't want no trouble. You hear what I'm saying? Just passing through.'

The big one dropped down to the muddy bank on the far side of the puddle, then stood up straight on its hairy legs, eyeing Maroto with the air of an unsympathetic witch-hunter. It pointed a long-clawed finger at him and made a series of rather serious-sounding chirps.

'Um . . . yeah, so I don't know what that fool told you,' said Maroto, pointing at the one he'd run off from the tree in the first place. At least Maroto thought it was the same monster, hard to tell them apart in a lineup. He kept his tone friendly. 'But you gotta know it was just a misunderstanding. I'm lost, is all, and figured he was coming at me, otherwise I wouldn't have rolled up on 'im. I'm not a bad guy.'

The first one chattered furiously but was shushed by a wave of the big one's hand. It jutted its gnarly chin out at

Maroto, pointed at its hairless face, and enunciated a quick burst of chirps. Then it pointed at Maroto and cocked its head expectantly.

Well well well. Whatever he'd expected, this wasn't it, but Papa Ruthless hadn't raised no dummies.

'Maroto,' said Maroto, pointing at himself. 'Ma-ro-to. Maroto.'

'Marrrrrrrotto,' the head monster said thoughtfully, rolling the word around its maw. All the other creatures were watching in solemn silence. It pointed at Maroto again and said, 'Marrrrrrrotto?'

'Yeah,' said Maroto, daring to hope he was on the cusp of something absurd but not necessarily fatal. 'Me Maroto, you, uh Chirp-krip-blurp. Yeah.'

'Maroto,' the apish chieftain said, its doglike lips pulling back to show its full array of teeth. They were the same size and shape as the fangs lining the creatures' clubs. 'Maroto, yeah.'

'How 'bout that?' breathed Maroto. He'd never paid much mind to the sagas of the Horned Wolf Clan, but this right here was *exactly* how shit would've gone down for Old Black or Rakehell – he was going to hook up with a savage tribe of beast-people, and a week from now he'd be their champion, leading sorties against some rival gorilla-dog clan. If he could whip a bunch of soft nobles into shape he could damn sure become king of the jungle folk, and the next thing Hoartrap and Zosia knew they'd be looking up to see an army of monsters led by none other than—

'Maroto!' the chief barked, but instead of pointing at Maroto this time its finger was aimed at the first monster he'd encountered. As if transfixed by its boss's gesture, the creature jerked upright to its full stature on its branch, the other ape-things bounding away to other trees. The monster swayed in place for a moment, then started furiously jerking off. Not entirely out of character for simians, if a little uncouth with company present, but then the creature abruptly launched itself out over the pool, and as it plummeted it howled a familiar name:

'Hoartraaaaaaap!'

It hit the water, splashing Maroto and causing the assembled beasties to fall all over themselves, slapping their cudgels and hands against their branches, howling with something rather a lot like laughter. As the monster surfaced and splashed its way to the far shore where its chief waited, it cried out in a whiny voice, 'Maroto, yeah, Maroto, yeah!'

Maroto couldn't believe this shit. While the initial dive had obviously delighted its fellows, this finale brought the house down. In his youth Maroto had worked the shadiest stages on the Star and knew a ham when he saw one – this fucking ape-thing was overplaying his role, but the audience was eating it up. Even the chief was chattering with mirth, slapping its fellow on the back as it emerged from the pool, still croaking, 'Maroto, yeah!'

'He's good,' Maroto called, trying not to let his irritation show. Nothing worse than handing an amateur a role beyond his abilities. 'Real funny. Now, can we skip to the part where you welcome me to the tribe with food and drink? Not snake, though, Maroto don't eat snake. Unless it's cooked, I mean, I'm not too proud to—'

Except the fickle chief was clearly bored with Maroto already, waving him silent the way it had previously quieted the mob. Now it chattered to its people, punctuating its jibber jabber with several instances of *Maroto*. Well, whatever got the message across.

Something hard cracked Maroto in the back of his knee. The bad one, which had already been pissed at him for the big battle at the Lark's Tongue even before he jumped out of a tree and probably tore it all open again. He tumbled forward with a cry, and would have gone down in the shallow pool again if numerous furry hands hadn't locked on to his limbs.

Maroto fought like the born fighter he was, but it was a rigged match. He slung one so hard it went skipping across the puddle but then another slapped him in the plums. He punched that one in its snout and sent the fucker flying only to have two more take its place, their cudgels singing through the air. The whistling clubs were even louder than the cacophony of monsters and, adding insult to injury, the beasts all cried his name as they beat him down. Better than dying nameless, maybe, but not by much.

Maroto's last stand didn't stay standing for long, the damn dirty ape-dogs taking him to the ground and working him over. Credit where due, as soon as he stopped fighting back they stopped clubbing him, and as he drooled blood and groaned they hoisted him up and carried him away into the jungle. Behind him, he saw the chief and the mock-Maroto ape-monster doing an admittedly fleet dance on the bank of the pool, shaking their rumps as they chanted.

'Maroto, yeah, Maroto, yeah!'

After that things got remarkably worse. Even en masse the creatures couldn't keep him high enough off the ground, so his head and arse kept banging into roots and downed trees, and his raggedy armor of padded vest and banded skirt offered scant protection from the errant thorns and nettles. At an opportune moment he tried to wriggle free, but that only resulted in another beating, so he limply allowed himself to be carried steadily between the trees and soggy dells until they abruptly descended into a dark grotto, which soon gave way to a lightless cave. In here the air was closer, hotter, saltier, the chirps of his captors echoing through unseen tunnels and the quasi-human stench of their manky bodies making it hard to think straight, and now when he bonked his noggin it was on damp limestone instead of mossy logs. If all this ended at some weird feast with him as the guest of honor he was still prepared to forgive their shoddy treatment of him as an initiation ritual, but he wasn't holding his breath.

They returned to light after what seemed like forever, and it must've indeed taken ages because by the time his eyes had adjusted and he had taken in the blue sky and green sea they were already swinging him back and forth in their arms, with obvious intent. The devil came alive in Maroto then, because if he was going to die then he'd damn sure take a few of them with him, but it was too late. Before he could get a hand on a hairy wrist or bite into a mouthful of fur they'd released him, and Maroto went sailing off into the heavens.

But only for a few seconds, like. After that, gravity caught him in her steady grasp and the natural balcony of stone that stuck out of the cliff face was lost to sight, and the crowd of dancing, laughing ape-monsters with it. Small mercy, sure, but he'd take what he could get. He was falling so fast he could feel the wind in his eyes, at the back of his throat, and he tried to twist in the air to avoid landing on his stomach like the last time. That he actually had the time to accomplish this small feat did not bode well, no it did not – as his gaze passed from the cliff zipping past to the crashing waves coming up to greet him, he saw he still had a few seconds to consider his imminent demise.

This was the time for a man to contemplate his life, to weigh his victories against his failings, alone with his actions at the end of everything.

Instead he cleared his mind, closed his eyes, and took a very deep breath, because at heart Maroto was an optimist.

Landing in that shallow pool had felt like dropping onto a rock; hard, yes, but also neutral. By contrast, coming down feet-first into the sea bore a remarkable resemblance to having mauls smash into his heels, and as Maroto shot deep into the surf he was sure his legs had snapped like chicken bones in the hands of a hungry glutton. He kept going, deeper and deeper, and as he opened his eyes he found himself boring down farther than the sun's rays. That was symbolism for you, Maroto Devilskinner diving to the places that not even the light could reach. Question was, now that he was slowing fast, was there any way he could come back up to the surface before his lungs gave out?

Only one way to find out. Maroto swam for it, his every limb throbbing, the air in his lungs already forcing itself out with him barely started on his long climb to the surface. He resolutely tried to keep his mind from what aquatic horrors might be swimming up beneath him in the inky depths, but didn't do a good job of it. Something hard brushed into his cheek, and having few other options he bit at it, hoping to dissuade whatever it was from investigating further. His teeth closed on a thin piece of smooth wood or bone, and he locked on to whatever flotsam had drifted his way, because a man with absolutely fucking nothing will cling to anything, at least until he can have a gander at it and judge its worth. It wasn't big, whatever he'd caught, and having more important matters on his mind, he focused on swimming all the harder. Up he went, lungs on the verge of implosion, but relieved to feel his arms and legs obeying him, however reluctantly – he might drown, sure, but if he did he'd do so knowing it was through no fault of his own.

For the second time that morn Maroto felt his raw cheeks plow up into the air and light, and keeping a firm grip on his unknown prize he gasped through his teeth. Looking down at it, he saw that of all the countless treasures of the deep he'd bumped into a pipe, and blowing out through it launched a tiny fountain of sodden tobacco and bilge into the air. Oh, but it was a fine thing to see those high cliffs and know that not only had the ape-monsters failed to kill him, but they'd inadvertently given him a new piece of briar for his trouble . . . but it would be finer still to contemplate his success on dry ground. Scanning about, he saw that the rocky cliffs yielded to a black beach a ways over there and, keeping a soft but steady chomp on the horn stem of the pipe, he started swimming.

It was farther than it had looked, and every stroke he expected some dagger-filled mouth or clammy claw or overly familiar tentacle to close about him, but at long last his numb arm slapped down into sand, and then the other, and then the wave he rode rolled back out, leaving him floundering on the shore. When standing proved too much for his jelly-filled legs he settled for crawling, blind but for the floor of black grains shot with seashells that wavered beneath his weary brow. Onward he went, dragging himself when crawling became too much, until the surf no longer tickled his toes, and he collapsed panting on the warm sand. It felt soft as any pillow against his cheek and, listlessly looking down the shoreline, he saw blue crabs and black gulls and all the other little hints of supper that fill a hungry castaway with hope and joy. Against all odds, against all comers, Maroto had once again saved his own hide, since no god nor devil would do it for him.

'There's something you don't see every day,' said an Immaculate voice from somewhere far away, but then a boot filled his vision and he realized he had his good ear planted in the sand. Another boot rolled him over on his back, which at least let him hear better. Through the blinding sunlight he saw a bedraggled Immaculate woman peering down at him, two more figures silhouetted behind her. He tried to speak but all that came out was another toot of sandy slurry from the end of the pipe he still held between his teeth.

'This just gets better and better!' cried the Immaculate girl, glancing back at her fellows. 'Take a look, this ugly merman's been good enough to bring me back my pipe!'

CHAPTER

6

In Diggelby's posh tent, Purna turned the barrel-shaped bowl around in her hand, inspecting the small letters engraved into the underside of the pipe. An M and a Z, etched into the briar with a sure hand. This was some juicy material history right here: the Cobalt Queen had carved this pipe for her captain a lifetime before Purna had even met Maroto ... before things had gone tits up between the old friends. It was heartbreaking, it was, to think how intently Purna had plotted to bring them back together, to repair those frayed bonds, only to be the catalyst for their final sundering.

'Nothing else?' she asked Digs, not looking up from the rusticated bowl of the pipe.

'Not really,' said Digs, sounding as run-down and heartsick as she was. They sat together on the cot where she'd finally escaped her fevered nightmares, awaking to a world every bit as mad as her dreams. 'A few weapons, a few fewer coins, a few more empty bottles, and enough dirty laundry to launch a stench offensive against half the Empire. I didn't even see a tubāq pouch or tools, just the pipe. Our fearless commander, the greatest hero of our age, left behind less of a legacy than a common thug.'

'One, he's probably not dead so stow the sob song already,' said Purna, sitting up straighter on her mountain of bedding to better boost her noble friend out of the doldrums they both stewed in. 'Two, a legacy's not the same thing as an inheritance, and even if he didn't leave a nest egg for the poor and the needy of the Star he left the world something far more valuable: us. And third, I wasn't asking if there was anything more in his tent, I was asking if you remembered anything else from their fight.'

'Oh,' sniffed Digs, pacing around the tent that had always seemed so cramped to Purna when Hassan and Din were still around to share it. 'No, it's all a blur, like I told you. They were fighting, I was trying to stop you from bleeding to death – without any help whatsoever, I should point out – and to be perfectly frank I may have still been a teensy bit tipsy at the time. After it became obvious Captain Zosia's devil wasn't going to help you I had a heart-to-heart with Prince, and the next thing I knew . . . well, it doesn't bear repeating. Maroto was gone by the time it was all over, and Zosia told me he'd gone off somewhere with Hoartrap. And that's that, simple as sin.'

'Simple's the word,' said Purna, scratching at the bristly poultice they must have adhered to the wound on the back of her thigh. Digs and his talk of Prince being a devil who'd melted into her leg was straight up bug-talk, obviously, but anything that helped him come to terms with losing both his dog and his friends on the battlefield was peachy with her. She still hadn't brought herself to look under the sweaty sheets at what the barbers had done to her, but whoever had fixed her up must've been a butcher, 'cause it felt like there were dozens of threads holding her thigh closed, and they itched *constantly*. Annoying, but not as bad as her tongue, which was so swollen from whatever bugs they'd dosed her with that she couldn't enunciate very well, or close her mouth for more than a minute before she felt orally claustrophobic ... but otherwise she felt fine. No, that wasn't it – she felt better than fine, like she'd just got back from a weeklong retreat to the bath palaces of the Serpent's Circle. 'I tell you what, Digs, soon as the sawbones says I'm good to walk we have a chat with General Ji-hyeon, and Zosia and Hoartrap for that matter. And if the gang isn't back by then, we ask for permission to track down Maroto, Din, and Hassan – pour out a bottle for them if they bought it in the battle, or pour them three if they somehow made it out.'

'Capital,' said Digs, wiping his nose on a gilded sleeve, and Purna congratulated herself on a job well done – until they found out for sure what happened to the others, it fell to her to keep the emotional pasha from falling apart. 'But what's that about a sawbones and you walking places?'

'Don't tell me you got clocked in the ear, too – did the barber who worked on me say how long it'll take for the stitches to come out? And you've chewed a basket or two of creepy-crawlies in your day, so how long do you think it'll be till the swelling goes down? Feels like I've a mouthful of a fat man's undergarments.'

'Stitches?' Digs looked genuinely confused. 'Swelling? Purna, I don't ... I don't think you were listening, there wasn't a barber, it was just Prince. The doctor who looked at you turned grey and said we'd be better off taking you to a priestess.'

'Har har,' said Purna, wiping a snail trail of drool from her chin. 'This is no time for pranks, Diggelby; the sooner I'm able to walk the sooner we can find our friends so—'

Digs had fished out the compact looking glass he used for snorting rails of caterpillar powder and snapped it open in front of her. Purna drew back in horror, then laughed nervously. It sounded an awful lot like a growl. Commanding him to hold

the mirror steady, she leaned in close and tried to remove whatever gross black leech they'd applied to her tongue . . . and after
a few moments of poking and prodding confirmed that her life
had indeed become a waking nightmare, screamed at the top
of her lungs.

They must have heard the howl that came out clear across
camp.

'As I was saying—'

'Silence!' barked Purna, throwing off her blankets and twisting around to look at the back of her thigh. All those Raniputri
meditative stretches her aunt and uncle had forced her to learn
now paid off, because she was clearly able to see there wasn't
any kind of weird poultice stuck to her leg, but a patch of white
fur blooming out of her skin. Not just fur, either: dog fur, the
same exact ivory shade as Prince's. Maroto had been right all
along, then: devils were real, and they could indeed grant the
desperate wish of their master. 'Diggelby. You did this.'

'I saved your life,' Digs said warily, backing away across the
tent as Purna hopped out of bed naked as the day she was born.
There was no soreness in her leg, despite being stabbed the day
before, and she hunkered down to leap at Digs. Seeing what she
was about, he tried to flee the tent, wailing, 'I saved your life!'

Purna took him to the ground in a trice, pressing him
between her arms and legs, and her heavy mouth lolled over
his lace-trimmed throat. His eyes were wide as he stared up at
the monster he'd created, and she went in for the kill. Pasha
Diggelby screamed, but there was no one left to save him.

'Why . . .' he blubbered as Purna dragged her slobbery
tongue up one cheek and down the other, making sure to
wriggle the tip into his nostril on the return path. So she had a
dog tongue now. That was something different. 'Why, Purna,
whyyyyyy?'

'Just my way of saying thanks,' she told him as she relaxed her grip and let him wriggle away from her embrace. Sticking her new tongue out to its full length, she could clearly see it wagging in front of her face even without a mirror. At least she'd be popular with the ladies, and certain gentlemen. Those with a strong stomach.

'You are *so* common,' said Digs, wiping his face and then dusting himself off. 'If you're well enough to . . . to be disgusting, I daresay you're well enough to put on some fucking clothes and help me find our chums.'

'Right-o, old bean,' said Purna, craning her neck to see if she'd been granted a tail or anything else even remotely cool as part of her unorthodox healing. Nothing, and a quick sniff of the stale air of the tent confirmed her nose didn't seem improved from the icky transformation, either. Oh well, it could be worse – at least she wouldn't have to tailor her wardrobe to accommodate her changes. 'Why don't you slip into something more flattering? If we're going to be asking the general for a boon you don't want to show up covered in devil slobber.'

Purna tried to make the most of it on their hunt through the busy camp, but even after donning dark leggings to conceal her furry thigh she couldn't shake the feeling that everyone was staring at her panting tongue. It could be much, much worse – what if Digs's devil had been some sort of bird? Oh, or a crustacean? Ew. Ew ew ew. And besides, wildborn like Choi lived every day of their lives facing the same scrutiny, and often with far more visible . . . mutations? Transitions? Come to think it, she had no idea what the proper term for her condition was. She wasn't wildborn, obviously, because she hadn't come out of her dearly departed mother this way, but it wasn't like there was a term for postpartum wildness. Or was there and she'd just never bothered to learn it? Purna considered herself a thoroughly modern sort of person, progressive, even, and it made her burn with embarrassment to realize that she might have even met individuals who were in the exact same boat she was, only to assume they were different by birth . . . Hold on a tick, for all she knew even Choi wasn't born wildborn, so to speak. Maybe she was the victim of the same sort of unfortunate tragedy as Purna!

Victims. Unfortunate tragedies. That was the exact sort of shitty language Purna had always railed against when discussing the wildborn, back before she'd been cursed with a devil dog's tongue.

Cursed? There she went again! Or was it okay to think about things this way, since she was now a part of the unjustly maligned group? Sort of? Maybe? Urgh!

'She *what*?'

General Ji-hyeon's voice carried from a few tents away, and exchanging silly faces she and Digs broke into a trot – from her hostile tone it seemed unlikely the general would remain in the same spot for long. They came around the side of the command tent fast enough that the armed guards had their steel half-drawn before Ji-hyeon noticed the new arrivals and waved down her bodyguards. Behind the four intimidating goons, the general was huddled in with a weird trio: her veiled boy toy, Maroto's sour turd of a nephew, and Hoartrap the Touch. Not a one seemed remotely interested in welcoming Purna and Digs to their private party, but Purna had crashed far more exclusive bashes in her day.

'Top of the morning, General, Digs and I were just—'

'Not now,' said the general, turning back to her hushed meeting. Two of the bodyguards deliberately placed themselves in Purna's way.

'Come on,' Digs hissed, tugging on the vermilion sleeve of

Purna's doublet, but there wasn't a beggar's chance she was being turned down so coldly, not after sacrificing her very humanity for this woman.

'Yes, now, if you please,' Purna said in her most imperious voice, though the effect was somewhat compromised by her need to bob her head around to see the general past this great armored oaf. 'Diggelby and I are on a *desperate* errand, a matter of life and bloody *death*, in *your* name, but we can't get on with it until we've reported to our general, can we?'

The general slowly turned away from her conversation, the camp seeming rather quiet all of a sudden, save for the creaking of the bodyguard's armor as she looked over her shoulder, presumably waiting on the order to dent Purna's brainpan. Hoartrap sniggered and, with the solemn silence good and bally well dashed, the general rubbed at her eyes with her one good hand, the other looking a proper fright of bloody gauze.

'I'll grant you one breath's worth of blather,' said General Ji-hyeon. 'Come on, be quick about it.'

'With the immediate Imperial conflict resolved, Pasha Diggelby and myself seek permission to break ranks and launch a private search party for Maroto, Din, and Hassan,' said Purna, and though she'd already exhausted her breath, added for the sake of clarity: 'You know, our people?'

'Assuming they haven't turned up yet?' said Diggelby hopefully.

'They haven't, and no you may not,' said the general, already turning back to her cabinet. 'Your request is denied, so please stay out from underfoot until you're called upon.'

'Please?' Purna said it in the syrupy voice her uncle had made her practice until her throat felt like she'd been gargling glass dust, the tone reserved for the most intractable of traders. 'You won't even miss us, fast as we'll find them!'

'She's got a point about not being missed,' Hoartrap pro-claimed, but that Sullen barbarian was giving Purna a look that he probably thought was hard but just made him seem cowish and confused.

The general gave Purna and Digs a scowl that made up for Sullen's lack of ferocity, and then some. 'Do you have any idea where Maroto's gotten himself? No? Then piss the fuck off until I have a real use for you.'

'I know where Maroto's gone,' said Digs, crossing his arms petulantly. About time the pasha's pride responded to the gen-eral's slight! 'I mean, it's so obvious, isn't it?'

Good one, Digs! Of course, stalling for time is dandy, but it helps to have an end goal, or at least an exit strategy. As soon as the general demanded that Digs elucidate on the obvious, Purna knew both their tails were good and kippered: 'Where is he, fop?'

'He's headed back to Diadem,' said Digs smugly. 'I mean, wouldn't you?'

'Explain yourself!' the general shouted, enraged by Diggelby's admittedly vexing cadence.

'Well, I mean, because of his oath to the queen?' Oh no. Oh no no no no no, Diggelby, that fucking nincompoop, he wouldn't spill the beans, not after Purna had made him, Din, and Hassan all promise to keep it under their hats before letting them in on Maroto's big secret . . . 'After he spent the whole fight breaking his back trying *not* to hit any of the Imperials, I'm sure he's realized it's just not a sustainable lifestyle. So he must be on his way to the capital to see if old Indsorith will release him from his oath – it's the same reason we've come here, isn't it? To see if you'll release us from the pledge we made to stick with the Company and all that rot? We noble personages take our oaths dreadfully seriously, and unless we're released then—'

'Hoartrap, see that a hundred swords are sent after her immediately,' said the general, though her eyes were nailed firm onto Digs's dumb ass. 'Make sure they're young recruits, no old salts who might support her over me if it comes to that. And tell them to hang back until I arrive. As for you two, carry on as we discussed, and play nice.'

'We . . . what now?' asked Purna as Hoartrap bounded away with his ever-distressing ease.

'Not you, them,' said the general, confounding the matter further by still keeping her gaze on Digs, and by extension Purna. As Sullen and the Immaculate lad took their cue and hustled off in the other direction, the general advanced on the handsome and talented but decidedly unlucky Ugrakari girl and her blabbermouth friend. Now Purna knew why the general hadn't batted an eyelash at the sight of her newly canine tongue – with a smile that big and mean, Ji-hyeon must have something of the wolf in her as well. 'As for you two, I have an errand of the utmost urgency, just as soon as you tell me more about this oath Maroto swore to the Crimson Queen.'

'There's Zosia!' said Digs, and they broke into a trot to reach her before she entered the still-smoky battlefield. The silver fox in question was marching away from the stockade, a long line of manacled prisoners dragging their feet behind her. 'How long do we have to stall her for?'

'I don't know, Diggelby, after that display back there I just assumed you had all the answers,' said Purna, painfully nipping her tongue in the process. Jogging and talking was something that she'd have to get used to, with this great big lolling cut of roast beef hanging out of her mouth.

'I said I was sorry,' huffed Digs. 'I just assumed she already knew. You said he told you and Choi about it, and she's in thick with the general, so obviously—'

'So obviously you thought everyone was as free with their tongues as you are,' said Purna, though he did raise an intriguing point – it was nice to know Choi could keep a secret, even from her beloved general. Not that Purna had seen the wildborn since before the battle; for all she knew she might be just as lost as . . . well, it didn't bear thinking on. With Maroto missing and Hassan and Din's prospects even dimmer, she had too many lumps in her throat as it was, and too big of a tongue to easily swallow them.

'You don't think she'll really do it?' said Digs. 'If we can't delay Zosia until the general shows up, I mean, she can't possibly hold *us* responsible for what happens.'

'Keep telling yourself that,' said Purna as they stumbled their way over the uprooted palisades at the edge of camp. 'I certainly don't intend to find out. Besides, if we keep Zosia busy like the general ordered she won't very well be able to refuse our request, will she? Just you wait and see, we'll be relieved of duty by the afternoon.'

'One way or the other, I wager you're correct,' said Digs as they finally caught up to the gloomy caravan. To Purna it seemed like the few dozen Cobalt soldiers who flanked the procession of prisoners were all gawping at her as she slowed to a walk beside Cold Cobalt (who really ought to be called Hot Cobalt, fit as she looked).

'Top of the morning to you, Captain Zosia,' Purna called, and shivered with relief when the older woman didn't flinch upon seeing the mutant who accosted her.

'And to you two as well,' said Zosia, not slackening her stride but seeming amiable enough to company that Purna fell in beside her. The older woman was as radiant and cheerful as the morning was cold and gloomy, the snow serving as confetti for her personal parade. 'Glad to see your recovery's been so speedy, Tapai Purna. Any ill effects from your diabolical salvation?'

'Just the urge to plant my nose in appealing asses,' Purna said lightly, wondering if a little flirting might slow Zosia's pace.

'So nothing new, in other words,' said Digs, looking back at the dour chain of captives. 'Taking the Imperials on a constitutional, Captain?'

'Something like that,' said Zosia. 'I'm taking them on a sightseeing expedition to the new Gate.'

'We'd heard about that,' said Purna, dragging her feet but then picking up her heels again when Zosia kept moving at the same brisk clip. 'Just opened up out there, huh?'

'Like something out of a bad bug dream,' said Digs with a shudder.

'One mortal's nightmare is another's fantasy,' said Zosia, with eerie intensity. Between her fierce expression and wild, silvery hair she looked like a witch who would break into a cackle at the drop of a silly-looking hat.

'Yes, well, be that as it may ...' said Digs, but couldn't come up with anything more to add. Zosia had him good and spooked, no doubt about it.

'Before we go any further, Captain Zosia, I wonder if I might chew your ear a bit?' Purna tried not to let her anxiety show, even though they'd reached the edge of the stale cloud that lingered over the Lark's Tongue valley. This plume had already seemed ill-omened enough before Purna had been informed that a Gate had opened up beneath it. She remembered how abruptly the fighting had broken off the day before, several demented Imperial soldiers sucked into the earth before her very eyes ... Except they hadn't gone into the earth, had they? No, they'd gone someplace far, far worse, into the First Dark itself according to Ugrakari lore, and to date neither Hassan nor Din had emerged from this doleful fume. And while he'd obviously not been pulled into the Gate when it had opened, Maroto hadn't come out of the smoke, either. It was the baddest business this side of Diadem, no doubt about it.

'You were saying?' said Zosia, and Purna shook her head, as though that were all it would take to dispel the looming fogbank.

'I was, wasn't I?' Purna said, hoping her grotesque tongue wasn't spoiling her winning smile. 'But let's take a breather so we can talk properly without a mouthful of poison gas, shall we?'

'It's not poisonous, and you can either talk while I walk or you can wait for me to finish my business,' said Zosia, stepping into the miasma. Lazy tendrils of musty smoke caressed her throat and limbs as though they had a life of their own, and smiling over her shoulder at Purna, Cold Cobalt looked as though she welcomed the attention. 'Come on, girl, it's not every day you get to see something like this.'

The captain had a point. Shrugging at the reluctant Digs, Purna followed Zosia into the cloud, the clanking of chains following them through the mist as though the Azgarothian prisoners who wore them were already ghosts. Considering this woman had by all accounts cheated death and devils, slain kings and gods, how the deuce had Ji-hyeon reasonably expected a couple of Maroto's Moochers to stall her? Really, now.

CHAPTER

7

After the absolute worst day of Domingo Hjortt's entire life concluded with a visit from his old nemesis Cobalt Zosia, he lay awake all night, staring at the shadows on the ceiling of the tent until the lantern she'd left him had burned out, and then he stared some more. His sister-in-law, Lupitera, had given her nephew an Usban shadow box and puppets for one of his early birthdays, but Domingo had not stuck around to condone the frivolous gift with his presence. He wondered if Efrain had noticed his father's absence, if his delight in a new toy had been undercut by Domingo's disapproval. He hoped not. He hoped Efrain had laughed and laughed, never taking his stern father too seriously. Oh, how he hoped that was true ... but he also hoped the Fifteenth had somehow survived the engagement, had overcome the Chainite witchcraft, that this was all a dream and Captain Shea would wake him and they could get on with plotting the downfall of the Cobalt Company. Why not call hope what it was, a daydream that would never come true, the last refuge of the failure?

Shea. What was her first name? Had he forgotten, or had he never even asked? Most of the captains had failed to make much of an impression one way or the other, but Shea had showed genuine potential, there at the end. He'd pushed her, because good colonels must be as parents to their officers, strict and vigilant and always ready to offer correction, but that didn't mean he hadn't warmed to her company, damn it. Before Zosia had left the tent she had offered her broken adversary anything, but other than having the chains removed from his wrists and ankles all he had asked her to bring him was Captain Shea, if she was among the Fifteenth's few survivors. She had not returned, and now, with the dull blue dawn seeping in around the edges of the tent, Domingo had to accept that his most promising officer must be as dead as his only child. It had always been too late for Efrain, even before the boy got himself killed in Kypck, but Shea might have been something, someday, if only she'd had a different colonel, one who held fast to the principles they both shared instead of making compromises, a commanding officer who fought with nobility instead of stooping to Chainite trickery . . . yes, Domingo had received exactly what he'd deserved, but poor, unpolished Shea certainly hadn't, nor had the thousands of other Azgarothians he had killed with his spite-blinded actions.

That was the worst of it, then: the truth. It wasn't his broken arm or broken leg or cracked ribs that kept him awake, nor was it the fresh slash on his face that the Cobalt surgeon had stitched with deliberate slowness. It wasn't even the aching hatred that pulsed through him at seeing his archenemy Cold Zosia, alive and hale and, cruelest of all, looking down at him with pity. The worst was knowing that while she had indeed murdered his son she hadn't harmed a single soldier in the Fifteenth – their trusted colonel was solely responsible for their unnatural end. Pope Y'Homa had set the Burnished Chain's plot into motion, true, and the duly departed Brother Wan had helped give it that final push, but even nervous young Shea had known that a good commander takes responsibility for her failings, lest order fray into chaos through the caustic application of excuses and explanations, and there were no two ways about it: Colonel Domingo Hjortt, Baron of Cockspar, had poisoned his entire regiment, forcing them to be sacrifices in an obscene ritual. And all in the name of avenging a son he'd never cared for, a reckless lad who by all accounts deserved the death he'd received at the hands of Cold Cobalt.

A general must survey the whole field before beginning to form an opinion, and now that he'd had a gander it was small wonder that Domingo couldn't find rest. It would be a miracle if he ever slept again. But such hyperbole was better suited for the boards of a playhouse than a lumpy bed and, quite without his noticing, the thrum of the waking camp transformed into a lullaby that rocked Domingo off to a dreamless slumber, the sort from which he never wished to awake—

'Colonel Hjortt!'

Like any veteran startled awake by the invocation of his rank and name, Domingo tried to snap upright with a smart salute. It was difficult to say which parts of him hurt worse, the ones that had obeyed his instinctive movements or those that were physically incapable. Eyes watering through the pain, Domingo craned his neck up and let the rest of his aching body relax – he was a prisoner of war in a rebel camp, and there was nobody here whose authority he respected enough to salute anyway. In the dimness of the tent he squinted up at the girl who had hailed him, then noticed the figure behind her and slumped back on his pillow. He guessed the girl must be the Immaculate general whom Zosia had confirmed was leading the Cobalts, and Domingo was positive that the horned woman behind the girl was the same witchborn scout who had helped Maroto summon the monstrous wolves into the Fifteenth's camp back in the mountains.

'At your service, ladies,' said Domingo, closing his eyes and savoring the fleeting numbness of waking that must soon give way to sharp pain once more. 'Do I suppose correctly that you're the general our mutual friend spoke of? Ji-hwan?'

'I am General Ji-*hyeon* Bong,' said the girl, 'and may I inquire after the identity of this mutual friend? Might she be the same captain who removed your manacles?'

'I was attempting to be clever,' said Domingo, opening his eyes and staring up at this teenage punk his Fifteenth could have crushed into pulp without any help whatsoever from the Ninth out of Myura, to say fuck-all of the Chain. He could only tell her once about how he'd dispatched her fiancé up by the border and then sent the prince's head to the Empress of the Isles, and so decided to delay that pleasure a little longer; it didn't do to get off on the wrong foot with one's captors, as Prince Byeong-gu could have attested, if only Domingo hadn't decapitated him. 'Blue Zosia is no friend of mine, but yes, she is the first of your army to treat with me.'

'Treat with you, did she?' asked the girl, and as his eyes adjusted Domingo was delighted to see one of hers was dark and swollen, and her left hand was swaddled in rags. His troopers must have pushed all the way into the enemy command before ... before the Chain's deviltry betrayed them. 'What terms did she offer you, Colonel, and did you accept them?'

'Again, my clumsy stabs at humor go wide of the mark. Forgive me, General Ji-hyeon, but I have always been a sober and direct sort of man, and while I've recently come to appreciate the comedic appeal of the absurd, I appear to be doing a piss-poor job of it. I was not being literal when I said a *mutual friend* told me of your personage and that Zosia came to *treat with me*, I should have said my *hated* fucking enemy came to rub my nose in the fact that I allowed my soldiers to become burnt offerings for the Chain's black magic. Sorry, sorry, there I go again – by black magic I of course refer to the alleged return of the Sunken Kingdom, and the materialization of a Gate upon our innocent battlefield. Pray forgive a weary soldier his crude speech.'

He had only just met her, but Domingo already knew this sprat well enough to recognize the fury boiling up her throat to inflame her cheeks. The witchborn beside her must have seen it, too, but didn't speak or intervene, letting the general come to it in her own time. After a long breath, the color began to fade from the girl's face, and in a dangerously level tone she said, 'When did Captain Zosia tell you all of that, exactly?'

'Last night sometime, I couldn't say when,' said Domingo, relishing the second flush of wrath clouding the general's face – she must be greener than an underripe avocado! Never one to leave a hilt just sitting there when it could be given a good twist, he added, 'I'm sure you can find out the approximate time from the guards who were minding my tent last night; surely whoever admitted her without your consent would recall the hour of her visit.'

The general's nostrils were flaring like a bull's, and she seemed on the cusp of a genuine tantrum when the witchborn leaned over and whispered something in her ear, keeping her devilish red eyes on Domingo the whole time. One of the anathema's black horns was broken off midway, and he wondered if that had happened during one of her engagements with the Fifteenth. He certainly hoped so. Whatever the creature had said to her mistress had calmed her, or at least reminded her that there was something more pressing to attend to. Closing her eyes and taking a deep breath, General Ji-hyeon asked him a ridiculous question, the exact sort of thing to get a cheeky bastard's lip split before yesterday's events had thrown what was once an absolute fact into absolute doubt:

'Colonel Hjortt, do you value the lives of your soldiers?'

'Yes,' said Domingo without hesitation, because he knew that if he considered it for more than a moment he might never be able to answer honestly. 'Of course.'

'And that's why you sacrificed most of them? Because you're a born-again Chainite who thinks that real lives and the real world are less important than the promise of what comes after?'

'I was tricked,' Domingo growled. 'I made the mistake of trusting the Chain, yes, but if I'd known what they were actually planning I would've skinned them all alive before letting them hurt a single flag-bearer or drummer girl. They said they had a weapon, a weapon that would help us ... and because I believed them, most of my people are dead, aren't they? Or worse. And all because I ... because I let my hatred get the better of me.'

'Hoartrap was right about you, then,' said the general, giving Domingo a cold shiver – so the Witch of Meshugg was working with her, too. 'He couldn't believe you'd sacrifice your regiment for any reason, let alone to aid the Burnished Chain.'

'For once the Touch speaks true. To paraphrase Lord Bleak, the Fifteenth are my children in all but blood, and I would shed my own for them as readily as they would for me.'

He expected something snide to come out of her, something along the lines of the reproachful thoughts that plagued his heart as soon as the hypocritical words left his mouth, but instead she said, 'Good. It's a strange and frightening thing, isn't it, to be responsible for the lives of people who would never guess that you don't know what you're doing.'

He might have thought it a dig at his command if not for

the melancholic note in her voice, the way she looked at the foot of his bed instead of his face. This was plain old green officer whinging, and didn't the prats always make it sound like poetry? Domingo had never found command strange, it was the most natural thing in the world, and he'd certainly never found it frightening! Though maybe he should have, in retrospect . . .

'We don't have time to bandy clever words like two foes in a song,' said Ji-hyeon, looking him full in the eyes again. 'You're my prisoner, and I'll exploit that to stave off an encounter with the Thaoan regiment if I can. But there's something more, something important that only you and I can work out, but if we do it'll have to happen fast.'

'So get on with it,' said Domingo, all this talk of matters military making him feel more like himself.

'You will be far more useful to the Cobalts cooperative than reluctant, and so I have a proposal for you,' said the general carefully. 'If you agree to work with me, to offer your counsel on Imperial tactics and to play the model prisoner, then I swear every soldier we capture will be spared and, what's more, offered the opportunity to serve in my army as we march upon Samoth, on Diadem itself.'

Domingo would have laughed in her face if he could have, but he was no actor and her ridiculous terms transcended the amusingly ridiculous and entered the domain of the outright insulting.

'And if I don't capitulate? You won't last long as a leader of mortals if you start executing prisoners of war,' he told her. 'Certain customs are sacrosanct by all peoples the Star over. Not even your Cobalt mentor would sink to such barbarism a second time – after the Battle of Eyvind she strung up all the captured Imperials from the trees, but that evil act turned half of her own allies against her.'

'Ah,' said the girl, 'but she's the one who's going to murder your soldiers if I don't stop her. She holds the Fifteenth Cavalry accountable for past crimes against her, and intends to execute them this very day.'

'The Cavalry?' The unit his son had led into that Kutumban village, the unit that had followed Efrain's orders to raze the whole bloody town . . .

'What's left of them, anyway,' said the general, rather smugly for a puffed-up little warlord he would have mashed under his heel if he'd rebuffed Brother Wan and fought the Cobalts fair. 'Maybe thirty in all? It's not much of a valuable unit anymore, I'll grant you that, but I didn't come here to broker a deal.'

'No?'

'I came here to tell you what's happening, nothing more. Zosia holds those soldiers of yours responsible, and unless I intervene they'll all die. If I do step in, it will raise the bile in my best captain – I can't imagine she'll take my order graciously. So you can either ferment in here until I ransom you back to Azgaroth, knowing you as good as killed another three dozen of your troops, or you can consent to my reasonable terms.'

Domingo considered it. 'You expect me to believe you'd risk the wrath of the Cobalt Queen to have a more agreeable prisoner in your camp?'

'These days she's not the queen of anything, she's just one of many captains,' said the general. 'And I'm not just asking you to be agreeable, I'm asking you to help me in my campaign.'

'Your campaign against Queen Indsorith, you mean?' Domingo could barely believe his ears – this girl was either mad or water-brained. Possibly both.

'Diadem is my target, but we both know the Crimson Queen rules in name alone,' said General Ji-hyeon, and for the first time he saw some real iron flashing in her eyes. And more than iron, something every bit as hard – the truth, or at least what she believed to be the truth. 'I bear Indsorith no grudge, but she is either unable or unwilling to keep the Burnished Chain in check, and since she cannot then I will. Or do you think the Star would be better served with the Black Pope's word as law? Especially since you seem to be personally responsible for raising the Sunken fucking Kingdom, I'd have thought the repercussions of your actions might have occurred to you. With Chainite prophecies coming to pass, do you think the church will be content with what they have, or do you think they'll expand their control across the Empire, across the Star? You marched against me to protect your homeland, but now Azgaroth lies at the mercy of fanatics, as does every other Imperial province – how long do you imagine they'll let you keep what little autonomy you have left? How long until this world becomes a living hell for everyone who doesn't bow before the Fallen Mother?'

Damned if this rogue princess wasn't keener than she looked. Crazier by half, too, if she thought she had any hope of success, but crazy wasn't the same as stupid. If only Efrain had been a little more of the former than the latter he'd still be alive. Still, Domingo was a Colonel of the Empire and Baron of Cockspar, and those things still meant something. Clearing his throat, he said, 'You're even greener than you look, if you think—'

'Fine,' she said, and just like that she was done with him. 'I won't waste any more of your valuable time, Colonel Hjortt. If you'll excuse me, I had better be present for the execution – if it's going to happen, I can't have rumors spreading that I didn't order it. You will be safely kept in isolation until we've arranged the terms of your ransom, but we'll be moving on long before that happens, so don't make yourself too comfortable.'

She was almost to the flap of the tent when Domingo made

his decision. He'd already betrayed Queen Indsorith when he'd conspired with Pope Y'Homa, no question about that. And though the debt he owed his queen certainly wouldn't be paid by embarking on new collaborations with her enemies, this General Ji-hyeon was right: the Burnished Chain was the foe of all sane mortals, and Domingo knew better than anyone that the threat it posed to the Empire was far graver than that of any invading army or assassin. And more pressing than that, even, was the fate of the Fifteenth – thousands had laid down their lives at his order, and if he could save a few of those who'd survived the folly of his command then he owed them that much, damn it.

'She won't be happy, will she?' Domingo called as the witch-born lifted the flap for her general. 'If I agree and you spare my troops, Zosia will be furious.'

'I imagine so,' said General Ji-hyeon, looking back warily.

'Then I'm your man,' said Domingo, relaxing back into his pillow. 'You save the Fifteenth, and I'll never forget the debt I owe you. You have my word as Baron of Cockspar that I will help you bring war to the maniacs of the Burnished Chain.'

'Glad to have you with us,' said General Ji-hyeon, trying not to smile as she saluted him, the witchborn beside her raising a fist as well.

After a moment's hesitation, Colonel Domingo Hjortt returned the salute. It hurt to lift his arm. As it should.

CHAPTER

8

Zosia had lost everything: her husband, her town, her empire, her devil, even her way. But she was still grinning like a babyskinner in an orphanage, because she finally had her vengeance. Twenty-seven members of the cavalry who had sacked Kypck were chained together behind her, awaiting her judgment, and oh did she have something fitting in mind. The miasma still clung like swamp vapors over the frost-stiff earth of the battlefield, but here at the center the banks of smoke gave way to dark clouds above and darker matter below. Like all Gates, this newest hole in the Star looked almost mundane, a perfect circle of darkness punched in the ground. It might have been mistaken for a pond of oily ebon water, save for the weirdness it projected into the world of mortals – the snow turned black before it reached the surface of the Gate, some of the flakes sizzling away into steam, others contracting into hailstones. It was just the thing to cheer up an old widow on a dreary morning. She caught herself glancing down to her flank before she remembered Choplicker was gone; a pity, he'd have really enjoyed what was coming next.

' – all the more reason to, you know, slip off just for the

moment so you can show me where it happened, since Digs can't recall, exactly, and – whoa!'

The Gate accomplished what Zosia had not been able to – it put a cork in Tapai Purna and Pasha Diggelby, who'd been pestering her the whole walk out here. Gates were always impressive to mortal eyes, pools of gleaming midnight that simultaneously beckoned and repulsed, and this new one dwarfed all six of the originals, stretching wide across the center of the valley. Whoa, indeed.

'So everyone who didn't make it back from the fight or turn up as a corpse ... they fell into that?' said Diggelby in the hushed tone most people slipped into when they found themselves so close to something sacred ... or something dangerous.

'Yup, swallowed 'em right up,' said Zosia, remembering too late that she'd meant to adopt a somber attitude; their friends Hassan and Din were still missing, and a thousand more Cobalts besides. 'But it's not hopeless. They might be okay.'

'Really?' Purna didn't sound like she believed it.

'Well, not *completely* hopeless,' said Zosia. 'There's all kinds of songs about folk disappearing into one just to turn up someplace unexpected. It happens.'

'Poppycock,' said Diggelby, but it was a hopeful sort of poppycock.

'A long shot, sure, but like I said, it happens. I personally know several individuals who have done just that, coming out not much worse for wear halfway across the Star.' Zosia elected not to mention that those lucky few had all known what they were doing and passed through the Gates in some highly specialized fashion that involved the use of devils, versus having the ground just give way to the First Dark beneath their feet. Most sane people would choose certain death to involuntarily entering a Gate, Zosia included ... which was the whole reason they were out here. 'But diverting as our little chat's been, I do have to get on with my day – you two can bounce, or stick around so long as you don't interrupt.'

'Actually, if you spare me just, like, a couple minutes, there's something I *really* need to talk to you about,' said Purna, and from the frantic looks she and Diggelby kept exchanging Zosia figured the pair had deduced her reason for bringing the Imperial prisoners to the edge of the Gate and meant to dissuade her. If she hadn't known what these captives had done to a villageful of innocent people she would have found it an evil play, too. 'I mean, you're a captain, so if you tell everyone to wait they'll be happy to—'

'Time's up, children,' said Zosia sympathetically. 'You'll sleep better if you leave now.'

Diggelby didn't need further encouragement, hot-stepping it back toward the chain of prisoners and their guards, but Purna grabbed his gilded ponytail. For a moment it looked like he'd dart away, gecko-like, leaving her holding his wig instead of a tail, but then he went limp and turned back to Zosia with a sigh so heavy that the sailboats would be feeling a boost clear down at Lake Jucifuge. Signaling the squad captain in charge of the guards, Zosia watched in satisfaction as the prisoners were herded forward and lined up along the side of the Gate, a few paces separating each of them from the earthen rim.

Back at the stockade, this lot had been just as docile as the rest of the Imperial prisoners – whatever the Chainite clerics had done to make them go mad with bloodlust before the battle had left them perpetually dazed afterward. They'd come along a lot easier than lambs to the block, the woolly little bleaters actually taking quite a bit of wrangling in her experience. Now, though, confronted with the consequence of the Chain's ritual, a change came over the slack-faced prisoners. It was like they were waking up after a long sleep, some jolting backward away from the Gate as far as their shackles would let them, others looking all about in confusion, some falling to their knees and others calling out in hoarse voices, demanding to know what in the name of the Crimson Queen was going on. The Cobalt guards and the pair of nobles were clearly disturbed by the transformation, but it thrilled Zosia; she wanted the condemned to be alert and aware of what was coming next. Most of her did, anyway; there was a tiny part of her that was appalled at what she was doing, and that inner voice of dissent was actually growing louder as she beheld the panic of the prisoners. It was a queasy sensation, to feel the pull of regret for a crime she had not yet committed but hotly anticipated.

'Friends!' she cried, loudly clapping her hands together. 'It's so good to see you all here!'

A few remained wide-eyed or inconsolable, but that got the attention of most.

'Zosia, if you could just wait a few—' Purna began to whisper, but Zosia gave her a look that warned she'd be next through the Gate if she interrupted again.

'I don't think we've been formally introduced, though I'm an old friend of Colonel Hjortt. Both of them, in fact.' Some murmurs at that, and Zosia looked from face to face, some maidens and some middle-aged men, some boys and some grown-ass women, all looking like they'd been dragged over a league of rough country, with stained uniforms and matted epaulets. She wondered if one of them had been the asshole who'd stuck a spear in the back of a fleeing child, her hands still feeling sticky with the blood of Pao Cowherd a year on. She chose a woman whose back was straighter than most, and stared into the woman's hard face as she said, 'I am Captain Zosia of the Cobalt Company, lately of Kypck, and I can't tell you how good it feels to be reunited with the heroic Fifteenth Cavalry. I've been dreaming of this day ever since you murdered my town last autumn. Your colonel and fellow soldiers who didn't live long enough to join you here are the lucky ones. Justice has come for you, and her name is Cobalt Zosia, widow of Leib Kalmah.'

Even the weepers and the teeth gnashers looked up at that. Eyes bugged out and jaws dropped. Out of the frying pan and into the volcano, eh you fuckers? The woman Zosia had focused on blanched, then looked at her feet . . . which meant looking at the Gate. Zosia knew that expression well – hard a soldier as she appeared, the woman was on the verge of puking.

'Bullshit.' The declaration arose from about halfway along the chain, from a man even older than Zosia. His white stubble stuck straight out from his leathery cheeks, and he said it again, looking across the curve of the Gate to stare Zosia dead in the eye. 'Bullshit.'

Under normal circumstances she would've marched right over and got in his face, but that would mean putting herself between the line of prisoners and the Gate, which definitely wasn't happening. She settled for taking a bow instead.

'The one and only Cold Cobalt, risen like the shade of your past crimes,' she called as she straightened up. 'I reckon you in particular might have recognized me from the bad old days, when Domingo was harrying me from pillar to post. Or did you enlist in your dotage, and only know Blue Zosia from the ghost stories of—'

'Oh, I know your fucking face, all right!' the old-timer shouted, veins bulging in his neck. 'I know you, Cobalt Zosia, that I do! And I say it again: bullshit!'

'Do you, now?' Zosia felt something very cold turn over in her belly, like a bed of hibernating ice pythons twisting around in their glacial nest.

'You tear the Star up for years on end, kill more folk than I've set eyes to in seventy years, and now you got a claim to cry about a few lousy peasants? You gonna bring us a fate worse than death for a crime so heinous you used to do it twice before breakfast on a slow day's march for the Cobalt Cowards?' His voice was rising like a squall. 'Bullshit! *You're* bullshit, *Cold* Zosia, the same fucking fraud you were back in the day – all mouth and no fucking trousers!'

And then he started laughing, a thick, wet sound akin to a cough, tears streaming from his eyes as he shook a manacled fist at her.

It wasn't true. It wasn't. Zosia had never taken out a town the way they'd taken out Kypck, never; she'd always had a reason, and she'd never ordered innocents put to the steel … but innocents had died all the same, hadn't they? Throughout the campaign, surely, and even more once she'd become queen – her attempts to dissolve the crooked feudal game and disperse the Empire's wealth among the people had led to work camps and worse in some of the provinces. As soon as she learned of the horrors committed in her name she had tried to reform the reformation, of course, but not before countless souls had paid the price of her slack oversight. That was why her successor had come for her head, after all, Indsorith's people having met a fate not dissimilar to the one the Fifteenth Cavalry had administered to Kypck. So no, this old Azgarothian hump wasn't telling her anything she didn't already know, but that icy knot in her guts pulled so tight she wondered if she'd ever get it untangled. And all the while a man who'd taken part in the slaughter of her village laughed in her face.

'Thank goodness ... you caught the baddies!' he managed between gasping guffaws. 'Cold Zosia ... to the rescue! Bulllllshit!'

Zosia was a calm woman, she really was. But before Purna even realized that the older woman was moving on her, Zosia had snatched the girl's pistol out of its holster, cocked the wheel back, and took steady aim at the loudmouth. Purna was calling her name, Diggelby was prudently slinking away to the side, and still the man cackled, even as the gun went off.

The smoke cleared in a hurry, sucked down into the Gate, and Zosia saw she'd shut the man up, but not in the way she'd intended. He was slumped over, pulled to the side by the chain that tethered him to the soldier Zosia had accidentally hit instead of her target. She couldn't tell if her wide shot had struck a man or a woman, only that she'd blown their face wide open.

'Reload that for me,' Zosia grunted, shoving the smoking pistol into Purna's shaking hands. She'd never been as good a shot with guns as she was with her bow, but wouldn't miss twice, not at this range. 'Now!'

'Well that's just typical, innit!' the old man howled, looking up from his fallen comrade. 'She wasn't even there, you stupid fucking arsehole! She just enlisted, ain't been in the Fifteenth more'n five months! And you killed her all the same, 'cause that's what justice means to Cold Zosia! You're worse than us, *Your Majesty*, 'cause we follow orders, but you're the one giving 'em!'

Zosia closed her suddenly stinging eyes, took a deep breath. *Stop*, her internal dissenter pleaded, *stop stop stop*, but she tried to ignore her doubts, to stifle her growing self-loathing. She wasn't here to debate her tactics or justify her actions to anyone, not even herself, and certainly not an Imperial cutthroat. She was here for justice, to fulfill the oath she had made to avenge

Leib and Pao and all the rest. And contrary to the final desperate shit-talking of a condemned man, she didn't want blood for blood's sake – if he spoke true and the soldier she'd inadvertently shot hadn't been part of the massacre, that was on Zosia, and she'd carry that burden to the end of her days. It could go on top of the pile.

'I'm a fair woman!' she shouted, cringing at how desperate the words sounded. 'I won't hold any accountable who weren't at Kypck! So if you enlisted after, you're free to go!'

She realized her mistake even before the first soldier piped up, and sure enough there was a chorus in short order:

'I wasn't there!'

'Me neither!'

'I just got promoted to cavalry!'

'We came on after, after!'

'Swear on the Crimson Queen's life, I never been to Kypck!'

'Shut up!' Zosia cried, what was supposed to be a triumph fast becoming a fiasco as most of the chained soldiers protested their innocence. They were probably all lying, they had to be . . . 'All of you, be quiet!'

'What's the problem?' the old-timer called, drops of his comrade's blood caught in his stubble. 'If you were there to know the whole Fifteenth's responsible, should be easy enough to recognize the culprits! Course you could always raze all of Azgaroth, just to make sure you didn't miss any! Or play it safe and hang the whole Star!'

'Fuck this,' Zosia muttered to herself, trying to drown her doubts with the memory of Efrain Hjortt peacocking around her house, her husband's head in a gunnysack. It didn't really work – her sweet dream of revenge had become a nightmare, in which she was a miserable prisoner condemned to carrying out an execution she no longer desired. 'Fuck all of this.'

'Let's wait, Zosia,' Purna murmured, putting a hand on her shoulder. 'We can interrogate them back at the stockade, find out for sure who was there when—'

'It's too late,' said Zosia wearily, the cold, bitter, hate-filled part of her heart knowing that if she paused for another moment she would lose her nerve entirely. 'It's too late for any of us. Soldiers! It's time! Push them in!'

The Cobalt guards didn't look much happier than the captives with the prospect, but good soldiers that they were they followed her order, shoving the line of Azgarothians closer to the Gate. There was some struggling, but the fight had been preemptively sapped from most of the prisoners, their bodies enfeebled after weathering the Chain's witchery of the day before. As the first pair of boots teetered on the edge of the Gate, though, a voice rang out over the whimpers and cries of the doomed:

'Stop! Your general commands you, stop!'

And so they did, guards and prisoners and the pair of nobles and Zosia herself all turning as one to see Ji-hyeon burst out of the smoke astride a charger, her retinue hot on her hooves. A dozen more horses wheeled and stamped, having come in so fast through the fog they might have ridden straight into the Gate if they hadn't instinctively shied away from the looming blackness.

'Just what in the holy fucking of the horny gods are you doing?' Ji-hyeon demanded, swinging down from her stamping horse.

'You know exactly what I'm doing.' The cold in Zosia's belly broke apart, melting into magma as white-hot fury boiled down from her heart, all of her doubt and guilt incinerated by the wrath she felt at Ji-hyeon's interference. In spite of her heat, or perhaps because of it, Zosia kept her tone perfectly civil as the girl advanced on her. 'I promised you my guidance and aid in exchange for something very small: vengeance against those who killed my people. This is what we agreed to, General.'

'I never gave you permission to murder lawful prisoners!' Ji-hyeon wasn't yet as good at masking her rage as Zosia. She might learn the trick, in time, assuming she didn't force Zosia into tossing her through this very Gate, which is exactly what she'd do if this treacherous brat tried to renege on their deal. You don't spend half a lifetime around devils without acquiring a taste for absolutes. 'Did you think I wouldn't notice, *Captain*?'

Zosia's control slipped a few more notches toward total fucking release; it was a strangely satisfying sensation. 'A deal is a deal. They're mine, *Princess*.'

'Zosia, *please*.' Ji-hyeon was so close Zosia could smell the stale saam smoke on her breath, see the little bits of white that still showed through the thicket of bright red veins clogging her eyes. 'The Thaoan regiment's moving in on us, *now*. With Colonel Hjortt and the rest of the hostages held according to the laws of the Crimson Codices, we can talk them into a temporary truce, stall them if nothing else. But if we start executing prisoners of war there's no fucking way they'll agree to talks. They'll attack us as soon as they find out!'

'Better make sure your people don't talk, then,' said Zosia, and when Ji-hyeon's face tightened Zosia leaned in real fucking close, her lips nearly brushing the girl's ear as she said, 'You don't have a choice here, Princess. They go into the Gate, now, and if you say another fucking word I'll toss you in after them and take your army for myself. I imagine most of these sellswords would be happy to have the real Cobalt leading them instead of a devildamned teenager who'd rather strike truces than blows.'

Forget saucers, Ji-hyeon's eyes were as big as bucklers, but she knew better than to push Zosia. Smart girl. The general nodded forlornly, then turned back to her waiting guards, all the tension gone out of her shoulders. Zosia had hoped to postpone that little showdown until after the execution, but at least the bridge was crossed and she could get on with—

'Arrest Captain Zosia,' Ji-hyeon called to her bodyguards, too chickenshit to look at Zosia as she gave the order. 'And take the Fifteenth Cavalry back to camp. This is not how the Cobalt Company treats prisoners.'

The guards moved fast, but Zosia moved faster. If she'd gone for Ji-hyeon she might not have reached her in time, but Zosia wasn't after the general. She barreled into the captive at the end of the chain, a baby-faced man with a dazed smile turning up his tear-muddied cheeks at the unexpected reprieve. Her shoulder caught him in the side, and he flopped into the Gate before the smile even left his lips. And just as she'd hoped, instead of going slack the chain that connected him to the next prisoner jerked taut as soon as the man disappeared into the liquid emptiness of the Gate. A second soldier was yanked off her feet and slid screaming into the darkness, the next in line bracing himself but unable to overcome the pull of the chain cutting into his wrist, blood welling out around the iron bracelet as he was pulled forward, heels kicking up dirt as he gasped, too scared to scream, and that's when Zosia was decked in the face, only realizing that the shrill laughter that filled the air was her own when the fist snapped her cackling mouth shut.

Shaking off the halfhearted blow Zosia started to laugh again, because mercy of mercies, it wasn't a guard who had engaged her, but Ji-hyeon herself. The girl hopped in place, clutching the maimed hand she'd thoughtlessly clocked Zosia with and yowling in pain. Instead of looking after their general, the guards had rushed to the aid of the chain of prisoners, locked in an unwinnable tug-of-war with the Gate. Cracking her knuckles, Zosia stepped forward to teach Ji-hyeon her last lesson: how to throw a decent punch. It was long past time for Cold Zosia to resume command of the Cobalt Company.

CHAPTER

9

It was almost a relief, to have it come to this. It was certainly clarifying, the jolt of pain in Ji-hyeon's mangled hand bringing the chaotic, blurry morning into perfect focus. Even the reminder that her strong left jab was out of commission for the foreseeable future didn't worry her; run-down and wild-eyed as the biddy looked, Ji-hyeon could've probably taken her with both hands tied behind—

Zosia came at her so fast Ji-hyeon barely got her arm up in time to deflect the first blow, and then the second popped her in the throat, a third snapped her chin, and the chain of punches would've laid her out flat if Ji-hyeon hadn't snapped her knee into Zosia's crotch, buying her a reprieve. Ji-hyeon stumbled backward as Zosia rocked in place, fists still raised but unable to immediately pursue her quarry as she rode out the pain. It was a low blow, but Ji-hyeon wouldn't think twice about burying her foot in the woman's snatch if she rushed in like that again. Choi called such attacks a Villainous Move, but what could be more fitting for the former Arch-Villain?

'Piece . . . of . . . shit,' Zosia hissed through her teeth, shaking her legs out. 'You're going in the Gate for that.'

'General!' A pair of guards let go of the prisoners' chain

to come to Ji-hyeon's aid, and the line of struggling captives slipped another meter, the one closest to the Gate shrieking as his bound wrist inched down to touch the black surface. The kneeling guard who had finally fitted a key into the man's manacle cursed, and then hand, iron band, and key were all pulled into the Gate, the prisoner's forearm disappearing into the darkness.

Zosia took advantage of the distraction, charging in at Ji-hyeon again, but a pair of bodyguards came between the two women. Zosia stalked to the side, deftly twirling her war hammer. The screams of the man being drawn into the Gate obliterated whatever shit Zosia was talking, overwhelmed the frantic questions of the bodyguards, drowned out even Ji-hyeon's thoughts . . . and then Tapai Purna jerked the kneeling guard away from the Gate, taking his place beside the hapless prisoner. Leaning perilously far out over the rim, she raised her kukri, and with no hesitation at all swiped it down into the man's elbow. The blow cut off the man's ear-piercing wail, but failed to do the same to his arm; it hung bloodily on by a ragged hinge of meat. Before Purna could raise her curved blade for another blow, however, the pull of the Gate finished the amputation for her, ripping the tendons out by their roots as it carried off the forearm. The chained prisoners and the guards supporting them all fell back from the abrupt release of tension, and Diggelby seized his tottering companion and pulled her back from the edge. Sound flooded back into Ji-hyeon's ringing ears, and she returned her full attention to her mad captain.

' – fair fight!' Zosia was spitting like a trapped fox on the other side of Ji-hyeon's two bodyguards, a third moving around to cut off any possible escape. 'Think you can take on the Crimson Empire when you can't even take one old lady, you cunt-punting chicken?'

'General?' One of the bodyguards, Ankit, had turned to Ji-hyeon, her pitiless panther mask looking for the obvious order. This could be over in a minute.

'Drop your weapon, Zosia!' The old cow looked ready to say something smart, and then she must have seen Ji-hyeon unbuckling her belt through the screen of armed guards. 'I can't offer you a fair fight, you horrible has-been, on account of you being too fucking old to hang – but if you really want to try me, I'll beat your fucking ass with my bare hands.'

'Uh, General?' Purna still hadn't caught her breath, her panting, wolfish tongue darting in and out of her mouth as she spoke. 'I really don't think . . . '

'Nor do I,' murmured Choi from Ji-hyeon's other side. 'That woman has tusks instead of fists.'

'About fucking time you stepped up!' Zosia dropped her hammer as Ji-hyeon's scabbard and sword followed her belt to the rough earth. The woman's back was fewer than a dozen paces from the hungry black pit that had eaten a pair of soldiers this morning, and ten thousand more the day before. 'Here's the stakes, Princess – winner takes the Cobalt Company, loser kisses that Gate!'

'Fuck your stakes,' said Ji-hyeon, elbowing her way between her befuddled bodyguards. She was mad as a newly bound devil but wasn't about to get lured into some pissing contest with this cagey crone. 'You take me down and maybe I won't have you executed, but that's a big fucking maybe after all your bullshit.'

For some reason the word *bullshit* set Zosia off again, her pupils swelling to fill her eyes as she trembled with rage. In a deadly low voice she spat, 'Bold talk for a dead brat – I don't see your little owlbat floating around to protect you, Princess.'

'And where's your devil, Captain?' It was hard, talking trash on the fly, but over the course of the campaign Ji-hyeon had gained some experience in this field. 'Seems like a wasted wish, to send him back to hell just so I'd kick your ass in front of my crew. All you had to do was ask.'

Which wasn't great, sure, but Ji-hyeon didn't have time to think of something better before Zosia nodded thoughtfully and then bolted forward with her arms tucked in tight to her chest. She wanted to get in close, just like before, but Ji-hyeon was ready for her this time and—

Shit, fuck, horse piss, how did a woman that old move like that? She was past Ji-hyeon's blocks in a twinkling, fists wheeling in one after another, hammering a precise line up Ji-hyeon's torso. The rogue captain would've nailed her already bruising throat, too, if Ji-hyeon hadn't set her heel and shoved back into the onslaught, stumbling into the rain of punches and slamming her forehead into Zosia's. Ji-hyeon had wanted the woman's nose, damn it, both women reeling for a moment, and then, as if she'd read Ji-hyeon's intentions, Zosia whipped her arm around, the back of her fist crushing Ji-hyeon's septum with a pop the girl felt all the way to her feet.

The world went dim, the falling snow turning red as it filled Ji-hyeon's vision. She staggered backward, half-blind, and then snapped her hand up to catch the blow she couldn't see but knew must be drilling through the air to finish the job. Her fingers closed on a wrist, and only realizing what she was doing as it was happening, she pulled Zosia forward, yanking her into the left hook she'd fired without even thinking about it. Zosia struggled but Ji-hyeon held her fast, hitting her again and again. Each punch brought Ji-hyeon a little closer to reality, and by the time she felt the bones crunching in her already-crippled hand Zosia's face was beginning to slide under Ji-hyeon's two remaining fingers.

As her opponent came back into focus so, too, did a growing ache in Ji-hyeon's side. Zosia was matching her blow for blow, clumsy rabbit punches to Ji-hyeon's ribs as Ji-hyeon held her squirming right arm and battered her face. The old broad looked bad off, and Ji-hyeon knew she had her . . .

A leg that must have been prying at hers the whole time finally caught Ji-hyeon off balance, and they both went down, Zosia's bloody mouth splitting into a grin as she tackled her quarry. The frozen earth felt soft as a feather mattress as it caught Ji-hyeon's fall, Zosia lighter than a pillow propped on the girl's waist, and when fingers tightened around her throat Ji-hyeon pitched herself to the side, taking her rider with her. They didn't roll so much as stutter, Ji-hyeon coming up on top and grinding her elbow into Zosia's gut only to be flipped over again, those hands still crushing her windpipe, and then it was Ji-hyeon's turn to be on top again. She dove down like an eel in one of Othean's tide-pool gardens, biting Zosia's shoulder until the woman let go of her throat and set to battering her ears. Ji-hyeon felt like a drum under the rhythm of those blows, an angry war drum that never wanted the beat to stop as she choked on her enemy's blood and hair, and then she slipped under for a moment, because when she could see and think again she no longer had a mouthful of muscle, no longer saw an eyeful of silver hair; she saw nothing but the shimmering colors that lurked just beneath the shining blackness of a Gate. There was laughter down there, too, the shrill cackling of the deranged waiting for her to join the chorus. Fingers knotted in her hair and a knee dug into her back, and she gave up the struggle – it was time to see what lay beyond the rim when you didn't have a guide to lead you safely through . . .

Then, just as she was warming to the prospect, Ji-hyeon was hauled rudely backward, bright blossoms of pain blooming across her face and ears, her throat and ribs. She blinked the blood out of her eyes, staring past Choi's wide-eyed face. She had never seen her Honor Guard so upset, and she choked up with guilt at having so worried one of her oldest friends. She tried to tell Choi it was all right but only bubbled up blood, which turned into a coughing fit. Choi helped her onto her side and Ji-hyeon spat out a mouthful of bloody silver hair.

Zosia. She looked up, the mad chortling of the Gate still rattling through her throbbing ears, and she saw her former captain bucking wildly on the ground, landing a few blows even with Purna holding her arms and Diggelby wrapped around her legs, two bodyguards warily trying to help. Zosia laughed and laughed, her bloodied, mud-smeared face bearing only a passing resemblance to a mortal woman. She looked like one of the blade maidens from Ji-hyeon's first father's scrolls, a goddess so hungry for vengeance she would welcome a devil to ride her flesh instead of that of a beast.

As if sensing her gaze, Zosia abruptly ceased her struggles and her laughter, staring Ji-hyeon in the puffy eyes.

'I won, Princess,' she croaked, blood running down her chin. 'I won! And that means you grant my wish. You grant my wish!'

Ji-hyeon wanted to say something smart, wanted to say anything at all, but her head was as empty as Cold Zosia's wild stare. Instead she just shook her head, closing her eyes and trying to shut out Zosia's screams as the woman started up again, the words no longer making sense – Ji-hyeon's name was mentioned, but so was that of Queen Indsorith, the sole link between the two being the mantra of granting Zosia's wish.

When Ji-hyeon finally gained her feet, buoyed by something vinegary from Choi's flask, she opened her eyes again and saw that a ring of people were all watching her. Her bodyguards, the prisoners and their guards, Choi and Purna and Diggelby, and, lying at their feet, trussed up in somebody's repurposed reins, a finally silent Zosia. Ji-hyeon stared back at them, worrying a loose tooth with her coppery tongue. What the fuck did they expect her to do, give a speech?

'Ji-hyeon, we must return to camp,' Choi whispered, taking her sore elbow and steering her toward her horse, the wavering smoke and falling snow transforming the dismal valley into some ethereal cloud-kissed summit. 'Meeting the Thaoans must wait until you—'

'Fuck that,' Ji-hyeon rasped, startled by how hard it was to speak above a whisper. She spat out another mouthful of mucusy blood. Hard as it was to talk, to even breathe, she was so, so, *so* relieved this was finally taken care of and she could get on with her day. 'We flinch from a meet with those clowns, they come back with lances lowered. Help me on my horse.'

'General—' one of her bodyguards began, but she waved him silent with her contorted, two-fingered hand. It was almost certainly broken now, which was just brilliant.

'Let's do this shit,' she said, her voice sounding funny even to her own ear. 'And bring along these prisoners – since we apparently can't keep a few captured cavalry safe long enough to negotiate their ransom, we're handing them back to the Thaoans *now*.'

Surveying the shell-shocked line of captives who had survived Zosia's madness, Ji-hyeon saw a white-haired old man in the center nod approvingly, and then he took advantage of the slack in the chain to raise his fist. When his fellows didn't follow suit he barked something at them in High Azgarothian, and one by one arms raised until the whole chain saluted her. Zosia spluttered unintelligibly, and Choi whispered an immensely tempting proposition in Ji-hyeon's ear . . . but looking down at the former Queen of Samoth, she decided against it.

'No, Captain Zosia returns to camp. To the stockade. She's just lucky I'm not as insane as she, otherwise she'd already be in the Gate.'

Zosia glared up at Ji-hyeon, and spit a tooth in her direction. Ji-hyeon wished her own was loose enough that she could return fire, but settled for something almost as good. She turned her back on Zosia, and limped down the line of Imperial prisoners, meeting each one's salute with a bump of her fist.

Appealing as Choi's suggestion had been, it would be a warm winter in the Frozen Savannahs when Ji-hyeon let Zosia off with something as easy as being turned over to the Thaoan regiment as a peace offering.

CHAPTER

10

The Frozen Savannahs were melting beneath the Horned Wolves' feet, and it didn't take a poison oracle or a song-singer to guess why.

Best held the sea otter fur-lined helmet in her hands, debating. Then she swung it onto her head, twisting it about until it stopped pinching her braids, and buckled it under her chin. It would raise some brows, wearing her high-horned helm before the council, but when had her presence not? She knew why they summoned her, and what they must expect – she who left her gear behind on the morning of a hunt was no true hunter, and so Best had prepared herself for the longest chase of her life.

The last item to go into her pack was the blanket she had stripped from the cot and tucked into the rafters the morning she awoke to find both her father and her son missing. It was not a sentimental gesture, but a practical one; her brother had told her tales of Samothan hounds so wise of snout they could track a single mortal's scent across a thousand leagues, and with nothing more substantial than an old skirt or comb to get them started. Once she entered the Crimson Empire she would seek out one of these mystical beasts, knowing that even as good a huntress as she would need help pursuing quarry nearly a year ahead of her.

Best didn't need to give her hut a once-over before leaving, everything she required already in her heavy pack or hands, but all the same she looked a final time. Then she quickly stepped back into the center of the room and stabbed her spear through her father's mat, then pierced her son's, and with a flick of the wrist deposited both of them in the smoldering firepit. She should have burned them right away, as she had her brother's when he had similarly fled in the night so many years before. Instead she'd foolishly left Father and Sullen's mats there where anyone could see, quietly announcing to the clan her hope that the disgraced Horned Wolves would return to her hut. The woven grass pads caught quickly, and where once five seats sat in a close ring around the fire now only hers remained. It hurt, watching the mats writhe in the flames she had let burn very low in the unnaturally warm night, and she quietly prayed to the Fallen Mother for serenity. Most mortals would have succumbed to the curse that gripped her family, potent as it had proven, but Best would overcome it, for all of them, and when she finally reached the Fallen Mother's Meadhall she would beg her leave to go and retrieve her damned family from the Hell of the Coward Dead.

First she had to send them there, though.

Going to the bed, Best knelt down and lifted the edge, sweeping her head under the dusty cot. Teeth nipped her fingers, and she withdrew the snow lion-tooth necklace Sullen had made her from his first kill. She had never taken it off, showing the troubled boy that his mother still believed he could be saved, but when he'd run away with his grandfather she had snapped the cord and stuffed it under the bed, hiding it there like a sorcerer's fetish bag planted under its victim's doorstep. A spell to keep a mother's heart bleeding every night as she lay alone with her shame, and that of her family.

Outside, the afternoon sun was burning even hotter than it had the day before, icicles as wide as walrus tusks snapping off the eaves of huts, the whole village flooded in ankle-deep slush. She was sweating even before the first of her neighbors turned his back from her, the way they always had from Sullen when he carried Father out on his constitutionals. Oh, how they had fought, she and her father, when he'd come back in griping about the clan treating him so shabbily, and though she had always lectured him and Sullen both that there was no reason to provoke the village by strutting about, now she knew that sometimes it couldn't be helped. Sometimes you just had to walk proud through the place you were born, even when none understood your need.

As she crossed the close-knit village of old sod huts, newer longhouses, and muddy paddocks, Best saw the situation was even more dire than she'd thought: the walls of the church were melting, blocks of ice meant to keep the faithful warm until the arrival of the summer sun shrinking so that gaps could be seen around the posts and at the edge of the shingled roof. Not wishing to hunker down in what must be a drizzly mess, the council had pulled their benches outside and arranged them in front of the thorn tree, just as they had in Father's heyday. Another rough chunk of sorrow caught in Best's throat at the sight of the elders sitting beneath the barren tree like a coven of pagan witches. Above them, the murder of blackbirds that resided in the tree announced her arrival with their cry. None of the council looked up, and Best quietly dropped to her knees before them, the icy slurry splashing her ghost bear cape and banded leather armor.

' – flee the apiary even as we hold summit,' the poison oracle was saying from her perch in the tree's lowest branch, her woad-smeared cheeks dripping blue in the blazing sunshine, the web of woven sinew and knotted bone that crisscrossed the boughs beside her dribbling snowmelt. 'Convinced of summer, they migrate north, and even with my magics may never return to this cursed land. The dead gods rise from the Bitter Gulf, beleaguering us with their hell-breath, and all know the cause!'

A great harrumphing from the council avowed this, Father Turisa and his novice offering some *amens* from the red bench set off a few paces from the rest of the council. Best repeated their solemn confirmations in her heart, but kept her lips as still as her spear. The elders carried on for a little longer, debating which devils exactly had contributed to their current misery, and which ancestors were most wroth at the development, and all the while Best stayed as still as the effigy of Old Black carved into the living face of the tree, the ancient carving but recently anointed with painted wings and crown of daggers to signify her function as Fallen Mother. There had initially been some confusion as to whether the Allmother had come to Flintland in the guise of the moon goddess Silvereye or her niece Old Black, but under increasing pressure from the poison oracle, a recent revelation by Father Turisa revealed that in her inscrutable wisdom the Fallen Mother had assumed both roles, and that of half a dozen other ancestors besides.

'And lo, less than a full day and night since this plague has befallen us, She With the Blood of the Apocalypse answers our summons,' the poison oracle cried after no small period of blustery proclamation, and it took Best a moment to realize that she herself was the wretched creature in question. The older woman shifted in her perch, spitting down further disrespect.

'Tell us, oh Daughter of Ruthless, Sister of Craven, and Mother of Sullen, will you admit freely to the witchery of your kin, or must I force the truth from your lips?'

More grunts and murmurs from the council, but Best was relieved to hear that not all of the elders approved of the oracle's assessment of her character. Neither Father Turisa nor his boy issued an *amen*, which further calmed her fury at being spoken to in such a way. Finally raising her head, she launched her gaze like a sun-knife at the poison oracle's heart.

'I will not speak for cowards or witches!' Best shouted, but kept her voice free of the emotion that she felt, knowing the oracle might seize such a snarl and use it to upend her. 'I speak only for myself, as a named huntress of the Horned Wolves.'

'And what do you say, oh named huntress?' The oracle was not using her name, and Best's heart beat faster at the snub. 'You must be a wise woman, with many thaws beneath your pelt and a close kinship with the accused, so what say you of our current calamity?'

'I say only the Fallen Mother and the rest of our ancestors truly know the cause of this evil sun,' said Best, but only Father Turisa and the novice nodded at her words. Before the oracle could exploit this, she added, 'But I can see as plain as any that this is our first winter since two traitors turned their back on the Horned Wolves, and murdered our clanfolk in their escape. If the council believes their betrayal has angered the ancestors and brought this heat upon us—'

'*If!*' cried Hammerfist, the youngest member of the council, evidently still furious with Best for refusing to take him as a husband two years past, though in point of fact she had only rejected him when he insisted she cast out her crippled father and devil-touched son before he would move into her hut. '*If*, she says, but I say now, and say proud, that we *do* believe this, we do *know* this, because it is true! Unlike you, oh mother of devils, who—'

'I believe Best spoke thusly to avoid putting words in our mouths, a courtesy which you seem unwilling to extend to her,' said Saltgrinder. The old woman wasn't looking at her, but Best gave silent thanks to the one elder who had not voted to cast Father off the council ... for all the difference her dissent had made, and for all the gratitude the old man had ever extended to her afterward. 'I will remind you, Brother Hammerfist, that Daughter Best has proven herself time and again to this clan, to this council, and she is called before us not as an accused but as a witness. Do not slander her again, lest she rightly request you prove your allegations in the Honor Circle.'

Of all the outcomes of this meeting, battling one of the elders in the Honor Circle had never crossed Best's mind ... but having one of the council stand up for her was even less expected, and far more welcome. Before Hammerfist could force the issue – and force her to kill his fool arse in front of everyone – Best said, 'Forgive me, oh just and noble council, for I am not as precise with words as I am with spear and knife. I simply meant to agree that something terrible has come upon our lands – when dawn broke yesterday, grey and chill as it ought, I never suspected that come nightfall I should be sweating in my hut, shed of every skin but my own. That today burns yet brighter speaks of evil forces set loose upon us, and if my blood be the cause then my blood shall also be the balm.'

'*That* remains to be seen,' said Father Turisa, his apprentice issuing a quavering *amen* beside him. 'An early thaw is not unheard of, surely, and—'

'And *this* is not an *early thaw*!' crowed the poison oracle, shaking her clattering web at the priest. 'In all the years of our clan, *never* has the sun of summer struck us on the eve of winter!'

'True, true,' the council hummed in place of *amen*s, but Salt-grinder said, 'Warmth comes out of season for a day or more every year in six, and while I grant that never in my life has it come so hot so fast, that does not prove it will remain so. A week from now the tundra may be as hard as it was two nights past.'

'It will not,' said the oracle solemnly. 'The icebees do not quit their hives for a heat spell, nor do the oryx herds return from the coasts as hunters have attested. This is not a hiccup in winter's heavy breath, this is the catastrophe our ancestors warned of, the calamity sung of by both ancient songs and Canticle of Chains. Is it not so, Father Turisa?'

'I *did* have troubled dreams last night . . . ' said the old priest reflectively, as if trying to recall whether he had nibbled on some cheese before lying down to bed. 'But if it is the event foretold in the Song of Queens, it is not a calamity per se . . . '

'Enough!' cried the poison oracle. 'Daughter Best, was your son Sullen not born in this season? And was not the Proudest Shedding of Jackal Blood also of the late autumn, that fatal battle where both your progeny and progenitor proved their scorn for our ways? Was this not also the season of Craven's final betrayal? Is this not the season where Ruthless was cast from the council?'

'It is,' she said quietly, the reddish cast of the too-big and too-bright sun glistening on the dripping thorns of the oracle's tree. 'It is.'

'There it is!' Hammerfist shouted, rising from his seat. 'Proof! Proof that her wicked blood is the cause of all our sorrows!'

'Hardly,' said Saltgrinder, but her voice was lost in a chorus of *amen*s and *harrumph*s.

'What do you have to say on the curse your people have

brought upon us?' the poison oracle asked, leaning forward on her bough. 'Today you claim crudeness of tongue, but you forget that while but an apprentice at the time I was present for your previous petitions to the council. Eloquent was the huntress who came before her betters to beg mercy for her brother after his ignoble return, and for her father and son after theirs. What song do you sing now that all three have shamed us twice, Daughter Best, now that you have yet again steered us foul with cries for clemency, and all the Savannahs weep at the cost of keeping cowards safe from ancient justice?'

'Hear me now!' Best cried, her voice thick as snowmead with regret. 'I beg, O council, hear me! I was wrong to speak on behalf of my brother when he slunk back to us! And I was wrong to speak on behalf of my son! Wrong to speak on behalf of my father! Wrong to let this curse grow in my very hut! Wrong! But I will make it right!'

'How?' asked Hammerfist. The idiot. Everyone else knew enough to wait for her to continue in her own time, Best squeezing her son's necklace in her hand until the teeth bit her palm and fingers and blood welled between them.

'Justice,' she said evenly, raising her head high even as she remained kneeling, and shook her bloody fist. Her eyes were dry as she met the suspicious glares of the council, but her hand wept for her, crimson drops mixing with the slush around her knees. 'Grant me leave to hunt those who were known as Ruthless and Sullen, and if he still lives, the one you named Craven. Grant me leave to track them, to dig them out from whatever burrow they hide in. Grant me leave to show the Fallen Mother and the rest of our ancestors what mercy a Horned Wolf offers those who would betray our laws. I swear on my life and the honor of my ancestors that I will not rest until justice is served!'

Hammerfist didn't look happy but at last the *harrumph*s were for her, and the *amen*s as well. Even the poison oracle seemed impressed, strumming her bone web like a harp. Father Turisa stood from his bench and, clearing his throat, began to speak. Only the poison oracle seemed perturbed by his talking out of turn, though soon enough Best was chewing her cheek and praying for patience of her own.

'Daughter Best is a brave and worthy child of the Fallen Mother,' said the priest, tottering over and tapping her bloody fist with his chain-wrapped one, the inverted cross of his iron rosary nicking her thumb. 'Which is why I solicit the council's approval for her to escort Brother Rýt to Diadem as the first leg in her righteous quest. Of all the Crimson Empire, the Holy City is closest to the Horned Wolves' borders, and lest this curse require more than the sacrifice Daughter Best promises to deliver I should like to have my novice bring word of our calamity to the Holy See. The Burnished Chain must know that strange portents stir the wind, and while the Frozen Savannahs may be the first to feel this infernal heat it shall not be long before all the Star falls under its sway.'

A few *harrumph*s, though not many, and Brother Rýt seemed incapable of summoning a single *amen*, staring in shock at his superior. Best did not relish the prospect of babysitting a pimple-faced foreign boy who had never earned his name, but the ways of the Fallen Mother were inscrutable. Not even Hammerfist was gainsaying the proposal, though, and with the council's unvoiced approval all eyes now turned to the poison oracle, who closed her eyes and muttered to herself as everyone sweated under the thorn tree, waiting in respectful silence.

'I wonder . . .' the oracle said at last, opening one eye in Best's direction. 'Decked for a hunt as you are, Daughter Best, I wonder what course you should take if I gave this honorable task to another hunter? If I told you to stay in your hut while Swiftspear went in your stead? What then?'

'I would give you my son's token to add to your web, and do as I was told,' said Best, and though fear filled her heart it could not slow her arm. She cast the bloody necklace at the tree, and though the light trinket would have fallen short, a blackbird flashed down and scooped it up, delivering it to the pleased oracle. She held the red-smeared string of teeth up to the diabolical sun and, whispering a few more words, set it on the branch beside her.

'Very well, Daughter Best,' said the poison oracle, grinning as wide as a leopard seal. 'I grant your wish – you have the council's blessing to hunt your family, and see that their hot blood restores the righteous frost to the earth they defiled.'

'Thank you,' said Best, bowing her head beneath the weight of the honor. As the council chanted their approval and Father Turisa added his prayers to the chorus, she imagined Sullen's eyes widening with surprise as she stepped from the snow with her grandmother's sun-knife in her hand, her father spouting his nonsense from his grandson's back, her brother who had led them into temptation standing at their side with a drawn blade and an evil grin. She said it again. 'Thank you.'

CHAPTER

11

'I shware by Ord Brack's honor, I'll break it tween my treeth,' Maroto growled around the pipe he still held clamped in his mouth. Hardly a threat to intimidate anyone but a dandy, but Maroto was long accustomed to making do with what he had, and if the devils of the sea had seen fit to grant him a briar bargaining chip he'd be damned if he didn't use it. The Immaculate girl paused, her outstretched hand a few inches from the pipe, and then she straightened back up, crossing her arms and glaring down at the waterlogged barbarian. The only sound was the tide toying with his toes and, blinking his salt-burned eyes, he saw the other two figures were also Immaculate, a man and a woman whose deep tans hinted at seasons upon the sea.

'Is Immaculate the native tongue, then?' the girl asked, hunkering down for a better look at Maroto. Dyed-green hair hung in ropes from the side of her head that wasn't shaved, patches of her skin popping with ink so rich it glowed in the sunlight. She wore the baggy, drab trousers of fisherfolk, and the silver-and-gold embroidered shirt of a merchant queen. The former were in good repair, but the latter was coming apart at the seams, and seemed to serve mostly as padding to protect her chest from a heavy leather bandolier loaded with a couple of barbed darts and a good many empty loops for more of the same. Loose gold chains hung around her tatted throat, and the cutlass lolling from her coin-studded belt had tight brass basketwork. Cute in the freckled face, too, but since she was looking to be just Maroto's type he'd better give her a wide berth indeed. His type tended to be nothing but trouble. 'Ahoy, there, merman, you understand me?'

'Unnerstand.' Oh, Maroto understood all right – these punks were pirates, or hammy actors playing the same who'd gone overboard in the wardrobe department. And if they assumed he was a native they must be as lost as he was. 'I'm a freebrooter, too. I'm usefur.'

'Are you, now?' She turned to the woman and said, 'Pass that over, Niki.'

The thick, mop-topped woman brought a green coconut with the top hacked off, and Maroto's mouth flooded with saliva so quickly he nearly choked on it. The girl sloshed the coconut in Maroto's direction, and dead tired as he'd felt a moment before, he hauled himself up on one elbow. Reaching for the coconut, he said, 'Very usefur.'

'Well then, Very Useful, how 'bout we swap? Unless you'd rather sip an empty pipe than a full coconut?'

It wasn't even a question; he passed her the cutty with a shaky hand, but as he did his eyes flicked out of habit to the underside of the pipe. He froze, unable to believe it, but sure enough, there it was: a Z carved into the briar, and beside it, blurred by clinging sand, another letter. An L. His hand shook all the harder, and he looked up at this Immaculate girl in wonder.

'Where'd you get this?'

'A friend made it for me,' said the girl, her nut-brown eyes steady. 'An old lover, if you must know. What's it to you, Useful?'

This chippie couldn't be thirty years old, and she called herself an old lover of Zosia's? Not too long ago the thought of a pretty young pirate making out with Zosia would have filled Maroto with very different feelings, and truth be told, he might have conjured just such images to while away a lonely night . . . or morning or afternoon, far as that went. Now, though, his craw tightened, and so did his fist, the pipe digging into his hand. So Zosia had lied to him – she hadn't just been holed away in her mountain home with some loverboy; she'd also taken this Immaculate into her bed and, more importantly, her confidence. For all he knew Zosia had actually let everyone in on her big secret save Maroto, letting him carry on thinking she'd died because she trusted him less than some random fucking pirate . . .

'Careful there, Useful, you break my pipe I break your face.'

'Her name,' growled Maroto, because as bad as Zosia had hurt him he still wanted to believe her, to believe *in* her. Maybe he was jumping to conclusions, maybe this girl had hooked up with some random pipemaker who also just happened to etch a Z into their briar. 'Your lover who made this, what was her name?'

'Oh, I reckon we both know that or you wouldn't be acting so queer,' said the pirate, breaking Maroto's heart all over again with a wink. 'But I don't like to say it aloud, on account of an oath I made to keep her secrets. She betrayed me in the end, but I believe a woman's worth is in how well she keeps her promises, even to those who don't deserve it.'

'That's something else we've got in common, then,' said

Maroto, suddenly unable to get rid of the pipe fast enough. She plucked it from his trembling fingers and tossed him the green orb. There wasn't much in the coconut to begin with, and some of it splashed out when he clumsily caught it. But oh, what a prize, dear as any he'd ever won in all his days, the milky water washing the briny tang of Zosia's latest betrayal from his mouth like tears wiped away by a lover's hand.

'Boss, you think that's wise?' said the man, and Maroto looked up to see the green-haired girl offering him the hilt of a knife.

'This hunk owes us his life, think he'll be grateful enough to return my steel once he's cleaned that nut. That right, Useful?'

'Absolutely,' said Maroto, taking the pearl-handled blade and jamming it into the open top of the coconut, shaving off a few rough splinters of white meat. 'And what do I call my saviors, then?'

'I'm Captain Bang,' said the girl, 'and this slab of steak is my bosun.'

'Dong-won,' said the man, an Immaculate tarshirt of prodigious strength. Cocking an elbow at his equally broad comrade, he said, 'That's Niki-hyun.'

'Your name's Bang?' Maroto sat up straighter in the sand, remembering that the pipe had an L carved beside the Z, not a B . . .

'Bang Lin's the full handle,' said the girl, following his gaze to her pipe. She brushed it off and tucked it into one of the loops on her bandolier. 'But Captain Bang works just fine for a fellow freebooter like yourself. And what about you, merman – folk call you anything other than Useful?'

'Lots of things, but never more than the once,' said Maroto, and because he couldn't bear to be the laughingstock of some old song Zosia might have sung to this girl, he decided to stay incognito. 'You had it right the first time – the name's Useful, Very to my friends.'

'Then Useful it is, because I make a point not to get too friendly with my crew,' said Bang, extending a hand with the modern Immaculate character for *Eat* tattooed in sapphire ink on her middle finger and *Steel* in scarlet on her index. 'Let's get you into the shade to eat the rest of that, boyo, 'fore we all get sunstroked.'

'Press-ganged, huh?' Maroto popped another piece of coconut meat into his mouth, then dropped the small knife into the open nut and set them in the black sand. 'Ain't the first time, and knowing my luck it won't be the last, but I'm damned happy about it for a change.'

'Oh yeah?' Bang's crooked smile flashed silver and gold as Maroto took her hand.

'Truth,' he said, bracing himself for what would likely be a dodgy climb to his feet. 'Your ship far from here? And where is here, anyway?'

Niki-hyun and Dong-won exchanged a nervous look, and a forlorn expression crossed Bang's pleasant face, the constellation of indigo dots inked above her left eye contracting slightly. To banish whatever it was that troubled her, she set her feet and hoisted Maroto up. She got him most of the way up before he listed dangerously to the side, but then Niki-hyun and Dong-won came around on either side to steady him. They turned him away from the wide blue ocean and, as he tried to find his balance on the crumbly black beach, Bang finally answered him.

'My ship's the *Queen Thief*, but most of her hasn't washed up yet,' said the captain as they approached the bright jade jungle that rushed down from the high slopes of the coast to press in tight against the sandy cove. 'As for where we are, that's one hell of a strange question to ask, considering how far we are from anyplace else. Where do you think you are, Useful? How'd you come to wash up on this shore?'

'I'm not the sort to ask questions unless I don't know the answers,' said Maroto, reeling a bit in the sand as the two Immaculates swayed in place with him. 'I was dumped on this blasted coast by the blackest sorcery, and into yonder ocean by a pack of stupid monsters up there on the headland. So if you know just where the fuck we are, Captain Bang, I'd appreciate it if—'

'The Sunken Kingdom,' said Bang, trying very hard to sound cavalier about it. 'You've heard of it, maybe? Jex Toth? Place of legend what dwells in the heart of the Haunted Sea?'

'Uhhhhhhhh . . .' Maroto couldn't help but picture Hoartrap laughing and laughing, slapping his milky knee from the safety of his tent beneath the Lark's Tongue. 'Nah.'

'That's what I said,' grumbled Dong-won, steering their charge toward a small cooking fire and pile of driftwood at the edge of the jungle.

'We sailed straight into it, so it has to be Jex Toth,' said Niki-hyun from Maroto's other side. 'But for a kingdom that's supposed to be underwater this place is plenty dry, and from the height of the trees it has been for a long-ass time. That don't exactly put me at ease, though.'

Bang dismissed their concerns with a grin over her shoulder and a shrug.

'Worse places to be shipwrecked, my seawolves,' she said, picking up the pace to their meager camp, but Maroto couldn't even enjoy the sight of a tight posterior wiggling beneath salt water-stiffened fabric now that he knew that beyond it lay a realm he had never even believed in, a cursed land the likes of which made Emeritus seem as mundane as Flintland. He wasn't just exiled on a desert island; he was banished to a place that hadn't been on a fucking map in five hundred years.

Well, if Zosia and her errand boy Hoartrap thought that was all it took to get rid of Maroto they had another think coming. His fists, specifically.

CHAPTER

12

Back on the plateau that morning Sullen had been sure of but one thing in all the Star, and that was that he wanted to kiss Ji-hyeon. Now, as his beloved's boyfriend led Sullen all over the camp in search of an obliging blacksmith, even that certainty no longer seemed so, um, certain. It wasn't that he regretted kissing her, because come on now, she was gorgeous and clearly inclined. It wasn't even that he'd tripped over Grandfather and spoiled the mood.

It was that Ji-hyeon was already deeply involved with Keun-ju here, and whatever his feelings about this Immaculate boy, Sullen's mother had raised him better than to play the homewrecker.

As if reading his thoughts, Keun-ju stopped so suddenly Sullen nearly bumped into the smaller man. He turned to Sullen, his expressive brown eyes the only clue to his mood with the rest of his face hidden beneath a beaded veil of black lace. Those eyes didn't seem happy, and Sullen wondered if Keun-ju suspected what he and Ji-hyeon had been up to . . . or if one of the whispers Sullen had watched Ji-hyeon deliver to her Virtue Guard's ear before the two men had set out was a confession of their dalliance on the plateau. Sullen's heart quickened under the sad weight of the boy's eyes, the mallet of guilt banging on the drum of his conscience.

'I apologize,' said Keun-ju, far less bold now that he was alone with Sullen than he'd been in their previous interactions. 'I thought it was over here . . . '

'Oh,' said Sullen, realizing that quick as Keun-ju had been to take the lead he didn't actually know where they were going. The Virtue Guard had led them directly to the first smith, so after she'd been unable to help Sullen and they had set out for the next one he hadn't even thought to take charge.

'I've only been here a few days, of course . . . ' said Keun-ju, his eyes finishing the statement with *so what have you been up to with my beloved while I was gone*? Or so it seemed, but then the Virtue Guard added with a hint of sass, 'Considering how long you have been in camp, I am surprised you do not recall where the blacksmiths have erected their works.'

'Nah, I do,' said Sullen, and though he hadn't meant to be rude about it that apparently hadn't come through, because Keun-ju's nostrils flared, puffing out his veil.

'Might you care to lead on, then, Master Sullen?'

'Sure, yeah,' said Sullen, orienting himself and then pointing back up through the tents. 'A big shaman-blooded bloke up that way has an anvil, I'm sure of that at least. Sorry, I thought you must've had a reason for taking us down here.'

'Oh, I am just sure to have a reason for everything,' said Keun-ju, but low enough that Sullen wasn't sure if he was supposed to answer or not, so he just shrugged and led the way between the uneven rows. It was getting on in the afternoon, but the snow hadn't let up and few soldiers were outside their tents. Keun-ju carried on with his muttering about reasons, saying, ' – just like three blacksmiths must have very good reasons for being spread all over camp instead of building one big forge to share.'

'She did have a reason for that,' said Sullen, relieved to have an answer for once. 'Ji-hyeon tried having them all work the same fires, like you said, but it led to some fights, so she had them set up their own works away from one another. Think there was some other purpose for it, too, but that's the one I recall.'

'Well, that makes perfect sense,' said Keun-ju. 'If you keep several tools to do the same job you don't want them bumping into one another.'

Which had some venom in it, and Sullen kind of wanted to stop right then and there and try to talk this thing out with Keun-ju, but glancing back at the wiry, bright-eyed man he found that he ... that he was actually kind of scared of such a confrontation. He was in the wrong here, or at least sideways from right. Ji-hyeon was her own woman, and no man owned her, obviously, obviously ... but if she was holding the whole truth back from Keun-ju, was it Sullen's place to betray her wishes? Better to hold his tongue long enough to have a private word with Ji-hyeon and tell her straight that he wouldn't carry on with her until she'd sorted matters with Keun-ju.

Then again, Sullen had been the one to put the moves on her back at the plateau, and maybe if he brought it up to her she'd drop him flat. Then where would he be? Happier for having the truth out, he decided, but that was sometime yet to come, and for the present he was relying on a righteously pissed-off little Immaculate man to do him a solid and help work out an arrangement with a blacksmith, and make sure the weapon-maker knew this job had the general's blessing. All Sullen could do was make the best of it, for all three of their sakes – whatever came to pass, Keun-ju had done him no wrong other than a sharp word, and who knew, if he'd been in the boy's position Sullen might've had some sharp words, too. Among other keen objects.

'Ji-hyeon says you're into swords,' Sullen said, gesturing to Keun-ju's scabbard as they walked. 'She reckons you know more about 'em than even the smiths, which is why she said I could borrow you.'

'She said you could *borrow* me, did she?' said Keun-ju, and Sullen was beginning to see that he and his mistress had a lot in common, because half the time he couldn't tell if the Virtue Guard was seriously offended or just messing with him. Prolonged exposure to Ji-hyeon had attuned him to reading her actual feelings, but ancestors willing he'd never spend enough time around this touchy boy to learn his mannerisms that well.

'Turn of speech, is all,' Sullen said as placidly as he was able. 'My words, not hers. Sorry.'

'No need to apologize, I know your Immaculate needs some work,' said Keun-ju, which was just plain impolite. Sullen would like to see this runt so much as say hello in Flintlander, any dialect. 'And yes, I have educated myself in the riddles of steel.'

Riddles of steel? Sullen rolled his eyes. 'Cool.'

'Yes,' said the prim Virtue Guard. 'It is.'

'Say, here's a question,' said Sullen, finally hitting on a subject that would probably get the blowhard talking – himself. 'What is a Virtue Guard, anyway? I, um, guess a boy from the ice boonies like me doesn't understand what virtue means in a case like this.'

That got a quick and dirty laugh out of Keun-ju, and while Sullen wasn't sure why, it didn't sound very nice. 'No, I suppose virtue would be an alien concept to you.'

Ah, so that was it – some more cheap heat. Sullen was about

ready to let the Immaculate have it when Keun-ju amended himself, perhaps sensing the wrath he was on the verge of incurring.

'In this case, I mean; virtue might be universal, but you are correct, on the Isles it means something very specific.' For the first time since they'd set out, the boy sounded in his element, confident and patient instead of snotty or twitchy. 'Immaculate children born out of wedlock are of course every bit as legitimate as those born to married families. Yes?'

'Uh huh,' said Sullen, though he already felt a little out of his depth. 'No shame in being a bastard where you come from, sure.'

'Considering there are over a thousand noble families in the Isles, each with hundreds of years of history, marriages are more complicated than they might be in less civilized lands. Because a child brings together two families, if not more, the older generations seek to guide the course of their individual houses by carefully brokering strategic arrangements – Ji-hyeon, for example, was betrothed to Prince Byeong-gu, and had their marriage gone forward and had they borne a child together or through an appropriate surrogate, that child would bind the Bongs of Hwabun to the Ryukis of Othean.'

'And that's *good* for Ji-hyeon's family, 'cause the Empress of the Isles is a Ryuki?' said Sullen, hoping he hadn't lost the thread already. Outlander politics always made his head spin – even the nomenclature was impenetrable. Like, why did the Crimson Empire have a queen instead of an empress, while the Immaculate Isles had an empress despite being some sort of federation of island monarchies, near as he could tell?

'Assuming Ji-hyeon bore Prince Byeong-gu an heir, it would be *very* good. But if, for example, she had carried on a secret affair with another noble of another Isle, one out of favor with the court of Othean, and if she had given them a child, then Hwabun would be linked to this other family. And then the royal family would be displeased to have a long-agreed-upon alliance undercut – even if the marriage were to proceed, Othean would be tying itself not just to Hwabun, but also to this disreputable family who Ji-hyeon carried on with, for she would bring into the marriage a child with the blood of another Isle.'

'Complicated,' said Sullen.

'Not really,' said Keun-ju airily.

'So you keep Ji-hyeon from fooling around with anyone except the person her parents pick, and you call that guarding her virtue?' As soon as he said it Sullen felt bad for stooping to the man's level, but Keun-ju didn't seem to realize he'd been called out.

'Nothing of the sort. As a Virtue Guard my role is to guide my ward into leading a virtuous life, which entails many things. Grooming and etiquette are important, as are dressmaking, and the arts, and yes, the proper expression of romantic desires is also my province. My duty is not to stifle Ji-hyeon in any regard, but simply to see that she comports herself responsibly ... which is to say, with virtue.'

'And that's why you're so into swords and fighting?' Sullen asked. 'To beat back any illicit suitors?'

'I have my own interests for I am my own person,' said Keun-ju, 'and the martial tradition is chief among them. It is true, though, that my position requires me to be every bit as skilled in combat as Honor Guards or Spirit Guards, for while they may be obliged to help Ji-hyeon fend off attacks on her person, I may be called upon to put myself between the princess and the most dangerous foe of all.'

'And who's that?'

'Herself, of course,' said Keun-ju, and again there was that hint of mischief in his voice that set Sullen's heart to bouncing around with doubt; if the boy didn't know for sure that Sullen and Ji-hyeon maybe sort-of had a thing going on, he definitely suspected. 'A Virtue Guard must be willing to stand between their charge and any temptation.'

'Yeah?' Sullen had a lot of things he could have said right then, about where this particular Virtue Guard might put himself in relation to his mistress ... but betraying Ji-hyeon's confidence just to get a dig in on a rival was too low to contemplate for more than a moment, so he let it go. 'Must be a hard job.'

'Sometimes,' Keun-ju squeaked, and glancing over at him Sullen saw that without even trying he'd made the boy's rose-mallow cheeks bloom as pink as cherry blossoms. Sullen had to smile at that; he knew all too well what it was like to feel a burn that probably didn't even exist outside your own conscience.

'Come on,' Sullen said, clapping Keun-ju good-naturedly on the shoulder. 'See that tent over—'

'Dead fucking gods!' Keun-ju bellowed, wrenching himself away from Sullen's touch and doubling over. Before he could even wonder at the boy being so weak he realized he'd slapped the Virtue Guard on one of the many wounds he'd acquired the day before. A smear of crimson shone through the heavy cotton robes on Keun-ju's shoulder, and Sullen upbraided himself for being such a dunce. The boy had been walking so easily Sullen had totally forgotten he'd been on the threshold of Old Black's fucking Meadhall but the day before.

'Sorry, shit, sorry!' Sullen cried, planting his spear in the ground and taking a step forward to help Keun-ju when the boy's blazing eyes warned him off. 'Keun-ju, I swear it was an accident, I swear it on my grandfather's name, I do!'

And just like that some of the flames died down in Keun-ju's glare and he tried to shrug it off, only to grimace at the movement.

'I'm fine, I'm fine,' he said, though it didn't fucking sound like it. Then he straightened up to look Sullen dead center, took a step toward him, and said, 'And of course it was an accident. I don't know you so well as others might, Master Sullen, but I know you well enough to believe that if you wanted to hurt me you'd charge me straight on, instead of coming in from behind.'

Which bit Sullen about as bad as that slap to Keun-ju's wound must have, but it was a fair blow, and so he sucked it up and nodded, and held up his fist for the boy to knock. Even if Keun-ju snubbed him it was best to make an effort ... and then the Virtue Guard cocked his veil to the side a little and bumped knuckles with Sullen. The weird thing was a part of him wished Keun-ju had left him hanging; it would've made it easier to carry on thinking down about the man, but now that he knew the Immaculate just the tiniest bit better than he had before, Sullen felt even lower for continuing to chase Ji-hyeon.

What would Grandfather do in a situation like this? Sullen wished he knew, because then he could be sure of doing the opposite. Where Ji-hyeon was concerned, that seemed the safest play. Without any wisdom forthcoming from the back of his heart where his grandfather would dwell for as long as Sullen lived, he forced a smile at Keun-ju and set off toward the smith's makeshift hut. It might have been his imagination, but he thought that under the snow-salted black veil Keun-ju smiled back.

They crunched through the snow and ducked under the overhang of the browning pine-bough roof, the support posts dangling baskets of horseshoes and chainmail scraps. The smith had his broad, apron-strapped back to them on the far side of a cluttered table, sparks erupting from the anvil as he whaled upon it with an enormous mallet. After Keun-ju tried in vain to politely catch the fellow's attention, Sullen barked at him so loudly he startled himself. The blacksmith turned from his work, revealing Gate-black eyes with no whites at all and fleshy whiskers that bore more resemblance to a catfish's barbels than a pureborn's mustache.

Dealing with this second smith proved a good deal harder than the first one due to the language barrier, and Sullen's reluctance to bring Keun-ju into his confidence. He didn't have a lot of options, though, as the tendril-faced fat man scowling at them in the orange glow of the forge didn't seem to speak a lick of Immaculate or Flintlander. Sullen's Crimson had improved since he'd joined up with the Cobalts, but not nearly enough to get the point across without a fair bit of pantomiming. Given the subject matter, he was more comfortable asking Keun-ju to translate than acting out his request and risking something getting lost in the translation.

Keun-ju's eyes got bigger and bigger as Sullen told him what he wanted done with his grandfather's remains; he'd had the Virtue Guard wait outside the first smith's tent while he'd conferred with the Immaculate-speaking woman in private. Sullen was about to tell Keun-ju to forget the whole thing, seeing how shocked the boy was by the proposal, but then his veil fluttered in a long exhalation, and Keun-ju nodded sharply. Turning to the already-irritated smith, Keun-ju rattled off Crimson words like he was born to the crude tongue. By the time the lad was finished the smith was smiling, and through the sheer lace of his veil Sullen was sure he saw Keun-ju's teeth, too. The two exchanged a few more guttural phrases, and the Virtue Guard turned back to Sullen. Even with the veil his expression was unmistakably enthusiastic.

'He's heard of the technique – he calls it sainted steel,' said Keun-ju, and just as welcome as the news was the barely accented Flintlander rolling off Keun-ju's tongue. The Immaculate boy had never given any hint of knowing even the simple greeting of the Noreast trading tongue, but here he was speaking it like a spice merchant straight out of Reh. 'And I've read about it, so while he's never crafted one himself he thinks we can do it together.'

'Yeah?' Sullen looked back and forth between the beaming, sweaty blacksmith and the eager Virtue Guard. The smith raised his stub-handled maul and grunted another chain of Crimson.

'From certain qualities of the metal he believes that hammer he holds was forged thusly, and came to him but yesterday, just before the battle,' Keun-ju translated. 'It belonged to a Chainite war nun who died here in the camp. A guard brought him the weapon, among others, and recognizing its quality he cut the haft to make it a tool, and has only just now completed it. He sees our coming as a good omen, that a relic of the church was delivered to his hand, and the very next day we come here begging his service to forge a similar weapon – one that will be turned against the Chain.'

'Huh,' said Sullen, not sure how he felt about all this. 'So that hammer he's holding has an ancestor in it, but not his? Ain't that bad luck or something?'

Another staccato exchange, the smith waving the hammer around all the while, and Keun-ju explained, 'He believes once the dead enter the steel, they serve whoever wields it.'

'All right, then,' said Sullen, smiling along with these two unlikely allies now that he knew it could be done, that it was an everyday kind of magic and not just some long song of Grandfather's. 'I'll bring him down here, then, and we can get to work. If it takes me paying him something extra to see that it's ready by the morn after next I'll see if I can't scrounge some coins together.'

'Day after *next*?' Keun-ju said in a tone like he was the native speaker and Sullen was an ignorant foreigner who'd said one thing when he meant another. 'I'll ask him about it, if you insist, but I'd bet my ink pot such a blade will take weeks to craft. At the shortest.'

'Hmmmm,' said Sullen, considering what it would mean to give Uncle Craven any more of a start than he already had. 'Ask him, then, for I need this as fast as mortally possible. Please.'

More blather, and the few Crimson words Sullen recognized didn't bode well: *Insane. Foolish. Impossible.* That these were the terms Sullen had learned over the course of his journey across the Empire spoke to Grandfather's character, and the impression the old man had made on strangers.

'He says it will take more time than that,' Keun-ju said when the smith was finished and, while Sullen waited for the little man to deliver the rest of the fish-whiskered smith's harsh proclamations, nothing was forthcoming, save a mild, 'Quite a bit more time, probably.'

'Hmmmm,' said Sullen, unwilling to linger in camp a moment longer than necessary. In his wrath over Uncle Craven's desertion Sullen had thoughtlessly sworn an oath to remain in camp for but three days before hunting the coward, and voiced the pledge in front of Hoartrap to boot, otherwise he would have already left ... but he was also reluctant to deny Grandfather's remains the noble fate this shaman-blooded blacksmith promised, now that he knew such an internment was indeed attainable. Then he thought of the empty slot in Ji-hyeon's double-holed scabbard, the sword she had lost along with two of her fingers during the epic battle. 'I have to leave before it will be finished. What about instead of a spear point or a sun-knife, then, can he make a sword? One identical to Ji-hyeon's?'

Keun-ju sucked through his teeth, and too late Sullen remembered who was doing the translating here. Nothing for it now. Keun-ju bandied some more Crimson, and when the Virtue Guard looked back at Sullen there was a certain vulnerability there that confounded Sullen – what stake did Keun-ju have in Grandfather's funerary rites?

'He has made Immaculate-style blades before . . . ' Keun-ju spoke cautiously. 'And with Ji-hyeon still possessing the lost weapon's twin, it will be easier to craft a replacement. But . . . but he is your grandfather, so why not do as you first asked, and make a spear or knife, so that when you return he has become a weapon you can use?'

' 'Cause I might not come back,' said Sullen glumly, and lest this kid get his hopes up, he added, 'I'm *planning* on a comeback, mind, but plans have a way of getting twisted, yeah? And if they do and I don't return, well, I wouldn't want no one lifting him in death who wouldn't put up with him in life, so that means he goes into steel that Ji-hyeon can use. Ever since we left the Savannahs, she was the first person who treated him serious-like, instead of looking down her nose at him on account of his being a crabby old savage. Yeah?'

'Yeah,' said the Virtue Guard in a wistful voice, when Sullen would've expected him to have a laugh at the whole venture. This Keun-ju kid was weird as hell, no doubt. 'And if you do return from wherever you go, Sullen, what then? Your grandfather will be laid to rest in a steel blade that you cannot use with any skill.'

'Ain't too worried 'bout that – I'm a fast learner, especially where killing tools are concerned,' said Sullen, and if this hadn't been Keun-ju the pretty boy he was looking at, Sullen might have thought there was a little gleam of respect in those deep brown eyes. And seeing as how the tale had already spun way the hells out to the side from where he'd first seen it going, Sullen decided on the fly to offer another fist for this foreign fool to knock or ignore as he saw fit. 'Everybody got to get on with their day, I expect, so I'll head up there now and bring Fa back down so we can get started . . . I know the way myself and I know you're busy, but if you were able and inclined I wouldn't say no to the company while I fetch him.'

And not for the first time that day Sullen's one true rival for his one true love surprised him, because instead of Keun-ju jumping at the excuse to be shy of him, his eyes shimmered, just before his gaze dropped to the snowmelt inching its way under the canopy of the smithy. In a voice that was every bit as solemn as the occasion demanded, Keun-ju said, 'It would be my honor, Master Sullen, to see your grandfather Ruthless delivered to this place.'

'Shit, son, I ain't master of much, so let's just leave it at Sullen,' said he, trying a little bluster of his own to overcome the unforeseen emotion that tightened his chest. He almost slapped Keun-ju's arm again before remembering himself. From the way the smith roared with laughter at their emotional exchange, Sullen wondered if the fat bastard spoke Flintlander after all. Well, let him laugh – this world was dim enough without begrudging a man whatever light he could pry free from the darkness.

CHAPTER

13

Darkness would have been preferable, but the cold afternoon sun found Zosia even through the sheltering snow. Typical – it had been a long time since she'd received anything but the opposite of what she wanted. If she preferred water she'd find ryefire in her mug, and if it was ryefire she needed the bowl was sure to hold wine. Maybe if she'd prayed for death and destruction to descend on Kypck everyone she cared about would still be alive, and she'd just be a spiteful old broad looking out over a happy village with a hunger in her heart that was better not fed . . . Maybe many things, in the songs of mortals, but at the end of the ballad all you were left with were the choices you'd made and the luck you'd had, for better or worse.

Today, as with so many others, the shittiness of Zosia's luck was surpassed only by the foolishness of her decisions. At least she hadn't broken her hand on Kang-ho's brat, and the old sawbones who had tended her after she'd been brought back to camp didn't think the bite Ji-hyeon had given her was too serious. The grizzled barber had ground some itchy paste into her shoulder and given the guards leave to dump her in the stockade, which didn't sound like much, sure, but Zosia was relieved to have something burny rubbed into her wounds; be it girl or beast, an untended bite could cause all kinds of trouble. Considering Ji-hyeon's reckless temperament, rabies didn't seem beyond the realm of possibility.

So that was it, then: the most that could be said for Cobalt Zosia, veteran of a thousand battles, was that her wounds probably wouldn't have a chance to fester before she met some equally rotten end. The hundreds of other occupants of the stockade certainly didn't look inclined to pour her a cuppa or rub some liniment into her bruises. No, the only thing that seemed to be keeping the mob of Imperial captives from stampeding over the newest prisoner was a disagreement over who got first dibs on kicking in the Stricken Queen's face. She'd kept her head down and moved straight to the back of the repurposed corral, flopping down on the frozen ground with her back to one of the palisades that formed the southern wall, but word of her identity had evidently spread.

'Zit true?' a big man with distractingly small teeth called, separating himself from the nearest pack and strutting purposefully toward her. 'You her?'

'Your mom? 'Fraid not,' said Zosia, staying where she sat sprawled out in the icy muck. 'But I did meet her one time, at a Geminidean stock show. She won the red ribbon for Ugliest Cow in the Empire.'

Which was just pathetic, really, but Zosia was several blows to the skull past caring. Put some color in his cheeks, anyway. He came in huffing and blowing like a tempest, stepping between her spread legs with the clear aim of booting her guts out through her ass. As soon as his right leg came back for the kick Zosia cocked her own, and fast as a devil, slammed it into his left shin. His leg slipped out behind him on the icy ground, and the big man fell forward so fast Zosia barely had time to sway out of the way before his face connected with a thick pine post of the palisade. Rocking back to her original position against the wooden backrest, she shoved the man's limp body out of the way. As he rolled onto his back in the snow she saw a thickening smear of dirty blood right between his crossed eyes.

The big man's friends were coming in now, a dozen Azgarothians with murder writ in bold script on their hard faces. All she wanted was to stay where she lounged, denying these soldiers even a decent fight before they claimed credit for killing Blue Zosia, but when did she ever get what she wanted? She owed them a good story out of it, at least. Her body carried her lightly to her feet, or so it must have looked – inwardly, the creaking of her joints and the aching in her bones pained her worse than any of Princess Pumpkin's little lovetaps. A wave of muddy Crimson tabards rose up to engulf Zosia, and she ground her feet into the slick earth, bracing for the impact . . .

'Stop! That's an order, damn it! Stop! All of you!'

If there was one creature in the world that took commands more seriously than even a bound devil, it was an Imperial soldier out of Azgaroth. The squad halted as one, heads pivoting in unison. They looked confounded, and Zosia couldn't blame them – the man who had given the order was a wisp of a youth with a mustache so weak it looked like it might blow off in the first strong breeze. He walked stiffly over from where he and a gaggle of soldiers in slightly different tabards had watched the scene unfold, and then Zosia recognized him as the young Myuran commander Hoartrap had captured, along with the rest of his regiment, when they had tried to ambush the Cobalts by sneaking around the back of the Lark's Tongue during the epic battle of the day before. He'd looked so traumatized when Hoartrap led him down from the mountain that Zosia had wondered if he would ever get over it, but apparently she shouldn't have concerned herself. His gait and gaze were both steady as he approached her.

'Colonel Wheatley,' she called. 'To what do I owe this honor? Fancy a turn with the belle of the ball before the rank and file wear me out?'

'We're better than this, damn it!' cried Wheatley, ignoring Zosia entirely and addressing the soldiers who crowded around. Many of the captured Imperials still looked as slack-eyed and shell-shocked as the cavalry Zosia had led to the Gate, but those who had come out of their torpor – or been rattled out of it by the appearance of a hated enemy in their midst – all turned to the Myuran colonel. 'Of course this ... this war criminal deserves justice! Of course! But we must not sink to her level, not even in the name of doing what is right. A true soldier obeys the laws of the Crimson Empire not only when it is easy or convenient, but when it is hard, damn it, hard as steel in your belly! A true Crimson hero knows that order is only preserved when we hold ourselves to a higher standard, even when our hated enemy is cast at our mercy! A true citizen believes—'

And on and on he droned, but seeing that she wasn't about to be lynched after all Zosia sat back down against the palisade and pulled her hood low over her ears to drown out his insipid speech. Most of the soldiers were drifting away, too, but as a pair knelt to retrieve their concussed comrade from where he still lay beside Zosia, one of the stern Azgarothian women hissed, 'Wait until dark, fuckface. Just you wait.'

So at least now she had something to look forward to.

———

Ji-hyeon would have fallen off her horse a dozen times over if Choi hadn't insisted on squeezing onto the saddle behind her. Her head felt like it was full of bees. Big, angry bees that kept stinging the inside of her nose and throat with every hoofbeat of the charger. There were rather a lot of hoofbeats between the Gate and the meet with the Thaoan brass on the far side of the valley.

'Shoi ... shit.' Ji-hyeon flexed her jaw, willing herself to stop slurring before they reached the Thaoans. She'd sounded a little funny after her fight with Zosia, but that weird scaly bug that Diggelby had produced from a cigar box in his satchel and insisted she eat must be weighing down her tongue. Maybe her Honor Guard had been right and they should have delayed the meeting long enough for her to be tended by a barber, but refusing to show when Colonel Waits herself had ridden down from her regiment would make the Cobalts look vulnerable. 'Shoi ... Shhh ... Shhh. Shit. Chuh. Chuh ... Shoi. Shit!'

'Turn your head this way,' said Choi, the comforting weight of her armor on Ji-hyeon's back and the woman's arms around her waist the only things keeping the general on her horse.

'Shhh ... Shhh ...' Ji-hyeon kept trying but it just wasn't happening. She obliged Choi, craning her neck around, but her eyes wandered over the smoky vale behind them, looking for Diggelby. Cobalt guards leading the surviving Azgarothian cavalry away from the Gate, but no sign of the dandies. She was going to give that bug-barmy fop a piece of her mind, if not her boot, for giving her—

Black lightning blasted Ji-hyeon's skull and her mouth flooded with thick blood. She reeled, and Choi's hand slipped from her nose to her side, holding her up as she drooled red syrup into the trampled grass. Her face, Choi had done something horrible to her face ...

'What the shit, Choi?' she gasped, letting herself be pulled upright on the horse again.

'You sound better,' Choi said happily. 'Your nose won't display your honor as prominently now that I've set it, but your enemies will better understand your boasts and challenges. A necessary correction.'

'My nose?' Ji-hyeon still heard a little lisp in her voice, but not as much. 'She broke it, didn't she?'

'A misnomer, but that is how the injury is commonly described,' said Choi.

'Damn,' said Ji-hyeon, worried about how it would look when it healed but also a little thrilled to have reached this milestone in most every warrior's career. 'Aren't you going to tell me how I should've avoided it? What I did wrong?'

'No. You fought admirably.' Was that smugness in Choi's voice or pride in her pupil? 'You may not have been aware, but your right arm was rising to block the backfist that crushed your nose. You almost intercepted it. She was faster. That is the way of all opportunities to win honor. Next time you must be faster, but you do not need me to tell you that. And . . .' Choi seemed reluctant to continue, but then, though the rest of the mounted bodyguards were flanked out beyond risk of overhearing anyway, she leaned in and whispered in Ji-hyeon's ear, 'I believe if your left hand had not been injured in yesterday's large-scale opportunity, you should have overcome her.'

Coming from Choi, such a compliment meant something indeed. In nigh on a year of campaigning, encouraging words were rare as owlbats' teeth, and outright praise unheard of. Apparently all it took to impress her Honor Guard was getting herself choked out by Cobalt fucking Zosia.

Looking down at the reins in her right hand and the bloody bundle of rags that covered her left, she supposed she'd acquired some cracked bones to go along with the throbbing stumps where her pinky and ring finger had been bitten off . . . and the very next day after a cannibal tried to eat her alive, Ji-hyeon had tried to rip out Zosia's arteries with her teeth. Nobody could say she wasn't a fast learner.

The squeaky bugles of the Imperials began to sound from ahead and, walking their horse through the last thinning bank of lingering smoke, Ji-hyeon saw a cluster of red-caped riders waiting for them just where the edge of the valley began climbing the foothill that bordered it. Behind the delegation of envoys, the Thaoans had their whole damn regiment spread out on the snow-smudged slope. Metal glinted even in the dimness of the day, the cold wind burning Ji-hyeon's face, but she couldn't very well cover it without touching the skin, and touching the skin made her feel faint. The small herd of Imperials did not walk their horses to meet her retinue, forcing her to approach them instead of meeting in the middle. Typical.

Coming up on the handful of officers, dozen mounted guards, and one sketchy-ass Immaculate envoy, Ji-hyeon offered an Imperial salute, because it never hurt to be polite. Especially since a full Imperial regiment, even one with the ho-hum reputation of Thao, could squash the beleaguered Cobalt Company before nightfall, if they had half a mind. If Fennec was right and her second father was plotting to come after her with both swords drawn, she had to play it very, very professionally with these Imperials he'd conned into working for him. The tall woman with her steel mesh visor pushed up to reveal sharp, heavily made-up cheeks must be Colonel Waits, and Kang-ho was just whispering something in the ear-slit of her helm when he got a proper look at Ji-hyeon. The treacherous old bastard broke with the rest of the Thaoans, cantering his horse the last few meters and flipping up his owlbat faceplate to better gawp at his daughter.

'What in all the incontinent gods of the Golden Cauldron happened to you, child?'

'I told you, Kang-ho, you're to address me as General Ji-hyeon,' said she. 'And if you think I'm bad you should see the other girl.'

———

'I see it, but I don't believe it,' said a familiar voice, and Zosia looked up from the tarp she was fixing to the palisade to see Singh walking toward her across the makeshift prison yard.

'Hey there, sister,' said Zosia, turning back to her work. The light was fading fast and she was keen to get her lean-to completed before the snow-shrouded sun dropped behind the Lark's Tongue; an invisible sun still made for warmer work than a set one, and the weather must show no signs of slacking if the Cobalts were giving out tarps and tents to their prisoners. 'Don't suppose you've brought me a hot meal and hotter kaldi? Maybe peatfire and a packed pipe to while away the hours until my execution?'

'As a matter of fact . . . ' Singh set down her steaming knapsack and helped Zosia with the tiny cairn of scavenged rocks she was using to pin down the edge of her tarp. She was grateful for the help, her fingers too numb to balance the stones properly. 'Now that my queen's boudoir is in order, might we step inside for some privacy?'

They wedged themselves under the small lean-to like two girls squeezing into a fort they'd fashioned in the woods from an old sheet and a low-hanging bough. In most circumstances it might have felt cramped, but with Singh sharing her beaver mantle, an over-steeped press of spice tea, and a rich pot of curried roots, the low shelter seemed positively cozy. After she'd bolted down the food and tea and began sipping on Singh's meerschaum pipe and silver flask, Zosia let herself lean into her warm friend, one of the very last she had.

'I fucked it all up, Singh,' she said quietly, warming her

hands on the clay pipe and savoring the cedar-scented smoke rising from the bowl. 'But what else is new, huh?'

'Stuff and nonsense,' said Singh, squeezing her shoulder until Zosia reminded her of the bite with a hiss of her teeth. 'You've been in tighter spots than this, sister, and always came out free in the end.'

'Not much tighter,' said Zosia, making her point by brushing her head on the tarp that barely covered them both.

'So about that ... ' Singh pursed her lips. 'What are you doing here, exactly?'

'You haven't heard?' Zosia sucked on the pipe, then passed it to her friend, letting the smoke roll out with her words. 'I would've thought it'd be all over camp by now. I found out some of the cavalry who attacked Kypck survived yesterday, so I came here and talked the captain on duty into letting me take them out, so—'

'Oh, I know all that – what are you doing here, in an understaffed stockade in the middle of a snowstorm?' Singh took a pull at the meerschaum, and by the glow of the pipe Zosia saw her friend looking at her with the same pitying expression she had worn back in the Zygneman stinghouse when they'd first been reunited. In the old days Singh had never looked at her that way. Zosia supposed she'd never had cause. 'What's the scheme?'

'Scheme?' If it had been anyone else, Zosia would have faked a laugh. 'There's no scheme.'

'You expect me to believe the woman who single-handedly broke into Kaldruut's dungeons to rescue me can't hop over a wooden wall? Why are you here, Zosia?'

A fair question, but when Zosia tried to reply she found she'd lost her answer ... if she'd ever had one. The simple truth was she'd barely slept in two days and was just aware enough of her state to recognize she was in a very bad way, every thought that crossed her mind twisting into ugly shapes. She shrugged, and Singh leaned into her until their scalps touched, rocking sadly in place.

'Oh, Zosia,' she said quietly. 'I've been there. It's scary, especially at first, but it does get better. You get used to their absence, and you're able to go on with your life.'

Zosia shook her head, because while she had so much she could have said on the matter, she didn't trust her lips to let anything out but a sob. Even after everything she'd done to avenge Leib, to honor him, he was more remote than ever before, and fading all the time. Thinking of him every day, every hour, she had been able to cope with that . . . but now she had to remind herself to remember him, and that was what tore her heart apart, the guilt and shame so overpowering she couldn't even think straight . . .

'I knew you before you bound him, Zosia, and you were even more fearless then,' Singh murmured in her ear. 'Youth played a part, yes, but your bravery didn't come from immaturity, it—'

'*Bound him?*' interrupted Zosia, wiping her snotty nose on her sleeve. 'Hold on, who're you talking about here?'

'Choplicker?' Now Singh sounded as confused as she was. 'You loosed him, didn't you? And now you're unsure how to go on, without his protection to see you through?'

It felt good to laugh, after the day she'd had, but soon enough the ragged cackle trailed off. 'Oh gods no, I'm glad to be rid of the fiend.'

Saying it didn't quite make it true, however, and remembering the damn dingo-dog's happy bark when they'd both come through another scrape together choked her up again. If she wasn't the better blessed part of a decade past the last of them, she would've thought her moons were coming on, fast as her moods were shifting . . . and hell, she did almost miss the old monster, at least a little. She took another hit off the warm flask and chased it with one on the pipe; this peatfire was even smokier than the smoke.

'Your husband, then?' Singh asked when Zosia passed her back the pipe.

'Yeah, I guess . . .' It had gone unsaid so long she didn't even know where to begin, or if she even wanted to. But want and need aren't the same things at all, and clearly her brilliant strategy of figuring it all out on her own hadn't gotten her anywhere good. 'I miss Leib so much sometimes, and others . . . at other times I have to tap myself to even remember why I'm here. I know nothing can bring him back, knew that from the first, but it's the only thing I want, the only thing that could possibly make me happy. And since I can't be happy, here I bloody am, doing the last thing he'd want me to do – tossing more bodies on the scales, as though killing folk ever evened things out instead of skewing it worse than ever. He hated bloodshed, Singh, hated me even talking about the old days . . . so what in all the fucking devils of Forsaken Emeritus am I doing out here?'

'Right now? Talking to an old friend, one who's always ready to listen, and sorting through troubles that no one should ever have to face alone,' said Singh, but then she didn't say anything else, because the woman knew Zosia better than she knew herself, and knew sometimes more can be said in a warm silence than in a thousand thousand words. Then Singh cleared her throat, and asked, 'When was the last time you got laid?'

'That's not it!' Zosia elbowed Singh, but not very hard. 'I mean . . . yeah, it's been a while since I was with anyone. Not since . . . Leib.'

'Grandmother's mercy, no wonder you're so crazy,' said Singh. 'I thought a week was your personal worst? Remember that time we were all coming back up through the Panteran Wastes, and you were so hard up Maroto thought he had a shot, but then we hit that cult of cannibal lepers and—'

'I remember,' said Zosia, though she kind of wished she didn't. 'Not exactly my finest hour.'

'You did better than Maroto! I wouldn't be surprised if those demented cultists still have him on their shit list, after the stunt he pulled . . . but really, Zosia, as your friend, I'm begging you – get some play, and not just with yourself.'

'Easier said than done,' groused Zosia, a certain perfidious pirate blowing her a kiss in her mind's eye. 'But give me a little credit here – you think I'd be this fucked up over a lack of action?'

'Yes,' said Singh, sounding serious as a hedonistic friar of the Ten True Gods of Trve preaching against temperance. 'Absolutely, without a – ouch!'

Zosia let go of Singh's braid with a smile; she hadn't tugged it that hard, and her friend went on: 'Alright, alright, you want me to be serious? I can be serious. You lost your lover, your devil, your whole life, all in a year's time. That is *bad*, Zosia, the kind of bad some people never bounce back from. I saw you were in a bad way back in Zygnema, which was the whole reason I signed on for this foolish errand – I thought it would be good for you to get some blood under your fingernails again, chop up the Imperials who torched your town. But I'm going to level with you, girl – you are worse than when I found you.'

'You asked me to oversee your kid's rebellion out of *charity*?' Zosia didn't know if she should be touched or insulted.

'Don't use the C word,' said Singh. 'Even after all these years it immediately makes me think of Maroto's—'

'Oh wow, yeah, what was he even thinking?' The merry memory of Maroto melted into the decidedly less pleasant encounter of the day before, and Zosia already had enough to beat herself up over without adding his bugged-out hissy fit to the docket. 'So call it a pity-coup then, but it amounts to the same thing – that's fucked up, Singh!'

'You looked like you needed it. And you would have done the same for me.'

'Don't count on it,' said Zosia. 'I don't have that much imagination.'

'Speaking of beggaring imagination, were you as wide-eyed as I was when you found out who this Colonel Hjortt really was?' The dark shelter flashed as Singh fiddled with her coalstick to relight the pipe they'd both forgotten about. 'Call me naïve, but I never would have believed old Cavalera would put a Chainite curse on his own people.'

'He didn't know what the Chain were planning,' said Zosia, almost amused to hear herself defending the good name of her onetime nemesis. 'I went to see him last night, because I thought . . . well, you know who I thought he was. But . . . but the Colonel Hjortt who murdered Leib and the rest of Kypck is Cavalera's son. Or *was*, anyway – he never made it out of the fire I set that first day. All this time I figured the boy was out there somewhere, waiting for me to come back and finish the job, but I was too damned thorough for my own good.'

'You found all that out last night? No wonder you're having a shit day of it.'

'Yeah, I've had better . . . It was so *weird*, Singh, talking to Hjortt née Cavalera last night. Or Domingo, I guess we'd better call him, since that name hasn't changed. But seeing him laid out on that cot, beat all to hells and confronted with his worst enemy, *me*, and knowing he couldn't lift a finger to hurt me, even after what I did to his son—'

'What *you* did to *his* son?' Singh sounded angry enough to march into the crippled old man's tent to set him straight on the account.

'Yeah, Singh, *what I did*, because you know what? I cut off his kid's thumbs before burning him alive. And the boy deserved it, but you think that matters to a parent? If it came out Leib somehow gave Hjortt deadly provocation to do what he did, I wouldn't have been any less sore over it. It might have stung even worse, because I knew there was some justification to it.' Zosia shook her head. 'So anyway, there I was, alone in a tent with the biggest thorn we ever had lodged in our collective ass at my mercy, and do you know what I did?'

'It's no crime to gloat over a fallen foe,' said Singh, though Zosia knew the chevaleresse's code would prevent her from ever behaving so basely herself.

'You know, I think he might have preferred it if I'd lorded it over him,' said Zosia thoughtfully. 'Left him with his pride, at least, but instead I just . . . I felt so fucking *bad* for him, because we both knew it was all his fault that most of his regiment were dead. Shit, not even just dead, but sacrificed, right, and sacrificed to further the ends of the Burnished Chain. And so I . . . it sounds stupid, but I tried to cheer him up. Told him the day wasn't lost so long as he drew breath, that is was never too late to pay back the fuckers who wronged him. Told him, sure, you tore open a hole in this world leading straight to hell, to say nothing of summoning back the Sunken Kingdom, but hey, at least you've got your health. Everyone you cared about is dead thanks to your bright ideas, but don't let it get you down.'

'Sounds like you were maybe talking to yourself a little, too,' said Singh, offering her the pipe now that she had it burning again, but Zosia gently declined.

'That's all I ever fucking do, talk to myself,' Zosia spit. 'And end up even more lost than I was before.'

'You're not lost, Zosia, you just needed a break, some time to figure things out,' said Singh. 'And now that you've had one, let's get you moved somewhere more comfortable so you can plan your next move.'

'You don't think bedding down in the Crimson henhouse is poetic justice for a fox of my color?' Zosia flicked her silver hair in the glow of Singh's pipe.

'I thought the command tent might be more your style,' said Singh, having slipped into Rhinote, the obscurest Raniputri dialect that they both had some handle on. 'When one feels lost, it's best to return home, don't you think?'

'Even if I wanted to, you think Ji-hyeon would fold that easy?' Zosia touched the poultice on her shoulder and winced. 'Kid's harder than she looks, and popular.'

'Not for long,' whispered Singh. 'The word's been all over camp since this morning: the Empress of the Immaculate Isles has issued a bounty on our general's head, and the prize is nothing less than governorship of Linkensterne. If we don't move on this fast, someone else will.'

Zosia could barely believe what she was hearing. Not that Singh would sell Ji-hyeon up the Isles to install her old friend in the girl's place, that made perfect sense, but that Ji-hyeon had managed to enrage Empress Ryuki so badly that she'd pledge such a prize. A villain after her own heart, all right. Zosia considered the angles. 'You think Fennec or Hoartrap would go for it?'

'If you were the one stepping up to fill the girl's helm and claim Linkensterne for your own? I think Kang-ho himself would pat you on the back and help broker the exchange, if you promised him a window to do business in the Link again. Maybe the Sunken Kingdom's risen from the sea or maybe Hoartrap's just off his nut, but one thing's for sure, and that's that an opportunity like this doesn't come along twice.'

'No, I suppose it doesn't,' Zosia said quietly and, dark though it was under the canopy, she held the plan up to her inner light, turning it this way and that, examining every facet and flaw. Inadvertently or not, Singh had raised an important question this eve, and that was what exactly did Zosia want that was actually attainable? Was there something, anything, that could bring her contentment, or at least chase away her cancerous sorrow, if only for a while? Could governorship of Linkensterne be just what she needed? She'd given up on ruling the Empire, because it was too damn hard and frankly too damn scary to be responsible for so many people, but running a corrupt city couldn't be nearly that tough. And after tasting the yoke of Immaculate oversight for even a short spell, all and sundry would welcome a woman of her standing as the savior of Linkensterne ... In no time at all, she could have her own personal paradise, a city she already knew and liked well enough honed into whatever shape she cared for. An end to this bitter, thankless quest for vengeance, a mission that could consume the rest of her remaining years and bring her no closer to discovering if someone had actually sent Efrain Hjortt and the Fifteenth Cavalry to Kypck or if the whole thing had been a devildamned goof on the part of a pea-brained young colonel. To welcome old friends into the governor's mansion and not have to worry if they would all be dead on the morrow after signing on for some half-baked campaign to save the world when all the world wanted was to drop into the nearest hell just as quickly as it could, thank you very much.

'I . . . ' Zosia paused.

'Yes?' Singh's breath was spicy in the closeness of the lean-to.

'I think you'd better pack another pipe, because we may be talking a bit longer yet,' said Zosia, for the first time in a very long time liking the course that was mapping itself out across the inside of her skull. It was a nice feeling, to know what needed doing, and while that alone wasn't much, to the woman who had nothing the promise of *something* shone and sparkled like all the beacons of the night sky. A shame even that was concealed by the early winter storm, but Zosia knew a thing or three about weathering storms . . . and also the conjuring of them, as far as that went. After their little exchange at the Gate that afternoon, Ji-hyeon Bong had a great big surprise coming her way.

CHAPTER

14

Maroto poked and prodded at his knee. He hadn't noticed when he'd first come through the Gate, because the raggedy bandage still retained enough of its material to cover the nasty wound he'd doubtless reopened during the Battle of the Lark's Tongue, and the knee certainly felt weak and sore enough to be a gaping, bloody mess ... but when he finally worked up the nerve to peel back the filth-plastered cloth and examine it, he saw it wasn't even pink and scabby, like it had been the morning before the big fight. It was completely healed, a band of white scar tissue as thick as his thumb crossing the front of the knee. Moving about on it still felt strange and clumsy, but the more he got used to it the more he figured that was just the result of babying it ever since he'd first gashed it open fighting the horned wolf. Nothing short of deviltry could heal a wound that fast, so either Hoartrap had done him a favor on the sly or jumping through a Gate had unexpected side effects. Of the two possibilities, only one seemed believable.

So yeah, this day had been one big old surprise after another, but as the sun melted into the jungle on the western edge of the cove, he was met with the biggest one yet: these seemingly intelligent pirates shipwrecked on a legendarily weird shore showed every intention of keeping their fire lit even as the luxurious purple twilight settled around them. He'd spent the day drifting in and out of dreams, the toxic cocktail of a sudden Gate-trip halfway across the Star and the aftereffects of his buggy bender still playing hell with his brain, but now he was feeling alert and lousy. Feeling himself again, in other words, and that meant it was time to sort out these amateurs.

'With all due respect, Captain Bang,' he said from his sandy seat at the edge of the jungle, 'having that fire going while the sun was up was mad enough, but I won't sit by in silence and watch you feed a lure to every hungry monster with eyes in its head.'

'No?' Bang sounded disappointed but didn't look up from the bright blue crab she was roasting on a stick. 'A pity that you'll be going off on your own so soon, Useful, when we've finally gotten accustomed to your smell.'

That got a laugh from Dong-won and Niki-hyun, but they all knew it was as cheap as they came.

'Look, I'm not trying to undercut your command,' Maroto said, as patiently as he could manage with the darkness thickening around them. 'But—'

'What do I say about *buts*?' Bang said, turning her crab over, and before Maroto could crack the riddle Niki-hyun and Dong-won spoke in unison:

'Sew buttons on them, Cap'n.'

'Precisely,' said Bang. 'Cute as yours is, Useful, I'd be happy to assist if you can't reach it yourself.'

'You don't know what's out there,' Maroto told the fools, leaning in closer to the fire and lowering his voice to the appropriately dramatic level for his necessary embellishments. 'I do. I've seen 'em. Hungry ape-monsters the size of horses, and vipers longer than an Immaculate customs ship. Worse things, too, I don't doubt, and a fire like this on the treeline can be spotted for miles, drawing them out of their lairs with the promise of easy meat.'

Dong-won and Niki-hyun didn't look thrilled, but Bang dismissed him with that annoying moan kids use when telling ghost stories. '*Oooohooohoooo*, Useful's seen such horrors as turned his hair white overnight! Good thing I've got my prayer beads to ward off any devils, and where faith fails we've got something better: cold steel.'

Maroto was about to reply when what she'd said gave him pause, and he reached up, wrapped his finger around a few hairs in the middle of his unkempt flattop, and plucked them free. Grey as the greasepaint his old comrade Carla used to wear when doing her drag routine. He tried not to grin as the pieces fit together; his nephew must've gone through a Gate, too, but far more exciting than that random bit of intelligence was the fact that his formerly dull, dark hair must look as fleet as his nephew's. Between this development and his knee mending itself, things were looking up – who knew Gate-hopping could be good for both your health and your style?

'Maybe I'd feel better if I could hold on to that dagger again,' he told Bang when a pop of her crab shell brought him back to his immediate concerns. 'Because it's not a question of *if* a horde of hideous monsters attack us, it's *when*. First rule of being a castaway is not attracting the local predators, and that's on a normal isle – what in all the heathen gods of your ancestors and mine do you think we'll draw in here, on the Sunken fucking Kingdom?'

'Here.' Bang still wasn't looking up from her crab, but drew the knife from her belt and threw it into the sand between his bare feet. 'Happy?'

'No,' he said, trying not to groan as he leaned forward to

retrieve the paltry weapon. 'So maybe you'd care to explain why on a balmy night like this, with dinner about done, you're insisting on—'

'Useful, I'm going to give you one last chance to stop that gob of yours.' Bang was finally looking up, and the flames reflected in her eyes looked a mite cooler than the furious flush of her cheeks. 'Last night Dong-won spied from that far headland the fire Niki and I burned down here, and if we hadn't kept it going through the night I might never have seen my bosun again. I lost four and twenty more of my crew when the *Queen Thief* went down, and I'll gladly fight off every devil on Jex Toth if that's what it takes to keep a guiding star lit for any of my people who might've made it to shore. You want to hide in the dark, get on with it, so long as you're quiet about it. Aye?'

Maroto met her gaze, silently cursing the foolhardiness of the young ... then asked himself what he'd do if he thought Purna or Choi might be lost out there in the black jungle, or limping across the jagged tide pools at the rim of the cove. His eyes didn't drop, then, but he nodded once. 'Aye aye, Captain.'

'My favorite words in all the world!' Just like that, the fury and desperation that Maroto had kept company with himself a time or three fled her face, and after several finger-singeing attempts Bang snapped off one of her crab claws and tossed it to Maroto. Easy as she'd planted the knife between his bare feet before, the morsel went wide enough he had to scramble for it, then pick it out of the sand and brush it off when it bounced off his clumsy fingers. He sincerely hoped she'd done that on purpose to make a point, because the alternative was she didn't throw as well as she thought she could and the knife had missed his ankle by providence alone. 'Now since you're feeling so talkative, Useful, how about a song to while away the hours?'

'Not much of a singer,' said Maroto, punctuating this sad truth by cracking the claw between his teeth.

'Ah, so that's something we've learned about our new friend already,' said Bang, blowing on the far more substantial shell of her meal. 'Useful's not a singer, good to know come music night. Now, how about sharing a little bit more with your fellow castaways? Like who you are, and where you hail from, and what blackest sorcery brought you into our company . . . that sort of idle chatter what makes strangers close as lovers.'

'Hmph,' said Maroto, slurping the crabmeat out of the shell. It was only half-cooked and tough as a boot tongue, but it tasted sweeter than Usban baklava to his starving tongue. 'That's . . . that's not the sort of thing you want to hear. For your own protection, I mean, the less you know about me the better.'

'That's what I love about meeting new people.' Bang nodded knowingly at her fellows. 'You don't just get to learn about them and their foreign ways, but they also get to learn about you, and thus the Star is made a smaller, warmer place. For example, you've just learned that I actually *do* want to hear all about you, and damn the oh-so-sinister consequences. Considering we were the ones to drag you out of the Haunted Sea, Useful, I'd say we know more about protecting you than you do about protecting us – that's another neat thing about making new friends, you learn stuff about yourself, too.'

'Yeah, okay,' said Maroto, because he was too bushed to put up much of a fight, or even point out that he'd gotten himself out of the water all by himself and they'd just assisted him up the strand to their over-illuminated camp. 'Yesterday morning I woke up halfway across the Star, on the eastern slope of the Kutumbans a little ways west of Thao. Being precise, I was camped with ten thousand other folk at the base of a mountain called the Lark's Tongue, this ugly peak that sticks up on the edge of the Witchfinder Plains. Shall I be more specific still, Captain?'

'Only if it helps the story,' said Bang, resting her unsampled crab back on the coals. 'Who were these ten thousand friends of Useful you were bunking with?'

'No one you know,' said Maroto, though that was actually a bit of a fib, gauging from the pipe she'd spent an hour cleaning, and which now sat drying a safe distance from the edge of the fire. 'A mercenary company I was scouting for, nobody famous.'

'A freebooter at sea and a scout on land,' said Niki-hyun, some of the first words she'd had all day long. 'No wonder they call him Useful.'

'Come to mention it, Useful does look a bit like another rogue I knew,' said Dong-won. ''Cept his name was Bullshitter and he didn't do none of what he talked.'

'Bullshitter, right – you've met my cousin, then,' said Maroto without missing a beat. 'Other than good looks, better humor, and champion cocksmanship, we don't have much in common, though.'

That got a grin out of Bang, at least, and a smaller smile from Niki-hyun, but Dong-won must have missed the joke. Come to notice it, though, the sea-ox had been scowling at Maroto ever since he'd advised they quench the fire. Boo bloody hoo. Maroto had spent his night dangling from a eucalyptus in the snake-haunted high country and you didn't see him taking it out on sensible strangers.

'Like I was saying, though, yesterday morning I was in the thick of it with these mercenaries, when the nastiest regiment in the Crimson Empire came sweeping down from the foothills on top of us.'

'Which regiment?' said Dong-won.

'The, um, shit, I'm bad with their numbers,' said Maroto,

but the knowing look Dong-won gave his captain and comrade jogged his memory back to the smushed old walrus he'd met right after they brought the pack of horned wolves screaming down into their mountain camp. He recited it perfectly: 'The Fifteenth, out of Azgaroth, led by Colonel Hjortt.'

Neither Bang nor Dong-won looked impressed, but Niki-hyun whistled and said, 'They *are* supposed to be the worst. Or were, anyway, back when Kang-ho was reaving it up down south.'

'Kang-ho?' Maroto tried not to show his surprise, and figured he did an adequate job – he might not be able to sing, but he could act the pants off anyone, when he felt the need. 'Suppose he must be quite the local hero in the Isles. He's one of the Five Villains, right?'

'Is or was?' asked Bang, a shrewder critic than he'd anticipated.

'I don't know much about how the tale ends in Immaculate songs . . .' said Maroto, and then was pulled from the fire by Niki-hyun.

'You remember,' she told Dong-won, 'that's the regiment he'd start in about, every time we sighted the western shore on the way down to the Dominions.'

Dong-won tried to shush her but the damage was done.

'Sailed with the dread seadog Kang-ho, did you?' A terrible thought occurred to Maroto, one that damped what little fun he'd been having with the Immaculates. 'Was he on board? Did he go down with the *Queen's Sneak*?'

'*Queen Thief*, and no, I never had the pleasure of sailing with that particular living legend,' said Bang, though the warning look she gave Niki-hyun hinted at an interesting song. He was just relieved to hear that the one Villain who had always done all right by him was still drawing breath.

Probably. What a shame Kang-ho had never joined his daughter; it would've been something to have the whole crew back together, if only for a night . . . 'You were telling us of indomitable Azgarothians and your plucky band of ten thousand nobody-we've-ever-heard-ofs?'

'Sure I was,' said Maroto, getting up with a groan and hobbling over to the pile of green coconuts the Immaculates had cut down. It was a careful dance, with coconuts – they had the only drinking water you could trust on a new shore, but if you gulped down too much too quickly you'd soon be putting out more than you took in, and not in a pleasant fashion. 'Craziest fight I've ever come through. The Imperials went totally apeshit, killing each other instead of us, eating people alive, and all the while this rank smoke was rising from the field, till you couldn't see the shield in front of your face.'

'That so?' Bang asked as Maroto returned to his seat. 'You wouldn't happen to have a strong taste for drink or bugs, would you, Useful?'

'Too strong for my own good where the crunchy crawlers are concerned, and just right when it comes to drink, but that wasn't it,' said Maroto, and because he knew his tale was too wild to tell any other way but straight, he caught himself and amended the story to include all the gory details. 'Well, I'd had a sting or two beforehand, but it wasn't *just* that. Unless you've heard of a bug trip so potent it'll open a Gate under your feet and catapult you clear to the Sunken Kingdom.'

'Jex Toth,' said Niki-hyun, and when both Bang and Maroto looked at her, she looked down and said, 'That's what they called the kingdom before it sank, and it ain't sunk no more, so . . .'

'Let me get this straight,' said Dong-won, apparently not interested in semantics. 'You're telling us you fought some

Imperials down in the Empire, then you went into a Gate in a place where everyone knows there ain't no Gate, and Woo-chi's your uncle you land on the Sunken Kingdom.'

'On Jex Toth,' said Maroto, winking at Niki-hyun, 'and Woo-chi's who now?'

'It's an *expression*,' said Dong-won, crossing his ink-sleeved arms. 'Point being, your song's got more holes than a customs agent's pockets. You keep telling us this place's crawling with giant monsters, so how come instead of getting et you swam in on the tide, same as us? And why'd a smart guy like you jump into a Gate?'

'I may have had some help going into the Gate,' said Maroto irritably. 'Yesterday. And after spending a bad night on the headland I may have had some help going over the cliffs into the sea, too, by those very beasties. Lucky for you that I did, or you wouldn't be enjoying my company.'

Dong-won snorted, but Bang said, 'Well, I count it lucky that he brought my pipe back. How'd you pull that trick, Useful, did you bat those pretty eyes of yours at one of the sea monsters who wrecked my ship? Maybe employ that quality cocksmanship we've heard so much about to trade your stiff piece of meat for my stiff piece of briar?'

'Didn't see no monsters,' said Maroto, unable to stop himself from momentarily reliving the experience of sinking down into the cold, lightless reaches of what he now knew to be the Haunted Sea. He didn't need his consummate acting skills to shudder convincingly. 'Was just bobbing under the surface and I caught it in my teeth, luck is all, like you said. But back to your ship going down – how'd that happen, exactly? I didn't think even Immaculate pirates were brave enough to sail into the Haunted Sea.'

'They gutted us from below,' said Bang, solemn as an

alms-begging monk now that she was talking of her tragedy instead of mocking his. 'These ... *things*, great, big ... things. With pincers and hooks and all plated in shell, but it was a soft sort of shell, your cutlass passed right through it ... The queer part was they scarcely noticed us, even as we tried fending 'em off. All they wanted was to take the ship apart, plank by plank and bolt by bolt, but then our lookout, Hae-il, he must've come to in the crow's nest and lost his senses, because he cast his signal lantern at one of 'em, and then the whole ship went up in flames. We carry a lot of rhum ...'

Bang turned her face from the fire, but not before Maroto saw a familiar shimmer in her eye.

'We *carried* a lot of rhum,' she said, quieter now. 'I dove over the rail just as she blew, and even then I barely made it ashore, the water just teeming with ... things. Different than the ones that boarded us, smaller and meaner and hungrier. Sharks that weren't sharks and devilfish that were more to the devilish than the fishy, if you follow.'

'I lost my boot and most of a toe,' said Niki-hyun, which explained her limp when she'd helped Maroto up from the shore. 'And my sister.'

Dong-won didn't say what he'd lost but from the wracked frown on his face as he abruptly stood and turned away from the fire, looking out to the moonlit sea, Maroto supposed it had been a someone rather than a something. It got quiet around the fire, and then for some reason the words came spilling out of Maroto's mouth, like steam released from the boiling cauldron of rage and grief where his heart used to be.

'I lost people yesterday, too. A couple might've turned up after I left ... gods and devils, but I hope Choi is all right, and Din and Hassan, and my kinfolk, of course. Purna, though ...' His throat closed near as tight as his eyes, but he had to say it, because one of the many things that girl had taught him was that pain was a poison, and if you didn't let it out it would grow and grow until it was all you had; that was how he'd treated Zosia's memory all those years, not as something cherished and warm, but as an ugly, cold weight in the center of his soul. He would never, ever let Purna become that; instead he would share the glory of her song with anyone who would listen, not just until the day he avenged her but to the day he died. 'Her name was Purna Antimgran, Thirty-ninth Tapai of Ugrakar, and she saved my sorry life more than once. She was clever and quick and more fun than you ever had in *your* sorry life, and she died because I was fucked up on bugs when I should've been protecting her. She was my best friend, maybe the best person I ever met, brave and loyal and utterly mad, and she died because she trusted me. She's dead, and I was betrayed by my oldest friends, and now I'm here, and that's my whole fucking song. I told you I couldn't sing.'

It was even quieter, only the waves and the hissing of damp wood thrown on hot coals breaking the stillness. Maroto opened his eyes and wiped away the tears, because even with her pale, shuddering body bleeding out in his mind every time he thought he'd got a handle on his shit, just talking about her chased that awful image away, let him remember her the way she was before he'd gotten her dead. She'd have fucking loved this, stranded on the Sunken Kingdom and hunkered around a campfire with real pirates, and he laughed a snotty, tear-clogged laugh to picture her sitting beside him, cracking wise and coconuts in equal measure. Wave after wave broke upon the black sand, and Maroto looked out at a sight no citizen of the Star ever had, not in his time nor his father's nor any living folk's, not since the Age of Wonders: the stars lighting up over a tapestry-perfect beach on Jex Toth.

'I think . . . ' Bang said carefully. 'I think the crab's all right to eat, people.'

'Eh?' Maroto turned back to the Immaculates and saw them ravenously cracking into the electric blue crabs they'd roasted some time before but apparently hadn't touched the whole time . . . other than the crab claw Bang had tossed him. The tumblers clicked into place. 'Oh. Well, fair's fair, but I'm last in line far as testing fresh water and such goes, then.'

'Initiation test,' said Bang, tossing him a spindly leg and keeping the rest for herself. 'From here on out, we all draw straws when something's in question.'

'And let me guess who holds them,' said Maroto, breaking into the leg and getting a mouthful of shell and a matchstick's worth of meat.

'That was some song,' said Dong-won, still standing as he split a carapace between his thumbs. 'But there is no Thirty-ninth Tapai of Ugrakar.'

'What?' Fast and foreboding as lightning over a clear sky, Maroto slipped into his battle calm. Used to be he had to be in the thick of it for that hyperawareness to take hold, but here it was, and he was so disappointed he could have wept. The big man hadn't seemed so bad, but absolutely nobody got to besmirch Purna's memory and walk away with their lying mouth intact.

'Either your friend's a liar, or you are,' said Dong-won casually, but as Maroto floated slowly to his feet the pirate must have caught a whiff of his impending arse-beating and changed his tune but fast. 'Ask Niki-hyun, you don't believe me – our old boss's hubby was half-Ugrakari, so we had to learn all sorts of titbits about the place so's not to embarrass him or us. Ugrakar's got thirty-six Tapais, just like their Temple's got thirty-six chambers – one for each noble house, and the Living

Saint who founded 'em. Common knowledge to anyone with a real connection to the place.'

Maybe the burly pirate was speaking true and maybe he wasn't, but that was irrelevant to Maroto as he stepped calmly around the fire. That jab about having a 'real connection' just earned this loudmouth one of Maroto's patented scars, which were apparently all the rage down in the Serpent's Circle. Best of all, he wouldn't even have to pay for it. Niki-hyun and Bang began rising, too, but it was far too late for anyone to save Dong-won, barring something truly fucking calamitous like a giant monster running up on them.

Some lugs have all the luck.

The jungle had fallen utterly silent, when Maroto knew firsthand from his wretched night in the eucalyptus that this place was a regular Tennegarian concert hall of shrieks, howls, chirps, splashes, and swishing underbrush. Wild places only go that still when a predator stalks, and a dire one at that. The starlight shifted on Dong-won's slowly jawing mouth, the pirate still talking his shit, and Maroto's head snapped around to see the attacker moving through the underbrush behind him.

Except there was no underbrush behind him, nor an attacker disturbing the shadows as it crept forward. There was just the open beach leading down to the water, but the slippery shadows deepened over the pirates' firelit faces, wavering like palm fronds . . .

Maroto's eyes rose up, up up up, even as his arms lashed out in either direction, one hand pushing Bang into Niki-hyun and the other shoving Dong-won arse over teakettle. Maroto was diving over the fire, but seemed to be getting there in no kind of a hurry, the humid air turned to treacle, and his sluggish eyes finally caught the moon-slick edge of one of the enormous ivory wings that propelled the thing down upon its prey. It fell upon him, fast as sin, even as Maroto tumbled through the air with the speed of grass growing in a shady plot . . . and then it snatched him, crushing the wind from his frail mortal form as it drove him into the burning sand at the edge of the fire.

Then it was gone. Maroto spit up hot sand, scrambling away from both fire and starlight long before his rattled skull even realized that the monster hadn't actually touched him, that it was the force of its beating wings alone that had slapped him out of the air. As he slithered past the barrier palms and into the closeness of the jungle, he looked back. It wasn't to make sure the pirates were following his sterling example, because his brain wasn't up to thinking anything nearly that coherent, but just to make sure it wasn't right on top of him again.

It wasn't, the horror skimming out over the waves now, but when he saw its outline against the night sky, the amorphous, airborne behemoth white as sun-bleached bone, he felt more than a little like a field mouse sneaking a peek at an owl. The sight of it plunging into the surf and rising with what might have been a dolphin or a shark grasped in its slithering train of tendrils did little to dispel the sensation.

Far as sensations went, though, being in fear for your life beat apparently running into a mangrove tree at full tilt. He bounced backward, and for a moment there it really seemed like fright alone would keep him upright and moving. Sometimes not even terror is enough, and Maroto ate sand for the second time in a few dozen seconds. Though every fiber of his being wanted him to wriggle deeper into the shadowy undergrowth, all he could do was dimly register that the grit in his mouth was a little earthier and damper here, back from the beach a bit. Then the boughs overhead spread with sadistic slowness, and the shadow, the pale shadow . . .

'I take back what I said,' Dong-won hissed as he held back

the branches so Bang and Niki-hyun could reach Maroto. 'You *are* useful.'

'And let's try to keep him that way, yeah?' whispered Bang, helping Maroto to his feet. In low tones that did nothing to hide the quaver in her voice, she said, 'After lengthy consideration of your proposal, Useful, I have decided to suspend all nocturnal fires for the foreseeable future. Hiding deeper in the jungle also seems prudent. Any other advice you might offer to your captain during this unprecedented period of open suggestions?'

'Aye, Captain Bang,' Maroto wheezed. 'I suggest we all shut the fuck up till dawn.'

Her gilded teeth flashed in a patch of starshine, and though it may have just been a taut branch snapping back across as they helped one another hobble deeper into the dense undergrowth, Maroto thought the pirate captain might have swatted his rump.

CHAPTER
15

When the sawbones finally let Ji-hyeon leave the medical tent for the second time in twenty-four hours, her ass was about the only part of her neither bruised nor broken, nor swollen from injury or insect. Her left hand, as she'd surmised from the gross clicking sounds it made when she moved it, was broken in several places. The raw fucking agony that had slowly but surely replaced the queasy lightheadedness of Diggelby's bug was also something of a giveaway; she'd known it must be bad indeed, to even begin to compete with the hurt that radiated outward from where her nose had been. Of course, the barbers told her it was still there, but she wasn't convinced, and declined their offer of a mirror. The expression on her second father's face had been enough to convince her that she didn't really need to know exactly how bad she looked, on top of feeling as bad as she did.

What a garbage day, and, as Fennec reminded her when he ambushed her on the way out of the white tent, it still wasn't over – she had her interrupted morning meeting with her cabinet to resume, albeit several hours later than originally planned. And down a member of said cabinet, too, but Fennec was too polite or too cautious to bring that up, though if he knew enough to find Ji-hyeon at the barbers' tents he certainly knew what had precipitated her arrival there.

'Obviously you'll go over the main points with the principal captains,' Fennec said as he, Ji-hyeon, and Choi slipped their way up through the dark camp, the snow still steadily falling and the refreezing slush turning the avenues between the tents into frozen creeks. 'But if there was anything you wanted to run past me in private, I would be happy to offer my counsel.'

'Yeah, okay,' said Ji-hyeon, and in the shimmering torchlight bouncing off the snow and ice she saw him perk up. It had been so long since she'd taken him into her confidence that he probably made the noises out of habit rather than expectation. 'Do I execute her? I feel like I kind of have to, now.'

'Well ... ' He didn't look so happy to have her boxed ear anymore. 'You don't *have* to do anything.'

'Not an answer, Fennec.'

'That she went behind your back is certainly cause for concern—'

'Goes, Fennec. Not went, *goes*. Constantly. Murdering prisoners is fucking psychotic, but right now I'm less worried about her owlbatshit bloodlust than I am about her trying to run things under my roof.' Floaty and nice as the centipedes had made her, the specter of Zosia didn't bring Ji-hyeon down from the clouds so much as darken them into charged and flashing thunderheads. 'She and Hoartrap convening about the new Gate and Jex Toth and everything before I've even heard word one about it is so fucking wrong I could spit, but do you know who else Zosia talked to before she told me?'

Fennec thought about it. 'Singh?'

'What? No! Not that I know of, anyway, but I wouldn't be surprised – she told brotherfucking Colonel Hjortt!' Ji-hyeon nearly slipped but Choi caught her elbow, allowing Ji-hyeon to continue instead of breaking something new on the frozen ground. 'Zosia swore an oath to serve me, and I find out she's sharing the most crucial intelligence of this whole campaign with the enemy commander before I've even heard about it! What the fuck *is* that?'

'A very big problem, as you say,' said Fennec. 'It's even worse than I suspected.'

'Oh goodie! I wonder what the shit you're hinting at, Fennec – could it possibly be something your beat-up, bug-stung general would rather hear about directly than have hinted at all fucking night? Hmmmmm?'

He smiled at her massive side-eye, a smaller, more genuine smile than she'd provoked out of him in a very long time, and she smiled back as he said, 'While you've been doing . . . whatever it is you've been doing all day, I've done some digging on your behalf.'

'Annnnnnnnnd?'

'And Kang-ho's not the only one who's found out about Empress Ryuki's bounty on you. The only thing that spreads faster through a camp than the pox is juicy gossip, and this morsel's positively glistening. I'd be genuinely surprised if there's so much as a cart horse that hasn't overheard someone talking about it by now.'

Ji-hyeon's stomach flopped. As general, she attracted notice everywhere she went, and she had finally gotten used to the sensation of being constantly watched. Yet now the drawn faces staring at them from around what low fires they were able to keep lit under the taller pavilions took on a sinister cast.

'They can't be seriously considering it,' she said, telling herself as much as Fennec. 'I mean, from our first victory any Cobalt sellsword with brains in their hat has to have known they could sell me out to an agent of the Empire for crazy coin, but nobody's tried it.'

Fennec glanced past Ji-hyeon, and following his eyes she saw Choi blatantly pretending not to have heard what they were saying. Something even darker and colder than the snowy night occurred to her, and she said, 'Have they?'

'A few sloppy betrayals, all resolved by Fennec and myself,' said Choi, as though such a trivial thing hardly bore mentioning.

'Wait.' Ji-hyeon stopped walking, and looked around to make sure no nearby tents had their open flaps cocked in their direction. All were tied up tightly from the damp chill. Still, she whispered, 'A *few* betrayals? You're seriously telling me that soldiers who took the Cobalt oath have plotted to *kill* me, and you never *mentioned* it?'

'One was a kidnapping, not an assassination,' said Choi, always the stickler for details.

'You have enough to worry about without getting paranoid over a few rogue elements,' said Fennec. 'Treachery and sedition are occupational hazards of your post, I'm afraid.'

'So even you two are making moves behind my back, and I'm not supposed to be paranoid?' Ji-hyeon's already bruised throat threatened to pinch shut altogether, the harsh air seeming to freeze her lungs.

'It is an Honor Guard's duty to protect you from incidents that might bring you undue risk without the benefit of glory,' said Choi, who sounded even less guilty about the duplicity than Fennec. 'I would no more concern my general with the doings of oath-breakers than I would with the machinations of worms in a midden.'

'And what about you, Spirit Guard?' she demanded of Fennec. 'Didn't want to trouble my soul with the quandary of how to handle my fellow sinners?'

'In my professional experience, what is bad for the body is ill for the spirit,' said Fennec with a shrug. 'A dagger to the back, for example, can have an adverse effect on both your physical and emotional well-being.'

'Get stuffed,' snapped Ji-Hyeon. 'I mean it, both of you. I'm not a helpless little princess anymore!'

'You've never been helpless,' said Choi.

'Look, just don't hold anything back from me anymore. That's an order.'

'As you wish,' said Fennec. 'And on that exact topic, what I was attempting to tell you is that it's not the grunts and humps you have to worry about where Empress Ryuki's bounty is concerned.'

'Yes, I remember what you told me this morning,' said Ji-hyeon. 'But Kang-ho didn't try to snatch me during the meet, did he? If he plans on slapping me in irons and selling me to Othean he's got a long game.'

'One which may involve his old compatriots,' said Fennec, lowering his voice and stepping closer to her. 'The reason I asked about Zosia possibly talking to Singh is that the chevaleresse paid the stockade a visit this evening, and something tells me she wasn't there to chat with any captured Imperials. Can you see where this might be going?'

Oh, could Ji-hyeon ever.

'Your dustup with Zosia might have been just the push she needed to reevaluate her role in the new Cobalt Company,' Fennec went on, perhaps mistaking her furious silence for confusion. 'She's sat in the same command as you, and she knows you won't have much choice but to dole out some stern discipline after today's fiasco. A general has her reputation to think of, and there were a whole lot of witnesses to one of your officers trying to murder you in cold blood. How do you think

Cobalt Zosia would have handled a captain calling her out in front of the troops, and then—'

'That piece of shit,' Ji-hyeon snarled. 'After all I've done for her . . . and for Singh, too, paying her dragoons twice what any other mercs in the Company are pulling down. Grrrrrr. Come on, this is shaping up to be a very interesting council.'

'I'm not saying they're planning anything,' Fennec hastened to add as they resumed their slippery march to the command tent. 'Singh and Zosia have always been tight, and the chevaleresse could have gone to Zosia to advise her to throw herself on your mercy, or just to make sure she's all right.'

'Does that sound like either of their style?'

'Not exactly, no.'

'I didn't think so,' said Ji-hyeon. 'Hoartrap's always been a wild card, my dad's actively working with the Thaoans, and Maroto's deserted us, quite possibly to betray us to the queen. I'm beginning to think teaming up with you old-timers was a bad idea.'

'I don't believe I ever suggested collaborating with any of them,' said Fennec.

'Maroto is not working for the Empire,' said Choi, the first time she'd offered her unsolicited opinion all night. 'I stake all my honor on this.'

'Fennec, the fact that you're the most trustworthy of the lot speaks volumes,' said Ji-hyeon. 'And as for you, Choi, I think your perception of the Mighty Maroto has been clouded by all the steam rising from your panties.'

'My . . . panties?' Choi sounded vulnerable, but Ji-hyeon was far too fucking pissed to cut her any slack.

'You've been talking him up ever since you came down from the mountains,' said Ji-hyeon. 'Answer me plainly, do you or do you not want to make out with that manky old barbarian?'

'I . . . He . . . Desire would never compromise my judgment,' stammered the usually unflappable Choi, which was such a shady dodge that Ji-hyeon almost threw up in her mouth at the mental image of Maroto and Choi getting frisky.

'Keep telling yourself that,' she told her flushed Honor Guard. 'For your sake and mine I hope he isn't a spy, but we can't know for sure until we catch him. At the moment, though, I have more immediate Villains to deal with. I've got more than half a mind to have Zosia brought up from her kennel so she can hear what I have to say – there's a lot of deadwood in the Cobalt Company, and a night this cold calls for a bonfire.'

The Azgarothian jackals had just begun to gather around Zosia's lean-to when a hissing torch scared them off, and Zosia dropped back down from the palisade she'd been halfway up. Climbing up the icy posts with cold-deadened fingers was proving so difficult she was happy for a reprieve, shoving her hands in her armpits in case the guards were just making the rounds. Now that her talk with Singh had cleared her mind, taking on a gang of wrathful Imperials was sounding like a lot more bother than just going over the wall and cutting out on her own.

'Captain Zosia?' said the older of the two greybeards, rough-looking fellows who were either cousins or closer relations still. Then again, it might have been the clutch of long, thin scars that squirmed across their faces that gave them a similar aspect, the ancient wounds shiny in the torchlight.

'That's me,' she said, and the men exchanged wonderstruck looks. When they'd received their orders they must not have believed it was really her, and she impatiently stamped her feet. Earlier in the eve guards had delivered firepots and fuel for the prisoners along with the tarps and tents, but Zosia hadn't felt inclined to join one of the tight rings of freezing Imperial soldiers who'd clustered around the meager heat like flies drawn to warm shit. 'You got a message for me, or can I go back to freezing my hams off? Hard to get a nice case of frostbite with you boys waving that hot torch in my face.'

'The general wants you brought to her tent,' the slightly younger one said. 'And pull your hood down; she doesn't want the whole camp seeing you come in after what you done.'

'Heavens, no,' said Zosia, curtseying with the cold-stiff hem of her cloak.

'And I've got to put some bracelets on you,' said the older with the tone of a man trying to coax a spooked horse into a bridle. He held up the manacles for her inspection but had the sense not to approach her. She was about to tell these two to go back to Ji-hyeon with a nice big raspberry if the girl thought Zosia would march through camp in chains, but seeing how anxious they already were she decided to be obliging. That quick-tempered brat would probably blame these poor schmucks for failing to follow her orders, and Zosia figured she'd already gotten enough innocent soldiers in the hot seat for one day after talking the stockade guards into letting her carry off the cavalry.

'You don't have anything in silver, do you?' she asked as she stuck her wrists out for his irons.

''Fraid not,' said the older man, and with a surreptitious little bow of his head, added, 'Your Highness.'

Zosia returned the nod as he clicked the manacles into place, thinking back to Singh's scheme. How many of the new Cobalt Company were old-timers like these two, who might've served under another blue banner a quarter century past, or who at least knew who she was, what she'd tried to accomplish? Maybe some of these sellswords would be happier if she pulled a tidy little coup . . . but it wasn't about them and what they wanted.

At her age Zosia had learned it was hard enough to make yourself happy without getting overly concerned with the wants of strangers.

'If you'll be so good as to follow me, my lady,' said the younger man as he led the way with his torch, and Zosia was touched by the chivalry of two scar-faced career soldiers who extended what courtesy they could to the Stricken Queen, even at her lowest point.

'It will be my honor, gentlemen,' she said and, blowing a kiss to the nearest dark clump of Azgarothians, followed the Cobalt soldiers out of the stockade to have a word or two with her impostor.

———

It all came down to this meeting of her captains – if Ji-hyeon was usurped from command of the Cobalt Company, it would be tonight. She'd allowed herself the fantasy of somehow tricking them all into the tent and then setting it on fire, but even if such a dramatic ploy were actually tenable there was the annoying wrinkle that all of her potentially traitorous commanders were so damned useful. No, the only way to steady her tumultuous future and reaffirm her role as unimpeachable general was to meet these schemers head-on, with a steady voice, a level gaze, and a harsh ass-whipping, if it came to that. Hesitating at the entrance to the command tent where everyone had settled in while she reunited herself with her weak dozing devil and then swiftly scared up and appointed her two new captains, she took a deep breath of the bracing air. She could do this.

'All right, boys,' she whispered to the men behind her, 'if things go bad, you know what to do.'

Keun-ju blew his veil out and up to reveal a sly smile, fingers tapping the pommel of his four-tiger sword. Sullen frowned, looking down at the handle of the top sun-knife on his bandolier as though it were a stinging insect that he was hoping would fly away on its own without his needing to brush it off. She wanted to come in close and kiss them both, and so turned back to the trouble at hand without kissing either. She had to figure out what she was going to do about this ridiculous romantic mess she'd created, but first there was a slightly more urgent concern. Making sure Fellwing was sturdily nestled in the elbow of her now good and useless left arm, she pulled back the flap and entered the command tent as if she didn't have a care in the Star.

'So glad you could join us – and you've brought your gentlemen callers!' Hoartrap waved them over to the command table where he, Singh, and Fennec sat sipping ruddy pine liquor and snacking on sausages, puddings, and cheeses. Choi stood behind Ji-hyeon's empty chair, but instead of going around the side to take her seat the general walked to the front of the figurine-cluttered table with its crude map of the Lark's Tongue valley. Without addressing the three Villains, she scooted away a steaming platter that had invaded the edge of the map and began rearranging the red miniatures on the board to reflect the afternoon's movements of the Thaoan regiment. They were the same pieces she and her second father had used for their many war games back on Hwabun. Seeing the encroachment of the Crimson troop on the Cobalt camp, the pale sorcerer said, 'Oooh, that doesn't look good – fenced in, are we?'

'Interesting,' said Singh, leaning forward and popping one of her tiny betel leaf–wrapped packets of tubāq and bugnut into her mouth; apparently talking with one's mouth full didn't violate the chevaleresse's sense of propriety. 'They mean to hold us here but don't seem to be planning an immediate offensive. Why wait for reinforcements, though, when they have such a superior force and our troops are war wearied?'

'No doubt they see how well that strategy worked for the Fifteenth,' said Hoartrap. 'As I said this morning, it's likely yesterday's ritual was entirely the Chain's doing and not the Empire's, and so the Thaoan colonel may believe we were responsible. In such case, prudence—'

'I made sure the Thaoans knew exactly what happened yesterday,' said Ji-hyeon. 'I told Colonel Waits everything I knew, and offered her the opportunity to align herself with the Cobalt Company as we march on Diadem. She's taking it under consideration, but in the meantime she's ensured we can't slip away.'

There was a stunned silence from the table, and then Hoartrap hooted with fruity laughter. Fennec and Singh exchanged concerned looks, and the chevaleresse said, 'A bold invitation from an inferior army.'

'Our quarrel has never been with any one soldier nor officer, nor any single province,' said Ji-hyeon. 'Our enemy is the corruption of the capital, particularly the malign influence of the Burnished Chain. Now that the Chain has murdered an entire Imperial regiment in the service of their mad ambitions, it is safe to assume they are attempting to overthrow the queen and seize absolute power for themselves.'

'Unless the Crimson Queen actually gave her blessing to this unorthodox offensive,' said Hoartrap, all business again. 'If we're jumping to wild conclusions, why not just assume she's a born-again Chainite herself?'

'Because she isn't,' countered Ji-hyeon. 'I interrogated Colonel Hjortt, and he confessed enough that I am sure this plot to resurrect Jex Toth was not known to Queen Indsorith. Which means yesterday's ritual and its sacrifice of thousands of Imperial soldiers constitutes a declaration of war by the Black Pope, not just against the Crown but against all free people of the Star.'

'Interesting,' said Fennec, pouring his general a dram of the resinous red liquor. 'It's true that in every Chainite rebellion since Zosia's time, Thao has sided with the queen, not the pope, so this plan may have potential . . .'

'Only if my second father doesn't talk Waits out of it, in favor of ransoming me to Empress Ryuki,' said Ji-hyeon, turning her full attention to Singh. 'Or if someone here in camp didn't have a similar notion, selling me to the Thaoans in exchange for the rest of the Cobalt Company going free. If the Chain truly has the power to raise dead empires from beneath the oceans, perhaps resisting their reign is hopeless. Perhaps both the Thaoan regiment and the Cobalt Company would be better served by getting on the winning side, instead of standing in the way of destiny. What do you think about such a course, Chevaleresse Singh?'

Singh didn't flinch, eyes locked on Ji-hyeon's, mustache gleaming in the lantern light. From the corner of her eye Ji-hyeon saw Hoartrap open his mouth to say something smart, but he must have thought better of it. Without breaking Ji-hyeon's gaze, Singh slowly rose to her feet, and then spat a red blob onto the center of the table. If she hadn't been so insulted to see the blue general figurine dripping red from Singh's betel-stained spit, Ji-hyeon might have been impressed by the woman's aim.

'On your honor as a chevaleresse, Singh, what did you and Zosia speak of in the stockade?' Ji-hyeon demanded.

'Many things,' said the old woman with a crimson-toothed grin. 'But you wish to know if we plotted to usurp your command and sell you for a profit, yes?'

'Your intuition is impressive,' said Ji-hyeon, waiting for the chevaleresse to spring across the table, or for Hoartrap or Fennec to make a move. Then Singh's hand rose and slowly inched into a fold of her black sari, making no effort to conceal her movement. This was it . . .

'We talked of the potential for such actions, but ultimately Captain Zosia dismissed it,' said Singh, reaching down and picking up the soiled general from the table. She snapped a handkerchief out of the fold in her sari and quickly cleaned it, then set it back in the center of the map.

'Why?' Ji-hyeon tried not to let her relief show.

'She thinks highly of you, General Ji-hyeon, and said . . . how did she put it?' Singh tugged thoughtfully on her mustache. 'Ah, she said we were too old for such petty schemes, and even if we weren't, you are far more valuable than the price Othean has placed upon you. She thinks that what happened yesterday is proof that the Burnished Chain has become a bigger threat to the Star than any in memory, and if anyone can lead an army against them, it is you.'

Ji-hyeon didn't know what to say, but Hoartrap filled the silence for her:

'Cold Cobalt, the Banshee with a Blade, and the Heart of a Lamb. Who knew?'

'Let's not get carried away,' said Fennec. 'If Zosia thinks a few platitudes and the decision *not* to double-cross Ji-hyeon is all it takes to get herself off the hook for this afternoon's madness at the Gate, she may find herself gravely mistaken. How exactly is the general supposed to maintain order if she pardons a captain who tried to murder her?'

'I don't think that will be a problem,' said Singh smugly.

'And why's that?' demanded Ji-hyeon, having found her voice again.

'Because by now she's escaped the stockade and gone her own way,' said the chevaleresse. 'I did not ask where she intended to go, so that I would not be obliged to share that intelligence with my employer, but trust that Zosia can be a very hard woman to find. You would have better luck hunting a ghost.'

———

With her hood pulled low, Zosia slipped and slid her way through the desolate camp. The snow had picked up again, and the two guards kept a respectful silence. To most it would have seemed a somber march, the disgraced former captain of the Cobalt Company led to face her judgment by reluctant captors who knew her for the queen she had been, but Zosia felt better than she had all day. Sure, her wounds throbbed and the cold gusts that were picking up through the tents cut her to the bone, but she felt like she had finally bested a devil that had harried her ever since Kypck. Sneaking away before dawn would have been far safer, of course, but she was confident that she could talk the kid into letting her go, so long as she swore some cheesy oath to never turn against her, something like that. They both knew Zosia was far more valuable alive and contrite than dead and of any temperament.

'In here, my lady,' said the guard with the torch, though the tent they had reached was still a long way off from the one they'd met in that morning. Ji-hyeon relocated her tent on a semi-regular basis to forestall spies and assassins from having a definite idea of where to find her, so the placement alone wasn't the problem. What flooded Zosia with dread was the realization that the general's heavily armored bodyguards were nowhere to be seen, the dark path between the darker tents empty of anyone at all save her escorts.

Before she could do more than register the depth of the trouble she was in, the guard with the torch pulled back the entry flap of the unlit tent and the man behind her took a decidedly less respectful approach than he had previously demonstrated, shoving her bodily inside. She kept her feet, but just barely, pivoting into the dark interior as the guards stormed in after her. Her hands were in irons, yes, but there were only two of them, and if she kept her cool she could get past them, back outside where her legs could carry her—

Onto her back. Someone else had been hiding in the blackness of the tent, and they neatly swept her legs out from under her. She went buckwild, hurling herself into a roll that hopefully would take her to the edge of the now-torchlit tent and not a waiting boot . . .

No such luck.

The first kick was followed soon after by its identical twin, and then in the too-bright torchlight they had her, hands holding her down while others worked her over, and then her legs were bound as tight as her wrists, and a noose slid round her throat. She panicked, whistling for Choplicker before a hard slap to the face reminded her that she didn't even have her devil anymore. The noose closed and began to tug her upward, and then the blob of hands and boots and contorted faces retreated enough for her to make out her three attackers – two women and one of the guards, meaning the other man was behind her, pulling the end of the noose over whatever makeshift gallows they'd erected in the dingy tent. Bad as they'd beaten her and tight as they'd tied her, she still managed to get to her knees as the noose pulled her upward, and then to her feet, and then onto the tips of her boots. The bare, frozen floor of the tent seemed to reel beneath her, and she almost fell before her toes found their balance.

'I don't fuckin' believe it,' said the older of the two women, vines of scar tissue marring her face just as it did those of the two guards. 'Cold Cobalt.'

'You sure it's her?' asked the younger woman, the only one of the four without marks on her face. She looked more nervous than the others, who seemed positively ecstatic.

'Oh, I'd never forget that face,' said the guard behind Zosia, tugging the noose a tiny bit more and then coming around for a better look at her. 'Lucky for us the fucking monster's forgotten ours, or we'd never've got her out the gaol.'

Without him holding the rope Zosia tried settling onto her aching heels, but there was no slack at all – he'd tied it to something, and if she slipped but an inch she'd be choked out in short order. Her heart was hammering so swiftly she felt like it might explode before they could hang her . . . and the worst of it was they were right, she had no fucking idea who any of them were.

'That right, Blue Witch?' said the older woman. 'You really don't remember Karilemin?'

Oh, Zosia remembered Karilemin all right – that fucking prison farm was the whole reason she'd finally abdicated the Crimson Throne. As soon as she learned of the atrocities being visited on the captured Juniusian rebels she had traveled there herself to shut the place down, but not before the damage was done . . . and shortly after she returned to Diadem, one of the camp's survivors had paid her a visit in the throne room. Here was justice as ripe as anything a bard could invent, Zosia finally answering for the same crime Queen Indsorith had sought to avenge twenty-odd years before.

'I remember Karilemin, and I'm sorry. And I know it doesn't change things, but it's not what I wanted, not what I ordered . . . ' Zosia was finding it hard to keep her balance while talking, and while it didn't seem talking would do her much good anyway, she still wanted to explain, and to apologize. Something she had never given Indsorith.

'Not what you ordered?' sneered one of the guards; now that

her eyes were filling with tears, Zosia was having a hard time telling them apart. 'We were right there in front of you when you gave your little speech and passed out the whips!'

'When we joined up with this new outfit in hope of finally makin' you pay for what you did, only to find it weren't really you, I was grieved near to death,' said one of the women. 'This lot wanted to desert straight 'way, but I says, nay, we come all this way and it's easy coin – just like it was working for Cold Cobalt, 'fore she became queen and turned on us.'

Karilemin. Of course. *Now* she remembered these assholes, albeit vaguely.

'You were . . .' Zosia's legs were tingling, and she almost slipped. 'You weren't Juniusian prisoners, you were the fucking Imperial guards who tortured them, starved them.'

'We interrogated them, you mean, to find any loot they had stashed before we locked 'em up and put 'em to honest work,' said one of the men.

'Loot we was gonna turn over to our beloved Crimson Queen,' said the other. 'And keepin' that many traitors in line takes stern discipline, otherwise they gets ideas about another revolt. Hungry folk take orders better than fat ones.'

'We was doin' what was best for the Empire, but when you come down from your castle you wouldn't listen to them who'd served you faithful,' said one of the women.

'Treated the fuckin' enemy kinder than you did your sworn soldiers,' said the other.

Zosia remembered gagging at the sights, the smells that had met her in the flinty fields and repurposed barns of Karilemin, but also remembered blaming herself more than the Imperial soldiers who had worked so many Juniusians to death. Now that she knew who these assholes were she couldn't fucking believe they actually harbored a grudge, considering her clemency – she'd become so sick of death and killing by that point that she had executed only the officers who had managed the work camp, sparing the grunts. 'I showed you mercy, didn't I? More mercy than you showed your wards.'

'Mercy?' cried one of the men. 'You call lettin' those fuckin' Juniusian scum take the lash to us mercy!'

'Whipped by our own prisoners, on your orders,' said one of the women, 'and banished like traitors.'

'But justice'll be done, now that—'

'Justice? You want justice?' growled Zosia, because these justly forgotten monsters could take her life but they couldn't make her listen to their self-righteous mewling another moment longer. 'Justice would be my old devil eating you fuckers alive, but guess what?' Zosia whistled for Choplicker again to prove her point. 'Justice doesn't exist.' She whistled a third time, just to make sure. 'There's your justice, you fucking crybabies, a whistle in the dark.'

'Hey, you can't talk to us like—' one of the women began but Zosia was done. What a shitty end to a shitty day in a shitty life.

'See you in hell, losers,' she told them, and dropped her heels to the floor as hard as she could.

CHAPTER

16

Zosia's feet hovered off the ground as the noose cut into her throat and the tear-filtered torchlight sputtered and flared. She closed her eyes so her last sight wouldn't be a pack of blurry cutthroats who'd been lucky she'd let them off with a whipping way back when, and focused on keeping her treacherous feet from instinctively finding footing on the icy earth floor. She couldn't shut her ears, unfortunately, and as her mind tipped and slipped into darkness, she heard their jeering voices, and louder now, their heavy panting, and their shrill shrieks and guttural gasps, and the crackling and ripping and snapping and growling and—

The slap of the cold floor against her cheek told her she'd failed in this, the last venture of her whole life – the dirty bastards had untied or cut the rope before she could hang herself, depriving her of even that small agency. Either the torch had gone out or her eyes had, the blackness of the tent absolute, and all she could hear was that thick, humid panting. Then something wet rustled through her hair, pressing into the back of her neck, and with a tug the noose was pulled loose from her windpipe and she gasped in spite of her commitment to dying. The air was no longer cold and still, but pulsed with a hot tide of fetid odor, a stench that was so familiar it might have been . . . dog breath?

Nails clicked on the frozen ground beside her, and a furry head bumped hers with a plaintive whine. Zosia raised her hands to stroke his coat, and as she did the manacles clicked open and fell from her wrists. He felt warm under her fingers, but also thin, his bones protruding from his hide, patches of his mangy coat tarred and foul. Her hands reached the back of his head, and she scratched him weakly behind the ears. He responded by scratching her cheek with his dried-out tongue, and she pushed him away with a groan.

'Thanks, buddy,' she rasped, slowly sitting up. She couldn't see a damn thing—

Then she saw too much, the extinguished torch bursting into flames on the ground beside her. She shielded her eyes until they readjusted, too exhausted – and relieved – to be unnerved by such minor deviltry. No, what got under her skin was the sight of the empty tent, the armor and gear of the four who had tried to murder her strewn in greasy tatters around the room. Nothing remained of the mortals save their befouled trappings, even the metal gear warped and ruined by whatever it was Choplicker had done.

More startling than the state of the tent was that of her devil. He looked more dead than alive, and from the night she'd first bound him she had never seen him so bad. What remained of his coat was white and thin, pale boils and weeping scabs showing on his exposed hide . . .

'Oh, *Chop*,' Zosia whispered, her voice thick with unexpected grief to see him in such a state, and relief to see him again at all. Whether they deserved to be or not, they were both still here. Gently stroking his heavy head, she said, 'Where've you been, you old devil? And what've you gotten yourself into?'

He barked happily, and despite his decrepitude he almost sounded like his old self again. Then he began hawking like a cat coughing up a hairball, and a bulge moved up his throat. She would have been worried as well as disgusted, but recognized the ugly sight from the old days when he would swallow rare treasures he found on the battlefield, carrying them back to his mistress in his swollen belly and then regurgitating them at her feet. His method of delivery took a lot of the fun out of receiving the gifts, as did the creepiness in knowing he could somehow fit whole pieces of plate armor into his narrow form.

Now he produced a sizable hunk of metal, along with a frothy grey spray. Through the film it sparkled with red glass or gems, and then she recognized it, and gasped. It was bent near to breaking, perhaps smashed beneath a hammer, but to the woman who had once worn it there could be no mistaking the raiment. After their interrogation of Hoartrap the night before, she had told Choplicker to claim any prize he wished in all the Star, so long as it harmed no mortal, and he had brought her the Carnelian Crown of the Crimson Queen.

But why? And how had it become so damaged? Had something happened to Indsorith, and if so, was it Choplicker's doing? By retrieving the buckled crown he must be trying to tell his mistress something important, but as was usual with her devil, he'd given her nothing but more questions.

'Damn,' she said, gingerly lifting the warm, slimy metal in her shaky fingers and looking in wonder at Choplicker. 'Looks like we've both had one devil of a busy day.'

—

'The busiest,' Ji-hyeon replied as Keun-ju helped unwrap the bandages on her hand. It was so nice to just be alone with him, though watching Sullen quickly excuse himself along with the rest of her captains at the end of the meeting had filled her with longing. And guilt, plenty of guilt, too. 'I'm not sure I can remember a stupider day, either, for that matter. Give me a big battle over politicking every time.'

'What would you have done with Zosia, if she hadn't fled the camp?' Keun-ju asked, then hissed as he saw the fresh damage to her hand. The cauterized stumps where her pinky and finger used to be were cracked and oozing, and the entire back of her hand had bruised a deep purple.

'Assuming Singh was telling the truth and she's really gone, you mean?' said Ji-hyeon, stroking Fellwing with her other hand as the little devil crawled over the stained bandages to get at the injuries, pulling herself along with her hooked wings in that cute way she did. The owlbat looked much better after a day's rest in the tent, but her fur was still bleached a sickly yellow instead of its former black after her overexertion in protecting her mistress. 'I hadn't made up my mind what I was going to do, exactly ... or still might, if I have her tracked down and brought back. But ... ' She yawned. 'We can worry about that tomorrow. A snowy night on the run will do some good to cool her down.'

'Would you ... execute her?' Keun-ju sounded upset by the prospect, and despite her fatigue Ji-hyeon perked up a little. He had barely said two words about his long journey with Zosia, and both of those had involved the deplorable conditions and her worse manners. But after spending months together traversing the Star by foot, ship, and horse, it was hardly surprising that Keun-ju and Zosia had bonded a little.

'Don't you think I should, after she tried to push me through a Gate?' Ji-hyeon was far too tuckered to be mad about anything, even his concern for the crazy beldam who had smashed in his lover's beautiful face. Well, okay, if not beautiful Ji-hyeon had at least been kind of cute, and now she was as mashed up as a good beef bowl.

'I . . . I'm not saying she doesn't deserve it, after betraying you so, but . . . ' Keun-ju trailed off, and following his eyes, she saw Fellwing had crawled over to the seared meat at the end of her hand. The devil stretched her beak out toward the finger stumps, and Ji-hyeon tried to stop her arm from shaking as the devil's blue tongue brushed the wound. It didn't hurt as much as she'd expected; on the contrary, each stroke of the tiny tongue soothed the inflammation.

Averting his gaze from the spectacle, Keun-ju leaned over the table and poured them both a dram of peatfire. He used to hate the stuff the time or two they'd gotten into Kang-ho's liquor cabinet back on Hwabun, but must have acquired a taste while Star-trotting with Zosia – she wondered if the silver-maned dame had converted him to any other indulgences.

'But what, Keun-ju? What should I do? I'm not being facetious, I really want to know what you think.' She shuddered as Fellwing nestled in close against her hand, the devil's hooked beak gingerly prying at the charred scab of her bottom knuckle. 'Do I just pretend it never happened?'

'Everyone makes mistakes,' said Keun-ju, and even with his veil riding higher than usual she made out the blush spreading to the tops of his cheekbones. 'And if she truly regrets her mistake – sorry!'

In passing her the peatfire his trembling fingers lost their hold of the porcelain bowl, and he upended the smoke-scented liquor all over her chest. This was her last clean housecoat, too, but she couldn't be bothered to care, yawning again as Keun-ju frantically apologized and dabbed at her damp bosom with a napkin. It was the queerest thing, that fucked-up as she was physically, on account of her wounds, and mentally, on account of the bugs she'd taken for the pain, she felt a familiar itch come upon her as he delicately leaned over her, his rapid breaths making his veil pulse as he pressed the cloth into her chest.

She lowered her head to his ear, and whispered, 'If you want to touch them, Keun-ju, you don't have to create such an elaborate ruse.'

His palm froze, along with the rest of him, and she kissed him softly on the earlobe, her free hand rising to untie the shoulder flap of her coat and her left pulsing with a pleasant hum as Fellwing chipped away at her wounds. Before she'd felt far too roughed up to even think about cuddling, let alone something more vigorous, but now all she wanted was to have him again – the night before the big battle they had had the *best* sex, and she wanted more.

She nibbled on his ear as the tie on her coat came loose, and she thanked all the devils of chance that her lover had returned to her after so long apart ... and considerate soul that he was, he'd even brought her their favorite toy, an elegantly curved shaft of lacquered princess wood inlaid with mother of pearl peonies and chrysanthemums. She had forgotten to take it with her, in her haste to escape Hwabun, and there was something disgustingly romantic about her dear little poet risking life and limb as he crossed the Star to find her, and all the while carrying along her long-missed dildo. The surrogates she'd acquired on campaign had been nice enough, the pleasure artisans of the Raniputri Dominions creating marvelous devices of bronze and rosewood, but you never quite get over your first. When they had finally been reunited in her bed and Keun-ju had shyly produced their old playmate and its shark leather harness she had almost gotten off at the mere sight of it. Now, as her fingers rose from her coat to wrestle with the obstinate ties of his and she moved her lips from his ear down to the fine, dark hairs on his neck, Ji-hyeon knew they were in for an even better night, the best of their whole fucking lives, and—

And then Keun-ju practically threw himself to the other side of the cushion pile to be away from her, and Ji-hyeon flushed with embarrassment. He had never rejected her so harshly.

'I . . . I'm sorry, Ji-hyeon, I can't,' he said, clutching the peatfire-damp napkin to his own silk-cloaked chest and staring down at his knees. 'I want to, I do! But . . . I'm so sorry.'

Of course. She was being selfish, so, so selfish; his wounds were even graver than hers, and engaging in even such a tender sport as fucking would likely exacerbate his condition. Considering her own injuries, what had possessed her to even attempt such a thing? A good climax or two relaxed her like not even saam or spirits, but that alone didn't account for her lust; perhaps having come so close to death in the last two days had filled her with a better appreciation for the little joys of being alive, and a need to taste them as often as possible, since one never knew when one's luck would run out.

'I . . . I helped Sullen work things out with a smith, for the old man's ashes,' said Keun-ju, his voice so small it could have been trapped under a thimble. 'Took most of the day, but . . . He's not so bad, I guess, and he thinks the Star of you.'

Oh gods below, did they really have to talk this out now? It was just what she fucking needed, after the day she'd had . . . but as soon as her annoyance came, her heavy conscience chased it off. She'd created this situation, and it was time she owned it. But before she could, he was talking again, faster, desperate, but still as softly as Fellwing ministered to her hand.

'It's going to be perfect, the sword he's going to give you, but we'll need to take in the twin you didn't lose so the smith can know what to do, weight and everything is so important with balancing a new blade, and—'

'I have a stupid crush on Sullen, Keun-ju, and he's got one on me, but that hardly means we're going to run off together tomorrow and leave you all alone,' said Ji-hyeon, but guessing from the tears now racing down to the lace edging of Keun-ju's veil that hadn't been the best way to open the conversation. 'Shit, Keun-ju, I'm really, really tired, and I'm not thinking straight. I love you. Before either of us says another word, believe that – I love you, and I've never stopped loving you, even when . . . even when people were trying to convince me I shouldn't trust you, even when Fennec was lying about you, I still loved you. Nothing that happened between me and Sullen came from me not caring about you, I swear!'

'What happened between you and Sullen,' said Keun-ju, nodding to himself as though that answered all his questions, then seeming to take heart from something else she'd said. 'And what about Fennec, anyway? You forgave him for . . . for trying to keep us apart, didn't you? So you clearly don't treat all traitors and liars the same . . .'

'I . . . what?' Ji-hyeon let her head loll over to the side as she surveyed her choked-up lover. 'Look, do you want to talk about you and me, and me and Sullen, or do you want to talk about Fennec and Zosia? You have to pick one or the other, because there's no way I can stay awake long enough for both.'

Keun-ju didn't answer, then darted his hand out to the table and grabbed the bottle of peatfire. His other hand undid the knot on his veil, and as it fluttered down his chin he knocked back a swig of liquor in one wracked-face gulp.

'Keun-ju, really, this is getting ridiculously dramatic. Why don't we turn down the lamps, take off our clothes, and cuddle in bed until dawn? I promise in the morning, before I do anything else, we can talk about everything you—'

'Fennec didn't lie to you,' Keun-ju gasped, breathless from the booze. 'I did.'

'What are you even talking about?' Ji-hyeon snapped, desperate to have him reseal the chasm that suddenly opened up in her chest with a simple explanation. He must be referring to something stupid she, Keun-ju, and Fennec had all been arguing about at some point, some disagreement with Fennec that Keun-ju had concluded with a white lie. It would be just like him to take the slightest stretching of the truth as a high crime when—

'I did everything he accused me of, the day you ran away from Hwabun.' Keun-ju's voice broke but his gaze didn't, his wet eyes meeting her widening ones. 'I told your first father . . . I told King Jun-hwan of our plan to escape, and I led the guards to the dock.'

Ji-hyeon just sat there, slowly absorbing his words like a limp lump of bean curd soaking up sauce. He was still looking at her and she was still looking at him, but they'd both changed in a matter of moments. Instead of contorting her insides with regret, his tear-streaked face filled her with abject disgust.

'And you lied to me, after Zosia brought you here,' said Ji-hyeon, her voice as low as his. 'You swore you loved me, and you'd never betray me, and everything Fennec told me about you was a lie. You lied to me about everything.'

'Not everything,' he said, though he had the decency to hang his head in shame. 'I have always loved you, and everything I did was to keep you safe. I swear on my life I feared that stepping into the Immaculate Gate would be the end of you – everyone knows entering a Gate is certain death, or worse! Didn't I beg you not to, over and over again? Didn't I urge us to flee by boat instead? I didn't go to your first father until the very day we were to leave, and only then when you refused my final entreaty to take any route but the Gate – if I thought there was any chance it would work I never, ever would have done what I did. And even at the end, when it was clear you'd get away despite my confession to King Jun-hwan, I would have gone with you into that hellmouth, if your second father's guards hadn't slowed me down on the dock and—'

'I could have killed Fennec,' said Ji-hyeon, shivering with revulsion. 'I was that mad, when you came into my tent with Zosia and told me everything I wanted to hear, that of course mean old "Brother Mikal" and my second father invented stories to keep us apart. Of course you didn't go to my first father, of course you didn't betray us. I was so furious, Keun-ju, I actually imagined shoving my sword into Fennec's throat, and if my mood had been a touch different when I confronted him . . . ' Ji-hyeon laughed a little at the memory. 'You know, when you came back and lied to my face and cried into my hair and insisted it was all a plot, I wanted to believe so badly I stopped reasoning altogether. When I cornered Fennec and told him what you'd said, he didn't confess to anything you accused him of, he just said that he was sorry for trying to keep us apart. And I was so upset I almost did something stupid, hurting him or sending him away, and now that I think about it he never, ever lied to me about you, not once – it's like he's said from the day we left, *I can't trust you.*'

'You can!' Keun-ju cried, finally looking up from the cushions at his feet. 'I swear, Ji-hyeon, the whole trip with Zosia I planned out how to tell you of my deception, but when I saw you . . . I didn't want to hurt you, and so in my weakness I lied, yes. And I hated myself for it, for I knew I didn't deserve your love, which is why . . . which is why I had to tell you. I couldn't bear to live with my wickedness for another moment.'

'No, you just waited until I spread my legs for you again,' said Ji-hyeon, 'until I let you recite your *love poems*, until, come to think of it, my second fucking father rode into camp – that's the only reason you're telling me at all, isn't it? Because you're scared if me and Kang-ho and Fennec start comparing notes we'll see that we were right all along, that you're nothing but an oath-breaking traitor!'

'No,' Keun-ju whined, 'I swear that has nothing—'

'You've sworn enough for one night, Keun-ju,' she snapped. 'The hour is late and your general requires her rest. So get the fuck out of this tent and don't you dare come back until I call for you.'

Keun-ju didn't protest, quickly hopping to his feet. 'Where shall I stay until—'

'Don't give a fuck.' It took so much to hold in her furious tears that Ji-hyeon's chest felt like a crossbow string winched into position. One with a hair trigger. 'But I better be able to find you, Keun-ju, fast and easy – if you leave this camp without my orders I'll see that you're given no quarter as a traitor and a deserter, from this day until my last.'

'My . . . mistress,' he said, clumsily tying his veil back into place as he bowed in farewell.

'Not anymore I'm fucking not,' she said, desperate to wound him half as bad as he'd cut her. 'You are hereby dismissed as my Virtue Guard, Keun-ju.'

He reeled at that, as though intoxicated by his own crocodile tears, and for the faintest sliver of a moment Ji-hyeon wished he hadn't said anything, that he'd kept the secret of his deception until his dying day. He stiffly walked toward the tent flap, as though he could bear this with dignity, but in the end he evidently couldn't, turning back to her.

'But . . . but . . . ' Keun-ju's eyes were so big they looked like they might fall out of his stupid lying face.

'Yeah, like you did such a great job at that anyway,' Ji-hyeon snorted. 'I should have known about you, Keun-ju, I should have known. How far can you trust a Virtue Guard who drops his vows as fast as he drops his ward's knickers? Be gone from my sight, oath-breaker.'

Then she turned away, not so she wouldn't see his heart breaking but so that he couldn't see hers. Only when the flaps rustled and she faintly heard the guards bid Keun-ju goodnight did she let the tears flow, along with a frantic scream into one of her pillows. Then she nudged Fellwing away from her aching hand, barely impressed to see fresh pink scar tissue forming over the stumps where open wounds had loomed but a little earlier. She'd have preferred it turn gangrenous if it had meant Keun-ju had stayed true.

As she turned down the lamp and collapsed onto her bed, the bugs in her blood goaded her toward dreams, but Ji-hyeon's agony rebuffed the soporifics. Each time she nearly escaped her anguish a new memory would flash through her aching skull, making her heart race anew. All the nights on campaign she had lain awake, unable to sleep for wondering and worrying about Keun-ju. All the times she had conjured him through her lonely fingers or instruments, and later, when she had thought of Sullen while doing the same, only to bite her lip afterward as she wondered if a part of her wanted Keun-ju to be untrue, so she might love Sullen with an unburdened heart. The joy she'd felt when her Virtue Guard burst into her command tent before even Cobalt Zosia could gain it, and the relief when he'd later explained everything away with such convincing words. The taste of her first and one true love but two nights before, as she and Keun-ju reunited their bodies in this very bed. And on and on, until Ji-hyeon allowed herself an indulgence she had long denied herself over the whole, difficult campaign, something she had not done since the night her fathers had sat her down and told her she was betrothed to Prince Byeong-gu of Othean and must leave her beloved Virtue Guard behind on Hwabun: she cried herself to sleep.

CHAPTER
17

Diadem burned, and Indsorith burned with her.

Whatever the Chainites had stung her with after the poisoned wine had subdued her now filled her veins with magma, smoke belching from her every pore as they stripped her of even her steel nipple cups and satin underthings. Indsorith fought the poison in her blood, in her brain, in the chants of the unseen choir—the smoke wasn't rising from her skin, but from the enormous statue of the Fallen Mother that filled the apse of the cathedral, the ikon's coronet of burning flowers blooming orange and green as pungent black waves rolled out across the vaulted ceiling. Incense, the entire effigy was formed from incense. Stinking patchouli and sweet musk. Creamy sandalwood and hot clove. Sizzling hair and boiling blood. A familiar figure writhed in the smoldering lap of the statue, burning alive against the blistering monument, and for the life of her Indsorith couldn't tell if the screams Abbotess Cradofil emitted to join the choir were born of rapture or agony or both.

Indsorith closed her eyes, counted to ten, opened them again. And wished she hadn't. The scene was the same, and while the faces of the bustling clerics were blurry, the details smudged by drugs and bugs and whatever else they had given her, there could be no denying it – this was really happening. She was the unwilling participant in some heinous ritual taking place in the Lower Chainhouse. She was probably the next sacrifice.

From the first day of her rule, Indsorith had worked tirelessly to keep the Burnished Chain in check, thwarting quiet political machinations and raging civil wars with the same diplomatic resolve. The loyal old colonels of Thao and Azgaroth had counseled her a dozen times to eradicate the whole church, but having witnessed firsthand what came of such harsh solutions she had always refused, trying and trying and trying again to make peace with the Holy See and the Black Pope, to bring harmony to a fractured Empire. When she had forced Shanatu to step down as pontiff and his teenage niece Y'Homa had assumed the Onyx Pulpit, Indsorith had thought that Crown and Chain finally had a chance of raising a future together, instead of trying to wrest it from the other's grasp . . . and now she saw just how wrong she had been.

Pope Shanatu had been a truly evil man, willing to sacrifice anything and anyone to achieve his ends, but at least he had known that to cement the reign of the Burnished Chain he had to take the Crimson Throne by legitimate methods, lest the people rise up against the religious usurpers. Stacking her cabinet with Chainite stooges to undercut her authority was one means, open and legal civil war against her rule another, but he never would have risked such a blatant coup as this. This was assassination, plain and simple . . . or at least she assumed it was, as she watched Abbotess Cradofil burn alive on a smoldering effigy of her presumed savior. Now that Y'Homa had come this far with her revolution, Indsorith knew that execution would be preferable to any other uses the demented pope might find for the deposed Crimson Queen.

Indsorith swooned from the fumes billowing off the enormous incense ikon, and when she was next able to lift her heavy
head she saw she might not have to worry much longer. A
robed figure wearing a mask in the visage of a black goat knelt
over the weak queen, a red razor held in an iron-ringed glove.
Crimson steel flashed close in front of Indsorith, the light of ten
thousand candles and a burning god blinding her as the sacred
blade dropped with excruciating torpor until its edge found
where eyelash met lid.

The papal barbers had steady hands, shaving her with the
long red razors until her ample flesh bore not a single defiant hair, then they squeezed her into the hairshirt robe of a
penitent. The crowd dropped to their knees as one, and Pope
Y'Homa appeared through the field of the faithful, wearing
only her opal-crowned mitre and a cape of ebon satin shot with
diamonds, as though she wore the night sky upon her scrawny
young shoulders and the full moon upon her brow. Her naked
body was etched with an arabesque of sigils both dark and fair,
some long-healed scars and others freshly carved into her pal-
impsest of flesh. Indsorith tried to speak, or at least spit at the
Black Pope's bare feet, but she could barely keep her eyes open,
tendrils of smoke curling around her throat like a noose. The
mad girl kneeled in front of Indsorith and solemnly addressed
her, but she couldn't make out her meaning, the words sounded
like crackling flames, like a burning city. Then Y'Homa kissed
each of Indsorith's cheeks, and receiving a crown of grey roses
from a nearby cardinal, she firmly planted it on the fallen
queen's bare skull, like a garland strung atop a maypole during
one of the pagan festivals Indsorith's mother had allowed the
villagers to conduct back in Junius, in her youth, before the
coming of the Crimson Queen . . .

The Black Pope rose back up, towering over her former regent, and a great shadow fell over them all, as though some gross leviathan had risen up out of Desolation Sound, taken wing clear over the walls of Diadem, and now swam into the Lower Chainhouse. Y'Homa turned to face whatever hulking horror approached, but Indsorith couldn't make it out, for the surrounding bishops and cardinals rose back to their feet, too, and pressed in tight around her. They melted a blazing waxen horn to the center of her scalp, and kissed her feet with tear-stained lips. When all was ready the clerics carried her up hemlock stepladders, and using braided ropes of hair, lashed her onto the metal saddle at the head of the enormous wheeled idol they had dragged into the cathedral. The silver and brass idol was as long as a city block, an overtly phallic battering ram pulled not by mundane oxen but by black-scaled, fire-eyed gorgon bulls captured in the swamps of Meshugg and tamed by holy herbs that turned their toxic breath into a jasmine-sweet breeze. This was how the Last Crimson Queen met her subjects for the first time since losing the Carnelian Crown but a day before; half-blind from the mix of melting candlewax and blood drawn forth by the thorny new diadem the Black Pope had fitted for her, and weathering apocalyptic visions that she prayed were but hallucinations brought on by the potency of insect and ritual.

Out they came from the Lower Chainhouse, boring through streets clogged with the corpse-slack faces of her subjects. Through wasp-stung lips Indsorith gave silent thanks to see that while the crowds seemed to burn, too, the chill mountain air was sobering her up. The swaying mobs had initially seemed to belch smoke into the fire-bright night, but as she lolled her head around she saw it was not the citizenry who smoldered, but the city itself: many of the precariously tall buildings that bordered the avenues were aflame, waves of embers crashing upward to warm the freezing stars.

Yet no matter how firmly she told herself to see past the illusions of the ritual and the intoxicants, she found it nigh impossible to separate the fact from the fantasy of the nightmarish scene. The harder she focused the more convinced she was that this was all really happening, despite how impossible it still seemed. One after another figures detached themselves from the heaving masses, scaling the front of the slowly rolling contraption and ducking into the widely grinning mouth of the Deceiver that capped the tip of the lewd effigy she was lashed atop. Indsorith's mother threw another ring of drab roses at her before wriggling into the cavity, but others went less willingly, her younger brothers tossed up and into the maw by their chanting father. Zosia appeared from the crowd, and so did Sister Portolés, each nodding to Indsorith before taking their place inside, sacrificing themselves to the hellish rites of the Burnished Chain.

That wasn't real. It *wasn't*. It couldn't be, not even Chainites believed the dead could return, but knowing her bug-bitten brain was applying familiar faces to random strangers hardly made the reality of their sacrifice more bearable.

As each wailing innocent or ecstatic reveler disappeared into the opening, the entire idol shuddered with the twist of internal mechanisms, and spumes of blood ejaculated from vents beside Indsorith's feet. The reverberations of the heated metal coursing up through her seat might have felt nice, under different circumstances, but combined with the fumes baking her skull she would have fallen from her perch on the sculpted head of the phallic statue if the ropes hadn't held her tight, the cool cords biting into her burning flesh. The chants of the procession reverberated through the city as the Fallen Queen led them inexorably onward, and now Indsorith was sure their goal must be what the Chainite mystics called the Navel of the Star, the Gate at the heart of Diadem . . .

In all her years as Crimson Queen, Indsorith had hardly ever visited Gate Square, and never if she could help it. Whatever purpose the place had served for the architects of Diadem when they had first raised the city in the belly of the dead volcano was long since lost, as was so much else from the Age of Wonders, and the only ones who voluntarily came to the city's solemn center were agents of the Burnished Chain. It was hard to belive that only two years had passed since Indsorith had wondered aloud what purpose a window into the First Dark served for such holy-minded mortals, and an advisor had told her that before being fully welcomed to the breast of the Fallen Mother, reformed anathemas had to first march out to the very rim and cast in any devilish deformities the Papal surgeons had saved them from. The image of wretched weirdborn penitents being forced to empty buckets full of their own amputated body parts into a Gate before being granted the privilege of serving the very institution that had mutilated them was enough to make Indsorith reconsider her own position of not eradicating every trace of the Burnished Chain from the Empire. Instead she settled for issuing a decree that weirdborn Imperials were no longer subject to the brutal laws of the church, which resulted in Pope Shanatu crying bloody murder and accusing her of overstepping her bounds as sovereign ... which in turn led to the last civil war, when she wouldn't back down.

And what had it gotten her, or her subjects? Death as far as the eye could see. Famine in parts of the Empire, rampant lawlessness in others, every province and city-state at its neighbor's throat. To restore the peace and end the war she'd been all too happy to accept Shanatu's abdication of the papacy, but she'd also been forced to allow his batty niece to succeed him, and grant the girl all manner of additional powers to boot. The weirdborn weren't much better off than they'd been before, Indsorith had lost even more of her tenuous hold on the Crimson Throne Room, and now? Now Indsorith was blasted out of her mind on all manner of poisons, taken hostage in her own city, and more than likely about to go the way of a weird-born's amputated wing or tail.

Which all just went to show that she should have listened to Hjortt and Waits and her other veteran colonels when they'd suggested she march every fucking Chainite in the capital out here to this quiet quarter where not even gulls or owlbats took sanctuary in the ancient ruins that bordered Gate Square, and deliver the true believers to an immediate reckoning with their god. To think such a suggestion had struck her as barbaric, savage . . .

When they reached one of the iron-spiked hawthorn cordons that blocked each of the five boulevards that terminated in Gate Square, the great barrier was rolled back on its hinges to admit the stamping, slick-scaled bulls and their iconic cargo. Y'Homa left her roost at the yonic end of the construct, strutting down the wide length of the phallus and casting handfuls of ash into the crowd from a goat-hair satchel. From the vantage of Indsorith's lolled-back head, the wide-eyed Black Pope seemed to dance toward her across the gilded roof of heaven. Then the mostly naked girl steadied herself against the back of Indsorith's uncomfortable throne, and the expression on her wine-stained lips was as mad as any of the flame-winged angels the queen saw wheeling over the teenage pontiff.

This wasn't all real, but it was all too real.

'Witness the miracle,' the Black Pope whispered to Indsorith, the words echoing louder and louder behind them, and then the monstrous bulls dragged the phallic machine into the sacro-sanct courtyard where Diadem Gate pooled black before them, impervious to the firelight. Indsorith's limp head fell forward as they jerked to a stop, and she saw the overworked beasts were sweating flames, their glistening flanks alive with green and yellow wisps as they were released from their yoke and led away by their handlers. Icy fingers dug through Indsorith's blister-thin shoulder, Y'Homa repeating her entreaty as she pointed to the Gate directly ahead of them. 'Witness the miracle!'

Metal screeched and wood groaned and the back of the long idol raised jerkily into the air, the nose of the phallus shifting forward, dipping over the Gate, and even tied in place Indsorith groaned, feeling her body rebel against the bonds that prevented her from sliding down into the darkness. As the wheeled construct seesawed into position, a thick discharge gushed from the open tip that had greedily swallowed so many. Rather than disappearing into the Gate, the bone-flecked flood splashed and spread across the black surface and, clinging to the throne-backed saddle beside her former nemesis, Y'Homa gasped, holding her breath as the last few trickles dribbled out of the mechanical idol. Looking away from the skein of gore cresting the Gate like oil settling atop water, Indsorith saw even Y'Homa was afraid, and she laughed in the idiot girl's face, her lungs erupting smoke instead of breath. This wasn't happening, this couldn't be happening.

Yet it was. This was no dream of drug and insect; this was a nightmare made manifest. Indsorith had sought to make peace with her enemies, and now she would pay the ultimate price, as would her people.

A rich cobalt glow reached them both, and Indsorith turned in tandem with Y'Homa to behold the brilliance flaring up from the Gate that in all the years she'd presided over obligatory ceremonies of state had only ever swallowed light, never returned it.

It was not the Gate that glowed, however, but what lay beyond it. The sight would have made her swoon even if she hadn't been suspended over it, for the perspective was all wrong, as though Indsorith stood on the prow of a ship overlooking the horizon. And what a horizon it was: blue sky and bluer sea, and pinned between them at the border of water and air, a coastline of such rich emerald it made her eyes water, the steam hissing on her cheeks as she saw it. And she knew it for what it was even before the shore of the once-Sunken Kingdom raced up toward the Gate, protean towers of white stone distorting and wobbling as they thrust up from the verdant jungles, the view now that of a bird darting above the trees, then over quiet alabaster cities, toward what waited at the bowels of the long-lost land of Jex Toth, and Indsorith closed her burning eyes, as beside her Y'Homa whispered.

'Her will is done, sister, her will is done. Heaven is made real, and the faithful are called home to the cosmic axis. Behold, the Fallen Mother has delivered unto us an army that no sinner may stand against. We have weathered five centuries of iniquity, but we have kept the faith, and our reward is at hand. The Angelic Brood of the Allmother returns to cleanse the Star, to save us all.'

Even with her eyes closed, Indsorith still saw the swarming, jet-shelled nest of countless horrors, their almost-human faces staring at her from across the Gate, and she shed boiling tears not just for herself and her subjects, but for all of the Star, for she now knew that they were beyond all hope. The Black Pope had lowered the Burnished Chain into the deepest depths of the First Dark, and now drew it back up into the light, carrying with it nothing short of the end of all things.

PART II

AND THE
DEVILS OF DAYS

The belief in a supernatural source of
   evil is not necessary;
men alone are quite capable of every
   wickedness.
—Joseph Conrad, *Under Western Eyes*

CHAPTER

1

Choplicker whined and licked Zosia's face, his normally slimy tongue dry and flaking against her cheek, but she had begun drifting out of her dreams even before the infirm dog had doddered over to wake her. She was buoyed up to the light by the sound of bugles ... Imperials on the march, and close. As she blinked her eyes and her nose wrinkled at the hot garbage scent of her dog's breath, Zosia struggled to place herself – where was she? *When* was she? She had been dreaming of the lean old days, working with Singh and Kang-ho to rouse the rabble in some piazza in Rwake or maybe Intarma, when the Eleventh Regiment, out of Lento, had ambushed them, rivers of soldiers pouring in from every street and alley, brass horns announcing the attack ...

Another bugle, closer now, and Zosia pushed Choplicker away before he could deliver another rasping lick to her face, her mind finally catching up with her bleary eyes. An anxious devil, looking every bit as sickly as he had last night, and her dim, cramped tent – she barely remembered finding her way back here after Choplicker's rescue. With aching limbs she freed herself from the layers of blankets her devil must have dragged on top of her after she collapsed to the cold dirt floor, feeling like a defective caterpillar as she emerged from her sour-smelling cocoon of furs no better off than she'd been the day before. She felt worse, in fact. The only thing that ached more than her neck and her knees was the bite wound on her shoulder, and a skull-splintering headache rounded off the whole depressing portrait. She shuddered at the stamping feet outside her tent, the rising cries and banging metal and Cobalt horn after horn after horn drowning out the blasted Imperial bugles that had first roused her.

'What the absolute fuck?' Zosia mumbled as she used her thumbnail to scrape the patina of mold off a strip of buffalo jerky. On closer inspection, perhaps it was actually venison – or maybe just a scrap of rawhide? No matter, it went into her mouth as she limped over to her chamberpot, batting Choplicker away when he tried to nose her outside. He barked as she hunkered down, the sound like dull daggers being slowly pushed into her eye sockets. Hard to believe she'd missed the bastard. 'Yeah, I know, I know, we're off to war – just shut up and give me a minute.'

That calmed him down, at least. The devil poked his snout around the messy tent, retrieving her hauberk from a heap of clothes and dragging over the war hammer Singh or Purna or somebody must have retrieved after Zosia's dustup with Ji-hyeon and dropped off back here while she was stuck in the stockade. Her eyes settled on the crown that had been so bright and shiny when she'd first placed it on her brow but now lay bent and dull on the bare floor of her dirty tent: as fitting a metaphor as they came. She knew if she actually intended to turn over a new leaf and be a better woman she'd have to start with something simple, like helping out the less fortunate, and that meant taking the thing to Ji-hyeon and sharing her suspicions about something bad having befallen Queen Indsorith.

That was exactly the sort of intelligence a bright-eyed young idealist could use in her campaign to right all the Star's wrongs and cast down the corrupt and all that shit. But like an old drunk who'd sworn off spirits the night before only to wake up with a commanding thirst, Zosia found yesterday's easy and seemingly obvious resolutions to get on the path of righteousness sorely tested by the sheer amount of bullshit that would go into such a venture...

But who knew, the way Choplicker was ferreting around the tent and dragging her things together, she might not even have time to soften up this codpiece-tasting scrap of jerky before more pressing concerns made themselves known. The only thing that could make him this excitable in his current bedraggled condition was the prospect of a big breakfast, and a devil's meal wasn't the sort of thing that made Zosia hungry. She swallowed a mouthful of salty jerky juice all the same; we've all got to eat, even when we'd rather starve. At least the devil was so occupied rushing her out the door that he wasn't watching her do her business over the chamberpot, which had long been a bone of contention between them. Said a lot about their relationship that she'd take something like this as a boon. What a charming start to the first day of her new life as a new woman.

So far, this life looked even more miserable than the last one.

———

Just when she thought the morning had already reached the absolute pinnacle of dumbfuckery possible in a single dawn, Ji-hyeon noticed the spotting of fresh blood on the warm sheets she had just vacated. She dabbed a finger between her legs, hoping it was just one of her many recent wounds that had – mother of fucks. More distant bugles and too-close horns sounded, the impatient clamor of her bodyguards reaching a fever pitch right outside her tent; what period had ever arrived to such fanfare? She had to get outside and see what the merry hob was happening. Rather than embarking on what might be a long hunt in the cluttered tent for her box of lady's handkerchiefs, she tore a little strip off the already threadbare sheet, folded it into the appropriate shape, and after finally locating a clean pair of knickers, tucked the makeshift cargo into the crotch and stepped into them. All of which proved even more annoying with only one good hand, the underwear catching on her knee, and—

'I do hate to interrupt your beauty sleep, oh weary general, but I fear – oh shit, pardon me!' Hoartrap's usual devils-may-care tenor abruptly changed as the creeper rose to his full height in the back of her tent and caught sight of what she was up to, turning his head and shielding his face with his hand in belated decency. Ji-hyeon yanked her panties into place, too furious to speak, and so a long, uncomfortable silence persisted as she also turned away and began donning her armor. The only thing worse than the arrival of her cramps was the appearance of Hoartrap, who eventually tried again. 'I, um, never would I have—'

'I fucking warned you what would happen if you snuck in here again.' Ji-hyeon hated how close to angry tears he'd brought her, when she'd already shed so many the night before. 'You're fucked, Hoartrap, for serious this time.'

'Sure, yes, absolutely,' said Hoartrap, still not sounding quite like his old self. 'But first maybe you'd like to see to the Thaoan regiment marching on our camp. Evidently your father and his good friend Colonel Waits have decided to decline your invitation to work with us against the Chain.'

'I never would've guessed that, what with all those distinctive bugles getting closer by the second,' grunted Ji-hyeon, trying to get her sword belt buckled with only one and a half hands. 'Whatever would I do without you, Hoartrap?'

'I dare not even ponder it,' said Hoartrap, suddenly right behind her and reaching for her waist. 'Here, let me help you with that.'

'Back the fuck up!' Ji-hyeon shoved the two remaining fingers of her left hand in his face. 'You must really want to die this morning, huh?'

'I hadn't planned on it, actually, but my schedule's still open, so—'

'If you forget the general's bubble again, you get stuck!' Ever since her bodyguard Sasamaso had been swallowed up by the Lark's Tongue Gate along with so many other soldiers, Ji-hyeon had missed the woman terribly, and mourned her death as a friend . . . and now she couldn't help but be reminded of her again, because the Flintlander chevaleresse would've stormed into the tent to smash in Hoartrap's ugly mug as soon as she heard raised voices coming from her general's dark tent. Apparently the rest of her bodyguards had grown too accustomed to overhearing shouts from the command tent at all hours.

'Apologies, apologies,' said Hoartrap. 'I was only trying to help.'

'You want to help, you godsdamned freak, pass me my fucking pipe.' Ji-hyeon's cramps tightened along with her belt. 'I thought Colonel Waits was supposed to be cautious as a smuggler going through Immaculate customs, what the fuck is she doing rolling up on us like this!'

'Some might argue that attacking your trapped, exhausted, and outnumbered foe before they have a chance to recuperate is judicious to the extreme,' said Hoartrap, picking up Ji-hyeon's colorful glass bubbler from the table and offering it to his general. 'Or perhaps she's just seeing if you'll fold without a fight, and if you lead the Cobalts down to meet the Thaoans she'll call off the advance.'

'So much for my dear old fucking dad giving two shits about me,' Ji-hyeon grumbled, taking the pipe in her good hand and nodding at the candle burning on her table. In the past she'd avoided smoking in the mornings so as not to risk compromising her perspective when making important decisions, but since her second father and Colonel Waits hadn't left her with any options to weigh she might as well be as high as a majordomo's hat when she led her last charge. It would help her cramps, too. As Hoartrap dutifully held out the flame so she could hit the stale, half-burned bowl, she added, 'So much for all of us, if Waits isn't bluffing.'

'If she's not, I do have an idea of how we might discourage her with a minimum of casualties,' said Hoartrap as Ji-hyeon's lungs filled with deliciously itchy saam smoke. 'But I don't think you'll like it.'

'Try me,' Ji-hyeon gasped, holding in her smoke as the riot outside her tent grew louder and louder, her still-pale owlbat fluttering weakly down to land on her shoulder, and Hoartrap's thick lips split into a devil-eating grin.

'Your wish is my command, General.'

He was right; she didn't like it at all. By Hoartrap's own excited admission, it was such a risky gambit he'd never heard of anyone employing it since the Age of Wonders . . . and if the old crackpot described it as *risky*, she could rest assured it was probably more like *insanely dangerous*. It certainly sounded like a really bad idea, the sort of thing she never would have considered a few days before, no matter how confident Hoartrap sounded. But as Ji-hyeon followed him out into the too-bright, too-cold, and far-too-loud outdoors and saw the faces of her faithful bodyguards and the countless soldiers clustered behind them, some rattled and others grimly resigned, she knew she didn't have a choice anymore. A trapped fox will risk anything to escape the snare, even if it means gnawing off her own leg. She just prayed one leg would be enough.

———

'Don't. Move. A Muss. Ull.'

Not the words anyone ever wanted to awake to, and especially when sharing a tent with Pasha Diggelby. Still, it was better than if he'd stayed silent, because Purna was just about to brush the stray hairs or whatever they were off her face when she heard his voice, and more than the words, the tone. She did as he'd suggested, not even opening her eyes, the tooting horns and hollering that began to crowd her ears now that she was good and conscious barely registering over the now-distinct sensation of tiny, prickling legs moving down her forehead. One of the twiglike limbs slipped into her nostril, hopefully by accident, and the rest of the legs went dangerously still as whatever they were attached to steadied itself. Purna didn't breathe, but she couldn't bally well stop her heart from pounding, or, even worse, her nose from twitching as the sneeze built with evil inevitability. She thought of herself as a cool, collected veteran of a hundred horrors, but in the moment all she could think was *get it off get it off get it off get it off right now*, and then her face began to contort under the pressure of the sneeze, jagged, slightly hairy legs tensing hard against her skin as—

'Gotcha!' cried Diggelby, a rough hand grazing her cheek just as Purna sneezed. 'Naughty, naughty!'

Purna thought it went a long way past naughty, finally snapping her eyes open to see Digs leaning over her, clutching something in his silkmail gauntlet. It squirmed, and then she recognized it as the bright blue scorpion he and Maroto had dosed themselves with before the big battle. She hoped it was the same one that had escaped just before they'd headed out to fight, anyway, and that it hadn't reproduced in the interim. What with everything else that had gone wrong, she had completely spaced on the venomous land lobster being loose in their tent.

'Diggelby,' Purna gasped, cold sweat belatedly beading on her brow as she squirmed off her cot, putting some distance between herself and the foolish fop clinging to a spastically twitching scorpion that barely fit in his gentle fist. 'You have five seconds to crush that flipping bug before I crush the both of you.'

'Not on your life,' said Digs, snatching the cuff of the long, supple glove with his free hand and removing it with a practiced flourish, the scorpion an angrily twitching ball trapped at the end of the inside-out glove. 'What kind of a tapai are you? The Ugrakari worship a scorpion messiah.'

'The biscuit we do,' said Purna, grabbing up one of her riding boots to bash the bug out of his hand. 'The Raniputri might still cozy up with insect gods, but the First fucking Chamber of Ugrakar is the renunciation of superstition.'

'Renounce superstition?' Digs stumbled backward as Purna advanced on him and his arachnid-squirming glove. 'Is that what you call worshipping a lich king?'

'Shows what you know – the Living Saint isn't a lich *or* a king,' said Purna, swinging her boot at Digs's wrist but going wide of the mark when she stubbed her toe on one of the remaining prizes of the pasha's shield collection. 'It's not like he dances at festivals or anything; after he established the Last Chamber he sat down to meditate in the Cave of Amokkshan and he's been there ever since.'

'When you're right, you're right,' said Digs, maneuvering around toward the flap of their tent. 'Fallen Mother knows, basing your entire way of life on the teachings of an immortal wizard isn't superstitious at all.'

'That he might not be immortal is the whole point,' said Purna, giving up the chase when she nearly stepped in Diggelby's half-finished bowl of porridge and decided to settle for stealing his breakfast. 'The monks don't let anyone in to see him, and that's how he remains alive forever – because nobody's checked to see if he died. That's the Seventh Chamber, by the way, the impossibility of knowing that which you have not experienced.'

'Well, I'm sure to someone who eats the dead that probably makes much more sense than the Chain Canticles,' said Diggelby, warily watching as she sat back down on a chest and began shoveling handfuls of his salty, malty porridge into her mouth. 'That's yesterday's, by the way.'

'Is it?' Tasty as the mush was, she hadn't noticed the crunchiness came from ice crystals. She set the bowl aside and licked her messy cheeks clean; one nice thing about her bloated-feeling dog's tongue was the ease of post-meal cleanup. 'And whatever you're imagining we do with our deceased, it's wrong, I'm sure. There's nothing savage about it; we throw them a huge party, children running every which way with baskets of flower petals and bright-colored dyes, tossing handfuls in the air as the throat singers eulogize the dearly departed. And then they're carefully prepared by the local Gatechef, and they give us their final gift – the strength of their flesh. It's the only meat devout Ugrakari ever consume.'

'When you say it out loud like that, doesn't it seem a *little* weird?' asked Digs as he transferred glove and scorpion into the small terrarium that had previously housed his bamboo worms, and then popped open his makeup trunk and sat down to put on his face. Ever since Purna had slacked off on wearing her signature corpsepaint Digs had suddenly found the style quite in fashion; leave it to the upper crust to always want to bite the style of the street. 'And I don't mean weird in a bad way *per se*, but as a wee pasha I took the Chainite sacraments like every good little Imperial noble, and I'll be the first to admit chewing up some blood-drenched communion wafers at least *borders* on the superstitious. I mean, have you ever ... you know, *eaten* someone? Like, someone you knew?'

'Of course,' said Purna nonchalantly as she shook out both boots to make sure Digs's little friend hadn't deposited any babies in there. 'One of my first memories is my parents' homecoming, probably because it was the only time I sat at the head of the table. My aunt and uncle love to tell the story of how just when the Gatechef brought out the first platter I jumped up and ...' Purna felt an unexpected lump in her throat as she remembered Aunt and Uncle's stern but loving faces, and how she must have shattered their hearts into a hundred million pieces with her betrayal. '... Never mind. It's tradition, is all, not superstition.'

'Oh. Wow,' said Digs softly, and perhaps mistaking her sudden melancholy as arising from talking about the untimely death of her parents, which had happened so long ago it didn't much bother her at all, he tried to shift the topic a stroke or two to the left. 'So, yes, tradition not superstition, and perhaps not much stranger than those of the Burnished Chain, I'll grant you, but why are the officiants called Gatechefs? It's not like there's a Gate in Ugrakar ... or is there?'

'We all have a Gate inside us, Diggelby,' said Purna, pulling her boots on. 'Thirteenth Chamber. The First Dark's something we all must face, and we carry it with us from our first day to our last. That's why the Living Saint named the holyfolk who cook our corpses Gatechefs – they are the ones who complete the circle. Our ancestors draw us out of the First Dark, using the alchemy of flesh to usher us into the world of mortals, and when we die the Gatechefs prepare our flesh to be taken back into eternity through the mouths of our descendants. From the bodies of our family are we born, and into the bodies of our family do we return. Homecoming.'

Diggelby considered this as he finished applying his snow-white foundation and opened the pot on his black lip paint. 'I take back what I just said, and revert to my earlier position: that is *way* weirder than anything the Chain practices.'

'I didn't say I believed anymore,' said Purna, annoyed that an Imperial clown like Digs thought he had any kind of leg to stand on where ridiculous pomp and ritual were concerned.

'You didn't say you didn't, either!' said Digs, as though this were some great rhetorical victory.

'Yeah, well, according to the Thirty-six Chambers of Ugrakar the First Dark is at once unknowable and familiar to every mortal, a place of infinite tranquility, but the Burnished Chain is pretty fucking adamant that the only thing on the other side is straight up hell, full of devils and torment, and since a bunch of our buddies got swallowed by a Gate day before last, I know which possibility I prefer,' snapped Purna, but immediately regretted it as Digs banged his makeup case shut, his blackened lower lip beginning to tremble. Bad enough Maroto still hadn't returned, but yesterday's thorough canvassing of the barbers' tents had confirmed that Hassan and Din, like so many others, had probably never walked off the battlefield. She tried to think of something to console her friend, to console herself, but came up with nuts – what would Maroto do, at a grim time like this? Probably find a distraction, be it a bad pass or a worse anecdote, or best of all, a big honking fight to take their minds off the subject of Gates and dead friends and—

'Quickly, comrades,' Choi called from the mouth of the tent, the wildborn poking her head inside to reveal a sharp-toothed grin that Purna had learned could mean only one thing: what the woman referred to as an opportunity to earn honor. 'Have you not heard the song of war rising through the camp? The Thaoan regiment marches against us, and we must meet their disgraces with our tusks!'

'I did think it was a little loud,' said Purna, buckling on her kneepads as Digs slipped into his worn, stained battle caftan, 'but figured I was just hungover.'

'All the more cause to move faster now,' said Choi, then asked, almost cautiously, 'You have not discovered sign of Maroto, either?'

'Not yet, but if he's not back by tomorrow General Ji-hyeon said we might be allowed to join an expedition to find him,' said Digs, kneeling over the scorpion's terrarium again now that he had his kit on. 'In the meantime, I'd better take a double dose in his honor.'

'You should come, too, if you can – with your help we'll find our boy in nothing flat,' Purna told Choi as she stood up and cracked her knuckles. 'But save the scorp for later, Diggelbugs, you heard the lady – we're already late to the party, and I don't want to miss a single dance.'

Not the best catchphrase, and Purna knew she could do better, but all the same she thought Maroto would've approved.

———

'You *something*! Oi, runt!'

Sullen opened his eyes with a groan, the few hours of sleep he'd offered his aching body not nearly payment enough after two exhausting days without rest. He'd fallen asleep propped up against the side of the blacksmith's anvil, watching Grandfather burn, and his aching back and neck informed him in no uncertain terms this had been the worst possible bed he could've made for himself. The catfish-whiskered smith loomed over him, and continued in his guttural accent.

'You sleep *something something* not my business, *something something something* Cobalts *something* battle I cannot forge *something something* blade.'

It took a moment for Sullen's numb brain to parse what Crimson words he understood from the jumble, and the horns and cries and stampeding soldiers outside the makeshift smithy translated the rest. The Cobalts were under attack, and between the far-off bugles and the new Imperial regiment that had arrived the day before, even a sleepy Sullen could figure out what was happening. They'd had one whole day off from fighting, and now ten thousand more angry Outlanders were bum-rushing the camp, when half that number probably would've been enough to finish the job even if most of the Cobalts were better rested than Sullen himself. And while his beleaguered friends and their fresh foes were already marching to meet one another on the valley floor, he'd been snoring on the upper end of camp. Sullen was beginning to feel kind of like his uncle – never around when people needed him.

The bleakness of the situation brought Sullen immediately to his feet, though he still felt dazed and disoriented. Knocking back the bowl of raw eggs the gruff smith offered Sullen helped a little, but while he'd raided a lot of nests in his day, the slimy, sour yolks didn't taste like the produce of any fowl or lizard he recognized.

'*Something something* don't want to know, runt!' said the smith, perhaps reading Sullen's thoughts as he took back the bowl with a black-gummed grin – small wonder he favored such a breakfast; the shaman-blooded man didn't have a tooth in his mouth. Sullen muttered his thanks over a sulfurous burp and, shaking his legs out, quit the smithy but quick. Although the snow had stopped and the sun was out, the morning was cold as spring on the Frozen Savannahs. Just the way Sullen liked it.

The rows between the tents were mostly empty by now save for low banks of dirty snow, though a few other soldiers came slipping down from higher up the camp. As he picked his way down the icy slope toward the confluence of horns and bugles in the still-tent-obscured valley, Sullen saw more than a few haunted faces peeping out at him from dark tents. He felt a surge of revulsion at their cowardice in hiding from the clash that was clearly about to go down, but then remembered how he must have looked to the Cobalts when he came skipping along through the lists after he and Grandfather had helped Zosia protect the plateau behind the camp. For all he knew the soldiers he saw tying up their tent flaps from the inside had fought like seawolves at the Battle of the Lark's Tongue, and the wounds they'd incurred necessitated their sitting out this fight. Maybe, maybe not, but it wasn't Sullen's concern – the important thing was that he didn't avoid what was probably shaping up to be the Second Battle of the Lark's Tongue.

Coming around the side of a long cooking tent and entering one of the camp's clearings where drills were run and bonfires kindled, Sullen slid to a stop in the boot-packed snow. Without much thinking about it he'd been heading straight for Ji-hyeon's spot, but without a bunch of tents obstructing his view he could now see beyond the camp, where the curtain of smoke that had lingered around the Gate had finally been burned away by the bright winter sun. The last time he'd looked out over the valley floor he'd seen a column of swirling devils rising up from where the Gate eventually opened, an unwelcome vision someone born without a snow lion's eyes might not have seen, but while the sight that met his eyes now was decidedly mundane it was nevertheless equally unnerving.

The hill on the far side of the vale was a bloodred wave that poured down to flood the valley floor, the Thaoan regiment even more sizable than the Azgarothian army had been. And coming out to meet this Crimson horde were a number of far, far smaller clouds of blue banners, their raggle-taggle ranks as sloppy as the Imperials' were tight, their numbers even less than Sullen would have guessed – he had no head for figures, but it was clear that not even half the surviving Cobalts were marching out to meet their enemies. There were at least three times as many Crimson soldiers coming down already, and the torrent that breached the crest of the hill showed no sign of slowing.

Sullen's stomach dropped. How could this battle be anything but a slaughter?

'So do we just charge in there, or go to Ji-hyeon's tent and see if . . . ' Sullen trailed off midsentence as he looked over his shoulder and his eyes reminded his sleep-syrupy skull that he was talking to a ghost. Sullen was on his own, and it was time he got used to that . . . but some habits die as hard as some men.

Looking back at the advancing armies on either side of the Gate, he tried to figure out what he should do, and knowing every moment he dallied was a moment Ji-hyeon's danger increased wasn't helping. If he went to her tent and she was already at the battle he would've wasted more precious time, but if he just ran down into the valley he didn't have much hope of finding her before the Imperials swarmed the Cobalts. He took an unsteady step in the direction of the command tent, then looked back at the Crimson army, reminded of when the dread huntress Janus brought her legion of blood sisters rampaging down the fjords to overwhelm the nightmare fortress of the Skeletonwitch ... Well, except what was unfolding here was as real as real got, and none of that other shit had ever fucking happened outside of some singer's imagination. But some habits don't die, ever, maybe.

Sullen took off down the hill at a gallop, toward the imminent clash – Grandfather had always told him he needed to learn from his mistakes instead of bawling over them, and it was long past time he put that wisdom into practice. The last time he had gone toward Ji-hyeon's tent instead of the front line, Cold Zosia had ended up strong-arming him into helping her defend their rear, and that had cost Grandfather his life ...

Of course, if he'd just swung on the crazy old lady the first time he saw her, the way the Faceless Mistress had commanded, he'd still have Grandfather. Maybe the dead god of Emeritus had taken Grandfather from him as punishment for Sullen's failure to deliver on an admittedly simple errand, using her devilish wiles to guide the weakbow's bolt ...

Would that he could truly blame Zosia or the Faceless Mistress for the old man's death he would run with a lighter step, but Sullen knew that only one person was responsible for the tragedy, and that was the idiot grandson who rounded a corner too fast in a hotly defended camp. That failure weighed Sullen down more than his ancestor ever had in life, and he ran all the faster for it. He didn't think he could outrun his guilt, but the sooner he got to the fight the sooner he could forget it, if only for a little while. That, and all the other burdens he carried, from not knowing what to do about Ji-hyeon to not knowing what to do about his cowardly uncle to not knowing whether he could trust Hoartrap to have even told him the truth about Craven running away to not knowing what to do about Zosia and the Faceless Mistress.

There was a pattern there, and another constant, too: whenever he got stuck on one problem he found another one to focus on, like this here more niggling issue of a giant enemy army coming down to kill the girl he loved, and everyone else in the area besides. These Thaoans needed dealing with, sure, but this tendency of Sullen's to save his worries for another day had led to his acquiring a great heaping pack of night soil to cart around, and if he ever hoped to be free of it he needed to start resolving his old issues instead of burying them under fresh ones. The things folk figure out about themselves when they're in no position to do anything about it.

As Sullen splashed through the slurry around the broken palisades and saw the Crimson flood still pouring down the far side of the valley, he supposed he might not have to carry all his shame and indecision much farther, anyway. He had never seen so many soldiers in all his days and, unlike in the songs, fights this one-sided tended to be as ugly as they were quick. Well, if only one of the old legends proved true, Sullen prayed it was that of Old Black and her Meadhall, where he could lay his burdens at the door, go inside, and raise a horn of good snowmead with Grandfather. He'd soon find out, more likely than not.

For the first time all morning Sullen cracked a smile, and picked up the pace.

CHAPTER

2

Ji-hyeon gritted her teeth, then cut that shit out with a wince when a flash of pain ignited her jaw; with all the bugs and saam in her system, she'd managed to forget that she'd knocked a tooth loose fighting the Azgarothians and now the fucking thing was hurting like hell; or maybe Zosia had done it, she couldn't remember anymore. She looked down at the wide black expanse beside her, the oily surface of the Gate as menacing as a carpet of coiled vipers. Two days ago she might have been standing right here on the battlefield when the fucking thing opened beside her, and yesterday she had brawled with Zosia on its shore. If she managed to live out the day, she'd make a point of not coming back to this damn place tomorrow – she was beginning to feel like one of the Sisters of Sleep who laid out steaming bowls of black rice and harpyfish incense on the stoop of the Immaculate Gate each morning. The one time Ji-hyeon had seen the blindfolded nuns marching across the dawn pumpkin fields with their grey-ribboned robes billowing around them like jellyfish mantles, she had found the ancient practice extremely creepy, but it was positively quaint compared to what Hoartrap was now doing on the bank of this Gate.

Fellwing flapped her wings in Ji-hyeon's face, distracting her from the naked white giant and the cluttered, makeshift altar he had fashioned atop his wicker-framed pack. She hissed at her devil to calm down, the little owlbat fluttering frantically around her head, buffeting her aching cheeks with leathery wings. Ji-hyeon wasn't happy about going ahead with the warlock's scheme, either, but unless the Thaoans halted in the next thirty seconds Hoartrap wouldn't even have time to complete his sorcery before they were all overrun . . .

Yet even as the fear yawned as wide as a Gate in Ji-hyeon's stomach, the Crimson cavalry stopped a scant fifty yards in front of her and her small retinue of guards, the Thaoans slowing their roll in a big damn hurry as the Cobalt riders created a long line by fanning out on either side of the Gate. Chevaleresse Singh's hundred-odd remaining Raniputri dragoons and the fifty or so of Captain Kimaera's cavalry who had survived the Battle of the Lark's Tongue didn't make for a very intimidating front, but it would have to do until the few thousand remaining foot soldiers caught up with their general, or Hoartrap delivered what he'd promised. Holding any able-bodied soldiers in reserve for defense or reinforcement wasn't even an option; the Cobalt Company didn't have enough capable killers to defend a castle, forget an encampment whose pickets had already been dashed lower than the army's morale.

Beyond the flapping fan of her agitated devil's wings, Ji-hyeon watched the far tighter line of three hundred Imperial riders hold their places in the fetlock-deep snow. The chargers were too well trained to stomp or whinny; if not for the blasts of steam jetting from their nostrils they could've been statues. The massed Thaoan infantry remained hidden behind the cavalry's imposing front, and Ji-hyeon let herself hope the war was not yet lost, that their rows would part and her second father and Colonel Waits would emerge to convene with the

Cobalt general, their bluff called. No movement, save an angry red sea of flapping pennants held back by the dike of cavalry. Crafty Kang-ho, they called her father, the one who always told her to lead from the rear – if he came riding out the day was saved, but if he remained with the Thaoan command they were as good as dead ... unless Hoartrap was able to perform a feat that had not been accomplished in five centuries, an act of ancient witchery apparently so potent that not even he had ever seriously considered attempting it before.

Ji-hyeon glanced over her shoulder to where Choi and Sasamaso should have been waiting just behind her, but of course only her Honor Guard was there on her left flank, the Crowned Eagle chevaleresse who would usually have been on her right gone forever, along with so many others. Fennec held the woman's place now, not looking too happy about it. Nor should he, given the size of the boots he was expected to fill; Chevaleresse Sasamaso had been wise and kind, ferocious in battle and loyal as any devil, and now she was lost to the First Dark and whatever horrors dwelled there ... horrors that she had given Hoartrap permission to court in hope of receiving their aid. As Ji-hyeon looked back to where the nude sorcerer knelt over his rituals, Fellwing finally left her alone, shooting high into the cold north wind, away from the Gate and the tattooed, sweaty ogre who cooed softly to himself or the dark portal, it hardly mattered which. His pale arms were buried to the elbow in a plain burlap sack he had laid out on his altar, something squealing and hissing from within.

'General—' Fennec began, voice high and strained, but he was cut off as the Imperial bugles blared, all in a row, so close Ji-hyeon imagined the cold draft against her puffy cheek came from the horns. It was the signal to attack. Instead of turning to face the Thaoan regiment as they began their charge she looked farther back, past the pale devil in human form she had loosed to work his wiles upon this world, past her two oldest guards, to the decimated infantry limping after their general even now, following her back to the very place where they had lost all their friends, their comrades, their hope. She wanted to be proud of these brave ones who still answered her horn, wanted to sit high on her horse and salute them with her one remaining sword held high in her one solid hand . . . but all she could muster was pity for their doomed fate, guilt and sorrow replacing fear as she tried to pick out Sullen's bulk or Keun-ju's lithe gait amongst the yet-distant figures. She didn't see them, only bland, shambling corpses who didn't even know they were dead yet, the Imperial cavalry now so close she could feel their pounding hooves reverberating up through those of her mount.

Oh, how she had wanted to see Sullen before it came to this, her inevitable final blunder, but there hadn't been time for that, nor had there been occasion to confront Keun-ju again, nor her second father, nor to see her sisters or their first father or so many others; there wasn't time for anything ever again, not even Hoartrap's sorcery, and now fear and guilt were squeezing her so tightly between them that she thought she might be sick, but it could have just been the bugs or the faint buzzing of the Gate. Had it always made that sound and she had been too busy listening to the riot of the world to notice, or did it emit its call only when it was summoning home the newly dead?

Her guts pinched, and despite the cloud of saam in her head and the numbing toxins in her blood she started out of her reverie, because she might be about to die but she wasn't dead yet – she couldn't imagine any gods, however capricious, would make cramps part of the afterlife. Snapping her head around to face what must be her final foes, she almost laughed as her eyes passed over the absurd sight of a naked Hoartrap capering on the brink of the softly buzzing Gate, holding aloft the great terror he had promised to summon forth to save the Cobalt Company – a fat black opossum, which hissed but otherwise remained docile as the sorcerer nipped at its greasy skin with his teeth. Then all she could see was red as she faced the charging Crimson cavalry, snapping down her visor, planting her long, bearded spear in the ground, and drawing her sword. Choi and Fennec came up beside her, spears lowered and spurs ready for her order, and General Ji-hyeon Bong stood tall in her saddle to sound the attack, ready to seize what honor she could before receiving what most of the Star probably agreed was long overdue.

Choplicker bounded over another frost-locked body, this one a girl soldier no more than thirteen or fourteen years old. Beneath the thin, winding sheet of snow her eyes were open, as was her mouth, and gaping widest of all was her too-thin breastplate, a ragged hole as wide as a grapefruit punched through the beaten bronze, pure white powder filling the cavity. The wound must have been caused by a pick even bigger than the one on the backside of Zosia's war hammer. Whatever cheap heraldry the girl had worn had been torn loose in the battle, but Zosia knew she had been a Cobalt; the Imperial regiments didn't arm children, though they were willing enough to put them to the blade. This was the third such youth they had passed on their jog across the gleaming white valley, and Zosia doubted it was an accident that Choplicker had chosen this particular route. Then again, the frozen valley was pocked with corpses as far as the eye could see, the Cobalt soldiers who post-holed through the snow on all sides of Zosia moving around or sometimes on top of the dead, heedless to whether they had been friends or foes. All that mattered was reaching their general before the Thaoans did, though Zosia highly doubted it would make much of a difference either way – even if they'd been out here at dawn, well rested and better organized, the sheer numbers of a fresh Imperial regiment would like as not have trounced the depleted Cobalt forces within the hour.

Zosia ran even harder, and not because Choplicker led the way to a slaughter she was eager to take part in – she slipped and slid across the snowy battlefield because Ji-hyeon and her coterie of guards were less than a hundred yards away, and if she could reach the general before the battle she could show her the ruined Carnelian Crown that Choplicker had brought her, proof positive that something terrible had recently befallen Queen Indsorith ... and Ji-hyeon in turn could show it to the Thaoan command, buying them time, if not more. Of all the provinces in the Crimson Empire, Thao was second only to Azgaroth in their fastidious devotion to the queen, and if Indsorith had lost her crown that raised some very interesting questions of domestic affairs, questions that a cagey colonel like Waits would surely want to consider before committing to today's attack. No sense wasting a single resource defending the realm from without when you might soon be called upon to defend it from within.

The Thaoan bugles sounded again, this time in harmony, and Zosia would've cursed if she'd had the breath. She was close enough now to see past the line of Singh's dragoons, and those fucking Imperials had started a charge without even deigning to send out an envoy to ask for Ji-hyeon's surrender. Most veterans get cagier with age, but it seemed the notoriously wary Colonel Waits was experiencing a second youth, overeager as a horny teenager at her first spring faire. Fast as Zosia had been rushing up behind Ji-hyeon and her mounted guards, she now cut to the right, meaning to put the nearby Gate between her and the rampaging Imperial army before doubling back into camp and out the other side, into the mountains. No one could say she hadn't tried, but there was no way she could deliver the Carnelian Crown to anyone who could call off the battle now, and if she stayed for a fight this stupid she deserved exactly what she got. It was high past time she—

Slipped to a stop, nearly falling in the snow as she saw what Hoartrap was up to on the edge of the Gate. None of the Cobalts panting past her seemed to notice, preoccupied as they were with the hundreds of horses galloping straight toward them, but the old wizard captured Zosia's full attention, and not just because she'd never realized his tattoos flowed all the way down the crack of his ass. Choplicker had also noticed what the Touch was up to, coming back to her side with a whine, then looking back at Hoartrap with a growl, his patchy, washed-out fur bristling on his scabrous hide. Bad as he'd looked in the torchlit tent last night, in the clear morning light the old hound looked like he'd been boiled alive and somehow lived to wag the tail. Whatever weird shit the old warlock was doing to the squirming black animal he held in his arms didn't agree with Choplicker, and Zosia couldn't blame him – she didn't like the look of it, either, and the keening buzz rising from the Gate couldn't be a good sign.

With a triumphant hoot, Hoartrap spread his arms wide over his head. In one hand he held something that looked a lot like an opossum but probably wasn't by the scruff of its neck, and in the other he held the tip of its obscenely long tail. The poor devil squealed, and with quick flicks of his wrist Hoartrap began winding the tail around his arm, more and more of the bristly white length unreeling from the animal's rump like silk from a caterpillar.

Even by Hoartrap's grody standards it was a pretty fucking gross spectacle, but Zosia knew he must have some strong motive for doing whatever the hells he was doing, here on the edge of the Gate with an enemy army barreling down on them. She had looked the other way plenty of times during the old days when he'd employed similarly gruesome methods with the bound devils he fed on to fuel his sorceries, and it was surely a devil he tortured now, not a real animal, but all the same Zosia found herself plowing through the shin-deep snow toward the warlock. The creature's screams were too pained, Hoartrap's methods too grotesque, and Zosia wouldn't stand by and let him—

Fast as he'd been unspooling the devil's impossibly long tail, Hoartrap abruptly tossed the opossum away, over his altar and into the Gate. The animal gave a final, almost human wail, and then vanished into the blackness without a splash . . . but its tail still stretched from where it had disappeared into the dark surface to Hoartrap's outstretched arm. Choplicker began barking fit to wake the corpses that Zosia stumbled over as she finally reached the circle Hoartrap had cleared in the snow, and the warlock staggered forward, his knee cracking into the little shrine he had set up atop his pack and sending red candles, black fangs, and a pyramidal stack of white purity rings flying onto the disturbed earth at the rim of the Gate. The tail he had wrapped around his forearm was taut, a quivering bowstring that vanished into the black portal, his milky skin bulging as the fleshy tether bit into his wrist. As he glanced over his shoulder toward Choplicker's frenzied barks, Zosia didn't think she'd seen the creepy behemoth this concerned since they'd summoned their first devils together, back in Emeritus.

'Help!' the sorcerer cried, the frozen dirt crumbling around his bare feet as he slipped another few inches toward the waiting Gate, his crusty toes almost brushing the edge. 'Pull me back, pull me back!'

Tempting though it might've been to let him follow the devil he'd tortured down into the First Dark, the damage was done now, and there were worse things than having Hoartrap the Touch owe you his life. Ever since Maroto had saved him from the titanic devil queen their meddling had roused in Emeritus, the warlock had always looked out for the barbarian. Besides, on the far side of the Gate, the Thaoan cavalry had split to go around the supernatural obstacle, and on either side Singh's cavalry engaged the swarming Crimson riders, so icing her old friend when they were about to be overwhelmed by Imperials anyway seemed too cold a play to run on anyone, even a bag of moldy dicks like Hoartrap.

Bracing her boots as best she could on the icy grit, Zosia grabbed Hoartrap's free wrist, his mammoth fingers closing around hers – and then a powerful jerk from whatever force held the other end of the opossum pulled them both off their feet, and even if Hoartrap had released her instead of tightening his grip Zosia would have been lost then, the momentum too much. She had tried to save that wickedest creature in all the Star, an eater of devils, and now the Gate would have them both. Like any mortal, she had wondered what lay beyond these ancient doorways to the First Dark, but also like any mortal, she had dearly hoped she would never find out.

The hopes of mortals are such fragile things.

———

Sullen nearly stumbled when he heard a familiar buzzing sound, the wheeling, clashing, falling, dying blur of blue riders and red riders and horses horses horses suddenly forgotten, the wheezing Cobalt soldiers he had been easily outpacing suddenly overtaking him in the desperate charge to the conflict at the center of the valley. Hard as he'd been keeping his eyes off the open patch ahead that must be where the Gate lay, he'd run up almost beside it, and while it was issuing a quieter thrum than what he'd heard when the Faceless Mistress took him to her breast in Emeritus, there could be no mistaking the sound. She was coming for him, just as he'd known she someday would after he failed to carry out her will, and he turned to see her rising from the Gate, as radiant as she was terrible . . .

Except it wasn't the Faceless Mistress on the rim of the abyss but her sworn enemy, the one Sullen had to stop before she murdered an entire metropolis using fire and deviltry: Cold Zosia. She, her devil dog, and Hoartrap the Touch were not twenty paces away, their backs to him and, as he watched, the foul sorcerer began to slip precariously close to the edge of the Gate, and then Sullen saw what had happened – something dreadful had reached out of the First Dark and grabbed one of his arms, pulling him slowly but surely into the bottomless pit. Zosia slid across the slushy ground toward Hoartrap, paying no heed to the wild melee that had begun, the two cavalries weaving among one other, spears and swords flashing in the cold brilliance of the early winter sun. Both sides gave the Gate a wide berth, however, so there was nothing stopping Sullen from rushing over to help . . . or to help them both go over the side.

The buzzing of the Gate throbbed louder at the thought, and Sullen started to sprint before he'd even made up his mind which course he would follow.

———

After being mobbed and partially eaten alive by Chain-maddened cannibals two days before, Ji-hyeon would have thought she'd be glad to go back to fighting normal soldiers. Yet so far the Second Battle of the Lark's Tongue was shaping up to be just as nasty as the first one. It had started off surprisingly well, the charging Thaoan cavalry failing to anticipate how spooked even the best-trained animals became in the presence of Gates; Singh's riders had noticed the change in their horses as soon as they had arrived, and the chevaleresse had altered her strategy accordingly. Since Colonel Waits had not followed the proper protocols for declaring an honorable attack, the Raniputri knight had no compunctions about employing any method that would assist her employer; as well she might, considering Ji-hyeon's hasty agreement to pay her twice as much as originally negotiated, on the spot. And so instead of countercharging the Imperials, the dragoons kept their nervous horses as still as possible, nocking their short steel bows and firing several volleys in quick succession at the Crimson riders. Despite how organized their assault began, the Thaoan charge soon descended into chaos as any horses nearing the Gate violently shied away, colliding with their neighbors as the arrows rained down. So yes, a good start, but it didn't hold – there were simply too many Imperials bearing down on them, and not enough mounted archers to slow the flood.

Facing the stampeding line of Thaoan cavalry filled Ji-hyeon with such deep fury it was almost cathartic; she saw her second father's stupid fat face behind every rider's steel guard, and was no longer sad or afraid, only eager to teach the old know-it-all a harsh lesson. She couldn't rely on Hoartrap's promises of mystical powers to win the day, nor the strength or stratagems of any of her other captains – the only way to beat back the Crimson flood was to take charge and lead her people in the defense of the valley. She knew she'd do that best by falling back to meet her infantry while Singh's dragoons covered her escape, but the greater numbers of Crimson riders were already slipping past the spread-out Cobalt cavalry, engaging the general's small retinue of bodyguards.

How to best fight on horseback wasn't something Choi had taught Ji-hyeon back at Hwabun, the Immaculate Isles better suited to naval conflicts than mounted combat, but ever since they'd come out of the Raniputri Gate, Ji-hyeon had focused on little else, her Honor Guard and Captain Kimaera taking turns drilling her. Her instructors had differed on certain particulars but were in agreement that nothing could prepare her for mounted swordplay but relentless training. Kimaera had a soft touch when they sparred, but Choi was her usual merciless self. Every time the wildborn snapped the reins out of Ji-hyeon's hand, spooked her horse, or knocked her out of the saddle, the young general had cursed her cruel tutor, swearing she'd be sorry when her ward broke her spine or dashed out her brains, and Choi had always shrugged and told her she'd have a hard time mustering sympathy for a hawk who flew into war but didn't even know how to properly land.

Ji-hyeon wasn't cursing Choi anymore. When the Honor Guard alerted her mistress to the pack of Thaoans coming up fast behind them, the general's retinue abandoned their flight, wheeling their horses around before they could be struck from behind. Choi's horse rose up on its hind legs just in time to avoid the charge of the lead Imperial, the animal seeming a projection of the wildborn's will, and then the rearing horse kicked the rider's helmet in as she rode past. The next Thaoan knight seemed on course to drive his lance through Choi's armpit as the wildborn's horse dropped back down on all fours, but Ji-hyeon spurred her mare forward in time to intercept him; the Crimson lances were a good deal thicker and sturdier than bearded spears, but the Immaculate weapons were longer. The butt of Ji-hyeon's spear buckled against her saddle as she lodged its tip in the knight's armpit, the shaft of the weapon exploding from the shock of the collision and showering them with splinters. The knight fell but his ankle caught in the stirrup and he was dragged past them, the scraping sounds as he bounced along almost louder than the buzzing that filled Ji-hyeon's ears. More riders were coming in fast, and Choi whistled for Ji-hyeon; she looked over just in time to see the bearded spear her Honor Guard tossed her way, and caught it clumsily between the thumb and two remaining fingers of her devil-healed hand. Choi had an Imperial lance laid across her knee, and Ji-hyeon began to wonder if it belonged to the knight she had just unhorsed, if Choi had somehow caught the dropped weapon out of the air, but then she didn't have time to wonder about anything, because just then a far more important Crimson lance caught her notice – the one a Thaoan rider was directing straight at her.

Then the Thaoan woman was no longer a problem, two arrows skidding off her plate armor and a third popping her just under the chinstrap of her helm. She also rode on past the general and her bodyguards, dead or dying but upright in her saddle even as her steed cantered along, and in the great tragic way of war, another three mounted Imperials took her place, and just beyond them came the clomping masses of the Crimson infantry – Singh's dragoons had failed to even slow the enemy's advance, and now the full strength of Thao was marching past the Gate, ready to consume Ji-hyeon's dream like army ants falling upon a crippled salamander. The fastest foot soldiers in the Cobalt Company had finally started to appear in the midst of the stampeding horses, but that was like trying to put out a wildfire with a watering can.

For all his promises of a diabolical ritual that was so dangerous it would send the Thaoans screaming from the field and might even eliminate them as a threat altogether, Hoartrap had failed to produce so much as a parlor trick. Then again, Ji-hyeon hadn't delivered, either, so why should she have expected any more from one of her Villains? All that was left was to make sure she wasn't taken alive by the Imperials – she wouldn't give Kang-ho the satisfaction. Fortunately for her, finding death on the busy battlefield didn't look to be much of a problem.

———

Much as Purna loved Diggelby, she was rapidly coming to the unavoidable conclusion that if he hadn't been packing a devilish spaniel for the entirety of their adventures he never would have made it out of the Panteran Wastes alive. No, that wasn't quite right, he was a chum from way back and deserved the credit he was due – if not for the dearly departed Prince watching over him, Pasha Diggelby might never have even safely made it out of a bathtub. And since Digs had traded away the one thing keeping his sorry ass alive to save Purna, she was honor bound as a woman of, well, honor, to do her all to repay the mortal debt.

Which she did thrice over before they'd even gotten past the chaotic cloud of cavalry choking up the middle of the valley, deflecting two passes that would have spitted him and then blowing the bally brains out of the Imperial with the spear who had been so keen on piking the pasha.

It wasn't that Digs was high – Digs was always high as a string of Ugrakari prayer flags. Often higher.

It wasn't that Digs couldn't hold his own in a fight, because while he'd never be a champion like Purna he could hold his own most of the time, if only because people chronically under-estimated the ninny.

And it wasn't that Digs had choked up in a tight spot, which would have almost been understandable, what with the deafening shouts and crashes and a great red wall of infantry nearly on top of them, riders circling all around so quickly the pair of friends barely had time to see whose side they were on before the bastards had come and gone, and most of the Cobalt foot soldiers they'd dashed out here with had sensibly drawn up short a hundred yards behind them, leaving them on their own on a battlefield clogged with hostile types. Despite all *that*, Digs hadn't choked up at all.

No, the problem was that Digs didn't choke up enough, as it were, the corpsepainted ponce leaping straight into every possible clash without the slightest concern for his own safety. Obviously having Prince around to protect him had given Digs an inflated sense of his own ability, which, while respectable, couldn't very well make him invincible the way a bloody devil could. Purna loved a good scrap as much as the next hot-blooded hero, naturally, but there went Digs, skipping ahead in his smartest woolly boots to meet the charge of a mounted Thaoan knight, even though she'd told the idiot to watch her back while she reloaded. She barely got the pistol up in time, shooting the galloping horse straight through the scale barding covering its chest, and popping its heart like a tomato at target practice (though as a rule she went for the rider, if it could be at all helped. Not that she liked horses in particular, big scary-faced brutes, but it didn't do to hold any animal accountable for its master).

Purna knelt to reload again, unclipping another pouch of powder and shot from her belt.

'And that's forty-five for me!' hooted Digs as he jabbed his crystalline sword into the visor of the dismounted Imperial who had almost killed him. Considering how still the knight had lain as Digs approached him the Thaoan had probably snapped his neck when his horse unexpectedly folded underneath him, but Purna didn't debate the point. For one thing, Digs was just spouting off random numbers now, their wager officially a wash, and for another, she was too busy wondering just how the devils they were going to get out of this mess at all.

The plan had been to accompany Choi to wherever Ji-hyeon was, thereby proving their fearless devotion, etcetera etcetera, so the general wouldn't get second thoughts about letting them go off in pursuit of Maroto. That simple plan had officially gone tits up as soon as they reached the command tent and Choi discovered her ward had left for the Gate without her, on some errand with Hoartrap. The wildborn hopped on her horse and flew off to join the general, leaving Purna and Digs with little choice but to jog after her, and by the time they gained the valley floor finding Ji-hyeon was a lost cause – there weren't nasty clouds of smoke on the field like there'd been during the first big fight out here, but it scarcely mattered, with all the hordes of furiously fighting soldiers substantially more difficult to see through than dark fumes had been. Where the general could be in all this tumult was anyone's guess, and even if they did find her it seemed unlikely she'd even notice their selfless assistance. No, the only thing for it was to pull back to camp and ready their things for a speedy departure, whether they got official leave or not – they'd come and fought, so if Ji-hyeon made it through she'd have to appreciate their spunk, and if she didn't, well, then they'd be leaving in even more of a hurry.

'Digs!' she cried, hammering the ball home in her pistol and pushing her horned wolf hood back off her face. She was drenched in sweat despite the cold bite of the morning. 'About face, butter bean, we're needed back at camp!'

Purna didn't know if Digs was ignoring her or just couldn't hear over the strange buzzing sound that was getting louder by the moment, but regardless of the cause he wandered away toward the steadily advancing line of Thaoan infantry, waving his shimmering saber about less like a bloodthirsty mercenary and more like a child playing villain. Not having much choice, Purna followed after – he hadn't let her foolish ass die the last time they'd come out to this field, so she had to watch out for his. How Maroto had ever put up with them she'd never know, but he had, and that was what mattered.

As she slipped through the slush and the mush after her last real friend toward a foe they could never hope to overcome, Purna figured she might have finally done the old lug proud. If only he could've been here to see it . . . but then if he were, he'd probably be running in the opposite direction with Purna tossed over one shoulder and Digs the other. Either way, she wished he were still beside her.

———

If only Uncle Craven were here it would've been perfect, all three of Sullen's problems laid out for him on the rim of what the crazy-arsed Jackal People called a Hungry God. Sullen was sorely tempted to just sit back and watch as Hoartrap the Touch was drawn into the Gate by the thin white tentacle that had grabbed his arm; after all, killing the old monster was exactly what Grandfather had urged him to do the first time they'd met. Once Hoartrap was out of the song Sullen was pretty sure he could knock Zosia in before she knew what hit her, the devil at her side looking so run-down it probably wouldn't be able to stop him. Not that the older woman had seemed the great villainess the Faceless Mistress had made her out to be, but could he afford to take a chance, with the lives of a city so big it filled a mountain in the balance? According to every story he'd ever heard about her she was as cold as killers came, responsible for countless deaths on every Arm of the Star, and if all that weren't enough, apparently she'd just tried to murder Ji-hyeon for no reason at all. Even without the warning of the Faceless Mistress that Cold Zosia had yet to commit her greatest crime, all that surely added up to someone the world would be better off without. To her credit, she'd kneed his uncle in the nuts, and that hardly balanced out the rest.

His boots barely touched the snow as he closed the last ten yards. If he'd thrown down on them the first time they'd met, Hoartrap on the Samothan plains and Zosia back in camp, maybe things would have played out a lot different, a lot better. Maybe Grandfather would still be alive, and maybe they could have sorted things out with Uncle Craven. Fast as he was coming in and bad as Zosia was limping as she reached out toward Hoartrap, she didn't have a chance of shrugging off Sullen's blow, and he'd shove her and the great big naked witch into the buzzing Gate together. No more indecision, it was time to fucking act, to settle this shit once and for all, to—

Skid to a stop on the crunchy ground and grab Zosia's arm just as she and Hoartrap were yanked off their feet. Instead of falling into the Gate together, they simply slipped forward another foot, still being pulled inexorably forward but momentarily arrested by the addition of Sullen to the end of this chain of struggling mortals. Stupid, stupid, stupid. But throwing your enemies into Gates was what Jackal People did, fucking savages, and Sullen wasn't a savage . . . and here at the edge of the First Dark, his muscles straining against whatever power pulled Zosia and Hoartrap down, he reckoned he wasn't the sort of person to kill somebody for something they hadn't yet done, nor was he low enough to tell himself that watching Zosia be pulled in and not trying to help was any different from giving her a push.

She looked at him and he looked at her and his foot slipped and just as it looked like he'd gotten himself dead for his trouble all the tension went out of the tug-of-war, and Sullen,

Zosia, and Hoartrap fell back in a pile. They didn't stay that way for long, Sullen and Zosia wriggling out from under the crushing weight of Hoartrap, who just lay there gasping great big mouthfuls of air and shuddering. Picking himself up and seeing Zosia doing the same on the far side of the beached-whale bulk of Hoartrap, Sullen tried to think of something fleet to say, and failing that was about to settle on a knowing nod, when he noticed that the thin white tendril was still attached to Hoartrap's wrist, snaking across the few feet of frozen earth and disappearing into the opening of the Gate. He'd figured it had snapped off somewhere down in the dark, but peering into the Gate he could see the furry cord winding way, way down, into the bottomless depths. That he could see it at all seemed deadly queer, for the Gate in Emeritus had been impenetrable, just black as black could be, yet looking into this one was like gazing into a clear glacial pool, and he wondered if this Gate was different, or if his devilish eyes had adjusted to the First Dark, were showing him things no normal mortal could see . . . and there, just beyond the vanishing point of the slack, swaying rope, something very big came crawling-swimming-flying up out of the gulfs, toward the surface of the Gate.

Sullen had seen more than enough to know it was time to dip. The buzzing was deafening, now, and even as he turned to book it as far and as fast as he could the earth shuddered in anticipation, and Sullen went flying into Hoartrap just as the warlock finally clambered to his feet. They went down even harder than before, and, before they could untangle themselves a second time, the sun was blotted out by whatever god or devil Hoartrap the Touch had called forth from the First Dark as it burst from the Gate, into the world of mortals.

Upon further consideration, Sullen *definitely* should have killed that fookin' witch when he'd had the chance.

CHAPTER

3

Domingo started awake, consumed with a stark terror he had not felt since he was a boy. It was the sickening, heart-thudding panic of realizing you have overslept, that the bells are already ringing and you're still shivering under your thin blankets when you should have been up an hour before, polishing your boots and buttons, because the inspections begin with the first bell and any cadet who isn't spotless will spend their morning peeling turnips instead of fencing. According to Domingo's connections at the academy, his sluggard son eventually skinned enough turnips to feed the needy poor for a year, whereas when he'd been a student Domingo had never denuded a single tuber. And yet the fear was always there, yes it was. The one recurring nightmare of his life was being ten years old and still abed back at the academy in Lemi, and hearing the dreaded tolling of his doom ...

Except that nightmare was far, far preferable to this unthinkable reality – some maniac in his command with an obvious death wish had signaled the attack, and without even bothering to wake the colonel. The bugles were distant, too; they'd actually left him back at the camp, going on the march without their leader! Domingo's groggy head ached, and furious as he was with whatever usurper had seized control of his regiment, he was even angrier with himself for letting this happen. He should have seen it coming, but who could it have been? Who would dare? Certainly not Shea, she was better than that, and Wheatley didn't have the avocados to pull off a coup, so—

Cheaper, tinnier horns sounded closer than the bugles, and Domingo relaxed back onto the cot, returning fully to the waking world and all its pains and indignities. He was injured – maimed, really – and a prisoner of war in the Cobalt camp. He had failed everyone, himself most of all, and was too hurt to even pull himself out of bed; Zosia herself had removed his chains, that's how toothless he'd become. The man King Kaldruut had once honored by referring to him as 'the Lion of Cockspar' had first lost his mate, then his cub, and finally his pride, leaving him little better off than a lame old house cat, so harmless he could be trusted alone with an open cage of songbirds.

So an Imperial regiment was engaging the Cobalts. It had to be the Third, since the other closest able-bodied regiment was the Second out of Meshugg, and even if they'd started marching west at the same time as the Thaoans they were still weeks away . . . but it couldn't be the Third Regiment, because Colonel Waits still led them, and there was absolutely no fucking way she would come down so hard and fast on an unknown army. Why, a substantial part of Domingo's reluctance to wait for the Thaoans before launching his attack was his confidence that Waits would insist on receiving explicit orders from Diadem before engaging the Cobalts . . . and now she was plunging straight in, and without the support of a sister regiment to back her up! Madness.

Unless Waits already had her orders from Diadem, and not necessarily from the Crimson Queen – one of the few things he and Waits had in common was their staunch support of the Crown and their shared scorn for the Burnished Chain, but considering Domingo had compromised himself it obviously wasn't beyond the realm of possibility that Waits had also struck a bargain with the Black Pope. Maybe she had been duped, the same as he, and now led another religion-poisoned regiment down into the valley for some worse ritual yet . . .

Or maybe, unlike Domingo, Colonel Waits had actually grown smarter with age, and seeing how weak the Cobalts were after their rough treatment at the hands of the Fifteenth she'd decided to snatch the low-hanging fruit with both hands. The Third Regiment might not be as feared as the Fifteenth, but the Thaoans made up in numbers what they lacked in skill. The more he thought about it the more sense it made, and he sighed deeply, though he knew it would hurt his aching ribs. Sometimes a man has to take an unpleasant action. Kudos to Waits – for once in her career she was giving the most sensible order instead of the safest, and it was without a doubt going to win her the entire Cobalt Company, and a few Villains besides. He briefly flirted with killing himself before she could stride into the tent and gloat over his rescue, but even if he'd been of a serious mind, he was in no health to even try such a cowardly escape from his due. He had made this bed for himself, and until the better officer showed up to relieve him from it, here he would stay.

The strangest thing about it all was the disappointment he felt at hearing those bugles draw ever closer. He didn't relish being captive and accomplice to Cold Zosia or her Immaculate protégé, that would have gone without saying if only it wasn't damnably crucial intelligence that was worth saying twice. These Cobalts deserved the justice paid all traitors and criminals, nobody would hear Domingo argue different . . .

But at the same time, fat luck finding a soldier who doesn't have something dark coming back to them, and Domingo had known ever since he was a cadet that taking down the greater evil often involves making compromises with lesser ones. That philosophy was the only way you could survive as an Imperial officer, and while it had led him into some trouble of late as far as his ill-considered conspiracy with Pope Y'Homa went, it was also responsible for his allegiance with Queen Indsorith, from her first civil war against the Burnished Chain to the last. It was true that of late Domingo had done the realm more harm than good, but nobody could deny that over the last twenty years the Fifteenth Regiment and their godless colonel had preserved the Empire from dissolution, or worse, a successful Chainite rebellion.

And that right there was where the biting disappointment came from – the realizations that the fundamentalist revolution he'd always feared had as good as happened, and moreover that he'd played a significant role in the takeover. When General Ji-hyeon had come to his tent the day before to ask for his support, she had argued that Queen Indsorith now ruled in name alone . . . and given that even the legendarily loyal Azgarothian colonel had gone behind the Crimson Queen's back to collude with the Black Pope, he had to admit the Immaculate brat had a point. Preposterous a notion as it was, that blue-haired teenager had spoken more truth to power in a few minutes than he'd heard in his entire career as a military man – all sane Imperial officers agreed the Chain was a problem, but nobody else seemed willing to consider the possibility that maybe every single one of the lunatics needed to be cut down or cast out once and for all. And that was exactly what General Ji-hyeon wanted, to save Samoth and all the other provinces from a pestilence that had slowly been spreading across the Empire, a pestilence Domingo himself had helped flourish.

At first her speech had seemed as cockamamie as any other rabble-rouser's, but he'd been turning it over ever since she'd taken him at his word that he would help advise her campaign and gone off to save the rest of the Fifteenth Cavalry from Zosia's vengeance; it had kept him awake late into the night, no doubt the cause of his uncharacteristic sleeping in. And by the end he'd been almost convinced, crazy as that surely made him. General Ji-hyeon and her advisors were waging a damned impressive war for such a ragtag mob of mercenaries and peasants, she had some of the most cunning military minds Domingo had ever gone up against already on her payroll, and with only the Third Regiment and their dithering, noncommittal colonel to worry about in the short term it had seemed like the Cobalts had ample time to prepare, too. As much as he hated Zosia, he hated the Black Pope far more, and he couldn't think of a more perfect example of using one enemy to destroy the other – if he and Cold Cobalt pooled their strategies and worked together to help General Ji-hyeon, the campaign would be devastating for the Burnished Chain.

Or could have been, anyway, if Colonel Waits had hung back to let the Cobalts plot and scheme instead of uncharacteristically plunging straight into a confrontation. Who knew, with Domingo's influence at the negotiation table they might have even convinced Waits to join forces with the Cobalts against the Chain, assuming she wasn't already taking her orders from the Holy See. Now, though, Waits was seizing the obvious advantage, and not even a regiment as sloppy as the Third could mess this one up. General Ji-hyeon was about to wake up from her little dream, but closing his eyes as he began to drift back off to the trumpeting of bugles, Domingo had to admit it had been a nice one, while it lasted.

CHAPTER

4

You don't spend as many years as Zosia had in the acquaintance of Hoartrap the Touch without seeing your fair share of weird shit, but all the same this may have taken the razorcake. She had just helped the naked old creep to his feet, nearly as eager for answers as she was for his help in escaping the busy battlefield before things got any hairier, when the ground rocked beneath her boots and Sullen went flying into the big wizard. It looked like it hurt, the two stout men knocking foreheads as they went down together. It might've been funny, in a dickish way, sure, but then Zosia saw what had set off the Sullen kid and didn't feel much like laughing.

It corkscrewed up out of the Gate and into the air, though the curvature of its arc looked less than graceful and more like the accidental result of its furiously twisting spine and tail ... an exceedingly long tail that began as thick as Zosia's waist before gradually tapering to the thin whip that was still wrapped around Hoartrap's wrist, embedded so deeply in the skin that his swollen hand looked about to pop. *Oh.* That was about all Zosia was able to process before the spiraling black monster crashed down to the ground on the edge of the Gate, the shock wave knocking her off her feet. It was only after it violently rolled away from the Gate in the opposite direction that Zosia realized she had almost died – if it had come south instead of north it would have crushed her and Choplicker, Sullen and Hoartrap, and the foot soldiers she now noticed some thirty paces behind them in the bargain. It was that big, a monster twice as tall and four times as long as the elephants she and Singh had once ridden to war, and as it came out of its frantic roll in the midst of panicked horses and their yet more panicked riders, Zosia saw its bald, snarling face snapping all around to inspect the cluttered field, meter-long whiskers waggling as it hissed so loudly it drowned out the buzzing sound that came not from the Gate itself, but from this fell monster Hoartrap had called forth with his witchcraft.

The general shape of the titan was familiar, but it was as similar to the opossum devil Hoartrap had fed to the Gate as a horned wolf was to Choplicker. The buzzing behemoth shivered in the cold air, bristling long, jagged quills in place of fur, and she saw multiple rows of yellow fangs in its slavering mouth ... a mouth wide enough to bite off a horse's head in one snap, apparently, as it idly jerked its head to the side and decapitated the mount of a nearby rider. Zosia couldn't tell from here if the rider had been Raniputri dragoon or Thaoan cavalry, but she saw well enough to know the poor fucker was dead now, hairy claws as long as bastard swords raking out and sending the headless horse and its mangled rider skipping messily across the ground. The unfortunate pair skidded into several other members of the clashing cavalries, horses' legs snapping out from under them like wheat beneath a scythe. Then the devil king threw back its long crocodilian snout and squealed so loudly that Zosia flinched, and as the sound trailed off, a terrible humming quiet fell on the valley, even the most feverishly locked combatants distracted by the new challenger.

Choplicker broke the silence, barking and bounding toward the monster before Zosia could stop him. The giant's cannonball-sized eyes fixed on her happy devil, and Zosia turned to demand some fucking answers from Hoartrap when her legs were swept out from under her for what felt like the hundredth time in the last day or two. Even as her tailbone smacked painfully into the ground she saw that it was none other than Hoartrap himself who had upended her, but she couldn't rightly fault him – the daft bastard still had the end of the devil king's tail fixed to his wrist, and was being keelhauled across the battlefield as the monster bounded forward into the fracturing mobs of red and blue soldiers. Choplicker chased after them, merrily yapping as the colossal devil dragged the sorcerer behind it, pursuing mortal flesh for perhaps the first time in centuries, if ever. In the event they both got through this, the Touch's most epic clusterfuck yet, Zosia would have to ask Hoartrap just where exactly he'd learned how to summon up this particular specimen, and what possessed him to set it loose. First, though, she'd finally found something she was excited about doing – sending this rampaging monster back into the First Dark, having another long talk with Hoartrap, and, assuming she survived all that, bringing Ji-hyeon the broken crown . . . and, just maybe, an apology for trying to kill her the day before. That order.

'Uhhh . . .'

Zosia glanced over and saw Sullen still sitting on the ground beside her, one meaty palm pressed to the side of his head as he stared after the monstrosity.

'Yeah, I'd say *uhhh* about covers it,' grunted Zosia, getting up and hissing through her teeth at the fresh hell radiating from her bruised ass. Offering Sullen her hand and the sort of easy smile she'd given the boy's uncle back before things had gotten so tense between them, she said, 'Well, kid, now that Hoartrap's taught you one way to call up devils, what do you say I show you a fail-safe means of putting them back down?'

He didn't look happy about the prospect, but that just went to show that not everybody's as dumb as they look. Licking her lips and taking the first step toward the incensed devil king thrashing its bulk through Crimson and Cobalt soldiers alike, Zosia wondered just how much the fool she looked right about then, walking straight at a monster the likes of which she hadn't faced in a quarter century, and even then, never by choice. Seeing the silhouette of its long tail whip through a clump of soldiers, a pale, limp shape hanging from the end, she supposed she looked smarter than Hoartrap, anyway.

———

Ji-hyeon really hoped Hoartrap lived out the day, so she could plant her toe between his lily-white cheeks. It went without saying that in this scenario she came out of the fight, too; after the Thaoan arrows started dinging off her helm and embedding in her thick hauberk, she stopped feeling the warrior's death that had sounded so good in theory. That right there was why you always had to be careful what you wished for, and never the more so than when devils were about. Still, Fellwing must be flying close overhead, or else one of the barrages of arrows would surely have dropped her steed, at the very least, but so far she'd stayed ahorse and unharmed. Choi and Fennec were still on either side of her, but the rest of the bodyguards had fallen away or fallen altogether, the only riders around them now wearing Crimson tabards and unmistakable sabretaches, the saddlebags embroidered with the flower-ringed dragon-deer of Thao.

Then the last of the stampeding Imperials veered away from them, and through the canine teeth of her helm Ji-hyeon saw she had become turned around in the fray and was charging straight into the front line of the Crimson infantry. She yanked the reins and dug in her foot, but the wall of polearms was coming up so fast and the necessary turn so sharp that for a moment she was sure her galloping steed would break her legs. The mare didn't, a better mount than Ji-hyeon was a rider, and they dashed along in front of the Thaoan line, long, steel-capped shafts jabbing out as Ji-hyeon continued to goad her horse into the full turn. Seeing a nearly ten-foot-long polehammer come swinging down just ahead of her, Ji-hyeon thought, *what an absurdly impractical weapon*, and then it winged the side of her helm so hard she swore she felt her skull splinter. She dropped the Crimson lance Choi had tossed her after her third spear broke, and if her boots hadn't been so firmly lodged in the stirrups she would have toppled. Instead she slumped in her saddle, paralyzed, as the horse completed the sharp about-face and cantered easily away from the infantry. Still she didn't fall, but it was too late all the same, the field before her darkening to a deep ruby as blood filled her eyes, her ears buzzing as loud as a barber's icebee hive. She closed her eyes to stop the world from spinning and, still too stunned to think but feeling the sensation return to her clammy fingers, she drew the reins gently to her chest, feeling herself slipping out of the stirrups and wanting the horse to be at a standstill when she dropped from its side. The buzzing in her leaking brains intensified, traveling down to the raw nerve in her loose tooth, and then she was falling . . .

And was caught. Blinking through the stinging blood and the tight perspective of her helm, she saw Fennec on the far side of her horse, removing her boot from the stirrup with his soft white claws. He wasn't the one who held her, and queasily looking down she saw one of Choi's gloves digging into her armpit, hoisting Ji-hyeon away from her horse and onto the wildborn's.

It felt like they were still galloping, the ground moving beneath her even as the horses remained still, and then she was spun about in Choi's strong arms, her leg dragging over the neck of her Honor Guard's horse as the woman planted Ji-hyeon in front of her on the anxiously whinnying steed. She was facing the wrong direction, belly to belly with Choi instead of looking out over the horse's head.

Fluid as Choi's movements had been, the transition made Ji-hyeon throw up a little in her helm, but she hurt too bad to be embarrassed yet, leaning into Choi's chest and resting the chin of her heavy helm on her Honor Guard's shoulder. She could see the infantry behind them, a funny perspective to have on a horse, and even through the nauseating pain in her skull and the blood in her eyes she managed to smile, because the mighty Thaoan regiment had stopped advancing, the whole line of infantry hastily backing away. They tripped over themselves in their retreat, those who fell trampled by their comrades, and others just standing there slack mouthed, staring at the injured general and her last two remaining bodyguards. One fainted dead away, bouncing off his neighbor on the way down to the slushy field. It sounded like Fennec was shouting, high-pitched, pony-like screams, but she couldn't make out the words over the buzzing in her brains.

'Oh, Ji-hyeon,' Choi whispered in the ear-slit of her helm, and somehow, despite how loud it was, she heard her Honor Guard perfectly, even over the droning that had spread from her skull to her teeth and now vibrated along every aching bone. 'I have to release you now, my general, but slow. You must lie still and gather your strength, and let me take the honor for both of us.'

That was Choi for you. Basically incoherent. But then Ji-hyeon's world spun again as the wildborn lifted her off the horse like a baby, and passed her to other hands. Fennec, his paws so gentle as he helped her down and let her lie on her back. Even through the sheen of blood, she could tell the sky was blue, blue as the waters of Othean Bay.

Fennec said something, but she still couldn't hear what, and then Choi's voice cut through the humming noise again. 'I will tempt it away. Be swift, my friends.'

Friends? Choi was without a doubt one of Ji-hyeon's best and only friends, but she hadn't thought the word even entered the wildborn's vocabulary, and while her use of it should have warmed Ji-hyeon's heart, instead it chilled it. Something very bad was happening, and as Fennec's furry hands slipped the damaged helm off her aching head she rolled over to see where Choi had gone . . .

No. No no no. Choi was as tiny as a miniature rider pictured on one of her second father's tapestries in the foyer back home on Hwabun – the Samothan pieces that recounted heroic epics – and towering over the charging wildborn was a nightmare of black spines and drooling maw, sharp talons and lashing tail, a horror the likes of which belonged more to the hell scrolls her first father kept locked away in a chest of vermilion-painted ironwood. The monster was four or five times as tall as the soldiers who ran screaming from it, and even on horseback Choi would barely reach halfway up its greasy flank . . . and worst of all, her Honor Guard stood high in her saddle and blew the horned wolf hunting horn Purna had given her general, attracting the titan's wrathful attention as Ji-hyeon helplessly watched.

Tough as the Thaoan riders had been when they were all the heroes had to contend with, Digs had led Purna almost on top of the Crimson foot soldiers before he'd realized just how far ahead of their own infantry they'd run, only a handful of fellow Cobalts following their bad example. Horses still wheeled all around, making it blasted hard to orient themselves, and now a hedge of pikes and long hammers was only a few yards off. Sadly, this dismal turn of Diggelby's non-strategy should've been expected – if she'd been able to catch her breath long enough to pontificate, she would've remarked on the predictability of the pickle he had gotten them into.

But just when you think you've seen everything, a giant hell gerbil shows up to broaden your horizons. At least the appearance of the gargantuan gross-out distracted the Imperial front line and calmed Diggelby's happy ass down, the pasha stopping in his tracks and gawping at the fiend that came plowing through the cavalry. Apparently all it took to put his ego in check was a monster as big as a barn. This hesitation on his part was the main difference between her and Digs (well, other than her superior style and his superior breeding); he seemed to be perfectly happy ducking death at the hands of boring old Imperial soldiers, but it took something special to excite Purna these days, and enemies didn't come much more extraordinary than a colossal predator crushing and ripping its way through Crimson and Cobalt alike. She got that tight, pukey feeling in her throat, her heart accelerating from a brisk march to a sweat-glazing war dance, and, holstering her loaded pistol, she hooked Digs's elbow and yanked him after her, toward their new target. The big bruiser had just taken off a horse's head and sent both carcass and rider flying, so clearly a straightforward offense wouldn't work; they had to find a way to jack the beast ... but with all the surrounding Crimson infantry and riders either staring slack-jawed at the thing or outright retreating, they didn't have to worry about being poked in the back as they circled around it. Hopefully.

There was a dread moment when she thought it had spied their approach, leveling its icky grey face in their direction, but then a nearby Cobalt rider came charging in, issuing a trilling challenge from a distinctive horn, one Purna recognized with a sinking feeling in her tum ... except no, now she saw General Ji-hyeon lying on the ground between two horses a short distance off. Captain Fennec knelt over her and, focusing back on the charging Cobalt rider, Purna saw a flash of black horn in a white coif, and her ill sensation became positively plaguey – it wasn't Ji-hyeon who rode out to meet the monster, but Choi, the handsome wildborn badass who had helped Purna craft the horn as a gift for their general. Choi trilled the horned wolf trophy again as she came in fast.

Refusing to look away from what would almost certainly be a dreadful end to one of the select few people Purna considered a personal inspiration, she started running again, no longer trying to flank the monster but going straight for the fallen general and the two nervously stamping horses. Purna's careful feet carried her over frozen bodies and far fresher specimens, the field clearing out around the beast in a hurry, and she saw Choi veer her horse away, obviously meaning to lead the devil king on a chase, but the monster was already braced to pounce, and the wildborn had ridden too close ...

Just as it began to launch itself at the tempting rider, however, a fallen Cobalt piker who had been lying beside one of its muddied claws abruptly sat up, thrusting her spear into the monster's leg. It squealed fit to wake the dead gods of old, or at least make them turn over in their dreams, and instead of leaping at Choi the monster snatched up the piker in a front paw and reared back on its hind legs, somehow finding its balance despite its prodigious girth and comparatively spindly limbs. It took several toddling steps backward, the spear jutting from its elbow no longer than one of its spines, and stared down at the woman crushed in its claw, her screams louder than the buzzing that filled the air. Then, in a decidedly human movement, it rubbed the captured soldier against its leathery, spineless belly and, like some traveling conjurer charming the peasantry with sleight of hand, made the Cobalt piker disappear from its paw. The monster's long muzzle curled up in an unmistakable grin and, realizing what had happened, Purna looked away in horror – there was a pulsing bubble on its bald belly, where the unfortunate woman had been shoved into a slit or pouch and now impotently squirmed against the suffocating skin that trapped her.

Purna liked to think it took a lot to creep her out, but that did it. Killing this thing no longer seemed like an honor or an adventure, but a necessary step to ensure she could one day, someday, fall asleep again. Maybe. That wasn't going to happen so long as there was any chance this thing was still alive and out there in the world. Nope nope nope.

She skidded across the ice to where Captain Fennec was tending their bloody-faced general, giving her water or spirits from a calabash flask. Ji-hyeon's owlbat fluttered down to land on Fennec's thigh, the pale little creature seeming about as feeble as its mistress – a devilish matter, no doubt, for Purna had seen the animal a dozen times over and could have sworn its furry plumage had always been a rich onyx. She glanced back, mostly to make sure the Thaoan infantry hadn't decided to sneak up behind them after all. While they hadn't, she saw Digs trotting after her, bless his bug-stung heart, though he wasn't in quite the same hurry she was. And ahead of them, the fell giant had dropped back on all fours, and was tracking Choi with its long snout as the wildborn steered her horse to the north. That was the only direction to lead it, really, with the Gate at its back, the Cobalt infantry scattering back toward camp to its left, and General Ji-hyeon between it and the retreating Thaoans on its right. It wasn't taking the bait, though, a lone noisy rider less intriguing than the clanking, frantic mass of Crimson soldiers, and its black eyes seemed to settle on the injured general and her wards.

'Guard Ji-hyeon with your life, Digs,' Purna called behind her as she scrambled onto the back of one of the nervous horses that flanked the fallen general and her kneeling captain.

'That's my horse,' said Fennec, sounding more confused than angry by the development as he looked up to see Purna settling into the saddle and Digs jogging up.

'Well I can't very well steal the general's,' said Purna, wiggling around to get comfortable on the thin Usban saddle and frowning down at the stirrups, which dangled out of reach of her short legs. Oh well, no time for corrections, and people rode bareback all the time. Kicking the big bay as hard as she dared, she gave a hearty 'Hya!' which sounded right, and sure enough, the horse jumped forward so fast she almost fell off its rump.

In the mountain kingdom of Ugrakar, almost everyone walked wherever they needed to go, and those who rode favored dire yaks, the sure-footed beasts far nimbler on the sheer terrain than any Raniputri pony or Azgarothian mustang. The only people who learned to ride horses were of the Tapai families, the big beasts increasingly fashionable as an obvious status symbol; the roads to your palace must be wide and level to accommodate a horse, and while the merchant guilds had appealed the decision numerous times, the royal family remained firm that only the noblesse were permitted to ride them.

Purna had only been on a horse a time or two, and never under such intense conditions, but she had cruised around

on enough yaks in her day to consider herself something of
an expert rider. It thus came as something of a surprise when
the horse abruptly lurched to the right, wanting no part of
the great buzzing hell beast that reared up before them, and
she went flying out of the saddle. She wasn't surprised for very
long, however, since her world went bright white as she landed
face-first in the snow, and that was it for Purna.

———

One question needled Sullen as he and Zosia raced up behind
the hulking devil king: was this entirely his fault, or only partially? He'd never know if the monster would've still managed
to worm its way out of the First Dark if he'd shoved Hoartrap
into the Gate before it could emerge, but considering the end of
its tail was still tethered to the sorcerer it seemed plausible it had
been relying on that connection to cross over. And now the biggest, freakiest horror he'd seen since the Faceless Mistress was
tearing its way through the middle of the battlefield, attacking
anyone it could lay its jaws or paws to, while Zosia's devil dog
raced enthusiastically after it, looking a bit like an ermine
chasing a ghost bear. The Gate-spawned opossum monster had
slowed its pace to a faltering scuttle – Sullen never would have
thought something that huge could be described as scuttling,
but that was the only word for it – and as he and Zosia crunched
their way across the torn-up earth in its wake they saw why it
had altered its gait. Ever since it had first reared up on its hind
legs, it had started grabbing live soldiers and tucking them away
into some hidden pocket or mouth on its underside. From their
vantage point it was impossible to see where exactly the unlucky
folk were being stuffed, but all the same it was pretty fucking
dreadful to behold . . . and it probably never would've come to
pass if Sullen hadn't decided to save Zosia and Hoartrap instead
of pushing them through the Gate.

'Having second thoughts?' Glancing over at the woman trotting beside him, Sullen couldn't tell if she'd shouted or whispered, the buzzing of the beast louder than ever.

'Uh . . . nah.' Sullen hoped his embarrassment didn't show, tightening his fists around the shaft of his spear and sun-knife. 'We good.'

'I meant about ambushing the devil queen.' Zosia's smirk made him feel more the fool than his own mouth had. On top of that, how'd she known it was female, a devil queen and not a devil king? Before he could ponder the matter further, she said, 'You know anything about bringing down something this big?'

'I . . . nah,' Sullen said after a moment's hesitation, because little baby songs about Cormorant the Oath-breaker hunting hairless mastodons before the Coming of the Iced Earth were just that, and less than no help in the face of the enormous reality they fast approached.

'Let's start with one of her hind legs, trip her up, and once that drops her backend low enough for us to reach we'll stick something pointy in the ass or crotch, whatever we get a shot at.' That was actually *exactly* what Cormorant had done to fell the elephantine blind guardian of the Forest of Stars, but Zosia seemed to mistake Sullen's surprised expression for reluctance. 'Not nice, I know, but a lot of blood flows through there, and a lot of pain, too, and pain's what we need to bring, and blood's what we need to spill. With me?'

Sullen stared up at the lumbering backside of the beast, a waterfall of thick spines crashing down around the tree-trunk rise of its tail; whatever unspeakable part of the devil she wanted them to strike lay hidden behind that fat white root. It had stopped lashing the fifty-foot appendage, at least, having used most of its length to wrap Hoartrap up in tight, furry coils. It balanced the warlock over its back like a scorpion's stinger as it advanced ever more slowly toward the retreating Thaoan infantry, arching its back so that its pendulous pink gut wouldn't drag on the corpse-riddled field.

Sullen was no coward, but he was no fool, either, and he didn't have a high opinion of Zosia's scheme – poking this thing in the butt seemed way more likely to bring its full wrath down on them than to do it any substantial injury. It was just . . . so . . . *big*, and between its epic stature and that numbing drone it emitted all he could think of was the Faceless Mistress, and he wondered if this might be another god, one long forgotten by mortals, if they had ever believed in such a fiend at all. And that was what scared Sullen – fighting an animal, however huge and dangerous, that was easy, and a necessary evil if it was causing mischief, but attacking a god seemed bad form, even if it was one you didn't worship.

'Deceiver wept,' whispered Zosia, stopping in her tracks, and before Sullen could try to parse that queer turn of phrase he saw what had brought her up short, and found he suddenly understood the expression perfectly. He skidded to a stop, too, despite being almost close enough to strike it.

'Old Black wept, too.'

The monster had danced all over the field in spastic dashes, foraying deep into the retreating Thaoan infantry only to dart back in the other direction, double-fisting the fleeing Cobalt soldiers into its belly, but now it stopped in the widening strip of vacated earth between the two armies. It began shuddering in place as it stretched farther up on the tips of all four paws, the pale pink surface of its dangling stomach bulging all over. There were people in there, writhing and pushing against the thin membrane, and other shapes that were almost human but weren't. At first Sullen thought the devil queen was carrying her brood in some kind of stomach pocket, that the hapless soldiers she had been stuffing in there were food for her young, but now he realized it was much worse than that. As he stared agape at the sick-making mass, a human face pressed into the edge of the rubbery, translucent flesh, and as its mouth widened in a scream its face ruptured, lengthened, the rest of its silhouette changing along with its skull. Throughout the gut-pouch, lashing tails and snapping snouts replaced scrabbling hands and mutely wailing mouths, the buzzing so loud Sullen felt it behind his eyes and vibrating through his taint . . .

'Move, boy,' said Zosia, slapping Sullen's biceps as if to remind him he wasn't dreaming. It only half worked, his eyes still stuck on the roiling stew of remade flesh that bubbled away inside its pouch. 'That left back leg, while it's up on tiptoes. Now!'

She darted forward, quick even with her slight limp, but Sullen couldn't move, his limbs locked up, his chest tight. It was going to put him in its pouch, he knew it, and he was going to melt away into the beast his clan had always told him he was – blood of devils or blood of shamans, it scarcely mattered, because soon he was going to be something else entirely, they all were, for who could hope to stand against a god? That's what it was, it had to be, to sow such chaos, transforming people into monsters . . . it wasn't even that they were all going to die that froze Sullen; it was that they might live on, remade in this devil queen's image. He never should have left the Savannahs, he never even should've stayed on the frozen field with Grandfather after the Jackal People maimed him, he should have been a good Horned Wolf and gone home with his mother, and then none of this would have happened, never never never—

A bark brought Sullen out of his dark reverie, and he saw

Zosia's dog back in front of him, wagging its tail, and as he met the devil's black eyes he took a step back, for there was something coldly intelligent in their depths that was every bit as intimidating as the new god behind it. It glanced over its flank to where its mistress had almost reached the devil queen's leg, and Sullen sucked in a breath of the bracing morning air. A god had told him to kill a woman, and now this woman moved to kill another god ... and at her beck and call was a creature that looked something like a dog and something like a devil but what Sullen was beginning to think was every bit as dangerous as any other power he'd met, from the Faceless Mistress to this marsupial devil queen. Maybe there was something to the ancient lore after all, maybe mortals were but characters in the songs of the Old Watchers, pushed this way and that by the caprice of the gods. If that were true, the worst mistake a person could make would be to bore them with indecision, especially by sitting out such a fight. Yes, all he needed was to start moving, to charge at the towering horror that was popping professional soldiers into its vile pocket like a child gathering teaberries in his skirt ...

Ji-hyeon. She was out there on the field somewhere, on the other side of this devil god or god of devils or whatever the hells it was. Her name jabbed him in the arse like a thorn, and then he was moving so fast he was halfway to the oblivious devil queen before Zosia had finished settling in for her strike, the woman standing beside its splayed claw and sizing up its enormous leg like a seasoned woodsman surveying a knot-riddled oak. She tensed her shoulder but didn't swing yet, looking back at Sullen with a mad grin on her face. The canopy of oozing, writhing flesh stretched thin just beyond her, the creature itself still shuddering in place, oblivious to the mortals rushing up behind it, and Sullen committed himself to something he never thought possible outside of the songs: he attacked a god, with a devil loping at his heel and a hero of legend fighting beside him.

He should have been excited, but it was all he could do not to throw up.

———

Ji-hyeon wiped blood and sick off her chin as she leaned against Purna's friend, Dangleberry or Dingleby or something. They were surrounded by the enemy. Fennec was trying to talk sense to the mounted Thaoan officer and the dozen Crimson infantry who had dared to go against the receding tide of their regiment, taking advantage of the gargantuan devil's sudden interest in the Cobalt infantry to dash forward and capture the enemy general. Another peril to having such a distinctive style as the one Ji-hyeon had borrowed: even the lowest enemy grunt knows what you look like. Still, she wouldn't have expected any of them to risk attracting the monster's attention by breaking from the Crimson mob, even for such a prize as her – her second dad must have put quite the price on her head. Easy enough to offer a king's ransom, when you'll turn around and flip your hostage for the price of an empress, and apparently there was nothing like greed to make even the craven bold.

Well, as soon as she got her strength back Ji-hyeon would teach them such rewards are easier imagined than earned. Whether it was the return of her weak devil to the crook of her arm or whatever sour, malty dram Fennec had poured down her throat, she was feeling stronger by the breath. Her head still ached and the buzzing in her ears made it hard to hear what harsh words Fennec and the Thaoan woman were exchanging, but she'd wiped the blood from her eyes, and realizing it had not welled out from inside her face but run down from a cut on her scalp came as a huge relief. If only they hadn't been

captured by Imperial soldiers while an enormous monster decimated the wrong fucking army and cut them off from any hope
of rescue, Ji-hyeon would have been feeling peachy.

'We're being abducted by sharks?' asked Ji-hyeon. She was
sure that didn't sound right, but whatever Fennec had just said
in reply to the cavalry officer had resulted in the ring of Thaoan
pikers tightening around them, spears pointed at their breasts
and polehammers raised. Fuck those hammers in particular,
looking at them made her eyes water anew.

'No such luck,' said the mounted officer, but her eyes
weren't on Fennec or Ji-hyeon, but something far taller that lay
behind them. 'Tell your guards to come peacefully, General,
or we gut them now and leave them to the warbeast. We'll
move faster if it's just you, but I'll give you one chance to save
your dogs.'

The fop propping up Ji-hyeon made an indignant sound at
that, but she shushed him and said, 'You heard her. They got
us, so let's all go quietly.'

She was surrendering to save Fennec and the dandy, she
told herself; she wasn't doing this because here at the moment
of truth she was scared to die after all. Besides, she deserved
something worse than death for ordering Hoartrap to loose
that thing on the world, didn't she? He'd promised her a great
weapon that would run their foes off or even intimidate them
into submission, and fool that she was she'd listened. Now even
more of her people were dead, she was captured, and the giant
monster was having some sort of fit behind her in the middle of
the field . . . but at least the Thaoans were retreating, and that's
what Hoartrap had promised her, wasn't it? A devil's bargain, if
ever there was one, exactly the sort of thing she should have—

Ji-hyeon doubled over, the air split by a squeal so loud and
raw it nearly made her puke again.

'Shit,' was the Thaoan officer's composed response, and then she wheeled her horse around and took off at a gallop. Ji-hyeon's mare jerked her reins out of Fennec's paw and followed fast on the first horse's fetlocks. Which didn't bode well, given the circumstances. A few of the Thaoan pikers ran after them, but the rest just stood there, too scared or awed to move, staring up at whatever it was that projected the increasingly loud humming aura as it slowly approached. Ji-hyeon still hadn't gotten a good look at the thing, but seeing how transfixed these soldiers were by its very appearance reminded her of how she'd felt hypnotized by the pumpkin devil back in Othean that fateful night she and her guards had snuck away from the Autumn Palace in search of adventure. Rather than risk becoming similarly enthralled by the grotesque majesty of the looming giant, she kept her gaze from its visage as she turned to confront it, instead focusing on the thick, furry legs that brought it forward in a faltering waddle. Here was death, taking its sweet time but nonetheless certain for the sluggishness of its approach.

Ji-hyeon should have expected something like this, after ordering Hoartrap to go fishing in the First Dark for something big and scary to throw at the Thaoans. Gates were called gates for a good reason, because they were the portals devils used to enter the world of mortals, and it stood to reason that the bigger the doorway the bigger the visitor . . . and this new Gate the Chainites had opened up with their suicidal ritual was by all accounts the largest in the Star. She hadn't even fully understood the mechanics of what Hoartrap was saying after a certain point – she got the part about how in order to fully cross over to the mortal realm devils had to possess a living creature, preferably a scavenger, but everything after that had been too screwy to follow. Something about how by using a bound devil instead of a mundane animal he could entice a far greater power into entering a living vessel that was already fully in his command. To his credit, he had warned her there might be some collateral damage, for although such an entity could not harm him it would surely seek to feed on anything and everything else it could lay claim to ... but so long as everything went according to plan, the devil-eater would compel it to return to the First Dark as soon as it had run off the Thaoan regiment.

So much for everything going according to plan, she thought as the titanic devil approached them with impartial but obvious malice. Its obscenely distended stomach swayed so low it almost brushed the ground as it walked, and behind the salmon curtain of its drooping gut several small figures harried it across the field; she wondered if it even noticed the mortals lashing at its rear leg, and if they were Cobalts or Imperials.

It was approaching so slowly they might have fled its coming, Fennec and the fop each tugging at a sleeve and hissing urgent entreaties, but she shook them off and nodded ahead. Between Ji-hyeon and the leviathan lay some fifty corpses, some mauled, others trampled, and more than one dressed in a Cobalt winding sheet. She had called this horror up, so it fell to her to put it down, despite the pounding in her head, despite the exhausted owlbat sleeping fitfully in the curve of her elbow, despite how badly she wanted to follow the fleeing Thaoans all the way back to her bad second dad and certain death at the hands of Empress Ryuki, if only it meant she didn't have to face the consequences of trafficking with a warlock. Drawing her sword, she slapped the slackly held polearms of the five remaining Thaoans, startling them out of their torpor.

'Looks like it ate itself stupid, so let's take it down before it wises up,' she told the pale, shaky Thaoans in their native Crimson, holding out her sword like a torch to guide them toward glory. 'Stick that big belly if you can reach it, and its legs if not. And be swift! Honors like this do not come often.'

They all looked at her like she was crazy, but at least their eyes were on her instead of the shambling devil lord. Then the face-painted fop tapped her sword with his diamond-faceted blade, Fennec did the same with his scimitar, and after a serious double scowl from her fellow Cobalts, the five remaining Thaoans brought their spears and long hammers in, too. By then their weapons were no longer vibrating from the slight impact but from the proximity of the buzzing monstrosity, and taking a deep gulp of the sharp morning air, Ji-hyeon braced herself to lead seven warriors into a hell of her own making.

CHAPTER
5

Singh and Fennec had often argued with Zosia and Maroto on the merits of sharp weapons versus blunt ones, especially where attacking oversized enemies was concerned (Kang-ho usually sat out these debates, as he preferred to attack big targets the same way he went after small ones: from a distance). The line of reasoning went that even the sturdiest opponent possessed veins to slice, ligaments to sever, and flesh to puncture, whereas a dull blow might be shrugged off by a large or armored foe. To this Maroto and Zosia had always replied, usually in unison while bumping fists, 'Not if you hit them hard enough.'

Swinging her war hammer overhead as though she were going to split a log with an ax, Zosia found no cause to doubt that old wisdom. The devil queen's splayed foot was the size of a tower shield; the head of Zosia's hammer wasn't much bigger than a fist. Yet when it connected with the top of the paw it crunched bones into splinters, mashed muscle into stringy paste – she'd wielded this hammer for so long it was an extension of herself, and she felt the damage she'd inflicted vibrating down the haft, vindicating her argument.

Not that there was anything wrong with a sharp edge, a point Sullen proved as he severed the thick tendon at the back of its ankle with the leaf-shaped blade of his spear, but Zosia would always prefer her weapons the way she liked her women: thick, blunt, and capable of fucking up even the biggest devil in the First Dark.

From the way the thing squealed you would've thought they'd gone and killed it, and instead of the leg giving out and causing the backside to droop low enough for Zosia to nail it in the sweet spots, the monster took off in clumsy, plodding steps, fleeing across the field with a definite limp. So, not the quick and smooth victory she'd hoped for, but then she'd also half expected it to respond to the attack by spinning around to gobble them up. Pleased as she was not to have its giant, drooling mouth or agile front claws to contend with, having the thing immediately flee was almost anticlimactic. If the first soldiers it laid into had stood their ground instead of justifiably freaking out, would this big bully have just turned tail back into the Gate?

No telling now, but at least she and Sullen had herded it back toward the retreating Thaoans instead of the Cobalt camp, and all the carnage the beast had caused seemed to have put the spring back in Choplicker's step, and some color in his coat to boot. This nasty fucking devil queen wasn't the only one eating well out here. The dog ran after the giant, looking over his shoulder to make sure they were following, and after exchanging wary nods with Sullen, they did. It might be moving a lot slower than it had as whatever abominable incubation process took place in its belly, but with legs that long they still had to run all out to even hope to catch it, and catching it before whatever was transpiring in its gut-sack reached fruition seemed like a wise plan.

Sullen gave a choking shout, and then he was gone, five, ten, twenty feet ahead of her, closing fast on the devil queen. She'd been flattering herself to think they were keeping pace because they were equally swift; apparently while she'd been giving it her all he'd barely broken a sweat, but something had put the fire under him now . . .

Tapai Purna, lying flat on her face on the ground right in front of the advancing devil queen. It had to be her, she was the first person in twenty years Zosia had seen wear a horned wolf hood. Zosia pushed herself harder, doubting very highly the girl could still be alive, laid out like that on a field like this, and hating herself for remembering what she had told Maroto when he'd begged her to save his injured friend just two days earlier – that a wish would be wasted on a girl like Purna, who'd find another grisly end for herself soon enough even if she recovered from her wounded leg. By all the godless devils of the First Dark, Zosia hated being right all the damn time.

'No!' Sullen wailed; not a bellow or a battle cry, definitely a wail, and now Zosia saw why: it wasn't Purna he was worried about; it was the huddle of Crimson cloaks holding their ground just beyond the prone girl, in the path of the beast, half a dozen shaky-speared Imperial infantry led by . . . Ji-hyeon?

———

Ji-hyeon. Seeing her there, standing firm with her sword held high in the face of a creature whose mere backside had paralyzed him with fear, made Sullen feel all kinds of funny. Terrified for her but impressed by her bravery, straight up fucking wigged out but also kind of inspired? They would fight this thing together, they would turn it back or cut it down.

He'd sheathed his sun-knife when they ambushed the devil queen, figuring he only had one chance to surprise the monster and wanting to make it count; he'd always been better at jabbing a spear than throwing a blade. He considered throwing one of his sun-knives now, but what if instead of slowing the monster it only spurred it faster? He couldn't risk that, so put everything into racing the behemoth, desperate to reach Ji-hyeon before it did.

No mortal nor devil was as swift as Sullen when he needed to be – Grandfather always said he could've outrun Count Raven himself – and even with its lengthy stride Sullen overtook it, outpacing even Zosia's devil. There was no time to circle around it so he just ducked underneath it, noting with satisfaction that the rear leg it dragged was leaking thick grey sludge from the hurt he'd put on it. He darted to the side to avoid careening into the translucent belly-sack pulsing with new-made monsters, wove back inward so as not to collide with the back of its front leg, and then Ji-hyeon was twenty yards ahead, only a few corpses for him to hurdle over before he reached her, and—

Someone tackled Sullen face-first into the slush and the mud, someone fat and slimy and stinking like a dead animal left to bloat in the summer sun. Except this wasn't even someone, it was some*thing*, its teeth latching onto his shoulder, its claws scratching him, and through the blind panic and confusion a part of Sullen just knew what had happened ... and that part went utterly, utterly mental. Instead of rolling over to try to dislodge his attacker or pawing around for his dropped spear, Sullen slapped his palms into the slick, melting earth and shoved off as if he were performing the fiercest push-up of his life. Even with the squirming weight on his back, Sullen launched himself up far enough to pull his legs in, planting his toes beneath him, and from there he jumped as high as he could, pivoting in the air so that he came down on his back, and came down hard. As intended, the creature cushioned his landing, its squeal cut off with a crunching sound and sensation, its mouth falling away from his neck, its claws flapping limply aside ... but just overhead Sullen saw another of the foul, furry spawn pull itself free and drop over the lip of its mother's pouch, the man-sized monster landing on all fours in the slurry beside Sullen. Bad as their parent looked, these poor bastards were worse, for the eyes staring balefully at Sullen were still human.

Before he could even reach for one of his sun-knives it came at him, just as hard as its sister had . . . but not half as hard as he came at it, for while it had claws and teeth and a mother's love, all Sullen had were his fists.

———

Sullen. For one golden moment crystallized in time like a lightning bug in amber, Ji-hyeon saw him racing for her, running between the great devil's legs with a cry on his soft, sweet lips . . . then a lump of the living nightmare detached itself from the whole, dropping onto his back. Before her shock could even register, he made short work of this new monster, beautiful man that he was, but then another descended, and another, and then Sullen and his attackers were hidden behind the curve of the giant's teeming belly as the devil queen came for her, relentless and inevitable as grief.

'No!' She didn't even realize the voice was her own until she was moving forward and heard her echo reverberating off the wall of spines and muscle. Now she looked, because she'd be a fool not to track the position of her enormous enemy's maw, and instead of being bewitched by its hellish visage she almost laughed out loud at the manifest absurdity – it was a fucking opossum. Magnified to a dragon's stature and devilfied into loathsome cast, sure, but still a fucking opossum. If only they had wheeled out all of the camp's refuse to distract it this whole fiasco could've been avoided.

A horn trilled, her horn, and then Choi rode in between Ji-hyeon and the lumbering behemoth. It was reckless, Ji-hyeon was still thirty yards out, but her fearless Honor Guard put herself in harm's way all the same, charging straight into the path of the beast, but slowing her whinnying steed as she did. Then Choi half fell out of her saddle, hanging off the side of the cantering horse, clinging to the saddle horn with one hand, and Ji-hyeon realized the wildborn hadn't come to protect her, but another. Choi tried to scoop a body off the field but either the angle was wrong or her strength failed, for the white-cloaked figure on the ground flopped back out of her grasp. And insane as it surely was with the hulking opossum devil almost on top of them, Choi clumsily dismounted, dropping into a crouch as the horse bolted away … only to be slapped into the air by a massive claw.

Then the unthinkable happened, and Ji-hyeon went utterly, utterly mental.

———

Someone slapped Purna, a great big slap that covered her whole body, and while her natural inclination was to roll over and ignore them, drifting back off to dreamtown, the damp chill that began to intrude on her skin was too clammy to be ignored. Opening her eyes, she found herself splayed out on her belly, dirty snow and dirtier dirt the whole of her world, and with each smack of her gummy lips and lick of her dog-like tongue she found herself less inclined to appreciate being roused. Whether she'd been dead or only dreaming of being dead, it had to have been an improvement on this, a steadily increasing and nigh-universal sense of dread … and pain, she couldn't overlook the pain that was now manifesting in her face, shoulder, knee – heck, pretty much everywhere.

But then Choi rolled her over, and it seemed a small price to pay, because the wildborn cutie was flushed and sweaty, her fetching left horn and the stump of the right visible through her wide-brimmed mesh hat, and she was down so low Purna could have kissed her ... and dash it all, why not? You never know when your last grain of sand will drop, so you might as well make the best of every occasion. Maroto might not like it, but whatever he felt for Choi wasn't the same as his thing for Zosia at all; this wasn't poaching, and besides, Choi seemed like a sensible lady, she probably had no interest in boys, so why not seize the day by the horn, as it were, and—

But then Choi was floating away like the angel she was, her scarlet eyes widening with the same disappointment Purna felt at having her dream so rudely interrupted, the pointed teeth Purna wanted to feel nip at her thighs exposed as the flying wildborn said something that sounded awfully like—

'Fuck.'

The giant monster. Choi. The giant monster had Choi. As Purna's stupid brain finally registered what had happened, she saw the moon-big monster's face split into a thousand-toothed smile as it raised the wildborn in its fuzzy paw. And awful as it would've been to watch it eat Choi alive, the monstrosity did something even worse – it shoved the woman into a disgusting, lathered-up flap in its stomach, the border of the belly-mouth stretched wide by the emergence of smaller but equally disgusting monsters who swarmed out, some of them tumbling to earth, others crawling upside down along their mother's flanks and then disappearing around the bend, climbing up onto its wide back.

Some people would've gone mental at a time like this, seeing something that no nightmare could compete with. Like, utterly, utterly mental. But not Purna. No, seeing her friend Choi get pouch-swallowed by an immense devil, Purna felt herself go to an angrier, uglier, stronger, darker, sharper place – Purna went absolutely fucking Maroto.

Sidestepping a back-kick from the broken paw that could have squashed her flat, Zosia swung her hammer underhanded, battering a startled mutant under the chin and knocking it out of her way. The big barbarian was being dog-piled by the things – or opossum-piled, to be more accurate – but Zosia cleared them out in a jiffy, her hammer dancing in her hands, colorless blood and grey fur and white teeth exploding out of the horde with each strike, warm gore splashing her arms and face. Maroto emerged from the cloud of flying bodies, soaked in oily grey ooze but alive, and only when she saw his bovine look of surprise did she remember it wasn't Maroto but his nephew, Sullen. Kid looked a lot like his uncle, but Maroto would've grinned to see her, whereas Sullen mostly looked startled and kind of intimidated to be rescued by an old lady, clearly amazed one woman could do so much damage with one little hammer.

'Not if you hit them hard enough!' she shouted, not caring that he couldn't get the joke, and not caring that another newborn monster grabbed her from behind, because she just jabbed it off of her with the butt of her hammer and spun around, splattering its elongated skull with the pick end of her weapon before it could realize it had bitten off way more than it could chew. The monsters kept dropping from above and Zosia kept swinging and somewhere nearby Choplicker kept barking and Zosia couldn't stop smiling, so pleased she could pop. This is what she'd lived for, once upon a time, and what she could live for again, she realized through the haze of ichors and scratching limbs – she'd been overthinking life as usual, when the whole truth of her existence was that Cold Zosia was happiest when she was doing what she did best, and what Cold Zosia did best was kill kill kill, kill everything, then kill some more.

So it came as a profound disappointment when she was suddenly grabbed from behind and hoisted off her feet, into the air.

———

It was too late for Choi, and it was too late for Ji-hyeon. Fellwing had regained enough of her vigor to take off again, winging this way and that as she rejuvenated herself on whatever invisible spoils she scavenged from the plentiful battlefield, but even if the owlbat had been at full strength, her plumage black instead of a washed-out ivory, Ji-hyeon doubted one small devil could protect her mistress from a foe of this magnitude. And even if Fellwing had been up for the challenge, Ji-hyeon wasn't making her devil's job any easier by charging straight at the massive humming horror that had eaten her friend.

It was exactly the sort of attack her Honor Guard would have chided her for, an obvious frontal assault against a braced opponent when cunning and quickness would serve her better. But Choi wasn't ever going to chide her again, and that brutal truth robbed Ji-hyeon of every hard-learned lesson, leaving only a burning ball of fury in their place. The ground flowed under her boots like a river that washed away her fatigue and pain as well as her wits, and she let the current take her, so intent on vengeance that the creature's stature didn't even register; her will alone would carry her up on a wave that would crest in the horrible thing's horrible face, and she would plant her sword so deep in the glittering Gate of its eye that it could never be drawn free, a fitting tomb for Choi Bo-yung, Honor Guard of Princess Ji-hyeon Bong of Hwabun, and when Immaculate and Ugrakari pilgrims passed this way and saw the whale-sized bones of a devil queen bleached by the sun they would lay garlands of chrysanthemums around the pommel that jutted from the skull and—

The same claw that had snatched Choi came in so fast Ji-hyeon didn't see it until it was too late, and then the ground did indeed fall away, and her ambitions were left behind in the world of mortals as she was delivered to a reunion with her Honor Guard in the wet tomb of the devil's belly.

———

Things had almost seemed like they might be okay for a second there, which just went to show that Sullen never learned a damn thing. Zosia had saved him, and thick as the twisted, slippery monsters were coming down the wild old dame was bashing them open, giving Sullen a chance to catch his breath, draw a sun-knife, and try to find where he'd dropped his spear. But as soon as he began looking around, a flash of movement to his side caught his eye, and flinching from a blow that wasn't even directed at him he turned in time to see Ji-hyeon run straight into the devil queen's outstretched claw. It had her, it had Ji-hyeon, snatching her off the ground like a selfish child taking back a toy she had lent a friend, and he knew exactly where the abomination meant to put her.

Sullen didn't think, *couldn't* think, just dropped his weapon and seized the nearest monster in both hands, pivoting on his feet for maximum leverage, and hurled the wee fucker straight up into the air, at the enormous paw that delivered Ji-hyeon to its pouch. It wasn't until the silver-maned projectile flew from his hands that he realized he hadn't grabbed a monster after all, but something far, far worse.

———

Fast as witchcraft, Zosia returned to the harpyfish dream she'd endured back on Othean courtesy of a poisoning at the hands of Kang-ho and his husband, King Jun-hwan. It was a vision of flight and devils and desperation, Choplicker howling her on her way. The world had turned upside down, and she plummeted straight toward the border between a devil queen's black chest and her pink belly. An arm as thick and solid as an ancient oak branch slid underneath to catch her, and there was no time to think, but that was fine, because she was done with thinking until further notice. Cold Zosia did what Cold Zosia did best, the overhead swing she'd been about to deliver to a far smaller target before being snared by this dream now put to even better use. She slammed the pick of her war hammer into the monstrous arm, then crashed into a hard-ass bed stuffed with quills and bones instead of goose down, and the dream ended as quickly as it began, returning Zosia to the quiet blackness of the First Dark.

———

Purna skidded in the melting snow around the giant devil's back legs, congratulating herself for having evaded all the smaller monsters swarming beneath their mother.

Any fool could use her last pistol ball to fire a token of her regard into a giant's face or waste the shot on one of her savage brood, but the Mighty Maroto would take a more devious route, one that packed a lot more hurting. Purna planted her feet and aimed her gun straight at the fell crevasse of the devil's derriere, nicely exposed by its uplifted tail, and pulled the trigger. This is what happens when you eat someone you shouldn't.

And of all the devil's own luck, the shot went slightly off target. A satisfyingly large segment of white flesh exploded off the base of the thick tail, though, right where it met the body, and the monster screamed the way monsters ought to, when faced with a champion of Purna's quality. Then the whole ridiculous length of the tail came slapping down at her, the appendage seeming to have a mind of its own, and its coiled, bulbous tip looked like it packed a wallop; the knotted ball at the end of the tail was more than twice as big as Purna, easy, and came swinging toward her fast.

But big partners are easily given the slip, something Purna had learned well from her brief acquaintance with the Crimson court. She jumped and shimmied, using moves she'd picked up in Serpentian ballrooms to evade bad dancers who got too close. When the huge corded club thudded down beside her, she nimbly dodged it and hacked into the mass with her kukri.

The inward-curving blade might have been short but it was also sharp, just like its mistress, and it made an awful mess as she dragged it down the length of the balled-up tail-club. The sweet, pus-like stink of its thick grey blood wouldn't just gag a maggot, it would make the poor beggar lose his lunch entirely, but Purna was made of sterner stuff than a corpse worm; she'd been around Din and Hassan when they'd been smoking bugs not even Digs would touch and was thus well accustomed to fetid smells. No, it wasn't the stench that made Purna stagger back with a gasp, but what else emerged from the tall, widening gash she'd opened up in the knot of tail meat – *another fucking monster*, because of course it was.

Fortunately, this one was a stillborn, as the biggest pups often were . . .

Except no, as the injured tail lashed away from Purna and the hulking shape slipped out from the interior of its devilish chrysalis to lie steaming on the ground, she saw bubbles bursting in the monochromatic slime that webbed over its nostrils and mouth. Human nostrils, or close enough, and human lips, or close enough. Then its eyes fluttered open, and a retching gasp broke the film over its mouth. Even with her newfound, Maroto-like sense of calm, it took Purna a moment to recover herself and come up with a good line, but the naked, shivering figure gave her all the time she needed.

'Hoartrap the Touch, as I live and breathe – I'd heard sorcerers always appeared when they were needed most, but isn't this overdoing it?'

So it wasn't *such* a great line, but who was he to complain?

———

Sullen would've felt bad for launching Zosia at the enormous arm that delivered Ji-hyeon to its pouch, but he was too busy feeling claws and teeth and whip-like tails pull him back down to the ground. He grabbed one's downy throat and squeezed until he felt a crack; he kicked another so hard its ribs snapped under his heel. The only thing Sullen hated more than the idea of hurting kids was killing animals he didn't intend to use, but given the circumstances he wasn't getting too choked up about it. The hissing, squealing pack were slightly more bipedal than their parent, but only just, and to make the whole situation even worse many of them still wore partially disintegrated blue or red tabards, the armor beneath melted or rusted by whatever foul process had remade their flesh. He'd probably passed some of them on the field that morning, back when they were normal folks, and now they had suffered a fate so fucking horrible Sullen had never before heard it suggested as a possibility in any of the songs; people were either born with the blood of shamans or without it, a simple truth the Star round, and monsters were born that way, too. One becoming the other didn't seem natural, even in a world where mortals and devils still bumped shoulders from time to time, when the moon was full or your luck was shit.

These thoughts drifted somewhere at the back of Sullen's mind, but at the forefront nothing registered save the desperate need to execute extreme violence. At some point his bandolier had been ripped away, leaving him without a single sun-knife, but it took more than that to disarm a Horned Wolf. Punch, stomp, elbow, forehead, twist, break, punch again. Neither their teeth nor their claws were particularly sharp, which was why Sullen hadn't bled out already, and when he blinked away the tears that a blast of carrion breath had brought to his eyes he saw why: while their faces had stretched into snouts, some still had human teeth in their sickly white gums, and while a few of them possessed talons, most had spindly fingers ending in normal fingernails. This seemed like a blessing, until his strength at last began to fail long before the onslaught did; being slowly eaten alive didn't seem like much of an improvement on the hasty version of that fate.

Another fell from the living, heaving canopy above, landing on Sullen's belly and knocking the wind out of him, and then the giant mother must have taken a cautious step forward, because the drooping, partially deflated gut-bag now swung directly overhead, its mysterious interior still swimming with dark silhouettes undergoing dark transformations. Before, the overwhelming horror of the sight had robbed him of his ability to move, and that was when viewed at a distance. Now, so close he could have reached up and brushed the swollen pink wineskin with his fingers if he hadn't been half-buried in dully gnawing monsters, the pulsing dance of figures within mesmerized him absolutely.

Ji-hyeon. He easily picked her out from her squirming neighbors; the delicate curve of her bosom, the sway of her hips as she wriggled down to the bottom of the pouch. She pressed her face into the elastic membrane, as if leaning down to give Sullen a kiss, and through the grey-veined veil he saw she must be undergoing an even worse transformation than the rest, the teeth in her silently screaming mouth already as sharp as arrow points. She pushed harder, pressing her forehead into her womb-like prison, the mutating soldiers piled atop her weighing her down, scrabbling at her with lengthening fingers. Then her head bowed entirely under the rubbery pressure of the distended pouch as she resigned herself to the inevitable . . . and that was when her small, sharp horn popped right through the pouch.

Even seeing that, it took a moment for Sullen to realize the Immaculate face he glimpsed through the membrane didn't belong to Ji-hyeon, but then he figured it out – it wasn't his beloved who tried to escape the belly of the beast, but her body-guard, Choi. The woman's other horn had broken off halfway down before Sullen had ever met her, so it was a slow birth as Choi headbanged her way to freedom, her single sharp horn tearing the tough tissue wider and wider as boiling grey slime dripped down onto the oblivious monsters swarming Sullen. Her head slipped through, the shaman-blooded woman gasping as she desperately tried to widen the aperture by wiggling her shoulders. She managed to pop her left arm out, the fingers stretching down toward Sullen, toward the world of mortals . . . and then the heaving mass of half-formed monsters that filled the pouch above her began dragging her back inside.

Sullen had thought he was done for, slobbery mouths biting down on each of his limbs, his whole body scratched and bleeding, wave after wave of opossum devils crashing over him every time he tried to rise . . . but seeing Choi begin to slide back inside the belly of the devil queen transformed something deep inside Sullen. He'd die down here, sure, but he'd die a fucking hero, or close enough – it didn't matter if they ate him anymore, or if they did so fast or slow. All that mattered was making sure Choi escaped that living, pulsing, stinking hell. Maybe it was too late for her – it was almost certainly too late for him – but she was a wildborn, as the Immaculates called people like him and her, and he'd make sure they both went down together, with both feet set solidly in the world they'd chosen for themselves, hard a price as they'd both surely paid to be here. They were mortals, not monsters, and they deserved better than anything a devil could offer, even if the most they got out of their time on the Star was a clean death, fighting together against the First Dark.

Choi's head disappeared back up into the foamy pouch, her arm drawn in to the elbow, and then the wrist, her splayed hand all that remained ... and then Sullen heaved himself out of the pile, rising from the furry waves like a seawolf leaping out of the surf of the Bitter Gulf to snatch an albatross out of the air. His palm slapped hers, slippery fingers tightened around each other, and as he dropped back down she came slipping out after him ... only to become stuck halfway through, her waist lodged in the cavity. Sullen's feet bounced on the backs of the frantic monsters that awaited them, and looking up at the slime-coated woman he saw her sharp teeth grit in pain, her red eyes watering, and then a plop of the grey gut froth landed on the sleeve of his tunic, smoke rising as the acidic substance burned through the wool.

His heart broke, then, because he knew for all he'd tried to save her Choi had been dead as soon as she went inside the devil queen's pocket, the fluids that churned through the incubation organ as caustic as a poison oracle's potions. Hanging there by Choi's greasy arm, Sullen felt something give above him, and closed his eyes. He didn't want to see her arm come off at the shoulder, strings of dissolving sinew stretched to breaking as he fell away with her devil-softened limb and the rest of her was pulled back inside ... or worse, her entire upper half might be about to go, a slurry of acid-sizzling entrails following Sullen and her bisected torso to the ground.

And then it happened, and he fell, and kept his eyes closed even as he slammed back onto the dubious pillow of thronged monsters. Her remains crashed into his chest, harder than he'd expected, and finally he looked, but only because the fiends were biting and tearing at him again, and it was too late for—

Choi? The woman had seen better mornings, no doubt, but then Sullen supposed they all had. She was certainly quicker than he to stagger up and start laying into the devil-twisted creatures that mobbed them, her arms and legs a blur as she struck blow after blow. And looking down in wonder at his own unburned hand, and realizing the goo had chewed right through his thick shirt but left his chest unharmed, Sullen just had to smile, because it all made sense now. Choi had survived her passage for the same reason he would have, if he'd been stuffed in there and had the wherewithal to pull himself free – whatever evil the devil queen's fluids worked on the flesh of pureborn mortals, it must not affect those born with the blood of shamans. Never in his life had Sullen been so happy for his oft-cursed heritage, and he almost laughed as he backhanded a squealing mutant . . .

But then he remembered that the last time he'd seen Ji-hyeon, the devil queen had held her clenched in its fist, delivering her to that toxic pouch. He'd been overwhelmed by her brood before he'd been able to see if throwing Zosia into her path had done anything to help, and considering what a brilliant plan that had been, it seemed pretty fucking likely that all he'd accomplished was breaking Ji-hyeon's neck, or Zosia's, or maybe both. Ignoring his attackers, he craned his neck back to the ruptured pouch, trying to pick out Ji-hyeon's figure amid the contorted shapes, but if she was inside she wasn't even recognizably human anymore . . . and in that grim moment, Sullen found himself hoping Ji-hyeon had died instead.

Fast and dirty as Ji-hyeon's life had ended, it came back to her in a smear of fur and claws and a bloody hammer. The oozing chasm of the devil queen's stomach pouch lunged up to welcome her into hell, and then Zosia swatted her right out of the monster's hand. There must have been a moment when they were falling together, the former general of the Cobalt Company and her illegitimate heir, but it was over before Ji-hyeon could blink. They landed together, anyway, on a bed of squealing, biting, clawing monsters, and it said a lot about the day she'd been having that this came as an improvement. Ji-hyeon still clung to her sword and, more importantly, her rage, rolling and kicking and hacking until she was back on her feet . . . only to fall over again.

There were too many of them. The entire length of her blade was covered in clutching, almost-human claws, and while a few long fingers came loose and fell away in the struggle for the sword, the weapon was soon wrestled from her fist. It was over.

Except it wasn't. Foul gouts of grey blood rained down, and then he was there, just like a hero in one of his romantic verses, cleaving through a horde of devils to rescue his love. His hand, always so gentle with her, snatched her by the wrist and jerked her to her feet, so hard they bumped into each other, eyes meeting for only an instant before he reached past her and skewered another screeching monster. And even in this waking nightmare she saw the smile he tried to hide from her as he went back to work: not a proud, self-congratulatory grin, not a this-is-why-you-put-up-with-me smirk, but one born of overwhelming relief that he had found her in time.

Then another devil-spawned beast slammed into him, taking him to the ground, and it was her turn to do the rescuing; she kicked the teeth out of the monster on top of Keun-ju, and kept kicking until he was able to get back to his feet. Spying her fallen blade half-buried in bodies, she snatched it back up and turned to face the relentless tide of obscene horrors.

And then it was over. The four-tiger sword she had given Keun-ju winked in the sudden sunlight, and they both looked up to find the open sky above them instead of a furry firmament. The devil queen was on the move again, shambling back toward the Gate as fast as her battered condition would allow, her absurdly long, ruptured tail dragging behind her, and as she fled, her remaining brood followed. The monstrous progeny swarmed up her plodding legs to join their brothers and sisters who already huddled on her back, and as Ji-hyeon and Keun-ju sagged into each other's arms they watched the devil queen plunge back into the Gate, her mortal-born children riding her into the First Dark.

CHAPTER

6

As far as recent mornings went, this one was shaping up to be worthy of a song . . . if not a particularly exciting or up-tempo ballad. Sure, they'd spent half the night slinking through the dark, dangerous jungle, constantly peeking through the canopy to see if the milk-white horror from the skies still pursued them, but eventually they'd come out of a bamboo thicket and almost stumbled straight into a tranquil, starlit pool at the base of a gentle waterfall, and the sleep he'd had on the plush moss of its banks was the best Maroto had enjoyed since only the Old Watchers knew when. And what should greet his eyes when he awoke but a hard-edged Immaculate girl every bit as fit as any he'd met, offering him a coconut filled with fresh water. He knew Captain Bang was being so friendly only because she wanted him to take the first sip and see if it made him sick, but the joke was on her; he'd already drunk a gallon of the stuff while he was keeping the first watch, too thirsty to care if it ended up melting him from the inside.

'Thanks, Cap'n,' he said, draining half the nut and reminding himself with a wince that he wasn't supposed to be staring at the dark and appealingly puffy nipples that were visible through her damp shirt. 'Been in the pool?'

'I look fool enough to go swimming with my clothes on, Useful?'

'No, Cap'n,' he replied, because he'd already figured out her game, and was happy enough to play along – kids always thought they knew shit when they didn't know shit, but it never paid to call them out on it unless the need was dire. 'You just look wet, is all.'

'It's hot as a phoenix's cloaca, and some of us have been up and scouting around already.' She wiped the sheen of sweat from her tattooed cheek, and fast as he started imagining how rich and salty it must taste he woke up enough to remember that he'd left his bad old ways back on the Star. He was a new Maroto, a better Maroto, the kind who wasn't so hornish he started leching on the first woman he met. Even a sweaty green-haired one with fleet inkwork.

'Yeah, no doubt it's gonna be a scorcher, but I'm warming to warm weather.' He took another swallow, the water sweetened by the coconut meat. 'Coming from the Savannahs the cold was all we knew, but they say back in the day all of Flintland was hot as the south end of Usba, so maybe I've got some of the old blood in me.'

'And you've got the old skin to match,' said Bang.

'Old enough to know better, but too young to care,' said Maroto, though he regretted it as soon as Bang rolled her eyes – why had he thought that sounded clever? To cover his old-man-trying-to-act-hip embarrassment he finished the water and passed her back the coconut. Blinking in the bright morning sunshine, he saw Niki-hyun and Dong-won trying not to stare from across the roughly circular pool, licking their salt water-cracked lips, and he called over, 'Water's fine, if you're wondering. Drank enough last night that if it was bad I'd be feeling it by now. I hope.'

The two practically fell into the pool, lying on their bellies and greedily lapping up handfuls, but Bang played it a little cooler, dipping the coconut where a wide, shallow stream broke off from the source.

'Seeing's as I took poison taster duty again without even being asked, Cap'n, you mind if I take a few more minutes to compose myself for the day?' It was actually kind of fun to go along with Bang's obvious need to maintain authority, but he couldn't resist poking at its edges to see how much he could get away with.

'A few and no more, Useful,' she told him after she'd guzzled herself breathless. 'No lollygagging on this crew.'

'I heard that, Cap'n, and thank you for your lenience.' Settling back onto his mossy bed, Maroto looked up at the jade leaves and the sapphire sky, listening to the calls of strange birds and the tinkling waterfall. If he only had a bite to eat it would be the perfect morning, and just like that he heard a fish jump in the pool. Nice. He'd borrow Bang's cutlass to cut down a bunch of the black bamboo that grew against the steep hillside around the foot of the waterfall, and then enlist the others into helping him build a fishing weir at the mouth of the stream. Then they could leisurely wade out and chase some breakfast into the trap – or maybe it would be lunch by the time they caught something worth cooking, it scarcely mattered. He was in the middle of nowhere with nowhere to be, and for a few more precious, sleepy moments he was able to keep all the awful memories comfortably buried way down deep, where they belonged.

But then he reminded himself how much Purna would like this shipwrecked scene, and all of a sudden the morning didn't feel so great after all, and besides, who was he kidding? Warm weather never agreed with him anyway. Closing his eyes to the pleasant morning, he fell back into the darkest memories his mind could conjure, and when that didn't *quite* make him feel shitty enough, he started in on all the worst-case scenarios that had probably gone down during his absence from the Cobalt camp.

Choi. That was a good one, the thought of his wildborn friend clamping his throat like a sadistic lover with a bad understanding of hard limits. Why hadn't he made a play at her, let her know how he felt? Maybe it would've been awkward, or maybe they'd have had some fun together. Hells, maybe they could have had something more, now that Maroto had finally come to terms with the fact that his One True And Also Dead Lover was both very much alive and an enormous fucking arsehole. Now it was far too late, and even if she'd lived out the battle he'd probably never see her again in this life . . .

But maybe that was for the best. He was nothing but trouble to men, women, and everyone else, and Choi was better off without him. He'd probably misread those intense glances of her ruby eyes anyway, and then he'd have queered their friendship by fishing for something more, just like he always did. Except with Purna, of course; much as he'd thought he'd been mentoring her in the ways of the barbarian, or whatever the fuck it was she hoped to learn from him, he was the one who had actually taken away the valuable lessons. Without ever even seeming to try she'd educated him about appreciating people for who they are instead of what you want them to be, how to flirt with your friends without overdoing it, and basically being a decent person instead of the selfish bastard he'd always been.

There. Focusing on Purna put him in the appropriate state of mind, and from there he bounced back to Choi again, and then on to Din and Hassan – of all his crew, Diggelby was the only one he knew for sure had come clear of the battle in one piece. Good old Pasha Diggelby. What would the well-intentioned loudmouth do now that he was alone in a camp full of rebels who despised the Imperial noblesse on general principle, with every single one of his true chums dead or gone? He still had Prince, sure, but that cowardly mutt couldn't protect his master from anything larger than shin-height; without Maroto and the rest to look out for him, the pasha was going to be eaten alive by the brutes and bruisers who had rallied under Ji-hyeon's banner.

Oh, and now that he was on a roll Maroto mustn't overlook the bitter memory of his dad and nephew, whom he'd barely spared a thought for since arriving on this bizarre island or continent or whatever landmass it was that Jex Toth turned out to be. He'd genuinely intended to have a sit-down with them, see if they couldn't squash the familial beef. There was obviously a whole provincial playhouse's worth of drama to discuss, and now they never, ever would.

Well, unless those loony blighters decided to track him down again, and managed to follow his ethereal trail all the way here to a land he hadn't even thought existed, outside of the songs he'd sung to his nephew when the kid was four or five. Oh, how he'd loved sitting in the hut with Best and her husband, Keenear, and their dad and the little cat-eyed moppet . . . sure, Maroto had been floating around the rafters thanks to all the icebees he was banging, but nevertheless, nevertheless, they had enjoyed some real nice evenings. Like most bad singers, Maroto secretly loved to belt out a ballad or three, and Sullen had always hung on his every off-key note, staring up at his stoned uncle with his great big feline peepers.

Maroto had fostered so many plans to help his nephew come

up right, noticing how the other kids picked on him for being wildborn and knowing the boy would need a friend to see him through the inevitable bad times. An only child needed someone he could talk to the way you couldn't talk to a parent or, ancestors knew, your hypercritical, hypocritical, mean-arsed grandfather. Through the lingering grief of believing Zosia had died, the shame at failing to avenge her, and the final humiliation of limping back home to the Savannahs after all those years abroad, that dream of providing Sullen with a strong role model and confidant had burned bright, giving Maroto something almost like a purpose . . .

But then had come the battle with the Jackal People, where Maroto made what might just be the biggest fuckup in a life filled with a hundred times as many mistakes as he'd lived years, trying so hard to be a proper Horned Wolf he'd turned his back on his wounded father and seemingly helpless nephew. And now, just when he'd been reunited with those two, triggering all the memories he'd been fiercely suppressing ever since he'd given them up for dead, what did he do? He went and disappeared on them. *Again.*

And that was what finally got Maroto to shake off his torpor and get to his bare feet on the spongy moss. Like his arsehole dad always said, if a horned wolf is sleeping after the sun's up it better be dozing on top of the biggest kill of its life, safe in its lair. It was time to build a fish trap, and over by the waterfall's slope he saw the three pirates already busily hacking down the bamboo. They looked to be making spears, but with some gentle suggestions he was sure he could guide them into splitting them further to make a far more effective weir instead.

'Wish you were here,' he told Purna and Choi, Sullen and Diggelby, Din and Hassan, and even his dear old fucking Da.

He shook his head as soon as he thought that, though, because if anyone was tenacious enough to survive an epic battle and hound Maroto to the ends of the Star and beyond, it was his kinfolk and his running crew. Wouldn't surprise him at all if they were already halfway here, but wherever they were, he hoped their day was off to as fine a start as his was. They deserved it more than him, anyway.

CHAPTER

7

'I *seriously* think last night was the absolute *rottenest* night in the history of the *world*, and this morning is even *worse*,' Diggelby said as he hoisted the heavy canvas pack in the lightly falling snow. Due to the thickness of his mittens it took him a while to get the final bag tethered atop the pile of gear already strapped to the back of Princess, the diminutive Kutumban pony their party was reduced to sharing. Their second night out he had bestowed that name on the oblivious animal with all the solemnity and raw emotion of a bereft father elegizing a murdered child. 'We better catch up with Maroto but fast, girl, or I am going to have to whip that whelp into shape.'

'That I would dearly like to see,' Purna said around the clod of funky, partially frozen gorgonzola she was sucking like an intensely salted lozenge. Her thighs were already burning but she kept at her squats, warming herself up after another tooth-rattlingly cold night in their iced-over tent. Long as their marches had been since setting out from the Cobalt camp the week before, prepping one's drumsticks seemed a capital way to start the day; get the blood up, the lead out, and so on and so forth. Her shoulder still felt like a godguana had kicked it from when she'd been thrown off that poorly trained horse during their fight with the devil queen, but both gams felt as good as gold and twice as hard. She'd been a little worried that she might discover some other devilish aftereffect of the nearly fatal stab wound she'd received, but nope, just a dog's tongue and a fluffy patch of fur on the back of her thigh, and as far as distinguishing characteristics went she'd take those over a limp any day. Digs was still grumbling a big game about what he ought to tell their new captain, and Purna said, 'As soon as they get back you should give him a piece of your mind.'

'I mean to give him the whole bloody thing, and the back of my hand for good measure!' said Digs, striking a daring pose in his white angora bodysuit and matching babushka, a single pale stripe of the pigment he called 'philosopher's wool' smudged across his cheekbones and over the bridge of his nose like a second, ill-placed mustache. Against the washed-out backdrop of the blizzard-wracked Witchfinder Plains, he looked like some broke-ass lowland yeti with a bad case of face mange. 'I don't believe he's related to Maroto, I don't believe it for a moment. I never thought I'd say this about anyone, but he's even less fun than Choi!'

'Don't run down a chum, Digs, we both know if Choi were here we'd be having a grand old time – and even if she didn't let us build a fire, either, at least she'd be nice to cuddle up with,' said Purna. The cheese nestled in her cheek had finally thawed enough to chew, and she abandoned her calisthenics to bum a warm-up from Diggelby's flask. Through a mouthful of pungent clods, she said, 'I couldn't believe my luck, when the general told us she'd decided to send along one of her personal retinue. Woof.'

'You know what *I* heard?' said Diggelby as he passed the flask in his ridiculously long-haired mitten. 'It was *supposed* to be Choi, that she even *volunteered* for the mission, but Ji-hyeon asked her to stay and sent the sourpuss instead.'

'Horsefeathers,' said Purna, sipping the flask and getting a mouthful of gritty sludge. She'd forgotten Diggelby had taken to infusing his breakfast grapefire with kaldi grounds, oats, and powdered mare's milk, and wondered if he actually liked the grimy consistency and bitter taste first thing in the morning or if this was just his way to curb mooching. That the mealy swill actually tasted remarkably more appealing now that she had a devilish tongue she did not consider an endorsement of the beverage. 'Why would Sullen want to come instead of Choi?'

'Some sort of Immaculate mating ritual, I expect – did you hear what she told them when she sent us all off, about how they'd better both come back alive or she didn't want to see either of them? It's a sex thing, has to be.' Digs slipped off a mitten and reached up, fishing around in his powdery headscarf.

'Or it's practical,' said Purna, mulling it over and then lighting on the obvious. 'Of course it is. Choi's one of us, a Moocher through and true.'

'Quite right, quite right,' said Digs, retrieving his golden coalstick and silver smoking case from the folds of his babushka. His exposed hand already shaking, he uncapped the stick and lit two orange-papered cigarillos on the end of it. Passing one to Purna and sucking down a lungful of the other, he spoke while holding in the spicy blend of shade-grown vergin and cypress-cured latakiss tubāqs. 'Choi's an odd duck, but any interesting flock is led by just such a bird.'

'So if Choi had come along, it would be the three of us giving Maroto the benefit of the doubt, with only Sullen hating on our favorite Villain. By pulling one of ours out of the pack and subbing in her pet, it's two against two.'

'You really think Sullen's got it in for his uncle?' Digs blew a smoke ring that was promptly slapped down by the snow. 'I never would have guessed.'

'Yeah, he's about as subtle as a hobnail boot to the snatch,' said Purna, giving Princess a once-over to make sure the pony hadn't frozen solid beneath her blankets and the pink earmuffs Digs had gifted her.

'Here's a thought ...' said Diggelby, and from the angry plumes of blue smoke he shot out of his nostrils it didn't sound like a happy one. 'What if he ... what if Maroto ...'

'He's not dead,' said Purna, though repeating it to Digs didn't sound any more convincing than it did when she repeated it to herself. 'Hoartrap insists he's still alive, and besides, as big a boasting point as icing one of the Five Villains would be, if someone had got him we'd have heard about it.'

'Unless it was one of his fellow Villains.'

'Well, you wouldn't go with me to interrogate the Touch so you've just got my unimpeachable word to go on, but I'm telling you, I believe him,' said Purna, shuddering at the memory of that awkward exchange with the convalescing giant. 'First time I've seen him halfway serious, and he swore on every devil he ever ate that the last time he saw Maroto he was alive and well, and no more than a few paces away from that new Gate. Said our boy tried to swing on him, so he left him to cool his heels, and when Hoartrap went back the next day to look for his trail he couldn't follow it. He kept hinting at some old boon he owed Maroto, such that he'd never do him in, just like he'd never come at me or Sullen, now that we salvaged his spoiled bacon back at the devil royal.'

'Just because he owes you don't mean he'll pay, and it certainly doesn't mean he'll play you straight,' said Digs, as though she was too thick to see that for herself. 'I don't trust him. I say we toss both map and compass in the first bottomless pit we find and go see my connection in Thao instead.'

'I look dopey enough to trust a devil-eating creeper? No,

don't answer that,' said Purna, since she had been the one to accept Hoartrap's gifts when she visited him the day after the Second Battle of the Lark's Tongue. 'But I think he really wants us to find Maroto, why else give us the tools in the first place?'

'He really wants us to find *something* with those witch toys, but how do we know it's Maroto? Call me old-fashioned, but when a beastly old geezer whom I've personally seen ghost a room full of Imperial officers gives me a supposedly magic map with an equally magic compass and says just follow the needle, I don't immediately assume that's such a swell idea. My gal in Thao, on the other hand—'

'I heard you the first hundred times,' said Purna, which was admittedly an exaggeration. He'd probably only mentioned the woman ninety-six or ninety-seven times, tops. 'It's our fearless leader you need to convince.'

'Sullen doesn't trust Hoartrap and his tricks either!' said Digs, as though that were news.

'Well, he must trust him more than he trusts you, eh smart guy? Otherwise we'd have ditched the compass already and be en route to Thao to meet your dealer or whatever she is. The devil-noshing freak that you know, and all that – whoever this friend of yours is, she doesn't owe me and Sullen and maybe even Maroto her life, so I don't see her being instantly more reliable.'

'She operates on cold hard coin and a sizable commission, which I find far more dependable than our big bald friend with his inscrutable schemes and penchant for making people disappear,' said Digs, drumming his fingers on the tiny icicles in his mustache as if he were playing the world's smallest, grossest xylophone. 'Did he say anything else at all? Something that maybe didn't seem like much at the time, but I dunno, might hint at some ulterior motive?'

'Not really. The only other thing that really stood out was his usual nastiness,' said Purna, not happy to be reminded. 'Like, when I asked him about whatever this debt was that he owes Maroto he acted all wounded, and said didn't it just break his heart that the Mighty Maroto never talked about the Touch to his girlfriend – real talk, Digs, did you ever get that vibe from me and Maroto? Romantically, I mean?'

'*Ew.*' Digs wrinkled his nose.

'That's what I said – I think the goon was trying to provoke me with that one, even after I saved him from . . . whatever it was that devil queen was doing to him. But the rest of it? Shit, something about the way he said it all made me think he was being square for a change.'

'Well, even a curved knife cuts straight from time to time,' said Digs, which sounded kind of like a burn on her kukri but she let it go. 'And when I said it might have been another Villain, I was thinking less of Hoartrap and more of Zosia – she seemed mad enough to do it. You should have heard her and Maroto going at one another, like cats and cougars. No, like dogs and wolves. No, like—'

'Sorry, I was too busy bleeding to death to notice what lousy old saw they were fighting like. Maybe if you'd paid more attention to what they were fighting *about* we'd have more to go on than a devildamned map and a definitely cursed compass!'

'Sorry, I was too busy preventing your insides from getting all over your outsides to take notes – maybe if you hadn't let some Chainite poke you we wouldn't be in this mess!'

'Point, Diggelby,' Purna mumbled, not really able to taste the cigarillo with her nose freezing off her face but craving the almost peaty warmth of the smoke all the same. 'And between her rough-and-tumble show with Ji-hyeon and those prisoners at the Gate and then her going apeshit on that devil queen and her kiddos, we know Zosia's bazonk enough to throw down on Maroto . . . but nah.'

'Nah? What is this *nah*? She's batty, as stated, violent, as proven, and already had it in for Maroto before the big fight, as witnessed by the both of us – that's evidence, girl.'

'That's bunk, Digs, and I say it again: nah. Zosia wouldn't play him that cold.' Maybe. Hopefully. Purna wouldn't have expected Zosia to go kill-crazy on Ji-hyeon or hammer-happy on a horde of opossum people, either, but after the women's duel at the Gate and Cold Cobalt's unexpected appearance during the Second Battle of the Lark's Tongue, it was pretty blooming obvious that predicting Zosia's next move was best left to bolder gamblers than Purna . . . but she decided not to share her doubts with her emotionally feeble fellow, lest he snap like the delicate reed he was. When a second meticulous search of the Cobalt camp had failed to turn up Din or Hassan she had been devastated by the obvious implication, too, but while she was capable of grieving her Gate-gulped comrades and still keeping her head, Diggelby seemed on the verge of losing his altogether.

'*Anyway*,' said Digs, 'I wasn't asking what if Maroto's dead, because that's an easy one – if he's bought it we go our own way, and the faster the better. I was asking what we do if he's not, and we actually catch the king of the catfish.'

'Oh,' said Purna, deciding for the time being not to further interrogate Digs's suggestion that they abandon the Cobalt Company if they found a Maroto-shaped corpse; that pickle could wait for its own jar. Or something, she'd have to work on that one. What had immediate relevance was Diggelby's point: 'If we catch him . . . *when* we catch him . . . Well, we find out why he left in such a hurry.'

'And?' Digs pressed. 'What if our intrepid chief tells us that in addition to swearing an oath of peace to Indsorith back in the day he's actually been working for the Crimson Queen ever since?'

'Then I say it's bullshit,' said Purna, flicking her half-smoked (and thus still half-good) cigarillo into the knee-deep snow to punish Digs for the asinine suggestion.

'Well *okay*, let's say he hasn't been an agent for the Empire at all, up until now, but since Zosia rubbed him so raw he decided to punish her by going over to help her worst enemy. Maybe Ji-hyeon doesn't even enter into his thinking, and maybe he thinks you're dead so he doesn't have much of a stake with the Cobalts.'

'Even if he did think I died, which is stupid—'

'Girl, I'm standing here right now talking to you and I'm *telling* you, the Tapai Purna I saw back on the field was deader than dog doo.'

'Don't say dog doo,' said Purna. 'It's gross. And even if I was dead, you and Choi are still with the Cobalts, and he wouldn't just leave you two.'

'I'd like to think so, I really would . . . but word around camp is that Maroto has something of a reputation for cutting out on his fellows in times of stress.'

'The camp can say that shit to his face,' said Purna. 'My point is even if Maroto thinks I'm dead, and even if he'd turn his back on you and Choi after all the times we had, and even if this falling out with Zosia was as bad as you think, *and even if* he did decide to go work for the Crimson Empire . . . then . . .'

'Yes, what then?' said Digs impatiently. 'This is my question from the get-go, what do we do if we find him and everybody's been right about him?'

'We trust that they're not,' Purna decided. 'I'm not buying

any of this canard until you and me and Maroto have a sit-down and figure out what's what. And if that means fighting off his jerky nephew to buy him an exit or time to talk, I'm ready for it.'

'Me, too,' said Digs, ditching the butt of his own cigarillo and pulling his mitten back over his bluing fingers so they could bump knuckles. 'And let's not forget the Immaculate master swordsman while we're plotting betrayal. I do wish Choi were here to tip the scales in our favor.'

'I wish she was here to tip the velvet,' said Purna wistfully, recalling the rawboned wildborn, and wishing there'd been time to see what was up before they'd parted ways. Even in Purna's more colorful imaginings Choi had a reproachful look to her features, as though she rather suspected she was but a figment of an undersexed girl's fancy and was a little embarrassed about the matter. That was all right, Purna liked a little rose to the cheeks ... 'That's my luck, right there, us getting saddled with another icky boy.'

'Your loss is my gain,' said Digs, 'though I'll miss Choi, too.'

'Yeah?' That right there was an intriguing development. 'Which one do you fancy, or are you more of an equal opportunist? I have five dinars that says I can play matchmaker so craftily the target never—'

'*Ew*. Neither, thank you very much. When I said it was my gain I just meant you're a lot more fun when you're not drooling over another icky girl.'

'So if warrior women, brooding hunks, and romantic heroes are all out, what does that leave?' Purna knew she was being rude, pressing about a topic he'd never once addressed, but it was cold as a merchant's heart out here and talking about sex warmed everyone up, didn't it? 'What *are* you after, old sprout? What's Pasha Diggelby's type?'

'Oh, Purna, I'm *flattered*, really, but – ew. You're a dear friend, just not anyone I would ever, ever, *ever*—'

She socked him in the arm even harder than she had after he'd told her he survived the fight with the devil queen by 'playing opossum'.

'All right, all right, though I thought it was obvious,' said Digs, looking winsomely into the snowy wilderness. 'My type is Diggelby, but I've never been fortunate enough to meet myself, and I'm certainly not going to settle for anything less.'

That made a lot of sense, actually, but then something stuck out at her. 'But the bet back in the Wastes when we first started caravanning together, the big contest to see who could be the first to bed Maroto – you put down twenty dinars!'

'I routinely lay wagers I never hope to collect in order to test the full extent of my majesty – you'd be surprised how often the Fallen Mother rewards my pride by letting me win the unwinnable,' said Digs. 'And besides, I laid twenty-two on myself in the community kitty, yes, but I had *you* down for fifty dinars at three-to-one odds in private bets with Din, Hassan, and Princess Von Yung. You made me a tidy fortune when you conquered the beast.'

'I told you, we never actually did it!' Purna colored, far more annoyed at herself for eventually coming clean to her friends than she had been to rig that stupid bet in the first place. She'd needed cash in a hurry to keep up appearances, and it had been yet another of her brilliant plots that went off without a hitch, but while her close friends had previously kept a respectful silence concerning the perceived union, ever since she'd set the record straight one drunken night in the Kutumbans they had all given her endless hell about it. 'I told you so, Maroto told you so, and I even offered to pay you back half of what I won, so—'

'Shhhhh, our gallant compatriots return,' said Diggelby, snatching the flask back and waving it at the two silhouettes emerging from the snow. The first rule of this whiteout weather was staying in pairs, and so far Purna and Digs had been able to insist they always buddy up on the admittedly manure-rich grounds that they had a lot of experience fighting together. Given the other two's evident distaste for one another, it was only a matter of time before this wafer-thin excuse crumbled. 'Yoo-hoo, anybody need a pick-me-up?'

'Quiet,' said Sullen, which seemed to be his favorite word in all the Star. You'd think a few days on the prowl with Purna and Digs would've loosened him up, but instead you could practically hear the squeaking of his asshole as it contracted to maximum tightness.

'Oooh, silence is of the essence, is it?' said Digs. 'Did you narrowly evade some Imperial scouts? Or maybe wendigos hunt this bountiful glacier? Or—'

'There's nothing,' said the sad-sack Immaculate, taking the flask out of Digs's mitten and knocking it back like the seasoned drunk he wasn't . . . and then coughing most of it up like the green kid he was.

'Well, nothing is something, eh?' said Purna, because she was going to stay positive even if it killed her; Diggelby was doing a decent job of acting like his carefree former self around Sullen and Keun-ju, but he couldn't fool his best pal. From how assiduously he was *not* talking about Prince, she knew he must be missing his dog something ferocious, and she could tell that between Din and Hassan's awful end and the giant devil queen that had almost given them a worse one, her old chum was close to the edge. Hoartrap's compass was insistently steering them north on the map, but they'd found nary a Maroto-sized footprint to confirm their course, and a week is a long time to march on only the uncertain word of an evil wizard. Digs needed something he could latch on to, some sign that they weren't just wandering into an even uglier trap than the ones they'd narrowly avoided back at the Lark's Tongue. If they didn't come up with something soon, she worried all the banter, booze, and bugs in the Star wouldn't be able to keep him from melting into a wet and weedy puddle. Maybe they should try his connection in Thao after all – he'd presumably feel better, even if it did take them out of the way, but since their way currently seemed to be the middle of nowhere, what could it hurt? 'So what sort of nothing is it today?'

'Nothing,' said Sullen, looking at her like *she* was the one with a skull as thick as a cannonball. Then, as though perhaps he'd overlooked an important detail, he said, 'It's quiet out there.'

'Well praise the Fallen Mother for that!' said Digs, but the look Sullen shot him said that no, maybe they'd better hold off on doing that just a little longer yet. For once, Purna agreed with the lunkhead's disapproval – ever since they had learned who was responsible for the ritual that had opened a Gate underneath poor Din and Hassan and all the countless others, she didn't care to hear any mention of the Burnished Chain or its beliefs, however sarcastically they were invoked.

'Shall we try the compass and map again?' said Keun-ju, but his sad, flat voice and his sad, flat eyes told the sad, flat truth – even if Hoartrap's detailed map of the Star was accurate to scale, and even if the spiny black iron compass truly pointed them toward Maroto, they were currently lost in an absurdly vast tract of white wilderness, and the only one of their party who seemed good with directions was, as Purna had rather brilliantly put it, cartographically challenged. In light of Sullen's distaste for their only possible means of finding Maroto, Digs had suggested the barbarian was tracking his uncle by smell alone, which was good for a laugh, but even such a blistering burn couldn't warm them for long in the eternal snow.

'Don't bother,' said Sullen, turning back the way he and Keun-ju had come after completing their morning's investigation. 'We keep east, we find the Heartvein. Can't miss it – me and Fa seen it in our travels, and even if it's frozen solid it's too wide to cross without noticing you're on it. We follow the river north, we find Diadem. We find Diadem—'

'Yes, yes, I know the bally chorus by now, you and General Ji-hyeon think he's run off to the Crimson Queen just because he swore some stupid oath to her, like, a hundred years ago,' said Purna, pushing her horned wolf hood back on her face to remind their human bloodhound that she was, one, adorable, and two, hard enough not to mess with. 'But if the whole point is catching Maroto *before* he reaches Diadem, our taking the long way round doesn't seem wise, does it? He's fleeing in a hurry, and since he can read a map – unlike certain other barbarians I could mention – he's bound to take the most direct path, not the easiest. Which is probably why Hoartrap's compass is telling us to go north, not east.'

'I thought of that,' said Sullen, the very idea of him thinking of anything more complex than how best to skin a wild aardvark or some such similarly silly beast beggaring belief. 'But I don't trust Hoartrap's deviltry, and even if my uncle's plotting his flight according to some chart, this blinding snow has robbed him of his tricks. What good is a map in a world without form?'

'What good is a map in a world without form . . .' Keun-ju repeated it softly, with maybe a hint of admiration, and even Purna had to admit it sounded sage on the nose, but when you really thought about it that's what a world was, a place with form to it, so Sullen's faux-wisdom could kiss her tips.

'Well, this is perfect, then – if we've almost reached the Heartvein then we've almost reached Thao,' said Digs, startling Princess as he cleared the snow out from between her earmuffs. 'We take a few hours out of our busy day to go south instead of north and we're there. As I've been saying all along, if we just talk to my connection she'll be able to, you know, procure something that can help. It's what they call her, you know, the Procuress, on account of—'

'Nah,' said Sullen, for maybe the fifty millionth time. 'Told you, Ji-hyeon put me in charge, and that means we go where I say. And told you, too, I don't trust witchcraft to find my uncle, neither Hoartrap's charms nor the auguries of your *connection*.'

'None of us relish such means to our end,' said Keun-ju thoughtfully. 'But if you are unsure if your map is accurate, it is wise to compare it to another, one crafted by another cartographer.'

Sullen's brows furrowed, all these big words and talk of maps probably putting him out.

'Of course!' Diggelby made a funny motion with his mitten, and Purna knew him well enough to guess he'd probably tried to snap his fingers. 'We double-check what Hoartrap's compass is telling us with whatever the Procuress provides, and if they both point us in the same direction we know we can trust them to guide us true.'

'Hmmm . . .' said Sullen, which was better than the expected *nah*. 'I don't know if that follows.'

'But it's more than we've got now, isn't it, in this world without form?' said Purna. 'We've got no tracks to follow, no recent Maroto sightings by passersby – nor passersby at all, far as that goes – and what happens if we don't pick up something solid? Walk all the damn way to Diadem, hoping we bump into him? Or even better, arrive halfway across the Star, search a city so huge they had to hollow out a mountain to make room for everyone, and then walk all the way back here if it turns out he's not there?'

Purna knew her logic was sound, but even still was impressed by how wide Sullen's feline eye slits grew at the mention of Diadem's size; poor bumpkin probably didn't know villages came that big, and he almost looked scared to contemplate it.

'Even in this weather a side trip to Thao adds no more than a day or two onto what will be an *exceptionally* long march to Diadem,' said Digs. 'The worst that happens is the Procuress isn't able to help, though I've never even heard of such a calamity, and then we're still no poorer off than we were before.'

'And we won't have to worry about running into any grumpy Imperial soldiers in town,' said Purna, 'since we know exactly where their local regiment is.'

'And we'll be able to enjoy a hot meal, a hot drink, and a hot bath,' said Keun-ju, sounding more excited than he had all week.

'We have to resupply soon anyway,' Purna pointed out. 'Rations are low.'

'To say nothing of the purebred steeds I shall purchase our party as a token of our close friendship,' said Digs. 'We'll make up any lost time in less than a day, and reach Diadem twice as fast as we would on foot, at a *minimum*.'

'Horned Wolves don't ride,' said Sullen, but he wasn't looking at them, peering off into the blank haze as if he expected the return of spring at any moment. Then he said nothing, and when Digs began to pipe up with some other enticement Purna silenced him with a sharp motion; rusty as the gears in Sullen's brainbox were it didn't do to overload the equipment. Finally, Sullen nodded the slightest nod. 'We'll be much faster if you three have horses. And if I don't trust your sorceress, Diggelby, we don't listen to her, even if her counsel matches Hoartrap's compass. Agreed?'

'Agreed,' all three sensible persons said in unison, and Digs added, 'I'm sure this will help us find him, whether he's actually run off or is camped down somewhere to sit out the crummy weather. Maybe he even went to Thao, same as us, and we'll find him snoring in some dive tavern just like he was when my cousin Köz and I first hired him on as a guide.'

'Hmmm,' said Sullen, walking off into the falling snow, the blue woolen cape Ji-hyeon had given him just before they departed comically short on his tall, broad back. 'He's not sitting still, wherever he is. Uncle Craven's a rabbit, and that's all they do, rabbits. Run. But wolves run, too.'

That sort of wisdom was much more typical than the *world-without-form* line, and Purna, Digs, and even soppy Keun-ju traded raised eyebrows at the profound parables of Sullen Fathead, Moonfruit of the First Water. Then they pulled down hood or scarf, tugged up veil or trousers, and set off into the storm after their de facto leader. Sullen might have significantly more brawn than brains, but he was the one officially in charge of reuniting them with their old chumrade, the Mighty Maroto, Devilskinner of legend and bounder of experience.

Maroto had better be having the worst time of his life to make up for all the bother they were going through on his account; if not, Purna might just have to kick his ass in one of their so-called fight-pretends. The thought of showing up her old pal and mentor kept her balmy as the snow picked up, and they marched on like the dutiful soldiers they most definitely weren't.

CHAPTER

8

The sun fled from Best, the Bright Watcher hiding in the wiregrass to the west and pulling down the cloak of her sister Silvereye to cover her trail. Many years ago, when a young Father Turisa and the old poison oracle had first convened in the Honor Circle, they had wrestled on the ground for hours, hissing back and forth as though they were mating frost vipers, and when they had finally separated the oracle announced through split lips that the sun was in fact but an aspect of the Deceiver, and the moon a manifestation of the Fallen Mother ... but Best couldn't stop herself from thinking of them by their ancestral names. It had been easier when only Silvereye was associated with the Allmother, but the new poison oracle had proved more receptive to Father Turisa's wisdom than her predecessor had been, and so a dozen more ancestors in as many years had revealed themselves to be but different incarnations of the Fallen Mother. This led to much confusion if one didn't slip into the old titles when discussing a hunt, a song, or most anything at all, up to and including the weather.

And what weather it was, Best sweating through her thinnest skins despite the looming winter solstice, and it only got warmer the farther south they went. She marched on through the muggy, thickening dark, Brother Rýt trailing a distance behind her. They moved across the Samothan borderlands toward the point where the Bright Watcher had burrowed into the earth – Best's wicked kinfolk had bewitched the sun to burn up the Frozen Savannahs, and so if they followed the sun they would find her family. Thus spoke the poison oracle, and Father Turisa had not gainsaid the wisdom; Diadem also lay west of Flintland, so all roads pursued the sun.

As the barleywine-dark fringe of Silvereye's star-studded cloak slipped around the rim of the world, Best stopped, waiting. This was how she and Brother Rýt had traveled all the way across the Frozen Savannahs and down through the Raptor Wood, she walking and he seeming to limp on both legs, until she got so far ahead that she had to stop or risk the boy losing her trail. He could not hunt any better than he could walk, and did not appear to be much of a warrior, either, and would not have lasted long by himself . . . which must be why the Fallen Mother had braided their paths together. Leading this daft pup around reminded her a touch of rearing Sullen, back when the boy was four or five.

As she waited for the monk, she thought back to the Flywalk over the Agharthan Gorge, in particular the picture stone the Horned Wolves had erected on their side of the bridge over the summer. The engraved face of the limestone marker showed the outline of a four-armed monster harried by hunters, corpses splayed beneath the fiend's feet. That her ignoble brother had long ago disgraced the clan twice over had appalled Best, yes, but it had not stunned her the way Sullen and her father had. The man who had planted Best in her mother and the boy Best had planted in her husband were no longer mere traitors to the clan; their sins had grown so great the two were now bonded together into a single massive anathema, as the monks called those born with the taint of devils.

It must have been preordained, this taint, for the old poison oracle had attended Sullen's birth, smearing a mixture of crushed insects, nettle ash, and cockerel blood on the foreheads of both the pacing, nervous mother and the moaning, laboring father. Best scratched the keloid the caustic toxin had marked across her brow, remembering how when Sullen finally emerged from between Keenear's legs she had thought that she must be dreaming from the oracle's burning balm. She hadn't been, alas, but there hadn't been any other explanation for why their wet, mewling babe would be so obviously cursed.

From that first day forward, into the months and finally years that followed, Best had tried in vain to understand what she and her husband might have done wrong to invite in this devilish presence. She and Keenear were both model members of the clan, skilled hunters and warriors, respectful of their ancestors, the church, and the Horned Wolf way, and they were hardly the only couple who were both two-spirited (or hijra, as the Chainites called those whose souls the Deceiver had tricked into being born into different bodies than those the Fallen Mother had intended for them).

It wouldn't have even occurred to her to consider this last factor, for those most tested by the Deceiver are most worthy of the Allmother's love, except her father had made quite the racket about how she and Keenear were no more responsible for how their son came out than he and his wife were for Best being born two-spirited. *The Old Watchers just watch*, he'd said with his usual flair for the profane, *they don't mess around in the wombs of innocent men and women, so take your boy for the blessing he is*. When Keenear had demanded to know how a boy afflicted with the devils' blood could be a blessing, Ruthless had boxed his son-in-law's ear and told him any child that wasn't stillborn was a blessing, and a bairn born with the blood of shamans was far better than a pair of ancestor-betraying Chainite converts like them deserved. After this showdown the new parents had hurried to confess what the old man had said, and Father Turisa was predictably appalled that anyone would compare an anathema to a hijra, listing all the obvious ways it was different. He even went on to imply that maybe Best's father's looseness with his tongue was what had invited in the malign spirit that had lodged in the child's eyes.

Yet when they brought the matter before the old poison oracle, he had told the both of them as well as the priest that a proven elder like Ruthless was entitled to his own say in his own hut, even if it stemmed from antiquated beliefs held over from less enlightened times. All the same, Best and Keenear would have been within their rights as parents to let Father Turisa remove the devilish corruption from their child, but Best couldn't bring herself to let the Chainite carry out the painful act of cleansing, knowing what little chance a blind adult had of prospering in the clan, let alone a blind infant.

Even now she spat at the thought of disfiguring a baby, and then spat again at the thought of what her misplaced mercy for an anathema had cost her and her people. When spitting wasn't enough to expel the anger and fear and shame at what evil must lurk in the blood of her family, she hoisted the hem of her battle-dress and pissed into the darkness. As she did, she remembered how her exhausted husband had reacted to seeing those round cat eyes looking back at him from the slippery new-born's face, Keenear reluctant to even let the baby nurse lest the devil-touched thing bite his heavy breasts . . . and remembering this, Best couldn't stop herself from also recalling how as soon as she had seen Sullen in his father's arms she had known their offspring was incapable of harm or malice, imperfect, yes, but a child of the Fallen Mother all the same. After everything that had happened since, Best now wondered if that immediate attachment and trust came not from motherly love but something more insidious, the curse that apparently affected every generation of her family making her want to protect a creature that everyone else saw for the wicked entity that it was. Sullen was not to blame for his condition, for he had been doomed by birth, but Best was certainly accountable, for she could have done something to spare the clan from the anathema her son was destined to grow into. She had been overconfident in her ability to guide him into a life of righteousness, and now all the Savannahs paid the price for her hubris . . .

A scent on the warm lowland breeze distracted Best from her grim reveries, and she sniffed the night, turning all her focus to the teasing hint of wood smoke. It passed, leaving her with the dull smells of the grassland, but not before she pinpointed the direction it wafted from. When Brother Rýt tripped up through the grass behind her, she was impatiently whetting her grandmother's sun-knife.

'Can we please rest?' Brother Rýt sounded like a child mourning the death of a clanmate. 'Please, just for—'

'There is a fire ahead,' Best told him. 'We will see who burns it, and either ask the right to use it or take it for our own. Since we set out this morn I delivered four hares to my gamebag, and that is a meat best cooked. Come, and stay silent.'

Best needn't have worried about Rýt betraying their approach, for he again fell so far behind her that she stopped hearing his blundering approach altogether. Silvereye slept but her countless twinkling children lit the way, the heavens cloudy with the celestial litter, until a low star on the horizon crawled down from the edge of the sky and settled on the grasslands. Between the warm nights and their rations of beancake and saltfish, Best had seen no reason to risk kindling a flame since leaving home, and so this fire was the first she had seen in many nights . . . and where there was fire in the wilderness, there were friends to be made, or, more likely, foes to be fought.

Now that she had found the beacon she again stopped, but after waiting a shamefully long time for Rýt she was obliged to retrace her steps to see where he had wandered off to. Clear and starlit as the night was, the helpless monk had still gone astray, but she soon found him and forced him to pick up his sluggish pace until he could clearly make out the distant glow of the campfire. Then she told him to walk to it as quick as he could, and set off on her own at a swift trot. He could only make her look weak if they arrived together, which would do neither of them any boons, and this way she could come in as cautious or aggressive as the situation demanded.

Soon the smell of burning locust wood became as sharp as the stars, and then other distinct notes came into focus: scorched pepper and herbs, and the rich tickle of tubāq. She slowed her pace to a steady walk, for charging up to a campfire sends but one message, and Best was no more a brute than she was a coward. So long as no Jackal People or sorcerers tended this lonely fire, she would give them a chance to do the right thing and let her share their camp. She felt the tall grass rasping at her knees fall away as she came closer, entering a wide ring of short, blackened stalks that crumbled to ash beneath her boots as she closed the rest of the distance. The bare ground felt sticky under her heels, and she quickly crossed the clearing back into the grass, something about the place setting her teeth on edge.

As starlight gave way to firelight she saw but one figure, hunchbacked and hooded, sitting on the far side of the small blaze. Best stopped on the edge of the light, wondering if this were but a scarecrow erected to lure her in, but then a long-stemmed pipe was raised to the opening of the cowl, and an ember glowed in the bulbous bowl as the solitary fire tender puffed the tubāq. Behind the stranger stood a wooden hut with a small door set partway up its face and three ladder-like steps leading down to the grass. Not a traveler, then, but a hermit who dwelled in this desolate border between Flintland and Samoth, capital province of the Crimson Empire. Best waited, knowing she could be plainly seen, turning the sun-knife in her hand so it caught the fire and flashed her warning. When even this didn't provoke the evidently ancient stranger into offering either a friendly invitation or a hostile challenge, Best issued the universal Flintland greeting, though this far past the Raptor Wood it might not be understood; had she spoken the Immaculate tongue half so well as her son she should have opened with that, instead.

'The night is cold, your fire is warm, and I would have friends before me than foes behind.'

The figure didn't acknowledge her, blowing out a curl-ing serpent of smoke that slithered into the sky, and Best tightened her hold on the throwing knife, wondering if the stranger showed her disrespect or was simply deaf. Before she could decide, the hooded head raised to survey Best, and two glowing red eyes flashed at her from deep within the cowl. A witch or monster of some kind, obviously, and Best's arm flew back to launch her sun-knife at the creature when it called out, 'The night is cold, my fire is warm, and friends are made as easy as foes.'

This posed a significant problem, as Best had no desire to treat such an unclean presence to anything save her blessed steel, but there was no crime more heinous than attacking one's host after receiving the ancestral welcome, especially when she had been the one to request it. Perhaps sensing Best's reluctance, the figure used a twisted, feather-topped walking stick to climb awkwardly to its feet, as if to show that every slight movement was dearly won. Then it used the long stem of the pipe it held in its other hand to flip back the hood of what Best now saw was a gauzy grey coat.

As the cowl flopped back Best almost laughed at her own foolishness, for this was no monster with flames for eyes, nor an ancient crippled by age, but a young woman with twin rectangles of polished glass fixed across her nose with copper wire. Despite her unaccented Flintland greeting, the girl was of no tribe Best had ever heard of. Her long, straight hair was mousy by nature and ratty with neglect, her skin lighter than that of most Flintlanders but far darker than any Immaculate's, with scraps of metal, stone, and bone flashing from the hoops, chains, and studs set in her sneering lips, aquiline nose, thick brows, and sharp ears. More silver and bone girded her throat, necklaces that looked as heavy as shackles drooping around the high collar of the foreign, lace-frilled dress she wore under the hooded coat.

'I am Best of the Horned Wolf Clan,' said she, for she had no fear in her heart for little girls, even ones willing to riddle their faces with such bizarre heraldry or dress in such outlandish attire. 'I have a hare to offer for your fire, and not one friend but two, for my companion will join us in time.'

'Well met, well met,' said the woman, bowing though the movement clearly pained her. 'I am Nemi of the Bitter Sighs, a sorcerer of no small skill.'

Best had no love for any wretch so shameless they would stoop to deviltry, but she had never before met a witch who so openly admitted to her practice. This showed boldness that Best could respect, but it also put her further on guard – a sorcerer might voice the ancient greetings only to betray that trust, and if an attack took place she must be ready to murder the girl with cold steel before she could be bewitched . . .

Until such a time, however, Best had meat that would not cook itself. She nodded curtly to this Nemi and squatted by the fire, thrusting the central blade of her sun-knife into the earth beside her. Unslinging her pack, she retrieved the gamebag and iron skewers.

'Your companion is clanfolk of yours?' asked the witch, leaning on her staff and watching Best dress the hares.

'No,' said Best, knowing from all the songs Sullen was forever singing to himself about witches and treacherous poison oracles that she must be honest or risk their ire, but she must also be vigilant to reveal as little as possible lest they somehow trap her with her words, or worse, her desires. That was what made sorcerers so dangerous, they sought to duel with your heart or your head instead of your strength or your skill.

'Is he perhaps one of my kind?'

Best thought about that one before answering – did she mean an obvious Outlander, or did she mean a witch? Picking her words as carefully as Sullen picked his when repeating a story over and over until he had it memorized, she said, 'I do not know what your kind is, Nemi of the Bitter Sighs. Perhaps if you sang me the song of your days I could better answer?'

Best tried not to smile at her cleverness, and gave silent thanks to her son for the inspiration; Boldstrut or Skinflint or one of Sullen's other idols had thwarted a witch by keeping her talking about herself until dawn, when the sun's light transformed her into a swarm of mosquitoes that were promptly eaten by an owlbat.

'I will sing you a song, Best of the Horned Wolves, but not of my days,' said the witch, which just went to show that Sullen's stories were nonsense, just like his mother had always said. 'I will sing you the song of the black blood of the earth which flows beneath our feet, and how I came to hold my vigil at this place. I have been awaiting your coming for some time.'

Best's fist tightened on the skewer she rammed through the last hare, and hesitated before laying it above the coals. It wasn't just the witch's ominous words, but the unmistakable sensation that she was being watched by something yet more dangerous than any sorcerer, a ferocious presence that waited beyond the edge of her vision. Now that she had entered the bubble of firelight, everything beyond it was obscured to her. 'Before you begin, Nemi of the Bitter Sighs, I demand to know if you mean me harm, or if whatever watches us from the darkness is in thrall to your will.'

'From what I learned, I expected a warrior of the Horned Wolf Clan to show more respect to her host,' said Nemi, but as Best stood back to her full height the witch gave a petulant sigh, as if Best had spoiled her fun. 'I will grant your *demands*, Best, though I hope in the future you will do me the courtesy of simply asking. I mean you no harm, and while I cannot claim complete authority over the watcher from the darkness, I assure you she poses no danger save to those who would bring me violence. If that is enough to allay your fears, I will begin the song I have long waited to sing you.'

'I have no fear of you nor your familiar,' said Best, which was true enough – fear was for prey, and what Best felt was the wariness of a horned wolf approaching a potential trap. 'But what of my absent companion? Will he arrive unmolested?'

'I have no interest in any but you,' said Nemi, which did little to assuage Best's unease. 'Unless your companion also seeks the same quarry as you and I?'

Best considered this, but did not ask any of the obvious questions – she had already said too much, especially when this witch seemed willing to talk without prompting. 'I think you are right – the time has come for you to sing your song.'

'Only if you're sure you're ready,' said the girl, smiling wolf-ishly at Best before tottering back around the fire. 'Nothing I could offer my gracious guest before we begin? Some spice for your rabbit, or fresh water? Something stronger to drink, or smoke?'

'No,' said Best, not much liking what she'd already tasted of the witch's hospitality. As the feeble girl lowered herself back to the ground with a groan, Best returned to her squat, turning the skunky hares and keeping the hilt of her sun-knife within easy reach. After all that preamble, though, Nemi took her time relighting her pipe with a long blade of grass, sipping it slowly until the pufferfish-round-and-knobby bowl was putting off nearly as much smoke as the campfire.

'Three seasons past, your clanfolk made their camp but a hundred paces from where we now sit,' said Nemi at last. 'A boy and an old man. Kin of yours.'

Best nodded before it occurred to her that this last may have been a question, the firelight flashing off Nemi's teeth and glasses confirming the girl welcomed the answer.

'It was here that they met the most dire sorcerer who ever walked the Star,' said Nemi, and when Best did not rise to this bait the girl continued. 'It was an accident, but not entirely, just as our meeting here is an accident, though not entirely. We are their shadow, speeding along at their heels ... or perhaps the echo of their screams, after the sorcerer put his work upon them, opening their eyes to the devils that consumed them.'

Best did not like the sound of that one bit – obviously Sullen and Ruthless deserved judgment, along with her brother Craven, but the tenderness of witches and devils was not a Horned Wolf's notion of justice. Slipping her leather cooking pad onto the cooler end of one of the skewers, Best removed it from the fire, making a show of blowing on the crispy meat. If Nemi thought Best was distracted by a meal, the witch might make her move . . . and when she did she would find the skewer was made of good iron.

'This sorcerer is called many titles, but most mortals know him as Hoartrap the Touch, or the Witch of the Purple Hill, or of Meshugg,' said Nemi, eyeing Best over her pipe, but if she sought some sign of revelation she was disappointed, for the names meant nothing to Best. 'He is a danger to every living thing on the Star, and other worlds besides. And while he was hunting for another prey, he found them instead.'

'And what then?' said Best, telling herself the deep ache in her chest came from the possibility that another party had deprived her of the honor of carrying out the sentence of clan and Chain herself. 'He set devils on them?'

'The devils were already there, as they are already here,' said Nemi, and though Best hated to give the witch what she wanted she couldn't stop herself from looking all around. 'Hoartrap merely showed them what waits beyond the horizon of mortal sight. They recovered, you will be glad to hear, and before they did Hoartrap fled. And after going their separate ways for countless miles, they found one another again, on the far end of the Crimson Empire. Last I was able to scry, they were camped together, on better terms, one assumes, than they were when they shared a fire much like this one.'

Her father and son, willingly conspiring with a sorcerer? It was even worse than Best had feared. She devoured the first stringy hare, watching Nemi smoke in silence, and when the carcass was stripped of meat and no more words had come forth, Best snapped. 'Well?'

'Well?'

'Well what else? Where do you come from and what do you want? Why build your hut in this place, and why wait for me? What are my kinfolk to you? And what must I pay for you to tell me where to find them?' As soon as the last word left her mouth Best chided herself for not only losing her patience but bringing the subject of a price into the discussion; you didn't have to listen to more than a couple of Sullen's songs to be reminded of the fact that the spirits of wild rivers often mani-fested themselves as mysterious women or talking wolves who were eager to help the unwary in any way you could imagine, but the cost for their aid was always the same: the death of a family member. Then again, thought Best, if this Nemi actually was such a devil in disguise and not merely a witch it would find itself in a unique situation, for what Best desired most was that very price, which all others feared to pay. Still, she wanted to know where she stood, whether it was with a mortal or a monster, so she added, 'And tell me true, are you a spirit or devil or merely a sorceress?'

'So many questions!' The witch wagged her pipe at Best. 'We will have much time to discuss it all in the coming nights and days, but for now we are united by a common quest, you and I, just as your family is bound to Hoartrap. We are their shadows, as I said.'

'I am bound to none save my clan,' said Best. 'And were I to align myself with an Outlander, it would not be a witch who speaks in riddles.'

'I beg your pardon,' said Nemi, 'but the Horned Wolf Clan must have a very different definition of riddles than is usually agreed upon. I have spoken as plainly as I am capable of in your tongue, and will endeavor to speak plainer still: you seek two of your kinfolk, and I am in a position to help you find them. I do not ask any price for my services beyond your company. When we do reach them, they are yours to do with as you please. It is their companion I hunt.'

'Why not seek him yourself, then?' demanded Best, the gamey taste of the hare lingering in her dry mouth. 'If you know where to find him, why involve me in your schemes?'

'Because the Touch is far too dangerous and difficult for me to direct my attentions on more than I already have,' said Nemi, and now there was a hint of something more to her girly voice, something deep and dark and full of a rage that Best could not mistake for anything else. 'The last time I met him was almost my undoing, and I will give him no hint that I survived to seek vengeance. If I dare persist in focusing my sorceries to find him, he will surely smell the trace of my wiles long before I arrive, and be waiting. But if I direct myself not at the Touch but the company he keeps, we both may get what we are after, and he will be oblivious to my coming until it is too late. Do I make myself understood, Best of the Horned Wolf Clan?'

'You do,' said Best, preparing to seize the sun-knife and hurl it into the witch when this played out the way she expected. 'And I refuse. I am not fool enough to involve myself in the quarrels of sorcerers. You and I part ways in the morn, and you shall never approach me again. Do I make *myself* understood, Nemi of the Bitter Sighs?'

The night seemed to deepen with Best's challenge, the darkness thickening around their sphere of firelight, and the Horned Wolf felt all her hairs stand up – she had never been in such danger in her life, somehow she knew this, and decided to preemptively throw her sun-knife at—

'Alas, you do,' said the witch, sounding disheartened rather than enraged at being rebuffed, and just like that the pressure seemed to lift, the menace passed. 'I know what it means to have your hand forced by another, and I shall not repeat the very crimes I have suffered. Believe me, though, that if you do not help me reach Hoartrap in time the entire Star will be thrust into darkness eternal, and the endless night that comes will be the hunting ground of devils and worse things still. Have you not noticed the world undergoes a sudden change, that something powerful prods and tugs at the Star? I do not demand your help, Best, I beg it – together we have a chance to halt this slide into the First Dark before it is too late.'

Best snorted at the insane claim, ready to rebuke the witch's foul prophecy in the hardest terms ... but she could not dismiss the very event that had sent her on this quest. Some grave transformation had indeed beset the Savannahs, but what if it didn't stop there? What if every land felt similar upheaval, what if snow fell in the fabled deserts of the south and the west even as a supernatural thaw warmed the Noreast Arm? And worst of all, what of this witch's claim that Best's son and father were both in league with the sorcerer behind the catastrophes? No Horned Wolf in memory would ally herself with a sorcerer, true, but had not her ancestors deigned to work with the very devils on occasion, when doing so allowed them to combat greater foes?

And there, at the very tail end of it all, was something more – what if her devil-eyed, angel-hearted son wasn't actually to blame for what befell their homeland? What if this Hoartrap the Touch was the true source, and Sullen was innocent of any wrongdoing beyond his shaming of the clan? If this were true she wouldn't have to do anything but put Sullen out of his misery, instead of administering harsher punishments ... and while mercy was a sin, Best could not help but wish that when the time came the circumstances would allow her to give the boy a quick death.

'We can wait until dawn for you to decide,' said Nemi quietly. 'But I wouldn't have waited for you to come if I didn't believe you were my best hope. Trust that I am not so desperate for sport that I would set up shop in the wilds, wasting the last nights of my wretched life in hopes that I could dupe a Flintlander into some petty plot. Sleep on it, and counsel with your companion. For now I must rest – I have gone without for days, lest I miss your passage.'

Best didn't reply, but nodded shortly as the frail young witch hauled herself back to her boots and climbed the stairs to her tiny house. Looking back from the doorway, she said, 'Whatever your decision, I shall abide by it. And as long as you share my fire you will enjoy my protection. Whatever you may see this night, you will save your life if you trust in my word and keep your weapons sheathed.'

With this final ominous proclamation, Nemi of the Bitter Sighs disappeared inside the shack, bolting the door behind her. Best considered the three remaining hares on the fire with little appetite, waiting for Brother Rýt to finally arrive and turning the proposition this way and that. It went without saying that Best could not trust a witch . . . but could she afford not to, lest the girl spoke true? What if this Nemi were a closer cousin to the intimidating but righteous poison oracle than to the black-hearted warlocks warned of in the Chain Canticles? If only the Fallen Mother would give Best a sign one way or the other, and if the Fallen Mother was busy, one of Best's other ancestors could certainly provide . . .

The wiregrass crackled behind her, and she straightened up so that the already overly smug Brother Rýt would not catch her at prayer. Then her hackles flew up and her hand darted to the hilt of her sun-knife. From the heavy plodding sounds she knew whatever moved through the grass at her hind was far bigger than the monk, and walked on four legs instead of two. As her hand tightened on her weapon, a deep growl came from so close she almost spun into the beast, but caught herself, strong enough to remain still despite every instinct telling her to attack. Remembering Nemi's final warning before retiring, Best kept the blades of her sun-knife sheathed in the dark earth even as the white shadow reared up beside her ... and then passed her by, moving around the fire and stretching its prodigious length on the ground in front of the witch's hut, guarding the door with intent as obvious as any protective hound.

When Best could finally breathe again, she soaked up the miracle through eyes blurred by both awestruck tears and the smoky fire between her and the horned wolf. She had not met such a creature since she had earned her name as a girl of twelve thaws, and unlike the lanky, underfed creature she had stalked and killed on the steep green slope of a remote fjord, this horned wolf was massive, sleek of coat and bright of eye, with five twisted horns as long as her arms ... and unlike any such beast she had ever heard of outside of Sullen's most outrageous songs, it seemed almost tame, regarding her with bored disdain rather than rapacious appetite. This was what she had sensed watching her from the night, the guardian Nemi of the Bitter Sighs had spoken of.

Well. Best did not flatter herself for the cleverest member of the clan, but certain omens were too clear for even a simple warrior to mistake. For the first time since the Age of Wonders, a Horned Wolf would hunt beside her namesake.

When Brother Rýt finally wheezed his way into the dim rays of the firelight, Best was almost asleep, and was jolted back into consciousness by his frantic whimpers at the sight of the snoring monster. By the time she was on her feet the portly monk was running faster than she'd thought him capable of moving, and when she finally caught him and wrestled him to the ground he seemed on the verge of complete panic. Her annoyed assurances that the horned wolf had been sent by the Fallen Mother to guide them didn't convince him to return to the camp ... but her suggestion that if he went off on his own he might meet less benign members of the breed did the trick. In light of his stark terror at being led back to the monster-guarded camp, she decided to wait until the morning to inform him that Diadem would have to wait until after they had saved the world.

CHAPTER
9

'Not in a hundred years,' said Kang-ho, returning his unsampled bowl of kaldi to the Cobalt command table as though he suspected his favorite daughter might poison him. Former favorite, anyway. 'That stunt you pulled with the devil queen hurt you more than it hurt the Thaoans, and I know you're too smart to make the same mistake twice. It's over, Ji-hyeon, and the sooner you admit that the sooner we can go home.'

'The sooner she surrenders the sooner you can go to your new home in Linkensterne, I think you mean,' said Fennec from his seat beside Ji-hyeon. 'Or let me guess, you've already straightened out the whole mess with Empress Ryuki, and Ji-hyeon just needs to visit Othean to light some incense at Prince Byeong-gu's tomb?'

'As it so happens, Fennec, I did indeed send a full and accurate account to Her Elegance as soon as I heard about the bounty, but have yet to receive a reply,' said Kang-ho, betraying no sign that Fennec's full-scale defection to his daughter's allegiances perturbed him in the slightest. It made Ji-hyeon wonder if they were still colluding, if this was just another ploy in their long-game strategy . . . or maybe they were just so used to double-crossing one another that her second father had counted on this as a foregone conclusion. 'And I should add that I went through the swiftest channels known to mortals to get my message delivered with all due haste, so the . . . misunderstanding should be resolved in no time at all.'

'And the message said what, exactly?' Ji-hyeon's bowl was empty so she reached across the table to take Kang-ho's kaldi before it cooled. '*I have my murderous daughter ready to deliver to your justice, and only need to dupe her into trusting me again so that I may—*'

'You're out of order,' said Kang-ho furiously, hopping to his feet. The self-righteous gesture would have been more effective if Ji-hyeon hadn't called the same bluff twice already during this morning meet; they both knew he wasn't going back to the Thaoans until she'd either given him what he wanted or sent him packing in no uncertain terms. 'You hurt me, child, you truly do. I wrote to the empress to explain that you were framed for the murder of her son, because that is what you told me, and I still have faith that you speak the truth to your parent. A trust that does not seem to be returned, and *that* is what frightens me, for without my protection Colonel Waits would have already launched a second offensive and splattered you and your rogues all over the snow. You owe me your very life, and those of your entire company, and still you persist in this disrespect!'

'Kang-ho, when I've disrespected you you'll devil well know it,' said Ji-hyeon, putting down the bowl she'd been sipping while he carried on. 'You come in here, into my camp, into my *tent*, to tell me that the terms I offered are insulting to the Thaoans and all the rest? Fine. You claim there was some merry mix-up between Waits, her officers, and the commanding clerics, and that's why the whole fucking regiment came charging down at us, to, ahem, *relocate their camp closer to better facilitate negotiations*? Okay, sure, fine again. And even as I'm trying to swallow that totally plausible explanation, you can't help but add that it was your pointing out to Waits that our armies were clashing that got her to call off the advance, not, you know, because *we raised the fucking devil* – fine fine fine, whatever, because now I'm just nodding at any stupid stories you throw at me, aren't I? I'm *trying* to give you the benefit of the doubt, Dad, I am really, really trying. But please don't insult my intelligence with this bullshit about me owing you my life, because we both know that the only reason Colonel Waits hasn't marched in here for another swing is because she knows I can just call up another devil queen if I get nervous, so she's waiting for reinforcements or an order from Diadem that she can't ignore. If she actually thought she could take me she wouldn't send you to beg for my surrender, would she?'

'We're not begging,' snapped Kang-ho, and then, remembering his role as worried father, he resumed his seat and lowered his voice. 'I am begging, yes, because I'm your dad and I'll say anything if it gets you to see reason, but Waits is firmly of the opinion that if anyone ought to be groveling it's you. You're trapped, Ji-hyeon, cut off, and while I understand why you have to put on a brave front and threaten to call up another monster, we both know that wouldn't work any better the second time than the first . . . and that's assuming Hoartrap can pull off the same trick twice, which isn't exactly his specialty, in case you haven't noticed. Where is he, by the way? I hope he didn't overexert himself with that vulgar display of power last week. I can't imagine what sort of toll trafficking with such powers puts on the mortal frame.'

'I'll give the Touch your regards,' said Ji-hyeon. 'I'm sure he'll be sorry to have missed you, but perhaps he'll pop over to say hello one of these evenings.'

'Yes, well, that might not be wise, given the company I'm keeping,' said Kang-ho, and she noticed with satisfaction her father's eyes were flitting to the dark corners of the tent. Hoartrap only had to sneak up on you the once before you made a habit of checking all the closets and under the bed. 'Colonel Waits is a remarkably reasonable person, but you've put her in quite the bind – first with the criminal suggestion that she join your rebellion against the Empire, and then with your invocation of a devil straight from the First Dark. How can a woman of honor work with you when in less than twenty-four hours you committed capital sins against both Crown and Chain? I'm telling you, it's only a matter of time before Diadem gets off its duff and delivers the only order they could possibly give, after what you did to the Fifteenth Regiment, and Myura, and Geminides, and every other Imperial city and province you trashed along the way.'

'Except she didn't do anything to the Fifteenth, as we all know,' said Fennec. 'Or did you forget to deliver Colonel Hjortt's letter to your new boss?'

'Oh, she read it all right,' said Kang-ho. 'But until such a time as Hjortt is sufficiently recovered to appear before Colonel Waits in person there are certain questions as to its authenticity.'

'I would have thought Colonel Hjortt's colorful turn of phrase when it came to the lack of punctuality of the Thaoan regiment and their colonel might have been sufficient to prove its authorship,' said Ji-hyeon, taking a nice big hit from her saam pipe to remind her father that he wasn't allowed to puff his acrid tubāq in her tent. Holding in the hit, she added, 'And she's welcome to come here and meet with him herself, or you could – ach!'

It was hard to imagine her father looking any more put out than he already did, but as Ji-hyeon coughed, sending the musky smoke straight in his face, she thought she may have finally nudged him that extra bit.

'Yes, well, considering my relationship to you, I think Colonel Waits has some grounds for not trusting me as much as she used to,' said Kang-ho, waving away the pungent cloud she had enveloped him with. 'I'm not sure she'd believe me even if I met Hjortt myself.'

'I wonder whatever you did to make her question your loyalty,' said Ji-hyeon, already feeling better as the heat shivered out through her lungs.

'Arriving to find my supposedly willing and able mercenary army refusing to march on Linkensterne may have played a hand,' said Kang-ho. 'And if that wasn't enough, discovering the entire fucking Fifteenth Regiment missing and a brand-new Gate in its place certainly didn't help. And then there's the niggling matter that when she quite reasonably tried to move her regiment a tiny bit closer to your camp to speed along the negotiation process, my darling daughter loosed a devil queen the likes of which hasn't been glimpsed by mortal eyes since the Age of Wonders. So unless you do the smart thing and trust me on this we all just sit here waiting on Diadem to order Colonel Waits to stop stalling and eradicate the lot of you.'

'We might not have to wait that long,' said Ji-hyeon, trying not to smile. 'Our countryfolk might send down an assassin squad from the Isles well before that happens.'

'It's not funny, Ji-hyeon! And it frankly terrifies me that you're putting more stock in the counsel of Fennec than you are in me.'

'Terrified is good,' said Ji-hyeon. 'Shows you've actually been listening to me for a change.'

'It's as if you do the opposite of everything I say just to spite me,' said Kang-ho sadly. 'I warned you about trusting Zosia, but you didn't listen, and we see where that got you – oh yes, the prisoners you handed over to the Thaoans during our first parley had quite the song to sing. The ones who survived your little Gate-side tiff, that is. I'm just glad you lived long enough to learn that she can't be trusted, and pray that you come to similar enlightenments about the rest – they didn't call us Villains because we were the good guys!'

'No, they called you that because the Empire had all the printing presses before we got started, and anyone who stood up to Kaldruut was a baddie,' said a voice from the entrance to the tent. Before Kang-ho had recovered from his surprise, Zosia stepped fully into the command tent, confirming his worst fears. Almost two weeks had passed since their brawl at the Gate, and Ji-hyeon was pleased to see the older woman still looked rough as a sherpa's old shoes. She wore a fading necklace of bruised skin around her throat and some matching blotches on her face that made her look remarkably like a mouthy old maniac who had been worked over by a much younger and more talented opponent. As with Ji-hyeon, some of Zosia's injuries had been accrued during the brief but brutal Second Battle of the Lark's Tongue, but also as with Ji-hyeon, the worst of them had been delivered the day before, not from a devil queen or her brood but at the hands of another mortal woman.

'So this is it,' said Kang-ho, slowly standing for the last time. It must have taken some real work to look away from Zosia, but he directed his heaviest pout at his daughter. 'I suppose I shouldn't be surprised. You always did take after your other father.'

'Chin up, Kang-ho!' said Zosia cheerily, strutting over and throwing an arm around his shoulder. 'Hells, your daughter and me are living proof that it's best to let bygones be bygones, especially when there's fresh trouble blowing in. So you tried to get Singh to kill me back at the start of this adventure. It happens. I'm a bigger woman than to let a little thing like that get me down. Now what say I escort you out of camp, so we can catch up a bit?'

'Ji-hyeon, please—' Kang-ho squeaked desperately as Zosia began guiding him out of the tent.

'Give my regards to Colonel Waits,' said Ji-hyeon, blowing her dad a kiss. 'And see you back here at this time tomorrow, barring any unforeseen developments.'

———

As soon as they left the command tent, Kang-ho began spluttering weak excuses ('I had no choice!') and appeals to her vanity ('Of course I knew you'd see through it, just had to go through the motions'), but Zosia shushed him as she led him through the snowbound camp. More weather had come in the day after the Thaoans' aborted attack, and the white stuff had come down slow but steady for well over a week. While the blizzard had finally passed in the night, it remained to be seen if the Cobalt Company's spirits could ever be healed. Even with the noon sun high above and not a cloud in the sky, every tent was still glassy with snow and ice that refused to melt. There had been some cave-ins where canvas had yielded to the seemingly eternal onslaught, but few fatalities, especially given the circumstances, and the duration of the storm had discouraged even the most committed deserters.

Zosia knew that firsthand: when she'd woken up in a sawbones's tent the day after being hurled headfirst into the devil queen's arm, she had been more than ready to chase down Sullen and give him a harsh lesson about not throwing your betters at monsters. Yet while he and his crew only had a few hours' head start, the snow had already covered their tracks.

Besides, the whole point of their departure during the start of a blizzard was to better sneak past the surrounding Thaoans, and knowing Zosia's luck the weather would break just when she wandered into a sentry squad. So instead of going after Sullen for a little satisfaction, or ditching the Cobalts for good the way she'd daydreamed before her run-ins with murderous prison guards and slightly more sympathetic opossum devils, she'd hobbled over to Ji-hyeon's tent to make nice.

Well, nice was an overstatement, but at least the girl turned out to be every bit as soft as Zosia had hoped. Between Singh's vouching for her character and Zosia's intentionally enigmatic proclamation that something very big and very bad had befallen Diadem and its sovereign, something that only Zosia was in a position to immediately investigate further, she'd been pretty confident Ji-hyeon would cut her some slack for her minor rebellion. Zosia knew just what to give the brat, and in what order: a little contrition ('Look, obviously I fucked it all up, and I'm sorry'), a lot of flattery ('Nice hook, by the way – I think you cracked my jaw'), and some bullshit excuses that certainly wouldn't have washed with Zosia if their roles had been reversed ('I hadn't slept in days, mixed bad bugs with strong drink, and completely lost control – will never happen again'). She didn't even have to whip out the damaged Carnelian Crown to make her point, and so she decided to keep that secret in reserve lest she had need to further lean on Ji-hyeon for a little more leeway – and besides, what if the general tried to insist Zosia hand it over right then and there? No, better to be able to keep it up her sleeve, and then present Ji-hyeon with it at an opportune moment, such as when she was in need of proving her worth to the immature general: *why do you keep me around? Oh, I don't know, maybe because I'm the only person who can give you the Carnelian Crown . . . like so!*

Yet in the end it seemed what had actually won the girl over wasn't any of Zosia's apologies or praises, nor her explanations or promises to embark on a top secret mission of the utmost urgency. No, what had allowed the girl to so graciously forgive her treacherous captain was Zosia's selfless rescue of Ji-hyeon during their takedown of the devil queen. It took her a moment to even realize what the kid was talking about, but then it clicked, and Zosia resolved to let Sullen slide on his poor choice of missiles in light of how Ji-hyeon had interpreted the event. Slaying monsters that Zosia knew with absolute certainty were evil incarnate had been the most fun she'd had since before the Fifteenth Cavalry came to Kypck, and it was all the more satisfying to learn that the encounter had also eased her back into Ji-hyeon's good graces.

The general was a little savvier than Zosia had been count-ing on, however, and it wasn't until she'd sworn on the newly returned Choplicker's freedom not to ever come at Ji-hyeon again that the girl agreed to move forward. If Zosia ever did need to break that particular oath, Ji-hyeon might be in for a nasty surprise, since the recent fiasco with Choplicker just went to show that the subject of the devil's liberty might not be resolved with something as easy as carelessly spoken words. Claim any reward that harms no mortal, she had told him, and instead of choosing to slip free of his unseen fetters he had trav-eled across the Star in a single night, all to bring her Indsorith's broken crown. What did that mean, exactly? Did he want Zosia to be queen again? Did he just want to inform her that some-thing had happened to Indsorith? Or did he maybe want her to melt it down and retool it into a fancy-ass collar for his mangy neck? It was all very weird, was what it was, and made Zosia less certain than ever of where she stood with the devil she'd bound so long ago, what all he was capable of, and why exactly he still served her, despite being offered ways out of her service three times over now. Sure, maybe foolishly telling him to take any prize he wished hadn't fulfilled whatever arcane code bound devils are forced to follow in order to earn their freedom, but surely her original wish of decades past to keep her and Leib safe from harm should have been easy pickings for any devil, to say nothing of her request to save Purna on the battlefield, a wish so easy to grant that Diggelby's devil had jumped on it as soon as Choplicker refused. So . . . why?

'So . . . why aren't I swallowing my teeth already?' said Kang-ho, reminding Zosia that she still hadn't spoken a word as they neared the edge of the icy camp, he leading his horse by the reins and Choplicker bobbing along merrily at her side. The luster was returning to the devil's coat in equal pace to the fading of Zosia's bruises. 'I can't imagine it's going to be so easy as our just agreeing that I owe you one?'

'Oh you know me, I'm always easy with my friends – we'll call it square, no questions asked, if you help me with a play I'm working on,' murmured Zosia in the corsair's cant he had taught her near thirty years past, when they'd first met on the deck of the Usban privateer *Cadaveria*. Kang-ho looked all around but they'd passed the last of the camp followers' wagons and stood in melting slush with not a soul in sight save the sentries off in the distance, and far beyond, the red Thaoan camp spread along the rim of the valley.

'You know I'd do anything short of slitting my own throat to make things right between us,' replied Kang-ho in the same patois when he'd allayed his worry of being overheard. 'I couldn't live with myself if I didn't make it up to you, my horrible, horrible mistake – you don't know what it's like, when you have kids, you'd do anything to keep them safe.'

'Blech.' Zosia jabbed a finger at her open mouth, because

there were few things worse than old friends lecturing her about how she'd missed out by not spurting a rugrat or four out of her cunt. In all their years together the only time she'd let Hoartrap directly put his work on her was when she'd taken him up on his standing offer to permanently render his friends sterile and pox-proof – only she and Maroto had gone through with it, since Kang-ho and Singh always wanted kids, and Fennec said he'd take his chances rather than allowing the Touch to apply his namesake to that particular part of his anatomy. Seeing how well Kang-ho got on with his daughter just reaffirmed Zosia's commitment to a childless life. 'Funny you should mention kids, Kang-ho, because Singh and I have been talking about yours, and . . .'

She lowered her voice even more for the proposal, whispering in his ear an offer that must have been as tantalizing to the dyed-in-the-wool schemer as a wriggling nightcrawler dangled in front of a half-starved trout. His eyes widened the slightest bit, and his lips betrayed a familiar twitch that desperately wanted to break into a grin. He whispered, 'I'll send her an owlbat as soon as I'm back at camp – what time should Waits request her for a midfield parley?'

'Singh's dragoons can be ready whenever you need them, and even if she brings her full retinue of bodyguards they'll be no match for the Raniputri riders,' said Zosia, her heart sinking a little, sentimental organ that it was.

'Let's say dawn, then,' Kang-ho decided, no doubt thinking in the misty morning he'd stand a better chance of stealing off with whatever loyal Immaculate crew he'd brought along, cutting the Thaoans out of the ransom altogether. He gave Zosia's shoulder a light pinch, then mounted his horse with respectable ease for a man as aged as he was. Then again, he hadn't been roughed up by a devil queen, or worse, his daughter. Looking down at Zosia, he gave her the old Cobalt salute and said, 'It's good to be working with you again, Zosia, instead of against.'

Then he was off through the sparkling frozen sea, his horse kicking up a spray of white dust as it carried him toward the Thaoan camp that encircled the Cobalts like a bloodstained noose round a scrawny blue throat. Watching him go, Zosia let out a heavy sigh, but Choplicker barked his approval of the treachery. The devil had a point: after the way Kang-ho had screwed Zosia, it was nice to know the man was at least consistent in his willingness to betray those he professed to love the most. Turning back to camp, Zosia set off on her other errand . . . the one Ji-hyeon didn't know about.

CHAPTER

10

When Sullen had first come to the Crimson Empire, each new city had overwhelmed him with its majesty. From the countless glittering spires of Yennek to the humbly carved yet brightly painted blue doors that graced every home in Purson, each locale had brought fresh wonders to his wide eyes, thrilling them with their unique characters. As a boy he'd always pictured the Crimson Empire as a rolling expanse not unlike the Frozen Savannahs, but with fire poppies coating the land instead of tundra, and with each of its famous settlements more or less the same as his village. Discovering just how vast the Empire was, and how each province or city-state differed from her neighbor, Sullen found himself confronted each day with a fresh marvel, be it of custom or clothing, agriculture or architecture. He could scarcely believe the salt miners they met outside Geminides bowed before the same queen as the gorgon herders of Meshugg, let alone shared the same tongue.

Grandfather, as a counterpoint, had been decidedly and consistently unimpressed, sniffing his nose at all the myriad ways people had concocted of doing things completely wrong, and remarking that seals from every sea could bark the same but that hardly made them learned. The Horned Wolves may have lost their way, but these Outlanders had never found it in the first place. Sullen kept his staunch disagreement about the quality of the Crimson Empire to himself, whether Grandfather was pooh-poohing a damp, musty coaching inn off the Katheli road or the whole damn Serpent's Circle; leave it to Grandfather to find fault with one of the last remaining relics of the Age of Wonders, an entire shimmering city that slowly rotated atop its artificial island floating in the middle of Lake Jucifuge.

Maybe it was just a sign that Sullen was getting jaded, or that without Grandfather around to push back against he wasn't as obligated to see the flowers growing from the cowpat, but Thao failed to impress the way the rest of the Imperial cities had. The squat wood and stone buildings were certainly modern enough, and the miniature castles that cropped up from time to time to tower over their one-story neighbors had an interesting, almost organic design that Sullen could appreciate, but, being real here, the whole place was kind of a midden heap. Literally. Even taking into account that the blizzard had only broken a few days before and the ensuing warm spell was making everything melt, the place was filthy. Not that a Flintland lad like Sullen would turn his nose up at a bit of dirt or dung on the streets, but in Thao the streets themselves seemed to be paved in manure, even the rooftops he could make out through the melting snow covered not in tiles or shingles but in brown muck. Thao did have a lot more trees lining its streets than other cities; pity they all looked dead.

Just when Sullen had thought the place couldn't get any more depressing, or dirty, Diggelby directed them down a street that followed the sinuous course of an ugly ten-foot-tall embankment of packed earth. They turned again, through a short tunnel in the side of the mound, and emerged into an open-air

bazaar. Sullen got his hopes up that he might be able to replace the sun-knives he'd lost during the encounter with the opossum devils – he'd found his torn-off bandolier afterward, lying on the field near his spear, but only one of the knives – but after browsing around for a while it became obvious all the souk had to offer was a lot of junk and a late lunch. Purna and Keun-ju acquired steaming cones of chestnuts, Sullen borrowed a coin to buy the worst berbere snails he'd ever tasted, and Digs got impatient; whatever he was hungry for couldn't be acquired at honest markets. As they ate he hurried them along another serpentine road through a posh neighborhood where the stately homes had all number of terraced roofs to pile with dirt and, unlike the poorer citizens, actual heaps of refuse. They passed along and under several more of the high earthen walls and finally went over the top of one, climbing a sturdy wooden ramp that Princess obligingly clip-clopped across while Sullen paused at the top to overlook Thao.

It sprawled as far as he could see from this slight prominence, as expansive a city as any he'd seen. It might've been an impressive metropolis, but all the raised, chaotically branching rivers of dirt made it look as though enormous moles had burrowed through the region in ages past and the people who had settled here had just decided to build around them. Sullen was thankful that they had visited Thao just after a cold snap, as this place must be riper than good lye-fish once the weather warmed up. Diggelby sidled up to him at the rail, while Purna and Keun-ju tried to coax Princess to come down the other side of the overpass – the pony was apparently of a mind to stay at the top, and until she descended the slope, neither could Sullen or the pasha.

'Sorry we're not here in the spring,' said Diggelby, following Sullen's gaze over the dirty city.

'I'm not,' said Sullen, but remembering how Ji-hyeon accused him of not being able to take a joke any better than he could give one, added, 'If I wanted that kind of stink in my life I'd just pitch my tent outside the Cobalt latrines.'

From the look Diggelby was giving him, Sullen had better concentrate on appreciating jokes before he started making any of his own. Then the little man must have got it, because his eyes went wide, and he said, 'Oh! Ohhhhh.'

'Yeah, well . . . ' said Sullen, giving the stubborn pony a gentle push to get her moving down the ramp. She didn't budge, probably not liking how steep the descent looked from up here.

'You've never heard of Thao? The Garden of the Star?' said Diggelby, but unlike most of the times when he asked about Sullen's body of knowledge it didn't sound mean-spirited or rhetorical.

'Actually, yeah,' said Sullen, but he was unable to place the song, which hardly ever happened . . . and then he had it. It wasn't from a song at all, but one of Father Turisa's hymns to the Fallen Mother. 'I thought that was on the Sunken Kingdom, though? Like Old Black's Meadhall, but for Chainites.'

'They only decided that at the Council of Horisont, oh, twenty years ago, I guess,' said Diggelby. 'And my uncle says they only did it to punish Thao for supporting Indsorith's rule after she usurped Zosia, instead of siding with the Chain. I think to myself, Diggelby, twenty years is an awfully long time, but it really isn't, you know? For reality to be so shifted, I mean, that even clear out on the Noreast Arm people already believe things a flock of cardinals decided in my lifetime – we think history's this hard, intractable thing, but it's actually as stretchy as we want it to be. I wonder what people will believe in another twenty years, or even less. Things we thought were eternal can be forgotten so fast . . . '

'Diggelby,' Sullen said after the pasha trailed off, 'maybe if I was a bughead I would've understood some of that, but I ain't so I didn't.'

'Oh!' Diggelby shook his head, as if just remembering he'd been holding incomprehensible court. 'I only meant Thao used to be called the Garden of the Star, and had been for hundreds of years, but then the Burnished Chain decided that was wrong, that nothing so grand could be built from the hands of sinners, and so they made it official – Thao might have *some* gardens and be *part* of the Star, absolutely, but *the* Garden of the Star grows now and forever on Jex Toth, and only when the Sunken Kingdom rose up from the waves to welcome home the faithful would we know the true glories of the Fallen Mother's bounty, etcet, etcet. My uncle was there when it all happened, though he was only a clerk then, or he would've voted against it – a good man, Uncle Obedear, though prone to the loquacious, if I may put it as gently as possible.'

'The Garden of the Star,' Sullen repeated, looking back out at the snow-scabbed veins of earth snaking through the filthy city, at the dung-packed streets and garbage-piled roofs and naked branches of the stunted trees. 'What happened to this place, to make it become so barren? Just the will of the Burnished Chain?'

'Something far older and stronger,' said Diggelby. 'Winter. Like I say, we should come back in the spring or summer – it's like being a child again, running through Papa's tulip beds with the flowers waving in the wind all around you, only without the firm talking-to afterward. Every avenue's an arbor or an orchard, and they call these raised beds we're on the Rainbow Rivers for all the bright blossoms flowing down them. Oh, how I love a Thaoan bug hunt under a chubby summer moon, quaffing flagons of hibiscus beer and dandelion wine and perambulating through the fragrant streets, getting elbow deep in the verge in hunt of new and unusual creepy-crawlies until the pollen is thick as wig powder on your jacket . . . '

Diggelby sighed, leaning on the rail, and Sullen sighed, too, looking out at a city as drab as the Temple of the Black Vigil in Emeritus, but one whose brilliance would be reborn when the seasons turned. He wondered if the Forsaken Empire would ever find its color again, if one day the tomb of the Faceless Mistress would be festooned with all the hues of the mortal world . . . He hoped so, and in the meantime silently apologized to the grimy city of Thao for jumping to conclusions about its nature. 'You said it's hundreds of years old, this place – so it's from the Age of Wonders, like the Serpent's Circle?'

'No,' said Diggelby, smiling so faintly his makeup barely creased around his shiny black lips. 'Thao's old, but not so old as that. This miracle wasn't built by witch queens or bound devils, just simple mortals with two things that seem in short supply these days: beautiful dreams, and the patience to see them through.'

'Huh,' said Sullen, and was about to say something stupid about how maybe after they found Uncle Craven they could stop back through on their way home to the Cobalt camp, but then he remembered that Ji-hyeon would definitely have moved the Company by then, and besides, while there was no telling when that would even be, Old Watchers willing it wouldn't take clear till spring to find the missing bastard. So Sullen didn't say anything, and then Diggelby told Keun-ju and Purna to knock it off, he knew how to get Princess moving, and, sure enough, after squeezing past the pony on the boardwalk he led her down the ramp by enticing her with whatever he kept in his flask. Only once she was down did the pasha let her have a dram, the beast sticking her tongue out for a taste of the dark, oily liquid. It was the queerest thing he'd seen all day, a man sharing a round with a pony . . . but they hadn't met Diggelby's so-called Procuress yet.

Then again, if she was an acquaintance of a puffball like the pasha, how bad could she be?

———

'Fucking fuck fuck . . . fuck you! You fucking fucker! And anyone who stays can get fucked, too!'

This grand finale to Sullen's temper tantrum was said in Crimson, and was thus the only part of the diatribe Purna understood. Having so eloquently made his point, the wild-born barbarian stormed out, slamming the door to the shop so hard a small bird skull fell off one of the curio-cluttered shelves that lined the wall nearest the Procuress. The woman caught it in a black-nailed hand without even looking, which was so fleet Purna exchanged approving nods with Keun-ju. The Immaculate lad was all right, especially compared to the unhinged ox who had just embarrassed them for no reason at all, and who might have just ditched them altogether, it sounded like? Purna certainly wasn't going to walk out now that her curiosity was good and raised, even if the smoky candles that crowded every available surface were burning her eyes.

'I am soooooo sorrrrrrrrry, Vex Ferlune,' Digs said, even his unflappable self caught off guard by Sullen's freaking out before introductions had even been completed. That he addressed their host as *Vex* instead of *Lady* or *Mistress* did not put Purna any more at ease, either, since she'd only ever heard that ancient honorific applied to witch queens in songs about the Age of Wonders. Maybe Sullen had the right idea in cutting out . . . 'I swear, he's never done that before, I sweaaaaaaar. Would it help if I mentioned I have no idea what he was even saying? Obviously it didn't sound nice, and I caught the last of it, but—'

'Do not concern yourself, Pasha,' said the Procuress, displaying the freakishly sharp canines that seemed to have so incensed Sullen. Her eyes went to Purna, no, to the hood she wore pushed back on her shoulders. 'He and I have a history far older than either of us, even if we have never met. Isn't that so, Tapai Purna?'

'Apparently?' Purna wasn't sure what the hell this pale, spooky woman with her long dark hair and black pointy fingernails and way-too-perfectly-tailored black velvet gown-robe-thing was talking about, but she would bet her bottom biscuit that the woman's eyeteeth had become that sharp not by nature but with a file. Purna had spent a lot of time surreptitiously staring at Choi's mouth, and figured she had become something of an expert on dangerous-looking wildborn teeth; these chompers looked too sharp to have grown in like that. 'I barely speak Normal Sullen, and don't know a lick of Mad Sullen, so . . . oh.'

Now that she thought about it, Sullen must've been ranting in Flintlander, some of the clicking sounds he'd made an awful lot like the insults Maroto had reluctantly agreed to teach her – he'd told her any Noreaster tribe worth talking to would know a little Immaculate, but it never hurt to be conversant in cusses. The clans on the Frozen Savannahs would apparently insult you to your face if they thought they could get away with it, and if they thought they could get away with it they'd probably think they could get away with a lot more. There was only one tribe who didn't much use the same Flintland burns as the rest, and since they weren't going to open their mouths to you unless it was to take a bite, there was no point in worrying about picking up the insults of the Gate-worshipping crazies who called themselves—

Then it all came together. Black, sharp fingernails. Yellow, sharp canines. Far, far lighter skin than any other Flintlander she'd ever met, even Ji-hyeon's missing-and-almost-definitely-Gate-gobbled bodyguard Sasamaso – this woman was as fair as Digs's foundation. And there, poking out of the side of the Procuress's waves of black hair, an ear cropped on the side and notched on the top.

'You're a Jackal Person,' breathed Purna, taking a step back through the chaotic shop, afraid in a way she hadn't been even when she'd ridden straight at a rampaging colossus back at the Second Battle of the Lark's Tongue. The stories Maroto had told her about these savages made her think a devil queen would make more civilized company . . .

'I'm no more a Jackal than you are a Horned Wolf,' said Ferlune the Procuress, exposing her black-robed back to Purna as she returned the fallen bird skull to its place on the shelf. An act of deference, that, or a challenge? 'The difference is that I once ran on all fours with my pack, but I think you've always preferred to stand tall on your own two legs. If you'd ever been a real Horned Wolf, even one adopted by the tribe, you would have left with your friend.'

That was something of a relief, maybe? This Procuress was witchy as all get-out, sure, but in a sexy kind of way – sharp fingernails notwithstanding – and Purna really, really, *really* wanted to believe Diggelby's friend wasn't an active member of a tribe so deranged even clans like the Horned Wolves and the Troll Lions who never saw eye to eye on anything could agree they were out of control. Really.

'He's not really our friend, anyway,' said Keun-ju, who apparently knew a thing or twenty about sucking up. 'Our relationship is . . . complicated, but rest assured he speaks only for himself. To second the pasha, please accept our apologies on Sullen's behalf.'

'And to second my own words, Master Keun-ju, do not concern yourself further with the matter,' said Ferlune, turning her tawny eyes back to Diggelby as she spoke. 'I assume this isn't just the usual for you, then, Pasha?'

'No,' said Digs, waaaaaay too quickly, and beneath his cake of creamy makeup Purna caught a glimpse of a rose so rare no merchant nor grower in all of Thao had ever before witnessed its bloom. Now what in all the Arms of the Star and the devils that dwelled there could make Pasha Diggelby *blush*? 'I mean, yes, that too, of course, but today I also seek to put your powers of procuring to the ultimate test.'

'Do tell,' said the woman, ducking through the purple batik curtains that cordoned off the back half of the one-room building. 'And speak up.'

'Normally this is the part where we'd tell her, and then she'd come out with whatever we asked for,' Digs hissed to his pals. *'I have no idea what's going to happen this time.'*

'Would be nice if she just brought out Maroto,' muttered Keun-ju, but it didn't sound like he was holding out a lot of hope. He wandered over to a stack of dusty luggage piled against several rolled-up rugs and began rooting through them. From the way Digs talked about the Procuress, Purna had expected her shop to be something like an upscale mercantile crossed with a posh stinghouse, but this cluttered, ill-lit dump actually reminded her of nothing so much as a junk shop, or the storeroom of one. Well, she was living proof that shabby surroundings didn't mean there weren't treasures aplenty – or something.

'We seek Maroto, known by many names and deeds, a friend of ours, and uncle to Sullen,' announced Purna, though Digs didn't look happy that she'd asked instead of him, and Keun-ju glanced over, not looking happy that she'd implied *he* was chums with their quarry. As if the starry-eyed boy was worthy enough to win the Mighty Maroto's respect. When no answer came from the dark interior beyond the curtain and Digs began making incomprehensible hand gestures, Purna struggled to think of what else to add — they'd all agreed that not mentioning Hoartrap's tools was the surest way of testing both the prowess of the Procuress and the efficacy of the compass. After all, if the Touch's methods provided the same intelligence sight unseen as those of the Procuress, they knew where to find Maroto. And if they pointed them in different directions, well, fucksticks. Clearing her throat, Purna expounded a little, though if this Jackal Lady was as adept at devilish tricks as Digs had promised she shouldn't have had to so much as voice her need for the woman to provide. 'Maroto's gone missing, and we are unsure where to seek him — we don't expect you to magically yank him out of a chamberpot or whatever, but if you could point us in the right direction we'd be in your debt.'

'That's more like,' said the Procuress, emerging back through the curtains with a tray entirely woven of black-stemmed snow roses, their white petals drifting to her bare white feet. Steam rose from a statue or artifact nestled among the thorns. 'And you were in my debt from the moment you walked in that door. I am disappointed that your ultimate test was nothing of the sort, Pasha, but hardly surprised. I'll bring you what you need to find your friend, but first there are certain customs worth preserving.'

As the Procuress maneuvered out from around the counter in the back of the shop, Purna saw the curious steaming object was nothing more than a cast-iron teapot in the shape of a seabeast, and circling it on the tray of flowers were five black porcelain cups, a plain bronze snuffbox, and a small dish containing a pair of Immaculate sesame buns. Digs and Purna gave the Procuress space as she maneuvered past them into the center of the candlelit room, which was the only open area among the shelves and unstable-looking stacks, and then she slowly lowered the service to the bare planks of the floor. It was neither drafty nor damp in the windowless shop despite the lack of hearth, and hungrily eyeing the Jackal's haunch through her sheer robe as the woman set down her tray, Purna removed her hooded cloak and magnanimously spread it on the floor for them to share. The ploy didn't work, Ferlune moving to the far side of the service to pour their tea, but before Purna could feel too disappointed her devilish tongue positively burst out of her mouth of its own accord, hungrily licking her lips. She would've been ashamed at the reflex, but its cause moved her so deeply and unexpectedly that she didn't initially notice she'd drooled all over her own sweater. That tea ... Ferlune smiled as she raised the cup but not her eyes to Purna, and she had to wonder if the woman had kept her gaze low to spare her guest the embarrassment of suddenly finding tears rolling down her cheeks.

Accepting the cup in shaking hands, Purna took a sip to confirm what her nose already knew – this wasn't just spiced Ugrakari tea thickened with yak butter; it was utterly indistinguishable from the gingery brew her aunt and uncle used to make. She hadn't tasted it in so long, and, she realized, had never tasted it at all with her canine tongue. She was experiencing the impossible but impossible-not-to-crave dream of every intelligent tea drinker, to once again taste the greatest beverage known to mortals for the very first time. She choked back a joyful sob as the hot-but-not-too-hot chai passed over her delighted new tongue ... and then choked for real, coughing on the tea and getting it all over herself.

Finally distracted from the uncanny experience, Purna looked up at her friends. Keun-ju's eyes were locked tight as his lips, a rapturous expression on his bulging face, and glancing at the empty plate on the tray she realized he must have jammed both of the buns in his mouth at the same time. Digs was too fast for her, though, the pasha making a show of rubbing his mustache in a poor attempt to conceal his chewing whatever wee morsel he'd just popped in there, his eyes everywhere but on her or the open, empty snuffbox. Curious though she was, nosiness was no substitute for her family's tea and, taking another sip, she shuddered. It was official. Purna was marrying this lovely Jackal witch and never, ever leaving this room.

Keun-ju gulped like a funnel python swallowing conjoined twins, and once the buns were in his belly, spoke in a rightly awed voice. 'What debt do we owe you, Vex Ferlune, for this . . . thoughtful repast, and your aid in locating Captain Maroto?'

'Nothing you cannot afford, and who knows, before you leave my company you may think of something else you want,' said the Procuress, and while the teacup still felt as warm as home in her hand, there was something about the hungry smile of her host and the coldness of her yellow eyes that made Purna decide that settling down as the bride of a witch might not be such a great idea, after all . . .

———

They had been inside too long. Way, *way* too long to be shut up in a windowless house on a deserted street in an enemy city with the sun almost down. Princess didn't like it, either, though she was too polite to voice her reservations. Sullen paced back and forth in front of the post he'd removed her to, way, *way* down at the end of the block, watching the shop's only door like a lean wolf camped outside a rabbit warren. A wolf that was half-afraid a snow lion was going to explode out of the hole instead of an easy supper.

He stopped, stared, and started up again, this time walking back down the row of dark, silent houses that he was beginning to think were all abandoned, and not just the boarded-up ones. It was either stop mucking about and see what was what or start sharing his concerns with Princess, and the others gave him a hard enough time without his picking up a cute habit like talking to their pony. He stopped in front of the mundane stoop, the place so nondescript he had to double-check the dung at his feet for his own tracks. This was definitely it, all right, but it was dead quiet inside. What a great big fucking plop of a day.

He had spoken in anger, and he had been wrong. He never should have lumped his companions in with that fucking Jackal Person just because they didn't know any better than to shun her on sight, and he never, ever should have left them alone with one of her kind. He wouldn't leave Hoartrap alone with a Jackal Person, or even Uncle Craven. Well, maybe Uncle Craven ... but no, damn it, some things were too devil-loved dire not to take more seriously. What kind of a Horned Wolf was he, anyway, to bark like that at a Jackal Person and then turn tail instead of throwing down?

Not a Horned Wolf at all. His people had known that he wasn't clan material long before he had, and it was truer now than ever, hard as it was for him to remember, sometimes. Not a Horned Wolf, just plain Sullen, an exile of his own making come down from Flintland to look for his family and ...

And that's when his wits finally caught up with him. If Sullen had been any slower he would've clapped himself on the head. There was no such thing as a lone Horned Wolf, but there wasn't any such thing as a lone Jackal, either. To grow up on the Frozen Savannahs is to know the Jackal People were the most territorial and insular of all the tribes, more than the Horned Wolves, hells, even more than the Troll Lions, and everybody knew those moon-touched fuckers were one long winter away from losing their collective shit once and for all. Sullen had learned the ins and outs of the Jackal People with the intimacy reserved for one's most hated enemy, ever since that stark morning on the permafrost where his fate had been decided by three blades: the one that took his grandfather's legs, the one that took his father altogether, and the one that Sullen used to kill his first Jackal.

And knowing these monsters who took the shape of mortals nearly as well as he knew his own tribe, he could not fucking *believe* one of them had not only left her tribe and traveled to the Empire, but had set up business in Thao as a . . . as a . . . as a *shopkeep*. He would have been less surprised to see his own damn mom tending the store – what the living shit was happening here? He'd gotten so worked up at the unexpected sight of a Jackal Person that he hadn't taken the time to ask himself just what she could possibly be doing here, and instead had just acted like an angry beast and then fled into the streets while she implacably took his abuse and let him go.

She must be an exile, same as him, another traitor to her tribe . . . or a sensible person who wised up, depending on who you asked. And while it was evident from her lack of anger at his appearance that she'd left the fruitless, inherited hatreds back on the Savannahs, he'd carried his along on his back all the many leagues since he'd left home, spoiling for a fight with a stranger who'd done him no harm at all, and who one of his companions had vouched for, to boot. So much for Horned Wolves being less savage than their enemies. The only question now was whether to knock before he went inside.

He didn't have to decide, because the thin cedar door creaked open and Diggelby almost fell backward down the stone stoop. Sullen hurried to help him, the fop carrying the end of a planed, intricately carved log of white tamarind wood. The thing was as long as Diggelby was tall and as wide around as Sullen's thigh, Purna and Keun-ju holding up the back end of it. As soon as Sullen cupped his hand under the rounded point of the thing, Diggelby danced away from it, shaking out his hands and letting Sullen take the full weight of it – and as soon as he did, Sullen felt a pressure tugging the whole damn log to the left, as though it were alive and trying to get away from him. The sensation surprised him so much he almost dropped it, but then found with a little effort that he could hold the thing steady despite whatever force pulled its tip to one side.

'What the devils is this?' he asked Diggelby, as Keun-ju and Purna argued over how best to get the log out the door with all their fingers intact while it squirmed in their hands.

'It's exactly what we came here for,' said the pasha with obvious relish. 'The key to finding your uncle. It's going to take us right to him!'

'Yeah?' Sullen looked down at the design carved into the flowing grain of the wood, then averted his eyes with a shiver. Gawping at things he was better off not having seen in the first place was another old habit it was apparently hard to kick. The figurals that ran down the length of the post were unmistakably those of the Jackal People; they would scratch these jagged shapes into the bark of giant baobab nuts and mount them on whalebones to mark the borders of their hunting grounds. Sullen had been reluctant to rely on the arcane devices of a known devil-eater, and so in their wisdom the Old Watchers had done him one worse – could he really trust the wiles of a Jackal shaman any more than those of Hoartrap? Could he afford not to, at this point? 'Guess I better go in and apologize, if she's helping us out.'

'She made it pretty clear . . . that wasn't necessary,' grunted Purna, finally just muscling Keun-ju out of the way and bringing out the rest of the post by herself, Sullen walking backward with its other end as she stepped down to the soft street.

'But she did say if you wanted her help with anything, to get your buns in there and she'd be happy to assist,' said Diggelby.

'She didn't put it exactly like that,' said Keun-ju, following Purna out with a rectangular walnut case tucked under one arm. He definitely hadn't been carrying that when he'd gone inside. 'But if you intend to go, I suggest you make haste. Diggelby says most of the bathhouses get busier the later the hour.'

'You know . . . Maybe I will.' Sullen figured for a witch who could spontaneously produce a magic post that supposedly knew where to find his missing uncle, procuring a few answers for a confused and conflicted barbarian couldn't be too tough. 'She can help with just about anything, huh?'

'For a price,' said Purna, and from the dark look the girl gave him Sullen guessed she was talking about something other than coin. That was fine, though, since he'd never fully taken to the Outlander practice of dealing in pieces of metal and rock instead of goods or deeds, and it would be a nice change of pace to engage in some good old-fashioned Flintland bartering with someone who presumably shared some small smidgen of his philosophy. Even if they couldn't work something out, the least he could do was apologize for bringing old drama into her new life, hear out the woman's terms, and then make a decision. Sullen dumped the end of the post off on Diggelby, who kept switching it from hand to hand in an attempt to find the best way of carrying the long, heavy log that didn't involve holding it with both arms. Eventually he followed Purna's example and hoisted it up onto one shoulder as Keun-ju headed down the road toward Princess, holding his rectangular wooden box in both hands and looking more closely at its brass-clasped surface than he was at where he was walking.

Sullen stepped into the dark entrance of the shop, the faint scents of buttery tea and candle-smoke from the doorway now overpowered by something else entirely. Flickering light played behind the curtain that divided her shop from the rest of the one-room building, a few rays spilling out from the gap to guide his path through the clutter ... and wafting along the path of the candlelight came familiar, tantalizing aromas. Pepper fish soup. Plantain and puffin pottage. Yams frying in seal fat.

Even after the way he'd treated her, this stranger had not only told Digs she was still willing to help Sullen out, but was cooking them up a proper Flintland feast in the bargain. He took a hesitant step into the dim shop, considering how to phrase his request – he really didn't want to screw this up.

After endless doubt and waffling about the role he might play in the plots of the Faceless Mistress and Cold Zosia, here at last he had someone who claimed to be able to provide him anything. For a man who hadn't gotten a good night's sleep ever since he'd met a dark and angry god and then her mortal enemy, a nudge in the right direction sounded like a prize more precious than any artifact or treasure ... assuming the Procuress could deliver. She might be able to produce any sort of item, but could she give him something as enigmatic and ephemeral as a straight answer or two about what a mortal should do in the face of divine orders and moral uncertainty?

And what would he do with any information she gave him, anyway? Take it as the solution to all his problems, trust that a Jackal shaman knew his fate better than he did himself? Bad enough he was going to use a charm ensorcelled by one of the people who had killed his dad and crippled Grandfather to track down Uncle Craven, did he really need to further involve himself with her deviltry? She might no longer be a real Jackal Person and he definitely was no longer a real Horned Wolf, but hanging right there on the exposed beam above the curtains was an iron jackal mask the likes of which he hadn't seen since the last time he went to war with a tribe of deranged fucks who worshipped the Flintland Gate as a ravenous god.

He closed his eyes and huffed the strong smells of his mother's stewpot, then let them go, the way he had let everything else from his past go, save Uncle Craven. And once he found the coward and settled the score with him one way or another, he'd think no more of the Frozen Savannahs, but turn instead to the future only he could make for himself. No sorcerer nor talisman could steer him truer than he could guide himself, and once he finished up with Craven he would go straight to Cold Zosia and confront her once and for all. You can't ever really know what you need to do until you're ready to do it.

Of course, there'd be no harm in eating with the Jackal, in tasting the sweet yams and crispy plantains, the spicy broth and thick, salty rinds of fat ... no harm, but no time, either, for a man with burdens to shoulder and places to take them. He turned away and stepped back down to the dirty street, and, studiously averting his gaze from the silhouette he saw approach the curtain, he closed the door of cedar behind him. But gently.

CHAPTER

11

Ji-hyeon felt naked, strolling through the camp with neither steel nor hair to shield her puffy face. The busted-up helm hung by its canine jaws from the remaining fingers of her left hand, and she casually swung the heavy piece of armor as she walked. The wounded flesh and cracked bones had mostly healed from Fellwing's ministrations, but the appendage still felt weak enough that such exercises seemed prudent. The last she had seen of her blue locks the owlbat had been making a nest out of them amongst the tops of the tent poles, and with her free hand she scratched the short, ashen shag that remained. It probably looked terrible, but she had sent away the one man she would've trusted to give her a decent haircut, if not for much else at present.

Just the thought of Keun-ju made her queasy, and she looked back over her shoulder at the rolling white hills beyond the camp where he and Sullen had disappeared. She wished she didn't miss him, wished one part of her didn't begrudge the other for having banished him so soon after he unexpectedly returned to her. But when Choi had asked her permission to accompany Sullen, Purna, and Diggelby in pursuit of Maroto, it had struck Ji-hyeon as too perfect an opportunity to miss – Keun-ju kept swearing up and down how he'd do anything to atone for betraying them to her first father back on Hwabun, and here was a punishment she could sink her teeth into. She wasn't about to let him off the hook just because he'd saved her from a swarm of opossum monsters, obviously, and assisting Sullen seemed far more fitting than any test of his loyalty she could have devised around the camp. When Ji-hyeon had explained the situation to Choi and asked her to stay so as not to lose all her best friends and advisors at once, the wildborn had agreed, though when she congratulated Ji-hyeon on her sly tactics it had sounded a little forced. Not that her decision to send Keun-ju in Choi's stead was born from malice, of course, and she was far more concerned that both men came back alive than she was about their finding the treacherous old Villain, but all that withstanding, she was proud of herself for coming up with such an elegant solution.

Assuming it worked out, but even if not, she had at least removed the two biggest distractions from her daily running of the Cobalt Company, and maybe by the time they returned she would have sorted out all the tangles in her heart. She kept touching her hair, knowing that Keun-ju would be scandalized by the decision, but thinking Sullen might like it . . .

The sartorial choice had been the first thing to set her second father off that morning; even after all their many deceptions and duplicity, he still couldn't believe she'd cut off all her hair. He hadn't been there during the First Battle of the Lark's Tongue to watch her get yanked to the ground by her stupidly long tresses, nor seen a handful of it torn out when it became tangled in the teeth of a mutated monster. She had always cut a cool figure in the full outfit, no doubt, wild blue hair blowing out the back of her devil dog helm, chainmail two-piece shining, but Zosia had been dead right about trading the metal lingerie out for real armor, and it was high time Ji-hyeon did away with the rest of her shallow trappings – long hair on a battlefield was almost as bad as a helmet with narrow visibility.

'General,' Ulver greeted her as she stepped under the dripping eave of his warm works, the wildborn smith not rising from the stool upon which he balanced his enormous posterior. His lunch was set out on the anvil before him, a ploughman's of dried apricots, brown bread, and a mite-riddled rind of hard orange cheese all softening up in a pan of water. Then his black eyes found the steel helm in her hand and he rose to his full height, the craftsmanship apparently worthy of more respect than the woman who wore it into battle. 'Yeah, that ain't bad a'tall. Why you want to mess up a good piece like that?'

'I need something more practical,' she said, her heart feeling as heavy as the helm she laid on his crowded table. 'Like I told you, in the Immaculate style.'

'No visor?' Ulver sounded skeptical as he ran a grimy fingernail down the snout of her old helm.

'You try engaging a skilled opponent with a metal basket over your head,' she told him, poking through the rings and ingots cluttering the table. 'How's the blade coming?'

'Slowly. Alloy's made and hammered, but there's a lot of folding needs doing. And I didn't use it all – some of the steel I made out of the old man is left over, too, if you want me to put him in the helm.'

'Absolutely not,' said Ji-hyeon, imagining Ruthless's ghost whispering at her every time she donned her armor. Not that she believed in ghosts, of course, but this whole practice of putting a dead man's charred remains into weaponry was already intensely creepy, if also admittedly fleet. 'Is there enough to forge a spear blade? One like the Flintlanders use, broadheaded. For fighting, not throwing.'

'Hmmm,' said the smith, sucking thoughtfully on one of the fleshy fronds that drooped down over his lips. 'Yeah. Trace it on a hide like we done for the sword. Also got this back from the lass I told you about.'

Moving down to the end of the long plank table that separated his workspace from the front of the open-ended tent, he picked up a short, leather-bound rectangle with two brass rings protruding from its side. Ulver had farmed out this component to another artisan, arguing he was no good at mundane ornamentation, let alone something this specific, but he had helped her design it. Slipping her fingers through the rings, Ji-hyeon swiped her hand through the forge-muggy air, trying to feel the phantom weight of the sword at the end of the grip. It would definitely take some getting used to, even with the adjustments Ulver had made to the weight and design of the blade, but when the smith was done Ji-hyeon would have twin swords again, though they'd no longer be identical. When Sullen and Keun-ju had pitched the plan to the smith, they hadn't been taking into account her missing fingers.

'Can you fix this to something dull? I'd like to start practicing,' Ji-hyeon asked, clumsily removing the knuckle-duster-inspired grip from her hand.

'Oh sure, got all the time on the Star for you, General,' said Ulver, looking with unmistakable intention at his neglected lunch. 'What say I have my girl run it to your tent first thing anon?'

'That'll be fine,' said Ji-hyeon with a smile. 'I wasn't planning on beating anyone's ass before then anyway.'

'Yeah, well, I'll try to get to it sooner,' said Ulver as he returned to his meal. 'Plans have a way of changing on us, don't they?'

'That they do,' said Ji-hyeon, looking down at the old helm

that had saved her life almost as many times as it had endangered it, at the customized grip that would soon be stitched and welded around the tang of a sword forged from the ashes of Sullen's grandfather, and at the fresh scars where her two little fingers ought to be. 'That they do.'

One thing Zosia never felt good about was a double cross, even when it had to happen, even when the victim had it coming five times over . . . and Kang-ho had it coming fifty times over, if he had it once. She glanced down at her dog as he led them through the camp, his tail wagging as though he didn't have a care in the world, and not for the first time she envied his lack of concern. Or lack of scruples, as the case may be. Funny to think this time last year she was ready to kill him herself, and now felt warm with relief to see his decrepitude fall away like a winter coat shed in the spring, his bare and blistered hide glazed over with new skin and fur. Maybe a little creepy for those who didn't know devils and how they relied on battlefields, brothels, and anywhere else where mortal blood ran hottest to feed on whatever intangible substance nourished them, but to Zosia it was a sign that they still had an honest chance; if he had some fight left in him, then so did she.

If this wasn't all some grand trap of Choplicker's. If trusting the old fiend wasn't the single greatest mistake she'd ever made. If a thousand different variables all fell smoothly into place, one after the other, instead of slipping out of joint. If hatred and revenge were enough to carry the day this time, when all it had gotten her so far was a busted-up face, a busted-up devil, and a few more corpses under her belt.

'Level with me, Chop,' she said as he led her higher and higher through the snowmelt-flooded camp, 'this is a fool's hope that's going to get a lot of folk dead, isn't it?'

Choplicker looked back and barked, lips curling up over his teeth in an all-too-human smile, and then resumed snuffling his trail through the slush.

'Knew there was a reason you seemed so eager to help,' Zosia grunted, slipping on the icy earth. That she and her devil were finally seeing eye to eye did not portend well for the Star's prospects. But then they'd always been cut from the same cloth, albeit with one side in this world and the other in his – they were good at one thing, she and Choplicker, and as with any skill, the key was figuring out the most satisfying application.

In her youth, she'd done things that not even a devil would be proud of, but later, when she'd spent years starving along with her followers, risking her life every single day, there had been a furnace in her belly, a fire desperate to escape its vessel and burn the whole corrupt Empire to ashes. That furnace, long banked, had roared back to life the day Efrain Hjortt took Leib and all the rest from her . . . but even the highest, hottest flames die out, if they're not fed, and her long quest for vengeance had been one damp disappointment after another. Sitting in the Cobalt stockade that miserable night after she'd become the monster they always said she was, the last feeble coal inside her had begun to fade, only to have Singh arrive and blow a little on the embers, kindling it with her kindness. Then the piece of shit prison guards had tried to kill her but all they'd done was stir up the firepot, and when Choplicker gave her the broken crown the flames really began to dance, though it had been so long since she'd properly stoked it that she didn't even know what fuel it needed.

She found out when she laid into those monsters and their mother down by the Gate. It was as if she'd applied a gallon of blubber oil and a tornado's worth of air to the mix, the pleasure of utterly obliterating a foe combined with the certainty that doing so was for the well-being of all living things. This was the passion she had burned with when she set out to save the Star a quarter century past, the knowledge that she may be as cold and deadly as any devil, but if she applied herself she could put those qualities to a greater good. And now, nearly a fortnight out from its reawakening, that bonfire was raging fiercer than ever; it was hard not to imagine the dripping, ice-locked camp thawing from her presence alone as she strode toward one of the means to her end.

At last Choplicker stopped in front of a partially buried tent, a stained flap of canvas sticking out of a snowbank. There was a fissure in the dirty snow, with a ball of ice covering the knot that held the tent shut. Looking around and making sure no soldiers were loitering about this shade-chilled corner of camp, Zosia cleared her throat and called into the dark interior.

'Out with you, then, I know you're in there.'

Silence. Choplicker whined at the entrance, looking up at her with limpid eyes. You'd think she'd starved the poor dear.

'Last chance, friend, and then I send my devil in to fetch you.'

That did it.

'All right, all right, you rumbled me,' the man called from just inside the flap, and then a dagger flipped out of the darkness and sawed through the frozen twine holding the tent closed. As soon as the tie snapped, half of the snowbank collapsed inside the tent, to the loud cursing of its occupant. He picked his way out into the open, the drift up to his knees, scowling at Zosia with bloodshot eyes and dangling the naked blade from one rag-wrapped hand. The foul steam rising in his wake confirmed he hadn't left the shelter for days, but from the tidy pack on his back it seemed Zosia had found him just in time. 'So that's that, is it? Your style to let me stew long enough to get my hopes up, then come and dash 'em?'

'Your name's Boris?' Zosia asked, stepping back from the overripe fugitive. 'Or is that just what you told the sentries when you and the war nun rode into camp?'

'You can call me Heretic,' said the gaunt youth, licking a cracked and bloody lip as Choplicker nosed his groin. She had hardly thought it possible, but he looked even worse now than he had when she'd found him burying Portolés before the battle. 'Don't suppose you'll call your devil off 'fore I piss myself?'

'Come on, Chop,' Zosia said obligingly, swatting the devil's rump. 'Can't you see the nice boy's happy to help even without your encouragement?'

'So very happy,' Heretic agreed, still holding his dagger with the despondent air of one unsure whether he wants to cut his own throat or that of his enemy. Choplicker obliged with a final snuffle, then passed by the youth to root around for treats in his soiled tent.

'It's good to see you again,' said Zosia. 'I was worried you'd be long gone by now.'

'Yeah, well, I was,' said Heretic, finally sheathing the dagger. 'But I came back, didn't I?'

'To help the cause?'

'To buy a few more days from death, I reckon,' said the young man, wiping snot on a frost-stiff sleeve. 'Snow started, and when it didn't stop I knew I'd be finished if I didn't get someplace warm. So I come back here, though I almost couldn't find it in the dark. Another miracle, me finding my way back. And another example miracles don't exist 'cept to remind us how doomed we really are, you busting me just as I was fixing to flee the camp again.'

'You do strike me as the sort of creature slippery enough to glide past sentries whether you're coming or going,' said Zosia.

'Oh, I'm a greasy creeper, no doubt,' said Heretic, scratching a wrist that bore the faint scars of manacles. 'I get something to eat before the worms do? They'll probably prefer me with something in my bowels, and you're all about seeing the poor don't go hungry, yeah?'

'Listen, friend, I'm going to tell you something I've not told many people,' said Zosia, looking the grey and grubby man right in the bright pink eyes. 'That morning we met, while you were burying Portolés – you were right about me.'

'I was?' Heretic didn't sound pleased about the possibility.

'You were. I talked a big game in my time, and I didn't follow through on all my promises. Didn't follow through on most of 'em.' So far so good, nothing she hadn't told herself over a thousand sleepless nights, but the last took real effort. '. . . And you're also right that I shouldn't have attacked the wildborn nun as soon as I saw her in the general's tent. You're right that I should have heard her out before passing judgment. It was a mistake, and because of that mistake she's dead. She must have worked hard to come all the way here, and so she deserved better than I gave her. I'm sorry.'

At least Heretic had the decency to look surprised at the proclamation, and Choplicker must really be trying to stay on her good side, because instead of chuffing or ironically howling the devil squirmed out of the partially collapsed tent and licked her hand.

'So you came here . . . to apologize?' Heretic didn't sound convinced.

'Sure,' said Zosia, but it wouldn't do to give an innocent man false hope, so she hastened to get the rest out there. 'To apologize, and to ask for your help. Something's happened, something that bodes extremely fucking ill for all the people of the Star, regardless of their allegiances. Your little speech of the other morn convinced me that you're a principled fellow, someone keen to stand up for the greater good.'

'Lady, you got the wrong heretic,' he said with a laugh so fake it offended Zosia's ears. 'I'm just a squirrel trying to get a nut.'

'Bullshit,' said Zosia. 'You believed once, Heretic, and I think you'd like to believe again. I'm your miracle, the Stricken Queen returned, and I'm ready to listen to what you have to say. I'm ready to work with you to fix Diadem, to fix the Empire, but to do that first we have to get rid of the common enemy, the one force in this world that's worse than any devil, because they're mortal and still aim to drag us back down into the First Dark: the Burnished Chain. And you can help me with that, can't you?'

'Well . . . ' Heretic looked past Zosia, out at the blue sky and the white valley and the Cobalt tents just beginning to poke out of the snow like early crocuses. 'Would that I could, Yer Majesty, but I'd not be much use to you, I fear. What can I offer that your army can't, or your devil?'

'Diadem,' said Zosia. 'That's your home, isn't it? The place you were born, the place you know better than any other? The place where you might have some friends who share your sympathies, people who might be willing to help the Cobalts recapture the Jewel of Samoth?'

'Well hell,' said Heretic, looking back at Zosia with new eyes, or at least more interested ones. 'That's not the sort of thing I expected to hear from you, granted. But why should I? 'Cause you'll kill me if I don't?'

'Because you know as bad a mess as we might make of it, it can't be worse than letting the Black Pope steer Diadem and the rest of the Crimson Empire straight into a hell of the Chain's own making,' said Zosia. 'What do you say, Heretic? Will you help me return to Diadem?'

'Huh,' said Heretic, smiling a faint, scared little smile, as though he knew he really oughtn't but couldn't help himself. 'All right, Yer Majesty, I'll help. But only because they'd never believe me if I came home without proof I'd met the Cobalt Queen.'

'I'll do my best to live up to the songs,' said Zosia, offering her hand, and he took it with a cold and sweaty rag-draped hand. 'At your service, Heretic.'

'And yours, I'm sure,' said Heretic. 'I do got one condition, though.'

'One you held back until after I shook,' Zosia noted. 'But you'll find I'm an agreeable woman, when asked nicely, so what's your request?'

'You help me get Portolés down to the Gate what opened up in the valley.' He wasn't meeting her eye anymore. 'She told me once, 'bout what they did to her when she was a girl. Those Chain sawbones cut . . . cut bits off her, and then made her and all their other new pets march down to Diadem Gate and throw their own scraps into it. Imagine doing that to anyone? Imagine doing that to a kid, just 'cause they got funny ears or fingers or something? That's why I'll help you, not 'cause of what you're saying, not 'cause I trust you, but 'cause it has to stop. So the first thing we do is take the sister down to the Gate, reunite her with what they took from her as a girl.'

'That sounds real nice,' Zosia said, deciding after a moment's thought not to mention that his sentimental gesture hardly seemed heretical. It was the little efforts to play nice that added up to being a better person, or at least the start of one. 'But the ground's frozen solid; at this point there's no way you're getting her out of her grave until spring.'

'Um, actually, she's already out ...' Heretic sheepishly looked back inside the collapsed tent.

'You mean ...' Zosia wrinkled her nose, having thought Heretic was surprisingly fragrant for but one man in a cold tent.

'Yeah, it took me the week and a few stolen tools what kept breaking, but I finally got her loose just before dawn.' Heretic held up his raggedy hands. 'Think I might have some frostbite under the blisters.'

'Ah,' said Zosia, sort of touched by his devotion, but only sort of. 'I see.'

'I stole a sledge, too, was gonna drag her down there tonight when the coast was clear, then split out, but you being Cobalt Zosia and all I guess we can just take her now, huh?'

'First we'll clear it with our general, but I don't think she'll have a problem with it,' said Zosia, knowing the more meaningless respectful gestures she offered Ji-hyeon the better. 'Then we'll take her home, Heretic, you've got my word.'

'I'm glad to hear it. And I changed my mind. Call me Boris.'

It felt good, knowing she'd inspired this man to believe in something again, but before she could congratulate herself too much he added, 'Don't sound right, coming out anyone's mouth but hers. You've got some big boots to fill, Yer Majesty, I'll tell you that right now. Portolés may have been a nutter, but she gave me a fair shake. I hope you prove yourself as well as she did.'

The flames flared up in Zosia at that; prove herself to this runt? Prove herself *as good as the war nun who had led the slaughter at Kypck*? Before she could do yet another thing that she might regret, Zosia closed her eyes and took a deep breath and forced herself to remember why she was here, and what she was doing. And besides, the smart-mouth had a point – if she couldn't comport herself better than Portolés had, she didn't have much right to claim the moral high ground.

Not that a lack of such terrain had ever stalled her in the past; it didn't much matter where you planted your feet, so long as you were still standing after the battle.

'Come on then, Boris, I don't think the war nun's in a big hurry so let's get you fed and washed before we do anything else. One has to look presentable before being taken before the general, and I want her to officially pardon you before we get started.'

'Pardon?' Boris licked his nasty lips again. 'You think she's liable to do that, after I brought Portolés here?'

'I don't think we'll have a problem with Ji-hyeon,' said Zosia with a grin. 'If she pardoned me, she'll pardon anybody.'

—

Nobody spoke as Ji-hyeon desperately scanned the small letter, parsing the High Immaculate with some difficulty – she had never excelled at the tongue. Nor had her second father, apparently, which made the translation even more arduous. Once she was positive it did indeed say what she had hoped it would, she put it down with a sigh and looked around at Fennec and Choi, at Singh and Zosia. She couldn't stop grinning, and her voice even cracked a little as she told them the news.

'He's warning me of your betrayal, Zosia.'

'Or he's declining the bait in favor of a better opportunity,' said Fennec, reminding Ji-hyeon just how infuriatingly cynical he could be. Cynical and realistic are often bedfellows, he would argue, but it scarcely mattered, because for the first time in a very long time her second father hadn't completely failed her. It was a small thing, his not trying to collaborate with his old friends to sell her to Empress Ryuki, but if only for a moment it made her feel as warm and safe as she had as a girl back on Hwabun, when a typhoon battered the Isles but she and her family took shelter in the cave at the heart of the island, sitting together around crackling fires in the ancient hearth. Such warmth was fleeting here in the snowbound camp with the Thaoan regiment trapping them just as the storms had surrounded Hwabun, but with no hope that the threat would eventually move past them on southerly winds, leaving the horizon clear. Ji-hyeon savored it while it lasted.

CHAPTER

12

Maroto hadn't got a good look at the thing that was chasing him through the dark jungle, and he preferred it that way. The mango-sized eggs he and Bang had stolen from a nest in the sea-caves had been way too weird-looking for him to want any glimpse of their parents. While the small party was initially pleased with the haul, they had suspected supper was off as soon as they'd heard the echoing shrieks from the direction of the cliffs, and drawn straws accordingly. Once the inevitable fix was in, Bang, Dong-won, and Niki-hyun took to the upper branches of the banyan tree with spears, Maroto waiting with a torch by the sizzling frying pan Dong-won had fashioned out of a washed-up greave. He knew the smell of cooking eggs would lure the vengeful creature in, whereupon they could overwhelm it with their numbers . . . but then he promptly turned and fled when he saw its silvery carapace careening out of the jungle at him. No way a pointed stick was getting past that shell, and Maroto had been disinclined to see if one quick jab of a borrowed dagger would've done the trick. And so here he was, half sliding and half falling down the sheer slope, sling-bag bouncing in his face, nooses of vines trying to catch his throat, snares of roots grabbing at his feet, fallen trees out to bash his knees, wet leaves doing their damnedest to extinguish his torch, and an insectoid fiend crashing through the trees after him.

Which was to say, the Mighty Maroto was back in his element. His Gate-scarred knee was feeling more and more normal every day, but wasn't all the way there yet, and nearly buckled as he dropped the last few feet down the slope. But then he hit the straightaway through the underbrush and it was back on the job, propelling him through the final push. The enraged egg-layer was almost on top of him, bringing with it the fishy stench of its stagnant cave, and since it had ceased its shrill screaming as it closed in on its quarry, Maroto started shouting in its stead. Fast as he was moving, the torch was actually an impediment, preventing his eyes from adjusting to the night and only illuminating trees and other arboreal obstacles when it was too late for him to fully avoid them, but he clung to it all the same, hoping he'd aimed true . . .

The sea foam cresting the waves glowed in the moonlight as Maroto blasted out from the jungle, weaving between the palms as he raced for the shimmering black beach. One of the trees splintered behind him, and Maroto stumbled as slippery undergrowth and muddy earth gave way to loose sand. It was dodgy as all devils for a few frantic seconds, and then he reached the firmer sand at the shoreline, strafing to the side and running parallel to the water. Waving the torch over his head and howling in a manner fit to wake any and all sea gods, Maroto tore arse along the moonlit beach, racing the shadow he threw out onto the waves . . . and seeing a far larger, pointier shadow come up behind it, the monster almost upon him.

Still waving the torch but barely able to draw air into his burning lungs, say fuck-all of expelling it at volume, he wrestled the bouncing sling-bag back to his chest. He couldn't get it open, the obstinate satchel staying upright and shut like it was supposed to, and with the bright sky offering no salvation he knew it was all over, another brilliant scheme gone the way of the Sunken Isle. Except you couldn't really say that anymore, because Jex Toth was back and badder than ever, and as he felt the icy spray of the creature's breath on his back he upended the tangled bag. Success!

Except the cargo had broken during the chase, and instead of three round eggs rolling out for the monstrous parent to stop and retrieve, a rich, runny yolk poured out all over his pumping thighs, scraps of shell sticking to his leg. It would have been a hilarious turn of events if it had been Hoartrap or Zosia out here instead of Maroto, but it wasn't, and so it wasn't. Before his dread-stunned brain could concoct a backup plan, something that felt remarkably like a tavern bench covered in scratchy spider hair clobbered his legs out from under him. Maroto ate wet sand.

It rolled him over with distressing delicacy, and in the fading light of the torch that had landed on the beach a few paces away he saw far more of the angry mother than he had ever wanted; that his plan had failed and he was about to be eaten alive was bad enough, but being forced to watch the meal take place seemed a bit much. Yet he couldn't look away, his damnably curious eyes refusing to stop taking in the monster that towered over him, its mandibles tugging at the soggy satchel on his chest.

Except they weren't mandibles, but silver-furred hands that were all the more repellent for their similarity to a human's. Had those long arms been the only concession to humanity it would have been bad enough, but they protruded from the sides of an enormous, pale face of disturbing normalcy. If that face had been half as big it would have looked perfectly fine attached to a human neck, but between the scale of the features and their placement in the torso of a gigantic chitinous horror, the effect was nauseating.

As was the smell, the creature's enormous mouth panting its marine stench in Maroto's face as it gingerly opened the slimy sling-bag that lay limply on his chest, the man beneath it seemingly forgotten. Fat globs of grey ooze ran down its plump cheeks as its teary eyes inspected the satchel, but even if the bag hadn't been tied around his shoulder there was no way Maroto could have escaped – the creature loomed over him, its four thick, crab-like legs trapping him beneath it.

The torch sputtered and sizzled just like the monster's eggs in the frying pan as the damp sand slowly extinguished the brand, and then the weeping horror's soft black eyes grew wide, and it let out a soft hoot. Maroto was witness to a miracle, one of the horror's hands tenderly rising from the satchel, a bright blue crab resting in its palm. The small crustacean slowly raised a goo-dripping claw, and Maroto realized that not all of the eggs had busted open from jostling around during his flight; this one must have hatched as nature intended. He also recognized the luminous blue of the newborn's shell from the crabs they had eaten his first night here on the beach, and as the thing's giant, loving eyes rose from its innocent progeny to the egg thief she had pinned between her spidery limbs, Maroto supposed he kind of had this coming.

Still, deserving a fate and welcoming it are two entirely different devils, and Maroto tensed up to make his move. Before he could even figure out what exactly this move was going to be, however, the monster's heavy underside flopped down upon him, the all-too-believable weight of the thing crushing his legs and midsection, its mandible-arms shooting out and seizing his elbows. The infant crab scuttled up one of the hairy arms and disappeared into a fold of its carapace, and the huge face slowly came down to meet his, as if her tumescent lips fancied a smooch. She smiled, and he saw that the human resemblance ended at the teeth, her needle-toothed grin falling into shadow as the torch died, and his hope died along with it. As he locked his eyes shut and gave himself over to his fate, his last silent wish to any devils that might be listening was not for some impossible salvation or even a quick and painless end, but that he should see Purna on the other side, so that he might beg her forgiveness for failing to avenge her.

Instead of chewing his face off, the monster started grinding into him, screaming into his face as its arms slapped at him, and unable to help himself, Maroto screamed back. It was so much worse than he had imagined. Instead of simply eating him alive it intended to mate with him, so that he might help restore the chain of life that he had so egregiously sundered with his egg-stealing. Maroto was a consummate professional when it came to lovemaking, having earned more coin with his cock than he'd ever spent on the thing, but even still, he wasn't sure he'd be able to pay this particular debt. He'd pleasured his share of questionable partners before, sure, but never a creature so hideous, and certainly not without a few rounds of drinks to break the ice.

As if sensing his reluctance it raised its girth off of him, giving him the space he needed . . . but then slammed back down again, even harder than before. It was the worst dryhump in a long life overfull of bad dryhumps, each new blow of its shell-ensconced body feeling less like coitus and more like it was being hoisted into the air only to drop back down. It was even worse than the time he'd allowed a wealthy client at the bordello in Vuyvr to rig up that pulley system and – holy mother of fucks, it had worked! His plan had actually worked!

The torch hadn't gone out, and it wasn't actually humping

him – now that the crab-mother was wrenched up into the air again, he saw the ivory edges of a second monster's fleshy wings protruding out from either side of the first one's shell. The egg-layer's long, spider-like front legs were thrusting up at its attacker, and before it could pull itself free from the flying horror's grasp and slam down on Maroto again he rolled away, into the encroaching surf. It must have been a sight to see, an amphibious titan of the sea-caves battling a great hunter of the skies, but Maroto didn't stick around to watch. He crawled through the shallows until he could stagger, and then he staggered until he could sprint, and only when he reached the cover of the treeline did he collapse back into the sand. Finally turning for a look, he saw they had undone each other, both the silver-shelled behemoth and the gelatinous, winged predator lying beside one another, their great bulks shuddering with death throes. Maroto honestly couldn't remember the last time one of his plans had actually come together, and he looked all around for his audience ... but he was alone on the beach, and even after he cautiously called their names into the night none of the three pirates materialized from the darkness. It figured.

———

'He's alive!' Bang called from the upper branches of the banyan tree when Maroto finally lurched back into camp, too bushed to have even stopped off for a wash at the nearby waterfall. He missed being able to just flop out of the pool onto the moss and pass out, but agreed with Bang that the spot was too exposed to the sky and diligently carried out her order to find a more suitable camp. He'd done a bang-up job, if he did say so himself; here where the canopy was thickest overhead they could safely keep a night fire burning without alerting anything that might be flying far above to their presence. Said fire was now nothing more than coals, the frying pan smoking with blackened egg yolk. 'Is it safe to come down?'

'Nah,' said Maroto, plopping down on a soft log and blowing on the coals. 'Might be more, you'd better stay up there till dawn.'

'We would have followed,' said Dong-won as he descended, 'but it looks like you had it in hand.'

'I'll say he did,' said Bang, swinging down as deftly as one of those fucking monkey-men Maroto had met his first morning on the island. 'Take a look at his skirts – you stop to polish your privates on the way back?'

Looking down at the creamy yolk drying all over his crotch and legs, Maroto nodded. 'Usually it's a more impressive load, but your mom's been keeping me so busy I barely had anything left over for myself.'

'What a strange thing to say,' said Niki-hyun as she dropped down after the others. 'Do Flintlanders think it's insulting to imply one's parents enjoy the act of lovemaking?'

'Not at all,' said Maroto, taking up one of the coconuts filled with the wine they'd made out of fermented palm sap and cinchona bark. Oh, how he'd wished when he'd laid this stuff away that they'd find a way off the island long before it became ripe – which went to show how well Maroto and wishes got along. He drained the whole syrupy draught in a series of noisy gulps. Wiping his mouth, he explained, 'Just reminding Bang that she may be my captain but I'm still her father, and she should show me some damn respect after I saved all your arses.'

'Does that mean old man Useful will put me over his knee if I don't toe the line?' asked Bang, using a stick to nudge the hot fry pan off the coals and into the sandy soil.

'I don't hand out charity lightly,' said Maroto, and almost elaborated but caught himself in time – flirting with comely smart-mouths came as naturally as breathing to Maroto, but that was another thing Zosia had taken away from him. Ever since he'd learned how offensive she'd found all his clever lines and well-intentioned compliments he'd tried to keep that part of his nature in check lest he repeat the mistakes of his youth. He'd rather deprive the cute pirate of his substantial wit altogether than risk rubbing her wrong or making her feel self-conscious with an ill-timed ribald remark.

'Here,' said Bang, passing him another booze-filled coconut. They had a limited supply since it took forever to tap the sap and weeks to get it strong enough to even deliver a gnat-sized buzz, so he hadn't planned on requesting more than his ration, but he damn sure wasn't going to refuse it, either. 'Did you give the beast the slip, or strike it dead?'

'Led it down to the beach, and that flying fucker what almost got us the first night finished it for me,' said Maroto between gulps.

Dong-won whistled as he scraped the charred eggs off the frying pan with a stick. 'Next you'll be telling us that luring it to the squid-dragon was by design.'

'No, Dong-won, it was a happy accident I took along a few eggs as bait, and a torch to attract the squid-dragon, as you say, and ran straight down to the beach we know it likes to patrol,' said Maroto, his legs starting to shake uncontrollably now that his body had decided he was out of immediate danger.

'I think we should start calling you Madman instead of Useful,' said Niki-hyun, building the coals back up with scraps of driftwood.

'Two of the same,' said Bang, pouring the rest of her tubāq pouch into her pipe. 'Nothing's more useful than a madman. You've earned yourself a smoke, old timer, and you'll sit out the next three draws of the straw.'

'You honor me, Cap'n Bang.' Taking the offered pipe, Maroto tried not to let himself feel as happy as he did. A belly full of sweet palmwine and an appealing lass offering him first draw on her pipe was far more than he deserved, what with Purna's corpse barely cold. For all his talk of avenging her, had he promptly found a way to sail back to the Star, or had he whiled away the days and weeks playing castaway with his new friends? Granted, he didn't know the first thing about raft making, and they hadn't discovered any sign that the Unsunk Kingdom actually housed a harbor or even people who might build one, just thick jungle and treacherous swamps, precarious headlands on both sides and steep mountains behind them, so getting off the place was easier wished than done ... but that didn't mean he had to enjoy himself during his exile. All the more reason not to let himself slip into his bad old ways and start hitting on his captain.

But really now, beyond his commitment to be a better bloke he must finally be settling down in his dotage, because even though Bang was undeniably his type, usually in a state of partial undress due to the heat and their lack of a change of clothes, and prone to making bawdy comments herself, his mind wouldn't give up the ghost of Choi. It was getting so he couldn't doze off without bumping into her, and her bumping into him, and yet he could never remember a damn thing about the particulars, other than he'd seen her on the other side of his eyelids. And more than just seen, of course, a whole lot more, but even though the details eluded him he knew they hadn't just been sexy dreams, they'd also been sweet, as if he were finally getting to know her in all the ways he'd meant to, before they'd been separated. And maybe that had something to do with his not rushing the others to leave the Unsunk Kingdom as fast as possible and by any means necessary, because as long as he stayed here, cut off from any news from the Cobalt Company, Choi was still alive, she had definitely survived the Battle of the Lark's Tongue, *no question*, and he could cling to the hope of one day seeing her again. More than he could say for other friends who had relied on him.

'Do you really think more might come?' Niki-hyun asked nervously as Maroto got the pipe lit on a blazing palm frond.

'I hope not,' he said through a mouthful of sour tubāq. 'I've stolen a lot of eggs in my day, and only ever had whatever laid 'em come after me for it. We'll keep the usual watches, but I don't think we're in for more trouble.'

'The last words of many a better man,' said Bang, taking her pipe back when Maroto had just barely got it good and lit.

'Guess you didn't think to bring back any of the meat?' said Dong-won hopefully as he put the pan back on the fire and reached for their pyramid of piled eggs.

'Slipped my mind,' said Maroto, begging for another hit off the pipe with his eyes. Just thinking about the monster made him smell it anew, and there was nothing better for curing a lingering odor than some nostril fumigation. 'And you know, I think I'm good on eggs, too.'

'There something else you have a taste for, Useful?' Bang asked, holding the pipe out so he could lean in and take a smoky sip off the stem.

'Yeah,' said Maroto, meeting her eyes as he pulled on the pipe. Letting it out through his nose, he said, 'Normally I'd say vengeance against those what wronged me, but tonight I'll settle for another few hits on this sweet lat, and last watch if it pleases my Cap'n.'

'Nothing makes me happier than being able to grant an old man's wish,' said Bang with a wink so big they must've been able to see it clear back on the Star. Maroto rolled his eyes in response, wondering if he had some kind of sign stuck to his back that made flirtatious novice adventurers want to party up with him and come on like they were in heat despite having no intention whatsoever of bedding him.

Worse fates, he supposed, but still, hardly the role he'd seen for himself back when he'd decided to forgo the acting life and seek his fortune as a wandering hero.

Then again, who can really plan on being stranded on a monster-riddled desert island at the ends of the earth? If anyone could've, it would've been Maroto, but like his dad always said, he didn't have much foresight. Returning to his seat on the far side of the fire, he wondered for the first time in weeks how the old codger and wee Sullen were getting on – they were probably plenty miffed that he'd gone missing after the battle, and the thought of his dad waving his arms around and ranting about his escape-artist son brought a smile to Maroto's face. It had been good to see the both of them, and he wished there'd been time to actually set things right with his family, or try, anyway . . . but there'd be time enough in Old Black's Meadhall if not before, and until then Maroto would do his best to prove himself worthy of those who wanted him to lead a better life or, failing that, earn a noble death.

All the same, he was glad to have lived through another stupid night, and absent gods of the Unsunk Kingdom willing, there'd be a good many more to come.

CHAPTER

13

The snow had burned off the ground and they had left even the chill behind, an unseasonable temperateness draping itself over the western bank of the Heartvein, but the cautiousness that winter inspires in all sensible mortals stayed with Sullen even as they entered the deep wood northeast of the Witchfinder Plains. He couldn't help but wonder if they would have arrived here a week or more earlier, if he had just stood up to his doubt and trusted in Hoartrap's compass from the outset . . . but if they'd done that they never would've met the Procuress and received the weighty, wobbly carven log that all agreed came from a marginally more trustworthy source than the Touch. Just to make sure, they routinely double-checked the post against the compass, and between these two tools working in perfect harmony and Hoartrap's detailed map, it seemed certain Maroto was cutting way to the north from the Cobalt camp, probably to throw pursuers off his track before arcing east to Diadem. They might have caught him already, if they'd made better time, but Diggelby's promise to buy horses in Thao had proven as hollow as the pasha's pocketbook; he belatedly realized he had packed the jewelry case containing his collection of interesting snail shells instead of the box with all his money, and nobody else had enough to cover the difference. At least when it was their turn to carry the mystical pylon the tapai and the pasha quickly became too winded to jabber, but alas, it was Sullen and Keun-ju's shift when they entered the gloomy wood that Purna and Diggelby kept calling the Haunted Forest in warbling voices.

'Bewaaaaare the Hauuunted Forrrrrrest!' said Purna.

'Beeeewaaaaare!' said Diggelby.

'Be quiet!' said Keun-ju, shifting the post around on his sweaty shoulder, and Sullen found himself nodding in silent agreement with the Immaculate youth. Something about the bald cypresses and wide pools covered in dead leaves instilled a solemnity that he was loath to break, even to chide his companions for their noise. Besides, Sullen had learned admonishments did little good; he had grown hoarse from vainly telling them to shut up.

'Beeeewar—' Diggelby crowed louder than ever, but Purna thumped her companion in the chest, and said, 'Knock it off, Digs, can't you see we're scaring them?'

Keun-ju had learned not to engage the pair when they were acting like this, so instead of taking the bait he rolled a sympathetic eye at Sullen.

'They should be scared,' said Diggelby, taking off the silly orange admiral's hat he had traded one of his turbans for back in Thao and crushing it to his velour-ruffled breast. 'This isn't the Wonderful Wood or the Glorious Grove, it's the Hauuuuuuuunted Forest!'

'Haunted by knaves and loudmouths,' grumbled Keun-ju as they paused to let their pony drink from a still pool.

'Ooooh, that's a good one,' said Purna. 'I'll be feeling that burn for weeks!'

'Wherever did you come by your wit, Keun-ju?' asked Diggelby. 'It's as sharp as Sullen's wardrobe!'

Try as they did to make Sullen self-conscious of his unbuffed boots, armored skirt, greasy wool tunic, and opossum-torn bandolier, he didn't give them the satisfaction of even acknowledging their words. He wasn't about to take fashion advice from a man who looked like a dead clown or a girl who couldn't make up her mind if she wanted to dress like an Imperial prince or a Flintland trapper. The cobalt cape Ji-hyeon had insisted Sullen take with him only completed his ensemble, as Diggelby would say.

'I checked the map and there's not even a woodland by that name on it,' said Keun-ju. 'So you can stop making up stories anytime you want.'

'It's not on the map because *we're* not on the map,' said Purna, finally talking at a reasonable hush. 'The Haunted Forest is everywhere and nowhere, materializing to lure in unwary travelers, who wander forever in its shaded depths.'

'They say once you enter, the only way to leave is as a ghost,' said Diggelby quietly, and looking out over the tranquil, leaf-strewn surface of the woodland pool, Sullen shivered.

'Legend has it, the Haunted Forest springs up on the hundredth anniversary of a great tragedy, and won't go away again until it's drunk innocent blood,' said Purna, squatting down and washing her hands in the rust-colored shallows. 'Each tree was once a lost soul, just like us.'

'This place feeds on the mulch of mortals,' whispered Diggelby, his voice carrying in the stillness. 'Our only hope is to find the tranquil clearing at its heart, and petition the spectral wardens of the Haunted Forest to release us.'

'Even then they will still demand a sacrifice,' said Purna, nodding her horn-hooded head toward Keun-ju. 'One way or the other, the Haunted Forest will claim some of us ... maybe even all of us.'

'Is this true?' said Sullen, his hackles good and raised now, the point of the ensorcelled post shivering with potency against his shoulder blade. Perhaps he had been too hasty in dismissing the carefree words of these friends of his uncle; they had faced real horned wolves in combat and jumped right in against a devil queen Sullen himself had balked at battling, so maybe they just didn't take *anything* seriously, even mortal danger. Now that he was on the lookout, the high tips of the cypress branches seemed to move, though he felt no wind, and the hoary grey clumps hanging from the trees that Keun-ju had called Azgarothian moss looked almost like tangled human hair . . .

Purna and Diggelby shrieked in unison, seizing one another for balance, and for the first time since he'd left the Cobalt Company a genuine laugh escaped Keun-ju's blue satin veil. They were laughing at Sullen. At his gullibility. He turned his attention to the placid surface of the water, so they couldn't see the pain on his face – he felt just as small and worthless as he had back on the Savannahs, all the other kids jeering at their simple playmate. Old Black's toes, but people could be nasty. As Sullen looked out across the reddish water with its reddish film of leaves and reddish cypress knees and reddish sunset above, he struggled to make himself as flat and muted as the landscape, to not give them the satisfaction of seeing him crack.

'It would hardly be the strangest place in this Star, even if every lie you two fools told was true,' said the last person Sullen would have expected to stick up for him. But then Keun-ju was even less amused by the fops than Sullen was, so it probably just came from a desire to shut them down before their high-pitched giggles became unbearable. Or even less bearable, to be strictly accurate. 'I propose we make camp here. There is fresh water, dry ground, and these two can scout ahead to make sure we are alone in this quarter of the wood.'

'Much as I would relish a rest,' said Diggelby, 'we all know who gives the orders around here, and it's not you, sweet cheeks.'

'Do not call me sweet cheeks,' said Keun-ju. 'And it wasn't an order, it was a proposition.'

'Ooooh, Keun-ju's propositioning Sullen!'

'Quiet,' said Sullen, considering the twilight. It was true Ji-hyeon had put him in charge, but Sullen was frankly relieved to have someone else weigh in on their course of action. He was fit for many roles, but playing leader made him feel a bit like Little Hook when she was put in charge of organizing the sea queen's feast . . . in over his head was the idea, and curse him for a baby to always be spinning himself songs instead of thinking normal adult thoughts. 'If you don't see anything for a good mile, come back with kindling. Those hares I caught need to be cooked or we'll all get rabbit-belly.'

'Woot!' cried Diggelby and Purna, doing one of their silly dances with their arms raised and their palms touching as Sullen and Keun-ju lifted the tamarind log off their aching shoulders and slowly set it down on the ground. Much as it quivered with intention when it was in hand, as soon as one partner let go of it the thing was just so much fancy firewood again; it took two to work the sorcery.

'What is rabbit-belly?' asked Keun-ju, who had already turned his veil up at the suggestion they eat the rangy hares Sullen had caught on the edge of the forest before the others had awoken that morning.

'Never had it myself, but my mom told me stories,' said Sullen, turning back to his companions. 'A real bad sickness, and you all take too long during latrine breaks as it is.'

The fading bruises that crawled out from the top of Keun-ju's veil sharpened as he blushed, but the other two simply cackled and directed their dance back into the trees.

Purna called, 'You heard the boss – a roaring fire when we get back, then, and story time to boot! I want to hear all about your mother's bun belly.'

'You would,' said Diggelby, and then they pranced off together, leaving Sullen alone with Keun-ju yet again. They looked at each other, then both looked away, trying to find something, anything, to occupy their attentions.

'Is it all right if I bathe?' Keun-ju asked as the darkness settled in. 'I'm disgusting, and cold as that pool is it's probably a bit warmer than the snowmelt we've been trudging through.'

'Not a bad notion,' said Sullen, the prospect of washing the past few days' grime off his body the only obvious upside to the recent change in weather from comfortably chill to cloyingly clement.

'Do you mind if I go first?' said Keun-ju, and Sullen stopped stripping, Ji-hyeon's cloak limp in his hand. 'Until the others return it might be safest for one of us to stay with Princess, weapons ready and watching the other's back, rather than both of us romping naked in the spring? Or we could wait for them to come back, if you would prefer.'

With that damn veil it was impossible to guess what Keun-ju's actual mood was – the words themselves sounded almost flirtatious, but Sullen wasn't so thick as to think that was their intention. The Immaculate boy was probably just shy or something, or perhaps repulsed at the idea of seeing Sullen in the nude.

'Yeah, sure,' said Sullen. 'I'll get that fire started while you do.'

'Is that wise?' Keun-ju hung his cloak on a tree and began unbuttoning the shoulder flap of his starched Immaculate coat. 'Don't you want to make sure the others return to tell us it's safe first?'

'I want cooked meat and a fire to warm myself once I'm out of the water,' said Sullen. After considering it for a moment, he decided to try making a joke again. 'If you'll feel safer I can offer a prayer to the Old Watchers that any monsters take their time eating Purna and Diggelby, so we can at least have a wash and a meal before our fire attracts them.'

'Riiiiight,' said Keun-ju, who obviously didn't have a sense of humor, either. Sullen gave the priss his privacy, gathering downed wood in the gloaming. By the time he'd got the damp fire hissing to life with Diggelby's coalstick and the hares staked out around it the evening had fallen into full dark, and Keun-ju returned to the firelight dressed in a fresh linen veil, frog-buttoned shirt, and skintight trousers, his long hair wrapped in a soft-looking length of cloth. A towel was what they'd called it back at that weird bathing complex of hot pools that Keun-ju had treated them to in Thao, after circumstances mandated that Diggelby's generosity remain strictly theoretical. 'No sign of the others?'

'WoooooOooo!' came from nearby in the darkness, and meeting each other's eyes, Sullen and Keun-ju shook their heads.

After Sullen had bathed in the silty pool, he excused Purna and Diggelby to do the same and tucked into one of the hares. It was so lean as to hardly be worth the effort, but the gamey flesh and the juice running down his chin was its own reward. Watching Keun-ju shave tiny scraps of meat off the tiny bones with a tiny dagger he called a quill-knife and then pass them under his veil, Sullen supposed he must look like a real barbarian to the Immaculate ... but then why argue with your nature? Ji-hyeon seemed amused rather than condescending about Sullen's habits, so it hardly mattered that her paramour got so wide-eyed when he watched Sullen eat. What kind of person observed another dine, anyway? That was just asking to be disgusted.

'Okay, look,' said Sullen, because a hoot and a loud splash from the nearby pool told him Purna and Diggelby might be gone some time. 'Ji-hyeon.'

What little color he usually had fled Keun-ju's face, and the hand holding the hare's drumstick began to tremble. The one holding the blade didn't. In words so clipped they couldn't have been pared finer with that quill-knife, he said, 'What about her?'

'You need to know . . .' Sullen's mouth suddenly felt as dry as if he'd chiefed a beedi all to himself, but he hadn't taken a puff since the morning with Ji-hyeon by Grandfather's bier. 'You need to know I didn't try to queer things between you two. I won't lie to you, won't say I don't fancy her, but I never said a weak word about you.'

'Oh,' said Keun-ju, looking away from Sullen as if he were ashamed. Sullen knew how that quick look-away went from personal experience. 'Well . . . I cannot blame you for anything that happened between Ji-hyeon and I. I . . . I did an excellent job queering things all by myself, and even if she had not met you while we were parted, I am sure that when I returned it wouldn't . . . well. My mistakes are my own.'

'Oh,' said Sullen, relieved at the answer, and kicking himself for not broaching the subject sooner. The last week would've been a lot less tense if he'd just grabbed the wolf by the horns at the bathhouse in Thao while Diggelby and Purna were chasing one another around, snapping their rolled-up towels with obvious expertise. 'Well. Good.'

'But I will not lie to you either,' said Keun-ju, and now his eyes were back on Sullen's, and neither hand was shaking. 'I won't give her up just because I made a mistake. I'll win her back, if it costs my life and more besides. She is the sun that nourishes me, the moon that guides me, and if I have set the dark clouds of mistrust between us, well, rest assured they will soon be brushed away by the winds of my adoration.'

'Oh,' said Sullen, because fast as the Immaculate words had come he was pretty sure he'd caught it all. Spending so much time with Ji-hyeon had given him something more than just a bad case of the heartthrobs. 'Well, we'll just both have to do our best, then, won't we? She deserves the best.'

Keun-ju looked about as annoyed as if Sullen had got all insecure and stupid about the matter. Maybe more so. 'You love her, don't you, Sullen?'

'So do you,' countered Sullen, 'but it ain't about what you want or I want, it's about what she wants.'

'Of course!' said Keun-ju, right riled now. 'I never said otherwise! And if you think for one moment that I would ever go against her wishes, well—'

'They're coming back,' said Sullen softly, because he could hear the sharp snap of a rolled-up towel and the ensuing yelp. 'Do you want to give them more fuel for their gossip, or do you want to let the matter go until we're both back in her company? I don't think either of us stands a chance of winning her favor from such a distance, so we might as well put aside our rivalry until—'

'Yes, of course,' hissed Keun-ju, even more agitated than before. 'But there is no rivalry, only two honorable men seeking what is best for their beloved. Agreed?'

'Agreed,' said Sullen, who would have never guessed in a million thaws that the snooty boy would ever call him honorable. Raising his voice a little, since Purna and Diggelby were obviously trying awfully hard to steal silently up on the fire, he said, 'And that's why they call it rabbit-belly.'

'No fair, getting started without us!' cried Purna, lurching chatter-toothed out of the darkness with only a soggy towel to warm her dripping body.

'Yes yes, start from the beginning,' said Diggelby, his sodden loincloth leaving even less to the imagination than Purna's kit. 'I need all the gruesome details.'

'Sorry,' Sullen told them as he gave Keun-ju a knowing wink, 'I never sing the same song twice in one night.'

'Well, tell us another one while we dress,' said Purna, yanking her towel off and drying herself by the fire as Sullen and Keun-ju both tactfully averted their gaze and found each other's. 'Maroto always said the one who built the fire was the host, and the host gets the first boast.'

'He said that?' Just as Sullen had been enjoying an unusual mix of nerves and relief to have finally cleared the air with Keun-ju, the phantom of his faithless uncle arrived late as ever to spoil the mood. That the hypocritical coward would dare to speak of decorum to his acolytes was yet another mark against his honor. 'Bet he sung all kind of songs about his bravery.'

'They mostly involved his fuckups, actually,' said Diggelby. 'It got so soppy we started putting wagers on it, Din and Hassan and me, about whether his newest tale would be more pathetic than the last. And it got *so* ridiculous that Din, she . . . she . . . '

Diggelby trailed off, staring into the fire with such a sad look on his face that Sullen truly felt for the man, though he couldn't imagine how much worse this expedition would have been if there had been four fops instead of two. But then they probably wouldn't have appreciated Grandfather's company, either, and Sullen would have sacrificed all his fingers and toes to have the old man for just one last adventure together. To try to lighten the unexpectedly heavy mood, Sullen decided to go against his promise to himself, or at least bend it a little, and instead of leaving all his beloved childhood tales locked up tight in the back of his skull, he'd break one out for them.

'Fair's fair, and you're right, I'm the host so I'll sing first,' he told them, and then realized there was a substantial problem with that. 'Um, thing is all my songs are in Flintlander.'

'So says the barbarian who's been speaking Immaculate better than these two for the whole trip,' said Keun-ju.

'Not the same, not at all,' protested Sullen. 'The words are just a part of the song, it's also ... well, it's the rhythms, the rhymes. I could tell it in Immaculate, but it wouldn't be the song, it would just be the words, and not the right ones anyway.'

'So have Keun-ju translate,' Purna suggested. 'Don't all Immaculates speak Flintlander, and every other trading tongue besides?'

'Not nearly all,' said Keun-ju, his veil flapping as he leaned in to blow the budding coals into bloom. Sitting back, he added, 'But yes, I hold a working knowledge of the tongue, among others.'

'I'm telling you, it's not the words,' said Sullen. 'They need to rhyme, and it's tricky enough to hit the right beats in Flintlander, long as some of them go.'

'I have studied the greatest poets of Ugrakar, the Crimson Empire in its Golden Age, and over a hundred Isles,' said Keun-ju, seeming to take everything Sullen said as either an insult or a challenge. 'If called upon I can recite all six chapters of Lantlôs's final sonnet, or sing Dissektist's *Ode to Sacrifice and Salvation*. I single-handedly translated Svedhous's *Vindication* into modern Immaculate, and, I say with all due humility, that my own verse has been praised by no less a discerning critic than Lady Yunjin Bong.'

'Might she be any relation to our general?' asked Diggelby.

'Her elder sister, but that has nothing to do with it,' sniffed Keun-ju. 'I simply raise the point to prove myself more than capable of translating Sullen's *Song of the Bestial Hell Ax of the Sulfur Giants* or whatever it is.'

' 'Fraid I don't know that one, though it sounds tight,' said Sullen, trying to come up with a way out of this – what had he been thinking, offering to sing one of his songs for these people? There might be a more embarrassing fate somewhere on the Star, but if so he couldn't think of it. 'Look, let's just forget the whole thing – I'm not stopping every line so you can put it into Immaculate. And there's no way you can sort it all out if I sing through it in one go, which is how songs are sung, traditionally.'

Boos and hisses from the fops, and Keun-ju was on the offensive, obviously keen to have Sullen make an arse of himself. 'I'll make notes as you sing, and when you're done I shall render an approximation in the same meter – the key to translation is a free hand, especially if you want it to sound right. I have read a few Flintland verses in my education, and so know firsthand that the ... quaintness of the prose will make my task quite simple.'

'Simple?' So that was it: Keun-ju had a low opinion of the songs of the Frozen Savannahs. He'd probably heard a few limericks and thought it was all a load of bawdy jokes and violent fights. Which, to be fair, much of it was, but Sullen now felt compelled to teach the stuck-up boy a lesson. Instead of the silly song of Skinflint and the Twenty-three Girdles, these twerps were going to hear how Old Black turned her back on the world of mortals and founded her Meadhall beneath the earth. Every. Heartbreaking. Verse. 'All right, fine. But you two get dressed first, and if anyone laughs I won't stop singing, but I promise you'll have your gobs shut in a hurry. I'm a man who can beat arse and rhyme at the very same time.'

'Have it your way,' said Diggelby, neither of the fops as enthusiastic about the song-off now that there was a gag order in place. Sullen pretended not to notice Purna mooning him as she went to put on some clothes.

'Let me fetch my writing case and we can settle in,' said Keun-ju as Sullen finished his now cold hare. The lad soon returned with the long, fancy box he had received from the Procuress. None of the others seemed interested in talking about whatever had actually happened in the Jackal witch's shop after Sullen had stormed outside, and since he was too polite to go hunting for weak game he had no idea what else exactly they might have received, what they had spoken of, or just what it was about the experience that made the normally chatty fops clam up like tundra oysters in warm weather.

Case in point here – Sullen had assumed the brown-and-brass case housed some fancy weapon, or maybe an instrument of some design, but instead of opening it up Keun-ju began fiddling with its bottom. He unhinged thin telescoping legs so he could set the thing in front of him like a narrow table. Sullen tried not to gawp at this minor marvel, but from the cooing Purna and Diggelby made over it he presumed it wasn't such a common tool even among the world weary. No wonder Keun-ju had provoked him into a song: he just wanted an excuse to show off his new toy.

Now that the Immaculate was making such a big to-do over getting set up – opening the hinged lid and removing scrolls and weights and quill and inkpots, even lighting a narrow red candle despite the brightness of the campfire – Sullen felt the song shriveling in his throat before he'd even started. Oh, how he wished he'd picked up some more saam in Thao, having finished the last of it the night before; it didn't seem right, to sing of Old Black without a burnt offering of her favorite herb ... but before he could protest on this flimsy pretext, he saw the coughing Purna and Diggelby were passing an enormous beedi rolled from cigar leaf and packed with the skunkiest bud this side of the Raptor Wood. They took their seats on either end of the bedeviled tamarind post and the saam went around, even Keun-ju raising his veil to take a few impressively deep hits. There was some more small talk, and a good deal more trash talk, and then Sullen was out of excuses, out of time. His three companions all sat staring at him in stony silence, even the pony seeming impatient for him to begin. Nothing for it.

'Right, so ...' Sullen closed his eyes and returned to the sagas of his ancestors, one of the uncounted songs that had brought reason and happiness to his troubled youth. Even when every member of the clan turned their backs on Sullen, or did worse things than that, Old Black was waiting, watching, and she would judge them all, in time. And when Sullen's own doom came upon him, he would stride proudly into the Meadhall she had raised for her worthy heirs, and there he would see his father again ... and Grandfather, too, now that he had been delivered home, and in time enough, his mom, who he couldn't think of without hurting so he barely thought of at all ...

And then Sullen banished these thoughts along with all the rest, for there is a time for thinking and a time for doing, and while he had taught himself this saga and so many others, he had never before sung it for an audience outside his immediate family. At last the song was something he must do, rather than merely think about. Opening his eyes and staring into the low fire, he began to sing.

It was a longer song than he remembered, and he tripped a time or two in the telling of it, but by no more than a stuttered word or slipped beat, and his voice stayed deep and steady even when his throat grew as warm and dusty as the Jackal King's skull drying over the hearth in Old Black's hall. Even when it was finished he kept his eyes on the fire, basking not in the oppressive heat of the flames but the glow of knowing he had sung the song as well as he was able, and so honored his ancestors as well as himself.

Coming slowly out of the song, the nightbirds and swampsplashes and general hubbub of the forest reminded him he was not alone, and his audience had kept a respectful silence clear through to the end. He was all set to thank them for their politesse when he looked over and saw Purna and Diggelby sprawled next to each other beside the fire, eyes closed and mouths agape. Instead of being disappointed, he actually felt good to see his song had been a lullaby to these two miscreants – Sullen's mother had often dozed off during his songs, and bittersweet as good snowmead, his thoughts turned to her, and how well she must be doing in the clan without Sullen and Grandfather to make her look bad . . .

Then Keun-ju cleared his throat, and Sullen slowly directed his saam- and song-heavy head to meet the Immaculate's criticism, wishing he didn't have to, wishing he'd stayed quiet and sung it only in his heart, feeling about as vulnerable as a tortoise who just realized he'd stepped in a fire ant bed. The empty surface of the writing case in front of Keun-ju did not bode well of his impression.

'Didn't even need to scratch any of it down, huh?' said Sullen, feeling as much the fool as he could ever remember . . . which was saying something indeed. Instead of replying with one of his barbs, Keun-ju just shook his head.

'You were right,' said Keun-ju, and it must have been a trick of the light because it looked like there were tears in the man's eyes. 'That . . . that's not something I could translate.'

'That bad?' Sullen didn't care what this milksop thought of him, so why did the insult to his song sting worse than any blade? Before Sullen could come up with some cool way to play it off, or storm off into the night, if nothing else, Keun-ju reached down, snatched up a twig, and threw it at Sullen. Sullen looked down at his chest where the stick had bounced off, then looked back up at Keun-ju. He couldn't have been more baffled if his critic had stridden around the fire and kissed him on the mouth.

'You know it wasn't bad,' snapped Keun-ju, but now that he was getting used to talking to the man Sullen was beginning to realize that the Virtue Guard could be just as tricky to read as his mistress; tone wasn't everything with these Immaculates. And it stood to reason Keun-ju would remind Sullen of the object of their mutual affection – they'd grown up together, and obviously shared certain mannerisms and tics. And . . . and hold up, now . . .

'Hold up, now, you saying you liked it?' Sullen's heart was pounding, his hopes unexpectedly raised.

'*Liked* it?' Keun-ju's eyes bugged out and his veil flapped around like a pennant in a storm. 'That . . . that was an experience the likes of which I have never . . . never . . . *experienced*. Gah! I can't even use words anymore! That was better than . . . well, no, but my gods, it was close! Liked it?'

'So . . . yeah?'

'If you tell me you composed that yourself I'm going to cut my own fingers off,' said Keun-ju, and he sounded like he meant it. 'Go on. Tell me you wrote it.'

'I didn't,' said Sullen, now thinking he might have preferred an offhand dismissal from Keun-ju instead of this unsettling intensity. 'I mean, I can't even write, can I? And if I could, no way I'm smart enough to come up with something like that. It's an old song, the oldest, maybe, passed down from one Horned Wolf to the next, until me. And for all I know I'm the last one who knows it – Witmouth, the singer who taught me, he . . . well, it's another song for another night, and I'm not certain one way nor the other, but I might've killed him. I hope not, I do, but he was one of them what tried to stop me at the Flywalk, and we didn't have no choice but to cut our way out of the circle . . . '

Sullen let the words go, because now that the song was over he was just blathering, high on saam but far higher from the headiness that comes of singing a song of such grandeur. It was hard to steal breaths during a tale that intense, and the lack of air always gave Sullen the sways when he was done. He yawned, and when he could see again saw that the Virtue Guard had shakily risen and was quietly folding the legs back into the writing case. Sullen was about to suggest he take the first watch himself, bushed though he was, when a blast of light cut through his foggy brain, and not a moment too soon he realized he had committed two of the gravest insults a host could commit: he hadn't thanked Keun-ju for his kind words, and he had hogged the night, singing so long nobody else was able to follow him.

'I thank you for listening, Keun-ju, and for the mighty compliments you have bestowed upon me,' said Sullen, tottering to his own unsteady feet and trying to recall the formal words that he had never before had cause to utter. 'I beseech your pardon for my gross, um, my grossness in singing so long into the night, and pray that you will do me the honor of singing a song of your own, if not this eve then the next.'

This seemed to catch Keun-ju so off guard he almost dropped his heavy case, but then he stiffened up, and turned away to repack his bag and retrieve his bedroll. Smooth and swift as his movement was, he wasn't quick enough for Sullen to miss the faint firelight that played over the man's half-masked face, nor miss the fresh flash of wetness on his cheeks. Damn but this was strong saam, and some sentimental weed at that.

'Would you like to know something, Sullen?' Keun-ju said when he returned with his bedroll, his eyes again clear and steady as he stepped out of his polished black boots and wriggled into the bedding.

'Sure,' said Sullen, though he wasn't at all sure he could handle any more odd reversals or revelations in one night.

'I am beginning to understand why Ji-hyeon finds your company so agreeable,' said the Immaculate, rolling over so fast his back was to Sullen before he could decide whether or not he should confess the same . . . even to himself.

Long into the night Sullen stoked the fire and considered how different this trip was shaping up to be from the one-man hunt for vengeance he had envisioned. His grandfather murdered and his uncle fled in disgrace, this should be the Time of Dark Sullen, the confused yearling of his youth replaced by an unstoppable beast. He knew he should be consumed with hatred for his uncle, that his every thought should be of blood and fire, but instead he'd spent most of the march daydreaming about Ji-hyeon or fretting about the Faceless Mistress and Zosia . . . and now he was singing fricking songs to these dear friends of Uncle Craven, instead of keeping his austere distance. He hadn't even honored his word to fuck up the kid with the weakbow who'd shot Grandfather when the runt hadn't waited around to face Sullen's judgment back on the Lark's Tongue's plateau – what kind of a Horned Wolf was he, anyway, if he shied away from as simple an act of retribution as killing the Outlander who had murdered Sullen's blood relation?

No Horned Wolf at all was the answer he'd been trying to make stick ever since Thao, and even before. From the time he'd fled in the night and attacked the clanfolk who came after him, Sullen hadn't had any right to associate himself with those people . . . and maybe it went way earlier than that, maybe he hadn't been a Horned Wolf from the day he'd hauled Grandfather back into the village all those years before. And the more he thought about it, the more okay Sullen was about leaving all that baggage behind for good. He'd harbored fantasies of returning home a hero, having proved the whole clan wrong, but why should he ever go back? With the exception of his mother, every single damn thing he loved in this world wasn't just different from the Horned Wolf way; it was anathema to it. Even a little thing like what had happened here tonight, him making peace with a hostile Immaculate not with violence but with song, that made him feel a hundred times better than any of his futile efforts to impress his clanfolk, and what did he have at the end of the night? Instead of blood on his hands or a blade in his back, he had a friendship, or at least the beginnings of one . . . and with a man who had every reason in the Star to hate him, a man who'd helped him carry a magic post given to them by a damned Jackal shaman! So now and forever, then, say it loud, and say it proud:

'Fuck the Horned Wolves,' Sullen told the fire, having learned this night that words have even more power when spoken aloud . . . but saying it in Immaculate, because he didn't think the Old Watchers would like him burning the clan in their own language.

'Fuck 'em?' said Purna, licking her chapped lips with her long black tongue as she picked herself up from where she'd passed out by the fire. 'Hardly knew 'em.'

'Um . . . ' said Sullen, embarrassed to be caught out.

'Your business is your own,' she said sleepily, staggering a short distance off. Then, over the sound of her piss, she called, 'I'll take next watch. Anything weird happen while I was out?'

'Yeah,' said Sullen, lying down and looking through the screen of low flames to where Keun-ju slept. 'But it's not the sort of thing that translates.'

CHAPTER

14

Waits was even warier than Domingo remembered, the willowy Thaoan colonel dragging her stool even closer to the bed and looking all around the empty tent as though there might be spies lurking in plain sight. That she had agreed to enter the enemy camp at all was itself an unprecedented act of boldness, especially after her shameless attempt to storm the Cobalts had apparently resulted in a giant opossum devil wreaking havoc for all concerned. But just as Domingo had told General Ji-hyeon, if the bait was tempting enough even the cagiest bird might be induced to go against its nature in pursuit of an easy worm. Domingo blinked at her, as if only now recognizing the visitor to his deathbed, and as feebly as he could manage he coughed a pitiful cough.

'By Lord Bleak's banner, what have they done to you?' asked Waits, but she sounded less concerned for his welfare and more impressed by the Cobalts' gumption in laying him so low. 'They claimed you shattered your spine in the battle and that's why you couldn't ride out to the midway meets, but I didn't believe it. If I had I would have come sooner!'

'It's all true,' said Domingo with a groan that was all too easy to produce even though his bruised back was one of his few body parts that actually seemed on the mend. 'As I wrote in my very first letter to you, I believe, several weeks past.'

'Well, you know how it goes,' said Waits breezily, 'it's entirely too easy to forge those sorts of things, and until we'd settled on terms with the Cobalt command I couldn't risk it. For both our sakes.'

'Of course,' said Domingo, for the first time in their professional acquaintance stifling the urge to call her out on her bullshit. There would be time enough for that if he didn't convince her to go along with his proposal. And though he knew the answer already, he said, 'What changed your mind?'

'Your last letter, of course.' Which she supposedly doubted the veracity of, but no matter, no matter. Waits produced a cigar case that was almost as shiny as the medals on her breast, and drawing her even shinier dress dagger, clipped their tips and offered one of the light-skinned chisels to Domingo. 'Your assurance that General Ji-hyeon is committed to conducting a lawful war convinced me I could safely parley in the Cobalt camp. That, and we're finally signing terms with General Ji-hyeon, and at this juncture she can't afford to jeopardize her one chance out of this mess by doing something as monumentally stupid as taking me hostage.'

'Quite so,' agreed Domingo, too relieved to be annoyed with her malarkey. 'It's an affair I never would have predicted, but a lifetime coordinating joint operations with other regiments has taught me that one must often put aside smaller differences for the greater cause, especially when there's a greater enemy.'

'How's that?' Waits asked as she struck a match off Domingo's bed frame and held it up to light his cigar. 'Greater cause? Greater enemy?'

Domingo took his time getting the cigar going, giving his temper time to cool before he snapped something rash at Waits.

Fast as satisfaction had settled around his weary bones, it went the way of the smoke rising from the end of the chisel. When he could no longer believably fuss over the stick of tubāq, he quietly asked, 'What exactly are the terms you're signing with the Cobalts?'

'Signed,' corrected Waits, then took damn near eternity getting her own cigar lit.

'Signed?'

'Just before I came here, General Ji-hyeon and I met in her tent and put ink to vellum. We'll have you back in friendly hands by this time tomorrow, along with the rest of the Imperial hostages, and in exchange we allow the Cobalts safe passage past our lines. Everyone wins.'

It was a classic swap, but a very far cry from what Domingo had expected. Mistaking his confusion for disappointment, Waits leaned so close he could smell the garlic on her breath underneath the leathery smoke.

'Don't worry, old lion, I'm not about to let the fox escape the yard. I stipulated we'd grant them safe passage past our cordon, but didn't mention the Second out of Meshugg. Our reinforcements aren't two days out, and we'll pin the Cobalts between us – they've got nowhere to go, and without a nearby Gate to pull another monster out of they'll be as quaking bluebells before the scythe. A truce today, a friendly wave as they retreat tomorrow, and on the third day? Total fucking massacre.'

Domingo bit through the end of his cigar, spluttering on crumbling brown tubāq.

Waits furrowed her brows. 'I told you not to worry, you'll get a share in the glory – you helped broker the truce, after a fashion, and if you really insist I can allow any of the Fifteenth we liberate to take part in the slaughter, I just assumed they might not be up to—'

'The terms . . . ' said Domingo, clumsily dabbing the broken wrapper off his tongue and onto the back of his liver-spotted hand. 'The terms were you work with the Cobalts to save the Empire from the Chain. The greater threat—'

Now Waits looked as shocked and betrayed as Domingo felt.

'The *absolutely ludicrous* terms that we rejected? The literally treasonous invitation to launch a joint operation with the Cobalts? To invade Samoth, our mother province, to conquer Diadem, our Imperial capital? To dispose both Crimson Queen and Black Pope, ushering in a golden age of namby-pamby love and unity? You thought we accepted *those* terms?'

Of course she hadn't. Domingo wouldn't have, if he were in her saddle. Had there been any hope at all?

'I know how it looks, Waits, believe me, I do,' said Domingo, aware of how dotty he must sound but needing to convince her, needing her to listen more than he'd ever needed anything in the entire history of his command. 'But Pope Y'Homa is in open rebellion against the Crown. She sacrificed my regiment to bring back the Sunken Kingdom, and devils only know what else. If we don't stop her, and soon, it will be too late.'

'It already is,' said Waits with that damnable pitying frown all of Domingo's lessers seemed to be adopting of late. 'Indsorith is no longer queen. The Black Pope has arrested her.'

'*What?*' Domingo had never cared much for Indsorith, finding her entirely too much like a watered-down version of her Cobalt predecessor and only allying himself with her because even twenty years ago he had been sharp enough to see what a threat the Burnished Chain posed to the Empire, and knowing it would either be Queen Indsorith or the Black Pope in the throne room. Even when he'd gone behind Her Majesty's back and worked with Y'Homa to bring down the second Cobalt rebellion and avenge his son he had never dreamed it would come to this. Compared to whatever Chainite reforms Y'Homa's puppet would inevitably enact, the bank-breaking populist policies Indsorith forced on her provinces would look positively benign. 'Who's the new queen, then? Not even Y'Homa would dare put herself on the Crimson Throne without the approval of the provinces!'

'There's no queen at all,' said Waits in the resigned voice of a career officer passing on an unpopular order. 'I'm sure there was a lot of loyal blood spilled in Diadem during the coup, but whatever resistance those faithful to Indsorith were able to raise has been quickly suppressed. We received official notice that the Crimson Empire is now and forever governed by the will of the Fallen Mother, which is to say, Her Grace.'

'And did you stop to think those letters might be forged?' Domingo cried, desperate for some explanation other than the obvious one – that he had not only fulfilled the prophecies of an insane fundamentalist, but also handed her the keys to the throne room.

'As I said, it's too late,' said Waits. 'But only for enemies of the church, which is to say, the state.'

'We never agreed on much, Waits, but you and I always stood together against the Chain,' said Domingo, recognizing his dead son's plaintive whine coming out of his mouth. 'Every uprising, every civil war, Azgaroth depended on Thao and Thao depended on Azgaroth, and we stopped the Burnished Chain together! And now we have to stop them again! It's not too late!'

'Domingo,' Waits said patiently. 'The people of Thao depend on their regiment to protect them, and as for Azgaroth, well . . . I hate to bring it up at a time like this, but you seem to have mislaid most of your army.'

'That's why we work with the Cobalts!' Domingo tossed the cigar away, grabbing the sleeve of Waits's uniform and pulling her down to his bedside. 'Can't you see that? With Indsorith deposed you have no reason not to! We're at war with the Chain, and not for the first time! And we can beat them, just like we always do!'

'Release me!' said Waits, jerking her arm away. 'How dare you suggest Thao commit mass suicide – did you lose your mind as well as your regiment? I'm sorry to see you crack, Domingo, I really am. But unless you want things to go very, *very* badly for your now undefended Azgaroth, I *strongly* suggest you make peace with reality. There is no war – there's not a city-state or province in the Crimson Empire that's foolish enough to stand alone against the Chain. It's over. The Burnished Chain has won, but the only losers will be those mad enough to resist them.'

'We can beat them,' gasped Domingo, collapsing back onto his pillow. 'With the Cobalt Company, we can still beat them. They have soldiers, they have the old Villains, and if Zosia overcame King Kaldruut, by all the faithful stewards who came before us she can overcome a punk like Y'Homa.'

'Oh, Domingo,' said Waits sadly. 'You've really lost it, haven't you? Cold Zosia's been dead for over twenty years. Ji-hyeon Bong leads the Cobalt Company. General *Ji-hyeon*. You know this, you mentioned her in your letters. Zosia's long gone.'

'You don't know a devildamn thing,' said Domingo. 'I'm sharp as I ever was. Sharper. You're the one who's lost it if you think capitulating to the Chain will save you or your people. They've brought back Jex Toth, woman, doesn't that mean anything to you?'

'Yes, yes, so you said in your letters,' said Waits, standing in that unmistakable way of people who think they're being subtle but obviously can't quit the room fast enough. 'Assuming I didn't dismiss your allegations as the ravings of a lunatic, what makes you think they'd convince me to fight the inevitable? If the Chain was able to exterminate the Fifteenth from halfway across the Star and conquer Diadem in a matter of days, why in heaven's name would I try to tangle with them? Far better to become a feast day Chainite and tithe a little more than we used to than have a Gate open up under *our* feet. Who knows, maybe they'll even start calling Thao the Garden of the Star once more, and I know that doesn't sound like much to a foreigner, but—'

'Coward,' Domingo spit. 'Yellow-marrowed, chicken-livered coward.'

'A wise general knows that surrender is sometimes necessary, for that same greater good you were going on about,' said Waits. 'Your problem is you never let yourself admit defeat. No wonder you're falling apart. I strongly advise you to pull your shit together, Domingo, because once we've gotten you out of this . . . this mess of your own making, you're going to have to make some sacrifices, for the safety of Azgaroth. You can't keep spouting—'

'What do you know about sacrifice?' snarled Domingo, knowing he should shut up, he should let her go so he could regroup, but finding that even his mouth was betraying his orders. Or maybe it was his heart, it scarcely made a difference. 'You're finished, you hear me? Finished! I won't let you get away with this, I won't! If I have to crawl over there and gnaw your legs off I'll do it, because you know the real difference between us, Waits? I've killed more Chainites on my back than you have on your feet, you bloody coward!'

'Oh dear,' said Waits, and the worry on her face told Domingo he'd pushed the overly cautious colonel just a smidge too far. 'Oh dear oh dear oh dear. You seemed so lucid at first, I never imagined . . . well. This *is* a disappointment, but I want you to listen to me, Domingo, with whatever's left in that soft skull of yours – this isn't your fault. It was my mistake. I shouldn't have spoken so freely with you, and I certainly shouldn't have given you that cigar, your health being what it is. A coughing fit, and then . . . a final sacrifice, for the good of the Crimson Empire.'

Waits moved fast, but Domingo moved faster. It was almost like old times. She had acquired the nock in her left ear from a friendly duel with Domingo many years ago, the Thaoan never able to get a point on the Azgarothian, while he was able to rough her up even with a dull fencing steel. Those contests had been on flat parade grounds, however, and now the field was anything but level. So accustomed to dominating his opponent, Domingo didn't even think to cry out for the guards, and he was only able to weakly hold her off him for a moment before she wrenched the pillow out from under his head and planted it over his face.

He struggled, but there wasn't much for it – she was far too strong, and he was far too weak, his one good arm losing its grip on the wrist that ground the pillow into his face. And then came what might have been the worst shock of Domingo's entire life: he was wrong, there was a hell, and he must be fast on his way, for as Waits smothered him he distinctly heard a demonic chuckle rising up from below. He'd kept them waiting long enough, and now it was time for the devils to feast.

The pillow went limp and Waits's crushing weight fell away from Domingo. Yanking the pillow off his face, he saw what had drawn the colonel away from her victim – a huge, hairless creature was crawling out from under the foot of the raised cot, the left side of its almost-human face pale as clotted cream and the right as dark as blackberry sauce.

Waits opened her mouth to shout for the guards, as Domingo should have done from the first, but then the yellow-robed, piebald thing on the floor raised a bruised, tattooed hand and whispered too softly for Domingo to hear. Instead of a cry for help, Waits's mouth issued a rapid-fire chain of pops as every single one of her teeth exploded; it was as if each pristine white kernel had been packed full of black powder. Tiny wet shrapnel stung Domingo's cheeks, landed sweetly in his gaping mouth. Blood began slowly cascading from Waits's gums, and from there down her chin. She didn't scream, though, like Domingo would have; instead she just slowly raised a violently shaking hand to her ashen face, making a gasping 'uh uh uh uh' sound. Domingo would have preferred screaming, frankly. Then she toppled over without another sound, and the monster at the foot of his bed rose cautiously to a crouch, as though it half expected Waits to get back up for another round like some unstoppable villain in one of Lupitera's ghastly grand guignols.

When Waits stayed limp on the ground, the hulking figure turned and smiled at Domingo, and he saw its swollen face wasn't just the color of berries and cream; the skin actually had the same consistency, lumpy and seedy. The cream had evidently gone off, too, and the rich dark sauce was rancid, and then the misshapen grotesque did the worst thing in the entire world: it picked the pillow up off the floor, tucked it under one armpit, planted its large, scab-striped hands on the end of the cot, and slowly crawled up the bed to lie beside Domingo. It was a tight squeeze.

'Hullo, Colonel Cavalera,' said the creature that could only be Hoartrap the Touch, the Witch of Meshugg. 'Be a dear and lift your head?'

Domingo did as he was told, drooling out Waits's tooth crumbs since he didn't even dare spit without the warlock's invitation. Once the pillow was beneath his skull he relaxed back into it, and Hoartrap did the same, so they lay side by side looking at the snow-baggy ceiling of the tent. It was like being back in the wagon with Brother Wan, only even worse.

'I know what you're thinking,' Hoartrap said after they had lain in silence for a time.

'Do you?' asked Domingo, nearly retching on the aftertaste of Waits.

'It's an obvious question,' said Hoartrap. '*How long was he under my bed?* Well, don't you worry, I slipped under just before our visitor arrived – you think I have nothing better to do than play boogeyman for overgrown children? Tut tut tut.'

'Get on with it,' said Domingo, closing his eyes.

'*It?*' Hoartrap sounded genuinely curious.

'I won't play your games, monster – kill me like you did Waits, or make it even worse, I don't care anymore. Just do it.'

'You are just as cheerful as a cherub, aren't you?' said Hoartrap. 'And she's not dead, though she'll probably wish she was once she wakes up. And as for you, my boy, you're the last person in the whole camp I'd want dead, maybe the last person left on the Star.'

'I . . . *what?*'

'It came as a surprise to me, too,' said Hoartrap, sitting up on one elbow to gaze down at his trapped quarry, making it so Domingo had no choice but to look at his filmy blue eyes, his discolored, waxen skin, his tattoos that subtly pulsed like veins beneath the few remaining patches of white on his deeply bruised flesh. 'I'll admit it, I came here expecting to catch you collaborating with the Thaoan colonel. But instead of a foe I find a friend, and a fast one at that. Your oration was straight out of a tragedy, so dramatic, so spirited! And so true. Domingo, I – may I call you Domingo?'

Domingo gave the faintest nod. Was the witch toying with him? He had to be.

'No matter how hard I try to tell them, Domingo, nobody listens,' sighed Hoartrap. 'I mean, Ji-hyeon *kind of* understands, but not the way you and I do. All that talk of coming together to stop the Chain, crawling on your tummy if you have to – I got gooseflesh, Domingo, honestly. Here, feel my hand – I'm getting it again just thinking about it!'

Domingo obligingly touched the back of the sorcerer's massive hand. It was true, where the flesh wasn't bulging with contusions and rough with thick, crusty scabs it felt as bumpy as a freshly plucked chicken. His mouth dry and his teeth sympathetically aching for those of Waits, Domingo whispered, 'What do you want from me?'

'Nothing that you don't want for yourself,' said Hoartrap, raising his hand to cradle the plum-hued half of his face as he looked dreamily at his bedridden captive. 'You just *get me*, Domingo, and I swear on all the devils I ever ate and the few who got away, I get you, too. I never would have suspected it before today, but that just goes to show you never really know anybody until you've spent some time hiding under their bed, hanging on to their every word. We're kindred spirits, you and I.'

Kindred spirits? Domingo hoped his horror wasn't too evident as Hoartrap rambled on. The warlock was either oblivious to his confidant's discomfort or encouraged by it.

'I just wish you had been there when I called that devil queen down on the Thaoans – I know *you* would have appreciated the elegance, the irony, and not gotten hung up on a few minor miscalculations. Everyone just wants to whine whine *whine*, as if I were a line chef who oversalted the soup instead of a savant attempting to re-create miracles undreamt of since the Age of Wonders, and succeeding! Succeeding beyond even my most optimistic predictions! If I'd even considered the possibility I might *actually* tempt a queen into taking the bait instead of some lesser, middling royalty then you can bet your soul I would have taken more precautions. But next time, oh yes, next time . . . like Domingo Cava – I'm so sorry, like Domingo *Hjortt*, Hoartrap the Touch does not fuck the same goat twice!'

Hoartrap was breathing quite heavily, staring at his prisoner, and to his profound disappointment Domingo realized the warlock was waiting for a response. 'Erm . . . Or even the once, if we can help it?'

Hoartrap's eyes narrowed, and then he brayed with wild laughter, embracing Domingo as he shook with glee. The giant witch smelled a lot better than he looked, like jasmine soap, and discovering in such a fashion what fragrance Hoartrap the Touch washed with Domingo counted as a low point not just in his morning but his whole life.

'Seriously, Domingo, why didn't we do this *years* ago?' asked Hoartrap when his giggling subsided. 'Don't answer that; I know, I know, it wasn't the right time, we both had a lot of growing up to do. But now we're ready, aren't we? Because it's not enough to just know what needs to be done, it's not enough to want to do it, you have to *need* to do it – and you can't need it until you've seen firsthand how bad it can get. And we have. I can't imagine what it was like for you, looking out from the far side of the valley once their ritual really got swinging and you realized just what you'd done to your own people, the forces you'd set loose on the world. I'm sure you lost a lot of friends that day.'

Domingo's hands balled into fists, and he tried to tell the sadistic monster to shut its mouth, to stop making him relive the worst day of his life with the witchery of his words, but his throat was too tight to make a squeak. He didn't even realize until Hoartrap tenderly dabbed his cheek with the edge of his yellow sleeve that he'd begun to weep.

'It wasn't your fault, Domingo. *It wasn't your fault.*' Hoartrap's melodious voice was actually somewhat soothing. 'They tempted you with lies, bound you with promises. They turned you into their *devil*, Domingo, enslaved you to carry out their whims . . . but you're free now. You're free, and while you can't change the past or undo the crimes they made you commit, you can show them what happens when they piss off the wrong old man, eh? You can prove that the will of mortals is harder than any steel, more dangerous than any devil. You can take the vengeance that is your due, Domingo, because you are more than what they tried to make you.'

Domingo nodded, sniffed, and nodded again, looking down at the dirty blanket that only minutes before he thought was going to be his shroud. Then he remembered who was cheering him up, and shook off the last of his pathetic self-pity as Hoartrap continued; the fiend knew how to fill an awkward silence.

'The pope and her Holy See and the rest of those turds must think they've won the day, now that they brought back Jex Toth. They think the end of the Age of Mortals is a foregone conclusion, as if we didn't have any say in the matter at all. And I'm glad they think that, really I am, because it's going to make our victory that much sweeter when we utterly, *utterly* destroy them. Together we're not just going to snap a few links off the Burnished Chain, we're going to smelt the whole damn thing, then pour the molten mess down the drain. Sound like fun?'

'*Fun*'s not the word I'd use, necessarily, but of course something needs to be done,' said Domingo carefully, finding the witch's friendly attention no more charming than his hostility would have been. After Indsorith took the Carnelian Crown, the presence of Hoartrap in her inner sanctum went a long way toward discouraging Domingo from having any part of her court until after the Touch had quit it. Domingo didn't believe in the Fallen Mother or the Deceiver or any of that other fairybook nonsense, but these days he was a staunch believer in witchcraft, for he had seen it with his own eyes ...

'You're quite right, of course,' said Hoartrap. 'Though I'd love to just stay here and talk for hours, I'd better bring our defanged hostage to Ji-hyeon, along with this troubling news of *yet another* regiment closing in and the peace agreement naught but a ruse. She'll be *so* disappointed.'

'Sooner you tell her the better, I imagine.'

'You're right – but don't worry, I'll pay you another call as soon as I have a little free time.'

'Wonderful,' croaked Domingo.

'It's straight out of a romance, isn't it?' said Hoartrap, batting his lashless eyes at Domingo. 'Two former foes drawn together by fate, discovering how much they have in common, how closely their passions run? Except instead of a love so great it could set the Star on fire, ours is a shared hatred for those black-frocked cultists who would murder the world to save its souls. There's really nothing more dangerous than a true believer with absolute power, is there? Even if it costs every life in this army, yours and mine included, it's a pittance to pay if we can prevent the Black Pope from carrying out any more of her insane rituals – better the Crimson Empire burn to ashes than become the dominion of the Burnished Chain. Don't you agree?'

He did. And of all the myriad horrors Domingo had experienced of late, finding himself simpatico with Hoartrap the Touch ranked up there as one of the worst.

CHAPTER

15

Outside another bright, sunny afternoon continued its slow assault on the polar landscape at the foot of the Lark's Tongue, but inside the command tent it was as gloomy as a crypt. Ji-hyeon sat alone at the table, having dismissed everyone after Hoartrap's dismal news so that she could try to process this recent turn. That Colonel Hjortt was apparently completely genuine in his support of the Cobalts was a welcome surprise, even if it was only born of a pathological hatred of the Burnished Chain. But one old man hardly made much of a difference when weighed against yet another hostile regiment marching against them, and with the surrounding Thaoan army already overmatching the Cobalts. Ji-hyeon considered burning a little saam, but instead decided on the documents she had signed just that morning with Colonel Waits. The rolled-up vellum crackled and gave off oily black smoke but refused to burst into satisfying flames as she held it over the candle. Sitting by herself in the quiet tent, watching her hopes of leading the Cobalt Company to safety burn away, Ji-hyeon felt as sick and anxious as she had when Fennec had led her into the Gate at Othean.

There was still hope, her council said. With Colonel Waits

captured, the Thaoans would be even more reluctant to make a second charge at the Cobalt camp. Ji-hyeon could wait until the regiment from Meshugg arrived and then offer their colonel similar terms, and maybe this time the Crimson command would accept them. Not the invitation to work together against the Burnished Chain, of course – she saw now how naïve it was to even think they would accept such a proposal – but maybe the Thaoans and Meshuggans would let the Cobalt Company safely pass through their lines in exchange for the release of Colonels Waits, Wheatley, and Hjortt, and the rest of the Imperial hostages.

Maybe, but not likely, not very likely at all – unlike the secular province of Thao, Meshugg had always sided with the Chain during times of unrest, and the Battle of the Lark's Tongue had proven how willing the Chainites were to sacrifice their own soldiers in the service of their apocalyptic prophecies. All of Ji-hyeon's captains were in agreement that if they tried to break through the Thaoan cordon now, either by force or through the peaceable release of their colonel, the encroaching Meshuggans would simply catch them on the run. Before, when it was just the Azgarothian regiment bearing down on them, the thought of standing proud against a Crimson army despite their superior numbers had carried a certain valiant charm; now, not so much.

Devils below, but Ji-hyeon was an idiot, and while she was glad she had sent both Sullen and Keun-ju away so that they would be spared whatever hell she had called down on the Cobalts with her sloppy command, part of her wished she had kept at least one of them with her, so that she wouldn't be so alone. Now that he had been removed from her life for a second time, all Ji-hyeon wanted was for Keun-ju to be back by her side, so they could try to work through what had gone wrong, instead of her trying to fix their problems by sending him away.

She still loved him in spite of what he had done, in spite of her feelings for Sullen, but even after he'd rescued her from the brood of the devil queen she'd given him the cold treatment, and now she would probably never see him again to prove how warm she still burned. Would the Imperials execute her themselves, or send her back to Othean as a diplomatic gesture?

Ji-hyeon hissed as a vein of embers in the roll of vellum reached her finger, and she dropped the burning treaty onto the map-draped table. Feeling even stupider than ever, she plucked up the blackening scroll by one unburned corner and dropped it on the cold hard ground, stomping it to char and ash under her heel. Even after it was safely out, smoke rose from the center of the table, the map evidently more flammable than the vellum. A hole had burned through the center of it, just where the Gate had been added with a smudge of charcoal, and now a glowing ring expanded outwards across the map. Ji-hyeon was about to slap out the cinders before they reached the nearest figurines, but her hand paused, and then she slumped back in her seat, letting the pulsing red borders spread out across the Lark's Tongue valley, wider and wider like the smile slowly spreading across her face.

It was madness, plain and simple, but then the world had gone mad, too, so what choice did she have but to evolve to suit it? Better to die leading a charge so bold it made the old gods sit up and take notice than to be manacled by the Burnished Chain. If she couldn't see Keun-ju or Sullen or her family again in life, she would give them something spectacular to remember her by, a legend even more audacious than that of Cold Cobalt.

Rising from the table with its smoldering map, Ji-hyeon whistled for Fellwing, and when the devil landed on her three-fingered hand the Cobalt general stepped out of her tent to make one last turn around her camp. They had to begin preparations immediately if they were to be ready for another predawn march, and first she had to retrieve her new equipment from the smith.

———

Zosia was in the middle of archery practice with Boris when she noticed the first few tremors: lone heralds tearing ass between the tents both on horse and on foot. Horns summoning petty officers to their captains. A woman repeatedly shouting 'fuck' at the top of her lungs as she stalked along the back of the archery range. Choplicker's especially good mood.

She told Boris to keep at it with his crossbow since he needed all the training he could get, and set off toward the command tent. Normally she'd unstring her bow after practice, but given the hubbub decided to wait just a little longer on that. The activity level only increased as she moved through camp, units coming together in every clearing amid the tents, and by the time she reached her destination there could be no misreading the signs: the Cobalt Company was preparing for another imminent engagement.

The general must not have waited for her to get started, but that wasn't surprising – even though she'd been quick enough to formally forgive Zosia's betrayal after what had gone down with the devil queen, Ji-hyeon was still keeping her at arm's length. A pity, that; Zosia would have thought her indisputably selfless offer to infiltrate Diadem in advance of the Cobalts would have gotten her back into the girl's good graces, but the kid must be smartening up. At least the bodyguards admitted her to the command tent, which was a step up from Ji-hyeon's recent tendency to keep Zosia waiting on the mat for a few minutes before inviting her in.

' – understand your concern, of course I do, but with my help it will be perfectly safe,' Hoartrap was cheerfully telling the rest of the council, but Singh, Fennec, and even Choi looked upset, only Ji-hyeon nodding her approval. Not a good sign. Noticing Zosia's arrival, the jacked-up sorcerer said, 'Why, ask Zosia if you don't believe me – she's cautious as a twice-trapped wolf back in the wild, and she's willing to put her faith in me.'

'I'll put plenty of things in you, Hoartrap, if the price is right, but my faith ain't one of 'em,' said Zosia, noticing the stink of burnt parchment, the blackened tabletop, and, grimmest of all, the lack of fresh kaldi. 'What's the haps?'

'Captain Zosia,' said Ji-hyeon, 'are you still willing to carry out the mission we discussed?'

'I've just been waiting on your order, General,' said Zosia, though not an hour went by that she didn't reconsider the proposal. 'Got my inside man practicing at the range as we speak, and me and Chop are ready to go at the drop of a visor.'

One of the terms of Zosia's return to command was that her devil had to stay outside the command tent at all times, but from beyond the canvas walls she heard Choplicker bark his agreement. Not surprisingly, the devil didn't seem to share her reservations about the plan.

'Then it's time,' said Ji-hyeon, and Zosia didn't like how pleased the general was to give the order. 'Hoartrap will escort you down the valley and through the Gate, and once he's seen you safely through to Diadem he will return for the rest of us.'

'He'll ... what?' asked Zosia, though from the unhappy expressions of the other captains she thought she was putting together the answer all by herself.

'There's been a slight change of plans,' said Ji-hyeon, looking a little manic around the sunken eyes and trembling lips. 'Instead of marching on Samoth while you ride ahead to incite a rebellion, you use the Gate to travel to Diadem immediately, and the Cobalt Company will follow you through as early as tomorrow.'

It was so quiet in the tent that Zosia could hear Ji-hyeon's devil snoring in the rafters, and after considering it for but a moment, she said, 'Yeah, that's a solid plan. Thought of the same thing myself, back when your dad was telling me how you escaped the Isles.'

'Of course you did,' sneered Ji-hyeon, not doing such a great job of keeping up appearances now that the Cobalts had been painted into such an ugly red corner. 'You think of everything first, don't you?'

'Well, maybe not everything,' said Zosia. 'Like, I can't see why you still want me to go through first, if you're just going to lead the Cobalts through tomorrow. It made sense before, to have me rally the rabble and find a way to open the city gates for your army, but now you'll already be past the defenses, and there's no way I can put an effective revolution together in less than a day.'

'*That's* your objection?' cried Fennec.

'Shut up,' Ji-hyeon told him and, turning back to Zosia, said, 'You claimed Portolés's accomplice had ties to an existing organization, did you not? A day should be more than enough time to alert them to our coming, and more importantly, enable them to prepare a diversion. Hoartrap tells me the Diadem Gate is in a courtyard in the center of the city, and we will be able to reach our target much quicker if the municipal troops are drawn to another part of town. If you have them rioting an hour before dawn in some remote quarter, it will clear our path to Castle Diadem.'

'Huh,' said Zosia, frankly a little impressed. 'That's true, General, but—'

'But nothing!' Ji-hyeon slammed her fist on the table and

pointed at Zosia. 'You have your orders, Captain Zosia, now carry them out!'

Zosia didn't budge other than to cross her arms. She was willing to do the unspeakable in the name of thwarting the Burnished Chain, to travel through a devil-loved Gate, but she wasn't about to be treated like a heel-dragging hump. Perhaps sensing she'd taken the wrong tone with this particular captain, Ji-hyeon's fury fled so fast Zosia wondered if it had been sincere in the first place.

'Please, Zosia, we need you to do this, and every moment we spend belaboring the particulars is a moment that could be spent preparing for the attack. By this time tomorrow we'll have taken the capital and won the war.'

'That's not how it works, General,' said Singh, the old-fashioned chevaleresse who normally waited to be called upon by her employer unable to remain silent any longer. 'Assume for the moment everything goes as you propose. Zosia completes her mission, day breaks, and you lead your army into the new Gate and emerge in Diadem with no complications. You march through the city and take Castle Diadem. You even catch Pope Y'Homa alive. What then?'

'Then we rule,' said Ji-hyeon, as though it were as simple as that. 'That's how you did it when you became queen, isn't it, Zosia? Only you didn't even have your army inside the walls, did you?'

'And supposing it doesn't go as planned?' said Fennec, making a point of removing his gloves to flex his grey-furred claws. 'Suppose your soldiers are in no condition to fight after passing through the Gate?'

'They will be,' said Hoartrap, but though he sounded as confident as ever he still looked more dead than alive from his slipshod summoning of the devil queen. 'I will personally open the corridor between here and Diadem, and I know my business far better than you, Fennec my boy. It's true that repeated passage through the Gates can have certain ... side effects, if precautions aren't taken, but that's what you keep me around for – to *take precautions*, to keep you safe, in this world and any others.'

'Like whatever precautions you took before summoning the archdevil that almost killed all of us, yourself included?' said Fennec, which was an excellent point even if Zosia didn't remember seeing her Usban friend anywhere near the opossum queen during the desperate battle. 'Those kinds of precautions?'

'Apples and apple trees,' said Hoartrap dismissively.

'Not an expression,' said Ji-hyeon.

'Look, we've been over all this. I had never attempted that ritual before, and I made a whoopsie. It *happens*. I told you I had discovered a method for calling forth a great devil, I just didn't know *how* great. The sheer power of that entity—'

'You also insisted you could control it,' said Ji-hyeon. 'That was rather the idea, wasn't it, you summon something you can direct against our enemies?'

'Sometimes you have to do something the wrong way to learn how to do it the right way,' said Hoartrap with a shrug, but Zosia could tell he was getting annoyed, as though he were the victim here and not all the poor Cobalts and Imperials who had been either mashed beneath the devil's claws or literally transformed into monsters. 'And I did tell you to keep your soldiers back, didn't I? But did you listen? No you did not.'

'I didn't have a lot of choice, since you also told me your ritual might not work at all.' Ji-hyeon did not sound very pleased to be dragged into Hoartrap's blame game. 'And I initially ordered most of the company to hold back, but when the Thaoans charged us and you were still just having a naked make-out session with an opossum, I did what I had to do. Don't think for a fucking second you can pin this on me!'

'Even if I would have tried, which I wouldn't, the second is now passed,' said Hoartrap, 'which allows us to return to the actual topic at hand. If you just walk into a Gate willy-nilly, of course something awful will happen. Of course of course of course. But that's not what I'm suggesting, and I can't *stress* how much experience I have with using the First Dark as a shortcut around the Star. I've done it myself hundreds of times, and taken others safely through on dozens of occasions. *At least.* I don't even need Gates to get around anymore, it's that easy for me.'

'Easy,' repeated Fennec, tapping a claw even harder against the table.

'For me, yes; for a would-be apprentice who never showed up for his second lesson, not so much,' said Hoartrap, throwing his hands in the air. 'I understand all of your concerns, I truly do, but this is not something new or scary to me. This is ... this is walking across the fucking street easy. For *me*. And the reason for that is because I have put years and years and *years* into researching how to do it safely and efficiently, and more years on top of that experimenting with the intricacies of it all, because if there's one thing I care about it's my own back.

'Now, if it will assuage your fears, Fennec, that neither you nor Ji-hyeon will suffer further alterations so long as I guide you through, and since dear Captain Choi seems immune to the influence of the Gates anyway, that just leaves the rest of the Cobalt Company. It will be the first time for all of them, and the initial exposure is always very minor. I should hope soldiers willing to lay down their lives for your cause won't balk at having their coifs lightened.'

'That of course raises the question of how in all the world you convince threescore weary sellswords to step into a Gate, let alone three thousand,' said Singh. 'There are barely a dozen people alive who know someone who has entered a Gate and come out safe, and half of them are already in this tent. However much the rank and file may wish to believe their general's tales of harmlessly passing through the Othean Gate, you may find the company that readily followed you across the Star will balk at marching into hell.'

'That's why I need your help in making the most out of my speech,' said Ji-hyeon, pointing at the blank page of goatskin on the table. 'We need that classic Cold Cobalt rabble-rousing to get enough of them excited about the prospect that they'll herd in the less committed.'

'In that case I better leave you to it,' said Zosia, preferring the uncertain fate of entering a Gate to the certain horror of speech writing. 'See you all on the other side, I guess. I'll have the peasants revolting an hour before dawn in Diadem.'

'Better make it first light instead of the hour before,' suggested Hoartrap. 'The sun graces Diadem well before it reaches the Witchfinder Plains.'

'Oh,' said Ji-hyeon. 'It does? That's the first I've heard of it.'

'It's not the sort of issue that comes up much in this benighted time, but in the Age of Wonders when mortals frequently employed the Gates to travel across the Star—' Hoartrap began, and Zosia hurried for the exit before she could be roped into the debate. When it came to matters metaphysical, she'd trust Hoartrap to have done his homework better than an exhausted teenage general. A riot with the dawn, then.

'If I may be excused for a moment,' said Singh, rising to follow Zosia out, but Choi's hand shot over and rested lightly on her shoulder. Ji-hyeon must have told her Honor Guard to expect this and quietly prevent the Villain from having a final collaboration with Zosia.

'I'm afraid we'll need the expertise of your tongue,' said Ji-hyeon. 'You'll have plenty of time to catch up with Captain Zosia once you help us take Diadem. For now, Chevaleresse, your employer begs the wisdom of your counsel a bit longer.'

Zosia waved farewell to her friend for what would likely be a very long time; if the deeply superstitious Singh went through the Gate instead of sneaking away with her dragoons in the night Zosia would eat her boots.

'Fetch your lackey and I'll meet you down in the valley,' Hoartrap called after Zosia as she raised the flap, talking over whatever objection Ji-hyeon had raised to his timetables. 'And be quick about it, I want to be back here in time for supper.'

'Yeah, can't miss that,' said Zosia queasily, the prospect of actually entering a Gate not exactly stimulating her appetite. 'But let's give it another hour, at least, I need to find a smith and pick up a new piece.'

'You *still* haven't done that?' said Fennec. 'Unbelievable.'

'I figured some grunt had walked off the field with it after I got knocked out, and once I announced a reward someone would bring her home,' said Zosia, too damn old and tired to be self-conscious about how hard she'd tried to recover her lost war hammer. 'But I guess if anyone carried it off it was that devil queen – last thing I remember was sticking her something fierce with the pick-end, so who knows? But if I ever find some hump made off with my hammer and didn't take the opportunity to return it, I'll—'

'Just get a new one already!' snapped Ji-hyeon, too young to appreciate the importance of heirloom weaponry. 'That's an order, Zosia.'

'Okay, okay, I will, I just need to—'

'Right. Now,' said Ji-hyeon. 'Go see my grumpy guy, he runs the smithy on the southwestern side of camp, near the Raniputri temple-tents. Buy a new hammer, meet Hoartrap, and get this shit done. If we fall behind schedule because you dragged your feet on commissioning a new one and spend all night picking out the perfect replacement I may seriously lose my shit.'

'Never going to find a perfect replacement, ever, so I'll just grab whatever piece of crap they've got lying around,' grumbled Zosia, good and annoyed about the situation all over again. 'Like I'd commission a fucking weapon from some chucklehead around here anyway. Antique is the only way to go in this sorry-ass age – you know that hammer of mine came out of Emeritus? Six hundred years old, and never rusted or tarnished. Might've put a ding or two into her, sure, but—'

'Zosia!'

'Yeah, I'm going, I'm going,' she said, but on her way out caught the attention of Hoartrap, Fennec, and Singh, and with exaggerated slowness swung an imaginary hammer at them, making a *woooosh* sound as she did. Ji-hyeon would never get it, but they did – they'd been there when she'd risked her life to wrest the ancient war hammer from its guardian, after all, and whatever else their faults they could appreciate material history. Fuckings kids today.

The nervous sweat seemed to freeze on Zosia's clammy skin as she stepped back out into the cold, Choplicker bounding over and doing cheerful laps around her. Before she'd made her peace with the devil after the First Battle of the Lark's Tongue, Zosia would have stuck her face in a meat grinder before she'd have considered using a Gate the way Ji-hyeon had when she'd escaped Othean. And now? She would still prefer the meat grinder, if it accomplished the same end, but since it obviously didn't that left her with hoping that between Hoartrap's devils and her own she would pass through a Gate unscathed. Her only consolation was that Boris would presumably like the idea even less than she did, and that put a little spring in her step as she returned to the archery range – nothing to make you feel better about your own bad fortune like spreading it around a little.

CHAPTER

16

The Haunted Forest turned out to be a total bust, with nary a spook or spirit in the whole place. The village in the center of the wood was decidedly more pissant than puissant, a smoky burg called Black Moth that looked on the verge of turning into a ghost town. Until that came to pass, though, they really ought to call the forest something else, just so travelers didn't get their hopes up.

Or so Purna thought, until the announcement board by the public gallows gave her the nastiest start she'd had since waking up to find herself wildtouched (as she'd taken to thinking of her condition). It was a specter from her past, no two ways about that, so maybe this murky wood had come by its name honestly. She managed to rip it down and stuff it into the pocket of her baggy wool pantaloons before the others could notice; Sullen and Keun-ju were distracted by the poster advertising an Immaculate bounty for General Ji-hyeon, and Diggelby had already taken their pony straight to the sauna to see about a warm bath for the both of them. In Thao they hadn't let the animal into the bathhouse at all, and while Black Moth was more accommodating of the pasha, he was disappointed to discover that Princess was less obliging of bath time than Prince had been.

After that, their brief stay in Black Moth was less than ideal, with Purna obliged to keep her scarf high and her hood low for the duration; the poster bearing her likeness was far too new for her liking. She even went without a turn in the sauna for fear of being recognized once she shed her layers, a tragic development by anyone's reckoning. The one upside to the stopover was that she'd been able to score a traveler's pipe case, a cheap coalstick, and some decent flake tubāq from the mercantile, so she could properly teach herself how to smoke Maroto's pipe – she'd picked up a big pouch of shag in Thao, but had lost it all in an ill-advised wager with Digs before she'd been able to sample a single bowl. Only the Old Watchers of Flintland knew when next they'd pass through a frontier town with decent pipeweed, but she tried not to let her luck go to her head . . . and then sure enough, she'd almost immediately countered this rare spot of good fortune by foolishly mentioning the score to Diggelby, and in the same phrasing, and so for the past day and night he'd not said three words that weren't related to her learning how to smoke Maroto's pipe.

'Now it's true that I never cared to wrap my lips around Maroto's, but that doesn't mean I can't offer some valuable advice to a novice,' Digs told her after she'd told him to shut his pretty mouth for the umpteenth time. 'For one thing, Maroto's is bound to be a good bit older than most of the pipes I've tried, so you'll want to treat it delicately. Especially the tip, those can become quite vulnerable over the years; never know when the last smoker clamped down with their teeth!'

'Quiet!' The more she used Sullen and Keun-ju's mantra, the more she found herself sympathizing with the pair of sour-pusses. Unlike herself, Digs didn't know when to give a gag a rest, and the fact that she now highly doubted he'd ever sucked any cock at all and was just being childish wasn't helping.

Gesturing ahead to where Sullen and Keun-ju had paused and set down the Procuress's post in the dead leaves, she said, 'Can't you see they're trying to think?'

'I had noticed an inordinate amount of perspiration greasing their unscrubbed necks,' said Digs. 'Which is why I thought it the perfect time to coach you on your new hobby – with those two sages sizing up their subject we may be here for quite some time.'

This wasn't strictly inaccurate. The tamarind pylon had led them off the road and back into the wilderness shortly after leaving the hostelry in Black Moth, and on they had gone throughout the morning and afternoon, scratching themselves stupid on increasingly thick underbrush and getting cobwebby moss tangled up on the pony's pack. Yet despite it not being time for Digs and Purna's next shift nor to break for the night, Sullen had called a stop and fished out Hoartrap's compass to double-check their course. The problem was obvious – over the last few hours the open wood had become pitted with soggy spots, then more and more pools, and then the forest had contracted entirely, with expanses of bald cypress-studded stagnant water stretching out on either side of them. The ground had proved solid enough, at least, gaining a little elevation over the slough as they strolled along the narrow natural causeway. Fine and good, so long as it held . . . but of course it didn't. They had now come to discover that the avenue of dry, leaf-carpeted land was in fact a peninsula, with a final steep slope dropping down almost a dozen feet into the wide-open waters of the swamp. The curious thing was that from this point on the aquatic trees fell away, too, leaving a vast, wet hole in the middle of the marshy forest, but on the far side of the boggy clearing the trail looked to rise out of the mire and resume its course. A shallow pond or lake, obviously, with an abundance of beaver dams in place of trees out there on one side of the pool; hardly a thing to warrant a full stop.

If only to escape Digs's interminable needling, she marched to the end of the track and joined the other two, who were hunched over the soiled map and rusting compass.

'Soooooo, gentlemen, what's it to be? Do we ford the fetid fen in hopes yon swell of earth is a continuation of this shortcut our magic post led us on, or bite the bitter pill of regret and retrace our footsteps, lest it prove nothing but a mirage of weary wanderers?'

'Huh?' Sullen finally looked up from the compass, whose needle pointed straight across the depressing pond.

'Should we plunge ahead or turn back and try to find a way around,' translated Keun-ju. 'To which I still say we just go for it. I don't mind a little mess.'

'Long as I've awaited those words to leave your veil, I fear this is not the context I had hoped for,' said Digs, fanning flies away from their pony's face with his goofy hat. 'These boots are made for walking, sir, not wading.'

'It doesn't look more than ankle-deep,' said Keun-ju. 'It's no worse than a wide mud puddle, and much better than knee-deep snow.'

'Graveyard,' Sullen muttered, scratching his unkempt bloom of tight white curls. 'Old man at the inn said we shouldn't cut through the graveyard.'

'I believe his exact words were *mind the road, stay out the woods*,' corrected Purna. 'All that *beware the graveyard and the castle of the dead* business sounded like an afterthought. Besides, seeing as how both our post and our compass ignored the main thrust of the man's advice it seems silly to bring up the point about steering clear of cemeteries and keeps, when it's the only suggestion we're following. Unless you think by *graveyard* he meant *random patch of swamp*?'

'Begging your pardon, Purna,' said Digs, 'but I seem to recall it a mite differently. What he actually said was *beeeewaaaaaare the graaaaaaaaaveyaaaard and the casssssstle of the deeeeeeeead*.'

'No he didn't,' said Purna, in no mood for cutting up with him after his merciless ribbing of before. 'He said it normally.'

'I wouldn't go as far as that,' said Keun-ju, having inexplicably lightened up after their first night in the Haunted Forest. In a remarkably close imitation of the pinch-faced ancient who had sent them off that morning, he said, '*Mind the rud. Sty oot the wud. Bevarr the graveyurd und the cassel uv the deed*.'

'Old people aren't always as daft as they sound,' said Sullen, wagging a finger at them. 'I think we better turn back. If we ignore the post for now and then try it again a ways up the road it'll probably show us another path.'

'Sullen. *Baby*,' said Digs, which looked like it went down as well with the nephew as it had with the uncle. Undeterred by the man's scowl, Digs pointed out at the still expanse. 'I know Grampa Gingernut said we shouldn't take any shortcuts through graveyards or castles, but does that look like any graveyard you've ever seen? Or a castle, for that matter? Because I've been all over the blessed Empire, and I've yet to find a place where they dispose of the dead by feeding them to beavers, or refer to their dams as castles.'

'Beavers?' asked Sullen, and though it broke her ever-loving heart, Purna refrained from making a crack about how she'd thought he'd become familiar with that particular fur-bearing game after meeting their general. Among the many differences she'd noticed between Maroto and Sullen was a distinct lack of wit in the younger relation.

'Those ... things out there, the big piles of sticks? They're beaver dams,' said Digs. 'Or nests or whatever, I suppose there isn't very much to dam up in a swamp. Or do you think the good people of Black Moth come allllll the way out here to bury their kin under—'

'All right,' said Sullen, pointing at the far shore some hundred meters off. 'You and Purna take the post across.'

'I'm not going down there until you walk all the way out and make sure it doesn't get deeper,' Purna told Digs. 'For a man who didn't want to get his hose wet you sure worked hard to get us post duty for the crossing.'

'Maroto always lets us draw straws to see who goes first,' protested Diggelby, but then threw up his hands and marched straight down into the bog. He probably figured it would be quicker to just walk across than explain to Sullen what drawing straws meant. The coppery water only came to his calves, and he began poking the mud in front of him with Hassan's genuine dromedary-pizzle swagger stick as he advanced out into the open swamp.

'Who will give me two-to-one odds that he sinks to his chin before he's made it to the far shore?' asked Purna, but neither of the other two were of a sporting mood. Too broke, no doubt, and sensible enough to guess she never took a foolish bet. Now a dozen paces out into the shallow water, Digs waved them on, and Purna sighed. 'Well, come on then – I want to be close enough to throw him a rope if he steps in quickmud. Up, magic post!'

As many good grins as she and Digs had got out of barking that silly command at Sullen and Keun-ju when it was their turn to hoist the tamarind log, it seemed almost fair it now came back to haunt her – it was the right forest for it, anyway. Pointing at the heavy front of the post, Sullen said, 'Nah, think it's your turn to take the lead. I'll bring up the rear since your boy got ahead of you, but soon as we're across you two are taking an honest shift for a change.'

Purna blew her fearless leader the raspberry to end all raspberries; another advantage of her devilish resurrection. But when she went to lift it Sullen shooed her off with a dopey smile, taking the front while Keun-ju lifted the back, and she realized he had been messing with her. Sullen's sense of humor was like everything else about him – not stupid so much as just plain odd.

Taking Princess by the bridle, Purna led her down the soft slope, into the bayou after Digs. The water was only an inch or two deep, but so was the mud – this was going to suck in more ways than one. As she trudged ahead, Keun-ju muttered something that Purna didn't hear but somehow achieved something even rarer than one of Sullen's attempts at levity – it made the big galoot chuckle. Earlier in their quest she would have been overjoyed to see the two grumps getting along, but now it just exasperated her. Maybe it was the crumpled poster in her pocket that put Purna in such a lousy mood, or maybe it was the fact that even after all this time she couldn't stop her stupid tongue from hanging out of her mouth for more than a minute before she felt like she was drowning on it, but this day was a dud round, and picking her way across a half-drained beaver pond wasn't exactly improving matters.

She tried to fortify herself by remembering why she was out here, who she was doing all this for . . . and remembered Maroto as she'd last seen him: wild-eyed and buggy on the battlefield, talking too fast to be understood. It wasn't her fondest memory of her chum, but it was what came to mind as she trudged through the piss-warm water. The Mighty Maroto, probably running as fast as he could to Zosia's hated enemy Queen Indsorith just as soon as he found out his old flame was actually a cold fish . . . and like the dog-girl she'd become, Purna was hot on his trail, for reasons that were no longer quite so obvious, all things considered.

Ahead of her, Digs began to colorfully curse, pinwheeling his arms in vain as an overambitious step led to him falling with dramatic slowness. He went facedown in the muck. Purna gave a triumphant cry and looked back over her shoulder to grin at Hassan and Din, but of course they were dead and gone, and the two po-faced boys who had taken their place looked at Purna like *she* was the asshole for laughing at Digs's clumsiness. She turned back to their floundering scout, Digs acting like he was drowning in a few inches of muddy water and trying desperately to retrieve his boat-like hat before it sailed beyond the reach of his swagger stick, and shook her head.

Fucking Maroto. He better be down on one knee, praying for his old chums to rescue him, with big snotty bubbles in his nose and tear-streaming eyes, hoping against hope for salvation. It was only fair that he suffer some really, really stinky fate in the interim, considering all the bother they were going through on his account.

———

Maroto had suffered in his day; not even his most hated enemy would dispute that point. Some of it had been his own doing, he'd fess to that, but plenty of it hadn't; bad luck, worse luck, hells, worst luck, you name it and Maroto had endured it. Physical agony and emotional, the hurt of desire and harder still, the pain of attainment, he'd been there, he'd paid his dues ... overpaid, in most cases, and never been given any change. He thought he knew every kind of misery there was, a veteran martyr if ever there was one, but here on Jex Toth, as the days blurred into weeks and the weeks blurred into regrets that he hadn't better kept track of the days, Maroto had managed to discover a new kind of pain. Her name was Bang Lin.

It wasn't her flirting that got to him, though his commitment not to engage her on those terms could be a burden, fit as he found her and fine a pastime as flirting undeniably was.

It wasn't her giving him the hardest chores, or the way she'd sit back and make cracks about his glistening thews as he carried them out . . . though that could be severely irritating, too. Everyone likes a compliment, but there's a time and a place for such things, and someone doing you the solid of rigging up a hammock out of a salvaged sail is definitely not it.

It wasn't even her insistence that he always be the one to accompany her on expeditions deeper into the interior of Jex Toth, where the presence of quicksand, deadly snakes, and minor monsters incurred a slightly higher risk than came from staying near camp to watch the bay for ships, as Dong-won and Niki-hyun did.

What it was, straight up, was not even her doing, but Maroto's, and it was this – despite his refusal to even acknowledge her double entendres, despite his careful looking away whenever she bathed in the pool or otherwise exposed an appealing portion of her anatomy, despite his tender thoughts and intense dreams of Choi, despite his promise to himself not to get hung up on another girl who was obvious trouble, Maroto had developed a crush on the pirate captain. A crush can be uncomfortable, obviously, especially when one knows as well as Maroto did that the object of his affection has no genuine interest in him, that it was a passion that could never be quenched . . . or at least a minor infatuation that seems incurable until something better comes along.

But Maroto had been hurt by love before, obviously, and being sweet on a new acquaintance is not even in the same realm as spending twenty years punishing yourself over a woman the way Maroto had.

No, what messed him up so bad, what gave him palpitations

when he thought about it, and what he couldn't stop thinking about, even though it gave him palpitations, was how
utterly doomed Bang was. Ever since he'd first started rolling
with Purna he'd half known he'd be the death of the girl,
and surprise surprise, his gut instincts had been right for a
change . . . and as soon as he'd gotten her killed, he went and
met another feisty young woman. Bang was quite different
from Purna in appearance and personality, but bore close
enough a resemblance in certain ways to have her fate sealed
by Maroto's very presence. This one wanted to be a pirate,
not a barbarian, but Maroto knew the devil wasn't in that
detail, it was in him – he was the common link, and it was
only a matter of time before Bang bought it in a bad way. He
could barely look at her smiling, metal-studded grill without
envisioning some deformed jungle beast bursting from the
bush to decapitate her. Every rill they drank from and every
fruit they foraged was sure to be her last, and that would be
that – vomiting blood, she'd die slow, painfully, clinging to
his arm and gasping out words between heaves, making him
promise to look after Dong-won and Niki-hyun after she . . .
after she . . . and then she was gone, the shine leaving her eyes
as Maroto closed his in shame.

'You still with me, Useful?' she called down the ridge, and
Maroto shook off the vision, knowing as he did that it wouldn't
stay gone for long. The gut-pinching daydreams were faithful as
bound devils, always returning to his side. Even now another
one was coming on, as he looked up the wildflower-covered
saddle they climbed and saw her striking a cocky posture with
a knee up on a boulder, peering into the distance. It would be
just the opportunity for an emperor centipede to strike one of
her tan legs, and reeling back, she'd slip, tumbling over the
edge to— 'Shake a fat leg, Useful, I don't have all day! Looks

like there's something up ahead and I'm not inclined to take the lead when I can send you in first.'

He knew he must look crazed, but as he hustled up the narrow, treeless ridge after her he cuffed the side of his head a couple of times, as though his compulsive imagination could be dislodged like water from an ear. Well, you never knew until you tried. Bang watched his approach from her perch, her hands on her hips, the flower-scented breeze stirring her blood-coral hair around her tan, tattooed face. The hot color suited her better than the fading green had, and that gave Maroto a rush of satisfaction – he'd been the one who spent hours on the hunt, splashing through tide pools and risking a nasty case of coral burn harvesting the dangerous growths, and even grinding up the pigment himself, adding in kamala fruit and some ruddy beetles as a sort of sympathetic magic to make the dye as red as possible. Under Captain Bang's orders, it was all literally thankless work, but the vibrant results were their own reward.

'So what do you make of that, old salt?' she asked as he clambered up the flowering knoll to join her, and blinking the sweat out of his eyes, he saw what she'd been looking at. The bottom of the next valley over had previously been hidden by vegetation and the angle, but up here on the steeply climbing ridge he now saw a wide white river winding through it ... a frozen river, with the occasional tree rising from it.

'It's a road,' he decided. 'Alabaster, or white marble or something.'

'That's what I thought,' said Bang, and pointed far up the exposed saddle to where the grass- and flower-ornamented ridge rose to a summit crowned with similar white stone. 'And I bet my bottom we'll get a better look at where it leads from up there.'

'I'll take that bet,' said Maroto, so busy following the distant road with his eye that he didn't pay attention to the stakes. 'See how overgrown it is down there? We're in the sweet spot right here, soon as we climb up or go down the road'll get eaten up by the jungle again.'

'It's a wager, then,' said Bang, grabbing the hand he'd been using to shield his eyes and shaking the unholy hell out of it. 'Both our bottoms are on the line, but just you wait and see, Useful, you're not in the sweet spot yet! Now shake both your legs, all this talk of going down and eating jungles is getting me antsy.'

'That's not what I said!' It was hopeless, though, Bang already moving along up the ridge, and Maroto followed her. There was a time not so long ago that he would've relished going second up a soft climb like this, taking the opportunity to admire the way Bang's baggy cut-offs went taut against her thin, muscular legs and narrow rear as she picked her way up the saddle . . . but those days were behind him, and he intended to keep it that way. He kept his focus on the ground in front of him, and when that became impossible due to Bang pausing and wiggling her butt in his face as she fished around for a better handhold, he looked back at the panorama spread out behind them.

The grassy ridgeline gave way on either side to even steeper slopes, earthen cliffs, really, hung with trellises of orange and pink blossoms. Both sheer sides of the saddle eventually plunged into the interminable jungle, but back the way they'd come a band of azure now shimmered at the top of all that emerald as the Haunted Sea came back into view, a border on the manifest color wheel between rich green flora and pale blue sky. Once you moved inland from the gentle beaches and sheer headlands of the coast, Jex Toth became a series of incredibly steep but short and narrow mountains intercut with equally tight and densely wooded valleys, as though the jungle grew atop the splayed fingers of a titan.

Yet here at last they seemed to be moving into new terrain, the ridge they now followed the first they had encountered that rose above the treeline, and beyond it the miniature mountains loomed taller and wider, and the valleys spread out accordingly. It was pretty, this place, and he felt the old elbow of guilt grinding into his heart as he thought of how much Purna would have loved it, this scenic wilderness full of monsters he'd never even heard of and more adventure than you could shake a curved Ugrakari blade at.

'Answer me a question, Useful,' said Bang, and as was usually the case, it sounded more like an order than a question.

'Sure.' Turning back from the breathtaking landscape, Maroto found himself staring at a more immediate but nonetheless impressive vista: Bang still had her arse perilously close to his head, hanging from an especially sharp uptick in the ridge like a cat clinging to a curtain.

'Would it kill you to give me a boost? I know the thought of touching me gives you the fantods, but unless you help we may be at an impasse.'

'Right, of course,' said Maroto, his fingers far too quick to leap at her bottom for his liking. 'Sorry, Bang, my mind was elsewhere.'

'Sorry, *Captain Bang*,' she corrected, floating up to easier climbing with the help of his hands. 'So where were you, Useful? Someplace much more interesting than the Sunken Kingdom, with all its mundane sights that no mortal has glimpsed in ten lifetimes?'

'Sunken Kingdom,' repeated Maroto, digging his fingers through warm grass and the twisting stalks of tiny flowers, into the cool, black earth, each hand and foothold in the ridge taking them farther away from the old-growth jungle below. 'Tell you this much, Captain, Niki-hyun was right that first day we all met – wherever we are now didn't just rise from the seabed last month. If it went somewhere it wasn't under the waves, that much is obvious.'

'*Obvious* is the word, all right – that fact just now sinking into your doddering pate, Grampa Useful?' asked Bang, her boot slipping and almost bonking Maroto in the nose. He dug his toes deeper into the dirt, this unexpected climb up a soft and sun-drenched saddle the first time he'd been okay with his involuntary barefootedness since arriving in a jungle full of sharp rock outcroppings, prickly vegetation, and snakes snakes snakes. 'Or you just trying to dodge the question?'

'Okay, it's like this . . . ' said Maroto, because it was long past time he kept his promise to Purna's memory and properly told her story to the world that was poorer for her passing. 'That first night on the beach, I told you about my friend Purna, remember?'

'Your friend who died, just before some others betrayed you and wizarded you here, yeah?'

'That's her,' said Maroto, pausing to haul himself up and over another steep patch. His belly was nearly flat against the grass and itchy flowers, but if he leaned back too far he'd topple over and roll all the way down. 'Except she died after they sent me here. *Wizarded* is a good word for it, too.'

'Wait . . . ' Bang inched up over another hummock, seeming to climb straight into the blue sky. 'How do you know she's dead, if you got dumped here before she died?'

'She . . . ' It was Maroto's turn to pause, but not just so he could focus on the ascent. He ground his forehead into the cool, soft grass until his grief passed, then explained, 'She was hurt too bad to recover. Nobody could survive what happened to her.'

'Fuck that,' said Bang, pausing to look back down at him. 'You didn't see her die, you don't know she's dead. That's basic, Useful, as basic as basic gets.'

'You don't know what you're talking about,' growled Maroto, knowing she only meant to help but nevertheless insulted. 'False hope is worse than no hope, Bang. Believe me, that's a lesson I—'

'*Captain Bang*,' she growled back, kicking the earth beside his head. 'And I don't give a shark's shart what lessons you think you've learned, Useful, there's always hope for our friends, until we know for certain. I've met a woman who the whole Star swore was dead, and just before I dragged you from the water I dodged a doom that any sane person would think a foregone conclusion. Becalmed in the Haunted Sea, water full of monsters, boat afire, off the coast of the Sunken fucking Kingdom, and you want to tell me about false hope? 'Twas false hope what made me and Niki-hyun swim for shore instead of going down with the *Queen Thief*, and false hope that lit the signal fire Dong-won spied through the night.'

She went quiet, but while he couldn't see her face from down here Maroto sensed she wasn't finished, so he stayed quiet, too. After a spell, she cleared her throat and said, 'I'm not a fool, Useful, I know the odds are long for the rest of my crew, and I'll live my life accordingly. But I won't give up on them, not until their bodies wash in on the tide. And I'm not naïve enough to think you'll listen, but I'll say it all the same, because while I'd lie to my own mother's face I'll never bullshit my crew, nor spare their feelings at the expense of the truth, and this is the truth: you didn't see your friend Purna die, you don't know she's dead. Basic shit. Let her live in your heart, man, at least until you've gotten yourself off this rock and can start worrying about someone's skin other than your own.'

It was a good speech, so good, in fact, that Maroto was sure some new winged horror was about to snatch Bang off the ridge, the ironic punctuation to her youthful optimism. When that didn't happen, he tried to let her words actually seep in a little, instead of just washing over him. Oh, how he wished he could share her childish hope, but life had taught him that things were always worse than you feared, never better ...

But what then of Zosia? Bang just mentioned meeting someone the whole world thought dead, straight up confirming what Maroto already knew – that Zosia had been the ex-lover who had carved Bang's pipe. Zosia who Maroto had given up for dead along with everyone else, because even if he hadn't witnessed her death himself it seemed impossible she could have survived the fate everyone insisted had befallen her. What if instead of believing those who said she had died, Maroto had kept his hopes alive? He'd been mostly successful thinking that way about dear Choi, and Din and Hassan, so why not for Purna, too? What if instead of wasting every day since he'd been dumped out here mourning her death, he had let himself cling to the chance that all was not as it seemed?

You had to let the dead go, of course you did. Refusing to acknowledge their passing could only lead to your squandering your own life, possibly even madness ... but wasn't that what Maroto had done with Zosia, anyway? He'd given up all hope that she lived, true, but he hadn't moved on, hadn't accepted it. It wasn't Zosia's presumed death that had destroyed Maroto's life, but his refusal to let her go – he thought she'd been the one to die yet it was he who had become the ghost, driven only by sorrow and loss, existing only to grieve her ...

And over twenty years later, he discovered she'd never died, that his whole tragic-hero-with-a-bug-habit bit had been on account of a tragedy that had never actually happened. And as soon as he learned this, another beloved comrade seemed to fall, and he committed himself to avenging her memory . . . the same fucking way he had with Zosia. His pledge to find and kill Hoartrap and everyone else responsible for Purna's death bore a striking resemblance to his pledge to kill Indsorith after he'd heard about Zosia. And after the young queen kicked the living shit out of him, he'd been so scared of dying that he'd sworn that dumb oath not to lift a sword against her, and started on his steady descent into depression and addiction.

Thinking back on it, why hadn't Queen Indsorith just killed him when he stormed her throne room, demanding a duel? Why had she let him off with the oath? He hadn't much thought about it since finding out Zosia lived, but now it was starting to make sense – Indsorith saw the grief-maddened Maroto, a man willing to burn his whole life to avenge his beloved, and took pity on him, because she knew Zosia still lived but must not have taken him into her confidence. The Crimson Queen must have realized how wretched Maroto was long before he did; she must have been moved to mercy, to offer him a chance to start over, and what had he done with this second chance? Squandered it, the same as he did with every other good thing that had ever happened to him . . . that was what he had done with Zosia's friendship, too, wasn't it? Squandered it, demanding affection she never felt, poisoning their relationship with his selfish insistence that she give him something more, something physical . . . she might have viewed him as a brother, if he hadn't insisted on treating her as a bashful sweetheart.

With Purna he hadn't made that same mistake, he didn't think – she'd made it clear she wasn't interested, and he'd backed all the way off, hadn't thought about her in that way since the Wastes, really. But what about the other mistakes? What about honoring the memory of his friends with violence and hatred, instead of hope and happy memories? What about trying to actually live his life for a change, what about enjoying the thrill of exploring a land undreamed of rather than stewing in impotent revenge fantasies and daydreams of his new comrades dying just as horribly as his old ones? What about that, huh?

'Useful!' Maroto blinked, and peering up he saw the silhouette of Bang waving at him from what looked to be the apex of the ridge, some fifty yards ahead and above. This is what came of ignoring the pirate's acumen – he'd been left behind again. And missed an extended opportunity to check out her backside, but he quieted that ignoble inner voice.

'I know you're dead, Purna,' he told her, whispering to the sweet purple blooms that tickled his chin as he climbed. 'But Bang's right – I won't give up on you. I'll never give up on you. Never.'

—

'I changed my mind,' Purna called back to Sullen and Keun-ju as Digs splashed around in the beaver pond, blundering deeper into the pool as his hat floated away, just beyond his reach. The sun was dipping down into the trees, casting the dismal, damp scene in deeper shades of red. 'This is balls. I don't want to chase Maroto's sorry ass anymore. Can I go back?'

'For sure,' said Sullen, 'but you have to take Diggelby with you.'

Digs shrieked again, so shrill it made Purna squint her eyes shut, but when she reopened them to upbraid her tenor-hitting friend she saw he may have had something of a point this time. The closest of the small beaver dams was floating quickly toward him and, as she watched, the other mounds of branches were beginning to move through the water, too. All told, there were a dozen of the small driftwood islands moving in on them from the lefthand side of the shallow pool, each of them at least as big as a charcoal burner's bundle.

'Run!' Sullen cried, the first order he'd given all trip that made a lick of sense . . . but as with all his orders, Digs ignored it, still flopping around in the water instead of getting back to his feet. Purna pushed ahead, keeping her cool even as the strange woodpiles sped up through the water, and coming abreast of Digs, she saw the problem: in chasing his hat he'd moved off the ankle-deep path through the center of the swamp, and fallen straight into a small sinkhole that opened up in the shallow mud.

'Come on, Digs, I've got you,' she told her idiot comrade, grabbing one end of his flailing swagger stick. If he would drop either the pizzle or the hat he'd finally nabbed, he could easily pull himself out, but then he wouldn't be Diggelby if he didn't prioritize his possessions over his own safety. Hauling him out by the cane, she nearly backed herself into another of the narrow but deep pools that must pit the swamp, but noticed the trap in the nick of time. Letting go of the stick and allowing Digs to flop back down in the shallows, she saw the nearest dam was nearly on top of them. 'Move, Digs, move!'

It was too late, though – the other curious woodpiles had floated around to cut them off on either end of what she now realized was the only path through the swamp, both the way they'd come and their only way forward blocked by several dams. More of the mounds were moving in, too, and the one that had come for Digs now floated toward them over the sinkhole he had just vacated, close enough Purna could have spit on it. Despite the failing light and muddiness of the water, she clearly saw what it was that propelled the bundle of water-wobbly wood, dead leaves, and sundry detritus: a nearly skeletal human form, its eyes shining just above the surface of the pool, with the piled flotsam on its back making it resemble some monstrous turtle.

Well, Purna knew a thing or three about monsters, and before its grasping fingers could catch Diggelby she whipped her pistol out of her holster and fired. Some sticks broke off of its driftwood shell and a plume of mud clouded the water where she'd shot through its back, but it didn't even register the wound, closing its long-nailed fingers around Digs's boot. Her friend screamed as the thing began swimming backward, dragging him toward the deeper water, as oblivious to the twig-snapping blows of Digs's swagger stick as it had been to the ball of her pistol.

This wasn't just bad; this was Maroto Bad, as their friend used to joke about his luck. Grabbing Digs around the shoulder before it could pull him away, Purna tried to set her heels but began sliding forward in the muck after him. The fucker must be strong as all devils, to be able to tow Digs so hard without any footing, and her friend's legs lifted clear out of the water as their tug-of-war neared its inevitable climax, the pasha going taut in the air between the opponents.

'Slip off your shoe!' Keun-ju cried, seizing Digs's other shoulder.

'Have you given leave of your senses?' Diggelby cried back. 'These boots cost more than your life!'

'Do they cost more than yours?' Purna grunted, wondering if Digs had just issued the foppiest last words to ever grace an empty urn, but then Digs planted his free foot against the heel of his snatched boot, and all three of them fell back in the swamp as it came loose in the creature's grasp.

If it had continued the attack they would have been in bad shape, but as Keun-ju scrambled up and helped Purna out of the shallows, and as Purna helped Digs, they saw the corpse-turtle had retreated into the center of the sinkhole, holding the boot in both hands and gnawing at the white patent leather with its mud-oozing mouth. Purna began laughing hysterically, couldn't help herself, really, as Digs screamed in outrage at the spectacle. Both of their outbursts abruptly ended as Keun-ju grabbed one of their shoulders in each hand and gave them a mighty shake. The usually sophisticated Immaculate's methods were crude, but he had a point: the mound-covered monsters that had congregated on either end of the flooded trail to cut them off were now approaching, pulling themselves along the muddy bottom with water-softened hands.

There was nowhere to flee, they were outnumbered, and far more tragic than the loss of Digs's boot, Purna realized she'd dropped her pistol when she'd collapsed into the swamp. She fell to her knees, rooting around in the mud for it, and when her fingers miraculously closed on the butt she gave a victory cry, wrenching it free of the muck . . . only to realize she'd just pulled a Diggelby, worrying about her prized possession when monsters were almost on top of her, keen to deprive her of something far more valuable. Only their sleepy-eyed pony seemed unconcerned by their prospects, Sullen clumsily balancing the magic post on her broad back, and Purna called bullshit on all the tales she'd ever heard of animals sensing danger and bolting in the presence of devils and monsters. But most of all she called bullshit on Maroto, on whose account they were about to be assaulted by fiends that were even wetter and weedier than dear old Digs, no small feat. Sticking the dripping flintlock in its holster and drawing her kukri as the monsters closed in, she shouted her war cry to the twilit swamp:

'Fuck Maroto!'

'Fuck Maroto,' agreed Sullen as he stepped up beside her on the narrow, sunken path, and then Digs and Keun-ju took up the call, too, as the first of the corpse-turtles came within striking distance: 'Fuck Maroto!'

———

'You actually remind me a bit of her,' Maroto told Bang as he joined her at the summit. 'My buddy Purna.'

'Oh yeah?' asked Bang, swallowing a mouthful of the starfruit they'd foraged in the foothills and wiping the juice off her chin. She sat lunching in the grass, leaning back against a rectangular boulder of white quartz that jutted from the flowery shelf at the top of the ridge. 'Was she gagging for it, too?'

'Devil's delight,' gasped Maroto, partly disgusted by the implication regarding his friend but mostly awed by the unexpected view. The ridge continued down the other side of the prominence, but the grass and flowers were interspersed with more chunks of ivory stone. Peculiar, given how barren their approach had been, but not nearly so peculiar as the ruined city that filled the whole of the valley beyond, ancient white buildings rising clear up the surrounding slopes in place of trackless jungle. It probably would have been a little disquieting to any observer, stumbling across the remains of a settlement as grand as Diadem itself, but to Maroto the monochromatic wonder reminded him of nothing so much as that dreadful place Hoartrap had led them all to a quarter century past, in pursuit of eldritch powers: the Temple of the Black Vigil in Emeritus. Not a happy memory, that.

'Please pay close attention to yonder road,' said Bang, not rising from her seat but pointing to the north with a bare foot that was several shades lighter than the rest of her, boots cast off in the grass as she took her ease.

Taking a look, Maroto whistled – the track they had spied from below had angled away, as he'd assumed it would, but only to bypass a wide, shiny black lake that formed a border on the southern edge of the city, the road coming back around its shores and terminating in a mostly collapsed wall that must have once stretched a hundred feet into the air.

'Now then . . . Useful . . . ' said Bang, punctuating her words with slurping sounds as she licked off her juice-slick hand. 'I've obviously won . . . the bet . . . so we need to determine . . . what exactly it means. I've won your buns, but what to do with them?'

'How's that?' Maroto was still taking in the spectacle, his eyes catching on the sparkling undulations of the black lake; dark as it was, if not for the light bouncing off it he would have assumed it was a Gate.

'We bet our bottoms to see who was right about being able to see the road from the top, and I'm the victor,' said Bang, no longer cat-cleaning her fingers. 'So now you have to be straight with me, instead of playing the blushing virgin. Do you fancy girls, Useful, and how broad are your tastes?'

All of a sudden, the ruins of the Sunken Kingdom no longer seemed the most miraculous discovery of the day. Turning to Bang and seeing her lean away from the rock, arching her back in a stretch so pronounced that he could make out not only the nipples themselves but every contour of her areolas through her sweaty, sun-bleached shirt, Maroto gulped. 'Are you, um . . . are you saying you might . . . are you asking if I fancy you?'

'Oh, have I been playing too hard to get?' Bang relaxed back against the stone, eyeing Maroto. 'It's no skin off my bits if you're not inclined, in general or toward me in particular. My winning your bottom in our bet can mean anything, after all, from a bit of the slap and tickle now to a favor owed.'

Maroto must have looked as incredulous as he felt, because she sat up a bit straighter and said, 'My apologies, Useful, I've obviously misread the situation. I'll not bring it up again, and let's call the bet paid in exchange for a friendly foot rub – if that's not too unpleasant? No, I see that that's how it is, so we'll just say the next time I draw the short straw I get to pass it on to you, yes?'

'No apologies necessary, Captain,' said Maroto, a long-smothered heat roaring through him even in the nice breeze of the summit. 'And since in all the weeks we've been at it I've yet to see you draw the short straw, I think we'd better settle on some other prize.'

'Oh yeah?' The way she bit her lip made him lightheaded. 'Like what?'

'You're the captain, you tell me,' said Maroto, trying to act cool despite how flustered he felt; was this really happening? 'If it helps you decide, let me just list my credentials: my tastes are as broad as the Golden Cauldron, my skills legendary even among the Whores' Guild, and I long ago had my equipment blessed by sorcery to insure sterility in every sense of the word.'

'I've heard that last one before,' said Bang, rolling her eyes. 'And while it warms my loins to learn you consider yourself broad-minded and capable, there's still that last sticky question – do you fancy pleasing your captain, Useful?'

Maroto nodded the affirmative, too emotional to speak – he'd been unintentionally celibate for so long he could scarce remember the last time he'd pleased anyone other than himself. Now, at long last, with a beautiful young pirate on a mountaintop where they could see any trouble coming from a long way off, Maroto was being ushered back into the carnal fold.

'You don't know how bad I need this,' said Bang, color infiltrating her freckled and ink-speckled cheeks as she hopped to her bare feet. One hand rose and rested in the wiry hair above Maroto's heart, framed by his tattered, sweaty vest. Eyes smoldering up at him, she whispered, 'Are you sure you can handle me, Useful?'

He gulped his assent, too nervous to even return her touch just yet but pushing his chest firmly into her hand.

'You look like a fellow up for some rough stuff,' she murmured, 'spanking, hair pulling, what the screws back at the brig used to call corporal punishment. Sound nice?'

It wasn't necessarily what he'd have jumped straight into with a new partner, but whatever floated the captain's frigate sounded just fine to Maroto. He nodded again, finally daring to reach out and brush the fiery hair from her face. She nuzzled his hand, and Maroto almost lost it right fucking there, the front of his old skirt lifting like a pirate flag being hoisted up the mast of a conquered vessel. This was really happening.

'All right then,' she said, all business as she took a step back and rolled her shoulders a few times. 'If it gets too much say "banana," otherwise I'll keep going no matter what I hear out of your mouth. Now turn around, I want you there, palms on that stone, perfect bend in that back, skirt flipped up.'

Maroto did as he was told, bracing himself against a boulder overlooking the valley. He should have expected this, really. He'd been on this end of such things before, and though it wasn't really his favorite he was certainly game. He just hoped she'd let them switch before it was over, but knew better than to ask a pent-up captain with a frisky wrist. Once she'd worn herself out a little he'd—

'Fuck!' Maroto yelped, hopping in place. How could such a small hand deliver such a wallop?

'Three. For. Flinching.' Captain Bang punctuated each word with a slap, then poked the small of his back with another correction: 'Posture, Useful, posture.'

'Aye aye, Cap'n,' said Maroto, the wicked glee in her voice restoring a good bit of the stiffness the initial blows had robbed him of as the blood was redirected to his stinging backside.

The times Maroto had taken this role in the past he had been lukewarm on it, mostly doing it to earn a little bug money, but this time was shaping up to be a beast of a different pelt. Maybe it was not being touched out of passion in so long, or maybe it was Captain Bang's obvious excitement, but Maroto found himself getting good and into it, waggling his bottom cheekily to provoke further strikes even as he sensibly slipped a hand between his legs to shield his pouch from her palm. So *this* was what was up!

He'd always enjoyed doling out smacks to a juicy bottom, sure, but had never quite seen the appeal of being on the receiving end ... but that was changing, and in a hurry. That the encounter was proving as illuminating as it was satisfying just went to show that you never know yourself so well as when you're in the boudoir with an enthusiastic partner or three. Bad as the first few strokes had burned, the pleasure Captain Bang was taking in him was downright contagious – he was once again giving his captain exactly what she wanted, what she *needed*, and more than that, he was enduring no worse than he deserved, and with each hot spank he felt like he was slowly paying off the debt he owed the world by being such a fuckup. He didn't like being hurt as a general rule, but this specific kind of pain was something else entirely, maybe because it was the pain he deserved, the pain of knowing he would try to do better but still find himself in this position again, Old Watchers willing ...

'You. Brought this. On. Yourself.'

'Yes, Captain Bang. Sorry, Captain Bang.'

'Sorry's! Not! Good enough!' With this newest volley Maroto went weak in the knees, clinging like a drowning man to the quartz boulder in front of him. His arse fucking *hurt*, but he also knew that so far she was treating him way better than he deserved ... and maybe that was part of it, too, all of Maroto's flaws and failings and guilt driven out of him in a flurry of merciless spanks. Hard to think of much of anything as she kept working his increasingly tender bottom, and Maroto fixed his eyes on the black lake at the edge of the ruined city, concentrating all his attention on it to distract his shaking legs from another imminent blow. Perhaps he tipped her off by tensing or something, because she kept him waiting, and the expectation was almost worse than the slaps themselves. Or better, it was all getting very confusing.

'You're just lucky my treasure chest went down with the *Queen Thief,* or else I'd have some proper instruments to work you with.' Instead of another slap, he felt a delightfully cool puff of air on first one side and then the other, Captain Bang leaning down to blow on his inflamed posterior as though feeding its heat with the bellows of her breath. Cupping a thumb under each cheek, she squeezed and kneaded him, thoroughly inspecting her tender prize, and Maroto tried to stop himself from flinching out of embarrassment, or as seemed more likely, going off without her so much as touching his engorged Charity ... when the black lake he'd made his focal point began doing something weird.

Captain Bang murmured something, but his full attention was now on the distant lake and its rippling movement, the entire north shore flowing out and onto the white road they had first glimpsed coming up the ridge. How could a lake spontaneously overflow its borders and pour along a road, and uphill at that, it looked like, at least for a short stretch before—

The crack echoed out over the dead city, and it took Maroto several silent mouthings of the word before he finally managed to get it out with a little sound: '*Banana.* Banana banana banana.'

'Already?' Captain Bang sounded disappointed in him, but her hand settled on his lower back instead of his bottom. The palm felt burning hot under his skin, and as the fingers walked up his still-arched back she said, 'Such a shame, if you held out for five more I was going to give you a reward, but now – *what the shit is that?*'

Bang's voice went from husky to hard in a trice, and Maroto didn't have to look away from the sight below to know that she had seen it, too. 'Well, Captain, it looks like . . . it looks like what we thought was a lake is actually a giant fucking army in shiny black armor and tight formation, and now they're on the march, aren't they?'

'I can see that, Useless, why didn't you say something!'

'They just started moving out on the road,' said Maroto defensively. 'And besides, you told me not to speak until spoken to.'

Bang softened a little, and stepped up on a rock to give him a peck on the cheek. 'Good boy. But whatever orders you have, next time tell me when something this crazy happens.'

'So what do we do?' asked Maroto, the magnitude of this development finally sinking in as the fog of strange euphoria left his skull, leaving only a dreadful pain in his posterior and painful dread in his heart. 'Who are they? *What* are they? There's ten thousand of 'em down there, assuming they're the same size as normal folk, and they've got the look of an army heading off to make somebody sorry.'

'But who, but who?' Bang tugged on her ear as she thought out loud. 'We know that road doesn't lead to any of the beaches or coves we've found, but it's heading southeast, so they'll hit the sea before long. It must take them out somewhere on the other side of that headland you were tossed off.'

'Or under it,' said Maroto, remembering the sea-caves those

simian monsters had carried him through his first day on the Unsunk Kingdom.

'Either way, the road has to lead them to the southern shore of Jex Toth.' Bang tugged harder at her earlobe. 'What does an army want at the southern shore?'

'A day at the beach?' When Bang gave him a harsh swat on his sensitive arse, he said, 'Well, what do I know about it? Maybe they've got a harbor there.'

'And an obviously well-trained army of Jex Toth marching to a secret harbor on their southern shore can only mean one thing, right?' Bang didn't look away from the glossy black river of troops moving out from the assembly at the edge of the city's fallen walls. 'They mean to invade the Immaculate Isles.'

'*What*? No! I mean ... maybe?' The more he thought about it the more plausible it seemed – here was a marching army, be it composed of normal folk or something weirder, and the one thing all the legends agreed about was that Jex Toth was a downright wicked place before their war with Emeritus led to both empires meeting mysterious disasters. Stood to reason that as soon as they were resurrected they'd start up with their old ways again. Ancient evils were always doing that, weren't they, in epic songs and plays? Getting banished for ages and then creeping back in to make another go of it? 'So ... what do we do?'

'Now we run,' hissed Bang, and finally averting his gaze from the valley he saw his captain hopping on one foot, trying to pull on her other boot. 'We run fast, and we run far, and we think all the while. Once we're back to camp we're bound to have a plan, though I'm thinking we build a raft and head for Hwabun – that's the closest Isle.'

'Warn the Immaculates?' Maroto nodded. 'Smart.'

'Lucrative,' said Bang. 'They'll owe us big if we can tip them off before the invasion starts. Now move it, Useful, before ...'

'Before what?' asked Maroto, giving the black army a final scowl.

'Before something stupid happens,' said Bang, grabbing Maroto's arm and pointing down the ridge that led from their vantage point toward the city. 'Like that.'

'Oh,' said Maroto, seeing the problem and feeling his stomach drop down into his sizzling bottom. 'Yeah, we definitely want to leave before something like that goes down.'

They had only previously seen one great white flying horror – presuming the one that had swooped down on them their first night was the same beast Maroto had baited into attacking the egg-laying monster from the sea-caves – and it had only ever seemed to come out after dark. The four horrors that flapped their way up along the ridge toward Maroto and Bang looked even scarier by day, their pale, greasy skin somewhat translucent in the sunlight so that purple organs and black bones could be glimpsed as they winged ever closer, their wavering tendrils almost dragging on the ground. The creatures must not be able to fly as high with the ebon-armored riders on their backs, each white, droopy-winged monster saddled with a pair of the hulking humanoids. The squadron was not a hundred yards down the ridge from Bang and Maroto, but made no sound at all as they flew straight up the saddle toward them with dread purpose.

'Damn,' said Maroto sadly as the fiends approached. 'I was just getting into that, too.'

'Oh, you'll get into it yet,' said Bang, swatting Maroto's sore arse and bolting back down the way they'd come. 'But not if you're caught!'

'Right behind you!' Maroto called after her, but this was a lie, because while he knew he should climb onto the quartz boulder and await their coming, knew he should leap from the high ground onto the first horror that reached the peak and buy Bang a little more time to escape, because that was what a real hero would have done for the wonderful girl who had unlocked his heart with the palm of her hand, Maroto had already started running down the ridge, too, and overtook Bang before the words had finished leaving his mouth.

'Bad move!' she cried. 'You don't want me behind you, Useful!'

'That's where you're wrong,' he called back, but in looking over his shoulder to make sure the mounted horrors weren't too close he tripped straight over the first of the many sharp drops that punctuated the ridge. He landed on his side on the grassy slope, but the pain in his ribs and elbow were nothing compared to that of his rump as he twisted over on it. By the time he'd stopped rolling and resumed his flight, Bang was back in front of him, but that was okay, too, since he'd decided it was probably all right to start checking out her butt. Not the worst day he'd ever had, then, not by a country league.

They had almost made it to the treeline when one of their winged pursuers soared down and around out of the sky, hovering at the bottom of the narrow ridge and cutting off their escape. Up close and seen in the daylight, it looked something like a cross between an owlbat and a giant, fleshy jellyfish. Dong-won's description of the first one as a squid-dragon wasn't too far off point.

So not the best day Maroto had ever had, either, but he knew a thing or two about making the best of a bad situation. As Bang slid to a stop rather than run underneath the mounted squid-dragon, Maroto dashed past, giving her a light swat on the rump as he went by. He'd be paying for that later, with any luck, but for now he charged even faster at the enormous monster. Its black-armored riders were a blur on its back, fast as

Maroto was coming down the slope at them, but he clearly saw them hoisting what looked rather a lot like a net. But while they were clearly waiting for him to try to feint around the hovering horror at the last moment, Maroto had other ideas.

Taking advantage of his wild descent, the steepness of the grade, and a slight hump just before the base of the slope, he leaped into the air, leading not with a fist or an elbow but both his heels. He felt graceful as a cliff diver pirouetting through the air, and then his feet smashed into the gnarly sky-beast's face. He couldn't say how effective this move was other than as a distraction, because the next thing he knew he'd slammed down on his back in those lovely little flowers and warm little blades of grass. A wide black net drifted lazily down out of the blue, blue sky and settled on his limp body, the wind knocked clean out of him. Woof.

An appealing red-haired streak crossed his vision, but when he tried to throw off the net to follow her he found it was more of an incredibly heavy web, sticky to the touch and actually a little caustic, now that the sensation was returning to his rattled brains. The gross monster drifted over him, its cluster of pachyderm-like trunks unspooling from its underside, but Maroto let his head loll to the side, looking down the ridge to where Bang was running away without a backward glance, running to the trees, and then running through the trees, running on and on and on.

Maroto had but one hope left in him, and it was that she would never stop.

CHAPTER

17

'Don't sulk,' Zosia told Boris as they slogged their way through the increasingly chaotic camp, word apparently spreading like ... well, like bad news through a mercenary camp. 'You know, people are usually *excited* when their benefactor offers to buy them a nice new weapon. You need to be able to defend yourself.'

'Told you, I'm a lover, not a fighter,' said Boris gloomily.

'Say, there's an idea!' said Zosia. 'Since we both might die on the morrow and all that, what say after we get equipped we make a quick stop off at one of the brothel tents? My treat.'

'You got a queer sense of humor,' said Boris, and Choplicker barked in agreement.

'Sure, that, too, but why the hell not, eh?' Now that she had brought up the possibility under the auspices of altruism, Zosia couldn't even remember why she'd been so opposed to the idea of just heading over there by herself – Singh was right, she needed to get something, anything, and fast. 'Could be our last chance to have a few fun minutes with a comely wench or lad or what have you.'

'And since we'll probably be dead soon we won't have to worry about any poxes, right?' said Boris, not sounding any keener on it, but now that she'd let herself suggest it out loud there was no going back – she was going to fucking *get it*, albeit briefly, since they had an imminent appointment to keep with Hoartrap. Perhaps mistaking Zosia's excited flush for embarrassment, Boris said, 'Not that having a pox is the end of the world, I mean, or saying all whores is dirty. Like, my own brother's a whore, and he's, uh … well, *he's* got a few different poxes, so that's a bad example.'

'I appreciate the sentiment, Boris, but I'm clean as the driven snow,' said Zosia, then amended herself as Choplicker lifted a leg over a drift. 'Well, not that patch of it, but you get the point. Ever since Hoartrap set me up right the only thing I've picked up in a brothel is my husband!'

And *shit*. Fast as she'd felt the winds of passion blowing her toward certain relief, she becalmed herself with that little reminder of why she hadn't hired any lustworkers over the past year, and her shoulders slumped like limp sails.

'My, but that's clever,' said Boris. 'Certainly haven't heard that one a hundred times before. Or let me guess, you actually came up with that punch line back in the day before anybody else did, another of your many contributions to Samothan culture.'

'No, I didn't mean he … just, never mind,' said Zosia, feeling her chest get all tight at the memory of first laying eyes on Leib in that bordello in Rawg. He'd been winsomely sprawled on a paisley daybed in the common area of the Sixty-nine Eyes. Oh, how she had wanted that towheaded hunk with his boy-next-farm charm. And for a good long while, she had had him, too, and as so much more than just a favorite lustworker … but they could have lived for a hundred lifetimes in that cabin above Kypck and she never, ever would have had enough. Nobody knew her as well as Leib had, she'd never allowed anyone to get that close … but even seeing just how dark she was inside, even learning of every crime in her downright evil life, even then he loved her, and his love had been worth more to Zosia than empires or treasure hoards, more than living, if it meant living without him. When she was with him she felt . . . she felt *okay*, like as much bad as she'd done, she couldn't be totally irredeemable, if someone as good as Leib cared for her.

During the happy years in the mountains playing peasant and eventually mayoress, the cold, sinister blackness that had always squirmed and plotted inside Zosia's heart, inside her thoughts, that ugliness that had always driven her, it all went away. And if they sometimes quarreled or came down sick and had to tend the other or she sometimes found herself looking out across the valley and daydreaming of heading off for one last adventure, well, those were the little things that proved what they had was real and true, that they weren't both just dreaming of a perfect life, but actually living one, or as close as things came in the waking world . . .

'Hey, look, I didn't mean anything by it,' said Boris, sounding a little rueful, and Zosia realized she'd stopped walking, was just standing there between the grim frozen tents, on the verge of tears. 'I give everyone a hard time, it's what I do?'

'I . . .' Zosia cleared the lump out of her throat with a rumble and spat out all the grief . . . or as much as she could pack into a bit of phlegm, but it would have to do for now. 'I was just thinking that we're not going to have time for any brothel tents. Day's getting on.'

'Suits me,' said Boris, falling in beside her as they resumed walking. 'To each their own, but I don't know how you'd be of a mood for it, at a time like this.'

'Neither do I,' said Zosia, picking up the pace so they'd have no more wind to waste on talking until they reached the smith's tent. They must be getting close, because the rills of snowmelt that trickled down between the tents were flowing faster and wider, and this late in a cold-ass day the likely culprit was a forge . . . and then they could hear the clanging of metal, and followed it to its source.

The smithy was the only structure they'd passed on the way up that was completely denuded of snow and icicles. As they entered the wide ring of mud surrounding the rectangular tent at the front of the works, Zosia said, 'Now Ji-hyeon told me the smith was grouchy, so let me do the talking – the last person you want to piss off is the guy you're counting on to sell you a decent weapon. One smart word out of you and he might give us gear that looks reliable but shatters like glass the first time we need it to save our lives.'

'No smart talk, got it.'

'No talk, smart or otherwise,' said Zosia, lowering her voice as she approached the pinned-up flap at the entrance and the clanging stopped, replaced by furious cursing. This was shaping up to be just bloody typical. 'I'll get a hammer, we'll get you something simple yet intimidating, and then we're out of here before you have the chance to say the wrong thing.'

'Got it,' said Boris, eagerly rubbing his bandaged hands together as the pleasant warmth from the forge wafted out of the tent. For all his whinging about how bad they hurt during archery practice he still had all his fingers, the frostbite only taking off a few layers of skin here and there, but just the same Zosia decided to get him something he could hold on to with both hands. But first, a hammer for her, though whatever she picked up here was guaranteed to be garbage so there was no cause to waste much time on it.

'Greetings, friend,' Zosia announced as she led the way into the close, smoky front of the tent. A long table of northern oak barred their way, covered with junk – some of it was scrap and some of it looked to be finished weaponry or bits of armor, but junk it surely was. Might not be the fault of the big man who now turned away from his anvil and stalked over to them; smithing in a mobile army meant banging out quantity over quality, trying to fix armor and salvage weapons that were already rubbish to begin with, and so—

But then Zosia got a good look at the clearly irate wildborn smith on the other side of the table, took in his catfish whiskers and great big black eyes, and said, 'Well, *damn*. I've seen ugly and I know stupid, but I didn't know they had a baby.'

The smith was too taken aback to speak, his already enormous eyes seeming to swell from within, and Boris quietly sucked in through his teeth. Then the great, sweaty man swung on Zosia, his meaty fist easily reaching across the table, and swatted her on the shoulder so hard she felt the vibration in her eyeballs.

'Zosia girl!' he cried. 'Good to see you, though you're looking older than you already are. Which is old as hell! Heard you were in camp, wondered if you'd come and see me.'

'Nobody told me you were here! Why didn't you come find me?'

'I got time to chase ghosts?' Ulver shook his big bald head, just in case she needed an answer to the rhetorical question. 'I knew if it was really you you'd show up eventually. That's how bad news usually works.'

'Damn, Ulver,' said Zosia, feeling even more annoyed at herself for not asking around to see if anyone else from the old days had shown up to follow the Cobalt flag. 'How long have you been in company?'

'Close to the beginning?' said Ulver, tugging thoughtfully

on one of his dangling pink barbels. 'I lit out to the Dominions a few years back, once the Chain started rounding up wildies again. Had a shop in Gorgoro, and did all right, mostly tools and armor since I never took to Raniputri weaponry, but soon as I heard the Cobalts were tearing it up in the next Dominion over I packed my bags and my kid, and that was it. Still hoping for a Cobalt revolution to knock the Chain out of the Empire, so that shows I ain't got any smarter with age.'

'How about that,' said Zosia, marveling anew at how much hope and devotion she still inspired, even in those who'd known her well. Especially in them. 'So how long did it take you to figure out it wasn't me in charge?'

'Ha! I knew that much before I even signed on,' said Ulver. 'No way I would've joined up if I thought you were back in the general's saddle, not after the mess you made last time. But I figure, maybe someone young, someone who really seems to get it this time ... well, that's what's up.'

'That is indeed what is up,' said Zosia, not hurt by his candor so much as by the truth behind it.

'So listen, Zosia girl, I need to pull some blades in a minute here,' said Ulver, wiping a moist hand on the front of his leather apron. 'But make yourself at home, and – say, who's the runt? He with you?'

'Yessir, I am,' said Boris, looking up from the knives at the end of the table he'd been intently inspecting, or at least pretending to. 'I'm Cobalt Zosia's wisecracking sidekick.'

'Ugh,' said Ulver, his whiskers bristling as he looked back at Zosia. 'I think you owe yourself better than that, Zosia girl.'

'No no, he's definitely the man-boy for the job,' said Zosia, holding up a hand in peace. 'Boris, meet Ulver Krallice, an old friend. Ulver Krallice, meet Boris. He's ... he's all right, I guess, until proven otherwise.'

Boris puffed out his chest a little at that, and Ulver jutted a thumb over his shoulder as he said, 'Like I said, I got some buns that need to come out the oven before they burn, but if you want to get comfortable or come back in an hour we can smoke some brown, and talk some, too.'

'Ah, crap, I'm afraid we can't – hitting the road soon, and since Hoartrap's waiting on us we better not be late or he'll just show up to ruin the party.' Zosia was so fucking pissed at herself she could shout; for the past week she'd been so caught up in trying to recover her lost hammer that she hadn't wanted to look for a new one, but if she had she and Ulver might have been able to actually catch up ... and now, as usual, she realized her folly too late. 'So sorry, old friend, should've asked around for you. If I'd known you were here I'd have come running.'

'Yeah, well, next time, right?' said Ulver. 'What's twenty years, more or less?'

'It won't be that long this time,' said Zosia, superstitiously knocking on the table before the words were out of her mouth. 'And I know you have to hop to it, but before you do can I grab a war hammer and a battle-ax? That's why we came in, get something solid for me and the heretic.'

'I told you not to call me that,' said Boris.

'Hey, I like heretics, so you take that double-header ax hanging up there,' said Ulver. 'As for war hammers, Zosia girl, I'm sad to say I ain't got any handy – people don't seem to swing 'em as much as they used to. If you'd come in a week ago, maybe I could've slapped something together, or ... or ...' Ulver's fronds started wiggling the way they did when he was tabulating ingot ratios or trying to count cards, and then he pursed his thick lips in a satisfied smile, nodding to himself. 'Here's what's up: hammer's for you? And you still the sort of dame to traffic with dark and dangerous powers better left alone by mortals?'

'Yes and fuck yes,' said Zosia, figuring that as long as Choplicker was around the latter was a foregone conclusion. But speaking of the devil, where had he got to? Looking around, she noticed he hadn't come into the tent with them, and while that might just mean he was cruising around the barbers' tents for a snack it bugged Zosia that she was getting comfortable letting him wander off on his own. How'd she ever let his leash get so long?

'Check this shit out,' said Ulver, returning from the back with what looked to be a sawn-off sledgehammer, the dull black steel head easily three times the size of her old war hammer. 'I took the handle way down, right, to use it on the anvil, but it's—'

'Sister Portolés's maul,' gasped Boris, nearly dropping the battle-ax he had finally gotten down from its hook.

Ulver and Zosia both stared at the little man with the big ax, and Ulver shook his head and said, 'Well, there's another song I'd like to hear but ain't got time for, but at least it sounds like he'll be able to tell you more than I can about it.'

'Actually, that's about all I know,' said Boris, coming over to join them in examining the hammer Ulver held out to Zosia. 'For as bad a gambler as she was, she kept her cards tight to her tits. Um, so to speak.'

'So what I'm getting from both of you is that this is some kind of Chainite weapon?' said Zosia. 'I don't know about that ... and besides, if it was a maul you cut the haft off it's going to be all out of balance, probably break my wrist or send it flying the first time I try to use it.'

'Well, it's all I got, so take it or leave it,' said Ulver. 'But I'll tell you this much – it's made of sainted steel, without a doubt.

I've heard all about it, everyone has, and had fools show me bullshit they got duped into thinking was the genuine article but wasn't, but this, *this* is the real deal. Old magic, Zosia girl, and while a war nun was swinging it I'm guessing it's older than the Chain itself.'

'I thought to make sainted steel you had to have a saint,' said Zosia, but now her interest was good and piqued. Coveting weapons she should have never looked at twice was one of those bad old habits that were hard to crack.

'You need to burn someone to put them in the steel, and you know how the Chain does,' said Ulver, resting the hammer on the table. 'Anyone who ever died is a saint to them, so long as somebody somewhere thinks that's a selling point.'

'And you're ... you're giving this to me?' asked Zosia, touched but also suspicious. 'This thing has to be worth more than I could pay, you have to know that.'

'You'd be doing me a favor,' said Ulver, poking it at her. 'I thought it'd be perfect for hammering blades, but since I cut it down to working size it's been nothing but trouble, ruins just about everything I put it to. I've been sweating in a smithy since I was my girl's age and I never knew a hammer that could just wreck what you put it to, but that's what it does – had to melt everything I touched it with back down. Just 'fore you came in it broke this damn claymore I've spent *weeks* on. So I've come to the opinion it's just not meant to build. It's meant to destroy.'

'Well, that's something we have in common,' said Zosia, and unable to help herself after a pitch like that, she took the proffered weapon. It wasn't as heavy as it looked, and somehow the balance wasn't bad, either; she smiled as she saw the heavy iron cap on the base, realizing Ulver must have found a way to counterweight it.

'Only other thing I can tell you before I get back to work is that it ... it's weird,' said Ulver, watching Zosia experimentally give it a little swing. 'I mean, *of course* it's weird, but more than that ... now as a rule I don't discuss commissions with anyone but whoever hires me, but I'll tell you this – the only two blades it didn't ruin in the making weren't just steel, they were sainted, too. I made up a batch of it myself, since it seemed a rare opportunity, and I figured I understood the principles behind it, but ... no.'

'No what?' said Boris.

'Just *no*,' Ulver said firmly. 'I know steel, and I know working it's a kind of magic to those who don't understand. It's not though, there's nothing witchy about it, however mysterious it sounds. So when I heard about sainted steel in a song I figured that was all it was – simple good, strong steel made with a bit of bone ash, nothing more, but the kind of story that makes people feel good when they're holding it, right? But when I made those blades, Zosia girl ... I wasn't just working the steel, I was working something *else*. I felt it. I smelled it. And every time that hammer fell on those black blades I was making, the noise it made, it sounded like ... it sounded like there was something *howling* in the metal, I swear it on my girl's life.'

That put the chill on the hot smithy, and nobody said anything for a moment, everyone staring at the black hammer in Zosia's hand ... and then Ulver slapped her shoulder again, and said, 'Well hell, I'm about to ruin another batch on account of that fucking thing, so good riddance to it, good seeing you, don't be a stranger, and tell me what you think of it next time you're through.'

'Thanks, Ulver,' said Zosia. 'I obviously owe you a song, at the very least, about why everyone thought I died, and why I'm back.'

'Maybe someday I'll hear it, sure, but I don't particularly care,' said Ulver, popping Boris in the shoulder for good measure, and then lumbering away toward his forge. Without turning to see them off, he called over his shoulder, 'You came back, Zosia girl, that's what matters.'

CHAPTER
18

'And that's that,' said Ji-hyeon, rising stiffly from the command table, formally bowing to her two remaining guests, and then wandering over to collapse face-first into her pillow-padded bed. Somebody said something, but the cushions muted it. She rolled onto one side and gave the still-seated Fennec and the still-standing Choi her most ridiculous bug-eyed sigh. Fennec looked as tired as Ji-hyeon felt, and while Choi didn't betray her fatigue as badly there was no mistaking the circles under her eyes – the kohl-dark crescents had first appeared on the Honor Guard weeks ago, and no matter how early in the evenings Ji-hyeon dismissed her cabinet they had only deepened with each passing night. Yet Choi never complained, nor did Fennec ... not seriously, anyway. Ji-hyeon didn't know what she'd do without them, the last two people in camp she could be herself around. 'One of you say something?'

'I said I don't know if we can trust Singh,' Fennec said, launching into the last kind of speech Ji-hyeon wanted to hear right now: another sermon on one of her captain's inevitable treacheries. 'If you'd spent more time courting her officers we might have tried to set them against her, but you barely met with them, and so there's little chance of that. Plus she's their commander *and* their mother, so it would have been a long shot even if you'd buttered them up. Since you didn't, we can only—'

'So are you saying she'll probably betray us to the Imperials, or she'll probably desert with her dragoons?' asked Ji-hyeon crossly. 'If it's the former, keep talking, otherwise let it go. Even with this moving speech you've written me we're still going to have a lot of Cobalts decline our invitation to win eternal glory as soon as they realize how exactly we intend to claim it. Singh had a point when she said the vast majority of people assume entering a Gate always always *always* equals death, or something even worse – hells, we three traveled through one ourselves, more or less safely, and I know you're no more thrilled than I am to be trying our luck a second time.'

'It will be my third,' said Fennec, tapping his downy claws on the edge of the burned map. He was wearing the gloves less and less frequently these days, the light grey fur a sharp contrast to his dark Usban complexion. 'The first time was before we met. My hair went white, same as yours, but we all know how easy that is to fix with dye. The second was when I led us out of Othean, and obviously the effect was more . . . pronounced.'

'The Touch has pledged to keep you insulated from any further improvements,' said Choi, and with her it was hard to tell if this description of Gate-induced transformations was one of her quirks of language or quirks of humor.

'Easy for you to take him at his word,' said Fennec. 'If he's lying or screws up half as bad as he did with the devil queen, you won't be the one enjoying any more *improvements*.'

'It is true I am past the need for enhancement,' said Choi, cocking her head to the side and polishing her unbroken horn with her sleeve. Now Ji-hyeon was sure the woman was just messing with Fennec. 'But I believe Hoartrap knows the dance of the First Dark, or sufficient steps to pass through without effect. He has used the Gates to travel for many years, has he not? If he did not know a more cautious route than the one he taught you, Fennec, he would be much improved by now instead of remaining a simple man.'

'Hoartrap's many things, but simple isn't one of them,' said Ji-hyeon. 'I just assumed he was wildborn, too, and that's why he could use the Gates without anything weird happening to him.'

'I agree he is many things, and only some of them have words, but he is not wildborn,' said Choi, making Ji-hyeon wonder if they could all somehow recognize each other, even when their alterations were minor, or internal. 'I did not anticipate ever having cause to speak these disappointing words, but I believe Hoartrap will behave with more honor than Chevaleresse Singh on the morrow. I agree with Fennec's assessment of her nerves and inclinations. Whether she dishonors herself with treachery or desertion, she will not follow us into the Gate.'

'Which is all the more reason to just let her do what she's planning instead of confronting her or trying to strong-arm her into coming with us,' said Ji-hyeon. 'Pressuring Singh or any other reluctant parties will just make them more likely to rebel against us instead of quietly running away. Most people would rather die fighting than be pushed into a Gate.'

'That ... that's actually a good point,' said Fennec, smiling with approval. It was only sunset and already they were exhausted, the process of perfecting the short speech having taken far longer than anticipated – it was no small undertaking, crafting something that might convince weary, frostbitten sellswords to follow you into what some people whispered was the gaping mouth of a hungry devil king. 'Let those who go, go.'

'And may they outlive us by a thousand years,' said Choi, 'to have sufficient time to contemplate their shame.'

'We're really doing this?' Ji-hyeon asked them, sitting up on her bed. 'Like, both of you are okay with my plan?'

'It is the boldest opportunity to win honor in my lifetime,' said Choi, her arrowhead-sharp grin missing a few teeth of late. 'There is no question that I am *okay*.'

'And it's the maddest one I've taken part in,' said Fennec, retrieving a black bottle from the saddlebag he had brought to the meeting. 'Considering all the owlbatshit schemes Zosia had us running back in the day, that's some honor. Congratulations, Ji-hyeon, you have officially surpassed the legend.'

'And I only had to risk all your lives to do it,' said Ji-hyeon, working herself up to the last thing she had to do before launching this deranged invasion of Diadem. 'Choi, Fennec, I . . . I officially release you from your duties to Princess Ji-hyeon Bong of Hwabun. Choi, from this day forward you are no longer my Honor Guard, but a free woman. And Fennec, or Brother Mikal, or whoever you really are, I release you as my Spirit Guard.'

They both looked taken aback, but then Fennec and Choi looked at each other, smiling like proud parents, and honored her in their own ways: Fennec removed the wire cork cage from his bottle and then opened it with a festive pop, and Choi took a deep bow, arching her neck as she did to keep her claret-colored eyes on Ji-hyeon the whole time.

'I know I should have done it when we first came out of the Gate in Zygnema,' Ji-hyeon confessed. 'But I was still such a little kid then, I . . . I guess I was scared? Not that you'd leave or anything, just . . . scared. I couldn't have done what I did, what *we* did, if I didn't know at the back of my mind that you were still my guards, that something remained from our time on Hwabun. But now I see that what remained was a kind of bondage, if only in name, and I won't have it, not anymore. You're my friends and you're my captains, but you're not my servants.'

Nobody said anything for a spell, Fennec pouring a golden draught into three bowls on the table, Choi cracking her knuckles, and then Ji-hyeon's former Honor Guard said, 'Thank you, Ji-hyeon, it has ever been an honor to serve you. Now that my service is complete, I shall depart the Cobalt Company in pursuit of he who has claimed my heart, the one called Maroto Devilskinner.'

Ji-hyeon's heart sank, and over Choi's shoulder she saw one of Fennec's bowls overflow as he stared slack-mouthed at the wildborn. Then Choi stepped around the table and tousled her former ward's newly shorn hair, giving her a wry smile.

'A joke, General Ji-hyeon. I would have left long ago if I did not think you worthy of my teeth, and I believe you will need them more than ever in the days to come.'

Not caring how childish it might be, Ji-hyeon jumped up and hugged the older woman, who remained stiff for only a moment before returning the embrace. Fennec thought it was a lot funnier than Ji-hyeon did, or maybe it was just the concept of Choi singing a long song that set him off into uncharacteristic giggles. It was a strange sound, coming from him, but so natural Ji-hyeon had to wonder if this was the first time in all the years she'd known him that he'd actually laughed in earnest.

'Come, ladies, and sample my liquid courage,' he said when the fit had passed, offering them a bowl with each furry hand. 'I know you've turned your noses up at my sours before, but this one is guaranteed to impress – I brewed it during our initial stopover in the Raniputri Dominions, and it's been mellowing ever since. One must always drink ale before a battle, so sayeth the Ten True Gods of Trve, and who are we to contradict such benevolent deities?'

'Ale?' Ji-hyeon sniffed the golden bowl cautiously. 'I thought you always drank cider?'

'I drink according to the season, and the stars, and the quality of the ingredients on hand,' said Fennec, holding his bowl up for a toast. 'Have you any fitting words of war to lead us in, Choi?'

'Confusion to our enemies,' said the wildborn, bumping bowls with them, and they repeated it before knocking back a mouthful.

'Definitely not cider,' said Ji-hyeon through her puckered mouth. 'Way too tart for cider.'

'Are you sure it is supposed to taste like this?' asked Choi skeptically. 'I have had sweeter limes.'

'You have to have a second bowl to appreciate it,' groused Fennec, refilling all three of their cups. 'Your turn, Ji-hyeon.'

'To ... to Chevaleresse Sasamaso, and all my other body-guards and soldiers who went missing at the Battle of the Lark's Tongue,' said Ji-hyeon, tearing up a little. She knew Sasamaso came from the Crowned Eagle People of Flintland before winning renown on the Star, knew the fallen chevaleresse preferred drinking mead to smoking saam, roasting tubers to meat, and a dozen other little things about her ... but the woman had hardly been the only one to never return from that desperate battle, and Ji-hyeon couldn't even honor the rest of the dead by recalling their names. 'No, not just to her, and not just to our fallen comrades, but to everyone who perished when that damn Gate swallowed them, whether friend or foe. To everyone.'

Choi and Fennec repeated the toast, then bumped, then swallowed.

'You're right,' said Ji-hyeon, the tart brew sterilizing the sentimentality that had been creeping up her throat. 'I'm definitely getting more of the nuance now. Is that a hint of ass I taste on the back?'

'I do not think so,' said Choi. 'Ass is much sweeter than this.'

'Just you wait and see,' said Fennec, wagging a finger and refilling his bowl but not theirs. 'You don't have to like the taste, but see if you're not feeling fearless before I've finished this bottle.'

'So you're a thief, a confidence artist, a master of disguise, and a snake oil merchant?' Ji-hyeon sat back down on the edge of the bed. 'Is there no end to your talents?'

'Friend of many, lord of few,' said Fennec, reclaiming a chair himself and dislodging a burp in the process. 'And I've never been a thief, that was always your dad's purview. Crafty Kang-ho, the lovable rogue.'

'Or not so lovable, as the case may be,' said Ji-hyeon, noticing a beat too late how melancholic Fennec looked. She decided to perk him up with his favorite tonic: an opportunity to run his mouth. 'Here's a question, Fennec – what did they call you?'

'I've been called many things by many folk!'

'No, I mean your title, your epithet – my dad was Crafty Kang-ho, Maroto was the Mighty or Devilskinner, Chevaleresse Singh has all the other honorifics that go with knighthood, and Hoartrap has almost as many nicknames as Zosia. So what did they call you, other than Fennec?'

'I was lucky when they could remember that,' said Fennec, knocking back his third bowl in one go and topping it right back up. Ever a comrade, Choi leaned against the table and poured herself another bowl, too, so he wouldn't be drinking alone. 'Fennec's not even my name, you know? Somewhere along the line they must have forgotten I had a real one altogether. And why shouldn't they? I never did anything with it.'

'Oh,' said Ji-hyeon, unprepared for this confession. Even when he'd been warning Ji-hyeon against trusting his former companions, Fennec's tales of the old days never carried this glum tinge. 'Well, that's obviously not true, because you're in most every song of Cold Cobalt and her Five Villains, aren't you? Even if they call you by an alias, that counts for something!'

'I'm in the songs for the same reason I was one of the Villains.' Fennec sounded as sour as his beer. 'Because I was Kang-ho's boyfriend back when Zosia started the original gang, and she wasn't such a shit as to kick me out after we split.'

That was unexpected. Choi's eyes widened and glanced at Ji-hyeon for confirmation, but Ji-hyeon's eyes must have been even bigger – Fennec and *her dad*? Remembering the fleeting crush she'd had on 'Brother Mikal' when her sooo mature Spirit Guard had first come to Hwabun, Ji-hyeon felt a little queasy.

'So I tagged along all the way to the end, but did I deserve it? Hells no. Zosia had brains and brawn, and Maroto had the same in less equal distribution. Singh was the noble-hearted knight and Kang-ho was the thief, the knife-fighter, the escape artist. And Hoartrap was Hoartrap, who obviously contributes something more than just his effervescent personality.' Fennec puffed out his cheeks and blew. 'And since you can't have Five Villains without a fifth wheel, there was me.'

'You were a priest,' said Choi. 'What was the word you used? A cleric.'

'You mean, like a real one?' Ji-hyeon felt kind of disappointed that these two had obviously talked about this when she wasn't around, at least a little, but then felt embarrassed by her privilege – of course mere mortals interacted with one another, even when their brave general or noble princess wasn't there to overhear. 'Was your Brother Mikal act not totally phony?'

'Oh no, it was!' said Fennec, brightening a little. 'This was long, long ago. I'd forgotten I told you, Choi, but it's coming back now – too much of my own stout back in Katheli. And yes, hard as it is to believe, Ji-hyeon, your Spirit Guard was actually a keeper of the cloth, albeit of a different weft. Waft. Whatever. Back when I first met Kang-ho, I was a mendicant cleric of Korpiklani, Mistress of the Malt. For you heretics I should probably explain that Korpiklani is Fourth among the Ten True Gods of Trve, just as I was destined to be the Fourth Villain. Everything is destined and preordained and something more than dumb coincidence when you have faith, even if it's in a drunken goddess. Maybe especially then.'

Ji-hyeon scrunched up her face, trying to picture Fennec's meticulously shaved cheeks laden with a long beard like most of the followers of the Ten that she'd encountered. Catching her looking, he clambered up and refilled all their bowls, and maybe it was some minor miracle of Fennec's abandoned god, but the sour ale was actually growing on her. He returned to his chair and his story.

'So yes, in the early days I offered spiritual advisement, after a fashion – one of Korpiklani's many blessings was that I could consume any liquid you could think of, and it would turn to beer as soon as it passed my lips. Of limited use to others, but I found it highly efficacious. More importantly, the brews I cooked up could heal the sick and the wounded, so long as they weren't too far gone . . . ' Holding up his bowl to the candlelight for a moment, Fennec knocked it back and continued.

'Now, before you ask how such a thing is possible outside of a song, or how I lost Korpiklani's favor, I'll tell you that I don't have any earthly idea, or I'd still be in her service, wouldn't I? The important thing is that sometime after meeting Kang-ho and Zosia, I fell from the graces of my goddess, and not long after that the graces of my lover. Since I didn't wish to also fall from the favor of my employer, I offered to do whatever Zosia suggested . . . and that's how I ended up donning a dozen stupid costumes and infiltrating this cult or that encampment, the master of disguise, as you so succinctly put it. The most dangerous work of all, espionage, where the only reward you win is your life, if you're lucky, and even that comes at the cost of universal distrust, even from the friends who put you up to it. And you know the secret to my success in this one field, the reason it always worked, despite my inability to put on an accent even as well as Maroto? It's because I'm so bland and forgettable, most people don't look at me once, let alone twice . . . '

After this Fennec fell silent, and Ji-hyeon went over to pour him another bowl only to find the bottle was empty. She felt sorry for Fennec, then doubted that pity as something he'd possibly been angling for, doubted the whole story . . . and then hated herself for doubting him at all, after all they'd been through. At the edge of her tipsy thoughts was something else, though, a silver lining she could almost put her finger on . . .

'I do not know if it results from your skill or your forsaken god, but this bitter beer has indeed fortified my heart,' said Choi, putting her empty bowl down and patting the forlorn man on the shoulder.

'That's it,' said Ji-hyeon. 'I knew I felt something, too, and that's definitely it – I'm not worried about anything anymore. Not even going through the Gate sounds scary anymore.'

'It's hardly a miracle,' said Fennec wryly. 'I brewed this batch with fire poppy oil. You must not remember but I gave you some after you took a tumble fighting the Thaoans, right before you jumped to your feet and charged that devil queen. Has a way of taking the edge off, doesn't it?'

'That it does . . . ' said Ji-hyeon, thinking, thinking. 'How much of it did you make? And how much does it take to feel the effects?'

'Not enough to go around, if I anticipate your meaning,' said Fennec. 'Even when we captured that granary on the way out of the Dominions I barely brewed enough for a hogshead, and have put a dent in it all by myself.'

'A little can go a long way, if we make its effects known beforehand and give the genuine article to as many of our soldiers as we can before it runs out, and then give the rest ordinary ale,' said Ji-hyeon, remembering with painful embarrassment how once upon a time, before she sampled the real deal, her older sister had convinced her and Keun-ju to smoke dried gingko leaves, claiming it was saam. Both of them had reeled around, feeling positively wasted until Yunjin had confessed her prank through paroxysms of laughter.

'It is true that nothing makes a warrior feel so brave as being reminded that she is,' said Choi thoughtfully. 'A ruse, yes, but a necessary one to help them overcome their own cowardice.'

'That's my poppy sour you're giving away to the grunts,' said Fennec, but smiled. 'Another inspired stratagem, General.'

'I learned from the best,' said Ji-hyeon. 'Where would we be if a certain missionary hadn't told a little girl she was brave enough to walk through a Gate, even without the benefit of drugs?'

Before he could reply they heard a commotion from outside, and one of the guards stationed at the entrance to her tent called, 'The Thaoan emissary approaches, General.'

'Oh *shit*,' said Ji-hyeon, really, really, really wishing she didn't have to deal with her second dad right now. He would never, ever approve of her plan to use the Gate to invade Diadem, and so to save him the worry she had planned on simply leaving him a letter on her abandoned command table. Even had there been time to do so she wouldn't have saddled down her invading force with tents and other bulky equipment, nor was she planning on taking along any Imperial captives who didn't willingly accept her offer of amnesty and join her cause. As soon as the Cobalts disappeared through the Gate, Colonel Waits and Colonel Wheatley would presumably hop the wall of the unguarded stockade and hail the waiting Thaoans, whereupon they would find her long gone ... but now she apparently had to explain to her dad that she was leading her troops on what could only be a one-way trip through the Gate, to ultimate victory or absolute failure in the capital of the Empire. It would not be a fun conversation, but she couldn't bear to just send him away now, not after his warning her of the false plot Zosia had tempted him with had proven, if only fleetingly, his loyalty to his daughter over his old accomplices.

'Send him in!' she called to the guards, and he must have already been pacing outside, for he burst into the tent as the words left her tart lips. Flustered as he'd looked the night of his arrival, when she'd told him of her grand plans and then the dire news of Empress Ryuki's bounty, tonight he appeared positively unhinged. He'd been rending his hair out by the roots, to judge by the trickles of blood seeping down from his scalp, and his eyes were red from tears.

'Ji-hyeon!' Kang-ho came at her so fast Choi moved to intercept them, but Ji-hyeon saw her father's hands were empty save for a sheet of parchment, and she ducked around her protective friend to embrace her second father. He clung to her like a lost child reunited with its sole living relation, and she squeezed him tight, trying to placate him with explanations.

'I'm sorry, Dad, but I didn't have a choice. There's another

Imperial regiment coming down on us, from Meshugg, and if we didn't snatch Waits when we did she—'

'Waits? Fuck Waits!' cried Kang-ho, releasing her and waving the document at her. 'It's your first father! Your sisters! The empress! The Isles! Hwabun!'

'Calm down,' ordered Ji-hyeon, but even with the special brew in her belly her pace began to quicken – the worst had come to pass, just as she'd feared, Empress Ryuki punishing her family since the wrathful ruler couldn't reach Ji-hyeon herself. All her life she had been taught that the royal family of Othean were the most honorable mortals not just in the Star but in all of its recorded history, and this faith in their absolute honesty and love for their people was the only thing that had allowed Ji-hyeon to sleep at night. An empress so blessed by birth that no lie could even leave her lips would never take out her rage on an innocent party, Ji-hyeon had told herself over and over ... naïve child that she was. Of course the empress had done something terrible to her family, thinking Ji-hyeon responsible for the death of her son, and of course it was all Ji-hyeon's fault – if only she had stayed on the Isles and married Prince Byeong-gu none of this would have happened. She had to hear it, though, had to hear an account of her crimes from her father's own lips, in all its gruesome detail. 'What's happened?'

'The Sunken Kingdom,' he gasped. 'It's risen! Neglected gods of our ancestors take pity, Jex Toth has returned!'

Outside confirmation of Hoartrap's assertion was not very welcome in this instance; he had claimed to use his deviltry to confirm it with his own eyes, but she still wasn't taking everything the Touch said as unimpeachable. Ji-hyeon shuddered as she remembered the play of lightning over the Haunted Sea as she and her family looked out from the Mistward Balcony.

'Who told you, Dad?' Ji-hyeon asked, trying to keep calm. Fennec had lit his own pipe on a candle and passed the smoldering briar to Kang-ho, but he shook his head, too desperate to speak to waste a breath on tubāq. This was so unlike the man who had raised her that Ji-hyeon feared for his sanity.

'The empress. We've been communicating, using this new Gate,' said Kang-ho. When the others looked at him in shock, he held up his palms. 'Not my idea. It's one of the purposes they served in the Age of Wonders, apparently, passing letters back and forth almost instantaneously with devilish messengers. And the empress reached out to me, not the other way around.'

'You've ... you've been talking to her?' All of Ji-hyeon's fears of a paternal betrayal returned, but Kang-ho waved them away as though they were pipe smoke he'd rudely blown in her face.

'Only because of her news, her terms,' said Kang-ho, closing his eyes and trying to slow his breathing with deliberate focus. After he'd taken a few breaths – and Ji-hyeon was made even more breathless – he said, 'The Immaculate Isles are under siege. A monstrous navy has laid waste to the outlying islands and encroaches upon Othean. Hwabun ...'

But Kang-ho could say no more, his eyes filling with tears and his lip trembling, Choi's hand going to one of Ji-hyeon's shoulders and Fennec's to the other as she snatched the parchment from her second father's shaking hand. It was easier to read than the letters he had sent her from the Thaoan camp, for the High Immaculate was clean, the calligraphy precise. News, as Kang-ho had said, but also terms, and quite possibly the only ones she would ever see from Othean.

'Ji-hyeon?' murmured Fennec as Kang-ho fell into an empty chair, sobbing with his head in his hands. And for the first time in her memory, Ji-hyeon let her second father see her tears as well, not even bowing her head to hide them. Her hand clenched into a fist around the parchment as Fennec quietly repeated her name.

'It's as he said – the Isles are besieged,' said Ji-hyeon, hardly believing the steady voice she heard was her own when her whole body seemed to be crumbling from within, a steady drip of tears falling from her chin to where Fellwing clung like a brooch to the front of her coat, catching them in her beak. 'The empress does not know how long Othean can stand without help. She's called on the Black Pope and the Crimson Queen, the Tapais of Ugrakar and the seafaring Flintlanders, on the Raniputri Dominions and even Usba, but she fears none of them will send help in time to save the Isles. And so she . . . she *begs* me, despite the crimes I have committed against her family, to return home, to lead the Cobalts to the defense of Othean. If I do, all is forgiven . . . and if I do not, the Immaculate Isles will be overrun by an army of hellish creatures that has set forth from Jex Toth.'

'And . . . ' Fennec cleared a thickness in his throat, his fingers pressing gingerly into her arm. 'And . . . what of Hwabun?'

Kang-ho's wail at the mention of their ancestral Isle should have been answer enough, but lest there be any doubt Ji-hyeon repeated what she had just read.

'The Isles nearest to the Haunted Sea were the first conquests of Jex Toth. Hwabun . . . Hwabun is no more.'

Fennec and Choi closed in around her, their arms warm, their breath warmer, but instead of finding comfort in their gesture she felt like boiling water trapped in a kettle, growing hotter and hotter, her teeth grinding so hard she felt the loose one pop free entirely, the lancing pain and taste of blood barely registering.

Little Hyori, trembling against Ji-hyeon's side as Yunjin sang them ghost songs against the backdrop of the Haunted Sea.

Pak, their majordomo who aspired to be like a third father to the children, but had only ever managed to be a stuffy uncle.

Lady Sung, her first father's valet, and Madame Kim-bo, the harbor mistress, and all the rest of the staff . . .

And towering over the rest, her first father, Jun-hwan, his beetled brows forever judging her, even in her memories.

Except he hadn't always been like that. She now remembered when she was younger, and her other dad's business ventures were still prosperous, how her first father's smile was so infectious she couldn't see it without grinning back at him. She remembered the ease with which he had led her on her first dance at the Festival of Servants on Othean, making his insecure daughter relax by cheekily critiquing everybody else's steps as they crossed the crowded room. And going even further back, she remembered the way he had comforted her when she would run crying into the house with a skinned knee or elbow. No matter how fine his robes or how perfect his makeup, on those occasions he would rock his grass-stained girl in his arms and kiss her cheeks until her sobs became cackles of delight, and and and . . .

'Zosia,' Ji-hyeon finally managed through a mouthful of blood from where her tooth had split loose from her jaw. She broke out of the shell of Fennec and Choi's arms and went to her second father's side. 'Stop her. Bring her back here. Don't let her go, no matter what. Not until I figure this out.'

Choi and Fennec vanished from the tent, and kneeling beside her second father Ji-hyeon wept with him, mourning the people they loved most in the Star, people they had never meant to hurt, though hurt was surely the only possible result of their selfish plots. Fellwing crawled between them, up Ji-hyeon's arm and down Kang-ho's shoulder, back and forth between her old master and her new one. With each sweep between the two the little devil's coat grew darker, richer, shinier, and her belly swelled bigger and bigger, until the last candle guttered out in the command tent of the Cobalt Company.

CHAPTER

19

Horned Wolves do not ride. The prohibition was far older than Best herself, but this, she told herself, was not riding. It was ... something else, and not something she liked, but obviously not the same thing at all as sitting on an animal's back.

The tiny house was roomier within than without, as was to be expected with witches. But instead of being built atop chicken legs or a turtle shell, as with the witch huts in Sullen's songs, this one rested on wooden wheels, and the horned wolf familiar of Nemi of the Bitter Sighs pulled the house behind her like an ox pulls a plow. Had any other beast propelled the hut, Best would never have agreed to join the sorcerer, but one could only question the Fallen Mother so far – a horned wolf was a horned wolf, and not the sort of message a Horned Wolf could ignore.

But that didn't mean Best had to like it. Even after weeks of sitting in the rattling, jolting, bouncing little house her stomach refused to become comfortable, reminding her in the worst way of the few times her father had marched her and her brother all the way out to the coast so they could paddle around on a coracle when they were young. At least on the boat there had been a rhythm to the rocking, but in the house it was unpredictable, with nary a bump for hours, and then hours more of it feeling as though they were being dragged over a giant's washboard.

It could have been worse, though – at least she hadn't gone blind, like Brother Rýt. He had brought it entirely on himself, so Best did not feel much sympathy for the chubby monk, especially since she now had to mind him more than ever. What kind of a fool does the one thing a witch tells you not to do? Brother Rýt, that was who.

Best had admittedly been curious, too, when Nemi had ushered them into the house that first morning on the plains and pointed out the strange birdlike creature sitting on a nest of woven hair and shredded parchment. It resembled a chicken, except for the black scales on its wings, back, and serpentine tail, and the white hue to its birdlike legs, chest, and beak. The small hood of stitched leather and iron had actually been the last thing she had noticed, but it was the first thing Brother Rýt commented on.

'Never, ever take that off,' Nemi had cautioned them before shutting them inside and taking her position on the roof, from whence she steered the horned wolf. 'If you do, she'll make you wish you hadn't.'

This was the first of Nemi's prophecies to be proven true, and when Best was startled out of one of the few naps she'd been able to slip into on the journey by Brother Rýt's scream she had known at once that he'd gone against the witch's wishes. Fortunately the monk had only lifted the edge of the hood, and as soon as he'd met the creature's gaze he had stumbled back with a wail, letting the protective mask fall back into place. Best stopped berating him when she pulled his hands away from his face and saw his eyes had turned to gemstones, because even if it was his own fault Best could tell he'd learned his lesson.

What had he expected from such an animal, though? Even with its hood in place it seemed to always be watching them, and was this not the same creature that Nemi had used to divine their path? Best had decided she wanted nothing more to do with the thing after Nemi had insisted the Horned Wolf hold out her hand and let its sharp beak peck her palm, and shortly after it had tasted Best's blood it laid a crimson egg that the witch fed to the horned wolf. To guide them to Best's kinfolk, Nemi told her, but that did not explain the other eggs the creature laid, black flecked with gold. Before setting out each morn the witch would crack one of these eggs into her mouth, and Best paid close attention to how after this breakfast Nemi would seem spry and healthy, save for the slight twist in her back . . . but come evening the young witch was barely able to move without wincing, and instead of breathing easy she bought each breath with a wheezing gasp. If Nemi of the Bitter Sighs ever betrayed Best, she would strike the lizard-bird first, for it was clearly where the witch had hidden her heart.

Fallen Mother's mercy, it would not come to that. Other than being a witch, Nemi made better company than the increasingly whiny Brother Rýt, and at night she would draw her singing sword as they sat around their fire. Tucked into the scabbard beside the incredibly thin single-edged blade was a bow of the witch's own brown hair, and sitting on the stoop of her hut with the dull point of the sword planted between her feet, Nemi would bend the supple steel and run the bow along its dull side, drawing forth keening wails that made the flames bend and sway in time with her music. Brother Rýt quietly prayed all the while, but Best preferred the melancholy songs of the sword to the monk's low mutters. Nemi's playing made her think of the open Savannahs under a full moon, of the wind running through the summer grass, of what might be found at the bottom of the wide, sluggish river they crossed after several weeks of monotonous travel, but Brother Rýt's prayers only made her think of her dead husband, her disgraced family.

One evening as the Bright Watcher dressed herself in the evening's blood, the setting sun casting its last rays through the hut's narrow windows, they bounced over a final root and stopped, though it was always Nemi's custom to drive the horned wolf deep into the night. Brother Rýt moaned a little from his padded chair, as if sensing the avian familiar's presence on the cluttered shelf behind him where glass baubles, wooden puzzles, and countless tomes stayed in perfect order despite the chaotic movements of the house. The small door Best always bumped her head passing through creaked open, and Nemi's silhouette stood framed by the quiet red wood behind her.

'The trees are too thick for my wagon, but we are very close,' spoke the witch, and hauling herself up into the already cramped interior, she retrieved a gold-flecked egg from the nest. Best slid out onto the leaf-strewn ground as Nemi slurped the egg behind her, and the unusual hour of the witch's feeding brought a nervous hum to Best's throat. They must be right on top of her missing kin and their dread sorcerer companion, if Nemi felt compelled to eat a second egg in a single day. As the witch left her wagon, she said, 'You . . . you just stay here, little Chainite, and keep Zeetatrice company.'

As Best donned her horned hunting helmet and stretched her cramped limbs beneath the high boughs of the bald cypresses, she saw Nemi had clasped her singing sword to her pouch-laden belt, and while her gait was steady from the efficacy of the egg the witch also carried her feather-topped staff.

'Here we come to the end of our road, Best of the Horned Wolf Clan,' said Nemi, and Best saw worry and excitement and yet more worry on the girl's face. 'Perhaps. If Hoartrap is still in the company of your kin, we must strike him first, and hard, lest you not have the chance to face your family.'

'How will I know this Hoartrap?' asked Best, hefting her grandmother's sun-knife in her strong hand and balancing her spear in the other. 'And would you not prefer to claim your vengeance for yourself?'

'If he is here, you cannot miss him,' said Nemi. 'Taller than you, nearly as broad as my wolf, and paler than Zeetatrice's breast. As for claiming my own vengeance, I will consider the battle fairly won if we bring him down together – even with my wolf at our side, he will not fall without cost.'

'Who is he, then?' asked Best as Nemi unhooked the horned wolf from her harness. She had never asked, for it was not her place to pry, but if Nemi begged her help to slay the sorcerer then she had a right to know. 'This hated enemy not only of Nemi of the Bitter Sighs, but all of the Star, what is he to you? A rival to your power? An assassin of your people?'

'He was my tutor,' said Nemi with a smile that looked as mad and hungry as that of the horned wolf who bared her teeth and padded off into the shadows. 'But now it is my turn to repay his lessons with one of my own.'

Best nodded, knowing if they came through this hunt she would be within her rights to request the full song. For now, she accompanied an admitted witch into a foreign wood on the western edge of the world, knowing that whatever else lurked in the closing dark, her son, her father, or her brother waited among them, if not all three. Her palm sweaty on the handle of the knife forged from her great-grandmother's bones, Best followed the white shadow of a horned wolf as it stalked between the trees, and knew she would do what she must, when the time came.

CHAPTER
20

As the Lark's Tongue curled around the sun, swallowing another day, the winter valley took on the bluish pall of a drowned sailor. Away from the tents it was silent save for the crunch and squeak of boots tromping through the strips of snow and wider patches of frozen earth, and the tapping of claws on ice. The Gate looked even creepier without the smoke that had initially concealed it, or the heavy snows that had come after. Now it just loomed there in the midst of the winter landscape, like a hole poked through a holiday-themed tapestry. In the fading light Zosia led them right up to its rim, and while their destination must have been obvious as soon as they had left the camp, only now did Boris speak up.

'I was afraid of this,' said the man, staring down at the impenetrable void. 'Ever since we brought Portolés down here and watched it swallow 'er up I just knew I'd be following, and figured you'd be the one responsible. I'm your, what's the word ... test? You toss me in and see what happens? That's my big contribution?'

'For a godless bastard, you sure are eager to jump to conclusions,' said Zosia.

'Being a heretic's not the same as being godless,' he said.

'And looking at something like that it's hard to say there's not something more at play than the natural workings of the mortal world, but that don't mean I want any part of it.'

'Sensible fellow,' said Hoartrap, pulling his robe tighter around his barrel chest. He was looking a lot better than he had in the first few weeks of his recovery from the disaster with the devil queen, but something was definitely up with the sorcerer, his normally high spirits declining further and further with each step they took away from the command tent. He idly kicked a dirty clod of ice with one fluffy wool slipper, and they watched as it spun out over the Gate. Instead of skipping along the surface or sinking beneath it, the chunk of ice boiled away in seconds, leaving white vapor hanging over the black lintel.

'Oh fuck no,' breathed Boris. 'Really?'

'Really,' said Zosia, though she wasn't feeling much better about the situation. Choplicker was playfully running laps around the wide rim, as if stretching his legs before climbing into a rowboat for a long voyage. He barked at her from the far side, his coat again blending into the night, his gait strong, his eyes and teeth shining. He clearly wanted this, and shouldn't that be enough to put her off it entirely?

'You telling me you *don't* believe some higher power is looking out for you, and you're still willing to take a swim in there?' asked Boris.

'Having no faith at all is still a kind of faith,' said Hoartrap, but it didn't sound like his heart was in his contrariness. 'And besides, our Zosia has a guardian angel, don't you?'

'Yeah, my little wet-nosed angel, who smells like death warmed over every time his fur gets wet,' said Zosia, and Choplicker zipped past them on another lap, tail slapping the back of her hand as he went.

'I don't know, I don't know,' said Boris, wriggling his hands in the ginger mink muff Zosia had found him, along with the rest of his warm but similarly ostentatious costume of plush furs and brightly dyed leathers. She'd put it together from the leftover wardrobes of the recently deceased Duchess Din and Count Hassan; Purna and Diggelby had picked their friends' tent pretty clean before setting out, and so what had remained were the items that even the other fops found too flashy or gauche.

'Well, then this will be an educational experience for all of us, because I don't know if it's a great idea, either,' said Zosia. 'But we're about to find out.'

'No!' Hoartrap's outburst made Zosia jump, the Touch beginning to pace back and forth, rubbing his mostly healed hands together in the frigid air until the scabs on his palms began dusting the snow. 'I won't go. End of song.'

'End of song? Son, you haven't even started it,' said Zosia, an already dodgy prospect becoming downright nauseous. 'If you can't take us through now, how in fuck's name do you intend to bring the whole Company through tomorrow?'

'I'm deeply sorry, Zosia, but you'll just have to ask your devil to ferry you across,' said Hoartrap, keeping his eye on the streaking canine shadow instead of meeting her glare. 'I've been pondering a way to gird myself ever since Ji-hyeon gave the order to take you to Diadem, but I'm coming up empty. Here on the Star, your willpower keeps the fiend in check, but the rules are different beyond the Gates. It's too risky, exposing myself to his mercy like that, so you're on your own – I'm going back to camp.'

'Ji-hyeon gave you an order, Hoartrap, you can't just say no!'

'Watch me,' said Hoartrap, his mood already improving now that he had made up his mind. 'If I've learned one thing from watching the two of you bandy words, among other things, it's that our general is lenient even with those captains who break her nose.'

'We'd better go back, too, yeah?' said Boris hopefully. 'I mean, if *that guy*'s not willing to try it out . . .'

'Like the general said, every moment we're not in Diadem we're worsening our chances of success tomorrow,' said Zosia. 'If you don't do this, Hoartrap, you're actively helping the Burnished Chain.'

'Codswallop,' said Hoartrap. 'Keeping myself alive, sane, and with both feet on the Star is the most I can offer the cause. The church would love nothing more than to have me walk into a Gate and never come out again, and I have no intention of granting any of their wishes . . . nor those of your devil. I have no doubt he is more than capable of seeing you safely through all by himself, so don't try to blame this on me – stay or go, it's your choice, but I wash my hands of it.'

'So that leaves us where, exactly?' demanded Zosia. 'You going back to Ji-hyeon, hat in hand, while I let Chop lead me into a fucking Gate? How stupid do I look?'

'That depends if you trust him enough to follow him through,' said Hoartrap. 'In which case I'd say pretty fucking stup—'

Choplicker flew out of the gloaming, front paws buffeting Hoartrap's belly as he barked furiously at the wizard. Hoartrap squealed, slipping backward on the ice, and it was almost funny, seeing the gigantic devil-eater knocked onto his big ass by an average-sized dog . . . except where Choplicker and Hoartrap were concerned nothing was ever funny. Hoartrap sat sprawled on the ground, ink-runed hands hovering on either side of Choplicker's long snout as the devil growled, low and deep, holding the sorcerer's gaze.

'Come on, Chop, time to go,' Zosia called, trying to project an authority she no longer felt. Even though the devil was bound to her here, on the edge of the Gate, they wouldn't be *here* for very much longer. Choplicker's growl abruptly became a plaintive whine as he looked over his shoulder at her, and she got the impression that he was actively fucking with Hoartrap. '*Now*, Chop. Don't tell me you're not excited to finally get me into a Gate.'

Choplicker barked, whipping around so fast his tail snapped Hoartrap in the nose. The Touch picked himself up off the ground with as much dignity as he could muster, but his adversary had already forgotten him, the devil playfully pouncing around Zosia and Boris. He would drop his front legs and snout to the ground while sticking his butt up and wagging his tail, then feint toward them, yipping happily. Zosia indulged him a little, swatting his back when he flew past her, but Boris cringed and flinched every time the devil rushed him. Hard to blame him.

'Farewell, then, dear friend, and may this trip to Diadem be more effective in the long term than your last one was,' said Hoartrap, brushing slush off his bottom. 'Forgive me if I don't shake your hand, but I'm rather attached to it and don't want your devil taking it off. If you want my advice I'd invest in a far shorter lead than you've allowed him thus far.'

'I could say the same thing about you and Ji-hyeon, though I'm no longer so sure who's got the leash and who's wearing the collar,' said Zosia. 'See you tomorrow?'

'If all goes according to plan,' said Hoartrap with a bow. 'And with so simple a scheme, what could possibly go amiss?'

'Let's hope we don't find out,' said Zosia, too concerned with the enormity of the next few minutes to worry much about tomorrow's invasion. Would that she lived long enough to do so . . . 'Ready, Boris?'

Boris looked at her. Looked at Hoartrap. Looked at Choplicker. Looked at the Gate. Looked back at Choplicker. And doubled over, puking up his dinner biscuits all over his pink suede boots. Choplicker moseyed over for a snack but Zosia shooed him away. That gave Hoartrap a final giggle, at least, and then his battered bulk turned away into the night, a spirit fleeing from the Gate into a softer darkness. Choplicker sat down by Zosia's side, his frantic tail whipping up a slurry behind them, and she scratched his ears as he looked up at her, smiling.

'Through the Gate, sneak past any guards on the Diadem side, raise a rebel army, start a diversionary fire at dawn,' said Zosia. 'That order. Easy.'

'You think so?' asked Boris, wiping his mouth on his muff.

'Not really,' said Zosia, taking a loose hold of the nape of Choplicker's neck with one hand and reaching for Boris with the other. 'But why risk your life for something easy?'

'I wish I had some good last words, but I used 'em all up the last time I thought you were gonna kill me,' said Boris, taking her hand.

'Last words are for losers,' said Zosia, imagining she could feel the damaged crown pulsing through her backpack, as though she were a fairysong witch who had hidden her heart in the circlet. Her legs were shaking so badly she wondered if she'd even be able to take the final few steps to the Gate, when the time came . . . and then, as if he knew her secret heart even better than she did, Choplicker plunged ahead into the abyss, and clinging to his pelt, Zosia followed him in.

The last thing she felt was Boris's sweaty fingers crushing her hand as she pulled him along, dragging innocents down with her to the very last.

The last thing she heard was Hoartrap shouting her name, telling her to wait.

And the last thing she thought of was Leib, holding her in the darkness of their bed as they listened to the summer rain.

Then the Gate enveloped her, and all the tragedies and triumphs and loves and losses of the world of mortals became as remote as the farthest star.

CHAPTER

21

Sullen had known at a glance that the swamp was trouble, that they should have turned back and seen if the tamarind post could find them another path instead of fording the flooded trail, but had they listened? No, they had not. Now Diggelby had stirred up a nest of somebody else's vengeful dead, all scrabbling claws and snapping teeth, with piles of wooden debris armoring their backs as they swam or scrambled forward on their bellies, and it was too late for I-told-you-sos. Hells, there was barely time to shoulder the whole damn post himself as Keun-ju went to help the others, and Sullen awkwardly transferred the heavy pylon to the pony's back, hoping it stayed wedged against the packs – he figured he'd be needing his hands free pretty soon. Reluctant as Sullen was to strike the remains of anyone's ancestor, these things had not responded to his soothing words of peace, pressing their attack. Purna shooting one with her deafening hand cannon probably hadn't helped, and didn't seem to do much but surround them in a peppery plume of smoke that hovered over the sunset swamp.

The pony was surprisingly placid as a line of three aquatic ancients approached down the narrow path ahead of them, another four coming up it from the rear. Keun-ju looked ready for action, but the other two Craven hunters were acting the fool, as usual, shouting and splashing and looking at Sullen as though he could magically undo the mess they had dragged him into. Purna was down on her knees in the marsh, rooting in the muddy waters, and Diggelby was hopping on his left foot as though reluctant to put his bare stockinged right one back into the water. In addition to the things quickly dragging themselves along the submerged trail, the one who had snatched Diggelby's boot still bobbed in a pool of deeper water just off to the side of the shallow path, while yet more could be seen approaching from deeper in the swamp.

Sullen hated this kind of shit. It wasn't these foreign ancestors' fault that a band of interlopers had despoiled their burial ground, thought Sullen, finally remembering where he had seen similar heaps of wooden poles rising from a watery scene. The Walrus Folk buried their dead in a similar fashion, submerging their bodies in tidal estuaries and then planting a cage of wooden poles around them in the riverbed so that they wouldn't float out to sea, but would instead be kept in place to feed the fish and crabs that would in turn feed the tribe. That this was an ancient gravebog didn't explain why the restless dead still wore so much soft grey flesh on their bones, or why those bones should rise to attack any trespassers, but then in the songs Sullen's ancestors were always running afoul of such revenants, no explanation needed. And that old man back in the town of Black Moth had warned them not to wander through a graveyard, hadn't he? Sullen's ma had always told him that those who ignore the warnings of the wise get what they deserve.

His sword drawn and held in a funny posture, Keun-ju glanced back at Sullen, his eyes wide and scared though the rest of him was steady as a picture stone. Sullen wished there was time to reiterate how much he had liked the poems Keun-ju had shyly recited over the past few days when they walked off ahead of the two on post duty, the words so richly seasoned Sullen could actually feel the salt-kissed breezes of Isles he had never visited, taste steaming dishes he had never eaten, smell the scents of unknown flowers, hear the cries of exotic birds . . . and, with the last verse Keun-ju had shared despite the tint it brought to his cheeks, revisit the woman they both clearly loved. There was no time to tell him all of that, though, so Sullen just held Keun-ju's eyes and nodded, like warriors were supposed to do before epic battles, as though they were passing secret messages, sharing a deeper understanding.

And perhaps Sullen had been premature dismissing those old songs entirely, for as the fear left Keun-ju's eyes and his veiled chin returned the nod, Sullen thought maybe they had communicated something in that silent exchange, just as the heroes of old supposedly did. It was a simple thing, really, and putting it into words, not such a great revelation . . . but Sullen's heart began to pound even faster than it had when he'd first glimpsed the wood-shelled dead, and he tightened his grip on his spear, leaving his last remaining sun-knife in its bandolier lest he lose it in the swamp. What they had agreed without a word was that they would not fail Ji-hyeon, that they would return to the Cobalt Company with the other or not at all, and in that moment Sullen felt almost like he had when Grandfather was still alive – like he had someone he needed to protect, even more than himself, and commitment to this task overpowered his earlier dejection at their situation. While Keun-ju moved back around him to guard their pony from the monsters at their rear, Purna clambered back to her feet and Sullen stepped up beside her, the first of the risen corpses sliding easily toward them.

'Fuck Maroto!' cried the soggy girl, whipping her dripping hair around her face as she brandished a long, inwardly curving blade.

'Fuck Maroto,' said Sullen, smiling to consider how little he'd thought of his feckless kin over the past few days; to be forgotten even by those who hunted him was exactly the fate the ruffian deserved.

'Fuck Maroto!' shouted Diggelby and Keun-ju, and then the underbrush-coated corpses attacked, the boot-nabbing monster in the pool swimming back in and making another grab for Diggelby as the creature before them on the narrow trail darted forward.

The risen corpse pushed itself ahead through the shallows, the hump of debris on its back half as tall as Purna. Its belly slid across the mud of the sunken path, its mutely snarling face and grasping claws cutting through the filmy water. Sullen stepped forward and jabbed his spear through the corpse's water-softened skull, nailing it to the marshy trail. It hardly seemed to notice, pushing forward against the shaft of the spear until Purna stepped around it and whipped her long, curved knife into the back of its neck. The blow severed its pinned head and, as Sullen flicked his spear around to send the skull flying off into the swamp, he saw the strangest sight yet.

Its gaping neck-hole writhed with movement, pale grey knots coiling over one another. But fast as he'd glimpsed the activity the thing retreated deeper into its human nest, and Sullen understood what was happening here. Certain ancient devils were known to hide in rocks or trees or other lifeless things, causing minor mischief, and a pack of such fiends must have slipped into the corpses of this graveyard, employing the wood-interred remains to engender fresh suffering. That seemed most likely, anyway, because whatever was moving around inside the corpse's throat was the same distinct shade of grey as the devils he used to glimpse dancing around his bed as a child, the ones nobody else could see because they weren't born with the same eyes as Sullen.

Sullen was about to warn Purna that if there was still a devil in the decapitated corpse it might not be done fighting, but before he could their opponent proved that point for him. The headless horror lunged forward, and while Purna was slightly off to the side Sullen was directly in its path. Before he could spear it again, one of its hands closed round his right ankle, talons digging painfully into his flesh.

Sullen panicked, spearing its debris-armored back over and over and trying to kick it off him with his left leg . . . but agile though he usually was, the slick mud slid out from underneath his heels, and the spear slipped from his sweaty fingers as he fell.

He landed flat on his back, splashing into the shallow mire, and worst of all, the headless thing still gripped his ankle. It was quick, too, and before Sullen could reach the spear that lay beside him it had pinned his writhing legs beneath its soft, slippery belly, and slid its way up his body. Its claws scratched at his arms, the particular stench of drowned mammals rising from the stump of its neck and making Sullen gag as it tried to crawl completely on top of him. Sullen screamed, then, not a noble howl or a defiant battle cry, but a noise more appropriate for the occasion as the devil-ridden corpse mounted him . . .

And with strength he did not know he possessed, Sullen rolled the whole stinking bulk of it off of him, onto its woody back. Which would have been perfect, except it held fast to his shoulders and carried him along for the ride; being held atop the slimy-bellied monster was better than being stuck beneath it, but he was still trapped. Its ribs bent like a rubber tree's boughs as he struggled to get free, the bundle of branches moored to its back groaning beneath their combined weight. Purna reappeared, shouting things he didn't understand, swinging her flashing blade perilously close to Sullen's extremities as she tried to hack him free of its talons. Then he heard the snapping of overtaxed wood and half of the creature's shell-like backing of soggy limbs gave way, and they pitched to one side . . . away from the shallow waters covering the path, and into one of the deep sinkholes that bordered it.

It was colder here, and hard to see. Sullen grappled his opponent in the center of a maelstrom of mud and dead leaves as they sank into the pool, screaming a cloud of bubbles as its fingernails burrowed into his biceps. The darkness deepened, as did the chill in the water, but then Sullen glimpsed something through the haze, a twisting rope of shining silver. It was the devil that lurked inside the corpse's nearly translucent skin, wriggling in the dead man's chest; this was one of those rare occasions when Sullen was glad he had been born with the eyes of a snow lion instead of those of a man . . . and glad that it had grabbed his shoulders instead of his wrists, since he could still move his arms through the pain. Bracing one elbow against the corpse's cheese-soft breastbone, he used his other hand to find the hilt of the sun-knife on his bandolier.

The devil inside the headless corpse must have sensed the cold metal, for its spear-like fingers slid out of Sullen's upper arms and swam to his wrists . . . but not fast enough. Though the darkening water made Sullen slow, the multiple edges of the flanged sun-knife tore through the corpse's shriveled chest as though it were wet silk. Before the silver devil could flee deeper into its hiding place the tip of the main blade brushed its coils, and its faint glow went out as though Sullen had snuffed a candle. The hands that had reached for his went limp, but the legs, which had become tangled in his own, grew stiff, and as he continued to sink into the cold, lightless pit he was obliged to break the corpse's femurs between hand and knife before he could slip away from its heavy bulk.

His chest tight, Sullen kicked his boots, thanking Grandfather for making him learn to swim in the snowmelt pond that formed when the Frozen Savannahs thawed each summer. The old man insisted Sullen be prepared for the inevitable day when the Horned Wolves returned to the sea, a day that had never come. Before he could get too relieved, though, Sullen's face smushed into cold muck; half-blind from the stinging silt in his eyes, he'd swum into the floor or side of the sinkhole. He'd never drowned before, obviously, but Sullen reckoned this was how it felt, fire instead of air smoldering in his chest as the dark water claimed him . . .

He tried again, awkwardly twisting in the blind well, bumping off the floating corpse, and again brushed a rough, muddy surface. And again he kicked off, shoving the sun-knife back into the bandolier so he could snatch the water with both hands . . . again, and again, and again, and—

Sullen exploded up into the fading light, unable to do anything but flounder as he gasped in the foul pool. In the moment or two it took him to regain his senses, another of the possessed corpses swam up almost on top of him. Nothing moved behind its dripping hump of branches and leaves, the open swamp flat and empty – Keun-ju and the others must have already been pulled beneath the surface, too. Sullen's feet kicked for purchase but there was none, the wall of the sinkhole crumbling away beneath his boots, and as he groped at his bandolier for his sun-knife the shriveled face of a long-dead woman lunged for his throat, her carapace of sticks and filth filling his world—

And then exploding as a brown blur landed atop her, sending broken twigs and plumes of water high into the air, an enormous animal crashing into the sinkhole beside Sullen. He was washed clear out of the pool by the ensuing wave, and found himself back in the muddy shallows that bridged the deeper waters. Familiar bodies coalesced around him as he dizzily rocked back and forth. Purna was pulling him up before his vision had settled, and he saw Diggelby was almost to the far shore already. The girl pulled him forward, the submerged trail becoming hard to make out as the setting sun stained the water copper.

The disappearing path was bad – they had to get across the swamp fast, or it would become impossible to see where they could step without plunging into another pool. He turned to impress the urgency of their need to Keun-ju, but the Immaculate wasn't where he was supposed to be, wading through the shallows behind them. He was just gone. Then Sullen's mud-stopped ears popped as the water and muck drained back to their source, and he heard the screaming.

Before that day Sullen had heard Princess whinny and nicker, but that was about it. Now the poor beast sounded almost like a shrieking babe as she floundered through the deep mire behind them, circled by the wood-backed horrors, and atop the wallowing pony was Keun-ju. He had ridden the animal straight onto Sullen's assailant, and in trying to swim back out of the sinkhole Princess had gotten herself stuck in the deep mud on the far side of the pool. The full host of hungry corpses converged around the trapped pony, and its trapped rider. Sullen snatched himself away from Purna, even though he could see how hopeless it was, even though he could only get himself dead by trying to rescue his doomed friend. Keun-ju managed to raise his legs out of the water, knocking the magic post into the pool and crouching with his feet precariously balanced on the pack animal's back, but any moment he would slip into the ravenous swarm.

And then it happened: Princess's scream cut off as one of the things caught her bridle and jerked her long pinto face down into the boiling water, her shoulder and haunches sinking quickly after. Keun-ju now appeared to be balancing on an enormous, undulating raft of driftwood, the corpses' funerary burdens becoming entangled as they fought to get at the easy prey. Hands were rising from the water on either side of him, clawing the air, and before Sullen could throw his sun-knife into one of the monsters the brave young Immaculate flung himself high into the air. He hadn't jumped toward Sullen and Purna, but away from them into the swamp, toward what might be open water or might just be more mud, and while the frenzying corpses weren't as tightly clustered on that side, he still failed to clear their perimeter. The Immaculate punched a ragged hole into the rippling waves of wooden debris, which immediately closed on top of him as the corpses banged their baggage together, desperate for a fresh taste now that the pony was coming apart in grisly pieces.

And just like that Keun-ju was gone, slipping out of the song so easily you never would have known he was in it if you hadn't been listening from the beginning.

Sullen must've been shouting, screaming, even, but couldn't hear anything over the splashing, thrashing ruckus the corpses made as they butchered Princess. He was on the verge of wading out after his friend, when he realized Purna was clinging tenaciously to his waving right arm. He finally pried the girl off, as deaf to her pleas as he was to his own cries, and focused on the first corpse he was going to stick his sun-knife through.

Worse ways for a song to end. Better than a fucking weak-bow to the gob, anyway ... but before he could lunge into the haunted bayou, a dark shape surfaced far out in what looked like deeper water, gulped the air, and went back under. Sullen blinked. He couldn't believe it, but he thought he had seen the last ray of the winter sun catch on the edge of a lace veil. It must have been a trick of the light, a large fish snatching a bug ... but it was enough distraction from his fury that he finally let Purna drag him back along the trail. Whether or not there was any actual hope that Keun-ju had slipped past the monsters, wasting his own life wouldn't help the situation.

'Come *on*,' commanded Purna, hauling him by the elbow. The path was nearly invisible now that the light was almost gone, and they slipped and fell several times in their escape. When they finally reached the high bank on the far side they were too exhausted to climb the steep, slippery shore, and lay panting against the moldy-smelling mud bank, trying not to throw up.

Purna couldn't possibly take another step. Let the horrible fuckers eat her like they'd eaten Keun-ju and poor Princess, so long as they let her lie on her back while they did it. She'd done all she could, and Maroto himself wouldn't have asked more of his star pupil.

Then she heard the dripping, softly splashing approach of another monster. Sullen must've heard it, too, and lurched back to his feet beside the miniature cliff that cut them off from the presumed safety of the forest. Purna might not be able to scale the yielding, slick shore, but Sullen's tall, toned form provided better traction, and she scampered up the barbarian as if he were a sapling, planting a foot on his butt and hopping from there to his shoulder and then leaping for the top of the steep bank. She almost made it, knocking the air out of herself as she dug her hands into the soft earth, her legs dangling down where anything might grab them . . . and then she hauled herself up over the edge, rolling onto her back with a gasp.

The moon wasn't high enough to cast much light yet, and she could barely make out the dim trail through the tangled magnolia bushes. She was about to call out for Sullen, to see if he needed her to find a vine to lower down or something, when Digs appeared out of the dark underbrush, his face so pale she wondered if he'd applied more foundation after gaining the high ground.

'Purna!' It was a stage whisper, like Maroto had taught them, but still sounded bloody loud out here in the Haunted Forest, which was actually a pretty good name for the dump after all. 'Where's the others?'

Purna held up a finger to quiet him and looked over the side of the bank. Now that her eyes were adjusting, she could see that the water's edge was empty save for one of the stick-backed fuckers. Its mantle of wet wood gleamed in the darkness as it tried in vain to climb the slope after her, coming up a few paces before its weight dragged it back down the muddy incline. Digs poked his head over the edge beside Purna's, and seeing the abject efforts of their pursuer, let a long, snotty glob of spit descend from his mouth, its tether growing thinner and thinner, until it broke off . . . and the creature snapped its head up in time to catch the loogie in one of its cavernous eye sockets.

'Real mature,' Purna hissed, pulling him back out of sight of the monster.

'I never made any claims toward such a depressing condition,' said Digs, sitting next to her in the moldering leaves and slimy roots, and they hugged each other tightly, feeling one another shiver from more than their drenched clothes and the coolness of the evening. 'The others, though? Did they . . . '

'I don't know. Keun-ju went down bad, and I think it might've terminally messed up Sullen – he tried to go after him but I wouldn't let him, and then he was right behind me, and then he wasn't.' Looking down, Purna saw she'd also lost one of her boots to the monsters or the mud, so that she and Digs only had a pair between them. 'Just our luck, meeting desperate foot fetishists after we lost the count.'

'Hassan and his foot thing,' said Digs with a chuckle. 'He'd have fit right in.'

'Come on,' said Purna, the return of her breath also heralding the return of her common sense. 'Into the woods with us, Pasha, and keep an eye out for one of those big live oaks we saw on the other side of the swamp. I think this may be one of those circumstances Maroto talked about where you're better off sleeping in a tree than on the ground.'

Even along the supposed trail the brush closed in thick around them, and when the moonlight finally arrived it shone on barren brambles and poison ivy. Purna stopped them at the first suitable tree she spied, not wanting to get too far ahead lest Sullen reevaluate his suicidal ambitions and come looking for them. The live oak was as wide around the trunk as a dozen barbarians shoved in tight, and the low boughs weren't much thinner, long, swooping branches that looked made for sitting on, with tendrils of moss for cushions. Once Purna had given Digs a boost up to the tree's crotch he wiggled himself around and dropped a hand to help her up. Now that they were safely off the ground Purna laid out her horned wolf hood to dry on an upper branch, and Digs stripped down to his skivvies. Then they made themselves as comfortable as they could, wedging themselves into the crooks of branches in such a fashion that they were unlikely to slip out without a push.

Only then did they break the silence, this corner of the Haunted Forest every bit as still as the rest, and kept their talking to the absolute minimum, lest they be overheard by . . . well, pretty much anything. If it was out here, they didn't want it knowing about them. Still, there were essentials that had to be covered before resuming their tactical silence.

'Got anything to eat?'

'Some dried figs. Here.'

'Ugh!'

'Yes, they're not so dry anymore, I'm afraid.'

'Take 'em back, take 'em back. Anything to drink?'

'My flask.'

'Keep it. Still have a skin with some water in it, let me know if you—'

'Yes, please.'

'Here.'

'You said Keun-ju took a tumble, but you don't suppose he might have . . . '

'No.'

Some soggy sniffling.

'And Princess?'

'I'm so sorry, Digs.'

A wracked moan.

'Yeah, I know. She was a good pony.'

'The . . . the . . . the best.'

More sniffling.

'Yeah, I know.'

'I loved her,' said Digs, as brokenhearted as she'd ever heard him. 'Not like Prince, but in time . . . I miss Prince so much, Purna, as much as Din and Hassan and Maroto. I guess that sounds . . . well.'

'It doesn't sound anything, Digs,' she told him, the words thick as swamp mud in her throat. 'And . . . and thank you again. For what you did for me. I know Prince would still be here if—'

'*No*,' said Digs firmly. 'It's what he would've wanted. And what I wanted. I'm actually happy about it, or trying to be. I mean, he *was* a devil, not just a dog, and all devils want to be free, don't they? That's their whole deal. I'd have let him go sooner if I'd known that's what he wanted . . .'

'Oh Digs,' said Purna. 'You gave him your heart, what devil could want more than that?'

Now they were both sniffling, and then Digs gave a wet laugh. 'I'd pass you a hankie, but everything I had in the Star was on that pony.'

'Yeah. Me, too.'

'Damn.'

'Yeah.'

' . . . '

' . . . '

'The magic post . . . '

'The compass?'

'Keun-ju had it in his pocket.'

'Ugh.'

'Double ugh.'

'Triple.'

' . . . '

' . . . '

'Silver linings, Purna, silver linings – I got my hat back.'

'Bully for you!'

'No need to be ratty. Surely you didn't lose everything but your waterskin and your snark?'

'I've got my kukri, a mud-clogged pistol, and Maroto's old pipe.'

'See, that's not bad! Shame we don't have the means for a puff, I'm famished for a kiss from Lady N.'

'You know ...' In the growing moonlight, Purna carefully unbuckled her belt from her traveling pantaloons, and slid off the pipe box she had picked up in Black Moth. The woman had claimed it had a gasket around the side that made it waterproof, but here was the test ... and unclasping the cedar-lined silver case, she felt around and confirmed the contents were indeed dry. Taking out Maroto's pipe, she rubbed out two of the treacle-cased flakes of tubāq in her palm and fed them into the tankard-shaped bowl. As Digs watched in solemn silence, she held the pipe between her teeth, closed the case back up, and flicked the steel wheel of the coalstick a few times until it gave off a pleasant glow. Then she applied fire to weed, and puffed Maroto's pipe for the very first time.

'Remember, dearheart, "blow" is just an expression,' said Digs as she struggled to get it lit, her big stupid tongue in the way.

'I ... here, you do it,' said Purna, glad the darkness hid her blush and shoving the pipe and coalstick into Digs's hands. Never in a million billion years would she have guessed it would come to this, she and Pasha Diggelby sitting in a tree, P-U-F-F-I-N-G, but that was the way of the Star, wasn't it? Sometimes the last friend you're left with is the last one you ever expected. 'What are we doing out here, Digs?'

'Mmmm,' said Digs, the surface of the bowl now smoldering as nicely as the coalstick he neatly capped with an expert thumb. 'Dying, I suppose, but slower than all our chums, so maybe we're ahead?'

'Maybe,' said Purna, nervously plucking at hairs on the back of her neck. 'Do you think we'll ever catch up to Maroto without the post or compass?'

'Maybe,' said Digs, sounding obscenely pleased as he let out a cloud of smoke and passed her the pipe. 'The real question is do you think he wants to be caught?'

'Maybe again,' said Purna, trying not to be frustrated by how hard it was to smoke the pipe with her bedeviled tongue. 'Thanks for the help with this, Pasha.'

'My pleasure, Tapai,' said Digs, and that tore it – Purna had absolutely no regrets about what she'd done or the fibs she'd told, but considering the wanted poster she'd found back in Black Moth, she owed Digs the truth. Not for honor or friend-ship, but for something he prized even more dearly – his own protection.

'I have a confession, Digs,' she said, her voice sounding so loud up here in this silent tree, in an unnaturally still forest.

'Oooooh!' said Digs. 'Is it juicy?'

'Juicy as Maroto's bottom,' said Purna, passing him the pipe so she wouldn't drop it if he came at her. Now that she'd resolved to tell him, it occurred to her he might be angry. Very angry. Nobody likes to be made a fool of, not even a deliberately foolish fop from the Serpent's Circle. Nothing to do but go for it, like Maroto always said . . . 'I've been lying to you, Diggelby, for as long as I've known you.'

'Who doesn't?' said Digs, the rising silver moon getting caught in the blue smoke he blew up into the charcoal sky. 'It's the mode, darling, nothing to get your knickers twisted over.'

'*Listen*,' she said, and her tone finally got him to sit up a little straighter. 'My name's Purna and I hail from Ugrakar, but those are about the only things I've told you that are true. I'm a . . . I'm not of noble blood at all. I'm not a tapai, not even close – I come from a long line of Harapok rug merchants. And last year, when my aunt and uncle finally trusted me with taking the winter line to the Empire, I . . . I sold the rugs, like I was supposed to, but instead of coming home with the earnings I spent them all on passing myself off as a foreign noble. Three weeks before we set out to the Panteran Wastes I was slinging mats at the Serpentian Bazaar. I'm not one of you, Pasha, and never have been. I'm a merchant, and almost as bad, a *thief*, a two-faced girl who dreamed of making herself something she wasn't.'

Pasha Diggelby didn't say anything, which wasn't good, but he didn't tear off a glove to slap her, either, so it wasn't going as bad as it might, either. Then he let out a protracted sigh, and dramatically kicked his bare heel into the tree a couple of times. He let out another sniffle, and wiped his nose – was he actually crying over the news? Purna hadn't thought she could feel any lower, but what did Maroto always say about there always being a deeper hell to slip into?

'Well, *damn*,' he finally said. 'I never thought I'd go to pieces over losing a bet. I can practically hear Din shaking her purse at me from beyond the grave. I'd give anything to be able to see the look on her face right now, regardless of the expense.'

'Digs, have you been hitting the scorpion again?' asked Purna. 'Did you hear a word I just said?'

'I actually swore off scorpions after the Lark's Tongue . . . I traded that big blue blighter to Singh's son for one of his centipedes,' said Digs. 'Though now I can't remember for the life of me where I put that beautiful little bug. I had him in my turban pocket before I traded it for this hat, but I'm sure I would've remembered to take him out before—'

'Digs!'

'Of course I was listening, and of course you're not noble,' said Digs, though without the attitude she'd expected. 'There is no Thirty-ninth Tapai of Ugrakar, everybody knows that.'

'They do?' Of all the outcomes of her confession, this was the last one she'd expected.

'Well, maybe not everybody. But Din did, and that first night we met you, at the garden party – whose was it?'

'Zir Mana's,' said Purna sheepishly. 'I'd delivered a rug to the estate earlier that week and overheard the servants talking it up, so I gate-crashed it. That's how I got in with all of you.'

'Zir Mana's hedge maze, right!' Digs puffed the languishing pipe back to life before continuing. '*Anyway*, it was so obvious you didn't have the breeding – even for a foreign fop, the way you acted was just agonizing. Hassan pledged coin that you were a spy of some stripe, Zir Mana was convinced I'd hired you as a prank, and Princess Von Yung thought you were operating some sort of long con, but Duchess Din and I knew from the first that you were a middling class lass shooting for the stars.'

'What?' Purna felt as silly as a sincere coxcomb who'd worn the wrong wig to a powder party. 'Was there anyone who thought I was genuine?'

'Hmmmm,' said Digs, considering. 'Maroto?'

'Ha!' Purna leaned back in her arboreal seat, remembering all the times she and her noble friends had had, before, during, and after the Panteran Wastes. 'So why'd you all let me tag along? What I did's a crime, obviously, and a capital one at that in most lands.'

'Because you seemed fun, and we had a lot of money on the table at the outset.'

'Oh,' said Purna; even after all that time playing at being one of them, she'd overlooked the most obvious explanation of all. To think of all the times she'd had a secret laugh at their expense when she'd made some social blunder and they'd failed to pick up on it, thinking them too thick to realize the obvious . . . 'So if you and Din both had my number, how come you said you lost the bet?'

'Yes, well . . . ' said Digs, sounding a little embarrassed, 'Din wagered you'd come clean in your own time, but I bet you'd never reveal your secret. She gave you more credit than I, I'm afraid.'

'No, Digs, you gave me plenty,' said Purna, her new tongue no longer feeling so constricted in her mouth; it matched the tightness in her throat. 'But you're shortchanging yourself a bit, as usual. I'd have eaten poison buttsauce before telling Von Yung or any of the rest about my past, but not you. You're a chum.'

'So are you, Tapai, so are you,' said Digs, puffing Maroto's pipe and then passing it across to her as they watched the moon climb higher over the Haunted Forest. It was sort of beautiful, in a tragic way, especially with all their friends probably dead, Sullen and Keun-ju the newest in an increasingly long line of folks they'd met who'd then met a bad end. It was enough to make a girl think she was cursed . . . but Purna dismissed the silly notion with a boggy belch. Besides, there was no sense counting Sullen or even Keun-ju out before the sun arrived to shine a light on the subject; life's full of enough sorrow without weeping over tragedies that might not have even come to pass.

Take Maroto, for example – maybe he really was a double agent for Queen Indsorith or maybe he was just a dope who tried to fix every problem by showing it his back, but either way they couldn't know for sure just yet. And until they found him and the truth she sure hoped he was happy, wherever he was. Funny to think that of all the familiar names and faces on that wanted board, his wasn't – or maybe he'd torn his down when he came through, same as she had!

A merry thought, but one that reminded her of the whole reason she'd finally spilled her guts to Diggelby, and suddenly she didn't feel quite so merry anymore. Clearing her throat, she said, 'One other thing I need to tell you, Digs.'

'Do try to make it interesting this time,' he yawned. 'Unless you want first watch.'

'It's, um, well, you won't be able to read it now, between the dark and all the muck that got on it when I fell in the swamp, but I found a wanted poster in Black Moth.'

'Bounty hunting?' Digs sounded intrigued. 'Might be a lark, depending on the quarry.'

'No, dummy, I found a poster with my name on it! That aunt and uncle I told you about, the ones whose rugs I ripped off? They ... they've got a price on my head, either to bring me back alive to Harapok ... or to bring just my head back, for a smaller price. I know with the Star falling apart and lost kingdoms rising from the sea it hardly registers, but it gave *me* a nasty shock, and, well, you've got a right to know, seeing's how we roll together.'

'Mmmm,' said Digs thoughtfully, and after a long silence, asked, 'How much are they offering? I need a new pair of boots.'

'Goodnight, Digs,' said Purna, still scared and tired and more than a little crazed after the day's awful ordeal, but relieved to know that Pasha Diggelby had her back. Come what may in the night, when dawn broke they would set out again for their missing friends, and not even the absolute ugliest, grossest monsters in the Star could stop them. Not for long, anyway, though Purna needed a new boot, too. Settling in for her watch, she whispered a prayer to Maroto's ancestor Old Black that she lived long enough to get one, and while she was at it, either save her mentor or avenge his death, depending on the circumstances.

What barbarian could ask for more?

Sullen crept along the shoreline of the dark swamp, picking up every sneaking devil now that the sun had set and his catlike eyes were attuned to the night, the parasites pulsing silver through the withered skins of their hosts. By staying away from the pools and the deeper water beyond, he was able to catch and kill four of the devils in the shallows, or banish them back to the First Dark, anyway – who knew what happened after they faded away from the corpses they had infested. His arms were really stinging from where that first one had grabbed him on the trail, before he'd gotten the hang of driving his sun-knife straight into wherever the devil lurked. They soon learned he was a danger, unfortunately, and through some unknown method the word must have spread that Sullen was to be avoided – before the moon was out from the trees he couldn't entice another woodpile into approaching him, and blundering out into the open swamp obviously wouldn't help anybody. Keun-ju was gone.

He was trying not to freak out like he had after Fa had bit it, but it wasn't really working – every step Sullen took in this world brought him deeper into darkness. He could scarcely have been more upset if Ji-hyeon had been the one to disappear into a devil-haunted swamp . . . and Keun-ju hadn't just disappeared, he'd sacrificed himself so that Sullen and the rest could flee. It was the sort of selfless heroism Sullen always imagined himself performing, except whenever the opportunity arose he blew it, finding an easy way out, fleeing instead of fighting, a lifetime of softness in his village making him better at dodging fights than winning them.

Looking out over the dismal black water with its pathetic, scrabbling devils, Sullen felt himself slipping backward in his memories, to Emeritus, and the Faceless Mistress. Maybe all of this *was* his punishment for going against her will. Maybe if he'd confronted Zosia back in the Cobalt camp and carried out the goddess's command to stop the old woman then none of this would've happened, maybe Keun-ju would still be with him ... He wished she would materialize, right here and now, so he could give her a piece of his mind. What right did the gods have to harass innocent mortals, making sport with their lives? Or maybe this trap had actually been set by Hoartrap the Touch or the Procuress or the two working together; after all, both magic post and devilish compass had led them straight into it ...

Except Sullen was singing songs to himself again, wasn't he? They weren't out here because of the Faceless Mistress or Cobalt Zosia or Hoartrap's compass or the Jackal witch's post or even Uncle Craven, easy a scapegoat as the quick-legged beggar made. They were here, in this devilish gravebog, because Sullen had taken them here. Keun-ju had ridden a pony into a pit full of devils because instead of being the leader his friends needed him to be and turning them all back to find a different route, Sullen had gone against his better instincts and basically ordered Diggelby to blunder on ahead – and now he paced in an overgrown mud puddle, hunting simpleminded devils and blaming remote gods and sorcerers for his own damn stupidity. He had defied the command of the Faceless Mistress, and *nothing had happened*, but as soon as he started telling trusting people what to do things took a bad turn in a hurry.

Fuck Maroto, that had been Purna's odd but satisfying cry before the battle with the devil-ridden ancients, but being real, who was more to blame for their current situation? Who had used his influence to pressure Ji-hyeon into putting together this posse? Who had basically killed the smartest, noblest, most clever-tongued man Sullen had ever met? Fuck *Maroto*? No.

'Fuck Sullen!' He shouted it to the too-still waters, the too-quiet trees, remembering Keun-ju's downcast eyes as he recited one of his delightful poems. Hazelnut eyes he would never see again, above a veil that had begun to drive Sullen to distraction, wondering what exactly the man's nose and mouth looked like beneath it. And there at the end, when he could have at least joined his fast friend in a worthy death, he'd convinced himself that the turtle or fish he'd glimpsed out in the distant water was that very veil, and so he'd done the exact same thing he hated his uncle for doing when the going got grim: he'd run away, instead of trying to help.

'Fuck! Sullen! Fuuuuuuuck!'

'If that's your come-on, it needs some work.' Sullen felt his knees go weak, the voice of the dead man drifting down from the branches of the Haunted Forest . . . but then he turned and saw it was no ghost nor deviltry. Or if it was, he didn't care, not now, and weary as he'd been moments before Sullen bounded over and scrambled up the precarious bank, swift as any snow lion pursuing its quarry.

As Sullen gained the wooded high ground, Keun-ju detached himself from where he'd been leaning against a cypress, his dark lips and bright teeth shining in the moonlight. He'd lost his veil, and Sullen saw he'd misjudged the man as simply being pretty before; he could now see the smooth jaw that attached to the high cheekbones, the dimple at the corner of his smile. He was dead handsome, not something Sullen usually noticed in other men, or if he noticed it, not something that made his heart lurch around in his chest like a snared hare.

'You're . . . alive,' said Sullen, hating what a fool he must sound like as soon as the words left his mouth. All hearken to the pronouncements of Simple Sullen, Speaker of Things Plain as the Crescent Moon Overhead. Then, relief and less clearly defined emotions butting into self-consciousness and confusion, he asked, 'How long have you been up here, watching me stomp around the swamp?'

'I can barely see you now,' said Keun-ju, sounding about as mixed-up as Sullen felt. 'I heard a lot of splashing and grunting, but until you started propositioning the night I had no idea it was you. I . . . I didn't know if you got out of that pit, I thought Princess might have crushed you, or worse.'

'Yeah, what *was* that?' asked Sullen. 'I mean, you saved my life, so I ain't complaining, but damn, man, what were you trying with that?'

'I misjudged the depth,' said Keun-ju, that warmth Sullen had thought he'd heard in the boy's voice now decidedly cooler. 'I thought I could ride her out and around, drawing those things away from you and the others. But the edge of that pool gave way, and, well . . .'

'Oh,' said Sullen, that making some kind of sense, at least. 'So wait, you weren't even trying to mess up that one that grabbed me in the water?'

'A happy accident,' said Keun-ju, looking out over the moon-lit swamp with a shiver. 'I've never been so scared in my life. I was sure . . . I thought it was over for me, but it just kept . . . it just kept *happening*, and I never got away. It was like in a night-mare, when you're stuck somewhere and can't get out? Like time has stopped . . . I've been in fights, bad ones, the Lark's Tongue, others, but it's never . . . it's never been like that. When I jumped off Princess and saw them coming up to catch me, and then I went under, it was like this hungry ceiling above me in the dark water, and I knew I was dead, I knew it, and . . . Ugh.'

'I know,' said Sullen, wrapping his arms around Keun-ju as the Immaculate shuddered in his wet clothes, but as warm and good as it felt, the smaller man quickly pulled away, making

Sullen wonder what had compelled him to embrace his friend in the first place. He tried to apologize, but Keun-ju was already doing the same, so they said it in tandem, neither looking at the other:

'Sorry.'

'I thought I saw you swim free, but I wasn't sure,' said Sullen, trying to undo some of the awkwardness by focusing on the facts. 'Must've been one devil of a race, outswimming those things.'

'If there is one thing we know how to do on the Isles, it's swim,' said Keun-ju, finally looking back at Sullen as the moon inched over enough for both of their faces to catch the light. 'We certainly don't learn to ride well, as demonstrated. If they hadn't been so busy with poor Princess, I . . . I don't want to think about it. The only reason they didn't get me when I first went under was all the lumber attached to their backs – they were stretching down for me, claws everywhere, but the water's deeper out there, and I'd sunk too far for them to reach. Every time they dove after me the wood made them float back up just before they caught me, and then I went as far down as I could, swimming hard as I could, knowing that the first time I came up for air might be my death . . . but when I did, they were behind me, so I swam on, and as soon as I got to shore I tried doubling back to where I thought you were. But it got too dark.'

'Damn,' said Sullen, reckoning that such a chase was about the worst thing he could imagine, and seeing that the Immaculate still had his cherished sword on his belt, he said, 'I left my damn spear back there after carrying it clear down from Flintland and almost losing it to opossum devils, and you gotta make me look bad by swimming a dozen leagues with that on your hip.'

'I really don't mean to be such an epic hero,' said Keun-ju, getting that proud tone he put on whenever the weapon came up. Ever since he'd explained the four-tiger sword's rich historical significance as a blade whose Ugrakari maker traced her lineage back to the Sunken Kingdom, Sullen found Keun-ju's attitude about it kind of endearing instead of obnoxious.

'Yeah, well that's my good example rubbing off on you,' said Sullen with a wink. 'Hard not to be epic around a Horned Wolf. Maybe when the time comes we'll sing this song together, huh?'

Keun-ju grinned up at Sullen in the moonlight, and seeing his sharp, mud-spattered features unveiled at last, Sullen felt as though a glacier had just broken loose from the fjord of his heart. Or something like that; anyway, he wasn't thinking so much as feeling just then, and what he felt rocked him from his toes to his nose. Keun-ju had lived, despite all odds, but they had not anticipated this disastrous day, and they could not predict the next one. Old Black stand watch, they might not even live to see the morning, if worse devils stalked these woods . . . and so that was why Sullen leaned slowly down, giving Keun-ju all the time he might need to flee, and when he didn't, kissed him softly on the lips.

Well, because of all that, and because he really, really wanted to.

Keun-ju's eyes looked like they were about to burst out of his head and he stayed stiff as the cypress behind him, so Sullen backed off with the quickness, apologizing . . . only to have a smaller but firmer hand grab his chin and direct him back in for another try. Delicate, fleeting kisses melted into longer, firmer ones, lips parting slightly, Keun-ju tasting as sweet as his poetry even after a dip in a devil-soaked swamp, and when Sullen slipped his tongue into his friend's mouth Keun-ju parried it with his own. They leaned into one another for an hour or an instant, it was hard to say, and when Keun-ju gently drew back, his eyes were no longer wide with surprise, but sparkling with something else.

'I . . . I've never done that before,' said Sullen, and seeing the incredulous look on Keun-ju's face, clarified. 'With another guy, I mean.'

'Neither have I,' breathed Keun-ju, and in the inscrutable way of the flesh, hearing that made Sullen's heart jump, along with the sudden fullness under his skirt.

'Was it . . . was it okay?'

'You've obviously been taking lessons from Ji-hyeon, princess of the sloppy smooches, but it's nothing we can't sharpen up with more practice,' said Keun-ju, but light as he'd said it the invocation of Ji-hyeon's name gave them both a small start. For a spell there it had seemed like the future was as irrelevant as the past, but now, not so much. Not sure how else to handle this sudden pall, Sullen reached out and brushed Keun-ju's throat with his fingers, and that seemed to do the trick – the Immaculate sighed happily, and raised his mouth the slightest fraction as the Flintlander came in for another kiss.

And froze.

They were being watched, from just through the forest. Sullen couldn't see who or what was spying on him, but he *knew*, his eyes jumping straight to a patch of shadow that was all the darker for the moonbeams scattered through the trees. Instead of delivering his lips to Keun-ju's he held up a finger before them, then pointed it down at the pommel of his friend's sword.

'Just gotta piss is all,' Sullen loudly announced as casual as he could, and pretended to randomly blunder out of the moonlight's glare, so he could see who or what lurked just ahead . . . and laughed when he saw her, turning back to Keun-ju with a grin. 'It's just Purna! How you—'

But the words died in this throat, and what a miserable death they died, too. It wasn't Purna. What he had taken to be her horned hood poking above the underbrush stepped out from the magnolias, growling low in its throat, and for the first time in his life Sullen saw a real live fucking horned wolf.

And emerging from the shadows behind it was the only thing less welcome than a horned wolf: a Horned Wolf, dressed for war, sun-knife raised, stance low. Unlike Sullen, the tall huntress still had her spear in her off hand.

Behind him, Keun-ju's four-tiger sword gave the faintest hiss as it left his scabbard, and in the stillness of the night it sounded as loud as a temple bell tolling out through the wood. Knowing he had only one chance to stop his assassin, Sullen went for his own sun-knife. Despite how slow time had seemed earlier that eve, things now began to happen very quickly in the Haunted Forest.

CHAPTER

22

It was not yet light when Domingo was awoken by Cobalt guards, rolled onto a stretcher, and carried out into the blasting chill that slid down the Lark's Tongue. There they assisted him into the straw-filled bed of a wagon, and in the bobbing light of the lantern pole he saw that his new bosom buddy Hoartrap the Touch drove the cart. Weirdos and wagons had become the two constants in Domingo's life . . . if you could even call it that anymore.

'Good morning, sleepyhead,' said Hoartrap, turning back to look at Domingo. 'Your saber's under the hay there, if you like I can stop and help you put it on?'

'No, damn it,' said Domingo; the only thing he hated more than the witch's infantilizing was his charity. Rooting around under the straw with his good hand until he found it, Domingo felt a tremor pass through him, from braided hilt to callused palm. Just having the weapon in his hand invigorated him, even if he might never recover enough to stand and use it again. 'I suppose you expect me to thank you for it?'

'I wasn't getting my hopes up,' said Hoartrap, turning back to the pony rolling them steadily down through the camp. Propped up as he was, Domingo could see the camp must be almost ready, the motley soldiers flashing their allegiance on cobalt-colored scarves, hats, and shields where tabards or banners were absent. It would have been a nostalgic sight, all these grim-faced youths and grimmer-faced veterans preparing for a predawn assault, if not for the appalling fact that almost every soldier they passed was hitting a bottle or bowl.

'I never would've stood for *that*, I tell you,' Domingo told the back of Hoartrap's saffron hood. 'A tot of grappa to celebrate victory is one thing, but getting loaded before the march is even on? I wouldn't stand for it.'

Hoartrap cocked his head as though he had something smart to say, but then relaxed back on the board without comment. Something was gnawing at the warlock, that much was obvious, otherwise he would've leaped at the easy opening Domingo had left him. He would have pointed out how Domingo had granted *his* soldiers something very strong indeed the morning before he ordered them through the Gate, so why shouldn't General Ji-hyeon allow something a little more mundane? The difference was that these soldiers were probably enjoying their morning drunk more than the Fifteenth had appreciated their Chainite anointment, and once they reached the Gate they'd be going through voluntarily.

Not all, of course, not all – even here in the Cobalt Company fools weren't that thick on the ground. Many of the mercenaries would stay behind, releasing Waits, Wheatley, and the rest to the Thaoans in exchange for a pardon, which might be honored when the Meshuggans arrived, or might not. General Ji-hyeon had supposedly argued that taking their chances with the Imperial regiments would be every bit as dicey as going through the Gate, but evidently not all had agreed.

Not surprising, that. When Hoartrap had first asked Domingo if he wished to be left in his tent for the Thaoans to recover or brought along with the Cobalts through the Gate, into Diadem, it had seemed an absurd question, completely out of order, and he had almost declined ... but then he thought of lying in that cot, disgraced and destroyed, waiting for no less an officer than Colonel Waits herself to decide what to do with him. And then waiting for her to write down her order, since she probably wouldn't be saying much these days, and afterward going to whatever Chain-mandated cell awaited him, if not the stake.

Or even worse, what if the new junta hailed him as a war hero for initiating the ritual that had sacrificed his regiment? What if he lived for many more years as an invalid in Cockspar, knowing that despite the speech he'd given Waits, despite what he knew in his heart, when faced with a tough call he capitulated to the Burnished Chain, the same as everyone else? What if that frigid, damp, smelly tent was the last stop on his military career, and after that came nothing but ass-kissing his most hated enemies, people he despised even more than the woman who had killed both his son and his king? Not that he had cared much more for old King Kaldruut than he had for young Efrain, the regent as dotty as the boy was sloppy, but the principle was what mattered, always the principle.

Faced with such unspeakable fates or the minor matter of accompanying the Cobalt Company into a Gate, he chose the only sensible option. A colonel shouldn't order his officers to do anything he wouldn't do himself, if needs must, and if he'd sent Captain Shea into that Gate, then by blood and thunder he'd follow after her, wherever it led. Even when Hoartrap had furiously burst into his tent last night and told him of the last-minute change in destination, Domingo was barely able to muster much disappointment. He would have preferred to die in Diadem, but so long as he fell with two fingers raised to the Burnished Chain he'd come out better than he'd expected, and better than he deserved. Besides, he highly doubted even as witchy a bounder as Hoartrap the Touch could safely guide them into one Gate and out another, or else the Cobalts would have tried this tactic twenty-five years earlier, so whether the goal was Diadem or Othean scarcely mattered, since they'd probably never arrive – the point was that a noble military suicide was better than a limp surrender.

Maybe Waits had been right about him after all; Domingo never could accept defeat. No wonder he'd basically murdered his only son by forcing him into a command he was never cut out for – Domingo would prefer Efrain die as a miserable young colonel than live on as a happy old politician or scholar, and that was exactly what he had gotten. Who said wishes don't come true?

The wagon stopped, but Domingo couldn't see over the riding board to the cause. The sky seemed even darker than when they'd set out, but torches burned all around them, stretching out into the night – peering about, it looked like their wagon was afloat in a sea of candles. Hopping down from the board, Hoartrap strolled to the back of the wagon, but even flat on the ground he loomed over Domingo.

'Time for the big event,' said Hoartrap. 'I'll send someone back to drive you through once we're ready. You should be able to hear the general's big speech from here, which I imagine Fennec spent all night writing for her. As soon as that's in the bag I let the devils out of mine, and awaaaay we go.'

'I've never been to Othean,' said Domingo, wondering just what manner of monsters were besieging the Immaculates and frowning as he realized that in a best-case scenario where this Gate trick actually worked, he would soon find out for himself. Whatever they were, Empress Ryuki couldn't possibly hate them much more than she loathed the person who had assassinated her son, for he was a plain old mortal, same as she. He imagined what sort of reaction it would garner if he casually confessed to the crime during the formal introductions. Probably not the sort of impression he needed to be making, even though he was no longer feeling great about having so expertly framed Ji-hyeon to take the fall. 'Never dreamed I'd be saving Immaculate asses instead of kicking them.'

'Apocalyptic war makes for strange bedfellows, as I'm sure you've recently discovered,' said Hoartrap. 'But Empress Ryuki has agreed to join our cause against the Chain once her shores are safe, and that's just too tempting, isn't it? An armada of turtleships swarming Desolation Sound as we lead ten thousand Immaculate foot soldiers through the Othean Gate and into Diadem – I'm getting goose pimples again! A much more practical approach than leading a couple thousand frostbitten humps into Diadem now and hoping for the best.'

'Only if we win at Othean,' said Domingo. 'If we fall there, it's all over.'

'Don't be a gloomy Gus!' Hoartrap chided. 'If we fall *anywhere*, it's all over, that's how falling works. And what do we gain by taking Diadem first if all the Immaculate Isles are sacked in the meantime? Believe you me, I'd rather be taking us to Samoth, too, but war's all about making personal sacrifices, isn't it?'

'Hmph,' said Domingo, unable to hear that word without getting queasy. 'And what about Cold Zosia's personal sacrifice, then? Were you able to bring her back from Diadem, or send word of the change in plans?'

'I'm afraid not,' said Hoartrap, which went a long way toward explaining his ill temper this morn. 'As soon as Ji-hyeon convinced me of the tactical benefits of shifting our campaign to the Isles, I popped straight over to Diadem myself to tell Zosia, but she can be a hard woman to find, as you well know. Wasted the whole night there, when I should have been scouting out the Isles.'

Hoartrap's cavalier attitude about traveling through Gates was probably meant to inspire confidence, but it only made the freak seem freakier.

'So Zosia's going to expose herself, rally some rabble, and start a diversion, all for an attack that will never come?' At long last, some good news for Domingo to glom to! 'She'll be a sitting duck in Diadem?'

'In the best of all possible outcomes,' said Hoartrap irritably. 'Frankly, I have no idea if she ever arrived. Just because her devil took her into the Gate doesn't mean he led her out again. I warned her not to trust him, that he was too powerful to push around like the rest of his kind, but did she listen? We may never see her again, and all for the pride that made her push away my friendship in favor of a capricious devil. Tragic, really.'

'I'm on the verge of tears,' said Domingo placidly. 'So General Ji-hyeon has the Five Villains at her command and doesn't even have Cold Cobalt to worry about. Not a bad strategic development, from her standpoint.'

'Three Villains, actually,' said Hoartrap, getting more and more peeved the longer they talked. 'Chevaleresse Singh and her children deserted last night, along with their dragoons, and I seem to have misplaced Maroto. The lummox was making the sorts of noises that I worried might permanently cool Zosia's rage toward the Crown, and rage is quite the hot commodity when you're waging a war – pun intended, by the way – so I enlisted him to do some reconnaissance.'

'But you ... misplaced him?' That did not sound very good.

'It was a rash decision, I'll admit, and one I've come to regret,' said Hoartrap. 'I've snuck back over to look for him a few times, since our circumstances have changed and he no longer needs to be protected from himself, but sadly, without success. If I'd been thinking ahead I would have given him a little going away present so I could easily find him again, but to be honest at the time I wasn't sure if we'd ever be of any more use to one another. It was that kind of spat, Maroto jamming his foot into the gears of my grand design and then blaming me when he came away with a boo-boo. But I digress; it's a dodgy business, poking around where he's gone, but we may have ample time to try again in the days to come – think of Maroto as an advance Cobalt scout on Jex Toth.'

At times like this, Domingo really, really wished he'd kept his mouth shut and didn't provoke the witch into talking so much. As usual, the conversation was interesting, but it was also quite obviously the sort of secret intelligence that people would kill to protect. Being brought into Hoartrap's confidence made Domingo feel like the rodent drinking buddy of an adulterous cobra.

'Well, I suppose we'll all have a better idea of what's what on the other side,' said Domingo, and seeking to remind the deranged sorcerer of his allegiances, he added, 'And I'll trust that wherever you take us, and whoever you enlist, it's all bringing us that much closer to seeing every Chainite church in flames, and every cleric, monk, and nun swinging from a tree.'

'Ooooh, but you are just a man after my own heart,' said Hoartrap with an unwholesome grin, his yellowish face looking as fake as the dummies in that wax museum Efrain was so obsessed with for a summer. To Domingo's extreme displeasure, Hoartrap reached out and placed one of his paraffin-soft palms on top of Domingo's age-speckled left hand. 'I remember how dashing you looked all those years ago, and even now I see that haughty, handsome young colonel looking back at me – where do the years go, Domingo? Why didn't we ever make time for *us*?'

'Yes, well, you've got more important matters than molesting me,' said Domingo, pulling his hand away . . . and feeling such contentment that it once more had a pommel to rest on. 'See you on the other side of the First Dark, I hope.'

'I hope so, too,' said Hoartrap so somberly that Domingo wondered if the Touch had mistakenly assumed he was being poetically existential instead of simply literal, but there was no sense correcting the madman. 'Before we can be reunited, though, I have the supreme privilege of playing errand boy for our august general, as if I have nothing better to do with my time than courier love letters and baubles all over the Star. If I didn't owe the boy in question a rather sizable debt I'm eager to see paid and out of the way I'd tell her where to stick her oh so special delivery, but that's life, isn't it? Some days you're the devil-eater, but most you're just another bound devil, enslaved to the capricious whims of your intellectual lessers.'

'I think I know the feeling,' said Domingo, though most of Hoartrap's bellyaching went right over his head.

'Well then, I'll go my way and you go yours, and let's compare notes over tea when next we meet,' said the Touch, squeezing Domingo's shoulder. 'Oh, and I'd suggest you keep your eyes open when you go through the Gate – it's a once-in-a-lifetime experience, at least for most mortals.'

And leaving Domingo to ponder what he might see, exactly, Hoartrap the Touch scurried off into the torch-brightened morning to clear a path of a dozen steps between the Lark's Tongue valley and Othean's Temple of Pentacles.

CHAPTER

23

Ji-hyeon punctuated the end of her speech by thrusting her new sword high into the air, the ebon steel flashing in the torchlight. For but a moment the only sound was the crackling of pitch and Hoartrap's low murmurs behind the general, but then one girl up near the front started banging her gauntlet on her shield, and it caught like wildfire. Turning to Fennec, she cut the blade through the air, and, taking a deep breath, he stepped up to the rim of the Gate, its black surface flashing with lightning-like streaks as Hoartrap held his palms out over the edge. Behind Fennec was his squad of a hundred plate-armored meatheads, all knocking their fists into their shields. Pointing into the Gate with the sword in her left hand, Ji-hyeon saluted them with her right.

Maybe it was the speech that had convinced them. Maybe they really believed that the fate of the Star hung in the balance, and if this new enemy was not stopped at Othean it would not be stopped at all. Maybe they believed in a thing greater than coin or conquest, the notion that all people of the Star deserved to live, and with the same liberties they would seek for themselves.

Maybe, but not bloody likely. These two thousand soldiers

who had rallied behind her, who had followed her up to the very Gate and now made their support known with the clangor of heavy metal, these Cobalt heroes ... they were in it for the money she had promised them if they came, for the wages she wouldn't pay if they didn't. A few were brave from Fennec's special sour ale, and many more were fearless from the regular stuff they'd been told would gird them from cowardice. They were going to march through this Gate because they were trapped between Imperials who would almost definitely kill them and a devilish scheme that might not. They didn't believe anymore, if they ever had, except in something even stronger than ideals, sharper than faith: they believed in getting good and drunk before they died in a truly legendary fashion.

Except Fennec. He could have fled in the night like Singh, but here he stood, returning her salute with the inhuman hand he had acquired the first time he went through a Gate on her behalf. On the far side of Fennec and his squadron stood Ji-hyeon's second father. Over the mountain range of armored heads and through the forest of pikes, she saw Kang-ho watching Fennec, his former lover, his former friend, and when Ji-hyeon returned her attention to Fennec he had dropped his hand and turned back to the Gate. It was time.

Fennec had gone first the last time, too, when they had fled into the Othean Gate instead of arriving through it, but he had held her hand when they went, and she'd been pulled in too quickly to see what happened. Now she had the proper perspective and plenty of examples to monitor, as first Fennec and then his squad stepped briskly over the edge and vanished from her sight. Instead of dropping feet-first into tarry black nothingness, each individual seemed to swing stiffly forward and down, as though there were hinges in the soles of their feet. There was no flapping of arms, no trying to catch themselves as they fell onto their faces atop the Gate, even their stride staying steady, and she realized that was because they weren't falling forward at all, but rather the perspective had become impossible to process; despite it appearing to be flat on the ground, they weren't stepping out over the Gate, they were simply walking through it.

When the last of Fennec's soldiers passed over and Choi began leading another unit into place, Kang-ho cut through the gap between the squads, joining his daughter at the edge of the Gate. Overhead, Fellwing's plumage was once again blacker than the night sky as she circled them both, the devil staying very close to her mistress this near a Gate. Ji-hyeon didn't acknowledge her second father's appearance, though her bodyguards certainly did, moving slightly closer as well.

'Yesterday's fashions are out, I see.' He must have been too upset the previous night to notice the new helm resting on its peg, but he certainly noticed it resting on her head. 'May I?'

'Now what kind of fool would I be to take off my armor on the middle of a battlefield?' she asked him, but was already loosening the chinstrap. It was too cool not to show off to one of the few people who could really appreciate it. Swinging it free and handing him the open-faced Immaculate helmet, she gave the signal for Choi to go in after Fennec. While her dad cooed over the buckle work and glittering steel, Ji-hyeon kept her eyes on Choi's red ones, until her former Honor Guard led her soldiers into the Gate, too. As Faaris Kimaera and the remaining members of his cavalry dismounted to enter, she noted with satisfaction that the horses weren't shying away from the Gate now that Hoartrap had 'opened' it, just as he'd said they wouldn't. She turned back to her dad and snapped her new sword up under his nose, nearly making him drop the helmet. 'Want to have a better look at this, too?'

'That's close enough, thank you,' he said, handing back her helmet and giving the black blade a cursory inspection. 'Odd pattern on the steel – looks almost like a horsehair pot. You know if you deck someone with that knuckle-duster hilt it'll break the two fingers you've got left.'

'I *know*,' she said, reverting to the affectations of her younger years to mess with her dad ... and to cover up how devastated she was by the news of Hwabun. When the bearded vulture devil had flown into the command tent just after midnight, carrying the treaty Empress Ryuki had already signed and stamped, Ji-hyeon had read it twice before adding her own ink, and then twice more, hoping she had missed something. But while exactingly precise in the terms of the truce, the document had offered no further details concerning the fate of Hwabun, and had there been any hope at all for the Bong family, the empress would surely have dangled it to further entice Ji-hyeon home. Her hands were shaking when she'd held up the signed treaty and the intimidating courier had winged away with it, back to Othean via the Lark's Tongue Gate ... but they weren't shaking anymore, and she put her hand on her second father's shoulder.

'I'm proud of you, Ji-hyeon,' he told her, and looking into his bloodshot eyes, she actually believed him. 'Can I ... can I give you a hug before we go through?'

'Da*aaad*, not in front of the troops,' she said, fitting her helm back into place. And seeing that lower lip begin to tremble, she whispered, 'I'm going through last, so wait until then.'

'Where's my daughter?' said Kang-ho, looking all around. 'Where is she? You look just like her, but I know no child of mine would ever do a sensible thing like leading from the rear.'

'Don't worry, I'm not going last for tactical reasons,' Ji-hyeon told him, signaling another squadron forward with the sword made from her lover's ancestor, the cobalt feathers Hoartrap had found devils knew where swaying atop her helm. 'I'm King Jun-hwan's daughter, too, and that means I know how to make an entrance.'

———

And what an entrance it was, Hoartrap's pledge to see every single soldier, steed, and cart horse safely through the Gates proven once and for all.

Dawn was just breaking, lending its warm glow to the golden roofs and terraces of the Autumn Palace when Ji-hyeon Bong and her second father stepped out from the wide pearlescent doors of the Temple of Pentacles, Royal Guards standing at attention on every ivory step leading down to the terra-cotta path through the pumpkin fields. Hoartrap had other business to attend to after he sent them through, so they didn't have a ghoulish show-stealer trailing after them, and the entire Cobalt Company waited for her, lined up along the road. General Ji-hyeon Bong had returned through the Othean Gate, as no champion had since the Age of Wonders.

And hard as Ji-hyeon had planned her triumphant return to Othean, Empress Ryuki had still upstaged her.

The sovereign matriarch of all the Immaculate Isles sat watching their approach from atop a terraced mountain of mahogany and gold brocade that had been erected just in front of the temple, a dozen Royal Guards kneeling on each of the platform's dozen steps. The Cobalt Company was in formation beyond this dais, an obvious move on Othean's part to establish from the outset that Ji-hyeon's army was now entirely behind the empress . . . and behind the thick twin bands of blue that bordered the road were twin seas of emerald armor, the entire Immaculate army brought out to fill the fields and make an unmistakable impression.

As Ji-hyeon and Kang-ho stepped down to the terra-cotta road from which the majestic pulpit rose, the Cobalts were blocked from view by the temporary throne room; another heavy-handed symbol. The white-robed empress rose from her cushion of white fur with perfect poise, the cylindrical, meter-high white hat rising above her white face not shifting a single white hair, and then she held up a bone-white hand. Ji-hyeon didn't like the woman making her bow as soon as she arrived to save her royal ass, but dropped to her knees in the red gravel all the same. Wouldn't do to make a bad impression, especially since she now saw that every kneeling guard on the dais had a white bow on one side and a white-fletched arrow on the other, and Fellwing gave an unhappy chirp from her perch on Ji-hyeon's shoulder.

'Yes,' said Empress Ryuki after a cramp-inducingly long silence. 'I recognize you, even in such a state. Ji-hyeon Bong of Hwabun. Hwabun, which is no more.'

'Your Elegance, you honor me—' Ji-hyeon began, but it was not her emotion that cut her off, but the empress.

'I do no such thing.'

Ji-hyeon was utterly stumped as to the etiquette of how to respond to such a slight, but knew better than to look over to her second father for a clue. Obviously the empress had not believed Kang-ho's proclamations of his daughter's innocence. Well, let her be as nasty as she needed to be, if it made her feel better about the death of Prince Byeong-gu – now that she'd signed a treaty with Ji-hyeon, some petty court bullshit was the only toll she could exact.

'What do you have to say for yourself, murderess?' demanded the empress, a decidedly unrefined edge to her voice.

Ji-hyeon almost did something stupid. She wasn't sure what, but she really, really wanted to do something stupid. Instead, she held her tongue until the impulse passed, and looked up at Empress Ryuki as she tried to be diplomatic about this, the way her first father would have wanted her to.

'Your Elegance, I sympathize with your grief for the loss of Byeong-gu – I wear this white armband as a token of mourning for my fiancé,' she began, glad Kang-ho had talked her into tearing a strip off her sheet just before they'd set out that morning. 'But I am no more responsible for his death than you are for the fate of my family at Hwabun. We are bound not only by the inhuman threat to the Immaculate Isles but also by our mutual loss. And I swear that once the terms of our treaty have been fulfilled, once Othean is again safe and the twin threats of Jex Toth and the Burnished Chain vanquished, then I will help you find your son's assassin. I swear on the memory of Hwabun, I will bring Byeong-gu's murderer before you, and prove my innocence.'

No wind stirred the silence that followed, or perhaps the breeze was ensnared by the barricade of twenty thousand Immaculate soldiers that surrounded the rebel general, the Immaculate Empress, and the Temple of Pentacles. Then the empress smiled, so faintly Ji-hyeon might have missed it if she were not studying the woman's face for some token of understanding. Empress Ryuki said something too low for Ji-hyeon to hear, and the archer closest to her on the dais reached into his robe and held up a piece of parchment, his eyes never leaving Ji-hyeon as the empress stepped up behind him and retrieved the document.

'Ji-hyeon Bong, I shall extend you a courtesy you refuse me – the truth.' And just like that, Empress Ryuki's other neat white hand went to the other side of the neat white parchment and ripped it in half. 'I honor no treaties with traitors.'

At that instant, Ji-hyeon knew she was a dead woman. She didn't scramble to her feet, didn't shout her protests, but she did turn to look at her second father – and saw he had not even had the forbearance of his wild daughter, hopping to his feet with a look of concentrated rage and hatred contorting his usually pleasant face.

'What is the meaning of this deception?' he bellowed, and as if in answer each of the dozen guards that knelt on each of the dozen steps calmly took up their white bows and nocked their single white arrows.

'You will quiet yourself, Kang-ho Bong,' spoke the empress, 'or you will not even be granted the final mercy I offer your daughter. If either of you speak another word you will be executed immediately.'

Ji-hyeon couldn't believe this was really happening. She could not fucking believe it. An upbringing in the Immaculate Isles had taught her that no single person in the entire Star was as noble, benevolent, and honest as the empress, and that ingrained idiocy had just led to her absolute downfall. This time yesterday she had sat and smiled across the table at Colonel Waits as they signed a truce that Ji-hyeon soon discovered the woman had every intention of betraying, and yet when the empress offered her even better terms that very evening she had joyously put her stamp to them. That even her innately duplicitous second father had not suspected a trap demonstrated how insidious this cultural belief in the empress's trustworthiness truly was, but that didn't do either of them an ounce of good, now that they had led the entire Cobalt Company into an ambush.

And yet like everything at Othean, even the ambushes were refined and quiet, Kang-ho looking as though he might burst a blood vessel in his bulging eyes but as silent as his dumbstruck daughter.

'That is much better,' said the empress, evidently enjoying the sound of her own voice as much as she abhorred anyone else's. 'Each moment you stand here drawing breath Othean is further sullied by your vile presence, and so I shall not prolong this ugliness. The truth I promised you is this: Jex Toth has indeed returned, but her shores remain quiet. Our armada has formed a blockade along the Haunted Sea while I consider different petitions to explore the interior, but my ships have spied no monsters nor devils, only once-violent seas grown calm.'

Ji-hyeon let out a sob of relief, then slapped a hand over her mouth, waiting for the arrows ... but this was apparently not outrageous enough to provoke their bows. Hwabun had not been overrun. Her other dad was alive, her sisters, the staff, everyone was safe, the empress had just told her a tale of monsters to draw her out, and—

'Hwabun has been sacrificed to atone for your madness and cruelty,' Empress Ryuki announced. 'You removed my son from this world, and so I have repaid the debt one hundred fold. Every member of your family and every servant on your Isle has been cast into the Temple of Pentacles, so that no trace of your tainted line remains in the world of mortals.'

Empress Ryuki was still speaking with that nasty, smug expression to her tone, but for the moment all Ji-hyeon could hear were her sisters screaming as they were dragged up this very gravel path to the temple built around the Othean Gate. She imagined her first father's eternally calm, reasonable voice rising to breaking point as he pleaded for the lives of his daughters and their household, begging their regent to put the blame for Ji-hyeon's crimes on him alone. How silent the steps to the temple must have seemed, once the last whimpering member of her house was cast into the First Dark as punishment for a crime of which both they and Ji-hyeon were totally innocent ...

'... and the estate has been burned to the foundations, which have been unearthed and cast into the sea,' the empress was saying as the roaring wave of images in Ji-hyeon's skull receded, returning her to this calamitous moment. 'The stairway to the inner bay has been blasted, along with the harbor, and the grounds salted down to the smallest cliff garden, so that Hwabun is never again mistaken for a territory of the Immaculate Isles instead of what it is – a dead rock in the Haunted Sea, unfit for life of any sort. And that is all I have to say.'

In the lull that followed this pronouncement it was so quiet that both the Cobalt Company and the Immaculate army who surrounded them must have heard Ji-hyeon's heart shatter like a dropped teacup, and her second father's along with it. And then Kang-ho was screaming, screaming so loudly Ji-hyeon never heard the bows twang. She saw them release, though, and as the flying arrows cast her into momentary shade she leaped to her feet, not even thinking, just doing, as she had in this field a year before when she'd snuck away from the dull festival and her dull fiancé and found sport among the pumpkin devils.

But before she could fully draw her swords the arrows struck.

It was Empress Ryuki's cruelest trick yet, for not a single arrow was aimed at Ji-hyeon, the cloud of white-fletched shafts studding the ground around her ... and her father. Kang-ho had taken two steps toward his daughter, perhaps trying to shield her, and now he pitched to the ground, a dozen arrows sprouting from his slight potbelly, his gentle hands, his pleasant face. It happened so fast the blood didn't even begin to ooze out around the arrows until his spasms made the terra-cotta gravel click and clatter around him. Oblivious to the empress's shouts behind her, Ji-hyeon took a step toward her last remaining family member, her boots rustling through the grove of arrows embedded in the path, when Fellwing fell limply from her shoulder, landing in the gravel at Kang-ho's feet.

Ji-hyeon stopped, staring down at her shivering devil – when they'd come through the Gate together but minutes before she'd been as black and healthy as she'd ever been, but now the little owlbat was as white as a bleached skull, her roundness withered to a bone-showing gauntness. Then Ji-hyeon understood what must have happened, and snapping out of her torpor, snatched Fellwing off the path, because while it was too late for her father, the devil might yet be saved. Spinning back to face the empress, Ji-hyeon saw the wide gap in the carpet of white arrows where she had been kneeling, an island of red gravel that Fellwing had drained herself protecting from the volley of arrows. There had been so many, and all at once, that the faithful creature had overtaxed herself to the edge of death.

Empress Ryuki was peevishly giving orders, but her insistence on making a classy spectacle had undone her plan – Fellwing would no longer be able to shield Ji-hyeon, but none of the archers had extra arrows. Everyone looked embarrassed, and nobody knew what to do.

Clutching Fellwing to her chest with her good hand so that the devil might be sustained on her broken heart, Ji-hyeon pointed up at the empress with the two remaining fingers of her left hand, holding the pose until the older woman looked back down at the path and saw the silent promise Ji-hyeon made her. Then Ji-hyeon charged, and her sudden movement in their direction clarified the questionable circumstance for the Royal Guards stationed on the temple steps. If Ji-hyeon had tried to engage a single one of them the rest would have easily stopped her, but drawing her two-fingered sword and battering their spears away, she shot up the pearlescent steps between them. A spear struck her in the small of the back but glanced off her hauberk, and then Ji-hyeon Bong disappeared into the Othean Gate for the second time in her young life.

CHAPTER

24

Best knew exactly what she would do when she finally tracked down her disgraceful family, but she had not known how she would feel. As a true Horned Wolf, she always did what was right without hesitation, but that did not mean she carried out her every action without feeling or doubt. This frailty was the design of the Fallen Mother when she had turned her back on her children to live out eternity in her Meadhall in the land of Jex Toth; if making virtuous decisions always came easy there would be no glory to be earned in faithfully leading a Chainite life. No, what confirmed their path as worthy of being followed was how hard if not outright painful it so often was to do the right thing. Only by overcoming the weakness of the mortal heart could one aspire to live a truly just life, one where you knew you had overcome the mewling enticements of the Deceiver – the pleasures of such sins as mercy and forgiveness were fleeting, but the righteous who overcame these spiritual snares would find strength in the virtues of pride and hatred, and in the end all would be judged not by their thoughts but their deeds.

If Nemi of the Bitter Sighs spoke true and Best's family had helped a sorcerer imperil the world they must be killed. If Nemi of the Bitter Sighs spoke false and Best's family did not associate with a sorcerer, they still must be killed, for the crimes of abandoning the clan and murdering those who sought to stop them. It would not be easy, both because despite their sins her wicked heart loved them still, and because they were blood of hers, and thus would prove dangerous opponents. Best knew the pain of ending her son's life in particular would devastate her, quite possibly past the point of continuing with her own, but she also knew if she had any hope of successfully petitioning the Fallen Mother to release their spirits from the Hell of the Coward Dead, she must enter her maker's Meadhall with such honors to her name as to impress even the keeper of the Star and all its fragile children. Putting an end to those villains who threatened the realm of mortals seemed like it might provide just such renown, and for all her failings Best still nurtured honorable pride in her breast – not for nothing had she come by her name, and if anyone could put cold steel through the iniquitous heart of her own devil-blooded son, it was she.

Best had never considered herself an imaginative person. Sullen's interminable songs had never conjured waking dreams to her mind the way her father said they did, even if she had appreciated the musicality of his skill and feigned interest out of love. Yet ever since setting out from the Frozen Savannahs she had been unable to stop herself from picturing what it might be like, their reunion, even though she knew she could not possibly predict the particulars. Some scenarios ended quicker than others, but in all of them Sullen overheard her slinking approach, the boy too much her son to be taken unawares even by a huntress of her quality. But now that she had finally found him, even this seemingly obvious detail was proven wrong, the boy as deaf as those savages who refused to hear the gospel of the Burnished Chain.

He was distracted, consumed with the girl he spoke with, and as Best padded from tree to tree watching them, her disappointment in her son's final failure to live up to his heritage turned into stark fury, a virtue she had never before felt to such degree. Her son, the boy she had convinced her anxious husband to keep at his teat instead of giving over to the poison oracle to be trained as a possible successor the way devil-blooded babes traditionally were, her little Sullen ... he was actually kissing this Immaculate girl, as if he hadn't sinned enough against the laws of the Horned Wolf already. Not that any member of the clan would have ever let him into their hut, anathema that he was, but Horned Wolves did not mate outside their pack, this was sacrosanct. He could not have hurt his mother more if she had caught him consorting with a Jackal Person.

In her righteous anger, she misstepped in the unfamiliar leaves of this foreign wood, and her son looked up from his lover, and the fear on his face disgusted her. He said something in Immaculate, practically roaring the words, and she cringed to remember how she had encouraged him to learn that heathen tongue – every village needed a trader who could travel to the coast and converse with the seafaring Outlanders, and while that duty carried the least honor in all the clan she knew Sullen could hope for nothing better. She had encouraged his wanderlust, Fallen Mother forgive her.

Sullen's hair looked pale in the moonlight, as if his dishonor to his people had leeched him of even his vitality – it was as though his flesh already knew he had no future, and hastened his transition into the worlds that lie beyond the Star. His devil-cat eyes that had always been so keen when he had still struggled against his toxic nature passed right over Best, and she thought of something Father Turisa had told her after

Sullen and Father had left, when she confessed her shame at not being able to detect the growing impiety in her own hut: *the eyes of the just can no more detect a hidden sin than the unrepentant sinner can see the ways of the just.*

She would have killed him then, before he could tally another trespass to his name, when Sullen's next Immaculate exclamation cut off midway, and his fixed stare brought her attention to something even she had failed to notice – Myrkur, the horned wolf who served Nemi, had also crept forward through the forest toward their prey, and before Best could act the great beast announced herself with a low growl, stepping out into the moonlight. Another sign from the Fallen Mother, that, and another that Best could not ignore and still call herself a Horned Wolf. She would not commit the sin of mercifully killing her son quickly, then, but would pay him the slow, shameful death in combat he had brought down on himself. Stepping out into the moonlight, she let him find her with his corrupted eyes.

When he did he didn't even seem to recognize her.

But then she could barely recognize him, either.

The Immaculate girl noisily drew a sword, and glancing over at the ruckus Best realized she had been wrong; the Immaculate was a man, though he'd been born in a girl's flesh. There were hardly any tells in his posture or features, but Best knew without a doubt – having had her feminine soul born into a male vessel herself, Best could almost always tell at a glance when others shared her burdens, which was to say, her blessings. She wondered if Sullen saw anything of his father in this two-spirited Outlander, but then pushed the thought away, along with all the rest. Speculating into the motives of a sinner was itself a sin, and not one she had any time for, when—

'No!'

Sullen must have recognized her, then, just as the sun-knife sped from his fingertips, and debased sinner that he was, compassionately sought to warn his distracted mother. The black blur of the blades was too fast for any mortal to dodge if his aim was true. She knew it was, the sun-knife destined for the center of her chest. Yet Horned Wolves are among the chosen children of the Fallen Mother, and more than mortal when they need to be, and Best spun out of its path. A single outlying edge nicked her shoulder as it passed her, the mild sting all the incentive she needed to return her own sun-knife to Sullen.

The one crafted from the remains of his great-great-grandmother.

The one that never missed, and always killed.

Unlike her son, Best made no sound as she hurled the branch-bladed knife. It would be her final lesson to her son, and she prayed he took this one to heart.

———

Sullen went for his sun-knife just as the horned wolf lunged . . . but instead of crossing the short gap between the trees to bite his arm off or impale him on its crown of twisted horns, it spun around in a whirlwind of white fur, and disappeared back into the deep night. His arm was already drawing back the weapon, and his eyes flicked to the Horned Wolf huntress, hoping she'd have departed along with her namesake, but instead he saw her focused on Keun-ju, who had stepped boldly out from behind the cover of the cypress, his four-tiger sword in hand. The huntress was about to throw her sun-knife, but none were faster than Sullen when he needed to be, and he launched his own cold steel straight at . . . his mom?

'No!'

She was even swifter than he remembered, praise the quick

blood of Rakehell that flowed in both their veins. The sun-knife only grazed her a little on the arm as it spun off into the woods, but what had she expected, creeping up on him like that, what was she doing here, and why why why was her sun-knife coming straight at Sullen, unavoidably close before he even realized she'd thrown it?

Bad as dying like that would've been, what happened instead was even worse. Keun-ju stepped in front of Sullen, fast as moonlight reflecting off water, his sweeping sword even faster than the rest of him. The mad Immaculate tried to bat the sun-knife out of the air, but that kind of shit only played in songs, and only the most over-the-top ballads at that. A smart man like Keun-ju had to know that move was impossible for mortals, had to know the only thing that was going to catch that knife was his throat. It scarcely mattered whether he was trying to play the hero or the martyr, though, because the end result could only be the same.

Sullen's mind could be fleet as his feet, but not even his thoughts were a match for his mother's sun-knife. It had reached Keun-ju before Sullen had even finished his thought, so it was all just noise after the fact; he might think of himself as quick-witted, but at times like this it was pretty obvious he couldn't even keep up with what was happening right in front of him. It was over, it had happened, and he still couldn't believe it.

Keun-ju gave a pained grunt as the sun-knife connected, but that slight sound was immediately drowned out by the echoing clang of metal, and a thunk.

Even batted off its course by Keun-ju's legendary sword, the sun-knife had retained enough momentum to sink two of its thick black blades deep into the trunk of a nearby cypress.

Sullen gave a wordless shout of ecstatic relief, but it was

a little early to get carried away – Sullen's mom had started charging them with her spear as soon as she'd thrown the sun-knife, and Keun-ju was still swaying from the impact of deflecting the heavy weapon. Sullen dashed for the sun-knife that had almost ended his life, that should have ended Keun-ju's, and grabbing the leather-strapped handle he yanked it with all his might. It was so well lodged in the tree it almost dislocated his shoulder, but then it came loose, Sullen pivoting on his heel to fire it at their attacker before his chronically doubt-plagued mind could remember it was his mom and do something foolish like hesitate when she was clearly here to kill his arse dead.

Except he hesitated anyway, even with his mom flying straight at him, her spear lowered. She was paying no mind to Keun-ju despite his being closer, and then Sullen saw why – the Immaculate had crumpled to the ground, the bottom half of his four-tiger sword still clenched in his fist . . . and the rest of the blade jutting from his shoulder, blood spreading out around the edge of moon-bright metal. It didn't make any sense, it didn't . . . and then it did. Keun-ju had claimed his renowned weapon could shear lesser swords in twain, but it had been no match for the heavy steel of the Horned Wolves; though he'd deflected the sun-knife, the impact had caused his four-tiger to snap in two, the upper half flying backward and embedding itself just above his armpit.

Keun-ju had managed to be both a hero and a martyr at once, then, saving Sullen by knocking the missile out of the way, but at the cost of not only his life but the sword he seemed to value even more. The black-bladed sun-knife in Sullen's violently shaking hand had as good as killed Keun-ju after all . . . and now it was about to kill someone else that Sullen loved.

He howled, then, not like a mortal or even a devil, but like a horned wolf mourning the loss of its mate.

And as she leaped over Keun-ju's twitching body, closing the last few steps between them with her spear leveled, Sullen's stern mother committed her worst sin yet against the loving son who'd tried so hard to understand her: she smiled.

CHAPTER

25

'Okay, now that *definitely* wasn't an animal,' said Digs, and as Purna fitted her damp cloak into place she saw he'd been getting dressed, too, despite how dismissive he'd been when she'd first said she heard something out there in the woods. Squirming into wet clothes while balancing in a tree was hard work, even a nice big oak with wide, comfortable branches, but not so hard as fighting in their panties if the ruckus made its way over to them ... Or if they made their way over to the ruckus, as now seemed unavoidable, because if Sullen hadn't been the one to issue that furious-yet-forlorn howl Purna would eat Diggelby's hat. The pasha almost slipped off his bough but caught himself, muttering, 'Shitty shitty fuck fuck.'

'Shitty shitty fuck fuck *shitty shitty*,' she sing-songed back at him, because while Sullen didn't sound happy, that he still sounded like anything at all meant he was alive, and that was the best news she'd heard all night. 'Time enough for shitting and fucking in Old Black's Meadhall, Digs, so the sooner we get over there the sooner we'll get to indulge.'

'Have fun in your sorry Flintland dive bar of an afterlife, I've got a royal-class coach booked for the Garden of the Star, and I don't mean Thao,' said Digs. He took a small sapphire-studded case she hadn't seen before out of his vest and, popping it open, revealed not bugs or drugs but a stack of black discs. 'Care to take your first communion while you've still got time? My paradise's apparently very much at hand, but I don't think any of our recent adventures have provided reliable directions to any meadhalls.'

'That's really not funny,' said Purna, her heart lurching in her chest as Digs carefully removed one of the wafers and popped it in his mouth. Somehow the possibility that Digs might be sincere chilled her more than Sullen's howl. 'What is that, some kind of concentrated spider spit? A pregame snack?'

'Look, don't get uptight about this,' said Digs through a mouthful of blood-dark crumbs. 'Obviously the Black Pope's a total buttdog and obviously I'm not in favor of the direction the Chain's gone in recent years, but the church does a lot of good, too, or at least it has in the past. Nothing's all black-and-white, much as Ji-hyeon wants to believe it is.'

'Mother. Licking. Bastard,' gasped Purna, all the obvious fire bells she'd been rigorously tuning out now clanging in unison. Diggelby's repeated suggestions they cut out on the Cobalts if they couldn't find Maroto. All his talk about pride and vanity being virtues. His habitual petitions to not only the Fallen Mother but plenty of saints, too. How could she have missed this? His uncle was a member of the clergy, for crying out loud, why hadn't it ever seriously occurred to her? 'I thought all that Chainite shit you talk was ironic!'

'There's nothing more ironic than sincerity,' said Digs, obviously trying to distract her from the real issue by baiting her with nonsense in need of calling out. It wasn't going to work this time.

'You ... you fucker!' Purna felt more betrayed than she ever had in her life. 'The fucking *Chain*? Fuck you! Even after all they've done, murdering innocent people, murdering our *friends*, you ... you ... fuck!'

'I said I *don't* support the church, *Tapai* Purna, what more do you want to hear?' said Digs pissily. 'That I renounce the Black Pope and the Holy See? *Abso-lutely*, to the lamest hell with the lot of them. That I think their persecution of the wildborn is the foulest crime of our age? I do, because it is. That sacrificing countless people to bring back the Sunken Kingdom is a bit overkill? I'll go one further and say if the cost is kicking one puppy down a flight of stairs then we ought to have let Jex Toth stay underwater.'

'But ... but ...' Now Purna was just as confused as she was angry. 'But you said you're a Chainite!'

'No, *you* said I was a Chainite,' said Digs, and it sounded like the fight had left him, leaving only the despondency that looked so bad on him. His corpsepaint had smeared and run from their fight with the swamp monsters, and he looked like a weepy mime. 'Between you and me, I don't even know if I believe in the Allmother. But I do believe that no matter how far they've fallen everyone and everything can change for the better, that there's no such thing as a lost cause ... not even an easy target like the Burnished Chain. I was born to a Chainite family, raised in a Chainite family, and if the Chain hadn't proved a supreme disappointment once I grew old enough to think for myself I might have joined the clergy.'

That was such an insane image that Purna almost burst out laughing. 'You? Hair shirts and rosaries and hot-bottomed confessions?'

'Oh, please,' said Digs. 'With my family's connections I could have done far better in the church than as a pasha's second son – if you think our parties in the Serpent's Circle were lavish you should see the fetes the Holy See puts on in

Diadem. Orgies of food and flesh, and you want to talk high fashion? Those clotheshorse cardinals make me look like a court jester, and if there's one thing I know it's that I kill in the wardrobe department, especially when it comes to shades of black.'

'So why not join up?' jeered Purna. 'It's not too late to get on the winning team, and what's a little thing like bringing about the apocalypse if you get to live the good life?'

'You know why,' said Digs, no longer sounding like he had anything to prove. 'But if you really can't guess, I'll spell it out for you after we go help our friends. That is, unless you'd rather put off finding out if Sullen and Keun-ju are still alive so you can keep interrogating me about the private life I never shared with even my *best friends* because I knew that no matter what kind of a person I was and what sorts of actions I took, as soon as you found out I was even *mildly* religious you'd be a great big bottom about it.'

Sullen and Keun-ju. Shitty shitty fuck fuck. She'd been so surprised by Digs's confession she'd got up on a high horse instead of running to their aid and simply taking another one of her friend's idiosyncrasies for what it was.

'Shit, you're right – let's go,' she said, but he was already out of the tree . . . and waiting to help her down. He was right. She *was* a great big bottom. 'Damn, Digs, I shouldn't have freaked on you, especially after you were so great about my dirty little secret.'

'You're right,' said Digs as he caught her and almost fell over, not quite as strong as some of their other chums but still making the effort. 'You shouldn't have, but it's in the past. I forgive you, my child, and may safe havens keep you at your rest.'

'I didn't say I was sorry,' said Purna, shaking out her legs now that she was back on solid ground. 'But I am. Sorry, Digs.'

'As a great man once told me,' said Digs, 'I know you're sorry, now apologize.'

Then they hugged, as only great big bottoms can, and set off to find their friends . . .

And only got a few paces out from under the shadow of the live oak before they both saw the young woman standing right there in front of them, the moonlight glittering on the wire frames of her spectacles and all the metal hoops and loops and bars and studs set in her face, flashing off the stone-encrusted bronze crescent at her throat and steel thread embroidered into her blouse, and the scabbard at her side. Purna chirped in alarm and Digs jumped straight into the air. With her funky-looking staff, woven crown of twigs and berries, and sudden appearance in a dark and haunted wood, Purna would have pegged her for a witch even if she'd opened with a different question.

'Good evening, pilgrims. I wonder if you'd be so good as to tell me where I might find Hoartrap the Touch?' The girl sounded all business, and the hand that wasn't clenched on the twisted walking stick dropped to the pommel of the sword hanging from a belt bedecked with pouches.

Hoartrap? Purna looked nervously at Digs, and he looked nervously back at her.

'Whotrap?' said Digs, the eternal optimist. 'I think you have mistaken us for someone else, good lady, for we are, as you said, but humble pilgrims on, um, pilgrimage, and certainly don't—'

'I can be patient when I need to be,' snapped the woman, 'but now is not one of those times. That you try to protect him tells me all I need to know about you, but I will nevertheless give you one last chance to prove yourselves helpful to my cause. If you refuse me a second time there will not be a third opportunity.'

It didn't do to provoke obvious weirdos you met in deep, dark woods, but Purna had no tolerance for this crap, not while her friends were almost definitely in some kind of trouble. And even if she was a witch, Purna could tell she was a cupcake compared to someone like the Procuress Vex Ferlune or old Hoartrap the Grope – this chit was trembling like a nervous squirrel, but fronting so hard it was almost impressive. It was time to shut her down and get on with rescuing Sullen ... but now that she'd sized her up Purna had decided she was also kind of cute, too, in the spooky way of girls you only ever seem to meet in the moonlight, so she decided to be generous.

'Look, we haven't seen Hoartrap in weeks, and that's the truth – but the last we knew he was camped out at the foot of the Lark's Tongue Peak, down on the Witchfinder Plains. If you want to talk more later I'd be happy to burn a bowl with you, *after* we get on with our business, but I know it's a long walk south so if you have to get on your way I'll try to understand.'

The girl considered this, pursing her pierced lips, and then her eyes settled on Purna's hood with unabashed excitement. It *was* a fetching cloak, and Purna was glad its quality had attracted an appreciative stranger's notice, until she said, 'You're going to come with me. I know someone who's going to be very interested in asking you where you came by that skin.'

'Oh, *I don't fucking think so*,' said Digs irritably. 'We're not going *anywhere* with you. Weren't you listening? She *said* we have to get on with our business, so why don't you get on with yours, hmmm? I don't give a good devil's damn what you do *to* or *with* the Touch, so long as you leave us out of it. And with that, *madam*, we bid you goodnight!'

This was not the right tactic to take, apparently, for as Digs moved to step around the girl she stepped to the side, too, a dangerous smile on her lips, and that's when the moonlight rippled across her features as something large and silent moved behind Purna. Wheeling around and drawing her kukri, she felt all the blood drop out of her face in a cold flush.

The giant horned wolf looming over her made the ones back in the Kutumbans look like Zosia's dog, and its baleful eyes were fixed on a certain article of clothing that Purna was now having serious second thoughts about rocking. Behind her, Digs was giving the girl a real piece of his mind, oblivious to what was going on. That the monstrous snout hovering right in front of her face hadn't bitten her head off yet Purna was counting a minor victory, and a token that maybe she could still get out of this, if she didn't do anything too Maroto here.

'Digs,' she called, too anxious to blink, her voice cracking, 'on second thought, I think we better go with her. Meet her friend who's got an interest in horned wolf hides.'

Purna only prayed she wasn't looking at said friend already.

———

Now that she had reminded her son who he could have been, what he was by birth, Sullen wasn't proving to be quite as much the disappointment as Best had first feared. They circled each other through the bald cypresses, and while the soft ground was spiked with jagged roots around their trunks, the tall, slender trees were bare of branch most of the way up, giving the warriors plenty of room to maneuver. Every time she closed on him with her spear he backed away, holding up her sun-knife like a poison oracle brandishing a fetish. He couldn't know that the black steel contained his ancestor, and thus could not miss its target, and so he held back, rightly fearing that if he threw his only weapon and Best dodged he would die on the end of her spear in moments. She feinted to his left, then darted in and slashed the front of his shin with the broad edge of her spear. It sliced through skin and scraped against bone, but he didn't cry out, nor did he rush in out of anger the way she'd hoped. He just jerked his arm back to throw, making her shuffle backward. Good boy.

She had worried that when the time came he would make a weak show of it, pleading and making excuses. He did her proud, keeping his mouth shut and his eyes hard. No, not hard, apparently ... he was struggling to keep them open as tears began slipping down his cheeks. So much for him doing her proud. Furious at his fear, she came in hard again, jabbing at his knife hand. This time he tried to parry her thrust, probably hoping he could hack the blade off the end of her spear. It was exactly what she'd wanted him to do, and she flicked her wrists, the butt of her spear snapping around to catch him directly in the gash she'd opened in his leg. That made him cry out and stumble back, and then she had him, administering more superficial cuts to both forearms, and then his other shin. She would bleed the cowardice out of him.

'Stop!' he cried, and Best's heart broke for good – it was as she'd feared, as she'd known. He was going to make a fool out of himself instead of dying with quiet dignity. 'I don't wanna hurt you, Ma!'

'Too late,' she told him, though his cheap ploy was having the intended effect, rousing a mute howl of pain from the evil, bestial part of her heart that she had been able to keep silent as long as her son remained so as well. She jabbed again, slicing through the thick white hair on the side of his head and into the scalp beneath. Her chest felt full of furious ants, swarming and biting her with the grief and uncertainty that was the Deceiver's hallmark, but she overcame temptation yet again, and decided to turn his own favorite weapon against him: words that cut as sharp as any sun-knife. 'Did you love that boy, Sullen? The one I killed?'

This weapon of his provoked a far stronger reaction than any of her spear blows, his sad, frightened face transforming into a lupine snarl, and Best realized she was going to die. Sullen was hurling the sun-knife at her, and from this distance he couldn't miss even with a mundane weapon. In the last great mystery of her life, Best found herself profoundly relieved . . . until the sun-knife stuck into the forest floor between her feet. He'd held on too long before releasing it, but not even her son could be so inept as to throw a knife straight into the ground by mistake. He had given up.

'I love you, Ma,' he panted, blood and sweat running down every limb, dribbling from the side of his head, dribbling off his ear.

She didn't hesitate, because if she did her inner sinner would take over, make her cast down her weapon and take her sad, lost son in her arms. Then they would both be condemned to the Hell of the Coward Dead, and she had to believe their fate was greater than that. Even as she planted her feet and thrust her spear straight at her son's heart, she expected him to slap it to the side, to grab the shaft, or jump out of the way. And Fallen Mother forgive her, she *wanted* him to.

Instead he just closed his eyes, set his jaw, and accepted his mother's gift.

———

Sullen didn't feel a thing. He waited, wondering if this was some final cruelty, his insane mother waiting until he cracked a lid so he'd have to watch her kill him. She didn't, though, and through the soles of his feet he felt the little tremor as her spear dropped to the ground, the shaft rolling against his toes, and then Sullen let out a sob of relief, opening his eyes and his arms to embrace his mom.

Instead of his mom, he found Hoartrap. His mom was there,

too, but the giant warlock had come between them, and tall as Sullen's mother was, her feet were kicking a meter off the ground as Hoartrap lifted her up by the throat, his crushing fingers keeping her as silent as his approach had been. He turned his head from his captured prey and smiled at Sullen, watching for his reaction, and then slammed the woman into the ground so hard the reverberation almost knocked Sullen off his feet. Sullen tried to speak, to tell Hoartrap to stop, but before he could an enormous slippered foot slammed into his mom's side, the kick sending her sliding through the scratching underbrush, kicking up a flurry of dead leaves and mud in her wake, until the sharp-kneed trunk of a cypress abruptly ended her skid with a terrible thud.

'Oh, but I got here just in time,' said Hoartrap with a wink, the large, fading bruises on his face making him look even uglier than usual. 'A friend of yours from back home, I presume?'

'My mom,' whispered Sullen.

'I might have guessed,' said Hoartrap. 'You and that family of yours, Sullen, I swear. It will be most interesting to see what happens when your bloodline mixes with Kang-ho's; I imagine the progeny will be spirited, to say the least.'

Maybe it was blood loss or maybe it was everything that had just happened, but it took a moment for Hoartrap's implication to sink in. When it did, his brain staggered from Ji-hyeon to Keun-ju, and then his feet were staggering, too, carrying him away from Hoartrap to the limp body framed in a patch of moonlight. Keun-ju. Keun-ju Keun-ju Keun-ju.

'Of course, of course, Keun-ju,' said Hoartrap, outpacing Sullen's faltering steps and putting himself between them. He almost got a face full of Sullen's forehead when he said, 'With my aid he'll recover, Sullen, I checked to make certain the matter wasn't too urgent before coming to rescue my fairest Flintlander.'

'*What?*' Sullen couldn't believe it, but squinting ahead he saw the broken blade in Keun-ju's chest rocking back and forth as the Immaculate took shallow breaths. 'He . . . he's alive? He's going to be okay?'

'With a bit of elbow grease on my part, yes, though he'll be changed by the experience.' Hoartrap picked his nose and rubbed something between his fingers. 'But who doesn't undergo a little transformation after a brush with death, hmmm? I know I'm a new Touch after you and Zosia and that Purna girl all helped me out so much during that unfortunate incident with the mother of all opossums.'

'Let's help him, then,' said Sullen, noticing for the first time that Hoartrap's heavy wicker pack was set against a tree next to Keun-ju, and a black hafted Flintland spear leaned against it. For the first time since they'd met, Sullen had a powerful thirst to hear any songs Hoartrap cared to sing, about how Ji-hyeon fared and where he'd come from and how he'd found them, but first they badly needed to see to Keun-ju. Giving Hoartrap a genuine smile, Sullen raised his fist for the Touch to bump. 'Thanks, Hoartrap.'

'Anytime, my boy.' Hoartrap was positively beaming, and happily knocked Sullen's fist. 'Now, the first thing we do is *vomit up vipers.*'

Typical Hoartrap. But before Sullen could register just how girly and unnatural these last words had sounded, Hoartrap's eyes bulged and he slapped a hand to his potbelly, then doubled over and did exactly as promised. Sullen had seen plenty of bizarre, gross shit since leaving the Savannahs, and *definitely* since meeting the Touch, but this might've been the worst thing he'd ever seen in his life. He staggered back from the loosely knotted ball of bile-slick snakes that the witch hawked up into the leaves, a fat indigo serpent hanging halfway out of Hoartrap's mouth and striking him repeatedly in the bruise-yellowed nose. The Touch might have been trying to scream or might have been trying to pass another mass of adders, but whatever the sloppy sound was it signaled that something very, very wrong was happening, and then it got a lot worse.

Sullen had always wondered if he'd ever see a real live horned wolf, and what he'd do if he did. Obviously in the old days warriors of the clan had to kill one to prove their worth, maybe earn a better name, but even as a young daydreamer Sullen had preferred thoughts of taming one and keeping it as a pet. Now that he had finally seen one in the fur, and was seeing it again, at the back of his mind he realized just how absurd a fantasy that had been – the enormous white beast that bolted out of the darkness at them was a thing of pure horror, and thus not exactly domesticable. It went straight for the doubled-over wizard, its long muzzle snapping shut around one of Hoartrap's legs with a nasty-sounding crunch. Big as Hoartrap was, the horned wolf was far, far bigger, and began dragging him off into the dark forest. Hoartrap clutched vainly at cypress knees and saplings, his face darkening as he choked on the scaly coils hanging from his distended jaw. Sullen stared, and Sullen saw, and Sullen couldn't fucking believe it. Whatever was happening with the snakes notwithstanding, if it wasn't one devildamned Horned Wolf ruining his night it was another devildamned horned wolf ruining his night.

Then Hoartrap and the monster were enveloped by the shadows of the Haunted Forest, and the shock wore off and the panic set in. He needed Hoartrap or Keun-ju would die – the wound that hadn't much troubled the Touch looked pretty fucking mortal to Sullen, and he had no idea what to do to help him. At least the venomous snakes Hoartrap had produced were no longer an issue; the mess of vipers had stopped writhing and begun sizzling and smoking, dissolving into grey cords of slime. Whether this was the result of the deviltry that had summoned them or being soaked in Hoartrap's stomach acid didn't make much difference, so long as they all melted into the earth. Sullen hadn't been sure what to do about a nest of deadly serpents materializing a dozen feet from Keun-ju, but with that final concern assuaged he went to his injured friend. The man looked even worse up close, bubbles forming in the wide pool of blood that surrounded the blade with each ragged breath. It was lodged in his shoulder just above his right armpit, and so deep it probably pinned him to the earth, but at least he wasn't awake to feel it.

'I'm gonna fix this,' he promised his friend, then left his side, as hard a course as he'd ever set himself on, but it had to happen. There was no way this ended well unless he rescued Hoartrap from whatever fell witchcraft had summoned the snakes of the earth and the wolves of the fjords down upon him. Fortunately, the Touch had inexplicably brought him just the thing to help. He snatched up the black spear leaning against Hoartrap's pack, the steel blade even darker than the perfectly balanced shaft, and then Sullen set off to do something a member of his clan hadn't done since his mother's time – he was going to hunt a horned wolf.

CHAPTER

26

'What's she doing?' Digs asked, as if Purna somehow comprehended the weird girl's actions. 'Is that an egg?'

It sure looked like it, the witchy woman raising up the pale oval she had removed from one of her belt pouches, and completing whatever incantation she had been uttering, she dropped the unbroken egg into her mouth. The girl was clearly trying to swallow it whole, but struggling, and Purna made her move, scrambling out from behind the log where they'd taken cover and creeping up behind her. If you were going to roll up on a witch, waiting until their mouth was full was one of Maroto's many, many rules for throwing down on magic users; made it harder for them to spit spells or eat devils, and besides that, most people will choke if you swing on them when they're chewing.

This chippie was going to regret bowing up on them, even if she had brusquely turned and fled through the forest just when things looked dire, her horned wolf overtaking her in three strides and then shooting off through the trees. Digs hadn't been hot on the idea of following, but had agreed on the condition that Purna do the first stupid thing that was required of them. When they'd found the girl but not the wolf and watched her carry out her strange dance beneath an unseasonably flowering rowan tree it had gone without saying that the required stupid thing was taking her hostage before her pet monster returned. And now the dummy had an egg in her mouth, and Purna was only five steps away from seeing that it ended up all over her smug face.

Four.

Three.

Two.

Annnnnnnd . . .

One.

'Move and you're dead,' Purna hissed, rising up on her toes so her lips almost brushed the taller woman's iron-cluttered ear, the keen edge of her kukri kissing the front of the witch's neck. The curve of the knife fit the curve of the girl's throat perfectly, resting just above the wide crescent of her necklace, and this close to her Purna smelled stale tuba‾q, wet dog, and a pinch of sulfur. The witch swallowed, and Purna relaxed the blade just in time to not nick her as the bulge of the egg finally cleared her esophagus. Then, in an intense voice, the girl said:

'Vomit up vipers.'

Not a bad cuss, all things considered, but certainly not one that would enter Purna's rotation – too disgusting an image.

'Do it on your own time, missy,' said Purna, realizing with a shiver that by standing on her toes and pressing this close to the witch she could see down the front of the girl's lacy dress to the bulge of her breasts. Damn but it had been too long and too lonely a dry spell, when even the egg-sucking sorceresses started looking good.

'Hmmm?' The girl sounded sleepy, her warm body relaxing back into Purna's arms, which certainly wasn't helping things. But then she went totally stiff, sucking in air through her teeth and, sounding far more alert, said, 'Whoever you are, we can work something out.'

'Whoever *I* am?' said Purna. 'And here I thought we were such fast friends. But now that you mention it, whoever are you? Let's get a name to go with that pretty face, and then you can tell me allllll about your interest in Hoartrap, horned wolves, and anything else I might ask.'

'I am Nemi of the Bitter Sighs,' said the girl, 'and I seek to stop Hoartrap from destroying our world.'

'A noble quest,' said Purna. 'But what makes you think he's out to do that?'

'I thought you said you'd met him,' said Nemi. 'Does it sound so far-fetched?'

'Well, no, not entirely,' Purna admitted. 'But the last time I saw him he was working with our friends to save the Star from the Burnished Chain. Whatever else Hoartrap is up to, I don't see him buddying up with the church. Lucky for us, or they'd probably have raised Jex Toth a long time ago.'

The girl tensed up even more. 'What do you know of the Sunken Kingdom?'

'Plenty,' said Purna, which was a bit of a fib but so what? 'I'm Ugrakari so I've got the ancient blood of Jex Toth in me. More recently, though, I hear it's not so sunk, courtesy of a Chainite ritual that killed a bunch of my friends and opened up a brand-new Gate.'

'No,' said Nemi, as though Purna hadn't been there to see it all go down herself. 'Hoartrap brought back the Sunken Kingdom with his deviltry. I don't know why, or how, but it scarcely matters, for the result is the same. He must be serving some power of the First Dark, conspiring to sell our world for his own ends.'

'Hmmm,' said Purna, thinking it over. 'I'm hardly Hoartrap's biggest fangirl, but I think you're fingering the wrong guy this time. I was there when the Chain did their ritual – it made all the Crimson soldiers go blood simple, and then poof, Gate underneath their feet. We captured the enemy colonel, and the word that trickled back to me is he confirmed everything I already told you: the Chain carried out some stupid-ass ceremony, his regiment was a sacrifice big enough to bring back the Sunken Kingdom, blah blah blah. When it all went down Hoartrap was clear up the side of the mountain intercepting an Imperial ambush, but Chainwitches were all over that battlefield – I almost bought the yak shack from one of their war monks.'

'The Burnished Chain ...' Now Nemi sounded just plain confused, and Purna couldn't blame her – it was a lot to live through, let alone accept secondhand. 'But why would they seek to bring back the Sunken Kingdom?'

'Something something crazy prophecy?' Purna's arm was sooooo tired of holding her knife and her calves were aching from staying up on her toes, but she wasn't convinced letting the taller girl go was such a brilliant plan. 'Say, I know someone who can shed some light on this – Digs, what are you waiting for, a monogrammed invitation? Shake it but don't break it.'

A barren yew thicket ahead of them rattled, but instead of Digs that damn overgrown horned wolf came barreling out into the clearing in front of the rowan tree. It dragged something big and gross in its mouth, but as soon as it caught sight of its mistress being held at knife's edge it dropped its meaty prize with a growl. Its hackles flew up as it slowly stalked toward them through the moonlight-striped forest.

'Here's where you tell your pet to cool it,' said Purna. 'My hand gets shaky when I'm nervous.'

'Well, I have a hard time sounding authoritative with something sharp against my windpipe,' replied Nemi.

'Uhhhhhh,' groaned the yellow-wrapped meatsack the horned wolf had deposited on the ground. 'Nemmmmmi.'

'Oh *sugar*,' said the witch, trying to take a step back and grinding into Purna instead. She had a rump on her, this girl, but Purna stayed strong, not letting the power of the bottom distract her. Much, anyway. 'Hark, stranger: you don't know me and I don't know you, but surely we can agree whatever role he played in calling back Jex Toth, the Star will be a safer, saner place without Hoartrap the Touch. If you met the devil-eater but once you'd know that's true.'

'Hoartrap?' Tearing her eyes away from the approaching horned wolf, Purna did think the large, ugly shape it had deposited in the shadows looked familiar. A little louder now, she called, 'Hoartrap, you old so-and-so, is that really you? What the deuce are you doing here?'

'Nemi *Ilstrix*.' He sounded hoarse but a lot more awake now, and his bulk shuddered as he rolled onto his side.

'Ill's tricks?' Purna asked her captive as the witch flinched with a hiss. 'What's that mean? Some kind of incantation?'

'My old name,' growled Nemi, and the horned wolf made a similar sound, the creature getting perilously close for Purna's comfort. 'The one he gave me when I became his apprentice.'

'Well, listen, Nemi Ilstrix of the Bitter Biscuits, you better tell your mutt—' Purna began, but the witch interrupted her, as though she were the one holding a blade to Purna's throat.

'No, *you* listen, and listen carefully, stranger, for we are all on the cusp of ruin,' said Nemi, sounding about as rattled as Purna had felt when the girl had first threatened her with the big beast. She sympathized a little, but not a lot. 'Whatever you were planning to do with me is now irrelevant. If I am harmed my familiar will tear you all apart, and if Hoartrap is allowed to further recover he will most certainly harm me. It is as simple as that – if you let him live, we all die; me first, then you. Understand?'

'Now I *know* I saw you admiring my mantle back when we first met,' said Purna, repaying the girl's fronting with some of her own – not only was this beastie way bigger than any of the specimens they'd seen back in the Kutumbans, but her knife was all she had to work with, since her pistol was clogged with swamp slime and her black powder had turned into black mud. Still, what people didn't know and all that . . . 'I eat horned wolves for breakfast, and that's without Hoartrap's help. You're going to have to do better than threatening me with the same monster twice, and you better hurry, because I think he's about to sit up. Murdering Hoartrap's off the table, so let's get creative.'

Nemi shivered against Purna, as if she were the one with a queen-sized horned wolf impatiently watching her. It was blocking Hoartrap entirely now, so they couldn't see what progress the injured Touch was making with his supposed recovery.

'Make him swear,' said Nemi suddenly. 'Make him swear on every devil he ever ate to do no harm to Nemi of the Bitter Sighs or her familiars, from this day to his last. Do that, and we'll all be safe.'

'From him, maybe,' said Purna, marveling at how much stock some people put in an oath. 'But what about from you? What's to stop you from siccing your sidekick on us as soon as Hoartrap's promised to play nice?'

'I swear on every egg I ever ate and every devil I ever loosed not to harm you or your friends, not even Hoartrap the Touch, so long as you first make Hoartrap swear the same for me and mine,' said Nemi, sounding relieved even though nobody had sworn boo yet.

'Hey Hoartrap!' Purna shouted. 'You up yet?'

'Nemi . . . did . . . this,' his voice rasped from behind the wall of white fur and tense muscle, and the witch fairly melted into Purna's chest to put even another inch between her and her nemesis. 'Vengeance.'

'Nuts to vengeance,' called Purna. 'Swear on all the devils you ever noshed not to harm Nemi of the Bitter Sighs or her chums or pets or whatever, from this day to forever.'

The throaty chuckle did not bode well for negotiations, and Purna was stumped, when Nemi piped up with surprising clarity.

'Hoartrap! I'm counting to three, and if you haven't given your oath Myrkur is going to eat you alive!' That did not provoke a chuckle or anything else from the far side of the horned wolf, and the witch must have been in an awful hurry to get dead, because in a breathless rush she cried, 'One two three!'

And as if it had understood everything its mistress had promised, the great horned wolf slowly turned back around, swishing its bushy tail at Purna as it faced the Touch. Now that the beast was no longer directly in the way, she saw he hadn't even made it onto his elbows. Maybe this witch wasn't so crazy after all, forcing the issue the way she had, maybe everything was going to be okay, maybe Hoartrap would swear the damn oath and—

'To borrow a turn of the tongue from my dear friend Purna – nuts to your oath,' said Hoartrap, jerking abruptly and unnaturally to his feet, like a marionette at the hands of an overzealous puppeteer. Purna scarcely recognized him as he took a swaying step forward and the moonlight caught his face, his features contorted by massive pulsing tumors that wept luminescent slime. 'I am literally going to turn you inside

out, Nemi, and I am going to keep you awake the whole ...
bloody ... time.'

Nobody had anything clever to say to that, which was fine
because there wasn't time for quips, anyway, as the enormous
horned wolf lunged forward to carry out the will of her mistress.
Purna didn't want to watch but it all happened so quickly she
couldn't avert her eyes fast enough. It was too bad for Hoartrap
but he'd brought it on himself, so—

As the horned wolf bit Hoartrap there was a flash of white
light so brilliant it probably would've fried Purna's eyes, if the
bulky monster hadn't shielded her and Nemi from the worst of
it. Even still, she was blind for a moment, pressing the blade flat
against Nemi's throat lest the witch get any smart ideas about
squirming away. As Purna blinked away tears the moonlit forest
slowly came back into focus, but even as it did will-o'-the-wisps
danced through her vision, strobing orbs that gave off pulses of
light as they bobbed through the trees ... and only when one
hovered over the prone mountain of fur at Hoartrap's feet and
reflected off its gnarled horns and the wetness covering its face
did Purna realize the bright, blinking specters were really there
and not a residual trick of her eyes.

'Wooooo!' Deformed and leaking as his face was, Hoartrap
was obviously smiling as he rocked back and forth, flickering
in the inconstant light of the strange bubbles as he vigorously
shook out his right hand. Black smoke rose from his wiggling
fingers. '*That's* why they call me the Touch! And *that's* why you
don't *flex* with the Touch!'

'Myrkur!' Nemi screamed, sounding less like a sinister witch
and more like a frantic girl. She would have slit her own throat
on the kukri as she tried to go to her fallen familiar if Purna
hadn't already flipped her knife up so that only the flat of the
blade rested against Nemi's neck.

'Calm down, calm down,' said Purna, and Nemi stopped struggling, even though Purna had really just been saying it to herself. In the sputtering glow of the fox fire she could now see what he'd done to the horned wolf, even if she didn't understand it, and even though she immediately wished she hadn't seen it at all.

The animal was still alive, and made several faltering attempts to rise and turn to its distraught mistress. When that proved too much it fell back on its side, weakly scratching at its muzzle and issuing muffled whines. Its snout and most of its face were enveloped in an undulating, luminescent blob, and as Purna stared the radiant, tarry substance crept farther up its neck, toward its ears and bulging eyes. The horned wolf tried to howl, but couldn't open its jaws more than an inch before the pressure of the coating forced its mouth shut, a bubble forming at the end of its snout only to impotently be reabsorbed into the pulsing substance instead of popping. It was already one of the worst things Purna had ever seen, but then small black bulbs began to open all over the spreading ichor, and from the way they shifted about in their recessed settings she realized they were *eyes*. Whatever Hoartrap had touched the poor horned wolf with, it was alive, and watching them.

'If I can't stop him, kill me,' Nemi whispered, her plaintive whine finally diverting Purna from the grotesque sight. 'Let me go, let me stop him, or if I can't kill me, kill us both, please, but don't let him ... don't let him ... I beg you ... don't ...'

'Oh, tosh,' said Hoartrap, holding up his smoking hand and blowing on it as he grinned at them through his tumid boils. 'Purna and I are thick as thieves, Nemi, and we owe each other our lives, so I wouldn't count on her doing anything I might find annoying. You have only yourself to blame, so don't go trying to make Purna feel bad for doing what needs to be done.'

'Hoartrap ...' Purna managed through a dry mouth and chattering teeth, the burning oil stench of whatever it was he'd put on the horned wolf somehow chilling her marrow even more than the sight of it. Whoever this Nemi was and whatever she'd done, Purna really, really wanted this night to be over, and now, without any more of ... *that*. 'That's enough, Hoartrap. You made your point. And this is all a misunderstanding. Nemi thought ... she thought you were the one who raised Jex Toth, is all, and since you didn't that means we're on the same side, so just, you know, stand down and—'

'I will *not*!' Hoartrap bellowed, and as he did a growth that covered nearly half his face erupted, thick, steaming juice running down his bloated chin. 'I am no bound devil, to be ordered about, to be kept in my place! I! Am! The Touch!'

'Okay,' gulped Purna, seeing she'd taken the wrong approach. 'But I'm not ordering, Hoartrap, I'm asking you, as an old chum, like you said, an old chum who saved your life, just cut this kid some slack and—'

'Tapai Purna, in deference to the debt I owe you I shall magnanimously overlook your pathetic demands, your threatening posture, but only if you walk away right fucking now,' growled Hoartrap, and it took Purna a moment to realize what he even meant by threatening posture until she saw her kukri shaking at the end of her arm; without even realizing it she had stopped holding it against Nemi's throat and pointed it over the girl's shoulder, straight out at Hoartrap. No doubt it was just a subconscious ward to keep the incensed warlock from coming any closer ...

But closer he came, and as he took a step his right leg gave a nauseating snap, and through the shredded bottom of his robe Purna saw a jagged piece of shinbone protruding from the huge bite wound. Purna didn't know which was scarier, seeing him walk steadily toward her despite how impossible that should be with a messily broken leg, or the fact that in his rage he didn't even seem to notice.

'I am fucking *done*,' said Hoartrap, eyes bugging out of his disgusting puffed-up face as he strode toward Nemi and Purna, and while he was staring them down he seemed to be half talking to himself. 'Threatened by devil dogs, dragged about by giants, dragged about *and* threatened by *giant devil dogs* – enough, I say, enough. It's time to remind the Star who I am, what I can do ... and anyone who stands in my way feels the full wrath of the Touch.'

Well, that was it then, and too bad for Nemi of the Bitter Sighs – no fucking way Purna was dying or worse on account of some witch who had seemed all set to let her horned wolf eat a pair of well-dressed strangers who just happened to be in the wrong place at the wrong time. But as Purna was about to lower her blade and give the witch a good bump forward so she could at least have a chance to use her sorcery to fight or flee, she realized the girl was hyperventilating, near catatonic with terror. Understandable, all things considered ... Purna was close to pissing herself, and she wasn't the one who'd made Hoartrap so mad.

'Last chance to walk away, Purna,' said Hoartrap, only a few unhurried paces off. 'As of right now I'm considering the debt I owed you paid in full – if anyone else kept bossing me about and pointing their pig-sticker at me even after I'd made myself so clear I would have detonated every organ in their body. So you saved my life with the devil queen, and now I've saved yours from something far worse – me. And now that we're evensies, I can and will do unspeakably bad things to you, if you persist in this ... this insolence!'

Hoartrap was almost close enough to touch Nemi, now, and

in the flashes of floating light Purna saw that whatever had happened to his face was fading, albeit in repulsive fashion – where the big tumor had burst his ruptured skin was melting back together, restoring what passed for normal to the grotesque warlock's features. Who could stand against a monster like the Touch? Purna slowly lowered her kukri and her eyes, finally relaxing back on her heels, sheathing her blade and putting her hands on her hips with a long, sad sigh. So this was really happening, huh?

Now that she'd backed down, even if she hadn't yet backed up, Hoartrap turned his gaze to the shivering girl cowering against Purna. He stepped right up to Nemi, seeming to ignore Purna even as he continued to address her. 'Smart woman. Now you can stay and see what happens to those who cross me or you can piss right the fuck off, I don't rightly care. Little Nemi Ilstrix here is going to learn her last lesson, and what's more, before the end I'm going to make her watch what I do to her devil. I've never eaten one that big before, so we may be here all night, but oh, what a feast! I expect I'll be potent enough to – now *that*, that right there is a mistake, Purna. Don't let it be the last one you ever make.'

'That's a good line. In fact, I like it so much I might just have to bounce it back on you, right about nowish,' said Purna, the pistol she'd whipped up and pointed at Hoartrap's big fat mouth steadier than her knife had been. She cocked the hammer for effect, wondering if his eyes were keen enough to see the dried mud caking the barrel, marveling at her own insane impulse . . . but if this was how she went out, protecting a vulnerable stranger from whatever awful fate this monster had in store, well, Maroto would be proud. And not just because the stranger was cute, though he would've surely noticed that, too.

'You've had your say and you've made your point, so now

it's my turn,' said Purna. 'However much this witch kitten scratched you, I'm guessing you're going to recover, yes? And I know you're mad, and you've got every right to be, but think about it, man, what do you get out of killing somebody who's at your mercy, who offered you a truce even before you got the upper hand? That's some Chainite shit right there, dark as dark gets – you of all people know the church preaches that mercy's a sin, and so is humility and understanding your enemy and everything else I'm asking you to do, and if the Chain's against it it's got to be okay, right?'

As she talked, Hoartrap's greasy grin grew wider and wider, which was never a good sign, and so she rushed to find whatever secret words he needed to hear that let everyone walk away from this, even as she doubted such an incantation even existed . . .

'Look, just . . . look! Look! Both you and Nemi here seem *real* fucking sore on Jex Toth coming back, so you've got that much in common, maybe we can all work together? I'm beseeching you here, Hoartrap, and you know I ain't the beseeching type – give her another chance, see if she can atone for whatever she did to you. I mean, if I can believe a nasty old creep like you can do some good in this world, Hoartrap, then I can damn sure believe anyone can, even random wolf-girls I meet in haunted forests. And since we're all taking on the Burnished Chain and whatever forces they've summoned, maybe having a second sorcerer in our pocket is a better move than not having any?'

Purna gulped, out of words and not too convinced she'd found the right ones, but hoping, hoping . . . and then Hoartrap said, 'You have no head for figures, Purna m'dear – come what may of Nemi here, I'm not going anywhere, so there will be always one witch, at least, fighting the good fight.'

'No sir, my maths were solid the first time . . . because if you touch her I touch you back, and that's an oath, Hoartrap. I swear it on all the devils I never hope to eat or even meet,' said Purna, wondering if heroes always felt like throwing up when they were being all brave and shit or if it was just her. 'So . . . be a chum, Hoartrap, and make that pledge she pitched you? You know the one, not to harm her or her friends, and while we're at it why don't you swear a fresh one not to harm me or mine, now that I know how fickle your friendship can be.'

Hoartrap narrowed his eyes, and seemed to actually be considering it, and from the way Nemi sharply took in a breath and held it Purna supposed the witch might have pulled herself together enough to take stock of what was happening. Then Hoartrap gave a heavy sigh, raising his palms in a peaceful gesture, and said, 'Oh, you're Maroto's successor, no doubt about that. And I admire your spunk, I do . . . but I'm afraid your bluff is officially called. We both know that thing isn't loaded.'

And simple as that, everything fell apart as Hoartrap placed one of his enormous thumbs over the barrel of her pistol.

'I truly am sorry, Purna,' said Hoartrap, and actually sounded like he meant it a little. 'I *had* hoped we could stay friends. That's what I get for hoping, eh? Now, I'd understand if you wanted to close your eyes now, but this isn't the sort of thing even devils usually get the chance to see, so I'd strongly advise you watch, however painful an experience it – naughty naughty!'

Standing behind the taller girl, Purna couldn't see what exactly Nemi had been surreptitiously reaching for, but Hoartrap had, seizing her by the wrist in one hand and ripping something off her belt with the other. Everything went dark as all the pulsing will-o'-the-wisps blinked out in tandem, and when they flashed back on Purna saw a small pouch floating in the air between

Hoartrap and Nemi. As she watched, a small grey egg rose up out of the open mouth of the pouch, hovering right in front of Hoartrap's inquisitive eyes. He now held both of Nemi's squirming wrists in one enormous hand, scratching his wet chin with the other as the empty pouch fell out of the air and he continued to ponder the floating egg.

'Interesting,' he said to himself, making a gesture with his free hand that made the hovering oval slowly begin rotating in place.

Purna took advantage of the distraction to casually reach for her kukri with her off hand even as she made a show of holstering her flintlock. As she did, though, something hard barked the front of her shin, and in another flash of fox fire she saw it was the heel of Nemi's boot kicking back to get Purna's attention. The witch had stopped struggling against Hoartrap's grasp and craned her neck around as far as she could, and was mouthing something Purna couldn't make out before another pause in the flashing witchlights made the scene vanish ... but when it blinked back into focus she thought she had it sussed, especially when the witch's wide eyes flicked from Purna toward the hovering egg. Nemi was mouthing the words *crush it*.

'Oh!' said Hoartrap, just as the light failed again. 'Fuck!'

Purna took advantage of the darkness to make her move, her right hand snatching for where she knew the egg was floating while her left drew her kukri. Crush the egg, slash the wrist that held the witch, see if she could level the odds, and – oh fuck.

As the fox fire lit the scene back up Purna saw just how screwed she was; her extended fingertips were about to reach the hanging egg when Hoartrap nodded his chin to the side and the drab oval shot away into the sky, gone just like that. And focused as she'd been on remembering where exactly the egg was at when the light went out, her knife hand was coming down all wrong, poised to hack into Nemi's forearm instead of Hoartrap's wrist. She let go of the kukri just in time, the heavy horn handle bouncing off one of Nemi's pinned arms as the knife flew away, and while that probably hurt something bad it was a lot better than it had almost been.

Then it went dark again, and something decapitated Purna with a single stroke, her head flying off her shoulders.

Except no, her head was still attached, but she only realized this when another pulse of the synchronized fox fire lit up the night. Hoartrap had grabbed her by the throat and held her so tightly she'd instantly gone numb from the neck down, and the feeling of weightlessness came from his holding her several feet off the ground. Raising Purna even higher with his right arm and still holding Nemi captive in his left, the obscenely satisfied sorcerer was about to say something – and Purna was about to try to kick him in the armpit – when the entire clearing at the foot of the rowan was bathed in red light.

Purna couldn't help but look to the heavens, just as she heard the blast and felt the hot wind sweep down over them. At first it looked like the Immaculate fireworks Duchess Din was so fond of setting off at her garden parties, a scarlet bloom Purna glimpsed low in the sky to the west, through the screen of branches. Then it looked nothing like a pretty firework; instead of fading into the night the glowing red smear spread writhing tendrils up into the sky like a devil-fish composed of liquid fire, until it finally dropped to the earth. Instead of burning out the mass disintegrated as it fell, geysers of flame jetting up into the air from wherever its pieces had landed.

Extraordinary a sight as it surely was, Purna had more important things to focus on, like the giant freak choking her to death.

'Oh ho, you almost got me with that one!' said Hoartrap, letting go of Nemi's wrists and snatching her by the throat, too. 'I'm trying to think of a good egg joke to lay on you, but considering the circumstances that almost seems . . . overeasy.'

Purna would have groaned if he hadn't made that as impossible as breathing, and settled for kicking Hoartrap in the ribs, digging her nails into his too-soft wrist, begging the Old Watchers and the Living Saint and anyone else who would listen to cut her some fucking slack here. Prayer went as well as it usually did, and since she knew that in a few moments she wouldn't be seeing anything ever again, Purna kept her eyes open to the very end . . . tempting though it was to close them against the will-o'-the-wisps so that her last sight wouldn't be the strobe-lit Hoartrap the Touch gloating over her murder, the bastard-ass jerk not even deigning to finish her off with witchcraft instead of his meathooks.

But as the lights winked out again Purna felt his hand relax, and she was able to breathe as her wildly kicking feet brushed the ground. He still held her firmly by the neck but she was able to stand, albeit wobbly-legged, and gasp as he let her catch her breath. She hated herself for doing it, figuring she was playing right into his sick games, but she couldn't help herself . . . and then the flash of the fox fire revealed he had set Purna and Nemi back on the ground for less sadistic reasons than to prolong their suffering. Hoartrap seemed to have almost forgotten about his captives entirely, his full attention on the sparkling blade that had appeared at the side of his throat, the weapon's facets catching the light from the will-o'-the-wisps and refracting it outward in sprays of pink and purple.

'Well, Hoartrap old fruit, here's a question for you,' said Diggelby, the tip of his crystalline saber jabbed so firmly against the warlock's thick neck that a bead of blood had formed around the tip. 'Purna's pistol wasn't loaded and that egg may have been off, but what's your professional opinion on this sword of mine, hmmm? I think it's in shipshape Geminidean fashion, myself, but I suppose there's only one way to find out how sharp a blade really is . . . '

Hoartrap looked appropriately gobsmacked, and opened his mouth to speak when Digs leaned forward in his perfect post, and the initial drop of blood where the end of the sword pressed into the Touch's neck was lost in a minute trickle. Hoartrap closed his mouth, and with his puffy face almost returned to normal there was no mistaking the fury he felt at being out-fenced by Pasha fucking Diggelby.

'That's what happens . . . when you flex with the Moochers,' Purna rasped as she pried Hoartrap's now-limp hand off her throat, and saw Nemi similarly extracting herself from the grip of the simmering warlock. 'I think the point Digs is trying to make . . . is that the next words out of your mouth . . . had better be that fucking oath . . . or they'll be the last ones you ever say.'

And as if this situation wasn't dicey enough already Nemi chose this moment to start contributing to the dialogue, but thankfully instead of talking more shit that might've further provoked Hoartrap she just said, 'And Myrkur, he has to take it off her, he has to save her. *Please*, Hoartrap, please, take it off.'

'He certainly does,' agreed Digs. '*That* is nonnegotiable, as is the rest. And as my wrist grows weary, Hoartrap, what say you? Keeping in mind if it's not that oath, with all due caveats, you are one dead Touch.'

Hoartrap smacked his lips, his eyes orbiting from Diggelby, to Purna, to Nemi, and finally settling back on Digs, the strobing glow of the witchlights making even these minor movements seem somehow both too fast and too slow. Purna wondered what Digs was going to do when Hoartrap forced his hand, what she was going to do, what any of them could do, now . . . And then, without any further hesitation, and keeping his gaze on Digs the whole time, Hoartrap swore the oath. Easy as that.

Even after it was said and done, Digs was evidently so surprised Hoartrap had actually done it that he almost skewered him anyway when the warlock began to take a cautious step backward. Giving Diggelby a withering glare, Hoartrap said, 'If you will *excuse* me, Pasha, I have an oath to fulfill? Regarding a certain mortal-eating monster you demanded I save?'

'Of course,' said Digs, no longer meeting Hoartrap's gaze as he struggled to sheathe his blade. His hand was quavering too violently for him to get it in right away, which made Purna all the more impressed that he'd held it together as long as he had. 'Wish it hadn't come to all this, you know, I . . . well, you didn't leave me much . . . choice?'

Hoartrap was already gone, though, limping away – he seemed to be feeling his broken leg, now, if far less than any other mortal would. He went to the prone, heaving form of the horned wolf, where the pulsating, eye-covered ichor had spread over the creature's entire head, emitting a cold grey light that throbbed in time with the fox fire. Then Nemi took a deep, shivering breath, and without sparing a word of thanks for her saviors stumbled over to the side of her animal, burying her face and arms in its furry flank. Hoartrap made a point of ignoring her as he rolled up the sleeves of his robe and knelt over the mess he'd made of the animal's face. Not wanting to see whatever came next, Purna turned to Diggelby . . . only to find him laid flat out on his back, staring up at the will-o'-the-wisps that rose through the branches of the rowan tree.

'Damn, Digs,' said Purna, sitting down beside him and patting his shoulder. He was soaked in a cold sweat, and gave a faint moan at her touch. 'Hey, you okay?'

'I ... I did it,' he gasped. 'I wanted to, I did, but I was so scared, Purna, I was so scared I couldn't move, I just stayed behind that log, and watched ... watched him ... back in Myura, you and Maroto were locked up in that closet, but Din and Hassan and I, we all saw what he did to those Imperial officers ... and I promised myself that night, I said, *Diggelby*, that is the one person – no, the one *thing* – the *one thing* in the Star you are never, *ever* going to cross. And I did, didn't I? And now he's going to get us, isn't he?'

'He swore an oath not to, Digs,' said Purna, starting to get the shaky legs herself now, too. 'He can't ever get us, not now. Because you saved us. Because when the real shit happened? Diggelby jack move. You saw I was in trouble, and you swept in to the rescue.'

'I ... I'm sorry,' said Diggelby, closing his eyes before saying the rest. 'It was you, of course it was you ... but? But it was also that ... that poor dog!'

Dog? What dog? There was only ... Diggelby gave a wet whimper, covering his face with a gloved hand, and Purna smiled sadly, giving her friend a squeeze on the knee, even as she shook her head. 'One woman's wolf is another witch's pup, huh? And you saved it, too, Digs.'

She hoped that last was true, though she couldn't imagine even a monster of the horned wolf's stature surviving whatever it was Hoartrap had done to it, even if the living ooze had only been suffocating it and nothing worse ... Yeesh. No thanks.

Purna lay back in the cool dirt beside Digs, the rowan branches spread out above them to net the crescent moon. Odd to find one of these distinctive trees growing in the lowlands, she'd thought they only sprouted in the high country. She and Digs watched the fox fire floating through the black latticework above them, the bulbs of light winking as they wove through the boughs like gigantic lightning bugs. And one by one the will-o'-the-wisps began to go out entirely, some brushing into the branches and popping like bubbles and others just fading away, but before the last orb went dark and left them in the soft moonlight it illuminated one of the tree's star-shaped blossoms, blossoms that should only bloom in the late spring instead of winter, however unusually warm it may be . . .

And seeing that flower reminded Purna of how when she was a child who would climb trees from dawn to dusk, her aunt and uncle had taught her that she must be respectful when scaling a rowan, and never use a knife to cut or carve its branches. They claimed there was magic in these trees, and that the older generations had called them Gate-ash because their every blossom and their every berry contained a tiny star, proof that they had their roots in the First Dark yet spread their limbs toward the heavens, as all mortal things must.

Purna remembered how few shits she had given about any of that mumbo-jumbo, how bad a niece she must have been for her aunt and uncle, always raising hell, stealing and getting into fights. Tasting that familiar tea back in the Procuress's shop – before things had gotten all super intense and scary – had reminded Purna that for as hard as she had convinced herself she was miserable and deserved better than what her family could give her, she had left behind many happy memories as well as sad ones. They had tried so hard to understand their wild niece, and she had pushed them away . . . but just as she was feeling all nostalgic (and guilty all over again for running off with their rugs), she remembered they had apparently put a hit out on her, so there was no call getting all misty on their account. Messed up a person as she was, she'd done them a favor by not only running away but also doing it in such a way that they would never miss her, if they had any sense at all. Instead of putting a price on her head they should have chalked it up as a loss and thanked her for her consideration, but expecting a word of thanks from anyone in this cold, cold world was like looking for light in the First Dark.

'Thank you both,' said a voice that sounded a lot more confident than it had a little earlier, but not so cocky as it had the first time they'd heard it. It was a nice balance, and Purna and Digs both sat up to once more face Nemi of the Bitter Sighs in the pure moonlight of the Haunted Forest. The witch leaned on her walking stick, looking even more run-down than Purna felt. 'Myrkur will recover, or so the Touch claims. We owe you our lives.'

'Well, you owe us a song, at least,' said Digs. 'And . . . and maybe I could pet your wolf, once it's better?'

'Certainly,' said Nemi, rubbing the dark marks just above her heavy necklace that probably matched the ones on Purna's throat. 'I never thought to meet folk who would risk their lives to help a sorcerer and a horned wolf, so I am sure your song is just as—'

'Shitty shitty fuck fuck!' Purna scrambled to her feet, unable to believe what a jerk she was – granted, she'd had an epic distraction, but that was no excuse to plop down on her duff and think back about old times when her friends were still missing, and presumably in trouble. 'Songs soon, Nemi, most definitely, but they'll have to wait until we've found Sullen.'

'What's a Sullen?' asked Nemi. Then they heard Hoartrap give a hoot of surprise, and a silhouette broke from the shadowy yews on the far side into the moonlit clearing, the bloodied man staggering forward with a spear held limply in one hand . . . and then he wobbled, and fell face-first in the dead leaves.

'That's a Sullen,' said Digs. 'Or what's left of one.'

'Oh sugar,' said Nemi, standing a little straighter and staring off into the darkness. 'I fear I've misplaced one of those, too.'

CHAPTER

27

Sullen was the sort of lad who'd had some dreams in his day, both awake and asleep, but if he lived another fifty years he'd never have one as long and terrible as this. Ancestors attacking him in a lake that wasn't really a lake, kissing Keun-ju and being rumbled by his mom, then saved by Hoartrap, everyone dying, snakes turning into mud and a horned wolf stealing his heart, and finally wandering through a moonlit forest with Grandfather.

That part wasn't so bad, actually – though not as exciting as the Keun-ju bits – and he wished he could remember more of it. The old man's legs were working again, but at the expense of his tongue. You'd think a silent Fa would be no Fa at all, but it was almost perfect, the two of them together again, not having to say a word after all they'd been through together. He didn't want to wake up, because as the Bright Watcher lifted the cobalt curtain of the night Grandfather began to come apart in wisps of saam smoke, until all that was left was the old man's hand in his, lending his grandson strength even at the cost of his own.

And then Sullen woke up. And everything hurt. He'd heard people say that before, after a tumble, but those people had no idea what they were talking about. This was unbelievably bad, one ache and cut after another piping in as he blinked in the sharp sunlight, a shadow looming over him like Old Black come to take him home. A hand shaded his eyes for him, and he saw Keun-ju sitting on the forest floor beside him. He had a veil firmly in place again but was otherwise as exposed as Sullen had ever seen him outside of the Thaoan bathhouse, the boy as shy about going shirtless as Sullen was prone to strip down to just his skirt when it got a touch above freezing and the sun was out. Then Sullen saw why his coat was off, and tried to sit up only to have the world slip out from under him and send the back of his head cracking into the ground.

'I'm all right, I am,' Keun-ju said from somewhere far above in the swirling haze, and he actually sounded okay, despite how he looked. 'Well . . . no, I'm not, and I doubt I ever will be again. But I am alive, and so are you.'

When he could finally focus on Keun-ju again without having the earth twirl beneath him, he made himself look, though it hurt so much to see what he'd caused. It must hurt Keun-ju so very much worse, though, and the least Sullen could do was not shy away from his handiwork. If only he hadn't warned his mother out of the way when he'd thrown his sun-knife, she never would have had the chance to do this.

'This isn't your fault, Sullen,' said Keun-ju, sounding like he wanted to believe that every bit as much as Sullen did. 'Trust me, I'd rather live with one than be buried with both.'

Sullen's eyes filled with tears but he would not look away. A wound would have been one thing, even a grievous one, but the utter absence of Keun-ju's right arm filled Sullen with such sorrow he could not even speak. It was so . . . *wrong*. Keun-ju sat on the ground at Sullen's side, and from his waist all the way up to the top of the silk straps he used to smooth down the swell of his breasts he looked fine, he looked himself . . . and then his arm was just gone, with no bandages or anything, the naked shoulder abruptly terminating in a raw stump covered in a sickening yellow crust. Sullen must have revealed his dismay, because glancing down, Keun-ju shuddered, too.

'I know, it makes it seem even worse, doesn't it?' he said, sounding weirdly nonchalant about his missing fucking arm. 'But it's not infected or anything, that's all just some sort of mystical egg yolk. At first I thought Purna and Diggelby were pranking me again, but all I can smell is spoiled quiche, so they may be right. It's supposedly the specialty of the new witch they found.'

'Eh?' Apparently Sullen's dreams paled in comparison to what had happened after . . . after . . . he closed his eyes, feeling like he had the worst hangover of his life, one so bad he hadn't even experienced it before. It was coming back in painful bursts, and not knowing where else to start, he said, 'But this is real and you're alive, right? You're not dead?'

'I feel somewhere in between, at present, though Diggelby foraged some insects that have me upright, at least,' said Keun-ju, which explained why he sounded a little loopy. 'But I wouldn't have made it through the night without my dear friend going in search of aid, and the help of comrades both old and new.'

'What about everyone else? Are they . . . all right?'

'You took it worse than anyone,' said Keun-ju, as though Sullen was the one who'd *lost a fucking arm.* It was so hard to reconcile the tender concern of the handsome man with the smarmy snot who had insulted Sullen to his face right after the First Battle of the Lark's Tongue.

'Other than you, you mean,' said Sullen mournfully, wishing it had been his shoulder that had caught the blade.

'Well, yes, I meant other than me,' said Keun-ju, trying to smile, but Sullen saw that beyond whatever bugs he'd taken and however much the witchcraft had lessened his pain, the Immaculate was hurt so much more than he was letting on. Sullen vowed that no matter how much it pained him, he would get back on his feet and over his wounds with all due haste, so they could focus on Keun-ju and his loss. He just had to focus on sitting up without fainting first.

'I know you will find this hard to believe, but you don't look so great, either,' said Keun-ju. 'When you went to find help for me you very nearly bled to death, and you've been asleep for days. I thought ... they weren't sure if you would awake. But you have, and yes, everyone else is fine, except for poor Princess.'

'I remember that,' said Sullen, though he wished he didn't, the dying pony screaming in his aching skull. 'Everyone's fine?'

'Just about,' said Keun-ju. 'But I do have some good news and some bad news for you, what sort do you like to hear first?'

'Good news,' Sullen said firmly.

'So predictable,' said Keun-ju, but Sullen was warming to the Immaculate's teasing. 'The good news is Hoartrap and Nemi have established an uneasy alliance, and together they claim they can take us all to Maroto, no magic posts or compasses required.'

'That's good,' said Sullen, 'since we lost 'em both.'

'You lost the post, but I kept the compass,' said Keun-ju. 'I had it in my pocket when those swamp creatures attacked. That's how Hoartrap was able to reach us so swiftly – before giving it to Purna he imbued it with something that would let him locate wherever the compass was in all the Star. Good thing we didn't throw it away like somebody suggested.'

'Yeah, well, I bet he just wanted an easy way to find us, after the trouble he went through before, tracking down my uncle. So I was right about his having a shady reason for giving it to us.'

'It's nice when we're both right, isn't it?' said Keun-ju. 'And I don't doubt he has ulterior motives for bringing us to Maroto, either, but we don't have much choice – Ji-hyeon's in trouble, and the rest of the Star, too, of course, but if we can get to your uncle, we may be able to help our general win the war against Jex Toth. They ... the monsters of the Sunken Kingdom ...' Keun-ju looked like he couldn't make up his mind whether he wanted to be scared, sad, or angry. Maybe all three at once. 'They attacked the Immaculate Isles, and so Ji-hyeon led the Cobalt Company through the Lark's Tongue Gate, to Othean, to help defend our homeland from the invasion.'

'She ... she led the Company through a Gate? To a war with monsters?' Thinking of their fearless, wonderful Ji-hyeon in such peril made Sullen feel like he might throw up a nest of snakes himself. 'That's some serious bad news, Keun-ju.'

'Ah, that wasn't the bad news,' said Keun-ju. 'The good news was that Hoartrap and Nemi will help us find your uncle, remember? Hoartrap believes Maroto has already begun reconnaissance for the counterattack against Jex Toth, and if we find him we may discover a way to strike the enemy from within.'

'*What?*' Sullen closed his eyes again, because the world seemed poised to start spinning again. 'Never mind, we can go over it all later. So if that's all good news, somehow, then what the heck is the bad news?'

'It ... it's about your mom.'

'Oh.' Sullen braced himself, his hands tightening to fists. One of them was wrapped around something round and hard, and glancing down at his side he saw a vaguely familiar black spear gripped in his fist, the steel blade near his bare foot glittering like onyx.

'You really didn't want to let it go, so rather than risk breaking a finger to get it away from you I told them to let you risk nicking a toe,' said Keun-ju. 'I assumed if you did it might stir that thick head of yours.'

'My mom,' said Sullen, because intriguing as this mysterious new spear definitely looked there was something a lot more important going on. Nothing was more vital than family, either the ones you're stuck with or the ones you choose. He remembered the sound her body had made when Hoartrap had kicked her into that tree, and he knew, yes he did, but he still had to hear it. 'She's dead, isn't she?'

'Oh no,' said Keun-ju, placing his palm on Sullen's shoulder. 'She's alive. But I don't think she likes me very much.'

'That's okay,' said Sullen, finally letting go of the spear, flexing his aching fingers, and then reaching up to take Keun-ju's only remaining hand in his own. 'You're in good company there.'

'I hope I always am,' said Keun-ju. 'And once she meets Ji-hyeon she'll see that I'm not so bad after all.'

It hurt to laugh, but then it hurt even if he didn't, so laugh Sullen did, and only stopped when Keun-ju knelt down and softly kissed him. It didn't make the world stop spinning, but at least it let him enjoy the ride. Keun-ju squeezed Sullen's hand in his, and breaking off their sweet reprieve from their pain, sat back up. It looked harder than it probably used to be, Keun-ju's balance thrown off-kilter by more than just the bugs, and there was something about the look in the sweet man's eyes that made Sullen realize he was holding something else back, some deep, raw pain or fear or both that went beyond even the amputation of his arm. And because that was something else they had in common, Sullen thought he could guess what it was.

'I'm worried about Ji-hyeon, too,' said Sullen, feeling himself get choked up at the thought of her out there in the Isles, facing down whatever unspeakable army the Burnished Chain had called forth from Jex Toth. But there was something else tightening Sullen's throat, an old guilt for what all their lives might have looked like, if Ji-hyeon and Keun-ju hadn't been swept up in the Ballad of Sullen Sourluck – they would be together, at least, and Keun-ju wouldn't have lost his sword arm. 'And . . . and I should have said this before, Keun-ju . . . and I don't know where this will all end, but yeah: I obviously . . . Um.'

'Surely this fat-tongued fellow I see before me isn't the same singer who so beautifully sung me the Building of Old Black's Meadhall,' said Keun-ju, gently scratching Sullen's head.

'Okay, then,' said Sullen, Keun-ju's ribbing probably the only thing that could have ever forced the words to leave his lips. 'I feel . . . the way I feel about her, yeah, but I'm also feeling it for you, I guess? And I'm just *really* happy I got to know the both of you, but at the same time, well . . . I'm sorry I came between you and Ji-hyeon.'

'I feel the same for you, Sullen, and you haven't come between us,' said Keun-ju, making Sullen feel a lot better, even before he added, 'much as I think Ji-hyeon likes the idea, if you follow my meaning.'

He didn't, at first, but when he got it they both laughed again, bittersweetly, missing the woman they both loved so much more than words or songs could ever convey, but bound even tighter together by being able to share this saudade that only they could know.

'We're going to find her,' Sullen told Keun-ju. 'I swear by all my ancestors, even my ornery old Fa, we will find Ji-hyeon and we will go to her, no matter where she is in all the Star.'

Looking into Keun-ju's eyes, Sullen could tell they both believed it, too, with the confidence that only comes from desiring something truly beautiful ... even if it seems too perfect to be true.

CHAPTER
28

Worse than the drugs, worse than the rituals, worse, even, than Y'Homa's endless, breathless, teenage chattering was the Office of Answers. It wasn't that the tortures Indsorith endured in that austere chamber were any less bearable or more creative than what the Burnished Chain had already inflicted upon her. It was the realization that unlike the church's psychotic barbarism, this stage in her debasement was entirely her own doing. She knew about the Office, vaguely, had signed off on some advisor's paperwork creating a new department to investigate sedition in the capital, certainly, but she had never dreamed a place like this had been created in her name, and under her direct authority. Save for her, the spacious chamber was empty for the duration of her interrogation, but from the sheer volume of identical rusty gurneys and stained sinks set around the place she had a fair idea that more citizens of Diadem had been brought here than ever enjoyed her public baths, kitchens, or hostels. She had been so busy keeping the Crimson Empire from going over to the Chain or falling apart altogether that she had never realized her most enduring legacy was not the formation of the offices of Public Health, Grievance Resolution, or Tolerance, but a state-sanctioned torture chamber.

But what had she expected, really? Afterward, lying in the cold, dripping, stone cell in the depths of Castle Diadem's deepest dungeon, warmed only by a mummy's worth of soiled gauze, Indsorith suffered a greater pain than any of her enemies could inflict – she hadn't known what went on in the Office of Answers because she had been stupid, and she had been lazy, and here at the end of it all she hadn't been any better of a queen than Zosia before her.

Even now, even here – especially now, especially here – rare was the day when Indsorith didn't think about her predecessor, and how their lives had not only become linked but overlapped. Indsorith came to kill a monster, and found only a sad, overburdened failure, but one who still clung to her tattered pride, and still owned her obligations. Indsorith had never quite got over that particular enigma – why, when she had finally confronted Queen Zosia and told her exactly who she was, and why she sought vengeance, Zosia had not tried to make any excuses or argue that what had happened at Karilemin wasn't her fault . . . even though it wasn't. Indsorith only learned the truth when she became the Crimson Queen herself, and had unfettered access to a city block's worth of records. She had appointed an entire committee to help her confirm what the documents seemed to imply, and there it was, in plain ink on plain vellum: Queen Zosia had never done any of the things Indsorith had so hated her for.

What were supposed to be peaceful negotiations between the Crimson Queen and the noble family of Junius became an international incident when Lady Shels preemptively set the fields of their province ablaze and led her army out in open revolt against the Crown. And what the Crimson Queen had intended to be egalitarian farming communities where all citizens of the Crimson Empire were treated as equals became open-air prisons, and in the case of Karilemin, a brutal work camp. But according to the documentation, Zosia had never sanctioned such barbarism, and once rumor of it reached Diadem she personally traveled to Junius to shut down the farms and punish those who had so egregiously perverted her edicts to settle old scores or turn a profit.

That was what had haunted Indsorith for so long, the question of why Zosia hadn't just told any of that to the avenging teenager who demanded justice for Junius. Why not say *something*? The paper trail didn't leave any doubt; within a fortnight of when Indsorith escaped the prison farm and started her long march toward Diadem to assassinate the Crimson Queen, Zosia arrived at Karilemin and did what she could to right the wrongs committed in her name . . . they might have even passed on the road on their missions of bloody-handed judgment. So why not tell any of that to her accuser?

But now, at last, Indsorith understood. Zosia hadn't held her tongue because she assumed the murderous Juniusian girl wouldn't believe her anyway, but because she didn't believe it herself. Even though she had given no order or decree intended to cause the horrors she found when she liberated the farms, Zosia was too smart to believe that she didn't have a hand in it. It happened in the Empire, during her reign, and so she was accountable, to herself if no other – that was why she had agreed to duel Indsorith, that was why she had made no excuses before they fought, and that was why the only stakes Zosia would fight for were death or exile. Because no matter what justifications others could make for her, in the end it came down to her sitting on the Crimson Throne, wearing the Carnelian Crown, and knowing the magnitude of the crimes people had committed in her name, under her flag, carrying her seal.

If only Indsorith had solved this riddle years ago, she might have learned from Zosia's mistakes instead of repeating them. By trying to ameliorate relations and work together with the Burnished Chain she had only given them the strength to usurp her. By focusing so heavily of late on the church's vicious persecution of the weirdborn she had overlooked the exact equivalent that had grown like a tumor in her own house – how could she hope to stop the Chain from mutilating people when she had empowered officers of the Crown to do the exact same thing?

Once upon a time, a brave young lady had sought to cast down the tyrannical Crimson Queen ... but when she took the villain's crown and placed it on her own head, she became her. Over the blurry weeks of brutality since the Burnished Chain had carried out their coup, Indsorith had lost so many hours, so many days, time becoming a never-slowing flood of pain and degradation ... but even right this moment she could still clearly remember signing off on countless writs and forms that she barely glanced at, the memories as fresh as if she'd spent the morning doing nothing else, instead of what she'd actually been up to – shivering in the cold and the dark, waiting for her overtaxed body to grant her a reprieve she knew she didn't deserve.

This was the real reason why she had declined Y'Homa's invitation to join the fleet sailing for Jex Toth, though it had been immensely satisfying to look the little lunatic in the eye through the grimy bars of her cell and claim she preferred the comfort of her own gods to those of the Burnished Chain. The truth was that Indsorith had never believed in any gods at all, but she knew heresy would infuriate the girl-pope far more than outright denial. It would have been satisfying, to accompany Y'Homa to whatever devil-riddled hell she had mistaken for heaven and see the look on her face when she realized what Indsorith had known all along, that the Fallen Mother was nothing more than a devil with a complicated story, if she existed at all ... but when the time came, Indsorith knew she didn't deserve even a petty victory over the girl who had usurped her. She deserved nothing more than what she had now received, to be forgotten in an ancient crypt, dying not as a martyr, but a proud fool. Like her mother before her, Indsorith was effecting a passive form of suicide rather than capitulating to her conquerors.

Granted, if the similarities between her convictions and those that had led to the pathetic death of Lady Shels had occurred to her sooner, Indsorith would have begged Y'Homa to take her along, because she had governed her entire reign according to the principle that her mother had been utterly fucking delusional about what constituted responsible rule ... but it was too late for that now. Despite twenty years on the Crimson Throne, when Indsorith had found herself backed into a corner she made the exact sort of idiotic stand she had promised herself she would never take. Such were the revelations one found when cut off from food and light and anything to drink save the mouthfuls of salty water that pooled on the floor from the dripping stalactites. If only she could chalk up her failings to a hereditary deficiency, she might have been able to sleep better as she slowly starved to death, deprived of even the conviction of the rightness of her actions that a condemned Chainite would have possessed.

Yet there was hope in a godless life, for without the promise of a better world beyond this one, without the assurance that all wrongs would eventually be righted by a higher authority, mortals would strive to protect each other in this life, would seek to make a paradise of the Star instead of waiting patiently for a posthumous reward. It was one of her mother's few teachings that Indsorith had kept close to her heart throughout her reign, and one that she hewed closer to than Lady Shels, here at the end. Her mother had chosen to die as a symbol of resistance, after all, but Indsorith now realized the error in such a philosophy – a willing martyr has but one opportunity to send a message, hoping it is the right one, while a living woman can keep working to better the world no matter how many mistakes she might make along the way.

Indsorith had come to this epiphany too late to save herself, yes, but that was no less than she had earned – her dreams of escape, of revenge, were but more penance she paid for her absolute failure to do any better than the woman who had ruled before her, another tyrant deposed by another teenage idealist who thought she understood how the Star ought to turn. As she lay on the cold stone floor, lapping at a mineral-rich puddle, she had to ask herself if she was actually doing this out of an improbable hope that she might somehow survive and escape her prison, or if this was one final form of mortification, denying herself the quicker death of dehydration so that she might prolong her miserable, inevitable end.

Warm thoughts for a warm cell, the woman who had stood tall at the crown of Diadem now swallowed alive by the very castle, slowly dissolving in its belly to nourish the next phase in the Empire's life cycle.

A rat clicked its claws down the hall outside, and Indsorith went perfectly still, holding her breath. All her philosophical brooding was replaced by another single, shining hope, here in the place where countless hopes had blossomed, only to wither on the vine – if the rat thought she was dead, it might come into her cell to investigate, to see if she was good to eat, and if that happened, if she stayed so still it sniffed her crusty bandages, then she might be able to snatch it in her hand and squeeze the life out of it, and have something to eat.

This was what the Crimson Queen was reduced to, at the end of her reign: hoping that she could taste the warm blood of a rat in her lightless pit.

This must be how it felt to be a devil, desperately cocking your ear to the squirming, alien lives of mortals in hopes of a meal.

The tapping of its claws came closer, and stopped just outside the cell. It wasn't a rat, the sounds of its approach too loud, the panting of its breath too heavy. Before she could turn her imagination to what other creatures might stalk these dungeons, after Y'Homa had set all the other prisoners free before abandoning Diadem for a better world, her visitor informed her of its identity in no uncertain terms: it barked once, the echoes through the caves deafening after so long without any noise but the dripping of water and her own ragged breath. Indsorith thought she was long past fear, but the jarring sound so close to her head made her scramble back across the cell, crouching in a corner like the animal she had become.

Just as she was overcoming her base panic, taking the first hesitant movements toward the door, thinking a dog must be far more nourishing than a rat, if she could just entice it to stick its head between the bars so she could snap its neck, Indsorith's eyes began to burn. It took her time to realize the source, a faint glow coming down the passage, but her eyes refused to adjust, the torch burning brighter as it approached, tears flowing faster from her stinging face. At last a silhouette arrived beside the low shape that she was sure *hadn't* been a dog a moment ago, when the light first struck it ... shielding her face with her fingers, she saw a lone figure standing beside the dog, and she squinted harder, trying to make out something more than a black silhouette limned in fire.

'So this is what it takes to get an audience with the queen these days?' asked the woman, and Indsorith fell back on her ass, unable to believe. The torchlight fell full upon her bandaged feet now, and the woman's tone took a sudden turn. 'Fuck's sake, Chop, open the door!'

The lock Indsorith had blooded her fingertips futilely fiddling with clicked open, though there was no key, and pausing to slip the blinding torch into a sconce in the hall, the woman slowly entered the cell, cautious as a trapper approaching a snared wolf. Indsorith must have flinched, for the woman paused, and lowering herself slowly to her knees, she said in a whisper, 'Devils' mercy, Indsorith, what did they do to you?'

Indsorith couldn't answer, the shock paralyzing her tongue. It was her. She had come.

'I'm not here to hurt you,' she said, her silver hair coming into focus as Indsorith's eyes finally let her see, the scar on the woman's chin gleaming in the torchlight. 'Portolés found me in time, and . . . well, I got the message. I know you didn't send Efrain Hjortt after me. I know the Black Pope is to blame for what's happening. And I came here to bust you out, so we can go after her together. I'm here to save you, Indsorith.'

Indsorith knew her mother would have expected her to stand defiant before this last test of her conviction, but Lady Shels was long dead in a grave of her own making. Indsorith scooted forward on her scabbed knees, and Zosia matched each small movement, until they were face to face in the dark, two queens reunited in the bowels of the Empire they had both failed to save. Then Indsorith threw her weak arms around the neck of the woman who had burned her world, the woman who had as good as murdered her entire family, and she clung to this woman as she convulsed, so grateful she could do nothing but sob into Zosia's hair. Her hope had not been in vain.

———

Zosia had planned on gloating a little. She'd been looking forward to it, even; not something to be proud of, but then the truth cared nothing for pride. But when Choplicker led her down into the dark caverns of Castle Diadem's dungeons and she saw what the Burnished Chain had done to Indsorith, such ugly, petty thoughts vanished in an instant, and try as she did to offer soothing sounds and kind words, her mind boiled over with rage and hatred.

After what she'd seen after emerging from the Diadem Gate, she had expected absolute chaos in the castle, but while rioting mobs tore the city apart, the inner walls of the ancient volcano were as silent as a slow day on the Frozen Savannahs. Then again, the populace didn't have the benefit of a devil to unlock the complicated locks and gates that barred every entrance, but they would find their way inside soon enough. Compared to the hellscape of the streets, the slippery passage between the Gates had been a walk in Diadem Gardens. Before they were set on fire.

They hadn't gone three blocks from Gate Square before Boris and Zosia agreed that given the anarchic state of the city, any additional diversions might be superfluous, and she gave him leave to look for some friends of his instead of the original plan of fomenting a revolution. He'd tried to tell her something just before they parted, maybe something sincere, maybe something sardonic, or maybe just a time and place they should meet, after the Cobalts arrived, but a burning building down the block had toppled over as its supports gave out, and when the smoke and ash lifted enough for her to see again Sister Portolés's pet heretic was gone. Zosia would say her odds of meeting him again were long indeed, but she'd thought that the last time they'd gone their separate ways and she was too damn old to waste her time betting double-or-nothing.

Only when she slipped into the castle through the same door they'd used when Choplicker first cleared her way to King Kaldruut's throne room did the magnitude of Diadem's riot sink in. The whole palace was as empty as Emeritus, the silence spooking her worse than the tumult outside. After she rescued Indsorith from the dungeons she'd once braved to bust out Singh, Zosia spent half the night lugging the battered queen back up Diadem's endless stairways, finally collapsing beside the woman on her luxurious bed. Zosia was drenched in sweat, only some of it hers, and as Indsorith rolled and groaned in her fever, the former queen tried to reorient herself to the labyrinthine quarters. Choplicker helped, though Zosia knew him well enough to guess there was some self-interest to the attention he paid Indsorith – devils could only feed off the living, and if she died he would miss out on quite the feast.

After Zosia found and raided the kitchen, she ferried soft oranges, ghee, pots of water, and other supplies back to the queen's bedchamber. Indsorith was induced to swallow drams of buttery, watered-down juice, stinking rags were cut off her bruised body and tossed onto the fire, sick-looking wounds were cleaned out with a red-hot dagger as the queen squealed in her delirium, and then Zosia gave her a pungent absinthe sponge bath.

It took the rest of the night before Zosia was satisfied she had done all she could, and looking at the wan girl she rather doubted it would be enough. It was so unfair it made her teeth ache. Whatever else Indsorith had achieved during her long, rough reign, one simple thing proved she was a hundred times the queen Zosia had been: she hadn't given up, even when the odds seemed impossible, and kept fighting the malign influence of the Burnished Chain right up until the end. It should be Zosia lying on her deathbed, and this fierce, fearless woman standing over her.

Zosia wandered away from the bedchamber and through the obsidian halls, out onto the open terrace of the throne room. The gusting air cooled her clammy skin, but it was far too warm for the season. With the moon gone to the west and the stars lit overhead, Zosia was brought back to the mountainside above Kypck, where Pao Cowherd had died wrapped in Zosia's only bedroll. *My life for his*, she had thought then, but was too afraid to say it, lest Choplicker grant her wish.

'My life for hers.' She said it now, looking not at the impartial heavens but her impartial devil. In answer he started licking her hands, just as he had back then, though this time she'd had plenty of water to wash the blood away. As if she ever could. 'My life for hers, Chop, what do you say?'

He whined, a doleful sound, and she sighed.

'I hear you. Isn't much of an enticement, offering something I don't value myself, but it's all I got,' she said, and looking into his sharp dark eyes, she wondered if her desires were as inscrutable and strange to him as his were to her. She gave him another rub behind the ears, and wandered over to the fire glass throne she'd abandoned all those years before. There was a second, slightly smaller cathedra set beside it, and from the silver chains entwined in its onyx arms she could guess who had occupied it. No matter, there was only ever one throne for the Cobalt Queen and she collapsed into it, staring numbly back at the only entrance to the open throne room. In the morning she would rise, walk back through that doorway, and go pull the sheets up over Indsorith's slack mouth, her blind eyes, the battered crown she'd left on the queen's pillow.

For the hour or two that remained before the dawn and the arrival of Ji-hyeon's army, though, Zosia would sit right here in her old throne, watching the glow of Diadem's burning streets play over the lip of the precipice, and indulge a luxury she'd long denied herself: she'd hope for a better tomorrow than she surely deserved.

EPILOGUE

'I think this is a really bad idea, Cap'n,' Dong-won whispered in Bang's ear, but she shoved him gently back into the bright green underbrush.

'That's what you said about the mutiny that won us our ship, Bosun,' she reminded him.

'And what he said about that evasive maneuver into the Haunted Sea what wrecked her,' said Niki-hyun, forgetting whose pearl she was supposed to polish.

'And it's also what Maroto told us about lighting a signal fire on the beach, but without that Dong-won never would've found us again,' said Bang, crawling forward on her knees to get a better look at the alabaster ruins that sprawled across the valley.

'Maroto?' asked Niki-hyun.

'Yeah, knuckleheads, the *Mighty Maroto*. He said he was Useful and useful he'll damn sure prove – I'll bet my bottom barrel our tall, dark, and almost handsome captive is none other than the Villain of legend. He recognized Cobalt Zosia's pipe in nothing flat, and fits the songs down to his toes.'

'I don't remember any songs where Maroto Devilskinner had white hair,' said Niki-hyun.

'Those songs first made the rounds before you were born,'

said Bang. 'Our meal ticket got old, same as your whiny attitude.'

'Well, I don't remember Maroto being a total jackass in the songs, either,' said Dong-won, flicking a weird grey caterpillar off his wrist and into the succulent bushes. 'Meal ticket?'

'Why do you think I want to get him back so bad?' asked Bang, trying not to let herself remember how hot his bottom had felt under her palm, lest color creep up her cheeks and betray her ulterior motives. 'Every Arm on the Star's got a bounty on him, and the Empire will pay more than the rest combined. We get the squid with the golden beak back to Diadem we'll be up to our butts in doubloons, pieces of six, or whatever denomination most tickles your purse.'

Dong-won looked intrigued. Niki-hyun, less so: 'You sure you're not confusing an Imperial bounty with an impressive booty, Cap'n?'

'Sea gods damn it, I've told you a thousand times!' cried Bang, snatching off her handkerchief and snapping Niki-hyun in the nose with it. 'None of this!'

'Ow!'

'No booty jokes! None! We're pirates, not poseurs!'

'Sorry, Cap'n,' grumbled Niki-hyun, rubbing her face. 'They're just so easy, you know?'

'Easy pickings are overvalued. Would you eat a dead fish that washed ashore, or would you wait until you caught a live one?'

'Sorry, Cap'n.'

'Not as sorry as you're going to be if I hear that word again,' said Bang, and returned to the topic at hand. 'Now then, the sooner we're in the sooner we're out, as Dong-won's daddy puts it, so let's go.'

'Yeah, see, I don't know about that right there,' said Dong-won, pointing at the open fields of waving marsh grass and prickly ferns between their position on the treeline and the nearest heap of rubble. 'We have to cross all that open ground when you say they've got those squid-dragons on patrol, *then* we have to sneak through the ruins that looked about as big as Othean from back on the hill, and even assuming we do get that far without getting rumbled, we still have to find your boy and spring him from whatever clink they've got 'im locked in.'

'Assuming they haven't ate him already,' said Niki-hyun helpfully. 'Monsters do that, you know. Pretty much all the time.'

'Only one way to find out,' said Bang, getting up on her hands and knees to make a dash for it when the other two dragged her back down.

'No bounty's worth dying for, Cap'n!'

'No booty, either.'

Snap.

'Ow! Sorry, sorry!'

'Last warning, Niki,' said Bang, retying her bandana and looking around the too-quiet jungle to make sure her crew's racket hadn't attracted any inhuman sentries. 'Now look, you two, he's worth a fortune, for one thing, and he's crew, for another. We don't give up on crew.'

'Who's crew?' demanded Dong-won. 'You have to serve on the boat to be crew. You have to be initiated to be crew. He's not crew.'

'I may have, um, given him an impromptu initiation yesterday,' said Bang, squirming forward on her belly so they wouldn't see her seditious flush. 'And he definitely launched my dinghy, so I'd say that counts. He's crew.'

'Crew we're going to ransom to the Empire,' said Dong-won.

'I knew it came down to booty,' Niki-hyun muttered quietly, but not quite quietly enough for Bang to miss it. Forgetting where they were and what they were doing, she laid into the girl with a flurry of bandana snaps, Dong-won's attempt to interrupt earning him a few sharp cracks of his own. When Niki-hyun was finally crying auntie and swearing the word was forever stricken from her vocabulary, Bang rolled off her with a final snap for good measure. She bumped into Dong-won's boot, and was about to drag the idiot back to the ground when she realized he was still lying on his belly on the far side of Niki-hyun. Pursing her lips as she stared at the shiny black shell attached to the barbed leg and up to the rest of the spiny, midnight-carapaced humanoid, Bang came to the conclusion that she was good and screwed. And this was before the other hook-plated horrors emerged from the jungle around them, silent as sharks gliding through the Honeyed Deep.

As their captured crewmember would say, *woof.*

'Sorry for ever doubting you, Cap'n Bang,' Dong-won said as they were jerked to their feet by the grotesque, silent inhabitants of Jex Toth and shoved in the direction of the ruined city. 'I think you've hit on a foolproof way of finding out where they're keeping good old Useless.'

'All part of my cunning plan,' said Bang, although in point of fact it wasn't. Who knew, though, they might always put her in the same cell as Maroto, let her get in a few more good swings on his sweetness before they all met whatever gruesome end the monstrous army of Jex Toth paid to interlopers – stranger things had happened, and recently at that. It didn't do much good to daydream, true, but at trying times like these a woman had to focus on what she might win instead of what she'd already lost, and work like a bound devil to make her own good fortune.

Look out for

A WAR IN CRIMSON EMBERS

The Crimson Empire: Book Three

also by

Alex Marshall

Coming soon

extras

www.orbitbooks.net

about the author

Alex Marshall is a pseudonym for Jesse Bullington, acclaimed author of several novels in different genres including *The Sad Tale of the Brothers Grossbart* and *The Enterprise of Death*. He lives in Florida.

Find out more about Alex Marshall and other Orbit authors by registering for the free monthly newsletter at www.orbitbooks.net.

if you enjoyed

A BLADE OF BLACK STEEL

look out for

HOPE AND RED

by

Jon Skovron

*In a fracturing empire spread across savage seas,
two people find a common cause.*

*HOPE, the lone survivor of a village massacred
by the emperor's forces, is secretly trained as a warrior
and instrument of vengeance.*

*RED, an orphan adopted by a notorious matriarch
of the criminal underworld, learns to be
an expert thief and con artist.*

Together they will take down an empire.

1

Captain Sin Toa had been a trader on these seas for many years, and he'd seen something like this before. But that didn't make it any easier.

The village of Bleak Hope was a small community in the cold Southern islands at the edge of the empire. Captain Toa was one of the few traders who came this far south, and even then, only once a year. The ice that formed on the water made it nearly impossible to reach during the winter months.

Still, the dried fish, whalebone, and the crude lamp oil they pressed from whale blubber were all good cargo that fetched a nice price in Stonepeak or New Laven. The villagers had always been polite and accommodating, in their taciturn Southern way. And it was a community that had survived in these harsh conditions for centuries, a quality that Toa respected a great deal.

So it was with a pang of sadness that he gazed out at what remained of the village. As his ship glided into the narrow harbor, he scanned the dirt paths and stone huts, and saw no sign of life.

'What's the matter, sir?' asked Crayton, his first mate. Good fellow. Loyal in his own way, if a bit dishonest about doing his fair share of work.

'This place is dead,' said Toa quietly. 'We'll not land here.'

'Dead, sir?'

'Not a soul in the place.'

'Maybe they're at some sort of local religious gathering,' said Crayton. 'Folks this far south have their own ways and customs.'

''Fraid that's not it.'

Toa pointed one thick, scarred finger toward the dock. A tall sign had been driven into the wood. On the sign was painted a black oval with eight black lines trailing down from it.

'God save them,' whispered Crayton, taking off his wool knit cap.

'That's the trouble,' said Toa. 'He didn't.'

The two men stood there staring at the sign. There was no sound except the cold wind that pulled at Toa's long wool coat and beard.

'What do we do, sir?' asked Crayton.

'Not come ashore, that's for certain. Tell the wags to lay anchor. It's getting late. I don't want to navigate these shallow waters in the dark, so we'll stay the night. But make no mistake, we're heading back to sea at first light and never coming near Bleak Hope again.'

They set sail the next morning. Toa hoped they'd reach the island of Galemoor in three days and that the monks there would have enough good ale to sell that it would cover his losses.

It was on the second night that they found the stowaway.

Toa was woken in his bunk by a fist pounding on his cabin door.

'Captain!' called Crayton. 'The night watch. They found . . . a little girl.'

Toa groaned. He'd had a bit too much grog before he went to sleep, and the spike of pain had already set in behind his eyes.

'A girl?' he asked after a moment.

'Y-y-yes, sir.'

'Hells' waters,' he muttered, climbing out of his hammock. He pulled on cold, damp trousers, a coat, and boots. A girl on board, even a little one, was bad luck in these Southern seas. Everybody knew that. As he pondered how he was going to get rid of this stowaway, he opened the door and was surprised to find Crayton alone, turning his wool cap over and over again in his hands.

'Well? Where's the girl?'

'She's aft, sir,' said Crayton.

'Why didn't you bring her to me?'

'We, uh . . . That is, the men can't get her out from behind the stowed rigging.'

'Can't get her . . . ' Toa heaved a sigh, wondering why no one had just reached in and clubbed her unconscious, then dragged her out. It wasn't like his men to get soft because of a little girl. Maybe it was on account of Bleak Hope. Maybe the terrible fate of that village had made them a bit more conscious than usual of their own prospects for Heaven.

'Fine,' he said. 'Lead me to her.'

'Aye, sir,' said Crayton, clearly relieved that he wasn't going to bear the brunt of the captain's frustration.

Toa found his men gathered around the cargo hold where

the spare rigging was stored. The hatch was open and they stared down into the darkness, muttering to each other and making signs to ward off curses. Toa took a lantern from one of them and shone the light down into the hole, wondering why a little girl had his men so spooked.

'Look, girlie. You better . . . '

She was wedged in tight behind the piles of heavy line. She looked filthy and starved, but otherwise a normal enough girl of about eight years. Pretty, even, in the Southern way, with pale skin, freckles, and hair so blond it looked almost white. But there was something about her eyes when she looked at you. They felt empty, or worse than empty. They were pools of ice that crushed any warmth you had in you. They were ancient eyes. Broken eyes. Eyes that had seen too much.

'We tried to pull her out, Captain,' said one of the men. 'But she's packed in there tight. And well . . . she's . . . '

'Aye,' said Toa.

He knelt down next to the opening and forced himself to keep looking at her, even though he wanted to turn away.

'What's your name, girl?' he asked, much quieter now.

She stared at him.

'I'm the captain of this ship, girl,' he said. 'Do you know what that means?'

Slowly, she nodded once.

'It means everyone on this ship has to do what I say. That includes you. Understand?'

Again, she nodded once.

He reached one brown, hairy hand down into the hold.

'Now, girl. I want you to come out from behind there and take my hand. I swear no harm will come to you on this ship.'

For a long moment, no one moved. Then, tentatively, the girl reached out her bone-thin hand and let it be engulfed in Toa's.

Toa and the girl were back in his quarters. He suspected the girl might start talking if there weren't a dozen hard-bitten sailors staring at her. He gave her a blanket and a cup of hot grog. He knew grog wasn't the sort of thing you gave to little girls, but it was the only thing he had on board except fresh water, and that was far too precious to waste.

Now he sat at his desk and she sat on his bunk, the blanket wrapped tightly around her shoulders, the steaming cup of grog in her tiny hands. She took a sip, and Toa expected her to flinch at the pungent flavor, but she only swallowed and continued to stare at him with those empty, broken eyes of hers. They were the coldest blue he had ever seen, deeper than the sea itself.

'I'll ask you again, girl,' he said, although his tone was still gentle. 'What's yer name?'

She only stared at him.

'Where'd you come from?'

Still she stared.

'Are you . . . ' He couldn't believe he was even thinking it, much less asking it. 'Are you from Bleak Hope?'

She blinked then, as if coming out of a trance. 'Bleak Hope.' Her voice was hoarse from lack of use. 'Yes. That's me.' There was something about the way she spoke that made Toa suppress a shudder. Her voice was as empty as her eyes.

'How did you come to be on my ship?'

'That happened after,' she said.

'After what?' he asked.

She looked at him then, and her eyes were no longer empty. They were full. So full that Toa's salty old heart felt like it might twist up like a rag in his chest.

'I will tell you,' she said, her voice as wet and full as her eyes. 'I will tell *only* you. Then I won't ever say it aloud ever again.'

She had been off at the rocks. That was how they'd missed her.

She loved the rocks. Great big jagged black boulders she could climb above the crashing waves. It terrified her mother the way she jumped from one to the next. 'You'll hurt your-self!' her mother would say. And she did hurt herself. Often. Her shins and knees were peppered with scabs and scars from the rough-edged rock. But she didn't care. She loved them anyway. And when the tide went out, they always had treasures at their bases, half-buried in the gray sand. Crab shells, fish bones, seashells, and sometimes, if she was very lucky, a bit of sea glass. That she prized above all else.

'What is it?' she'd asked her mother one night as they sat by the fire after dinner, her belly warm and full of fish stew. She held up a piece of red sea glass to the light so that the color shone on the stone wall of their hut.

'It's glass, my little gull,' said her mother, fingers working quickly as she mended a fishing net for Father. 'Broken bits of glass polished by the sea.'

'But why's it colored?'

'To make it prettier, I suppose.'

'Why don't *we* have any glass that's colored?'

'Oh, it's just fancy Northland frippery,' said her mother. 'We've no use for it down here.'

That made her love the sea glass all the more. She

collected them until she had enough to string together with a bit of hemp rope to make a necklace. She presented it to her father, a gruff fisherman who rarely spoke, on his birthday. He held the necklace in his leathery hand, eyeing the bright red, blue, and green chunks of sea glass warily. But then he looked into her eyes and saw how proud she was, how much she loved this thing. His weather-lined face folded up into a smile as he carefully tied it around his neck. The other fishermen teased him for weeks about it, but he would only touch his calloused fingertips to the sea glass and smile again.

When *they* came on that day, the tide had just gone out, and she was searching the base of her rocks for new treasures. She'd seen the top of their ship masts off in the distance, but she was far too focused on her hunt for sea glass to investigate. It wasn't until she finally clambered back on top of one of the rocks to sift through her collection of shells and bones that she noticed how strange the ship was. A big boxy thing with a full three sails and cannon ports all along the sides. Very different from the trade ships. She didn't like the look of it at all. And that was before she noticed the thick cloud of smoke rising from her village.

She ran, her skinny little legs churning in the sand and tall grass as she made her way through the scraggly trees toward her village. If there was a fire, her mother wouldn't bother to save the treasures stowed away in the wooden chest under her bed. That was all she could think about. She'd spent too much time and effort collecting her treasures to lose them. They were the most precious thing to her. Or so she thought.

As she neared the village, she saw that the fire had spread across the whole village. There were men she didn't recognize dressed in white-and-gold uniforms with helmets and armored chest plates. She wondered if they were soldiers. But soldiers were supposed to protect the people. These men herded everyone into a big clump in the center of the village, waving swords and guns at them.

She jerked to a stop when she saw the guns. She'd seen only one other gun. It was owned by Shamka, the village elder. Every winter on the eve of the New Year, he fired it up at the moon to wake it from its slumber and bring back the sun. The guns these soldiers had looked different. In addition to the wooden handle, iron tube, and hammer, they had a round cylinder.

She was trying to decide whether to get closer or run and hide, when Shamka emerged from his hut, gave an angry bellow, and fired his gun at the nearest soldier. The soldier's face caved in as the shot struck him, and he fell back into the mud. One of the other soldiers raised his pistol and fired at Shamka, but missed. Shamka laughed triumphantly. But then the intruder fired a second time without reloading. Shamka's face was wide with surprise as he clutched at his chest and toppled over.

The girl nearly cried out then. But she bit her lip as hard as she could to stop herself, and dropped into the tall grass.

She lay hidden there in the cold, muddy field for hours. She had to clench her jaw to keep her teeth from chattering. She heard the soldiers shouting to each other, and there were strange hammering and flapping sounds. Occasionally, she would hear one of the villagers beg to know what they had done to displease the emperor. The only reply was a loud smack.

It was dark, and the fires had all flickered out before she moved her numb limbs up into a crouch and took another look.

In the center of the town, a huge brown canvas tent had been erected, easily five times larger than any hut in the village. The soldiers stood in a circle around it, holding torches. She couldn't see her fellow villagers anywhere. Cautiously, she crept a little closer.

A tall man who wore a long, hooded white cloak instead of a uniform stood at the entrance to the tent. In his hands, he held a large wooden box. One of the soldiers opened the flap of the tent entrance. The cloaked man went into the tent, accompanied by a soldier. Some moments later, they both emerged, but the man no longer had the box. The soldier tied the flap so that the entrance remained open, then covered the opening with a net so fine not even the smallest bird could have slipped through.

The cloaked man took a notebook from his pocket as soldiers brought out a small table and chair and placed them before him. He sat at the table and a soldier handed him a quill and ink. The man immediately began to write, pausing frequently to peer through the netting into the tent.

Screams began to come from inside the tent. She realized then that all the villagers were inside. She didn't know why they screamed, but it terrified her so much that she dropped back into the mud and held her hands over her ears to block out the sound. The screams lasted only a few minutes, but it was a long time before she could bring herself to look again.

It was completely dark now except for one lantern at the tent entrance. The soldiers had gone and only the cloaked man remained, still scribbling away in his notebook. Occasionally, he would glance into the tent, look at his pocket watch, and frown. She wondered where the soldiers were, but then noticed that the strange boxy ship tied at the dock was lit up, and when she strained her hearing, she could make out the sound of rowdy male voices.

The girl snuck through the tall grass toward the side of the tent that was the farthest from the man. Not that he would have seen her. He seemed so intent on his writing that she probably could have walked right past him, and he wouldn't have noticed. Even so, her heart raced as she crept across the small stretch of open ground between the tall grass and the tent wall. When she finally reached the tent, she found that the bottom had been staked down so tightly that she had to pull out several of them before she could slip under.

It was even darker inside, the air thick and hot. The villagers all lay on the ground, eyes closed, chained to each other and to the thick tent poles. In the center sat the wooden box, the lid off. Scattered on the ground were dead wasps as big as birds.

Far over in the corner, she saw her mother and father, motionless like all the rest. She moved quickly to them, a sick fear shooting through her stomach.

But then her father moved weakly, and relief flooded through her. Maybe she could still rescue them. She gently shook her mother, but she didn't respond. She shook her father, but he only groaned, his eyes fluttering a moment but not opening.

She searched around, looking to see if she could unfasten their chains. There was a loud buzzing close to her ear. She turned and saw a giant wasp hovering over her shoulder. Before it could sting her, a hand shot past her face and slapped it aside. The wasp spun wildly around, one wing broken, then dropped to the ground. She turned and saw her father, his face screwed up in pain.

He grabbed her wrist. 'Go!' he grunted. 'Away.' Then he shoved her so hard, she fell backward onto her rear.

She stared at him, terrified, but wanting to do something that would take the awful look of pain away from his face. Around her, others were stirring, their own faces etched in the same agony as her father.

Then she saw her father's sea glass necklace give an odd little jump. She looked closer. It happened again. Her father arched his back. His eyes and mouth opened wide, as if screaming, but only a wet gurgle came out. A white worm as thick as a finger burst from his neck. Blood streamed from him as other worms burrowed out of his chest and gut.

Her mother woke with a gasp, her eyes staring around wildly. Her skin was already shifting. She reached out and called her daughter's name.

All around her, the other villagers thrashed against their chains as the worms ripped free. Before long, the ground was covered in a writhing mass of white.

She wanted to run. Instead, she held her mother's hand and watched her writhe and jerk as the worms ate her from the inside. She did not move, did not look away until her mother grew still. Only then did she stumble to her feet, slip under the tent wall, and run back into the tall grass.

She watched from afar as the soldiers returned at dawn with large burlap sacks. The cloaked man went inside the tent for a while, then came back out and wrote more in his notebook. He did this two more times, then said something to one of the soldiers. The soldier nodded, gave a signal, and the group with sacks filed into the tent. When they came back out, their sacks were filled with writhing bulges that she guessed were the worms. They carried them to the ship while the remaining soldiers struck the tent, exposing the bodies that had been inside.

The cloaked man watched as the soldiers unfastened the chains from the pile of corpses. As he stood there, the little girl fixed his face in her memory. Brown hair, weak chin, pointed ratlike face marked with a burn scar on his left cheek.

At last they sailed off in their big boxy ship, leaving a strange sign driven into the dock. When they were no longer in sight, she crept back down into the village. It took her many days. Perhaps weeks. But she buried them all.

Captain Sin Toa stared down at the girl. During her tale, her expression had remained fixed in a look of wide-eyed horror. But now it settled back into the cold emptiness he'd seen when he first coaxed her out of the hold.

'How long ago was that?' he asked.

'Don't know,' she said.

'How did you get aboard?' he asked. 'We never docked.'

'I swam.'

'Quite a distance.'

'Yes.'

'And what should I do with you now?'

She shrugged.

'A ship is no place for a little girl.'

'I have to stay alive,' she said. 'So I can find that man.'

'Do you know who that was? What that sign meant?'

She shook her head.

'That was the crest of the emperor's biomancers. You haven't got a prayer of ever getting close to that man.'

'I will,' she said quietly. 'Someday. If it takes my whole life. I'll find him. And kill him.'

Captain Sin Toa knew he couldn't keep her aboard. It was

said maidens, even eight-year-old ones, could draw the attention of the sea serpents in these waters as sure as a bucketful of blood. The crew might very well mutiny at the idea of keeping a girl on board. But he wasn't about to throw her overboard or dump her on some empty piece of rock either. When they landed the next day at Galemoor, he approached the head of the Vinchen order, a wizened old monk named Hurlo.

'Girl's seen things nobody should have to see,' he said. The two of them stood in the stone courtyard of the monastery, the tall, black stone temple looming over them. 'She's a broken thing. Could be a monastic life is the only option left to her.'

Hurlo slipped his hands into the sleeves of his black robe. 'I sympathize, Captain. Truly, I do. But the Vinchen order is for men only.'

'But surely you could use a servant around,' said Toa. 'She's a peasant, accustomed to hard work.'

Hurlo nodded. 'We could. But what happens when she comes of age and begins to blossom? She will become too great a distraction for my brothers, particularly the younger ones.'

'So keep her till then. At least you'll have sheltered her a few years. Kept her alive long enough for her to make her own way.'

Hurlo closed his eyes. 'It will not be an easy life for her here.'

'Don't think she'd know what to do with an easy life if you gave her one anyway.'

Hurlo looked at Toa. And to Toa's surprise, he suddenly smiled, his old eyes sparkling. 'We will take in this broken child you have found. A bit of chaos in the order brings change. Perhaps for the better.'

Toa shrugged. He'd never fully understood Hurlo or the Vinchen order. 'If you say so, Grandteacher.'

'What is the child's name?' asked Hurlo.

'She won't say for some reason. I half think she doesn't remember.'

'What shall we call her, then, this child born of nightmare? As her unlikely guardians, I suppose it is now up to us to name her.'

Captain Sin Toa thought about it a moment, tugging at his beard. 'Maybe after the village she survived. Keep something of it in memory, at least. Call her Bleak Hope.'